P9-CTQ-799

Crumbs

DANIE
STIRLING

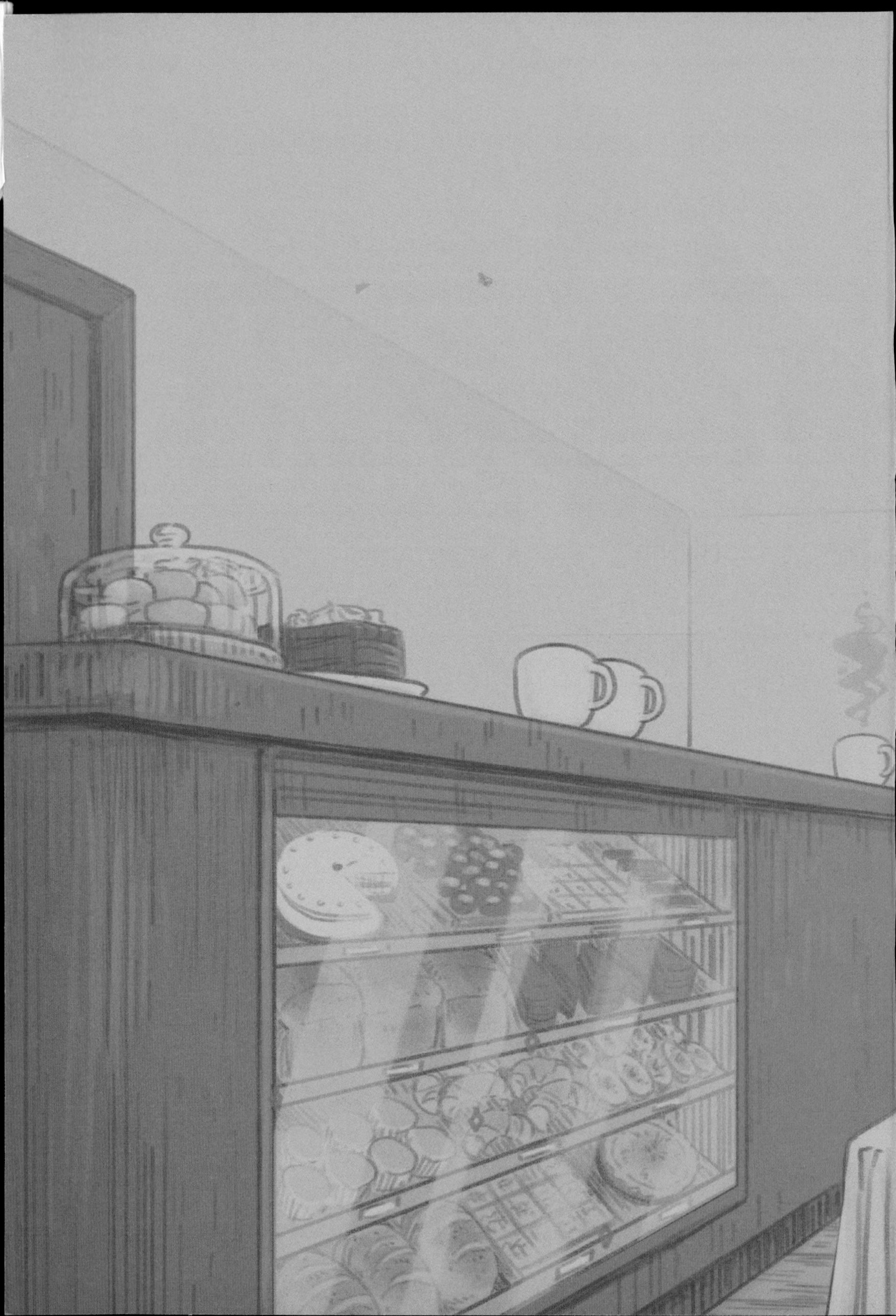

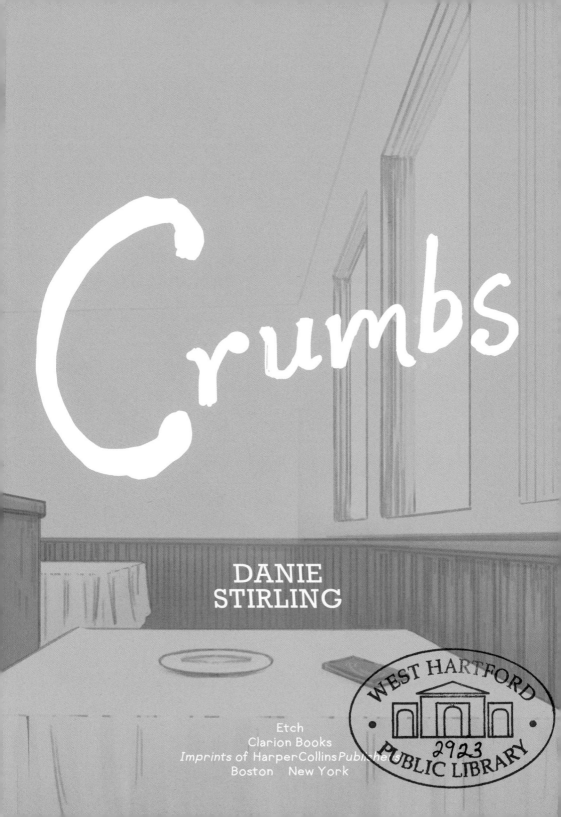

Crumbs

DANIE STIRLING

Etch
Clarion Books
Imprints of HarperCollins Publishers
Boston   New York

Etch and Clarion Books are imprints of HarperCollins Publishers.

Crumbs
clarionbooks.com

Library of Congress Cataloging-in-Publication Data has been applied for.

ISBN: 978-0-358-46779-3 hardcover
ISBN: 978-0-358-46781-6 paperback

The text was set in Gumball.

Manufactured in Spain
EP 10 9 8 7 6 5 4 3 2 1
4500844300

First Edition

A digital version of *Crumbs* was originally published on WEBTOON in 2020.

YA
GRAPHIC
NOVEL
STIRLING
DANIE

CHAPTER 1

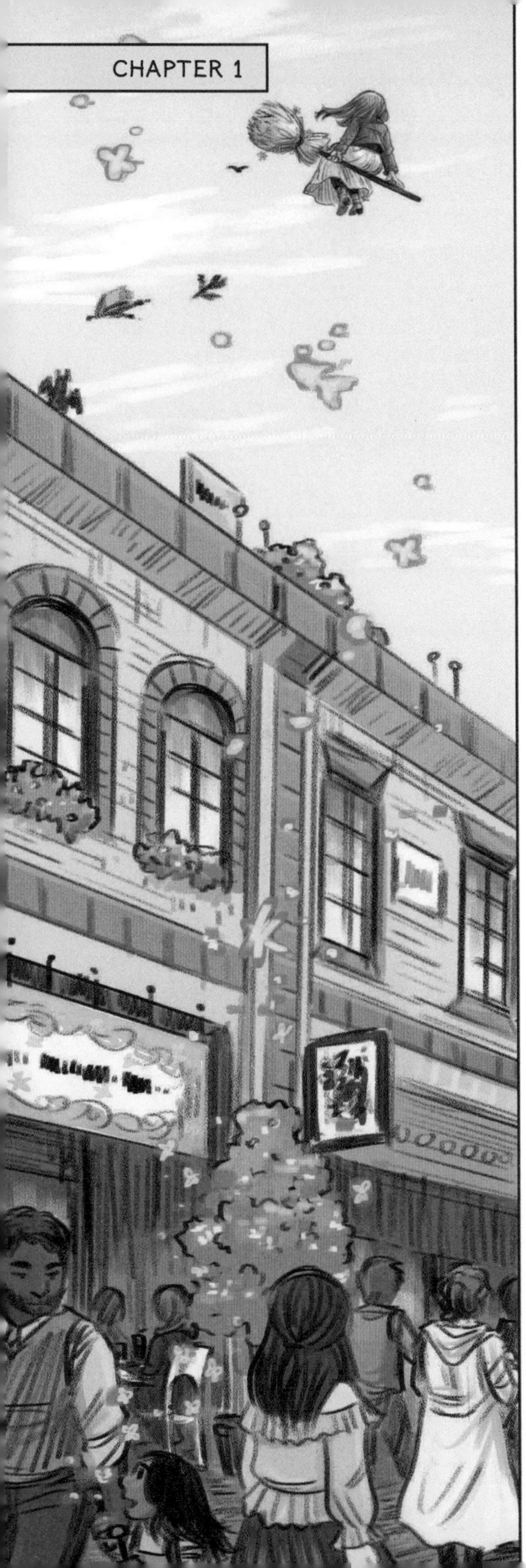

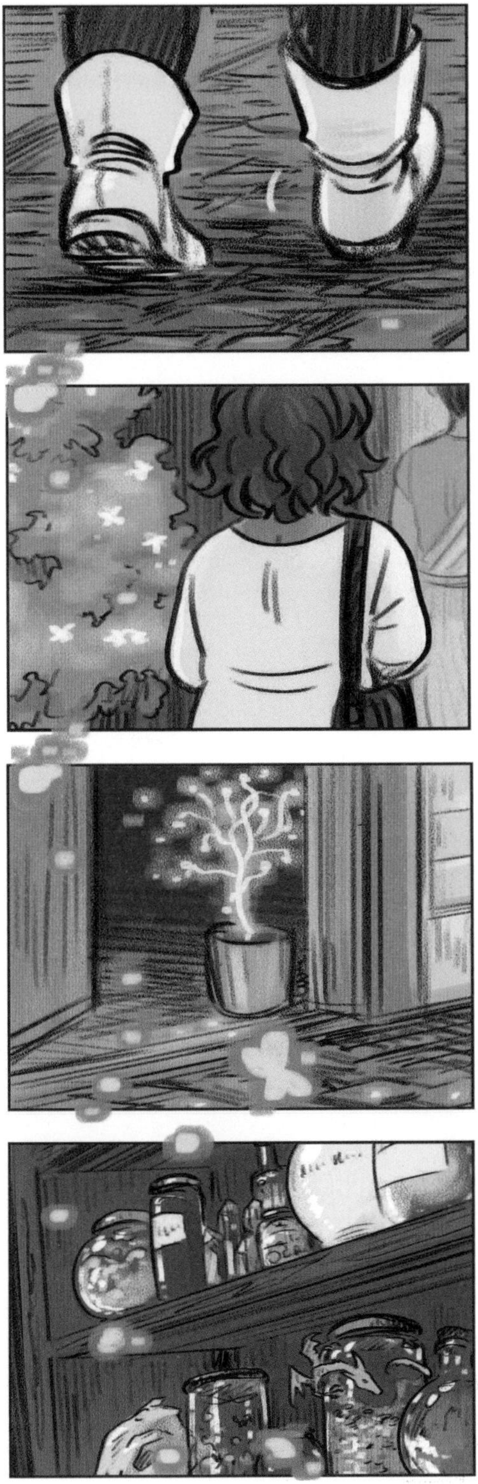

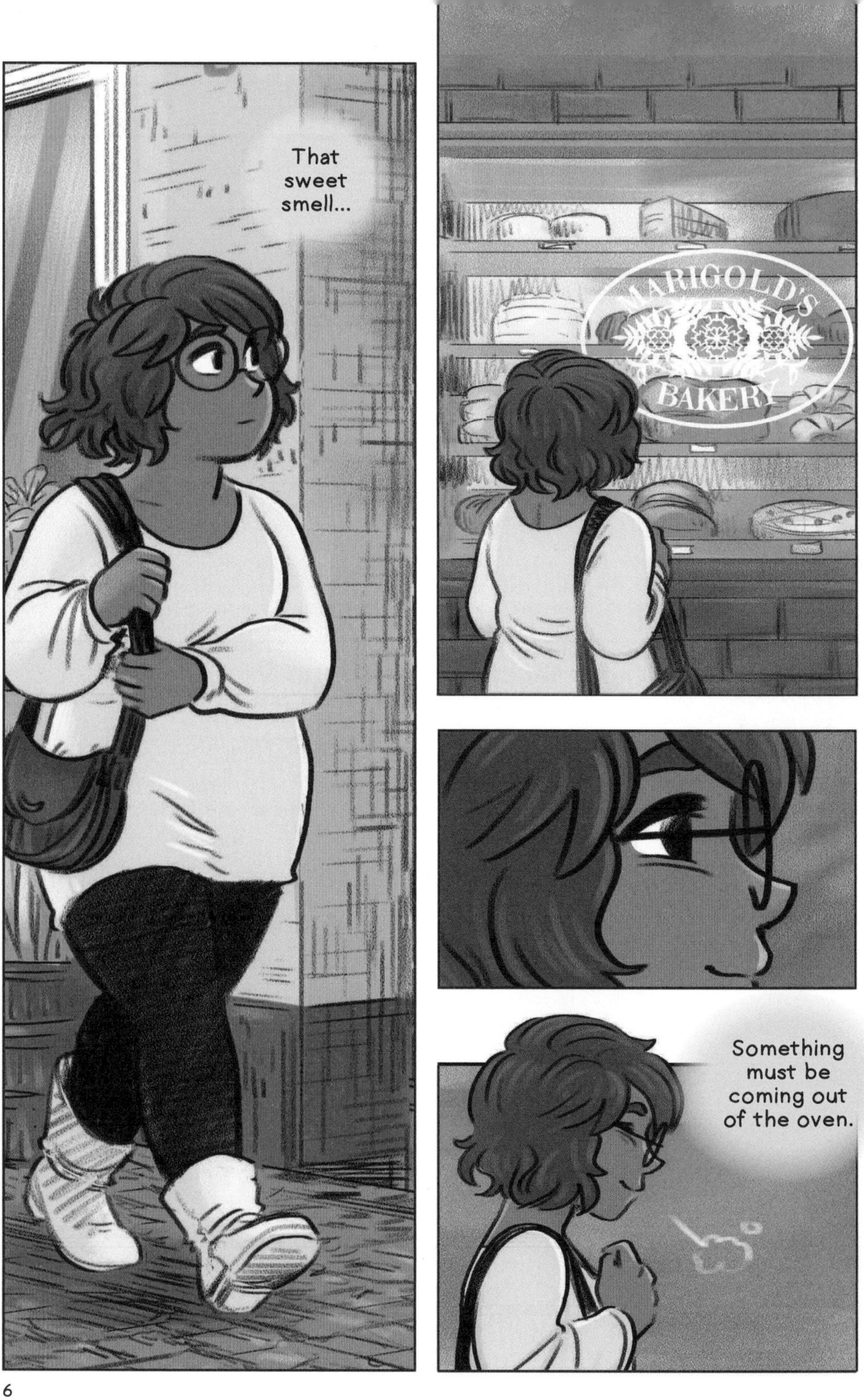
That sweet smell...
MARIGOLD'S BAKERY
Something must be coming out of the oven.

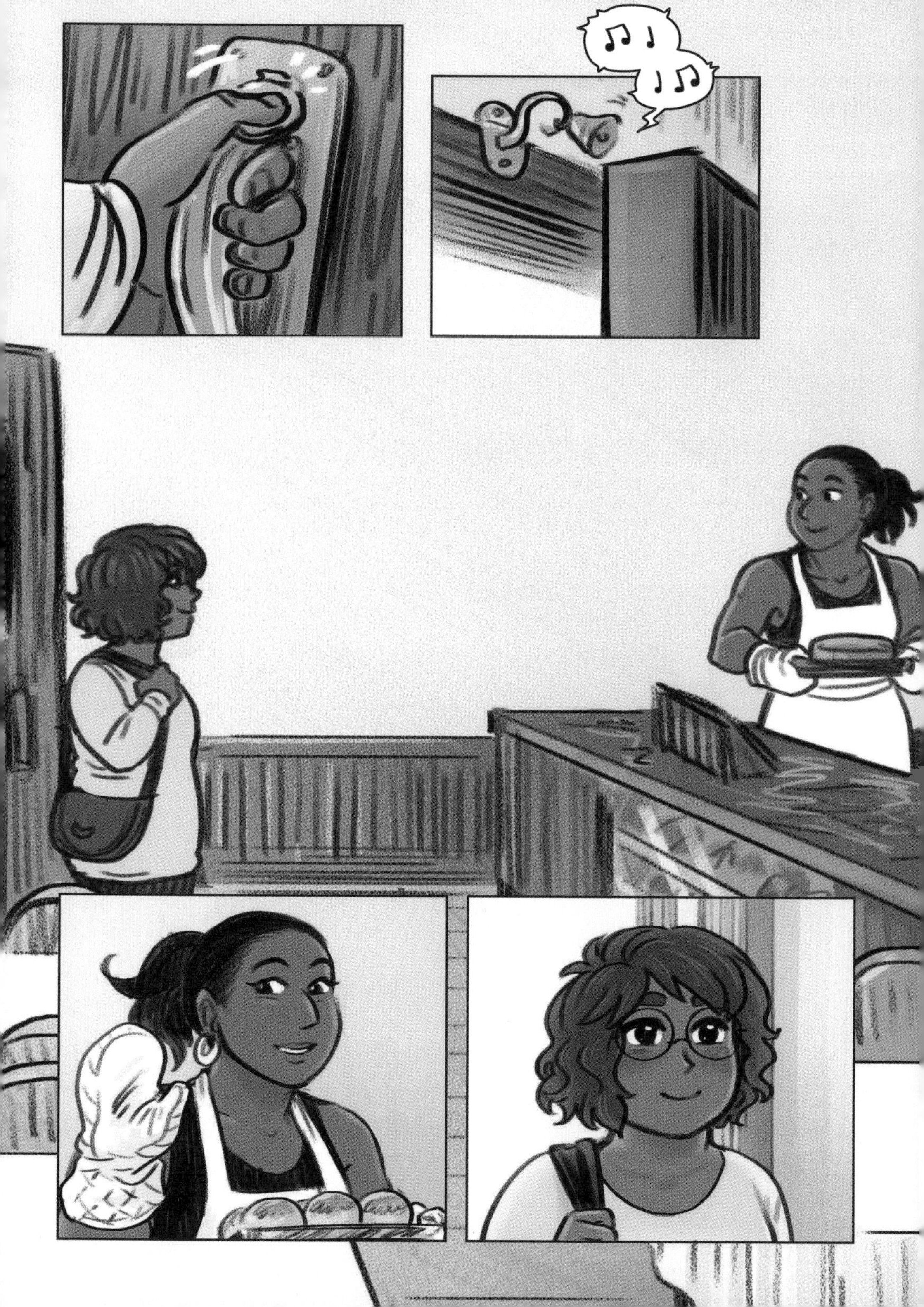

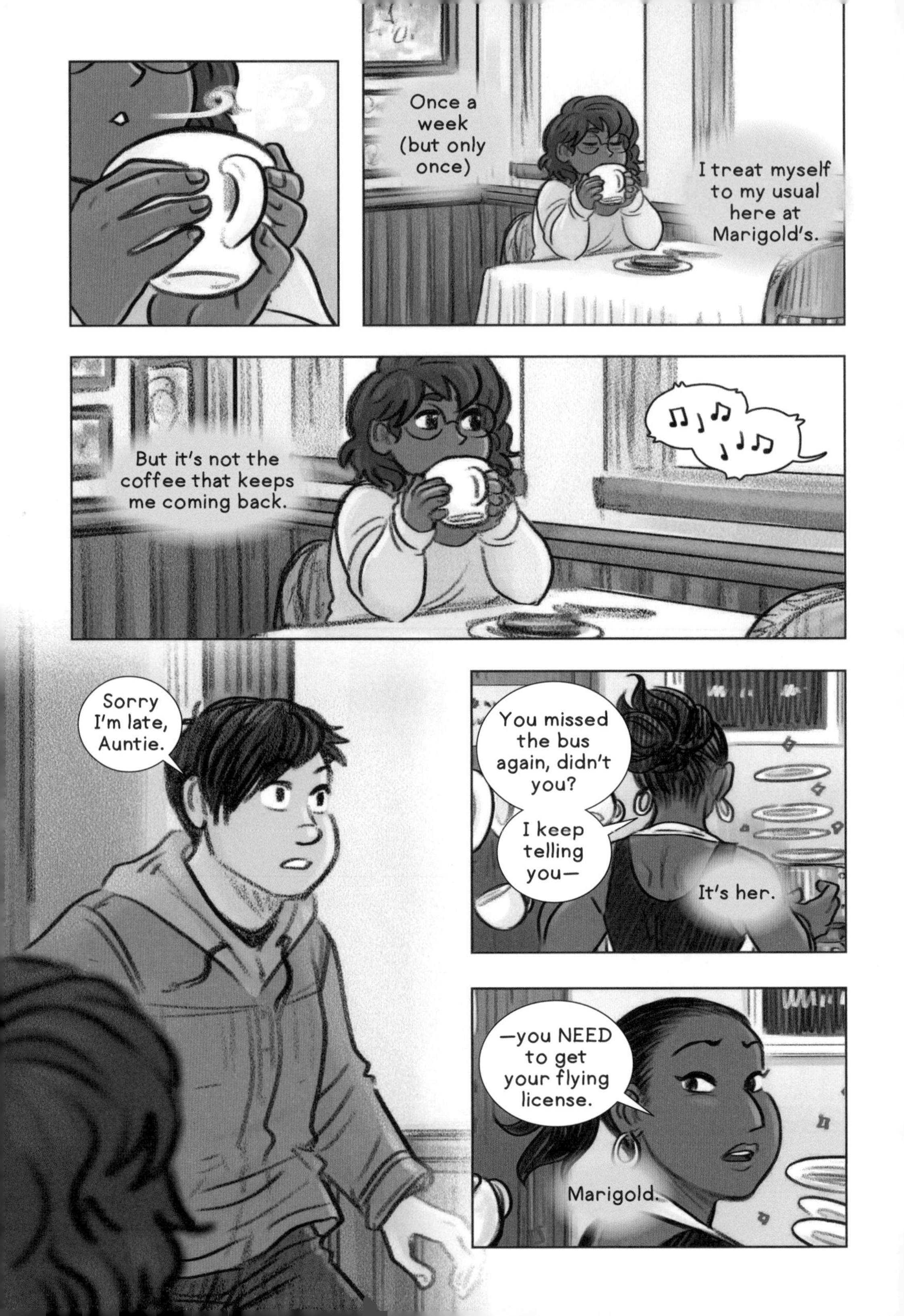
Once a week (but only once)
I treat myself to my usual here at Marigold's.
But it's not the coffee that keeps me coming back.
Sorry I'm late, Auntie.
You missed the bus again, didn't you?
I keep telling you—
It's her.
—you NEED to get your flying license.
Marigold.

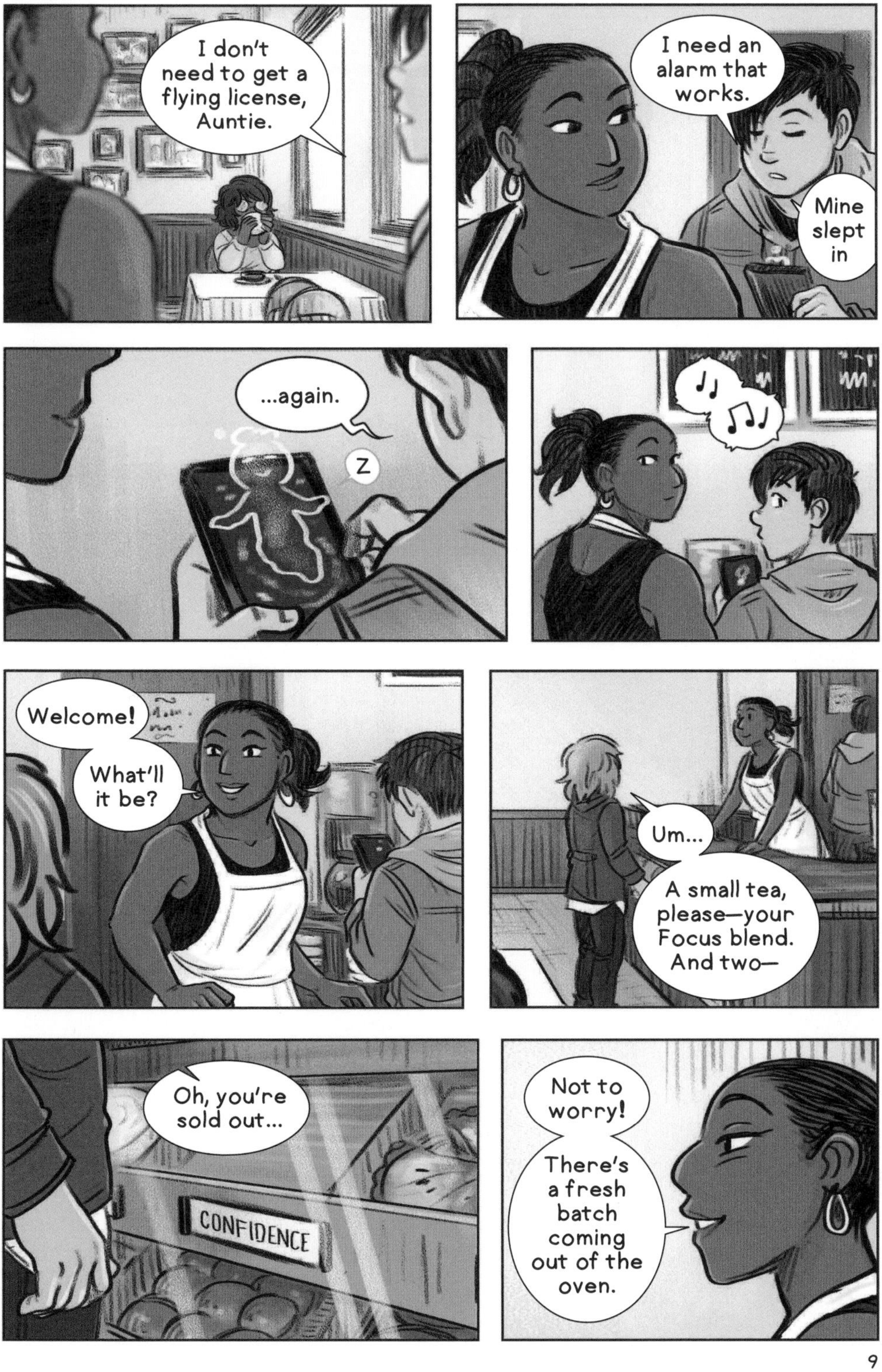
I don't need to get a flying license, Auntie.
I need an alarm that works.
Mine slept in
...again.
Z
Welcome!
What'll it be?
Um...
A small tea, please—your Focus blend. And two—
Oh, you're sold out...
CONFIDENCE
Not to worry!
There's a fresh batch coming out of the oven.

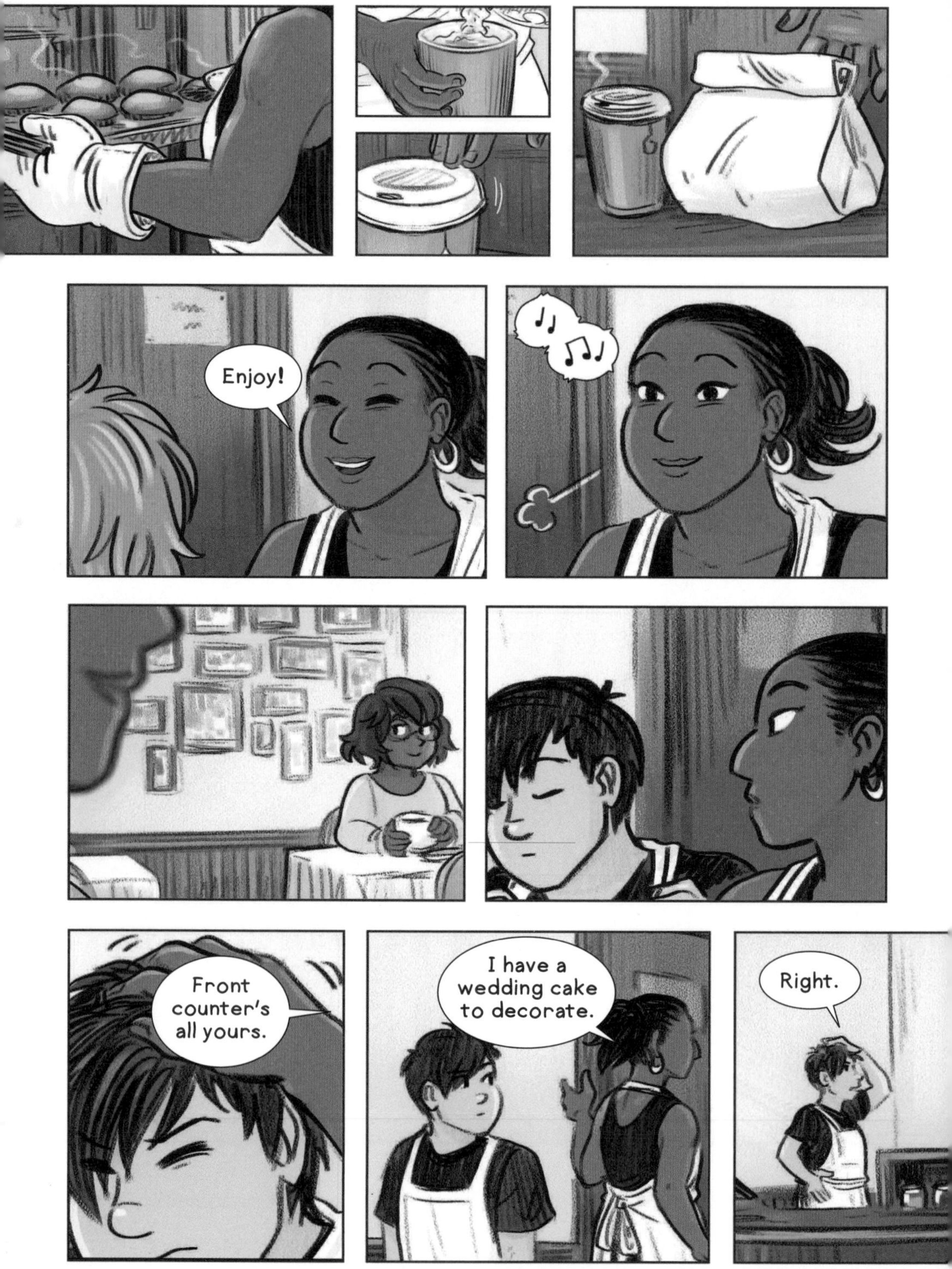
Enjoy!
Front counter's all yours.
I have a wedding cake to decorate.
Right.

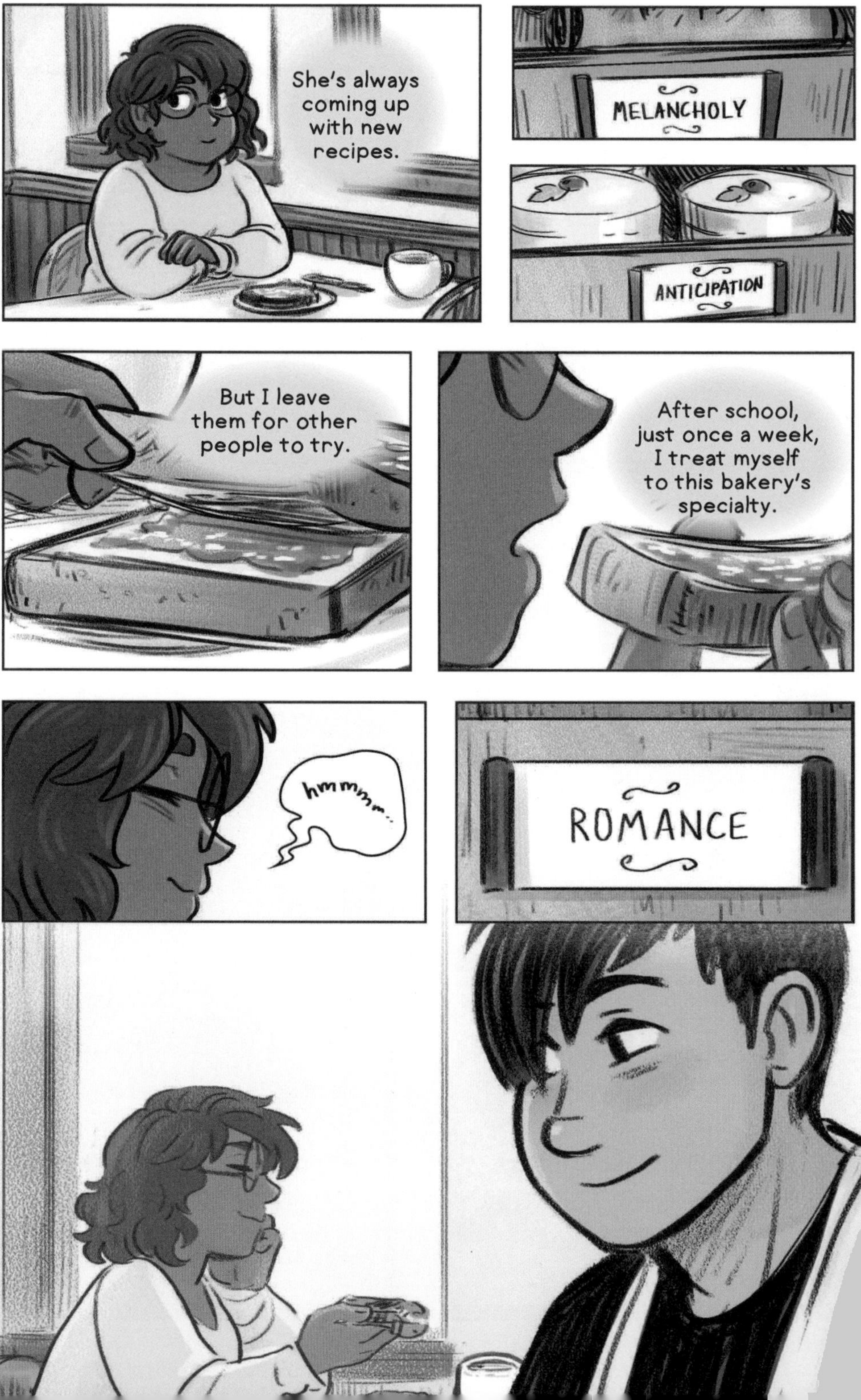
She's always coming up with new recipes.
MELANCHOLY
ANTICIPATION
But I leave them for other people to try.
After school, just once a week, I treat myself to this bakery's specialty.
hmmmm...
ROMANCE

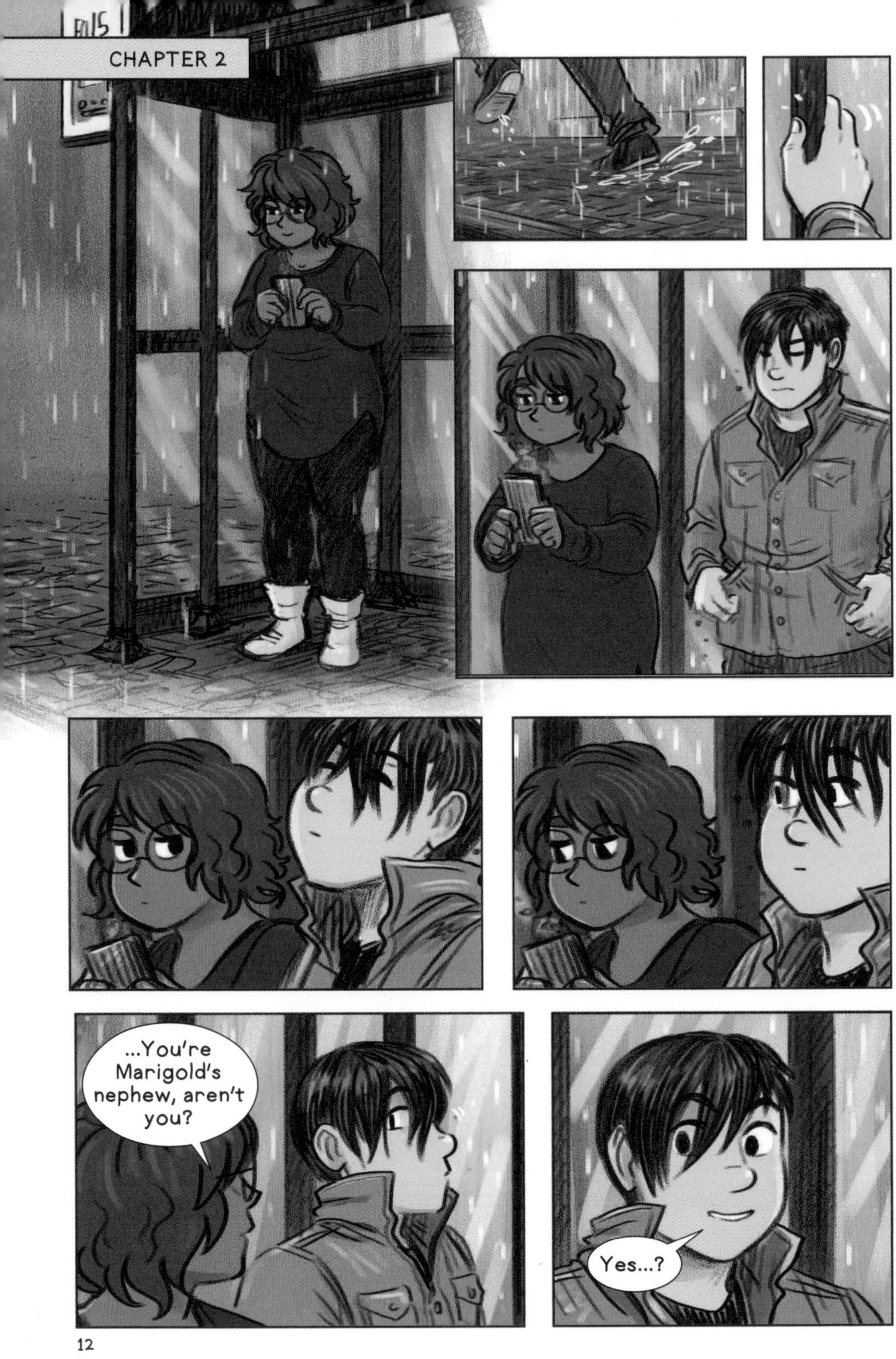
CHAPTER 2
...You're Marigold's nephew, aren't you?
Yes...?

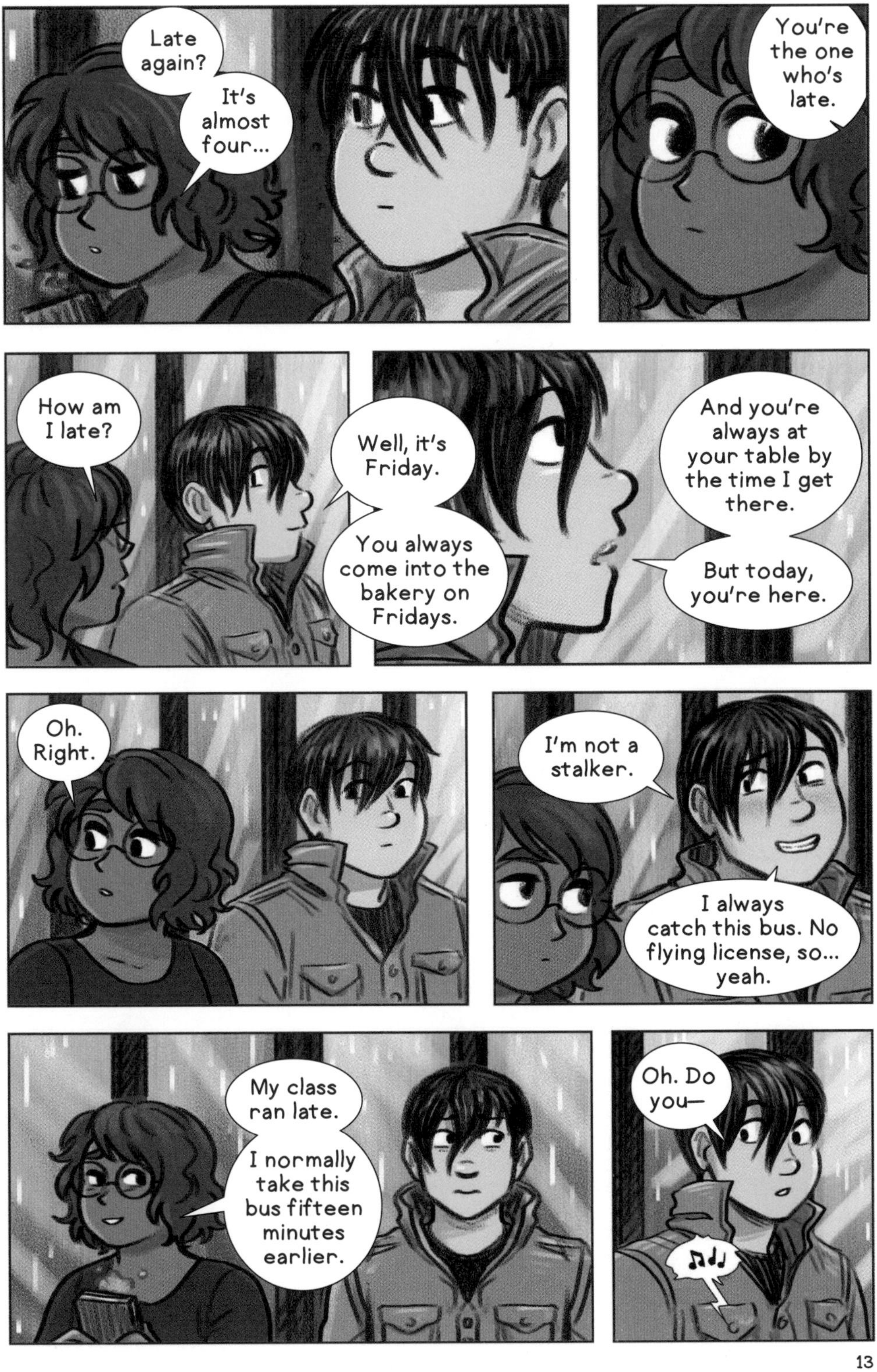

Late again?
It's almost four...
You're the one who's late.
How am I late?
Well, it's Friday.
You always come into the bakery on Fridays.
And you're always at your table by the time I get there.
But today, you're here.
Oh. Right.
I'm not a stalker.
I always catch this bus. No flying license, so... yeah.
My class ran late.
I normally take this bus fifteen minutes earlier.
Oh. Do you—

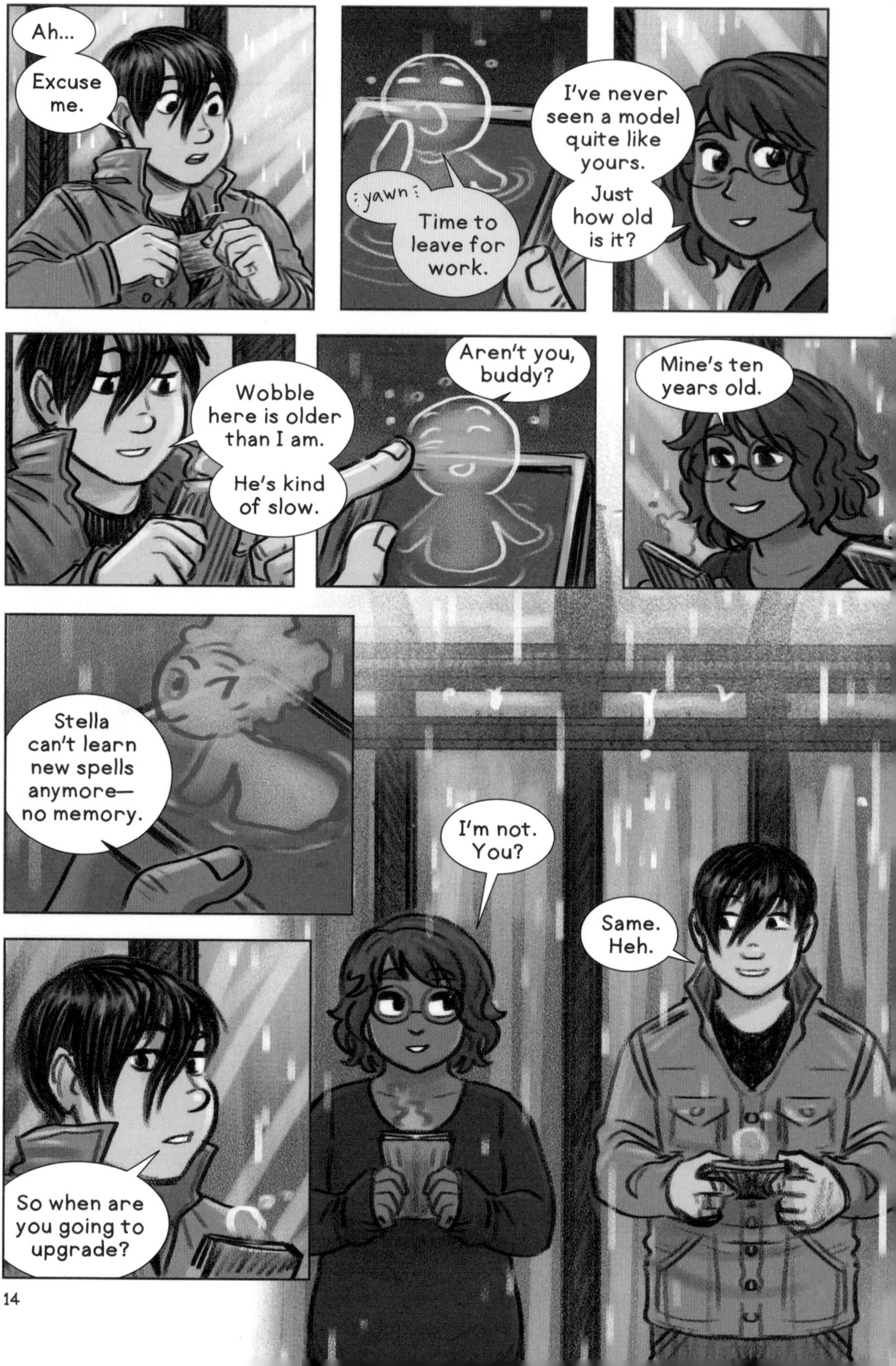
Ah...
Excuse me.
yawn
Time to leave for work.
I've never seen a model quite like yours.
Just how old is it?
Wobble here is older than I am.
He's kind of slow.
Aren't you, buddy?
Mine's ten years old.
Stella can't learn new spells anymore— no memory.
So when are you going to upgrade?
I'm not. You?
Same. Heh.

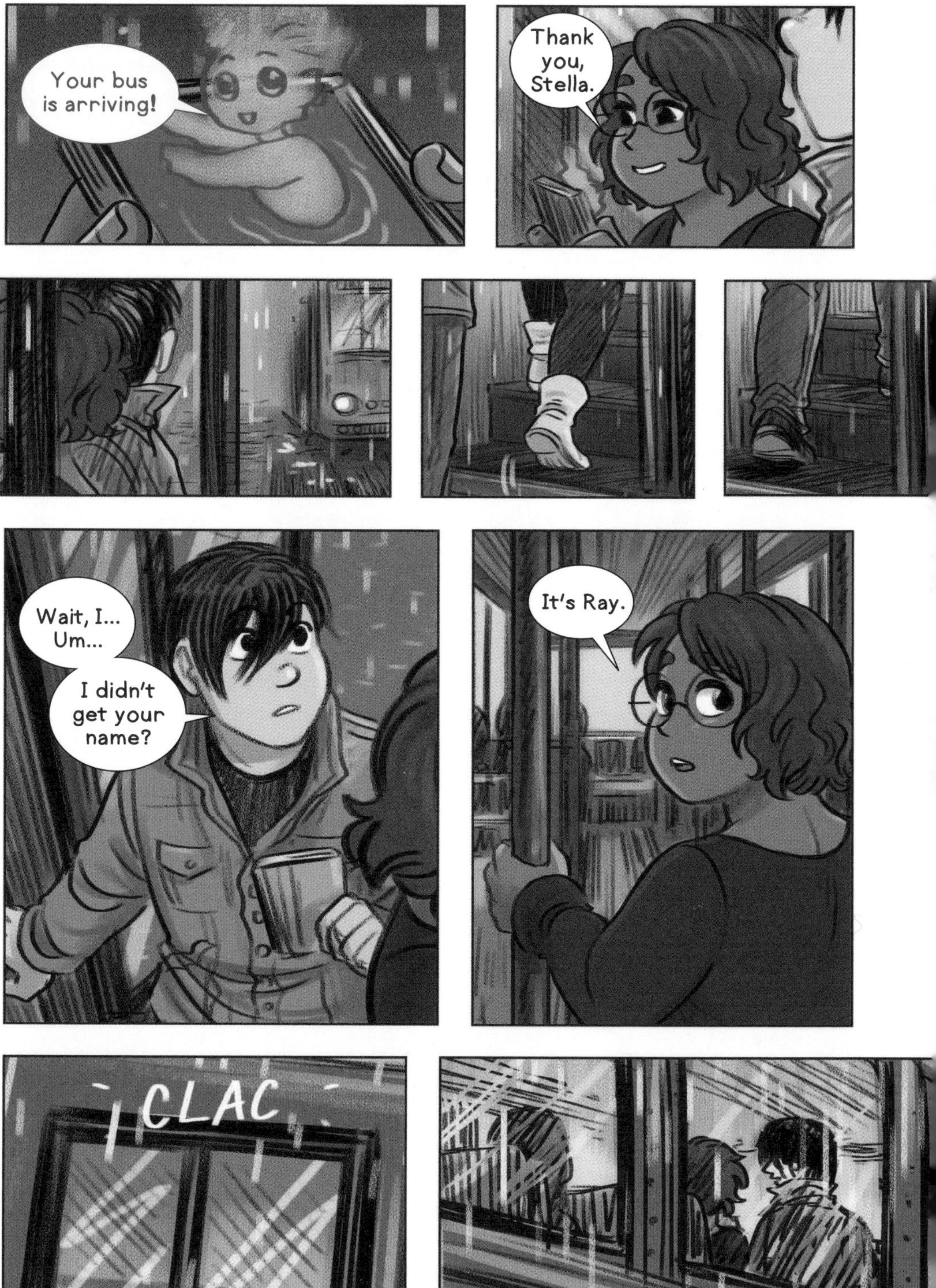
Your bus is arriving!
Thank you, Stella.
Wait, I... Um...
I didn't get your name?
It's Ray.
CLAC

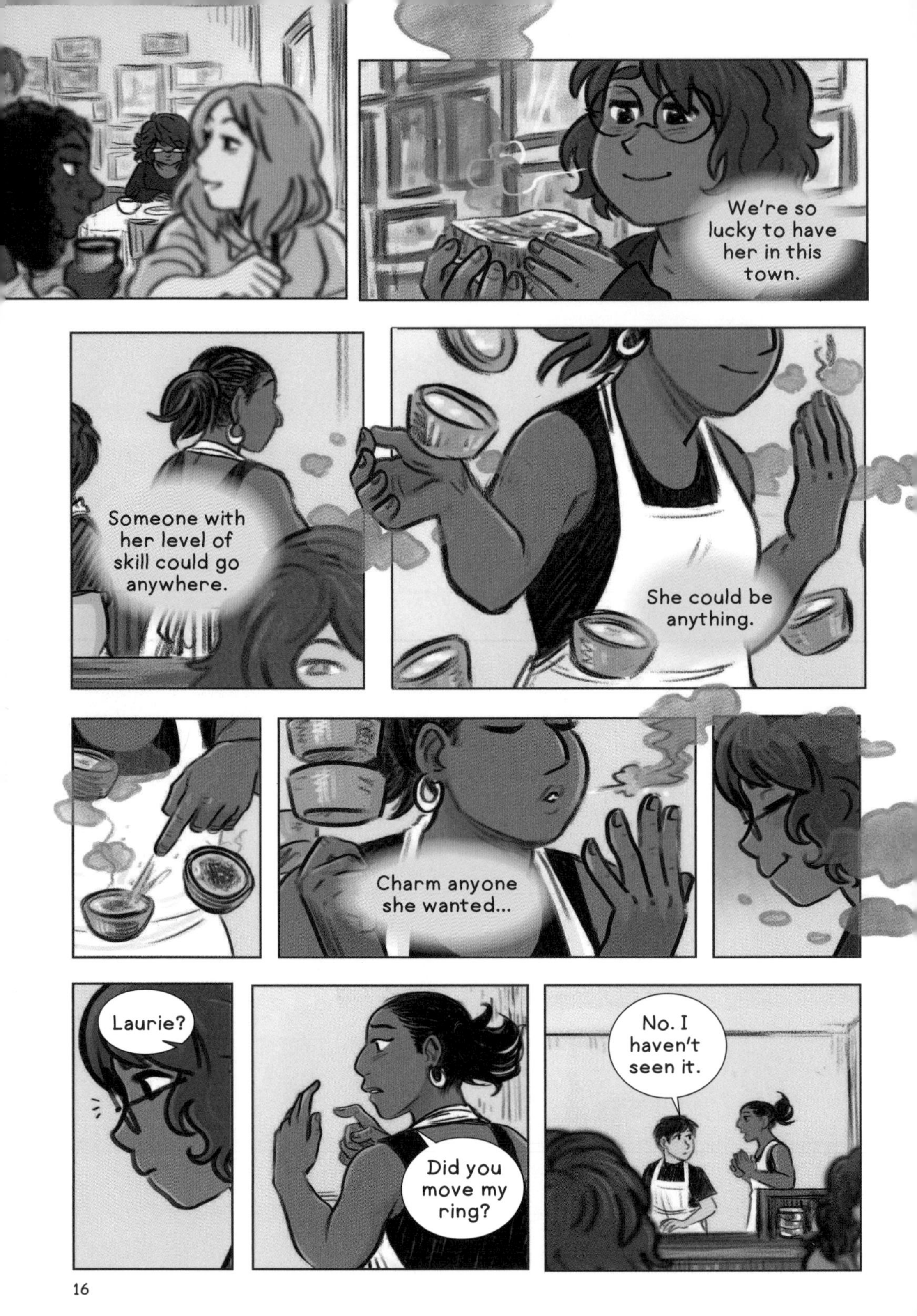
We're so lucky to have her in this town.
Someone with her level of skill could go anywhere.
She could be anything.
Charm anyone she wanted...
Laurie?
Did you move my ring?
No. I haven't seen it.

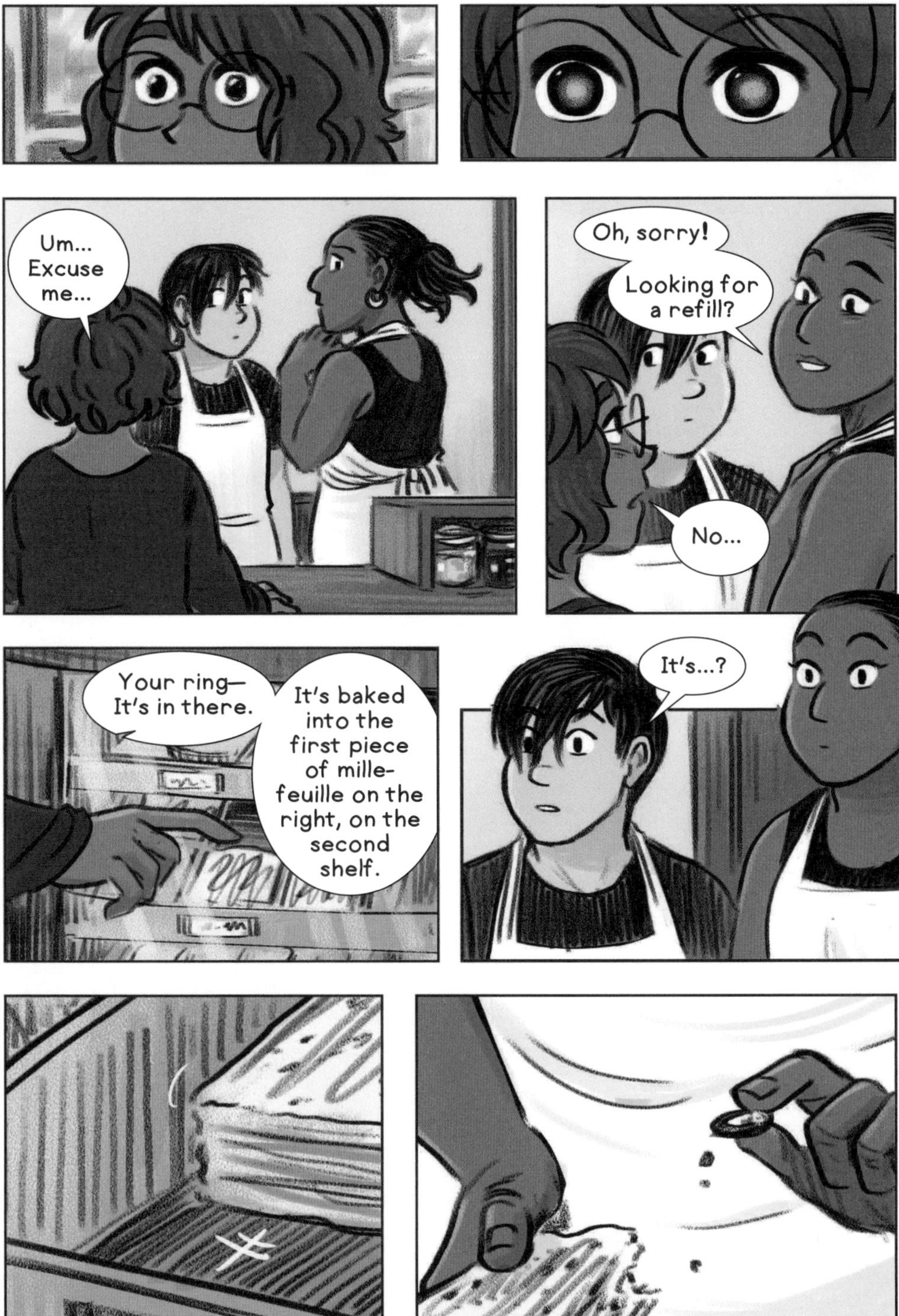
Um... Excuse me...
Oh, sorry!
Looking for a refill?
No...
Your ring— It's in there.
It's baked into the first piece of mille-feuille on the right, on the second shelf.
It's...?

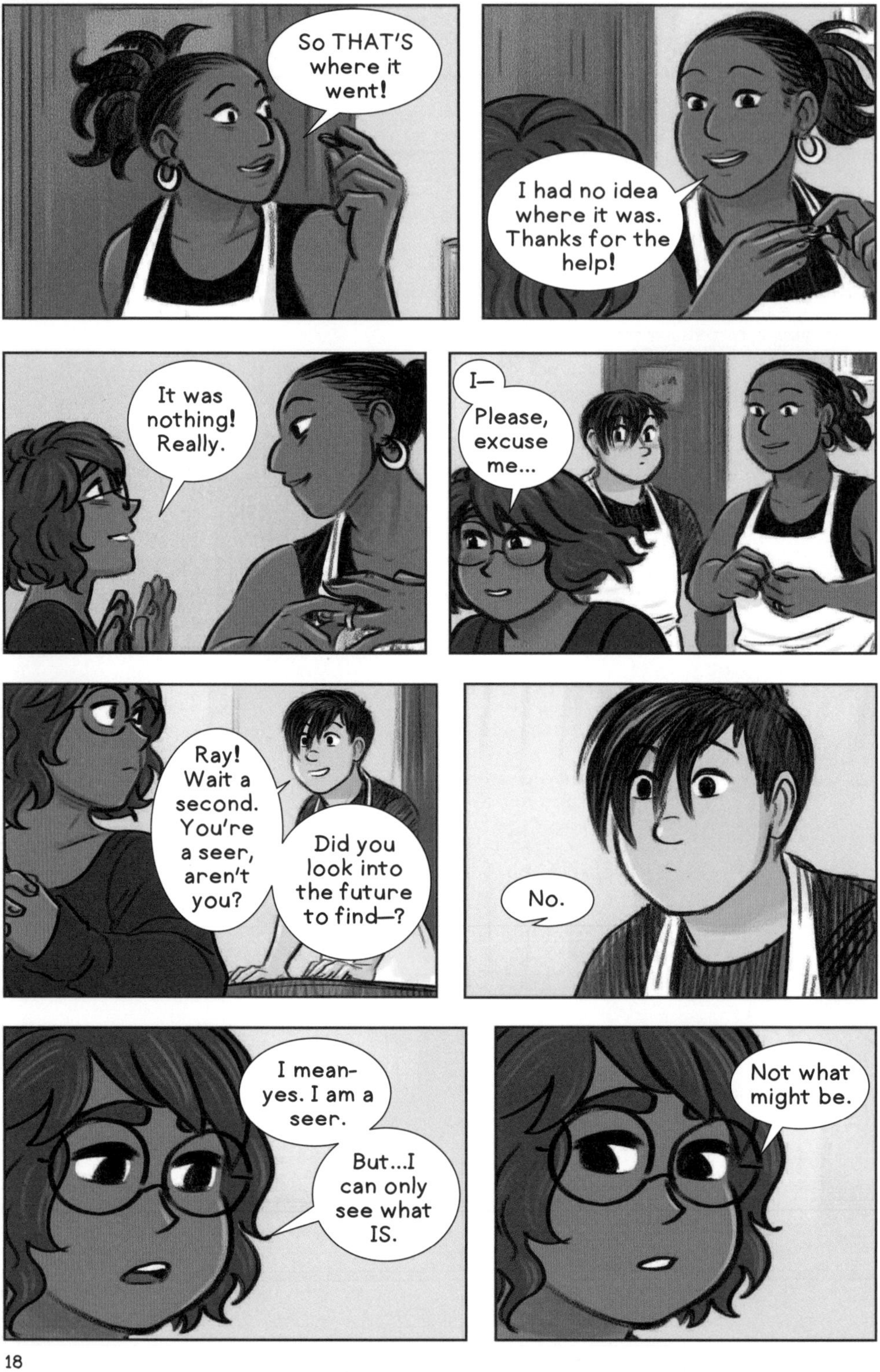
So THAT'S where it went!
I had no idea where it was. Thanks for the help!
It was nothing! Really.
I—
Please, excuse me...
Ray! Wait a second. You're a seer, aren't you?
Did you look into the future to find—?
No.
I mean- yes. I am a seer.
But...I can only see what IS.
Not what might be.

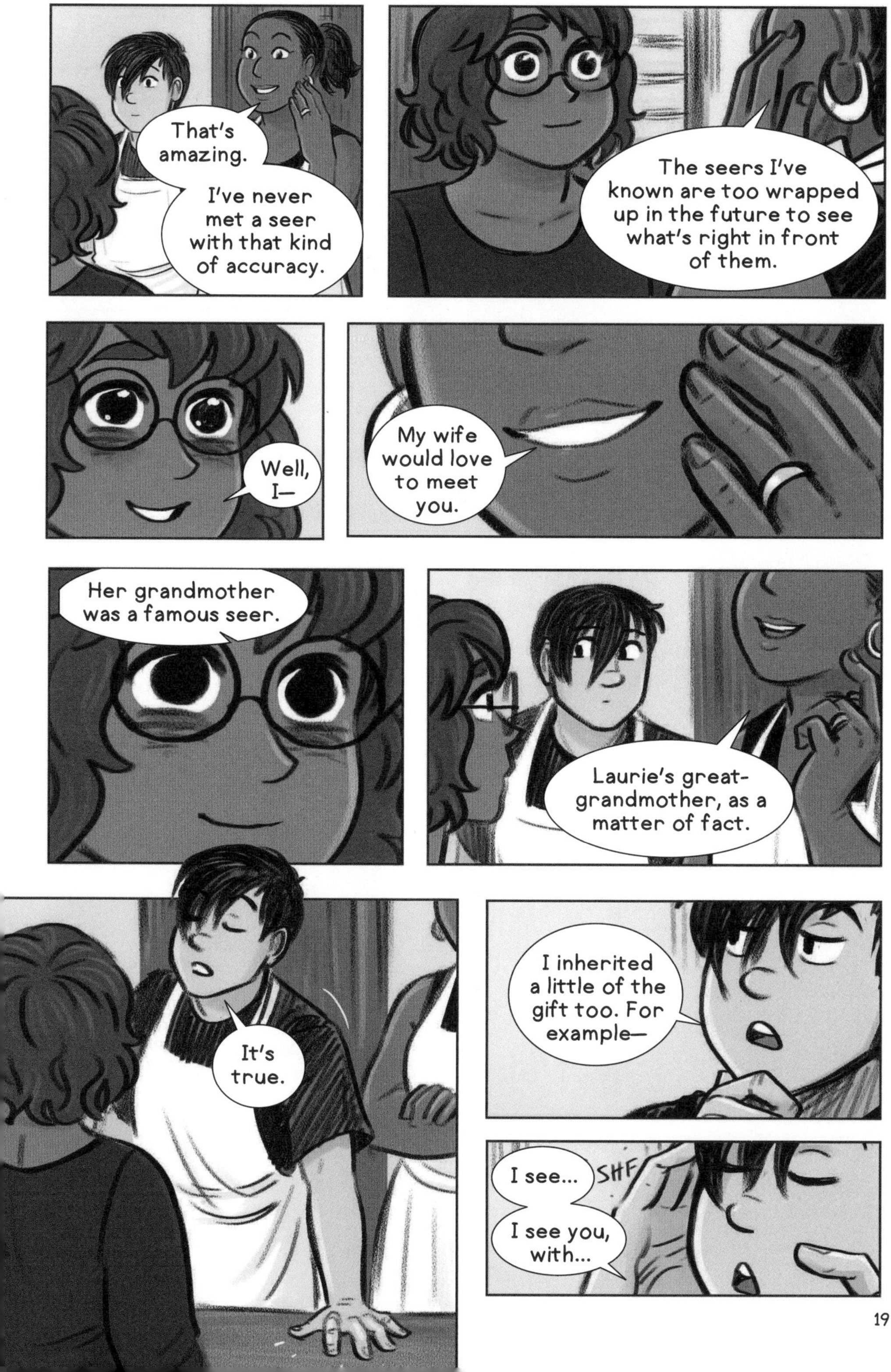
That's amazing.
I've never met a seer with that kind of accuracy.
The seers I've known are too wrapped up in the future to see what's right in front of them.
Well, I—
My wife would love to meet you.
Her grandmother was a famous seer.
Laurie's great-grandmother, as a matter of fact.
It's true.
I inherited a little of the gift too. For example—
I see...
SHF
I see you, with...

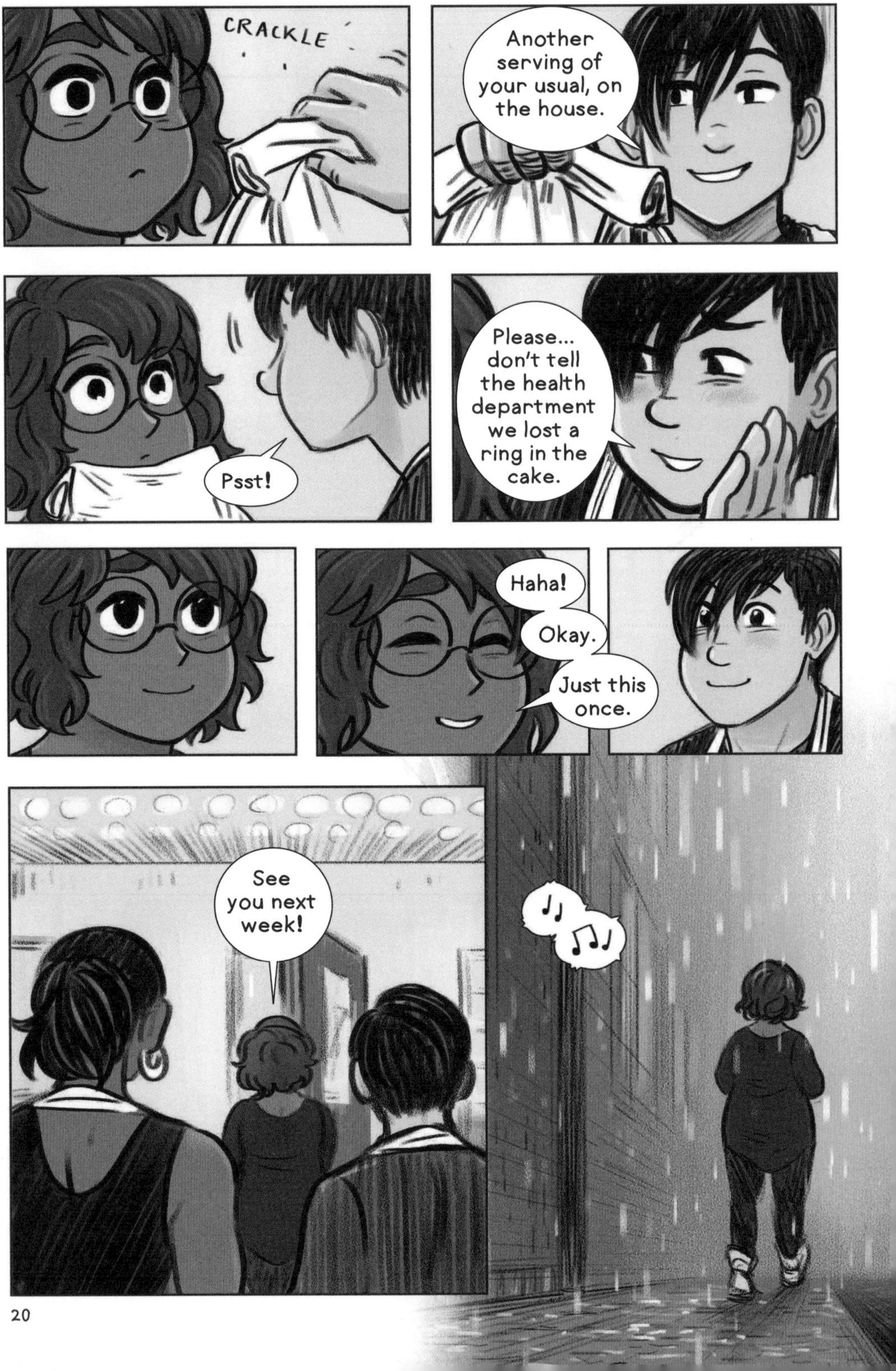
CRACKLE
Another serving of your usual, on the house.
Psst!
Please... don't tell the health department we lost a ring in the cake.
Haha!
Okay.
Just this once.
See you next week!

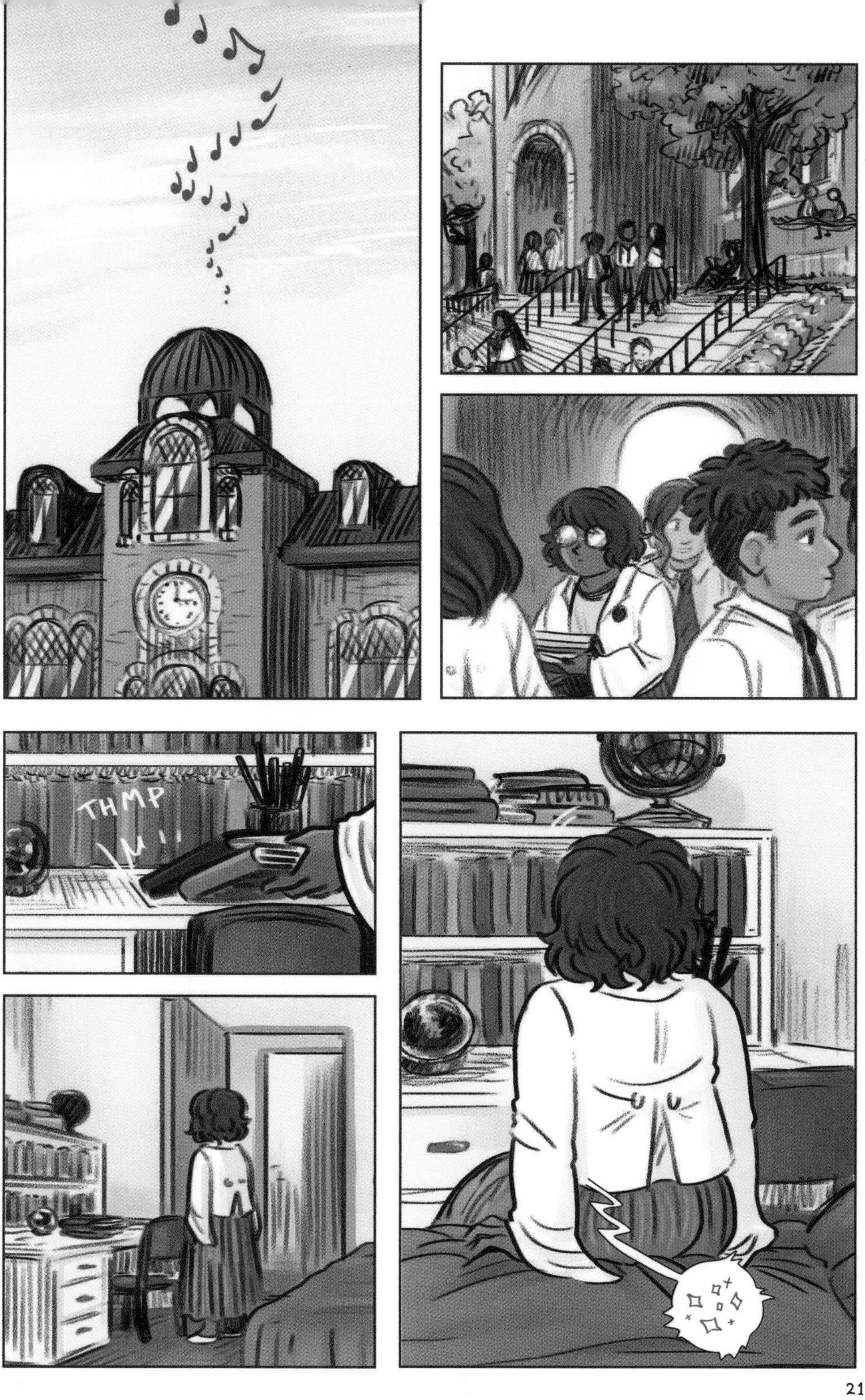
THMP

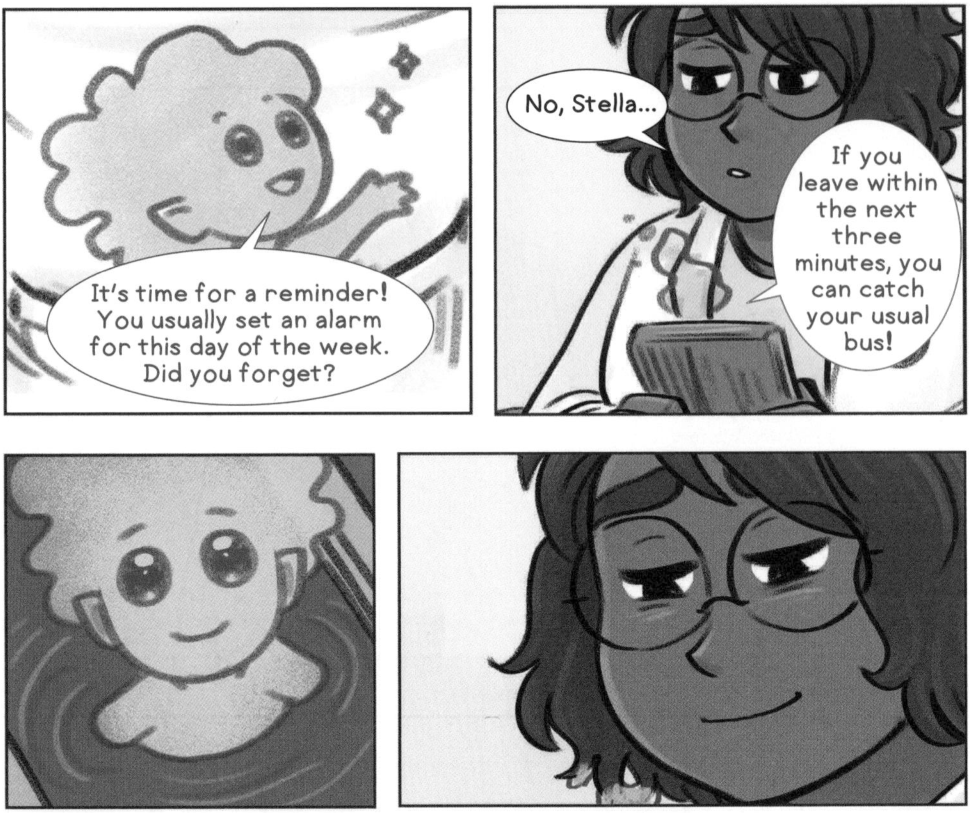
It's time for a reminder! You usually set an alarm for this day of the week. Did you forget?
No, Stella...
If you leave within the next three minutes, you can catch your usual bus!

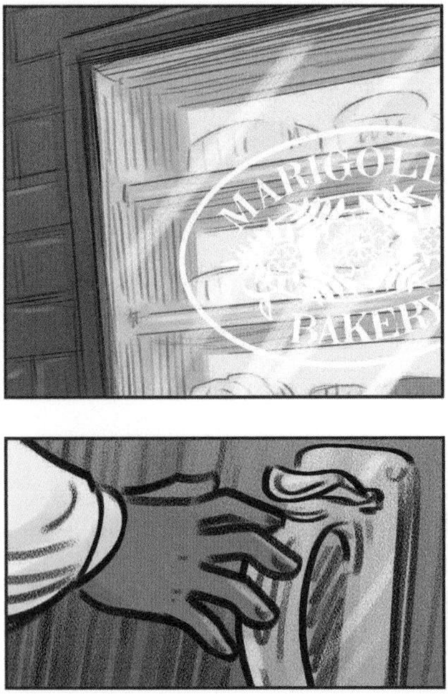

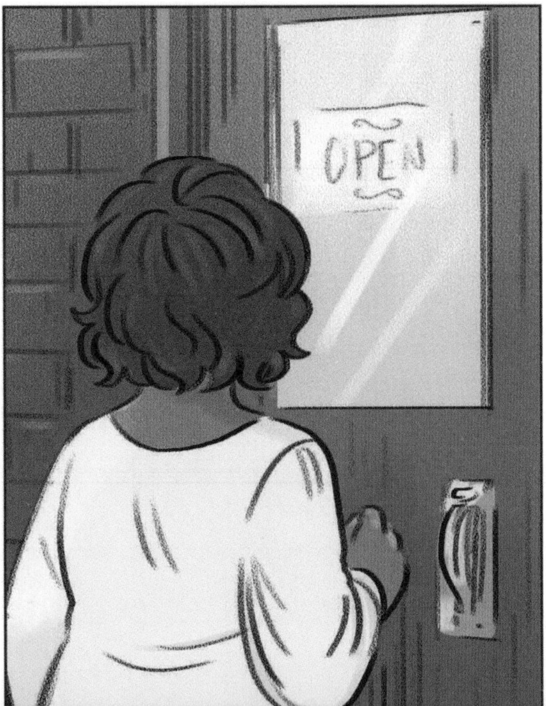
OPEN

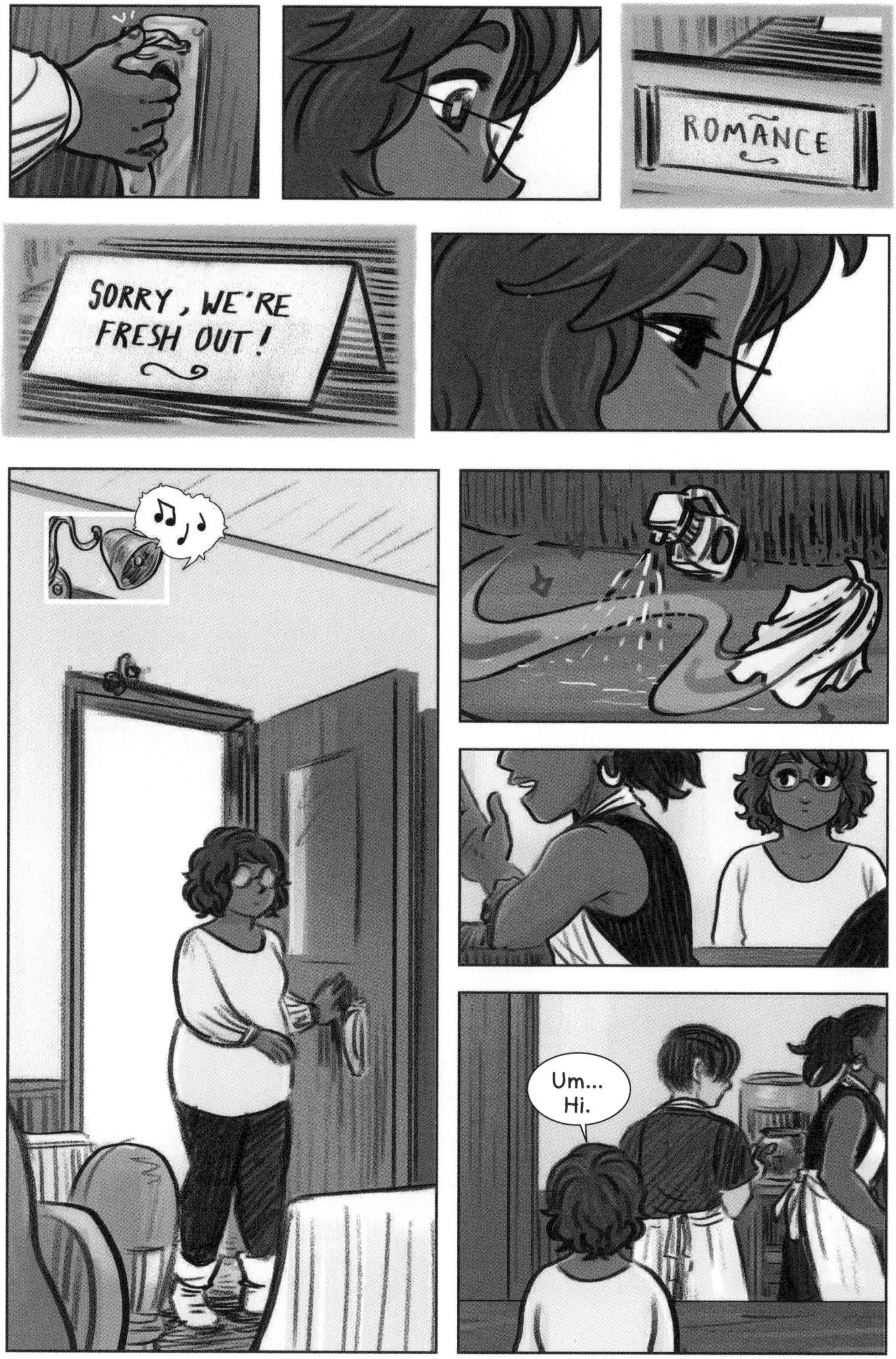
ROMANCE
SORRY, WE'RE FRESH OUT!
Um... Hi.

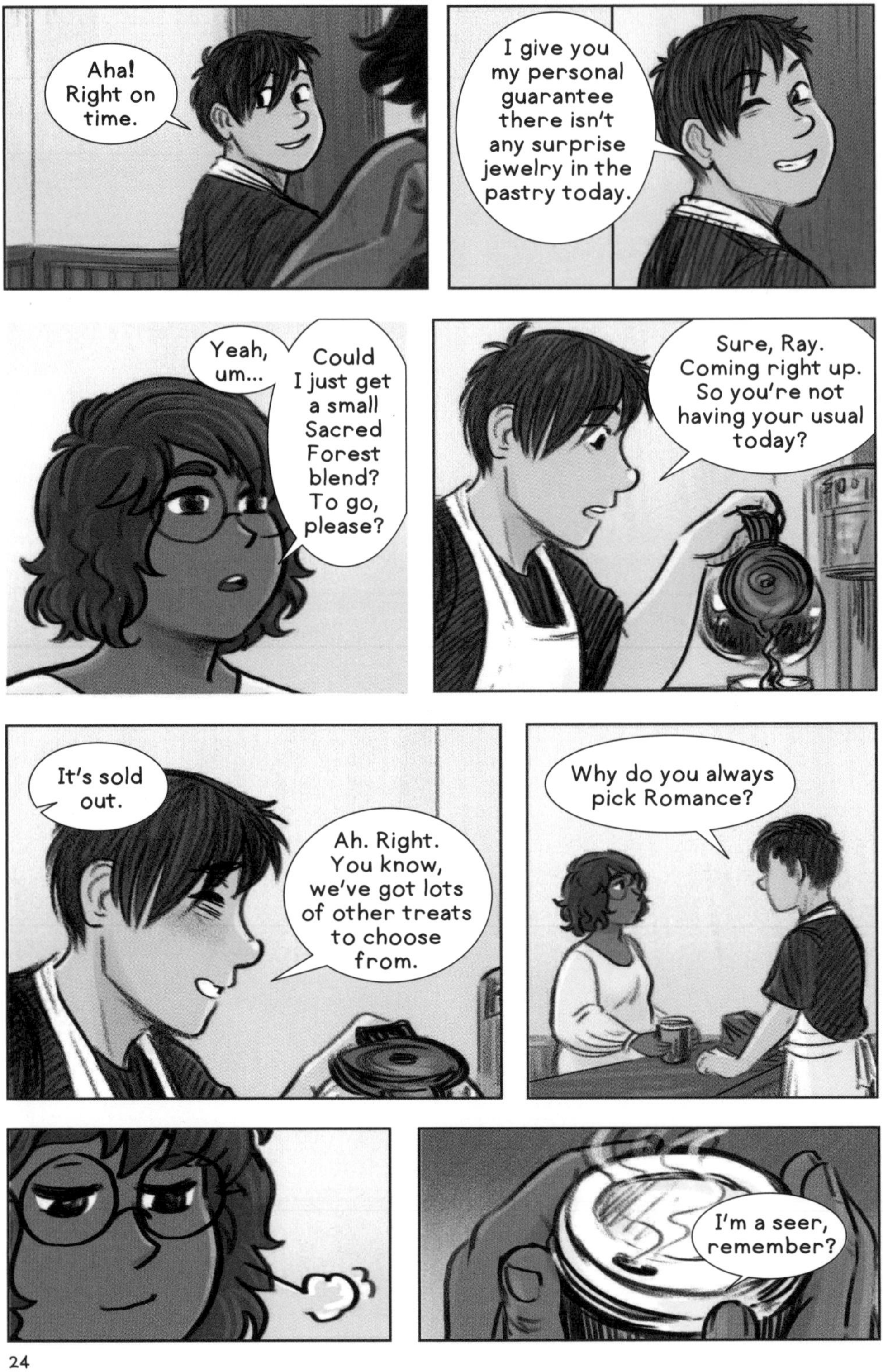
Aha! Right on time.
I give you my personal guarantee there isn't any surprise jewelry in the pastry today.
Yeah, um...
Could I just get a small Sacred Forest blend? To go, please?
Sure, Ray. Coming right up. So you're not having your usual today?
It's sold out.
Ah. Right. You know, we've got lots of other treats to choose from.
Why do you always pick Romance?
I'm a seer, remember?

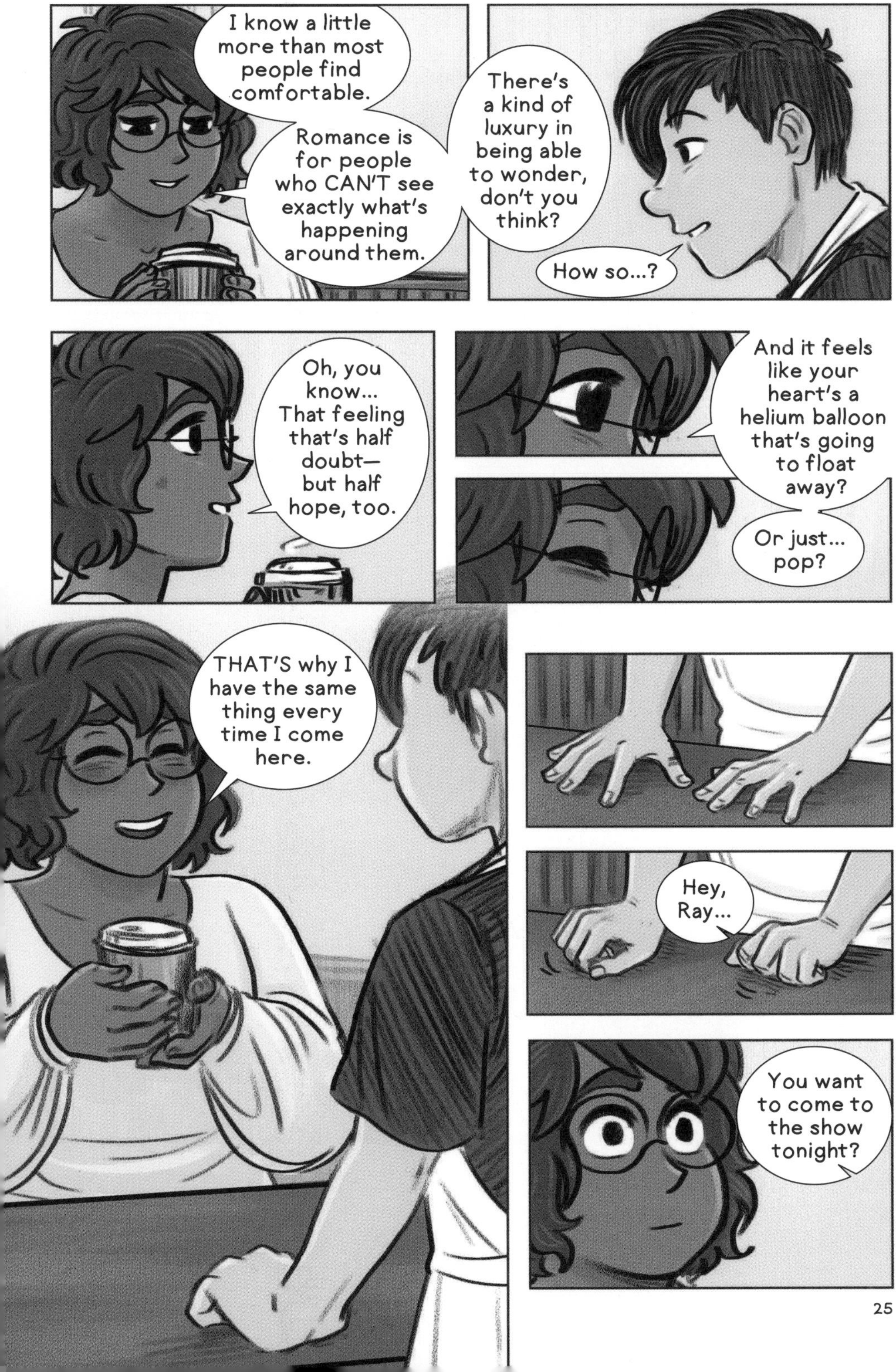
I know a little more than most people find comfortable.
Romance is for people who CAN'T see exactly what's happening around them.
There's a kind of luxury in being able to wonder, don't you think?
How so...?
Oh, you know... That feeling that's half doubt— but half hope, too.
And it feels like your heart's a helium balloon that's going to float away?
Or just... pop?
THAT'S why I have the same thing every time I come here.
Hey, Ray...
You want to come to the show tonight?

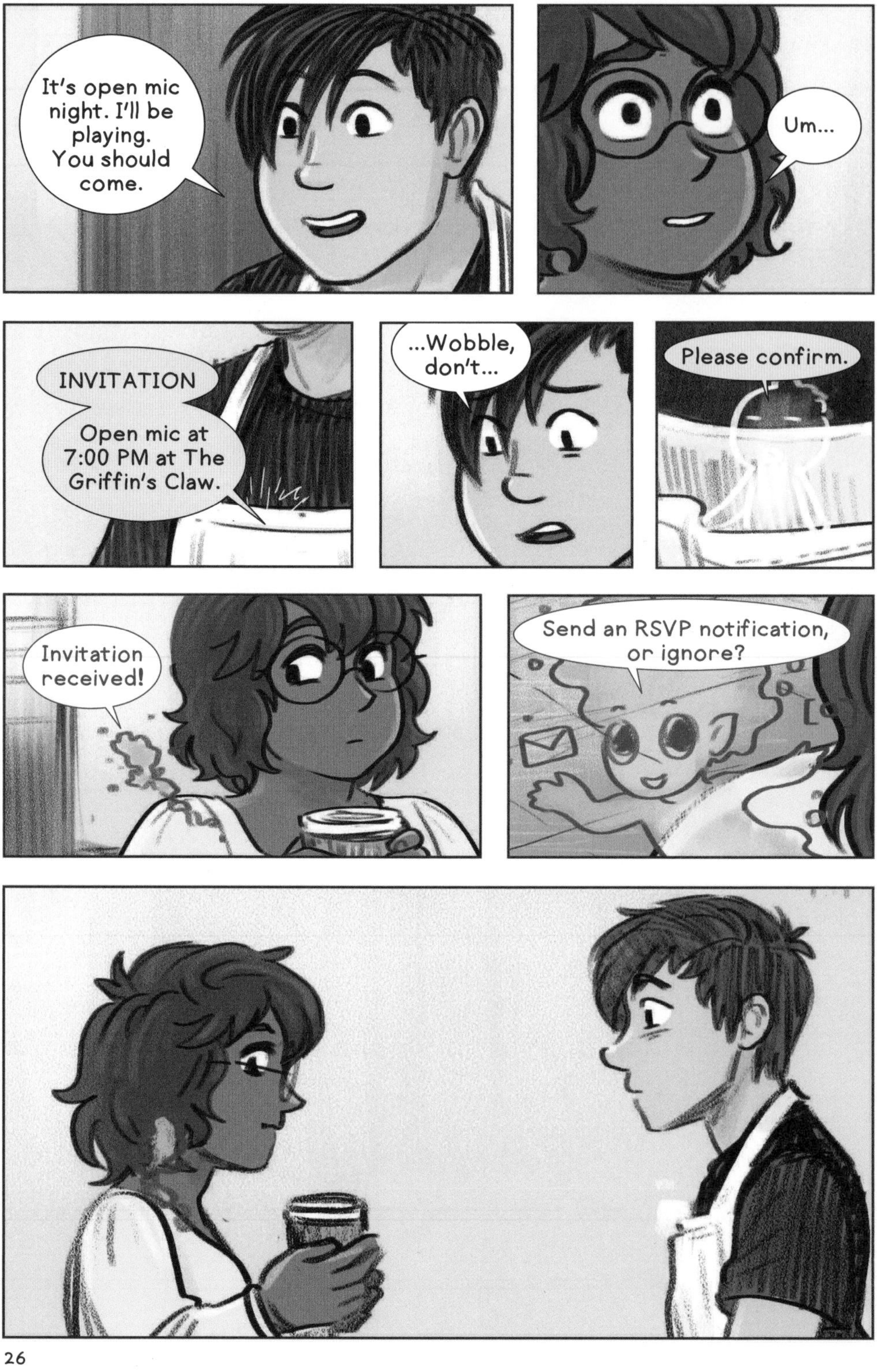
It's open mic night. I'll be playing. You should come.
Um...
INVITATION
Open mic at 7:00 PM at The Griffin's Claw.
...Wobble, don't...
Please confirm.
Invitation received!
Send an RSVP notification, or ignore?

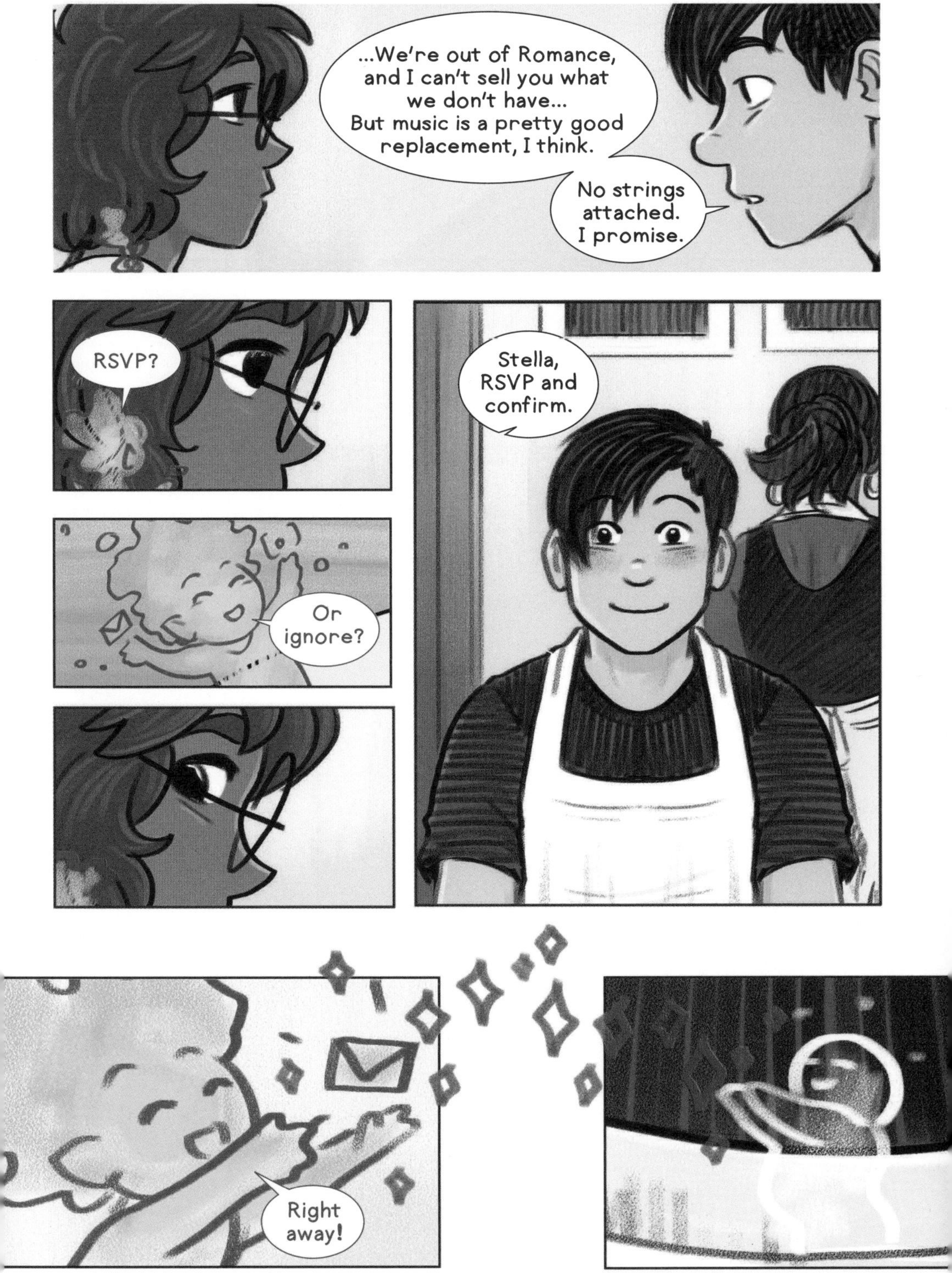
...We're out of Romance, and I can't sell you what we don't have...
But music is a pretty good replacement, I think.
No strings attached. I promise.
RSVP?
Or ignore?
Stella, RSVP and confirm.
Right away!

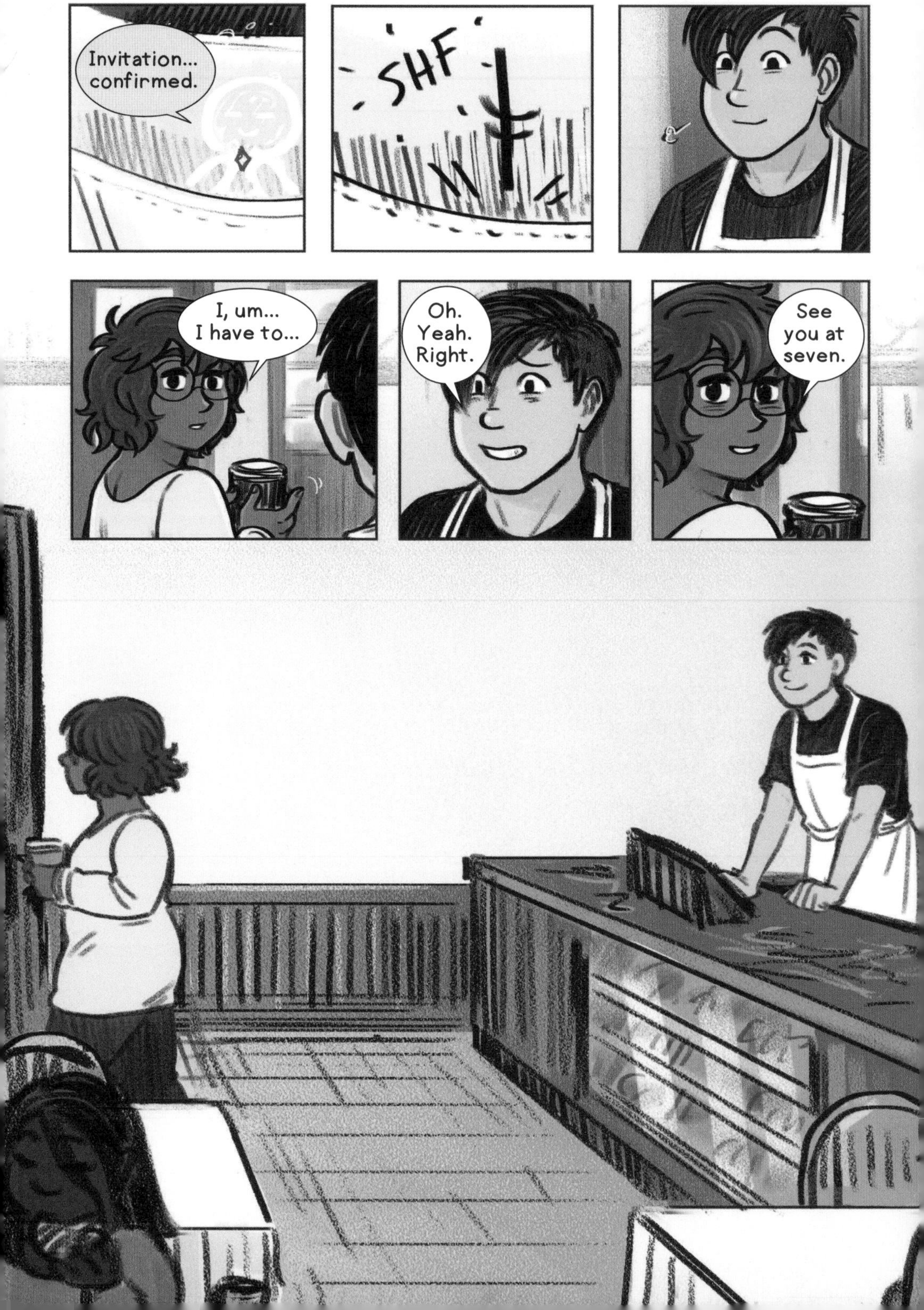
Invitation... confirmed.
SHF
I, um... I have to...
Oh. Yeah. Right.
See you at seven.

CHAPTER 3

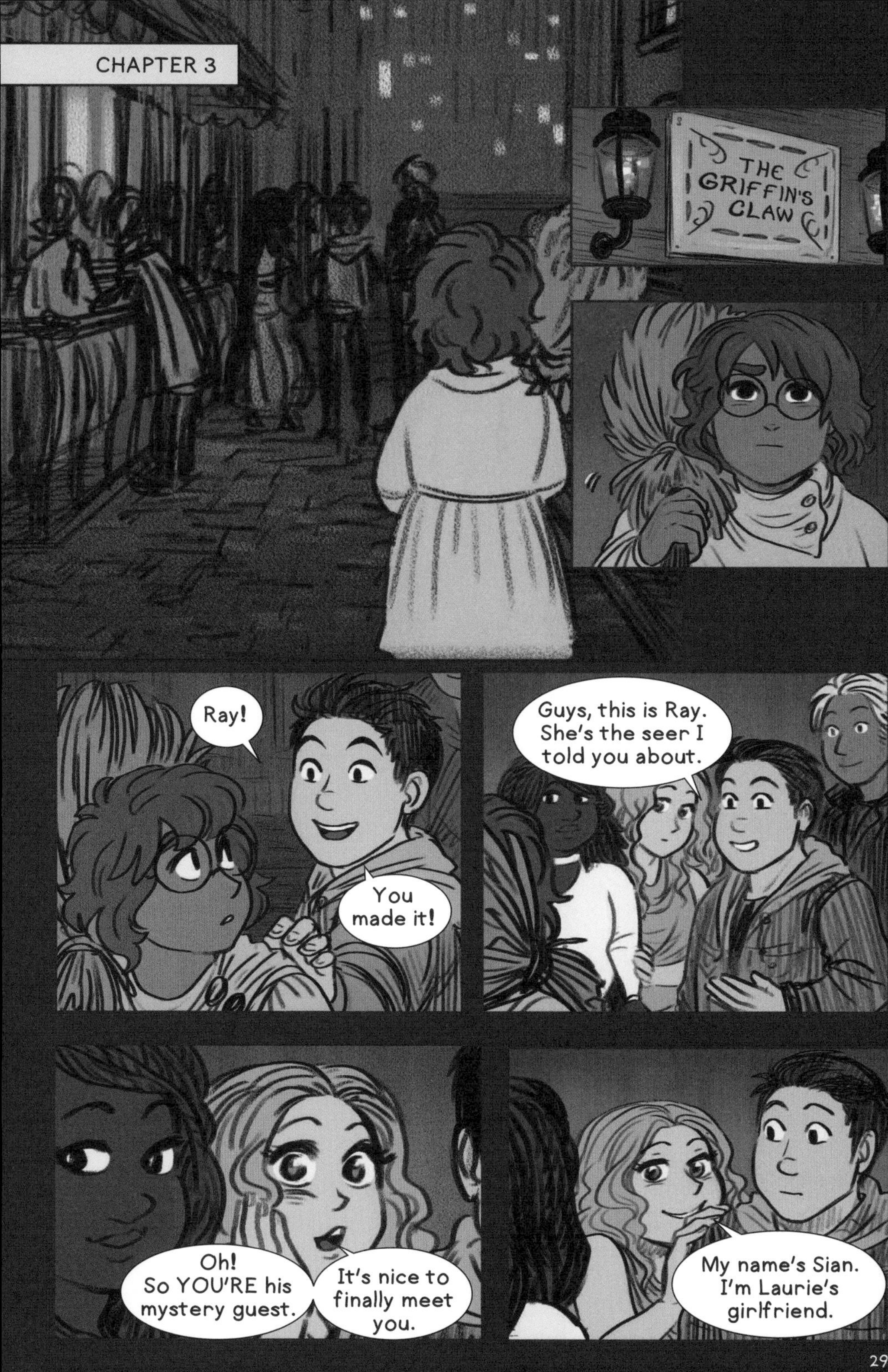
THE GRIFFIN'S CLAW
Ray!
You made it!
Guys, this is Ray. She's the seer I told you about.
Oh! So YOU'RE his mystery guest.
It's nice to finally meet you.
My name's Sian. I'm Laurie's girlfriend.

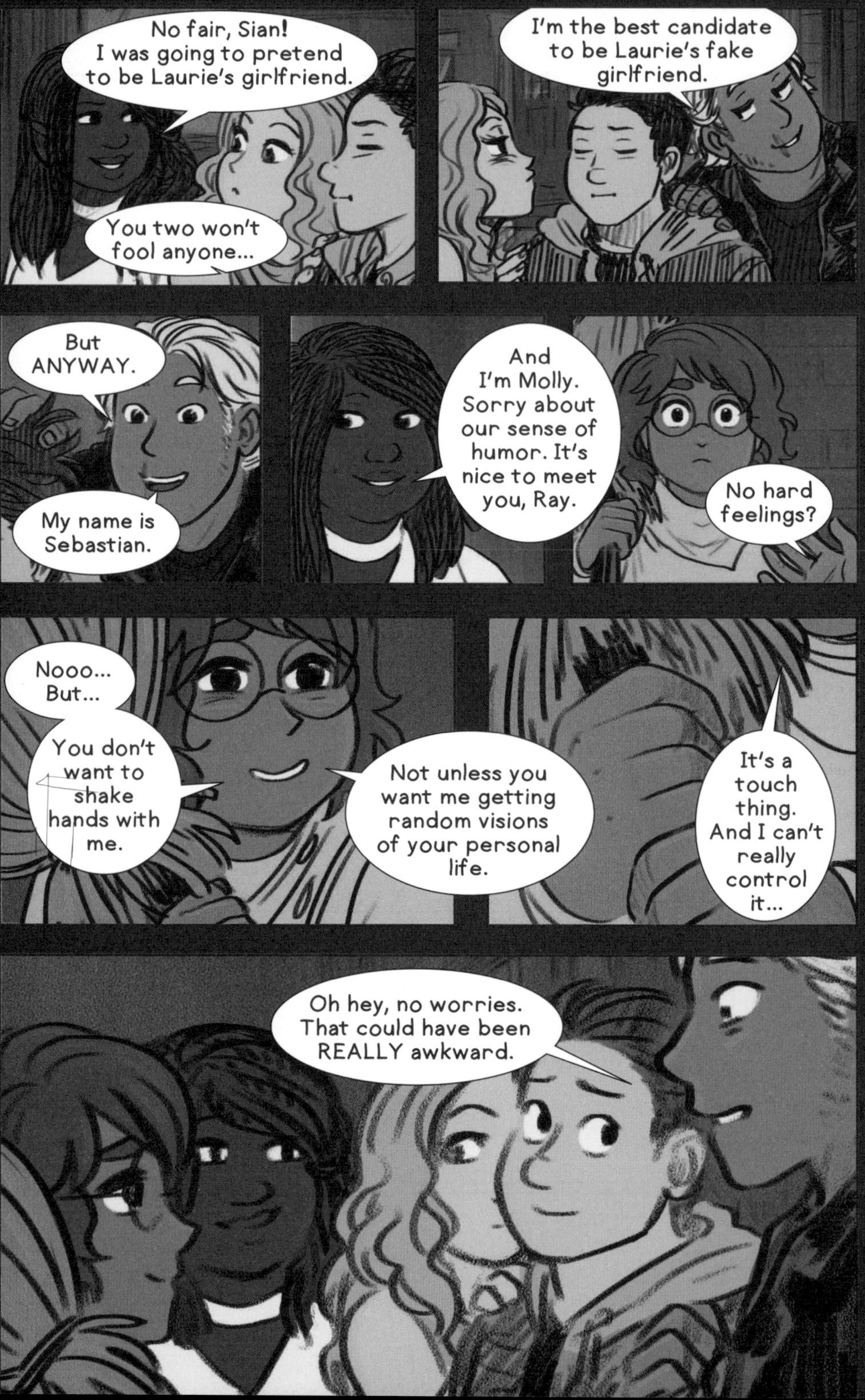
No fair, Sian! I was going to pretend to be Laurie's girlfriend.
You two won't fool anyone...
I'm the best candidate to be Laurie's fake girlfriend.
But ANYWAY.
My name is Sebastian.
And I'm Molly. Sorry about our sense of humor. It's nice to meet you, Ray.
No hard feelings?
Nooo... But...
You don't want to shake hands with me.
Not unless you want me getting random visions of your personal life.
It's a touch thing. And I can't really control it...
Oh hey, no worries. That could have been REALLY awkward.

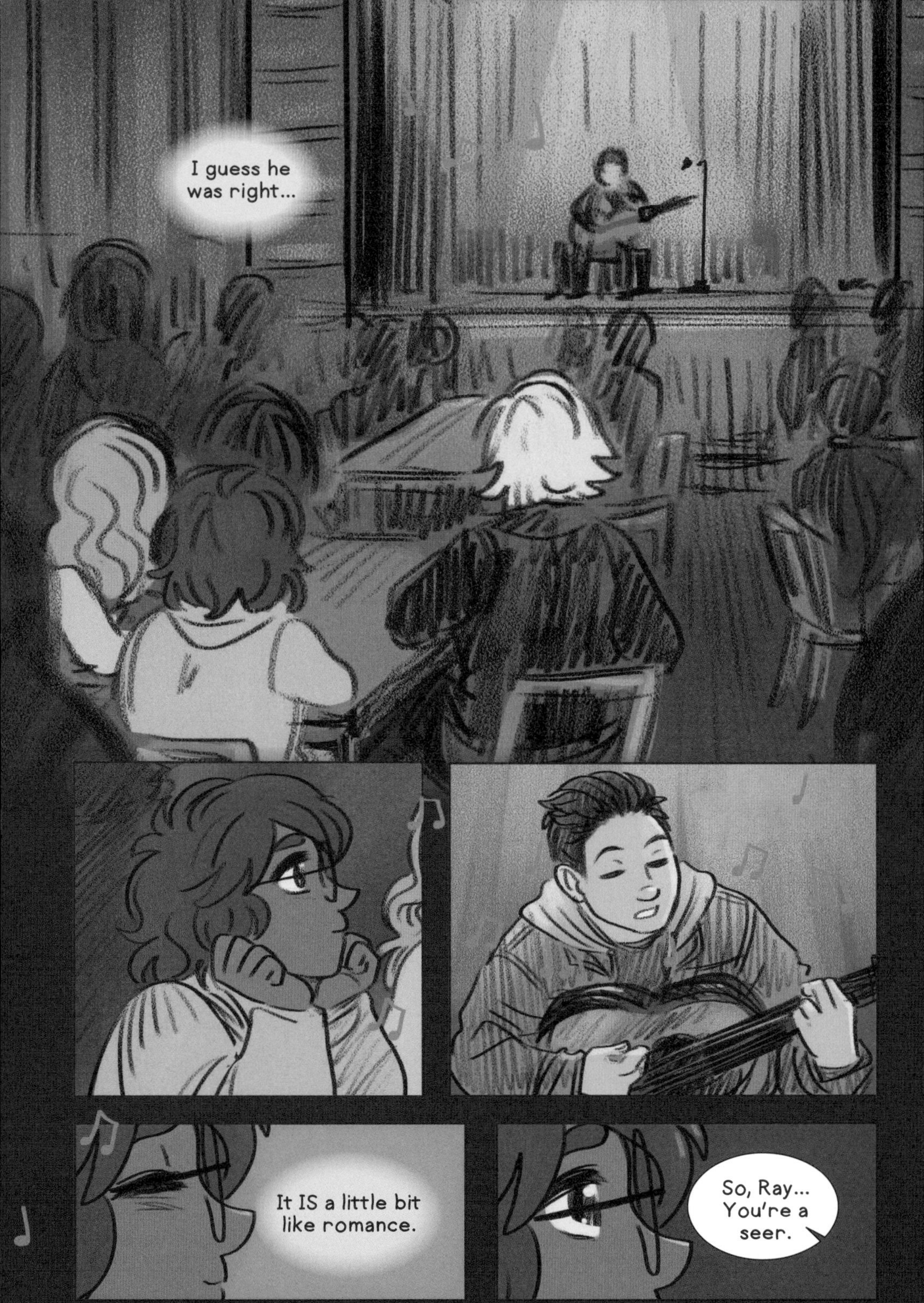
I guess he was right...
It IS a little bit like romance.
So, Ray... You're a seer.

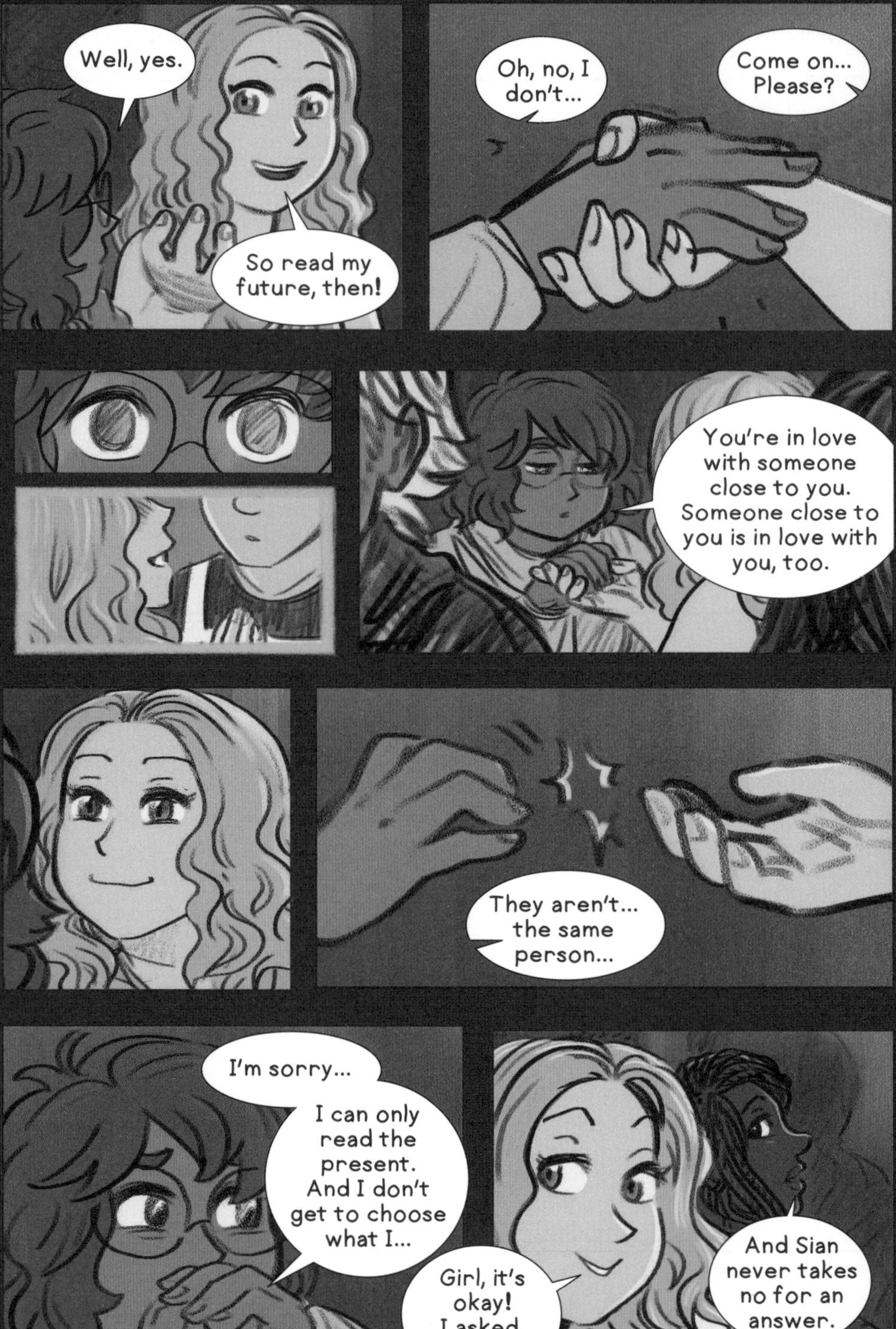
Well, yes.
So read my future, then!
Oh, no, I don't...
Come on... Please?
You're in love with someone close to you. Someone close to you is in love with you, too.
They aren't... the same person...
I'm sorry...
I can only read the present. And I don't get to choose what I...
Girl, it's okay! I asked, after all.
And Sian never takes no for an answer.

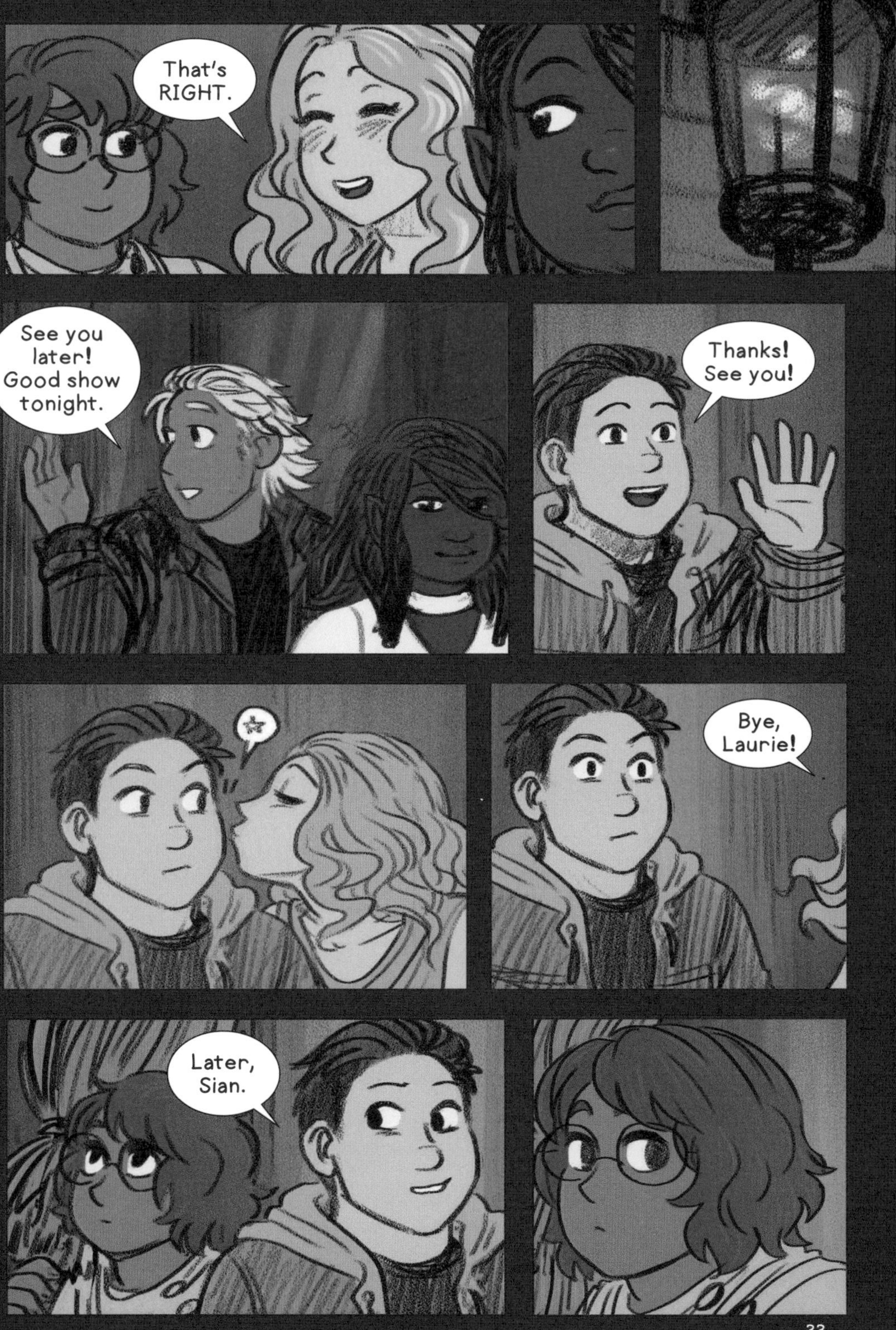
That's RIGHT.
See you later! Good show tonight.
Thanks! See you!
Bye, Laurie!
Later, Sian.

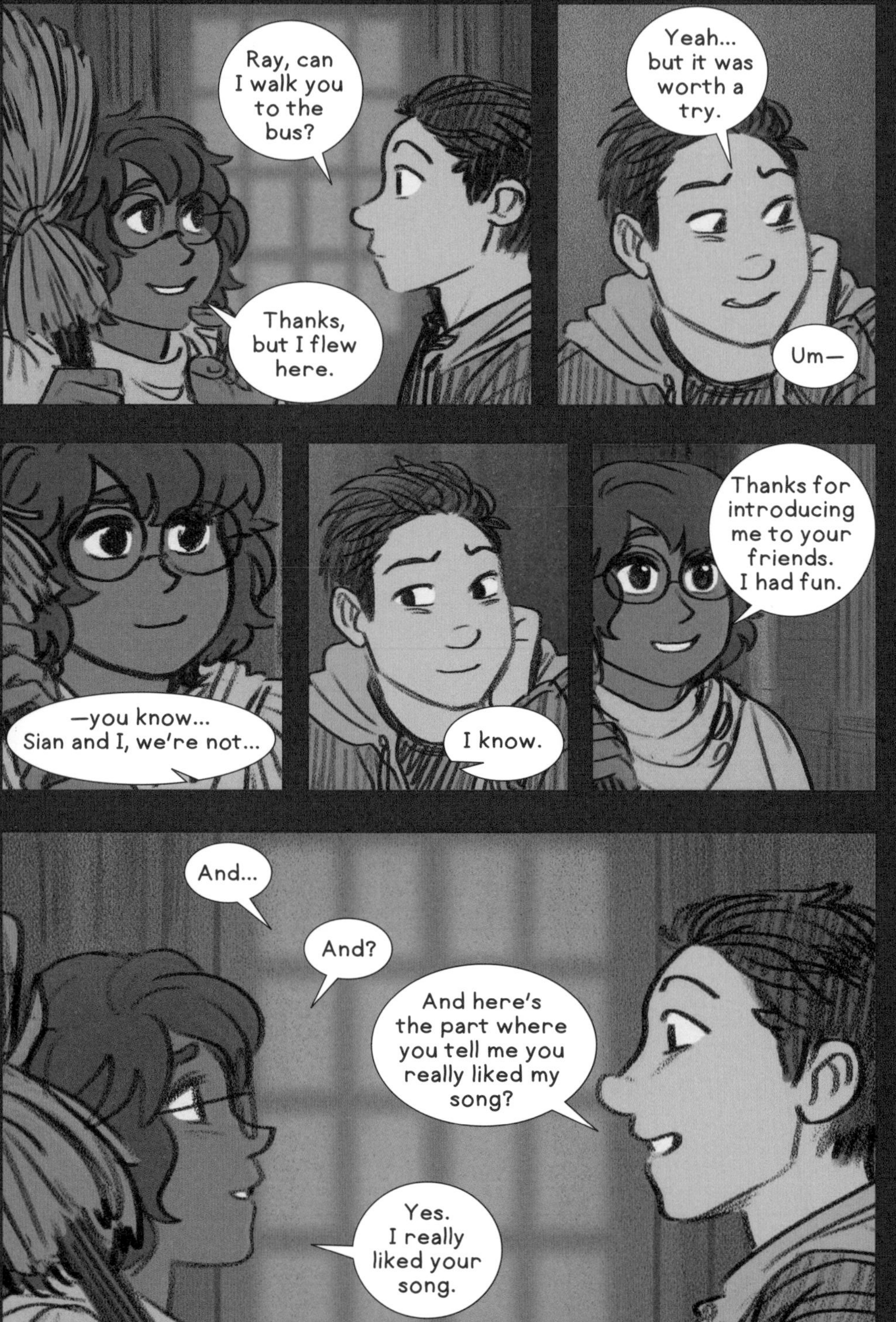
Ray, can I walk you to the bus?
Thanks, but I flew here.
Yeah... but it was worth a try.
Um—
—you know... Sian and I, we're not...
I know.
Thanks for introducing me to your friends. I had fun.
And...
And?
And here's the part where you tell me you really liked my song?
Yes. I really liked your song.

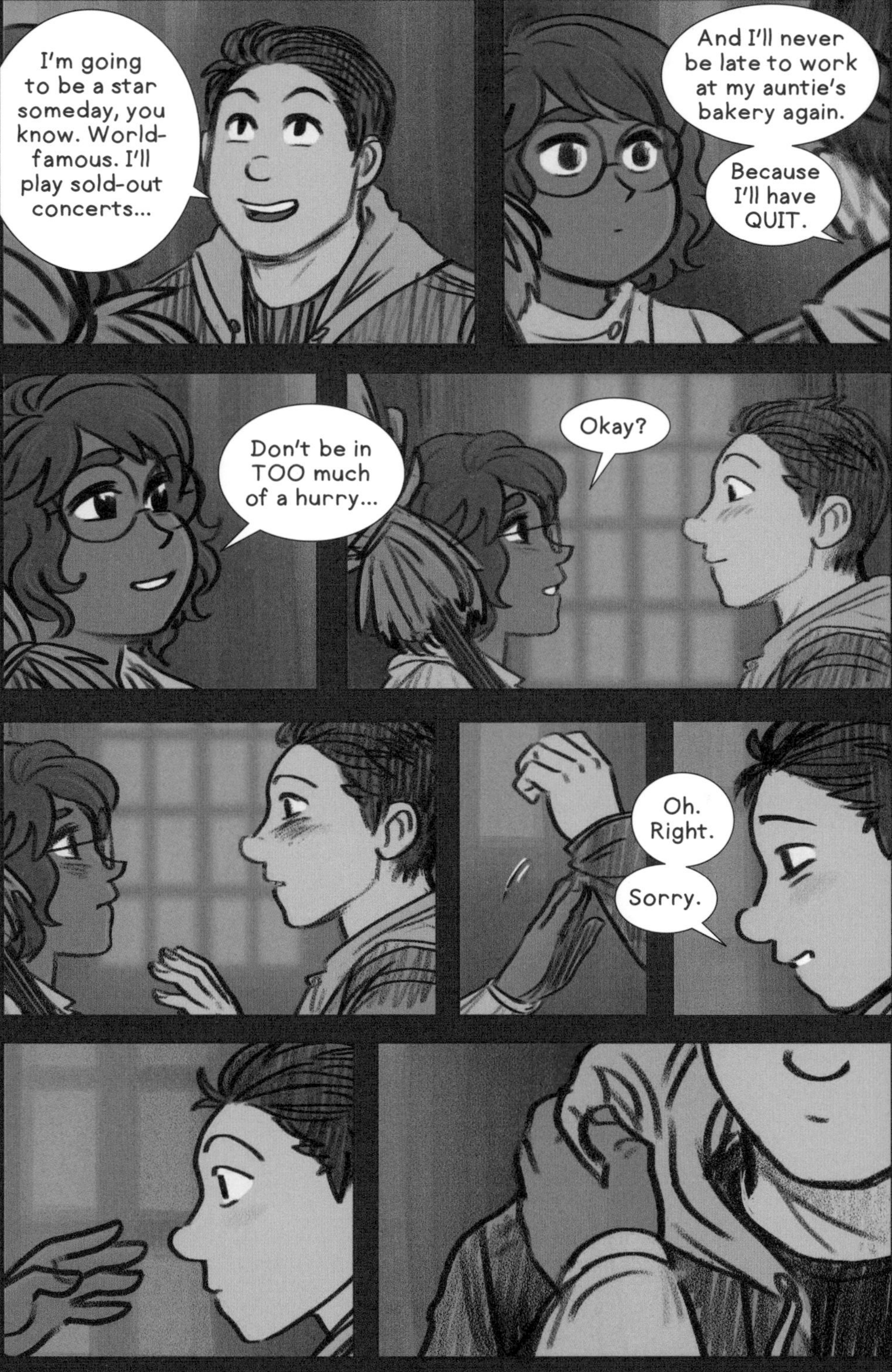
I'm going to be a star someday, you know. World-famous. I'll play sold-out concerts...
And I'll never be late to work at my auntie's bakery again.
Because I'll have QUIT.
Don't be in TOO much of a hurry...
Okay?
Oh. Right.
Sorry.

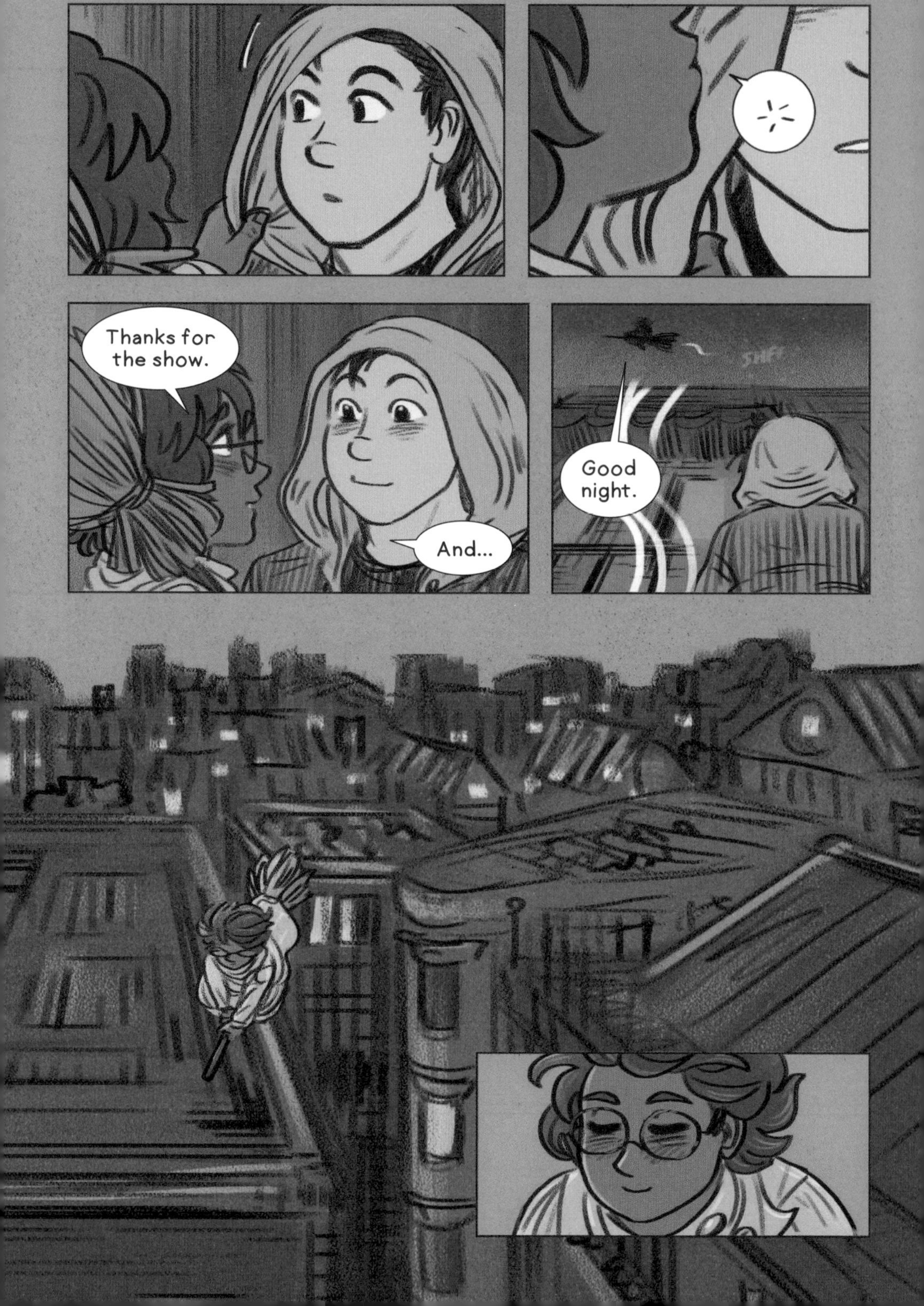

Thanks for the show.
And...
SHFF
Good night.

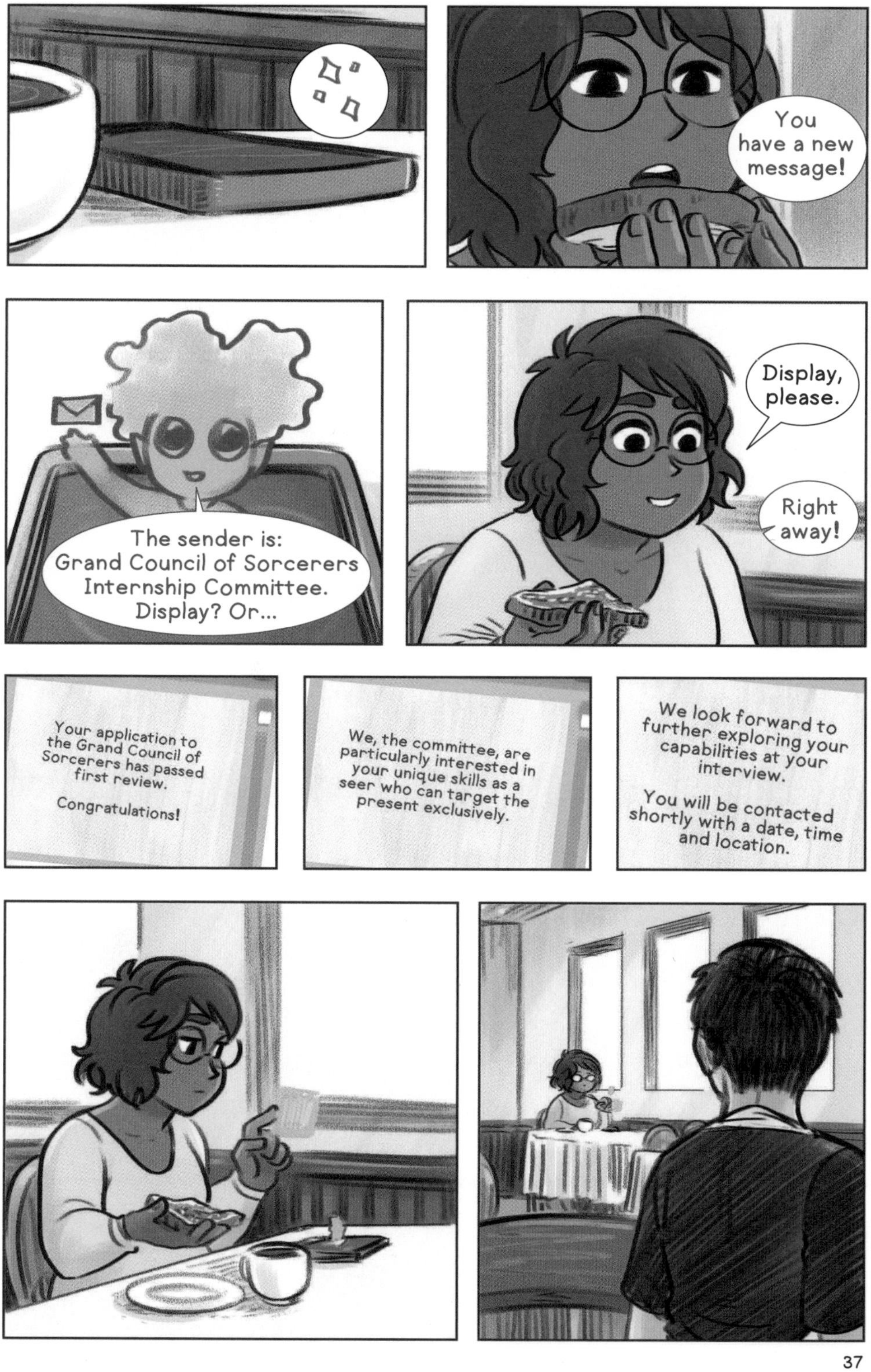
You have a new message!
The sender is: Grand Council of Sorcerers Internship Committee. Display? Or...
Display, please.
Right away!
Your application to the Grand Council of Sorcerers has passed first review.
Congratulations!
We, the committee, are particularly interested in your unique skills as a seer who can target the present exclusively.
We look forward to further exploring your capabilities at your interview.
You will be contacted shortly with a date, time and location.

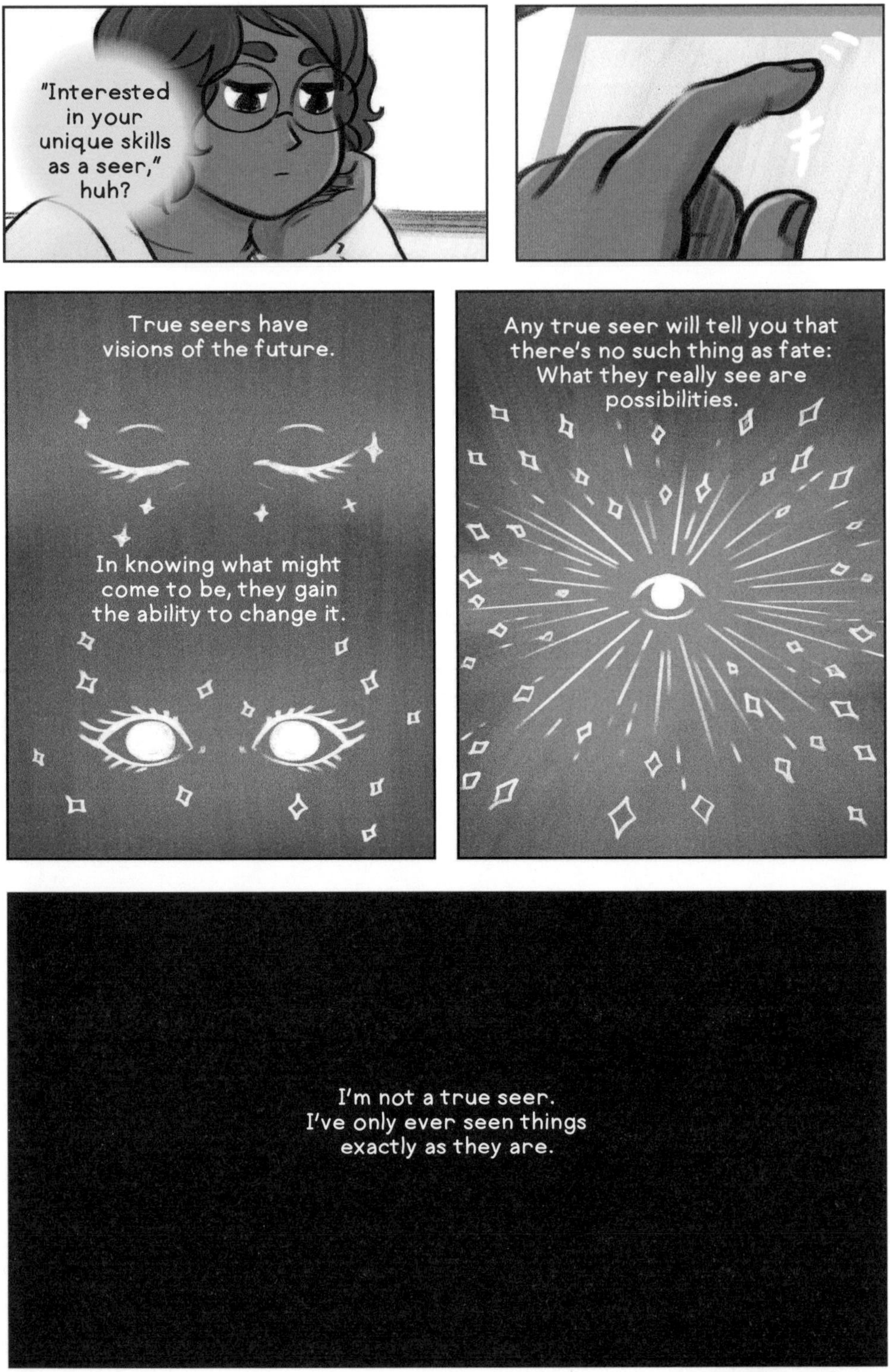
"Interested in your unique skills as a seer," huh?
True seers have visions of the future.
In knowing what might come to be, they gain the ability to change it.
Any true seer will tell you that there's no such thing as fate: What they really see are possibilities.
I'm not a true seer. I've only ever seen things exactly as they are.

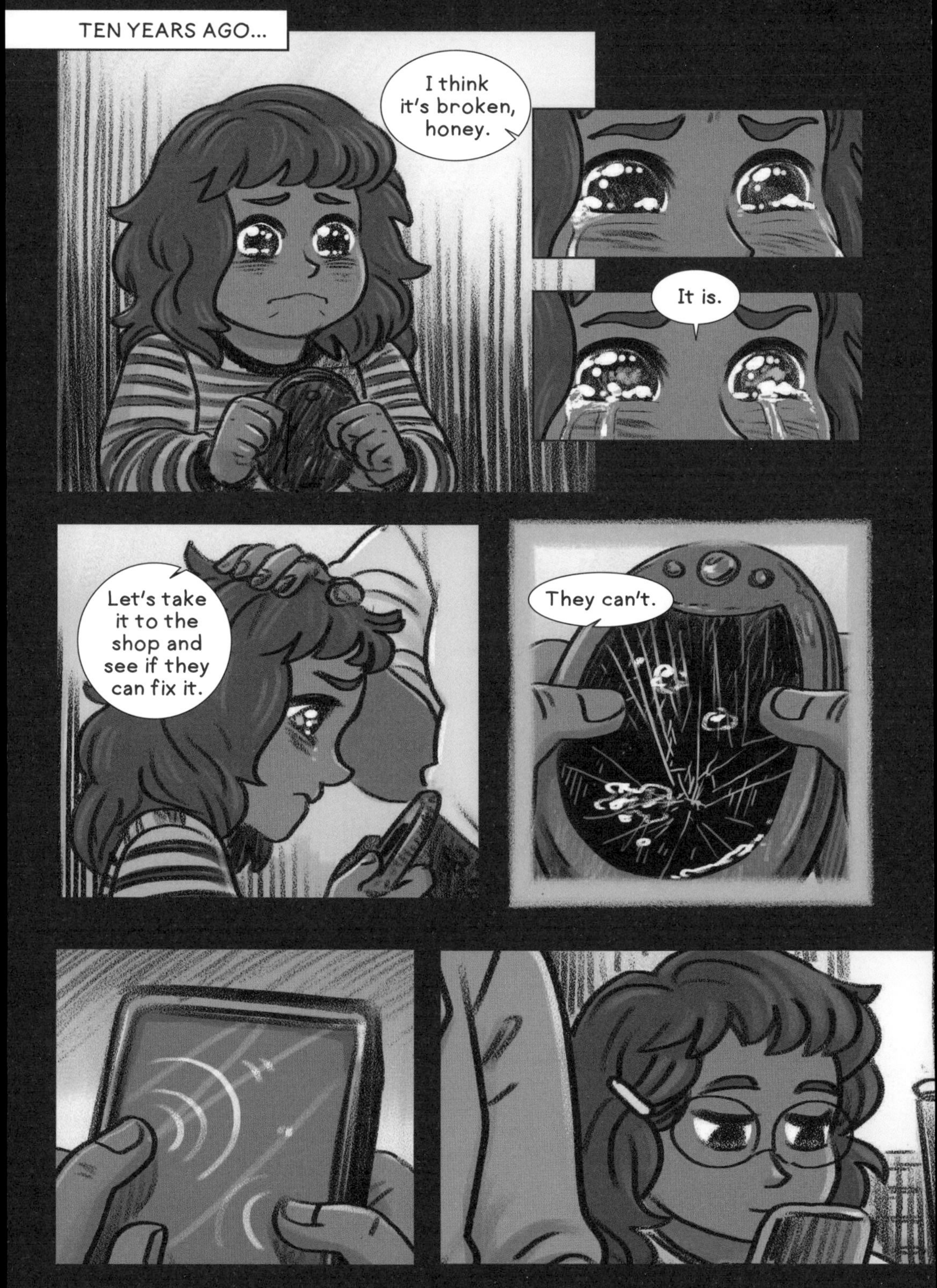
TEN YEARS AGO...
I think it's broken, honey.
It is.
Let's take it to the shop and see if they can fix it.
They can't.

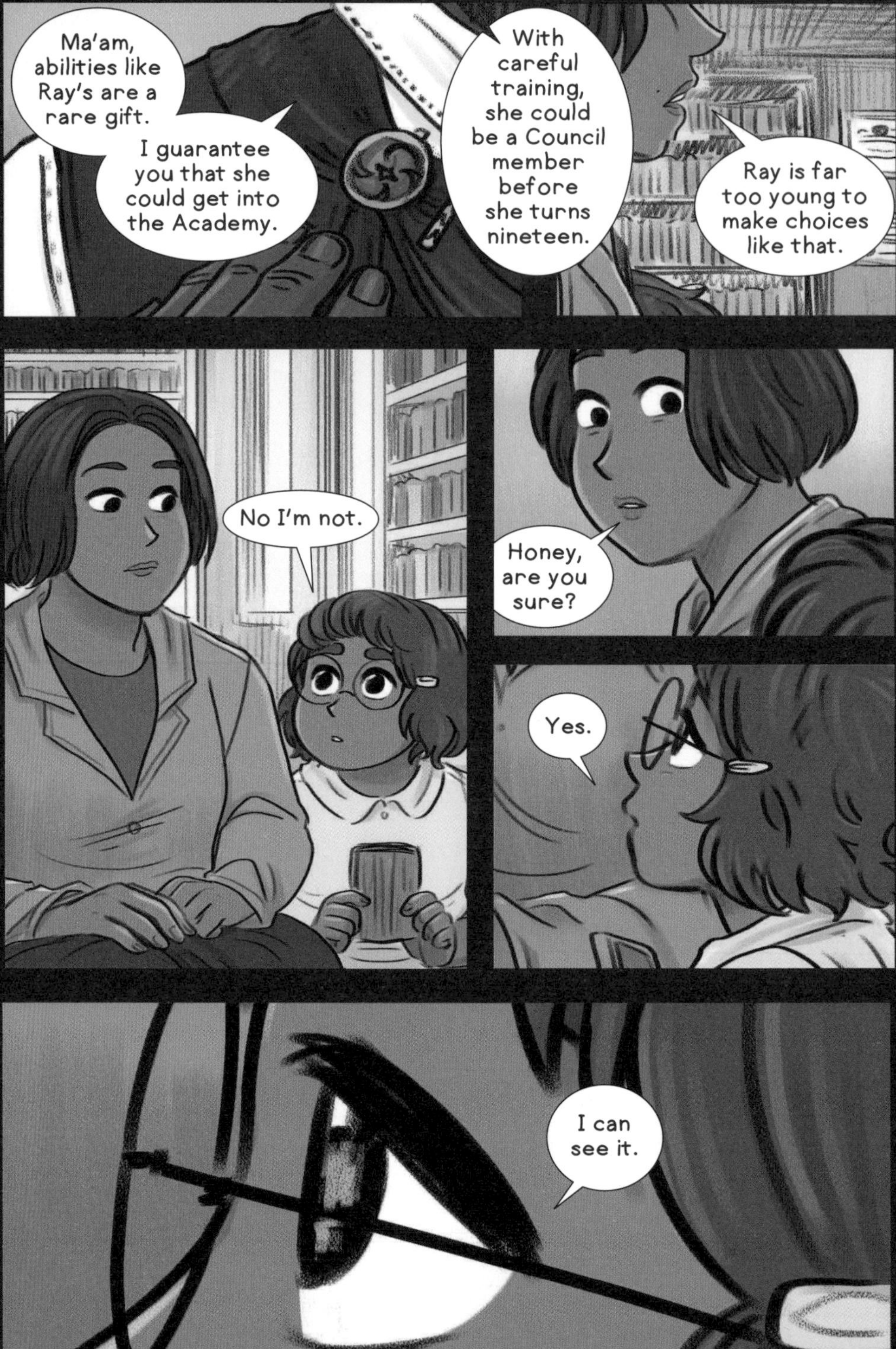
Ma'am, abilities like Ray's are a rare gift.
I guarantee you that she could get into the Academy.
With careful training, she could be a Council member before she turns nineteen.
Ray is far too young to make choices like that.
No I'm not.
Honey, are you sure?
Yes.
I can see it.

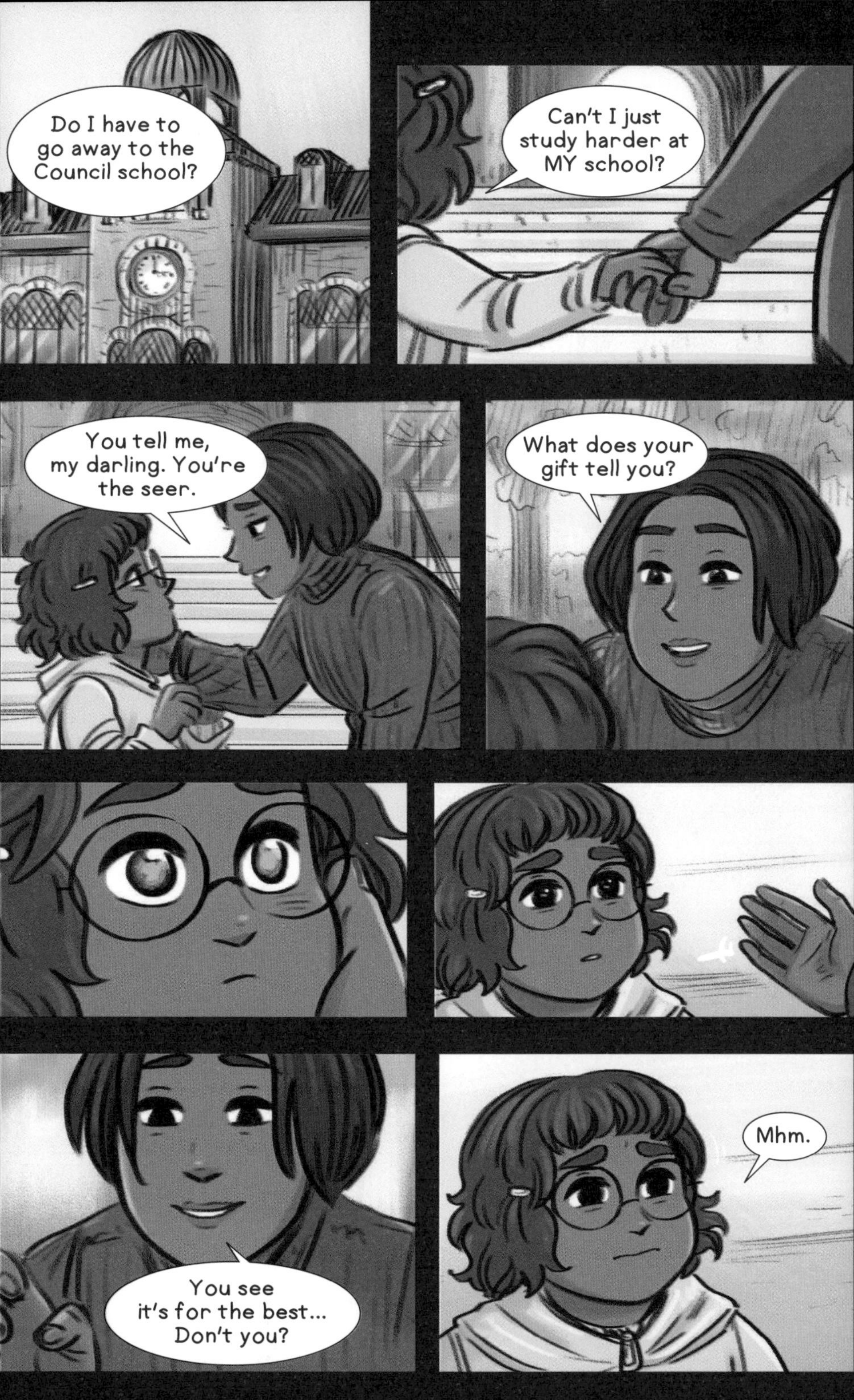
Do I have to go away to the Council school?
Can't I just study harder at MY school?
You tell me, my darling. You're the seer.
What does your gift tell you?
You see it's for the best... Don't you?
Mhm.

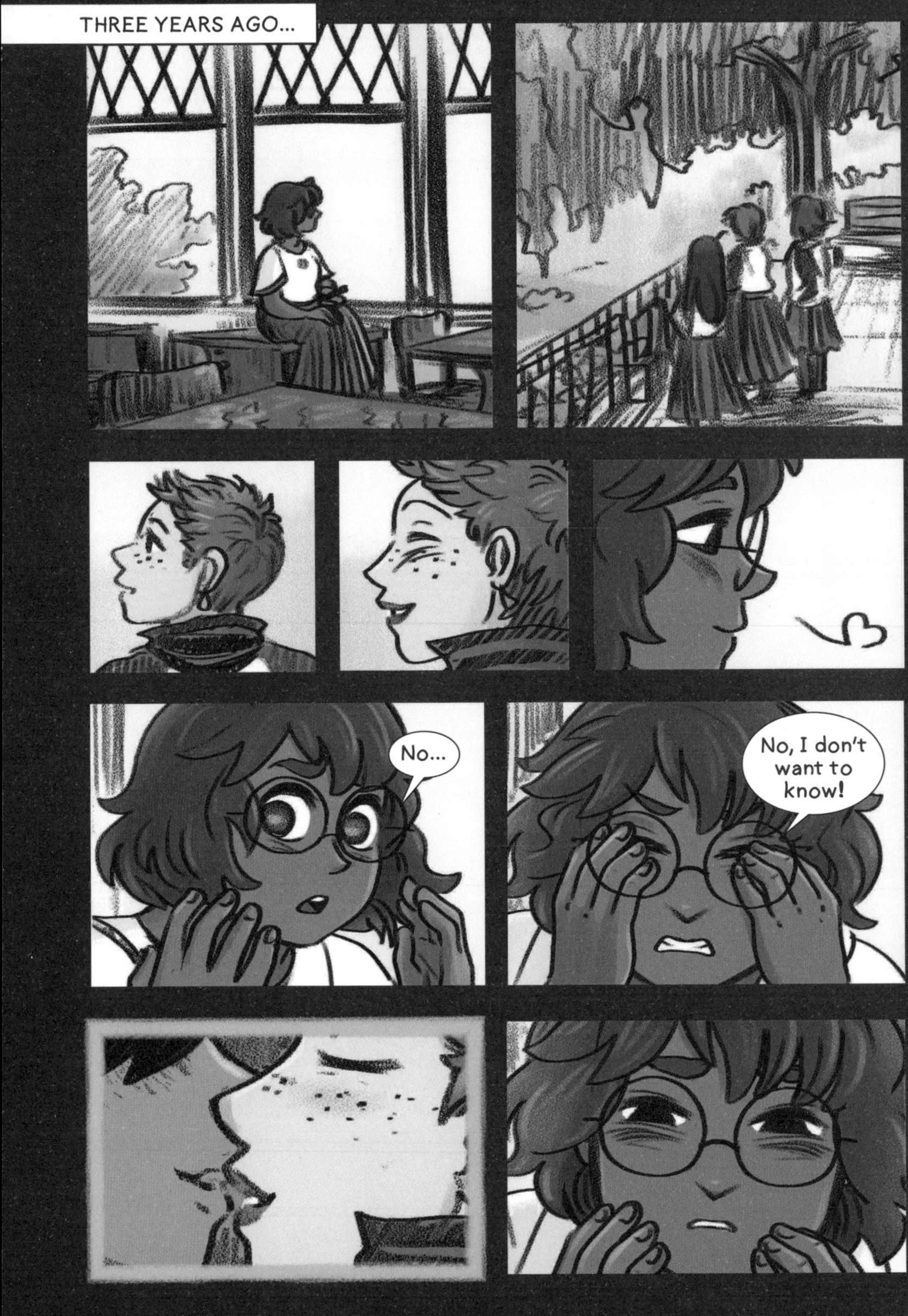
THREE YEARS AGO...
No...
No, I don't want to know!

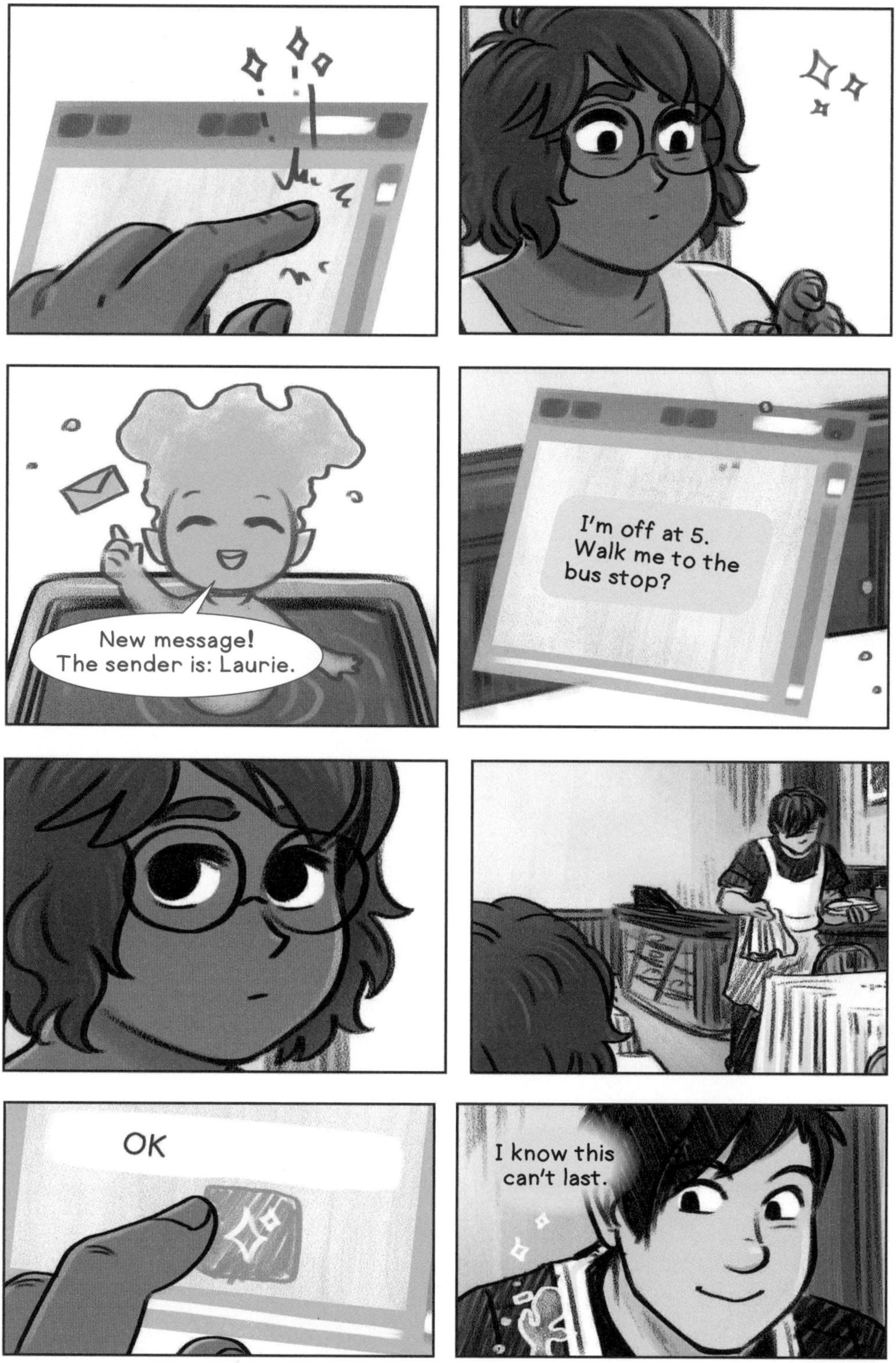
New message!
The sender is: Laurie.
I'm off at 5. Walk me to the bus stop?
OK
I know this can't last.

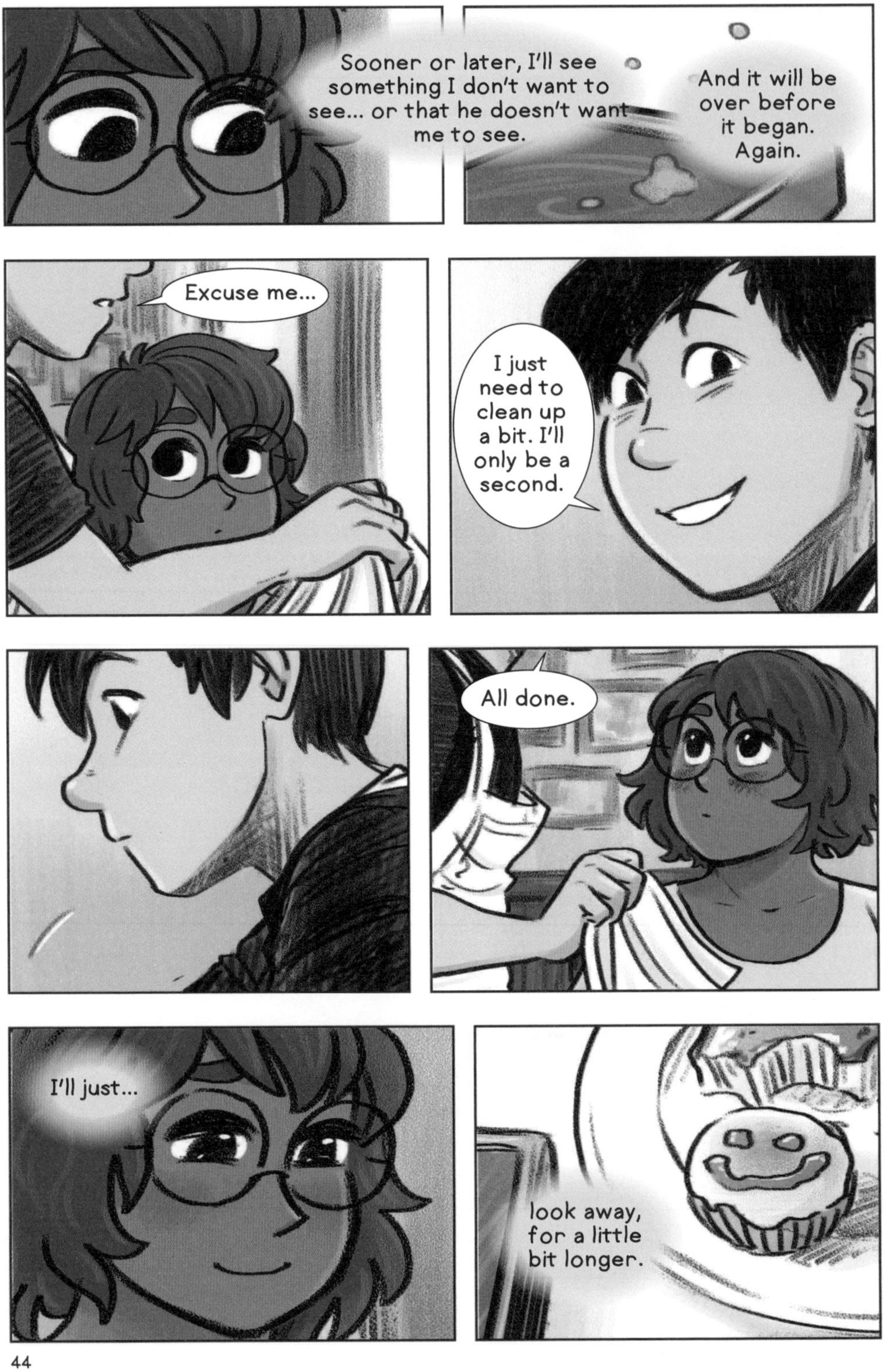
Sooner or later, I'll see something I don't want to see... or that he doesn't want me to see.
And it will be over before it began. Again.
Excuse me...
I just need to clean up a bit. I'll only be a second.
All done.
I'll just...
look away, for a little bit longer.

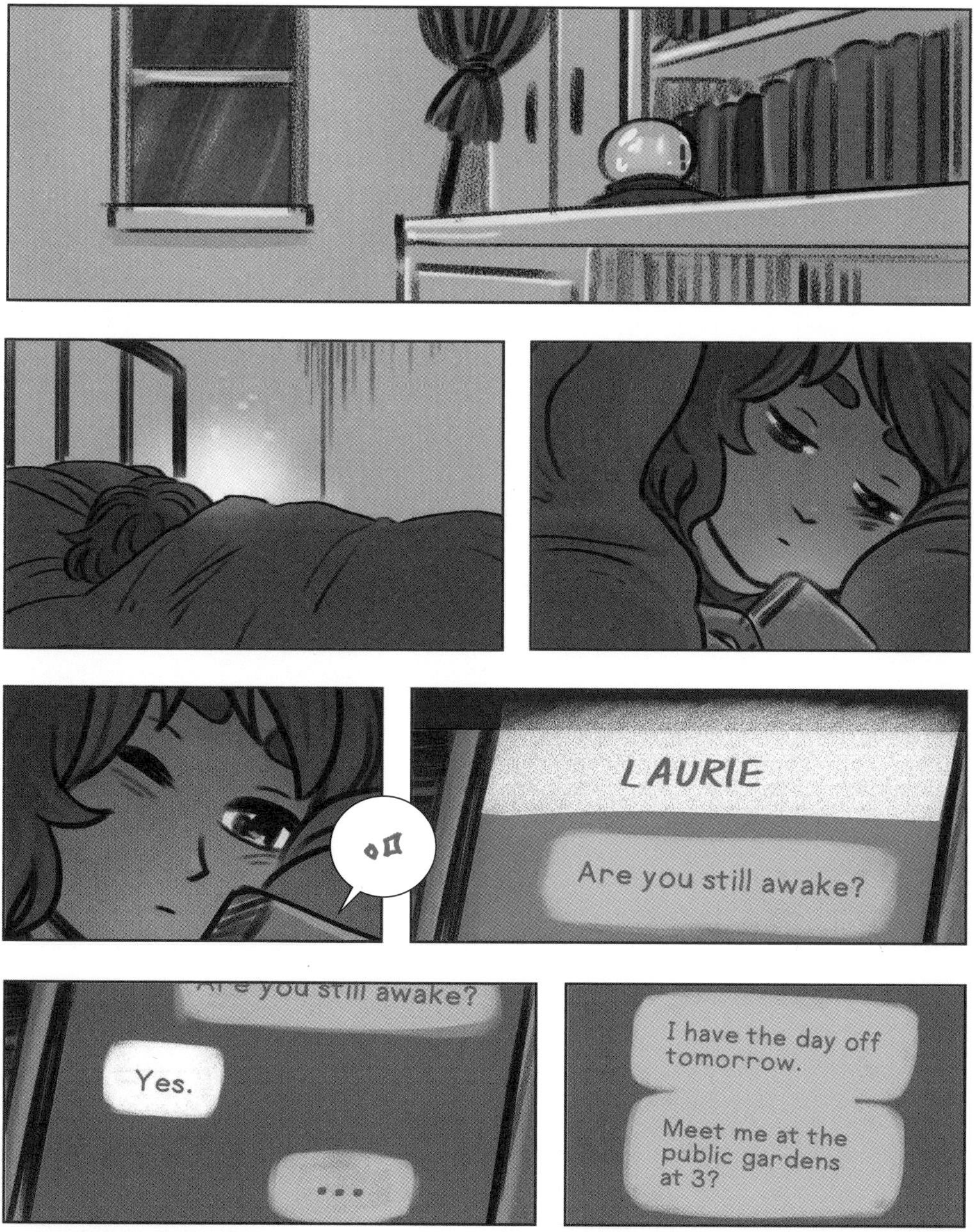
LAURIE
Are you still awake?
Yes.
...
I have the day off tomorrow.
Meet me at the public gardens at 3?
OK

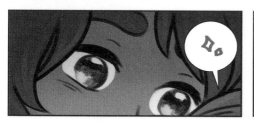

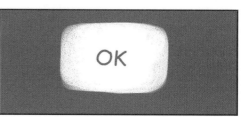

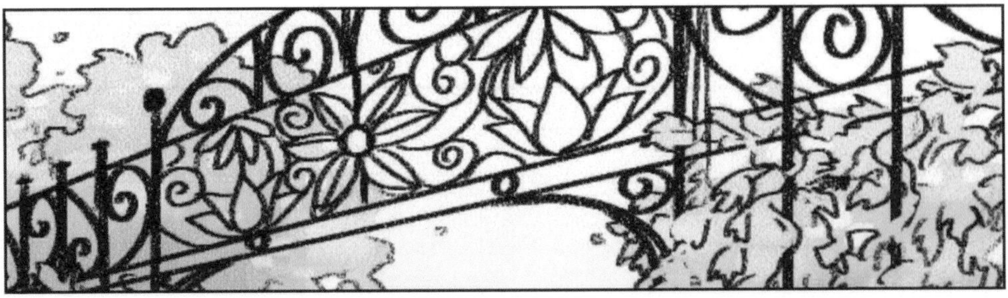

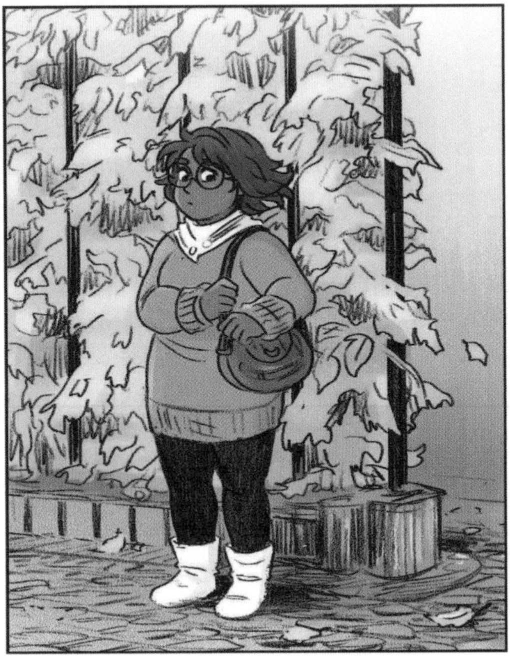

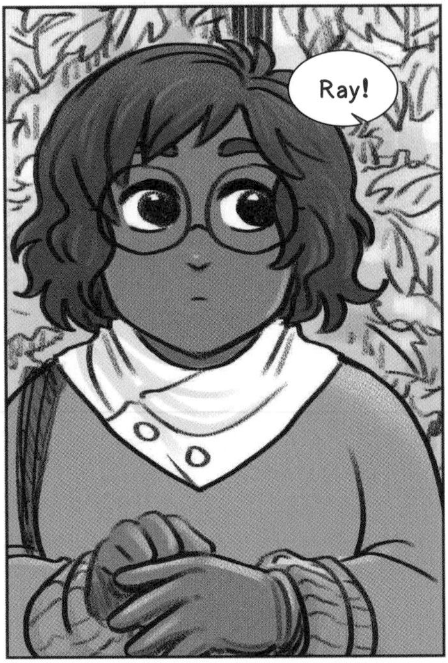
Ray!

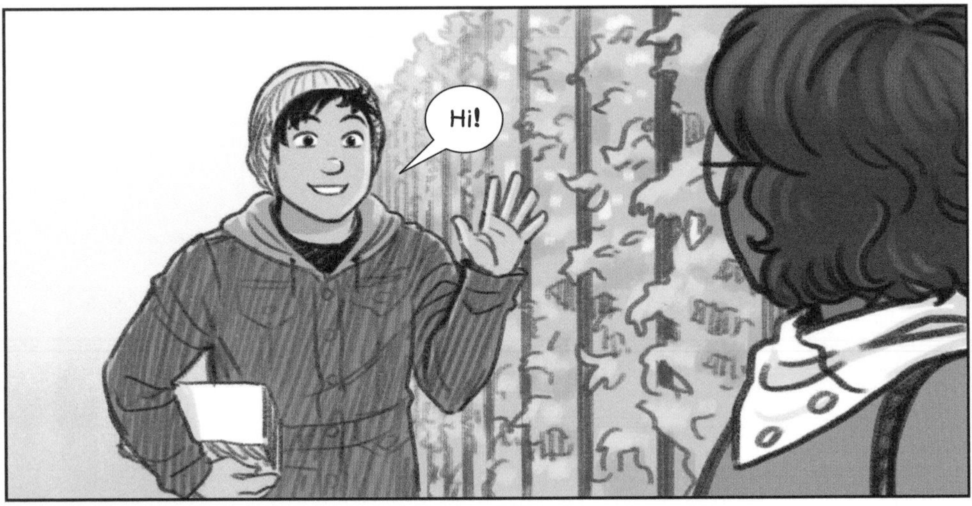
Hi!

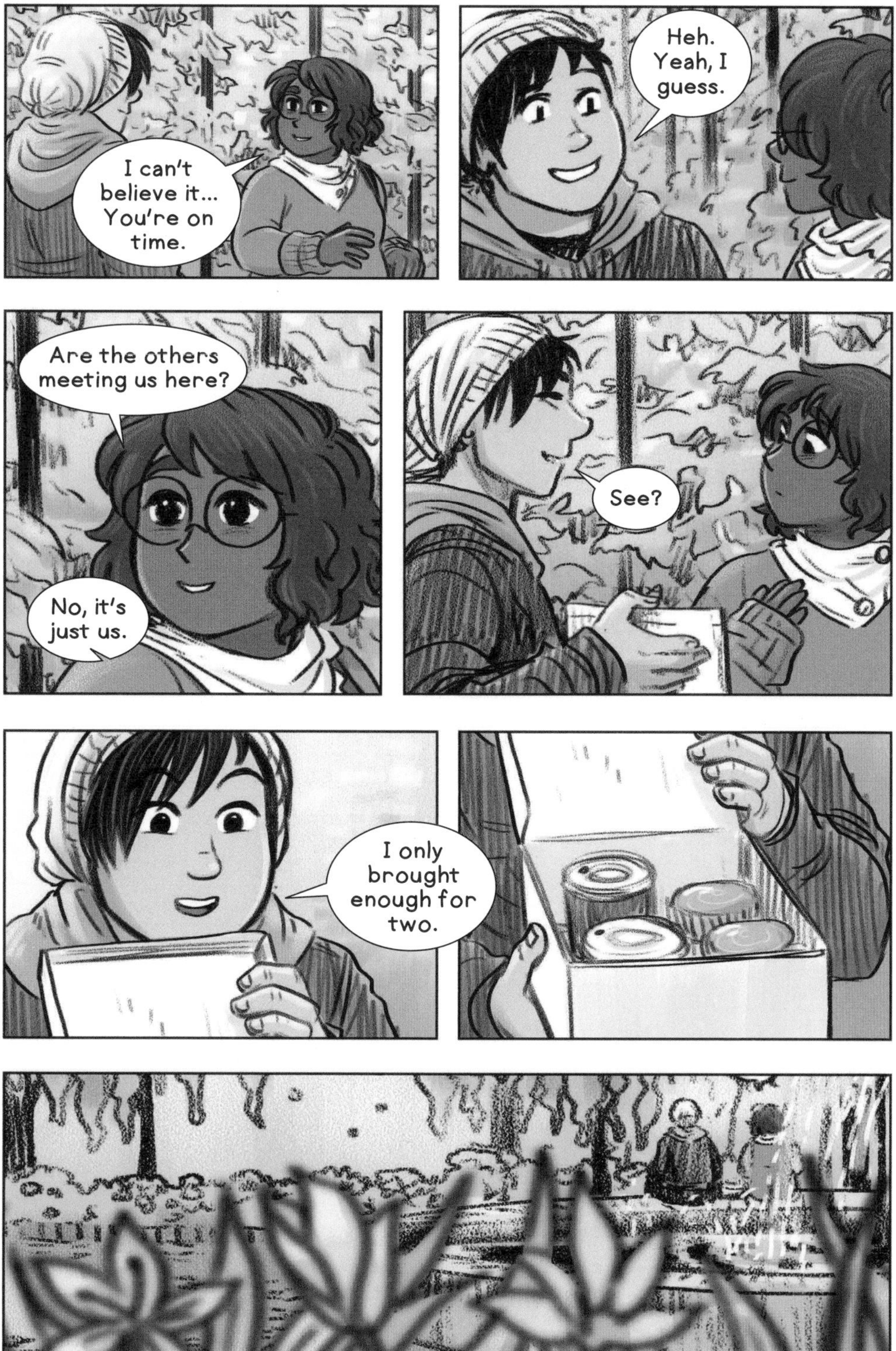
I can't believe it... You're on time.
Heh. Yeah, I guess.
Are the others meeting us here?
No, it's just us.
See?
I only brought enough for two.

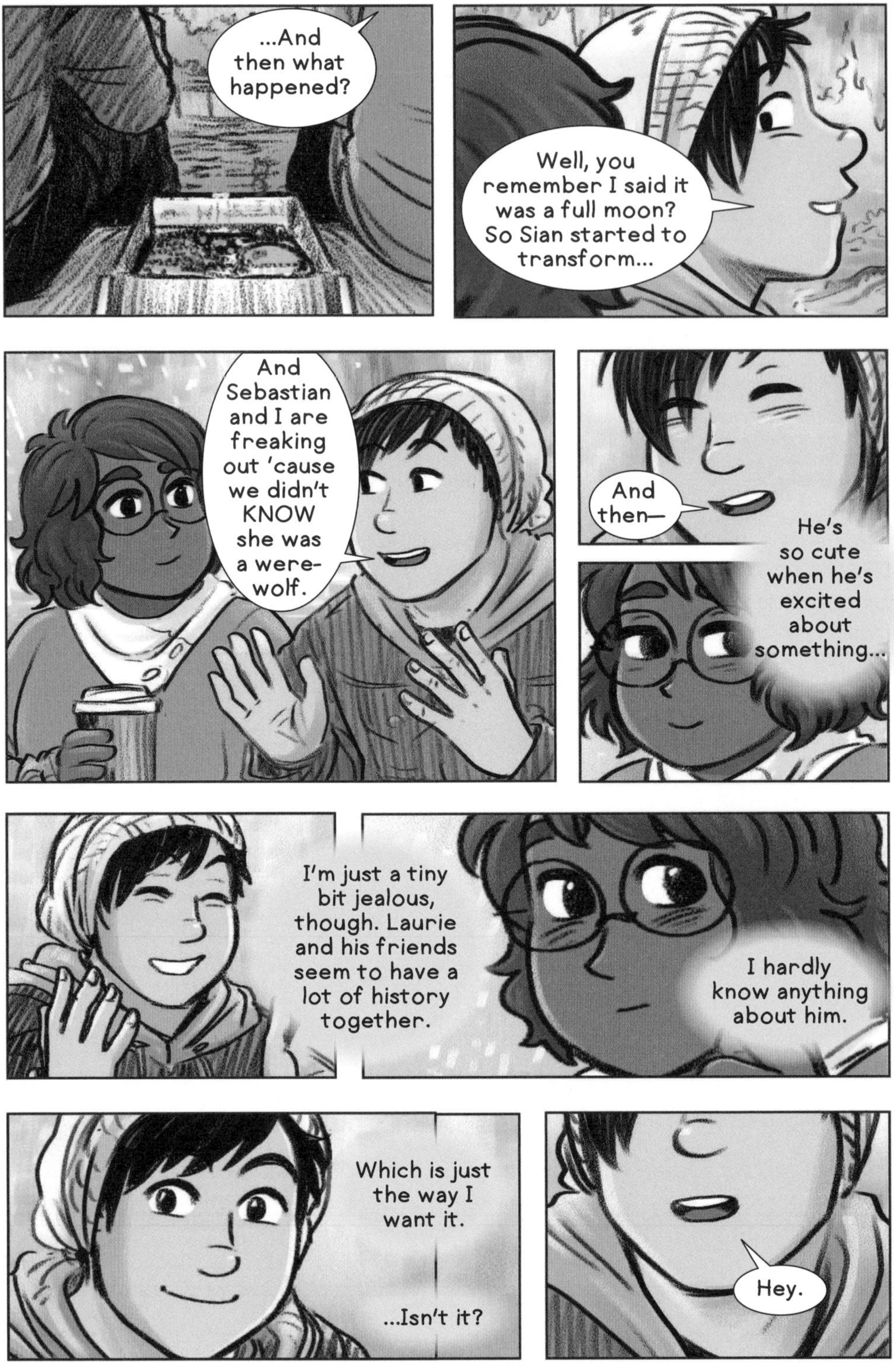
...And then what happened?
Well, you remember I said it was a full moon? So Sian started to transform...
And Sebastian and I are freaking out 'cause we didn't KNOW she was a were-wolf.
And then—
He's so cute when he's excited about something...
I'm just a tiny bit jealous, though. Laurie and his friends seem to have a lot of history together.
I hardly know anything about him.
Which is just the way I want it.
...Isn't it?
Hey.

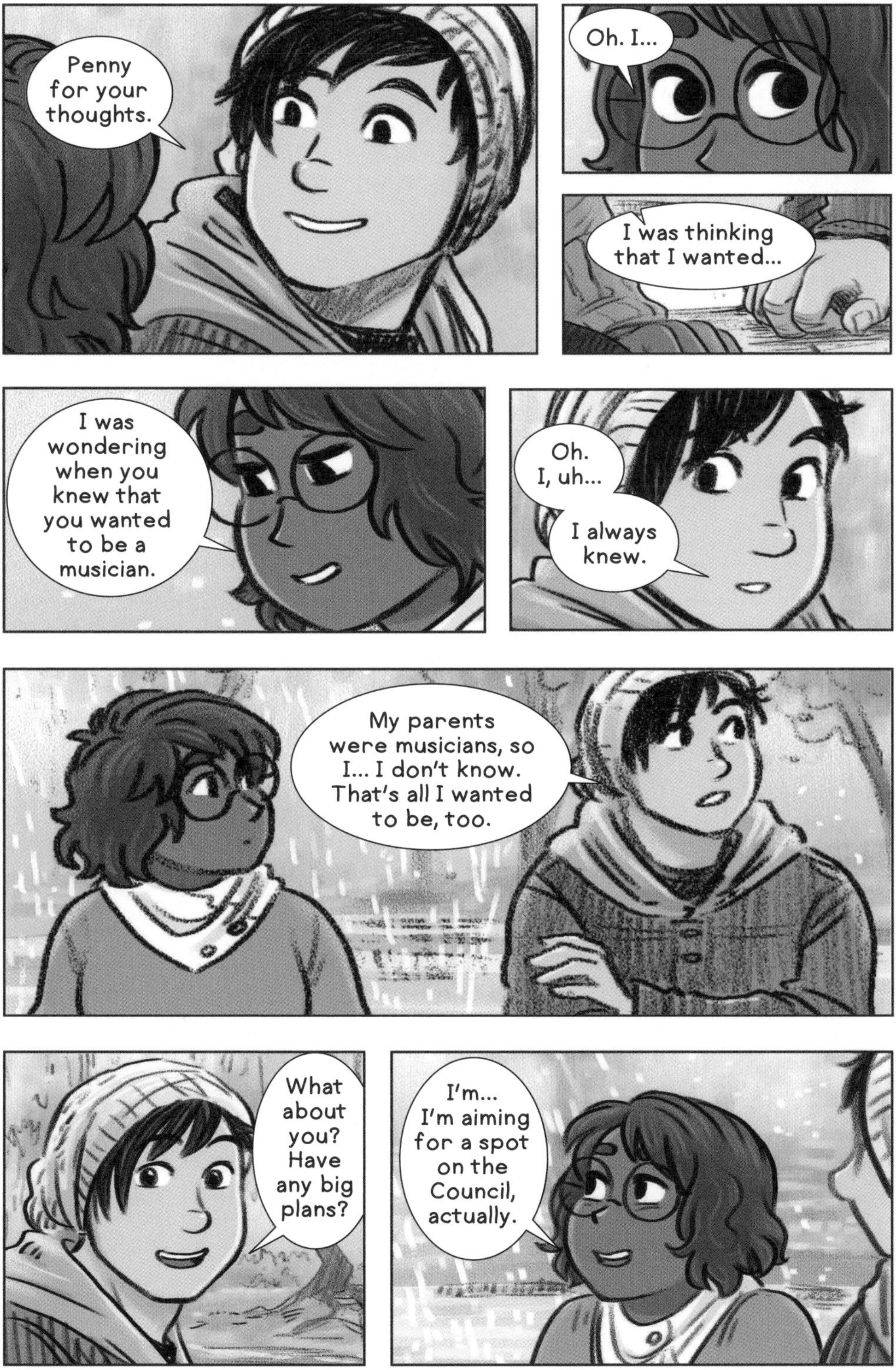
Penny for your thoughts.
Oh. I...
I was thinking that I wanted...
I was wondering when you knew that you wanted to be a musician.
Oh. I, uh...
I always knew.
My parents were musicians, so I... I don't know. That's all I wanted to be, too.
What about you? Have any big plans?
I'm... I'm aiming for a spot on the Council, actually.

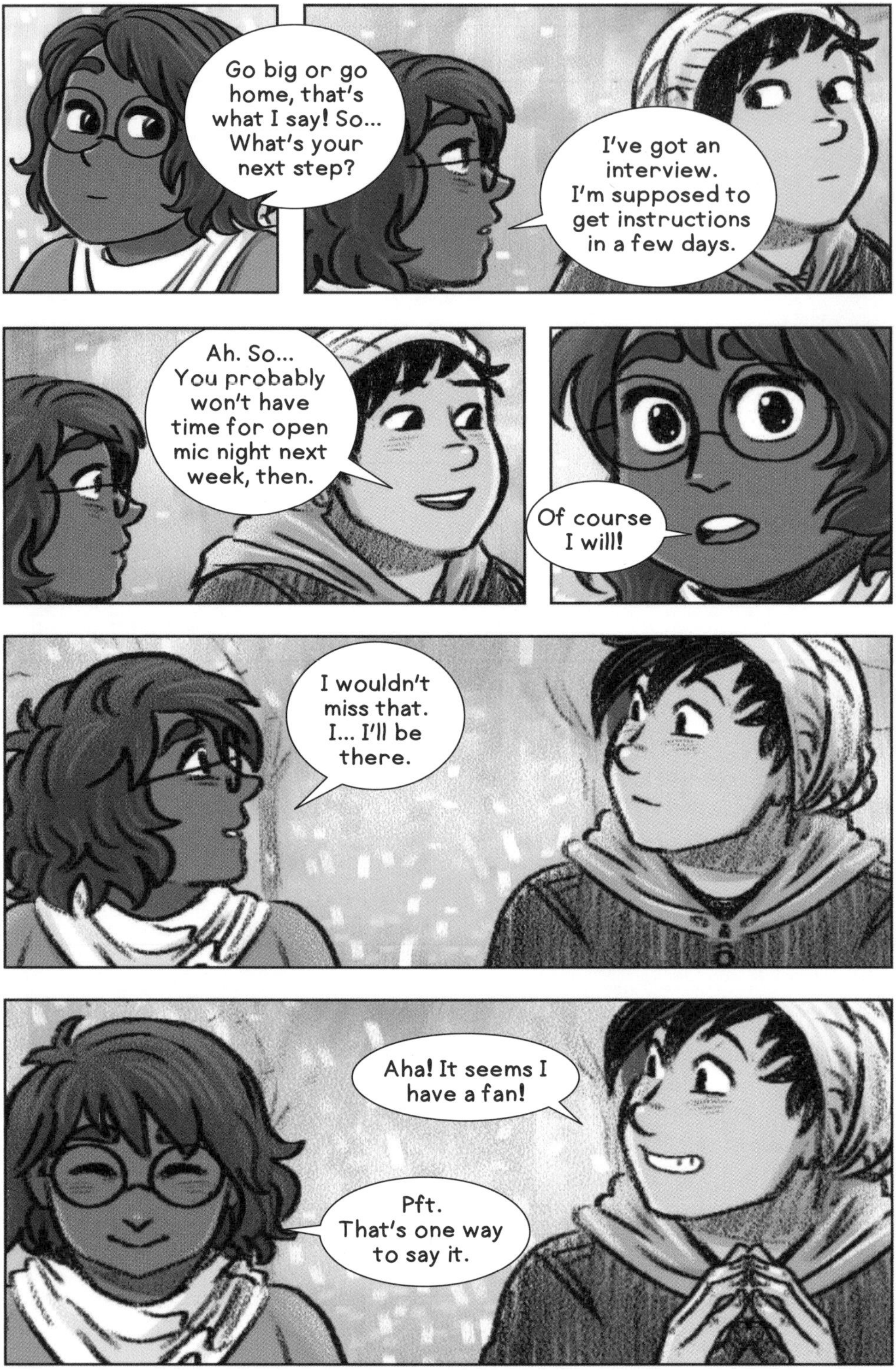
Go big or go home, that's what I say! So... What's your next step?
I've got an interview. I'm supposed to get instructions in a few days.
Ah. So... You probably won't have time for open mic night next week, then.
Of course I will!
I wouldn't miss that. I... I'll be there.
Aha! It seems I have a fan!
Pft. That's one way to say it.

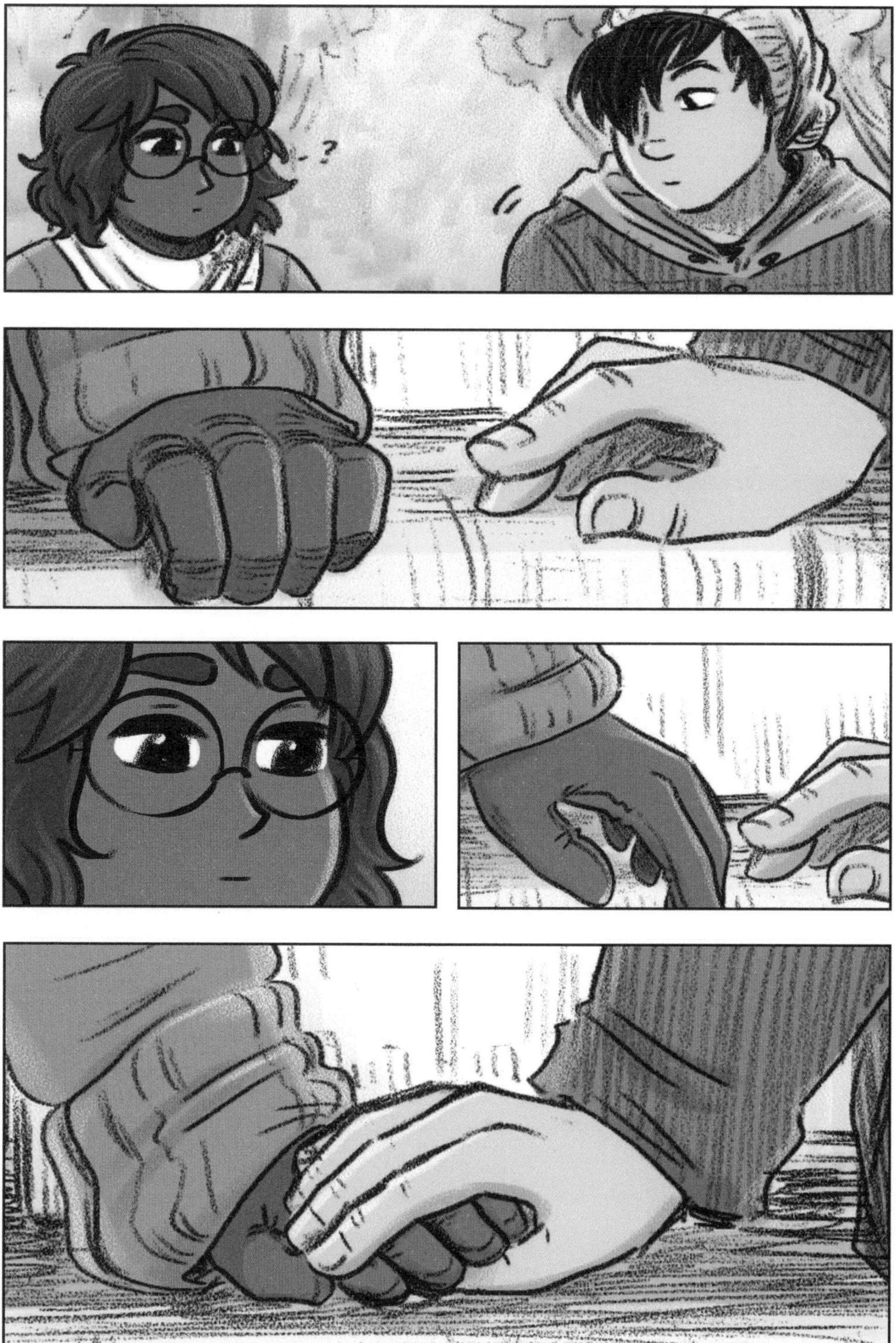
?

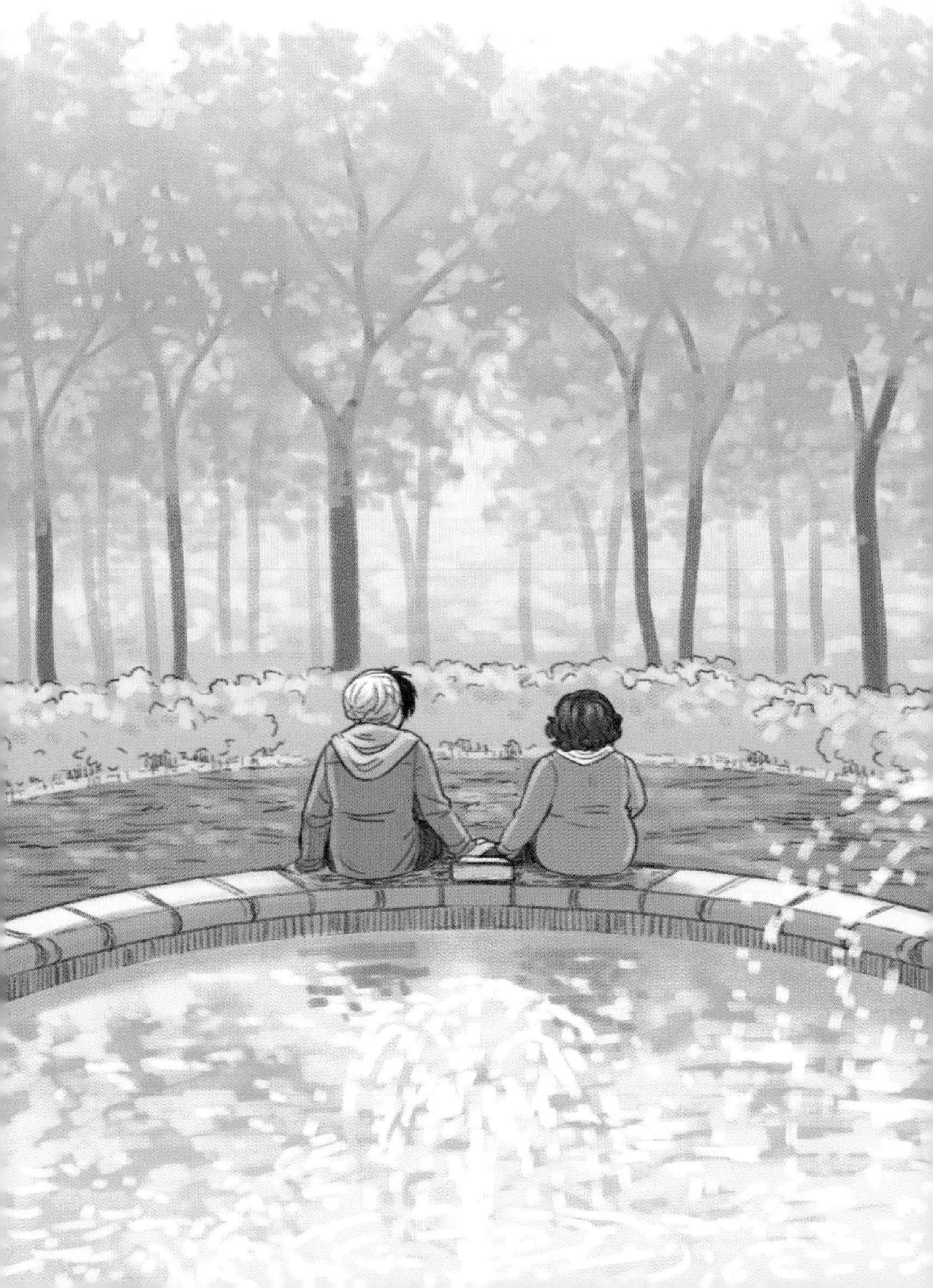

CHAPTER 4

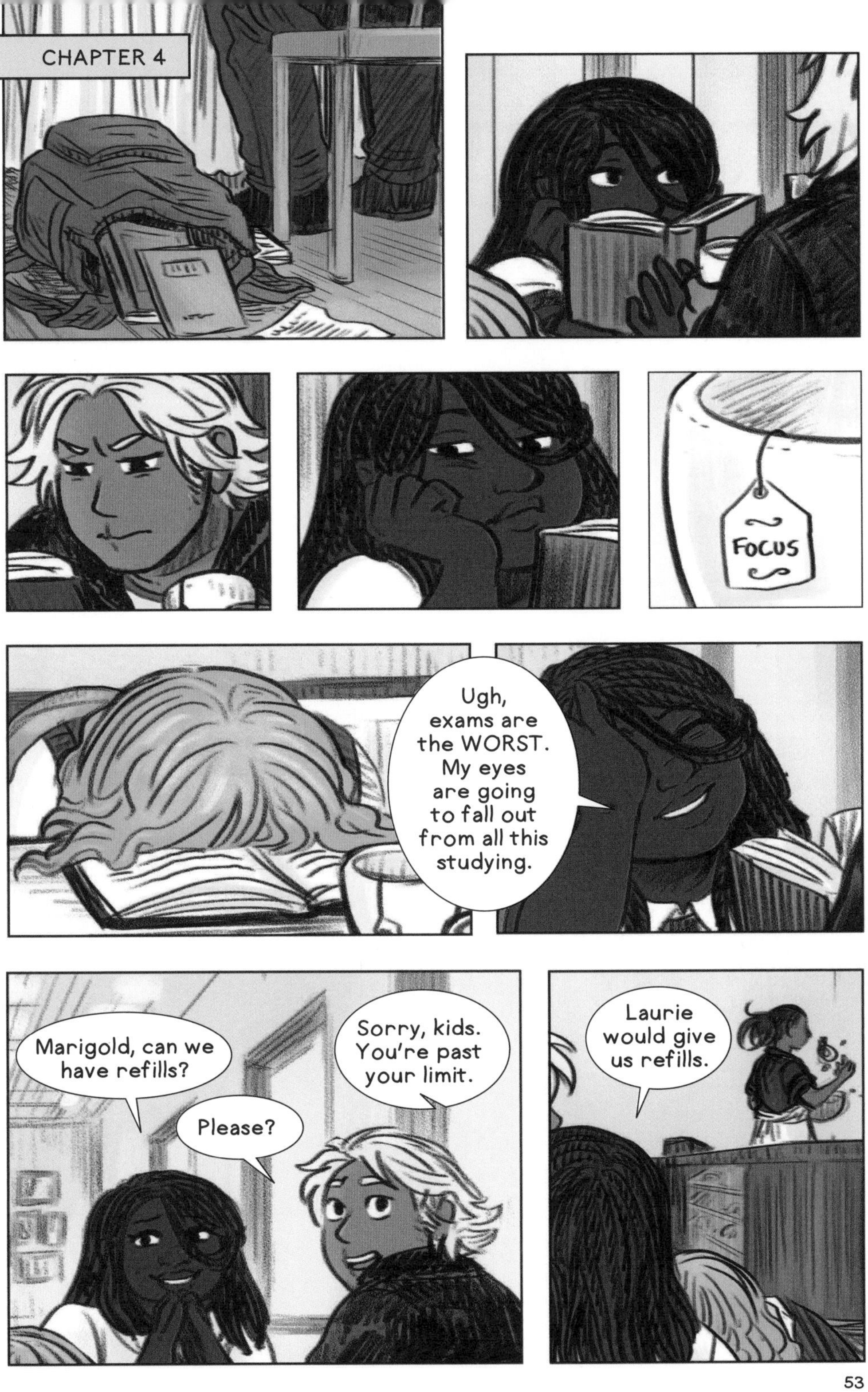
FOCUS
Ugh, exams are the WORST. My eyes are going to fall out from all this studying.
Marigold, can we have refills?
Please?
Sorry, kids. You're past your limit.
Laurie would give us refills.

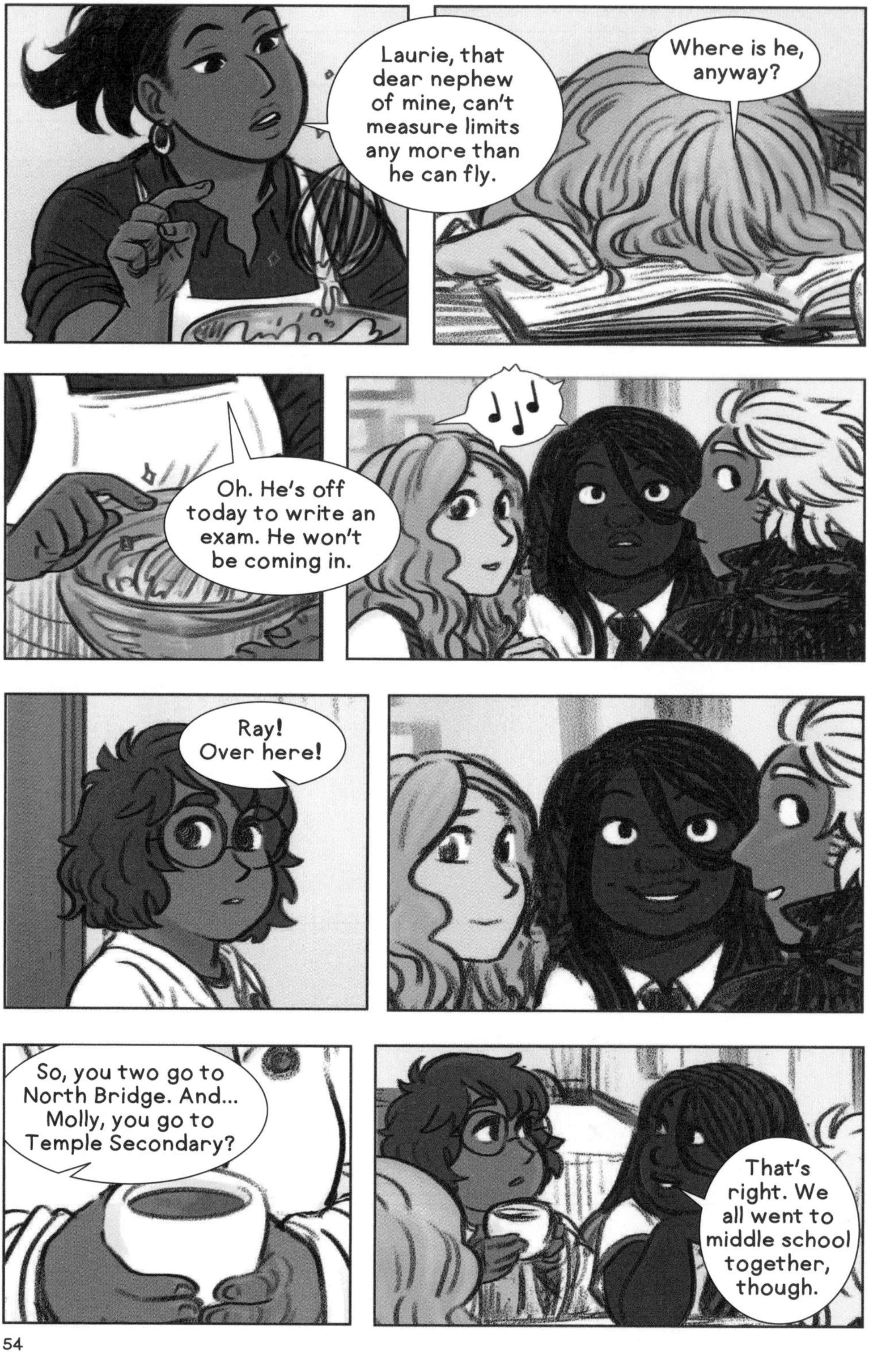
Laurie, that dear nephew of mine, can't measure limits any more than he can fly.
Where is he, anyway?
Oh. He's off today to write an exam. He won't be coming in.
Ray! Over here!
So, you two go to North Bridge. And... Molly, you go to Temple Secondary?
That's right. We all went to middle school together, though.

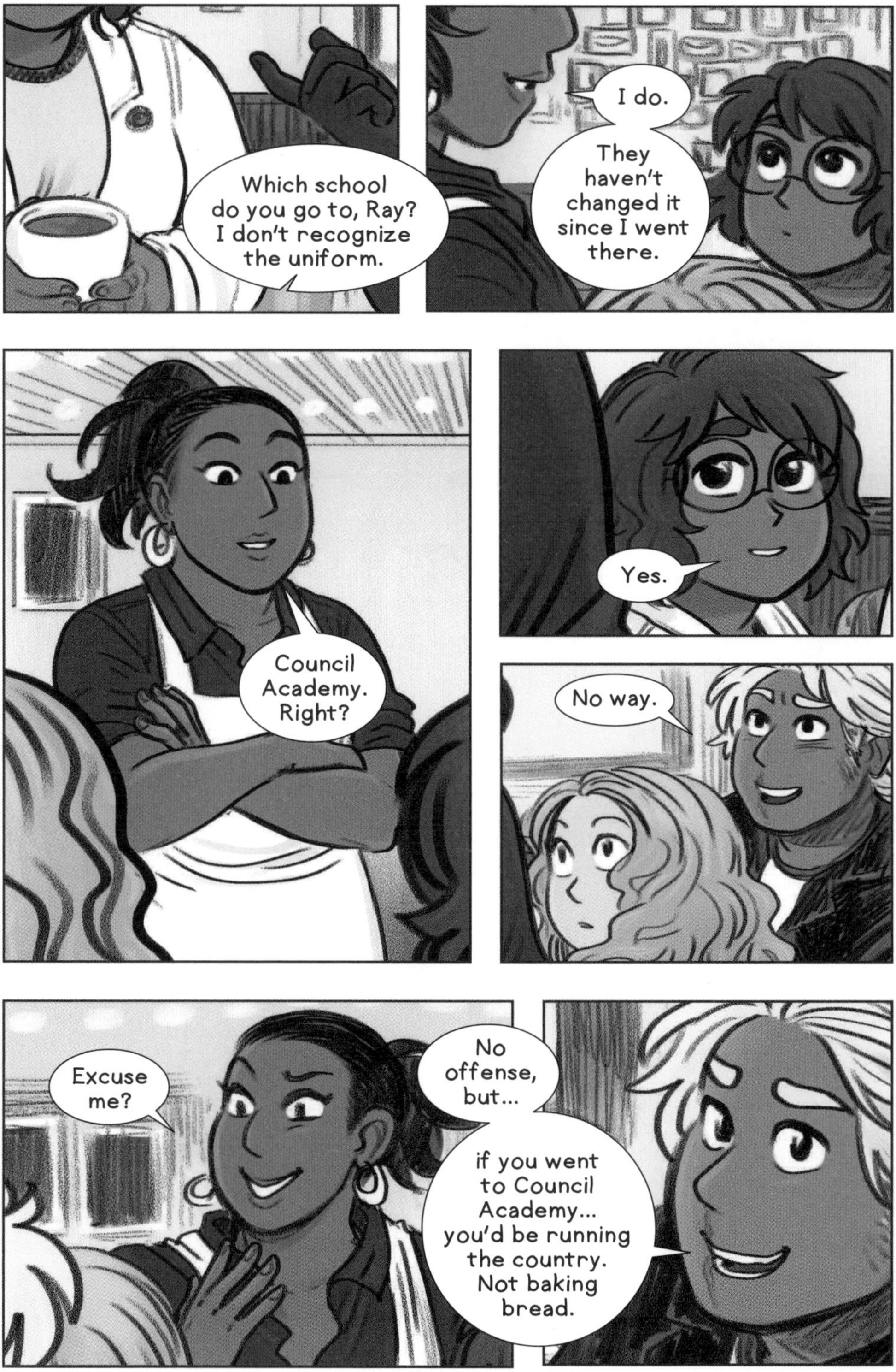
Which school do you go to, Ray? I don't recognize the uniform.
I do.
They haven't changed it since I went there.
Council Academy. Right?
Yes.
No way.
Excuse me?
No offense, but...
if you went to Council Academy... you'd be running the country. Not baking bread.

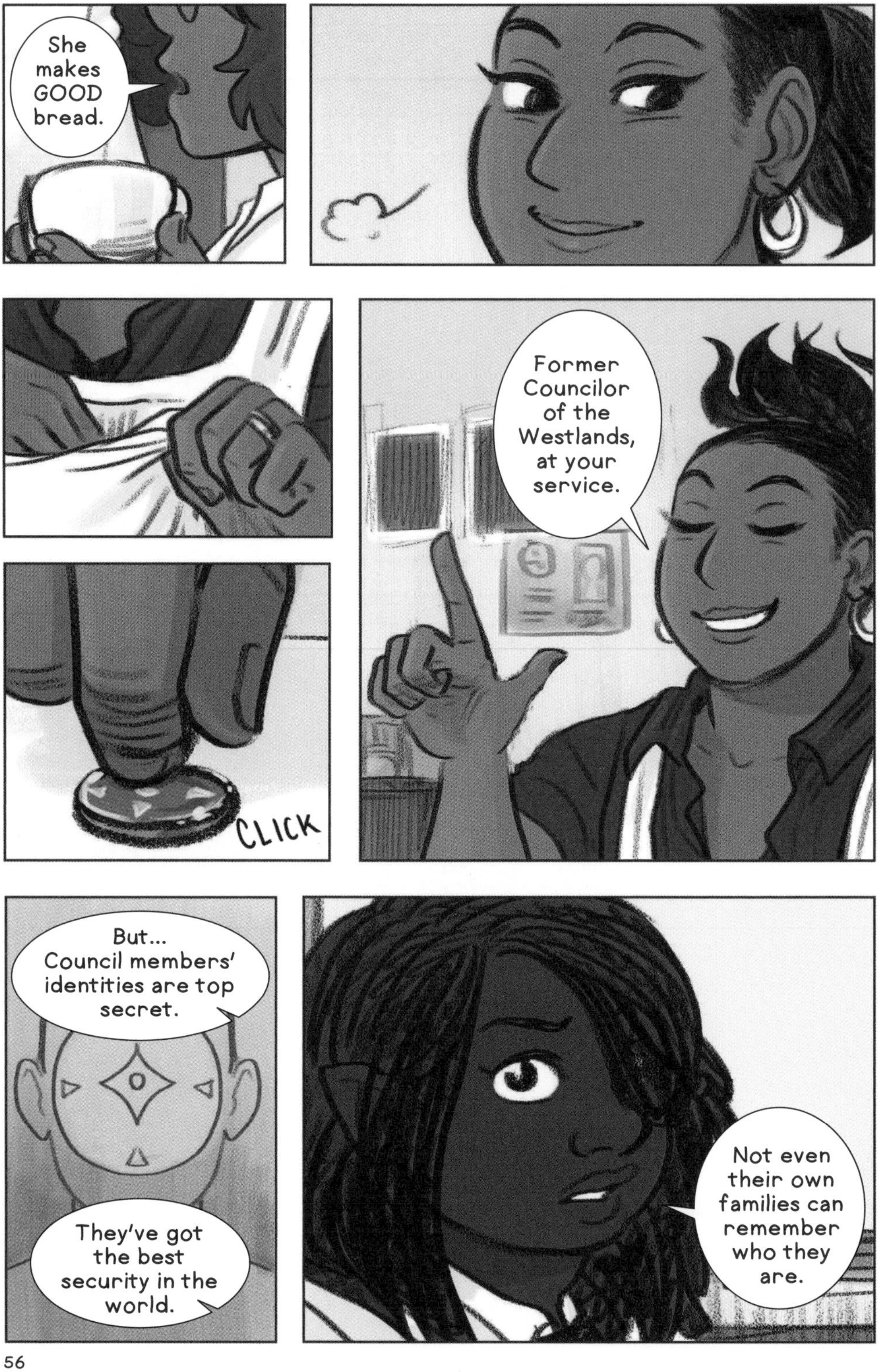
She makes GOOD bread.
Former Councilor of the Westlands, at your service.
CLICK
But... Council members' identities are top secret.
They've got the best security in the world.
Not even their own families can remember who they are.

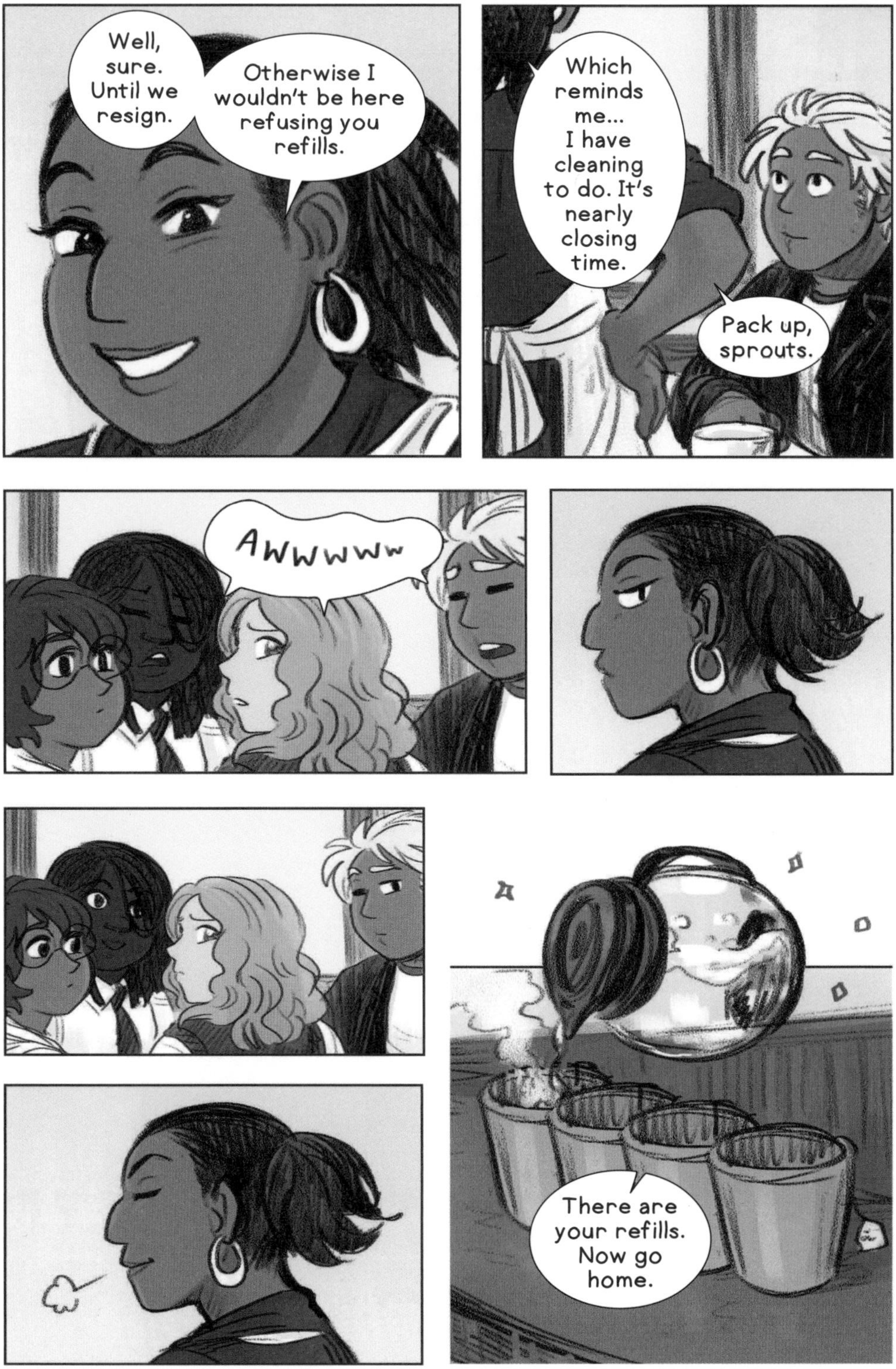
Well, sure. Until we resign.
Otherwise I wouldn't be here refusing you refills.
Which reminds me... I have cleaning to do. It's nearly closing time.
Pack up, sprouts.
AWWWWW
There are your refills. Now go home.

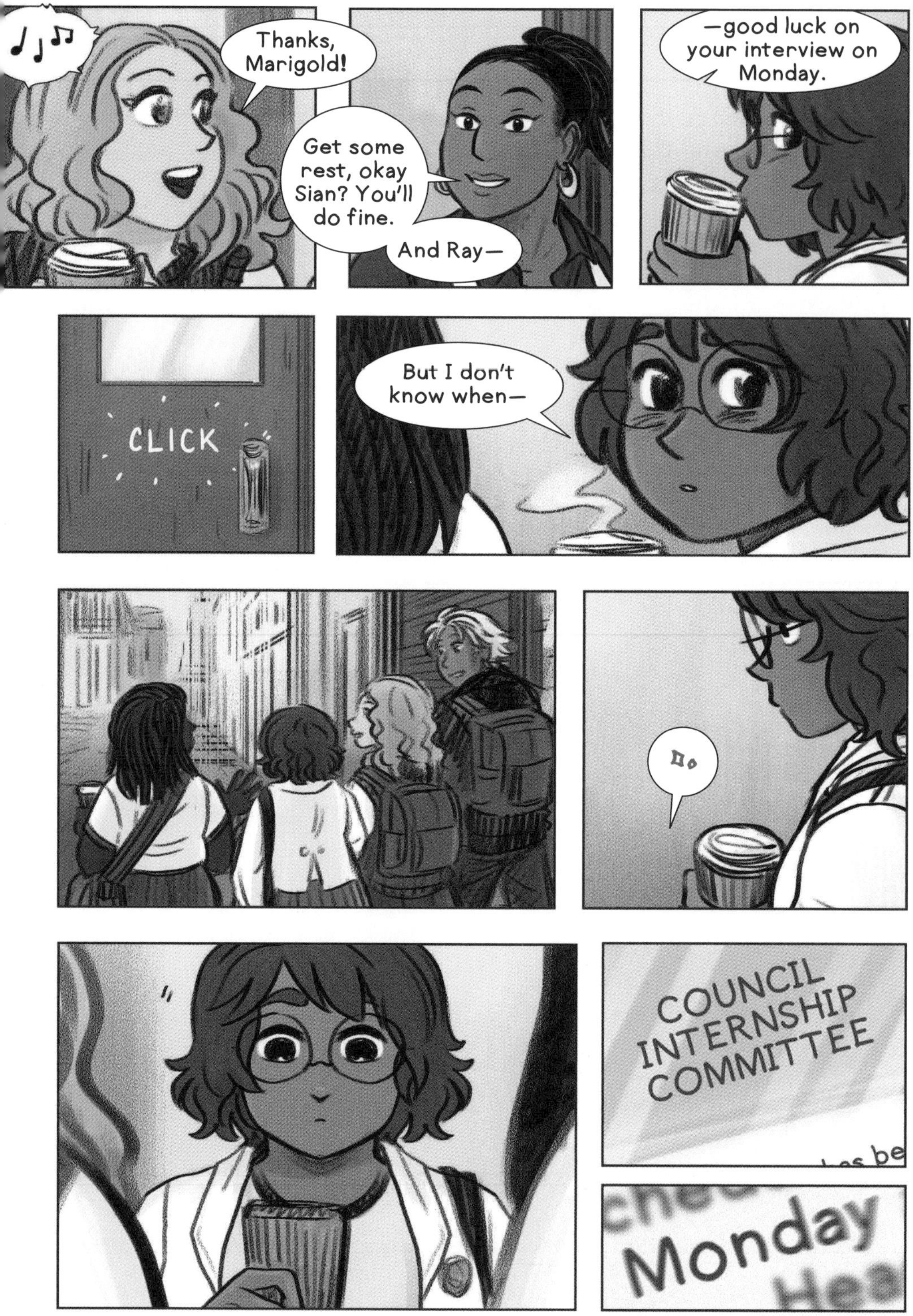
Thanks, Marigold!
Get some rest, okay Sian? You'll do fine.
And Ray—
—good luck on your interview on Monday.
CLICK
But I don't know when—
COUNCIL INTERNSHIP COMMITTEE
Monday

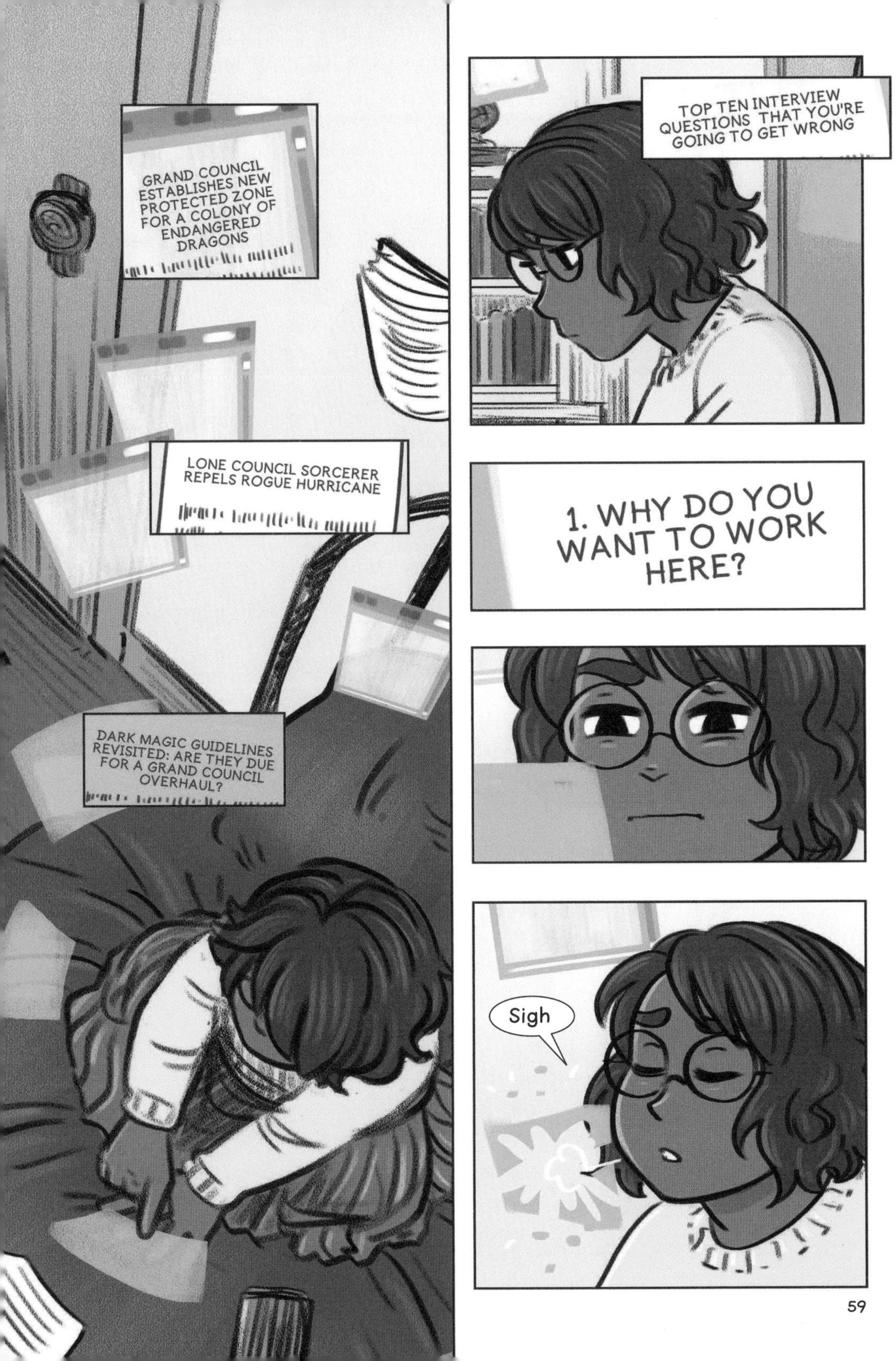
GRAND COUNCIL ESTABLISHES NEW PROTECTED ZONE FOR A COLONY OF ENDANGERED DRAGONS
LONE COUNCIL SORCERER REPELS ROGUE HURRICANE
DARK MAGIC GUIDELINES REVISITED: ARE THEY DUE FOR A GRAND COUNCIL OVERHAUL?
TOP TEN INTERVIEW QUESTIONS THAT YOU'RE GOING TO GET WRONG
1. WHY DO YOU WANT TO WORK HERE?
Sigh

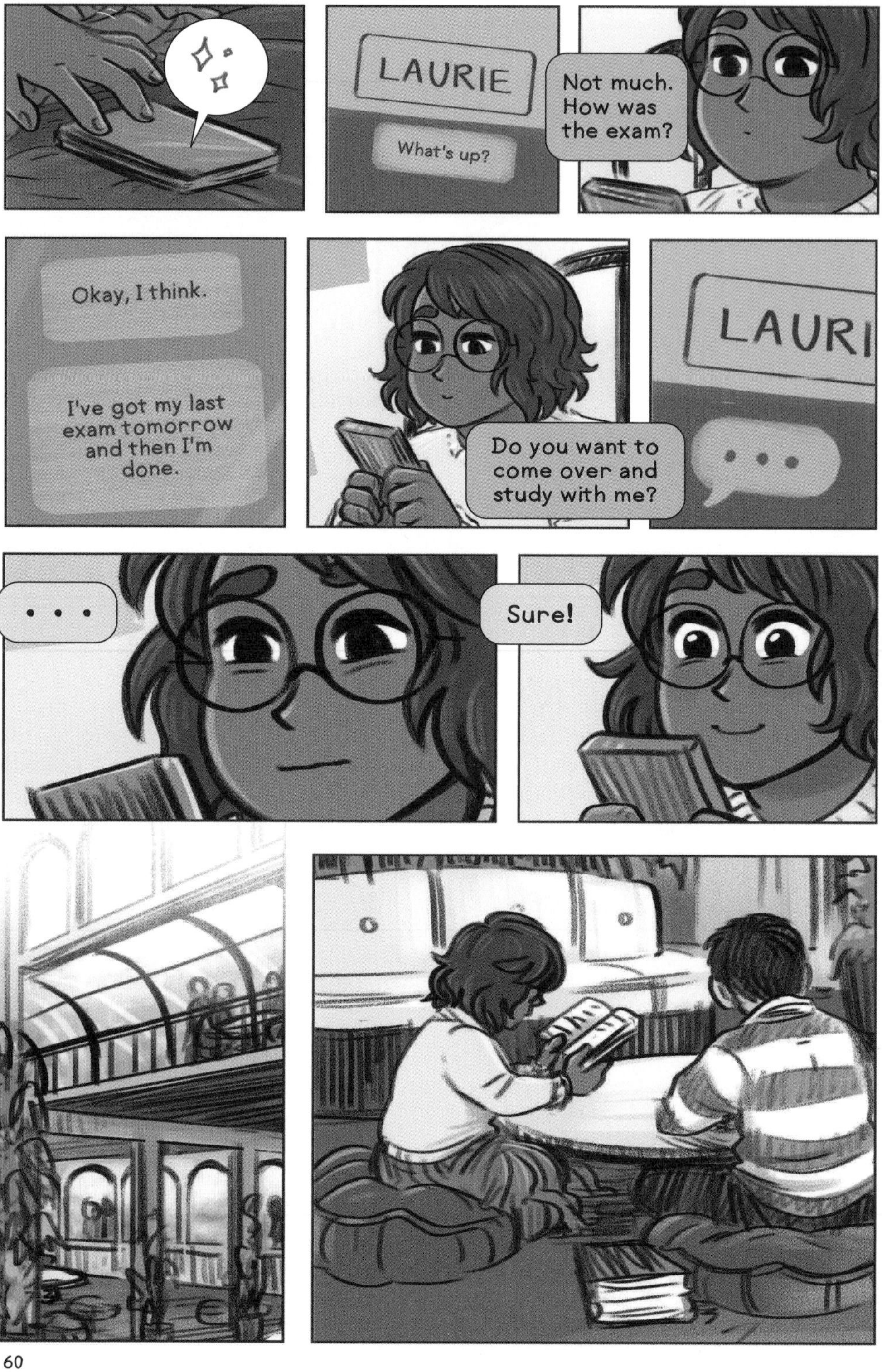
LAURIE
What's up?
Not much. How was the exam?
Okay, I think.
I've got my last exam tomorrow and then I'm done.
Do you want to come over and study with me?
LAURI
...
Sure!

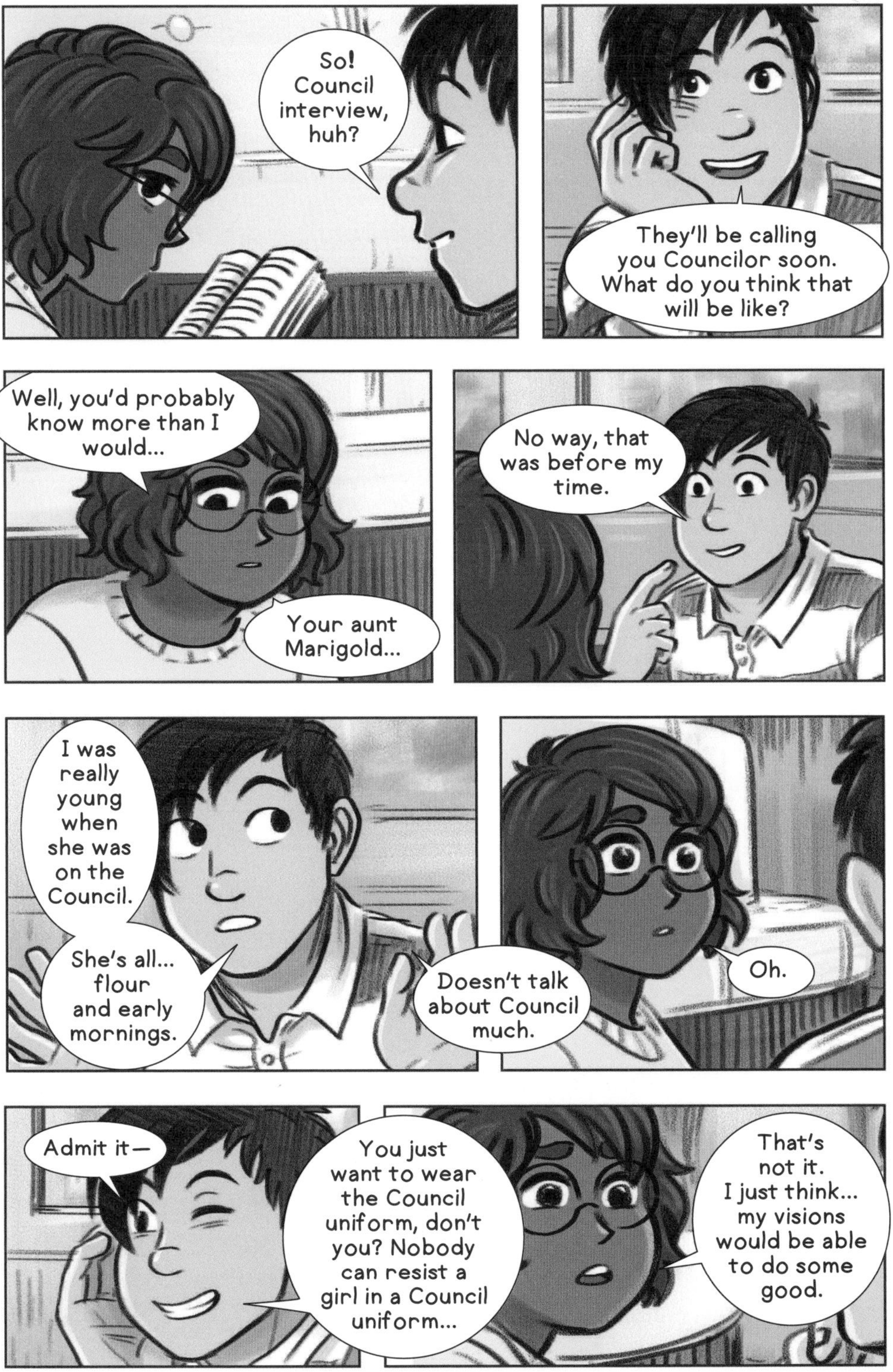
So! Council interview, huh?
They'll be calling you Councilor soon. What do you think that will be like?
Well, you'd probably know more than I would...
Your aunt Marigold...
No way, that was before my time.
I was really young when she was on the Council.
She's all... flour and early mornings.
Doesn't talk about Council much.
Oh.
Admit it—
You just want to wear the Council uniform, don't you? Nobody can resist a girl in a Council uniform...
That's not it. I just think... my visions would be able to do some good.

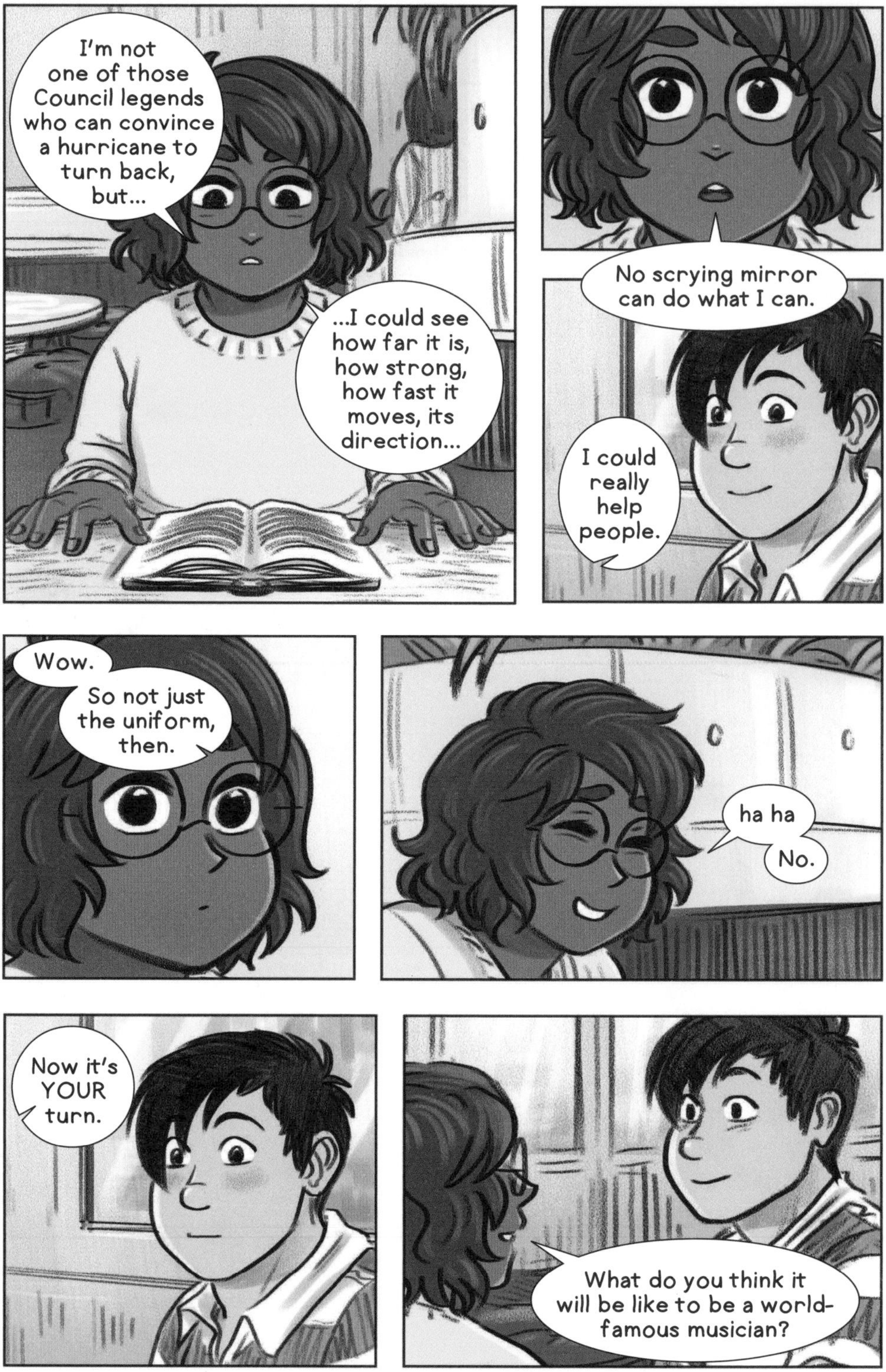
I'm not one of those Council legends who can convince a hurricane to turn back, but...
...I could see how far it is, how strong, how fast it moves, its direction...
No scrying mirror can do what I can.
I could really help people.
Wow.
So not just the uniform, then.
ha ha
No.
Now it's YOUR turn.
What do you think it will be like to be a world-famous musician?

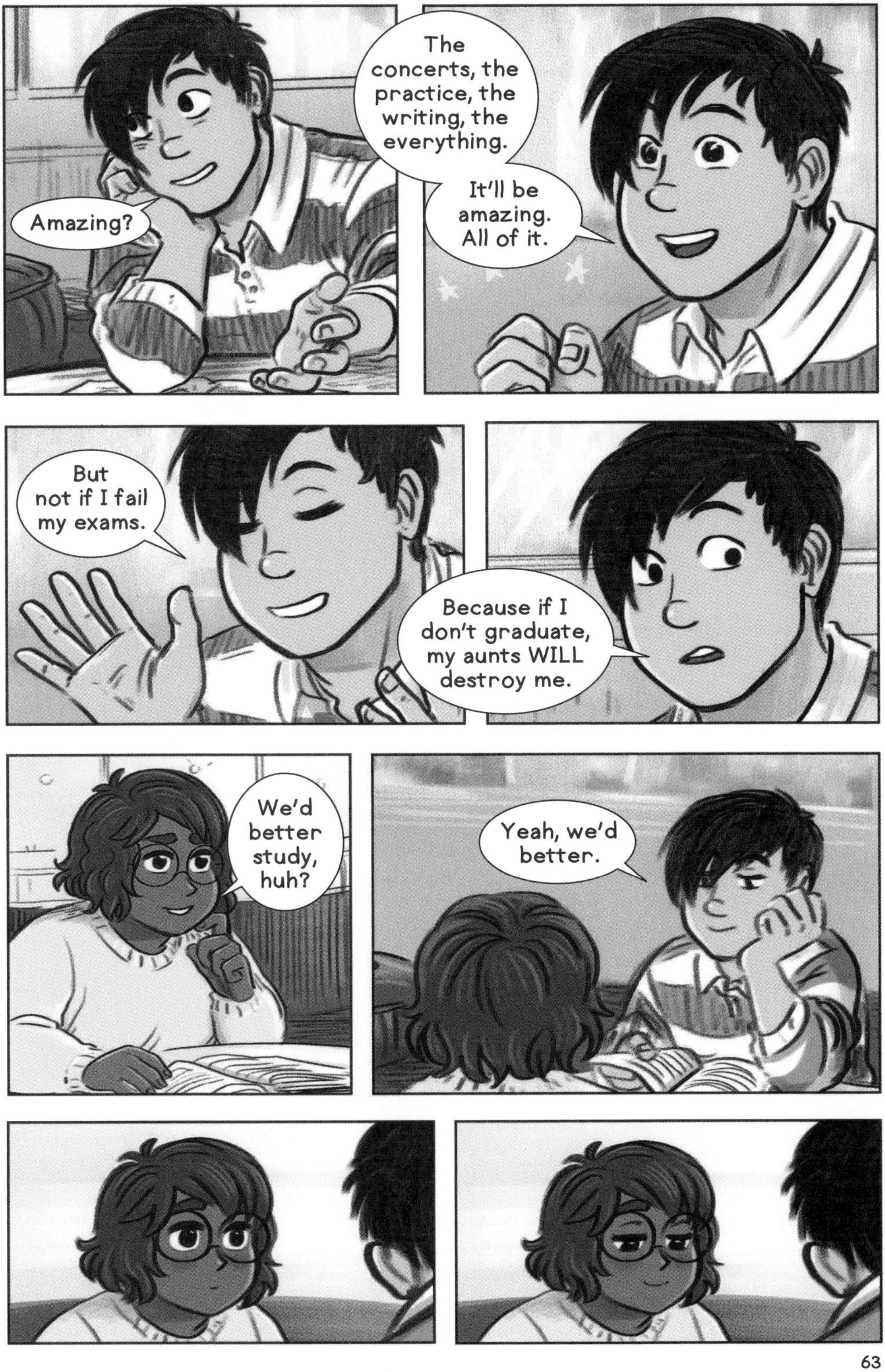
Amazing?
The concerts, the practice, the writing, the everything.
It'll be amazing. All of it.
But not if I fail my exams.
Because if I don't graduate, my aunts WILL destroy me.
We'd better study, huh?
Yeah, we'd better.

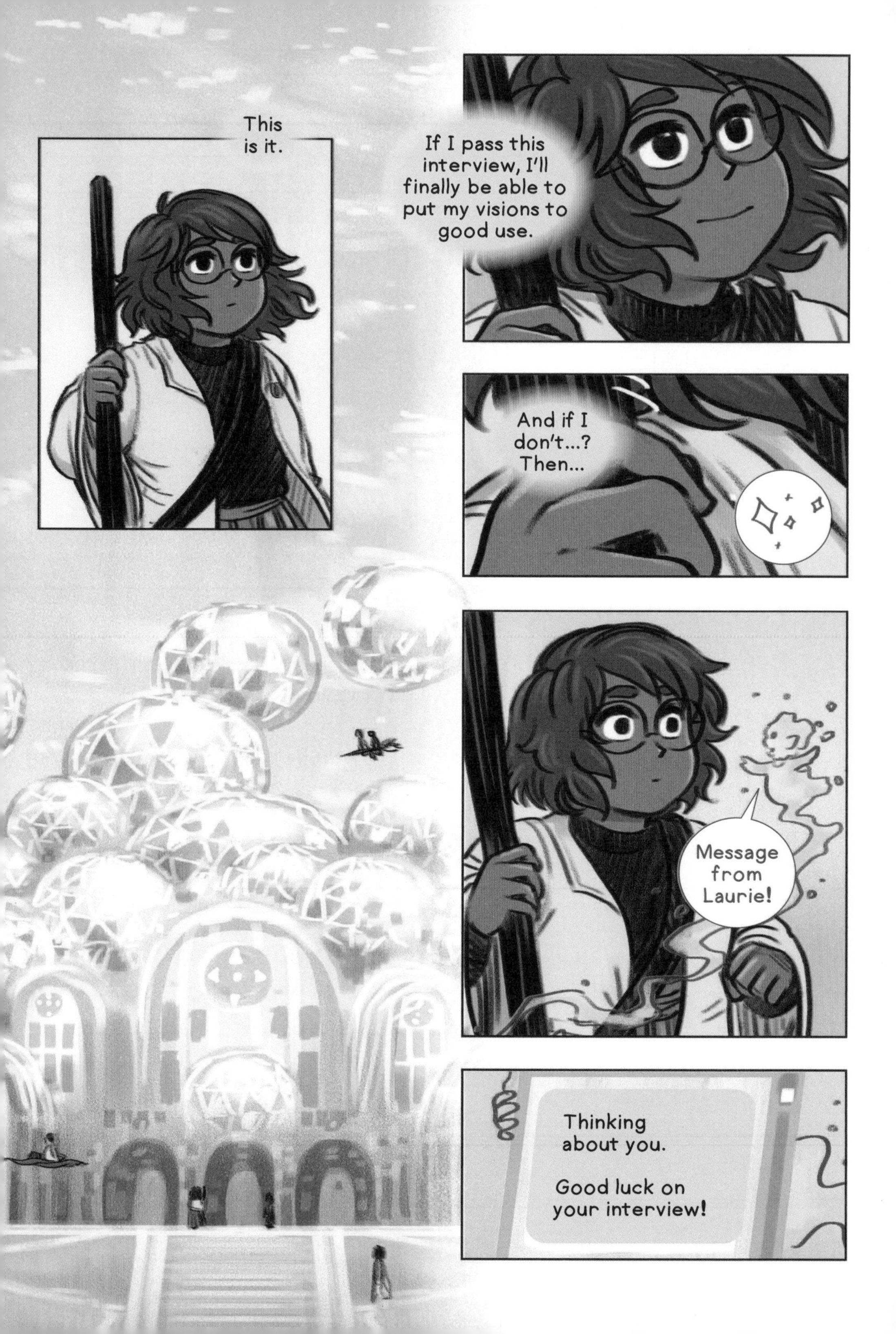
This is it.
If I pass this interview, I'll finally be able to put my visions to good use.
And if I don't...? Then...
Message from Laurie!
Thinking about you.
Good luck on your interview!

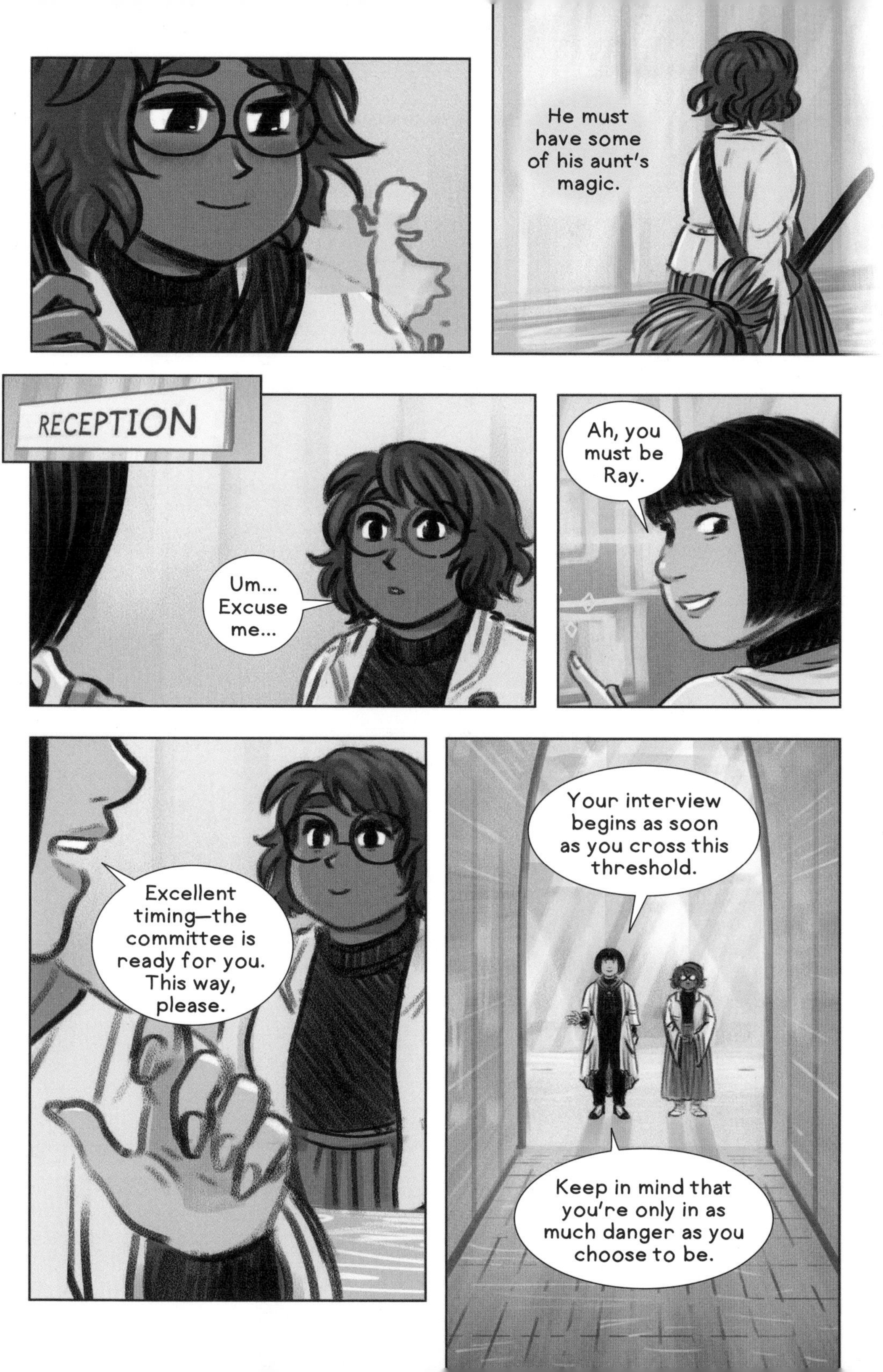
He must have some of his aunt's magic.
RECEPTION
Um... Excuse me...
Ah, you must be Ray.
Excellent timing—the committee is ready for you. This way, please.
Your interview begins as soon as you cross this threshold.
Keep in mind that you're only in as much danger as you choose to be.

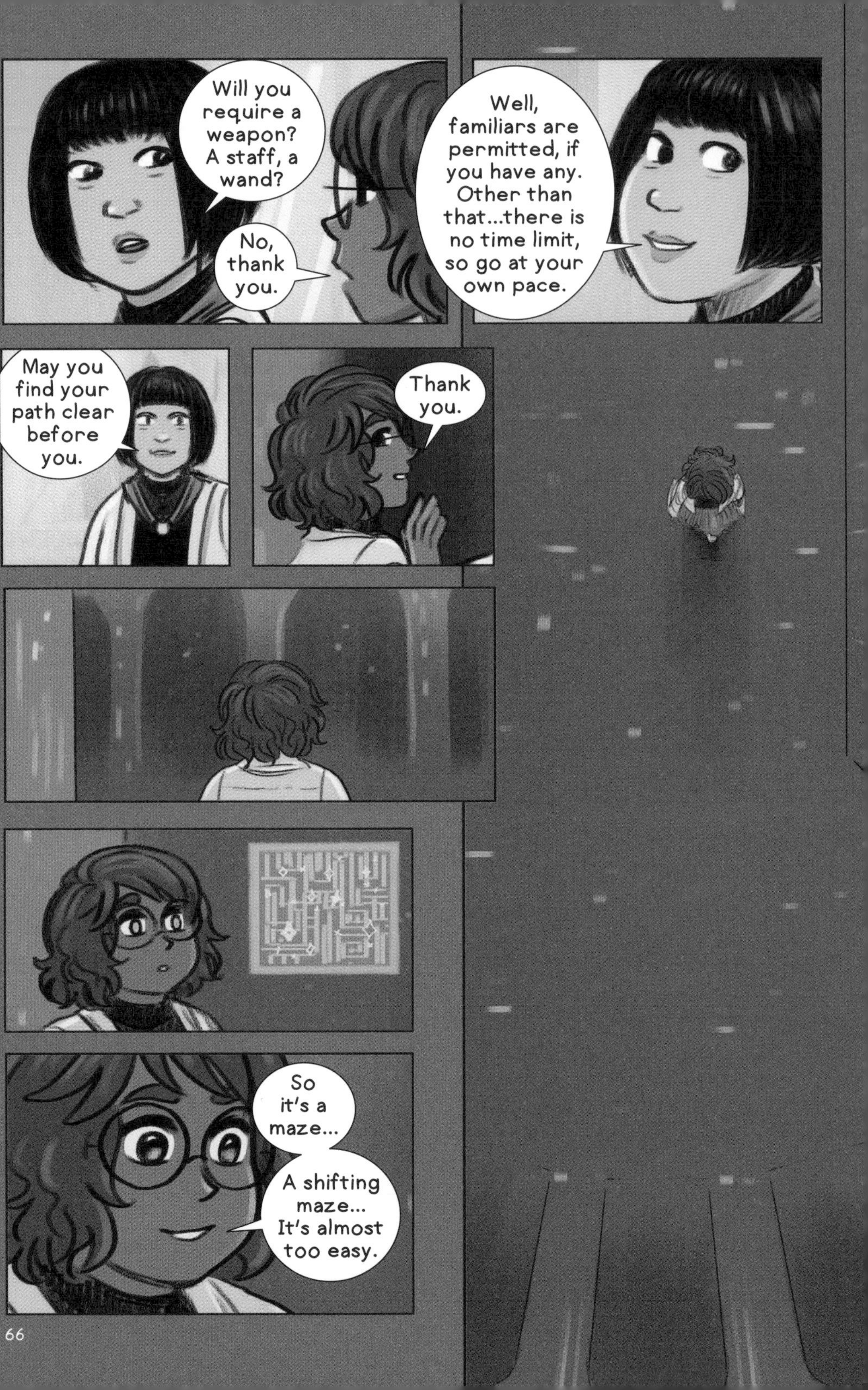
Will you require a weapon? A staff, a wand?
No, thank you.
Well, familiars are permitted, if you have any. Other than that...there is no time limit, so go at your own pace.
May you find your path clear before you.
Thank you.
So it's a maze...
A shifting maze... It's almost too easy.

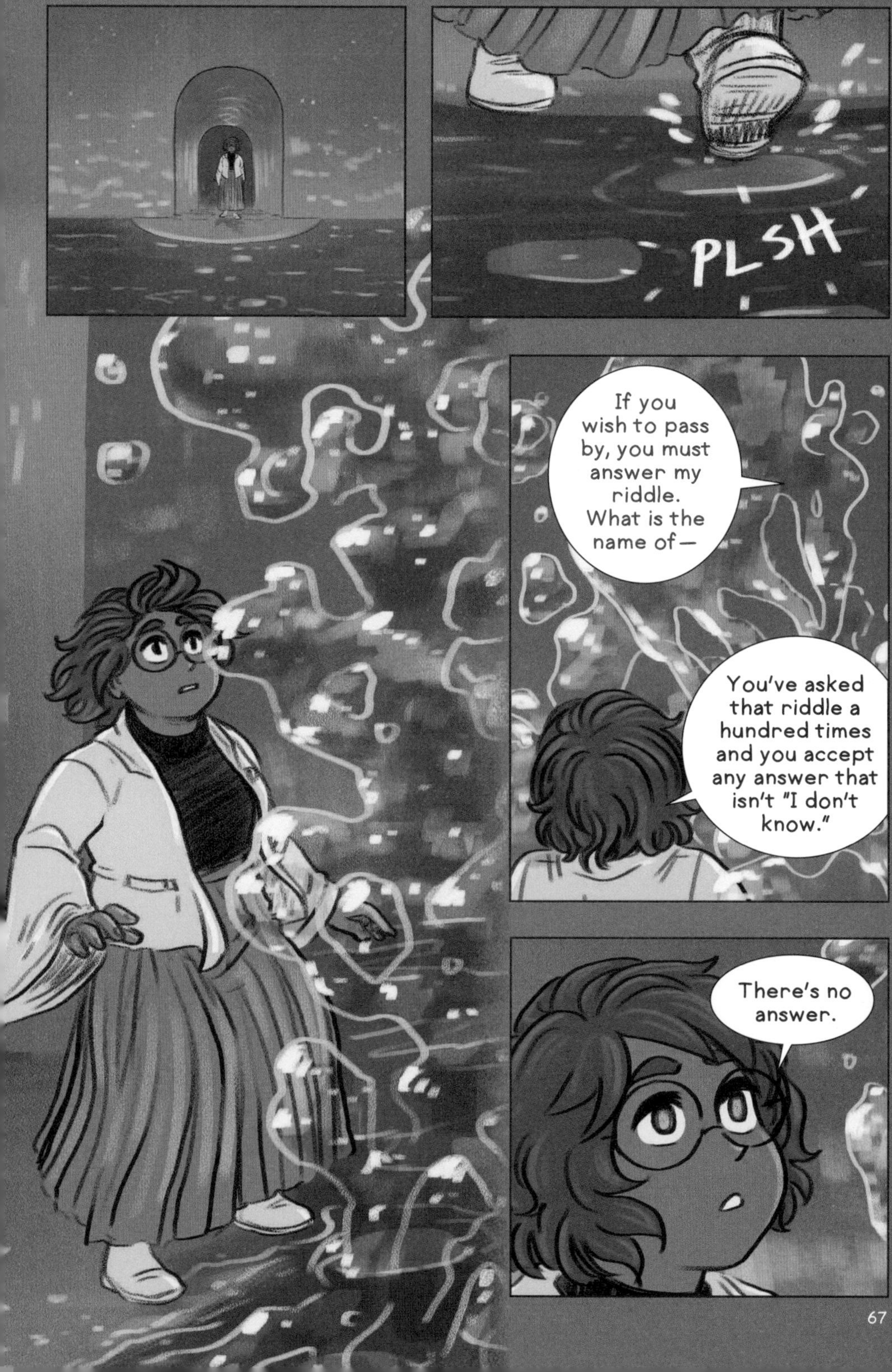
PLSH
If you wish to pass by, you must answer my riddle. What is the name of—
You've asked that riddle a hundred times and you accept any answer that isn't "I don't know."
There's no answer.

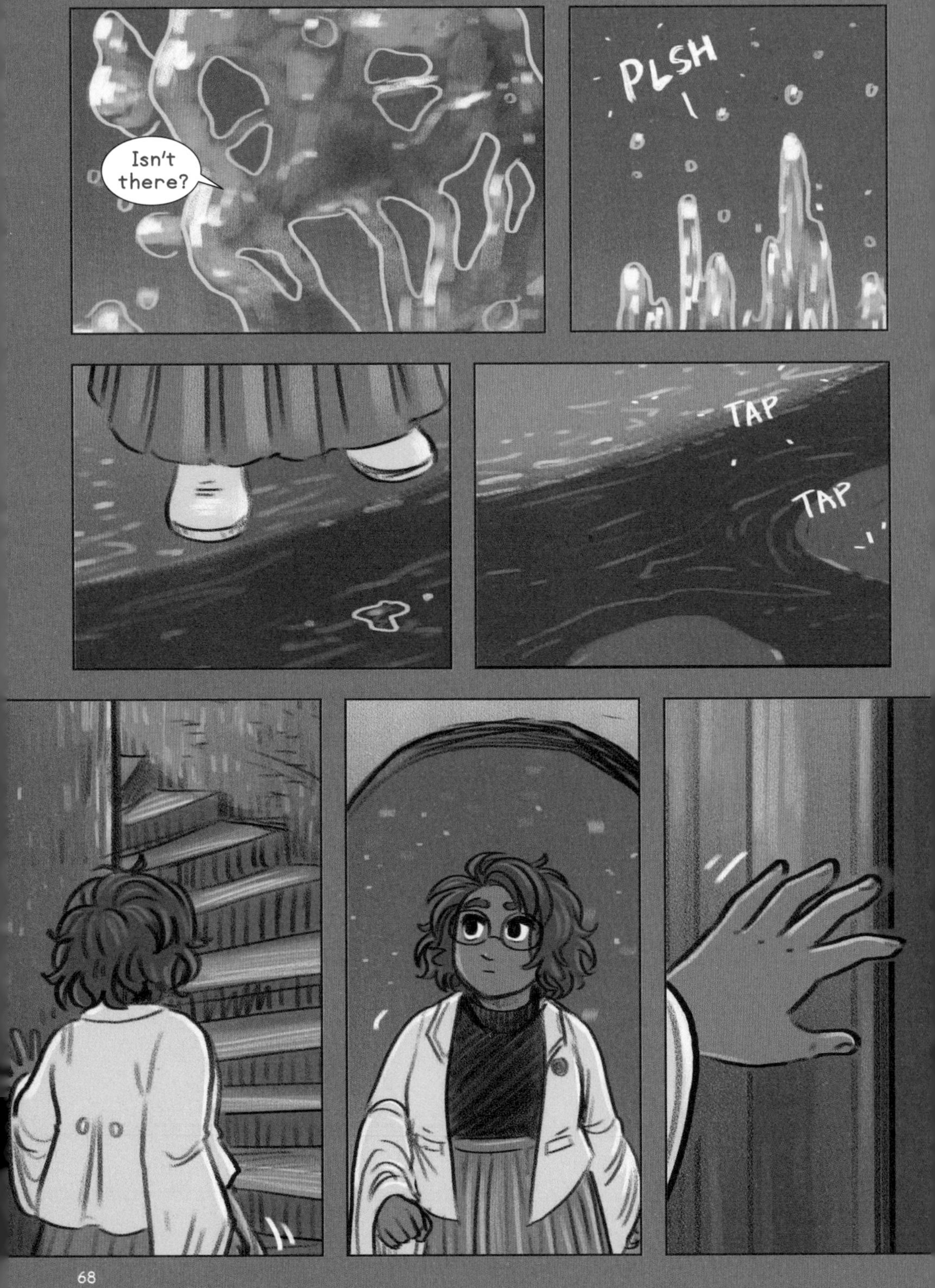
Isn't there?
PLSH
TAP
TAP

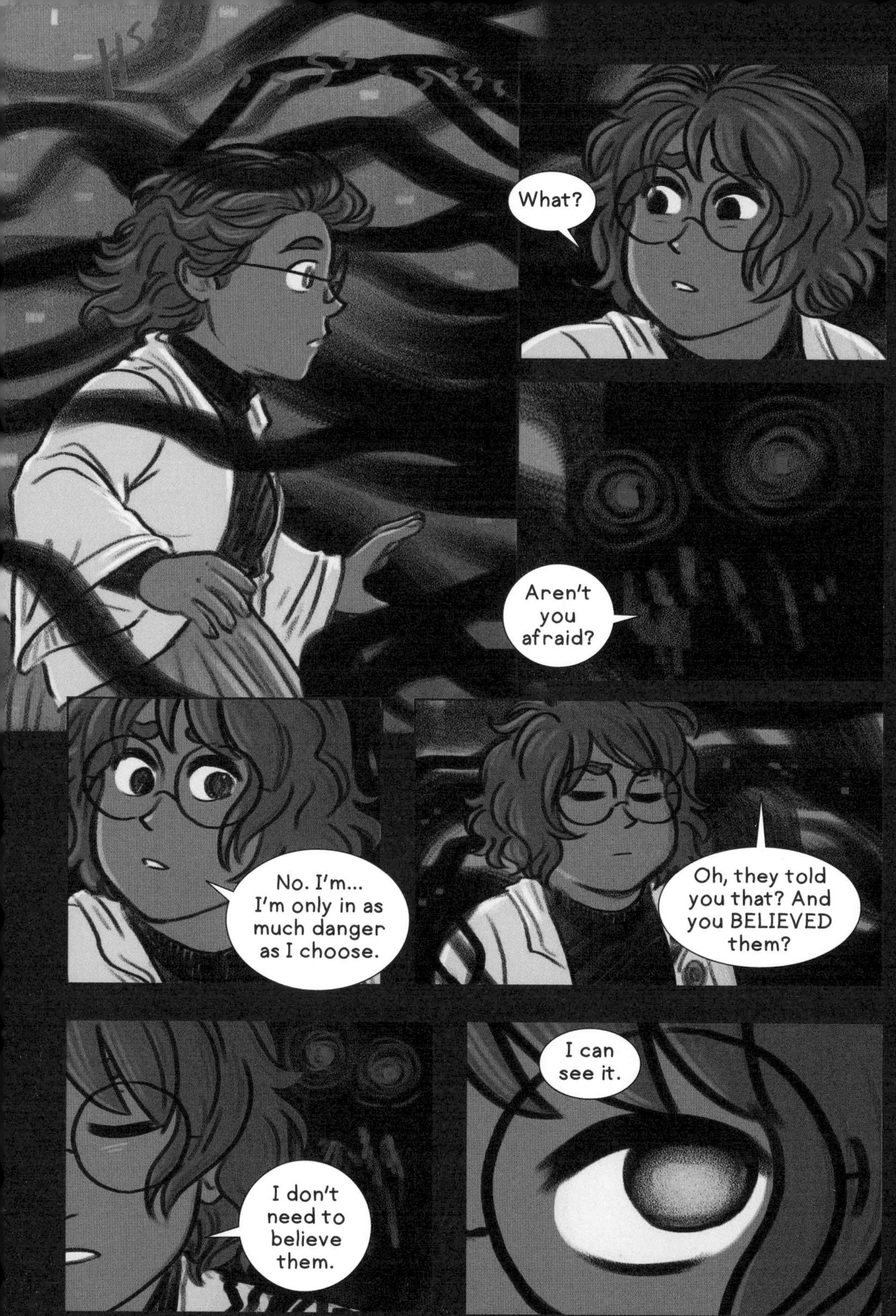
HSSSSSSSSS
What?
Aren't you afraid?
No. I'm... I'm only in as much danger as I choose.
Oh, they told you that? And you BELIEVED them?
I don't need to believe them.
I can see it.

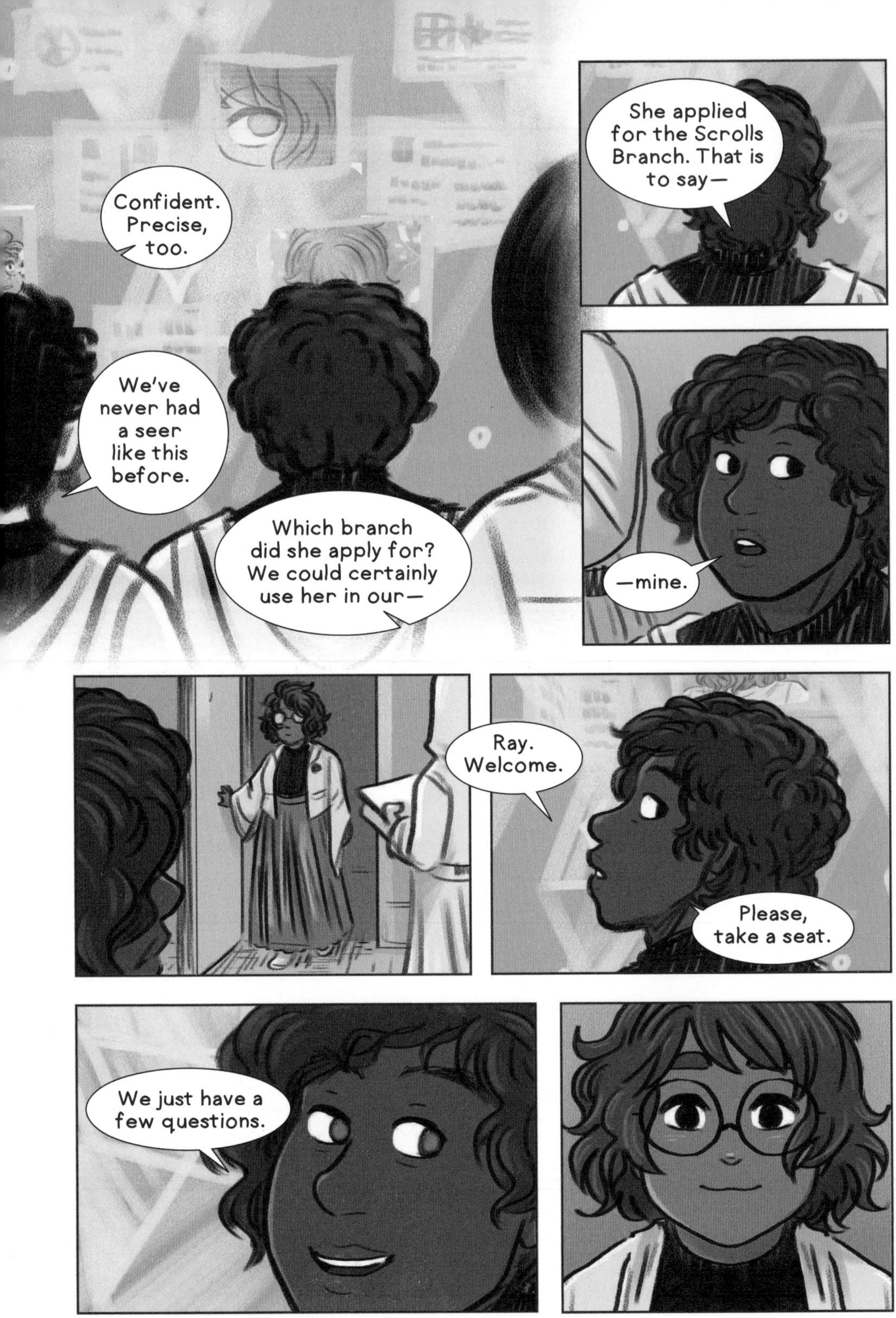
Confident. Precise, too.
We've never had a seer like this before.
Which branch did she apply for? We could certainly use her in our—
She applied for the Scrolls Branch. That is to say—
—mine.
Ray. Welcome.
Please, take a seat.
We just have a few questions.

CHAPTER 5

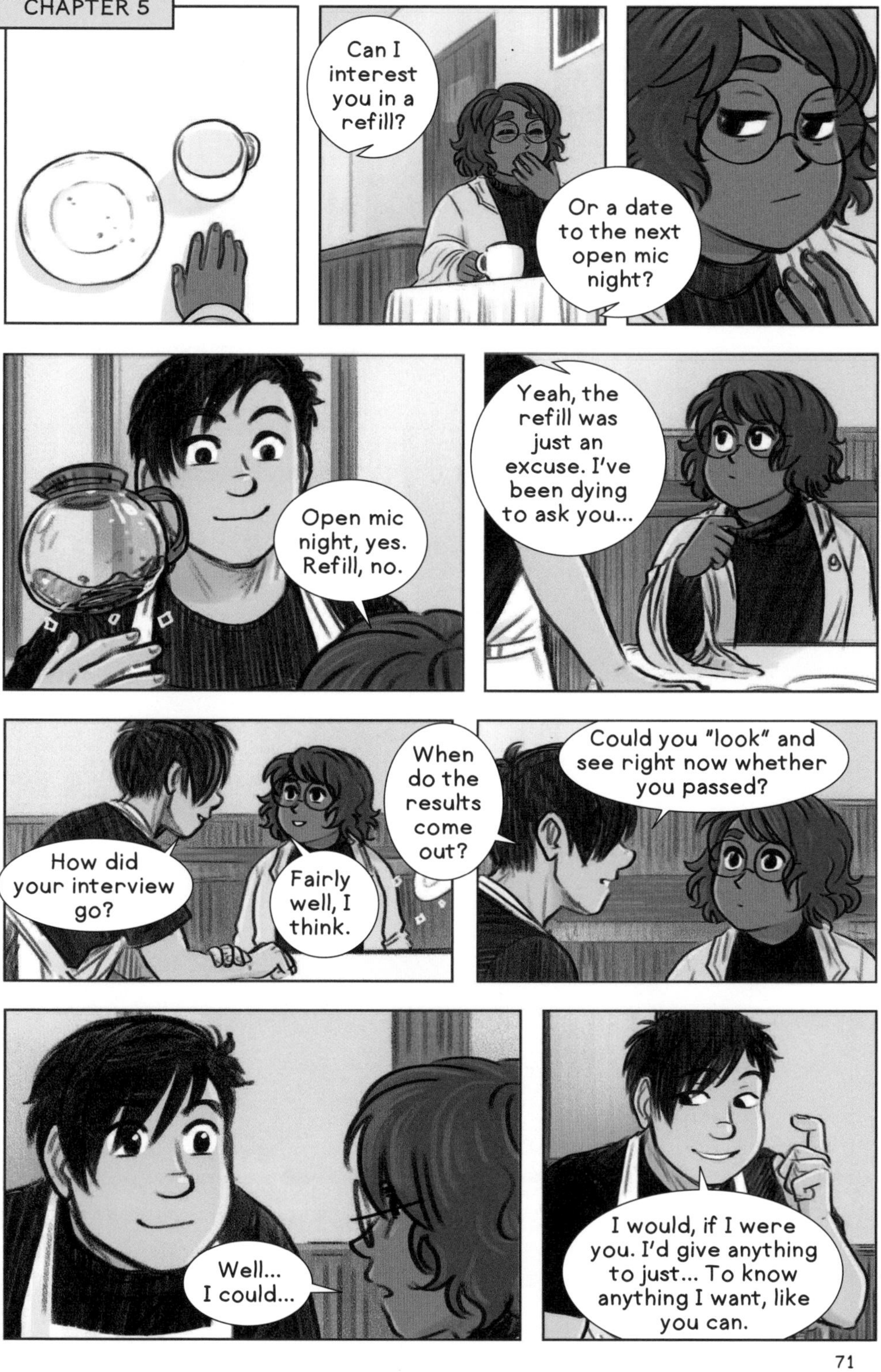
Can I interest you in a refill?
Or a date to the next open mic night?
Open mic night, yes. Refill, no.
Yeah, the refill was just an excuse. I've been dying to ask you...
How did your interview go?
Fairly well, I think.
When do the results come out?
Could you "look" and see right now whether you passed?
Well... I could...
I would, if I were you. I'd give anything to just... To know anything I want, like you can.

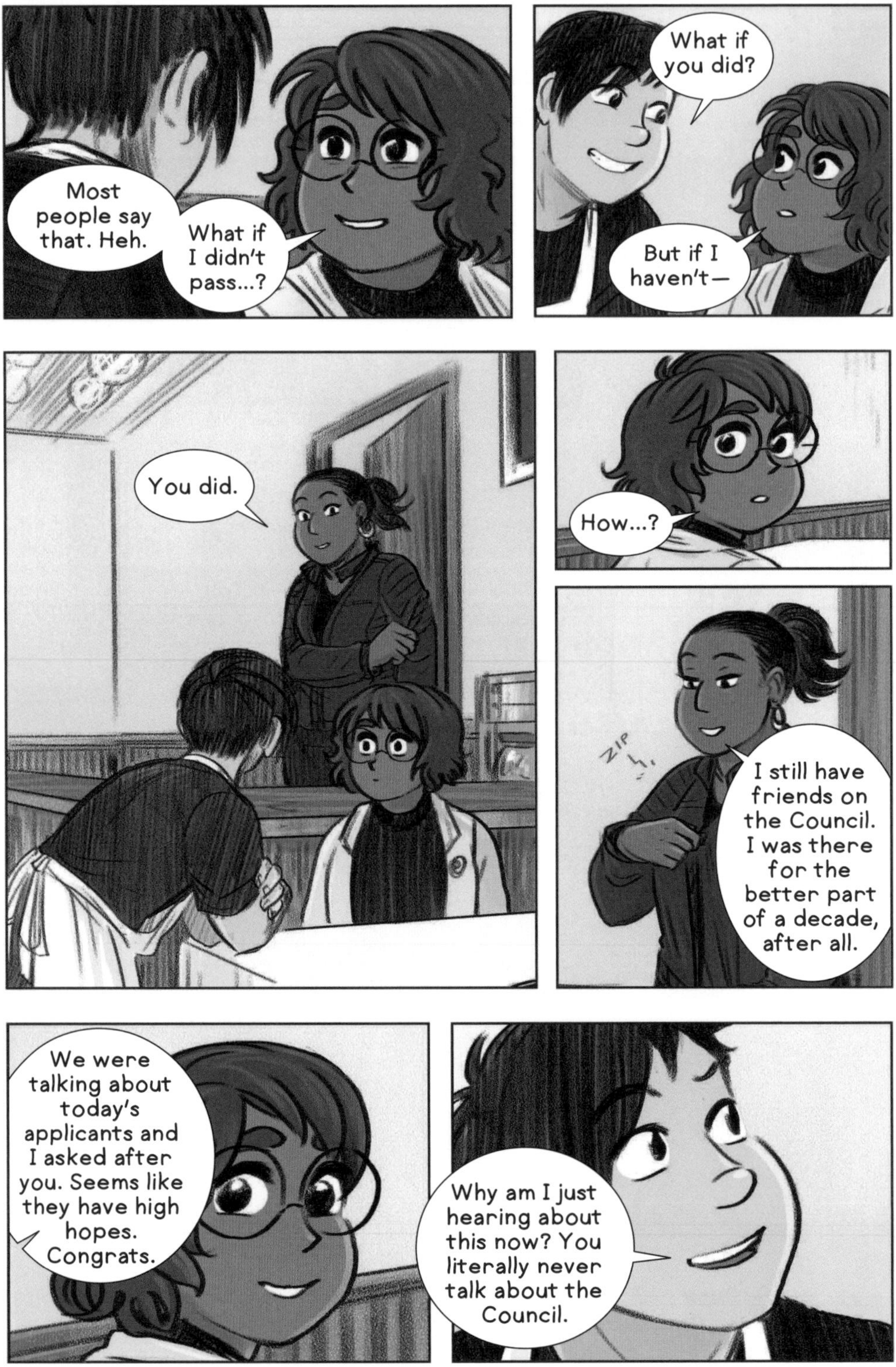

Most people say that. Heh.
What if I didn't pass...?
What if you did?
But if I haven't—
You did.
How...?
ZIP
I still have friends on the Council. I was there for the better part of a decade, after all.
We were talking about today's applicants and I asked after you. Seems like they have high hopes. Congrats.
Why am I just hearing about this now? You literally never talk about the Council.

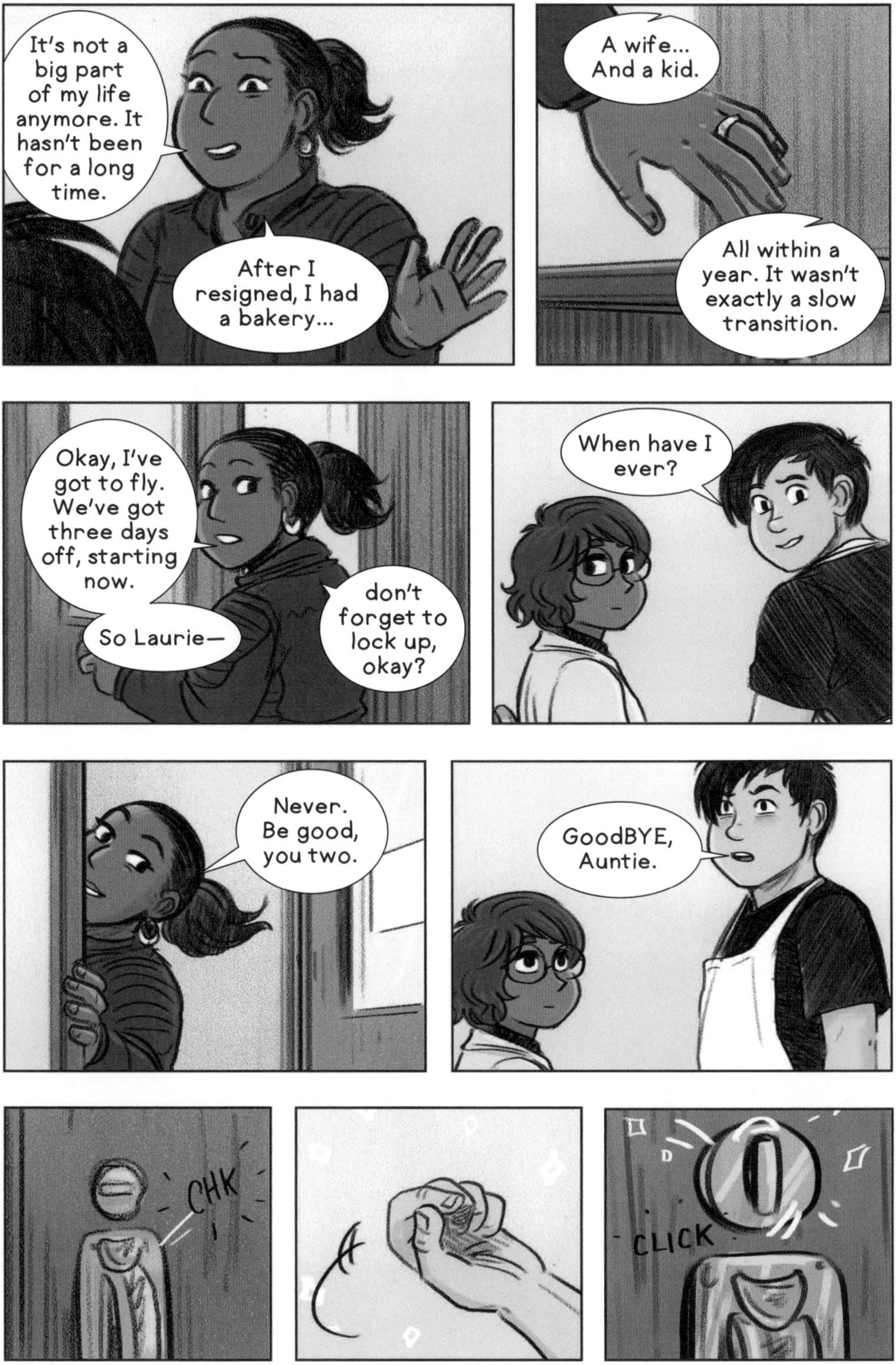
It's not a big part of my life anymore. It hasn't been for a long time.
After I resigned, I had a bakery...
A wife... And a kid.
All within a year. It wasn't exactly a slow transition.
Okay, I've got to fly. We've got three days off, starting now.
So Laurie—
don't forget to lock up, okay?
When have I ever?
Never. Be good, you two.
GoodBYE, Auntie.
CHK
CLICK

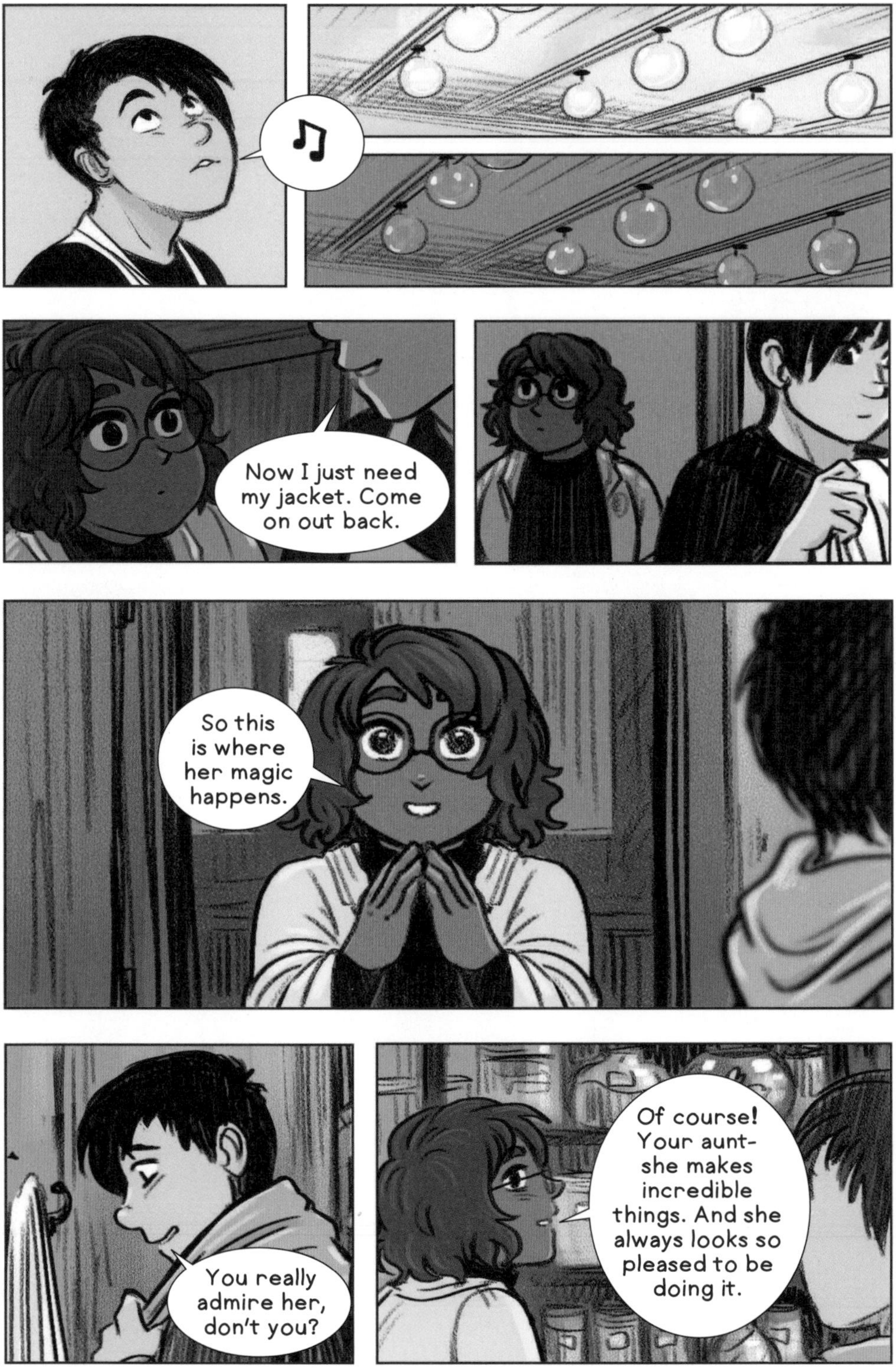
♫
Now I just need my jacket. Come on out back.
So this is where her magic happens.
You really admire her, don't you?
Of course! Your aunt- she makes incredible things. And she always looks so pleased to be doing it.

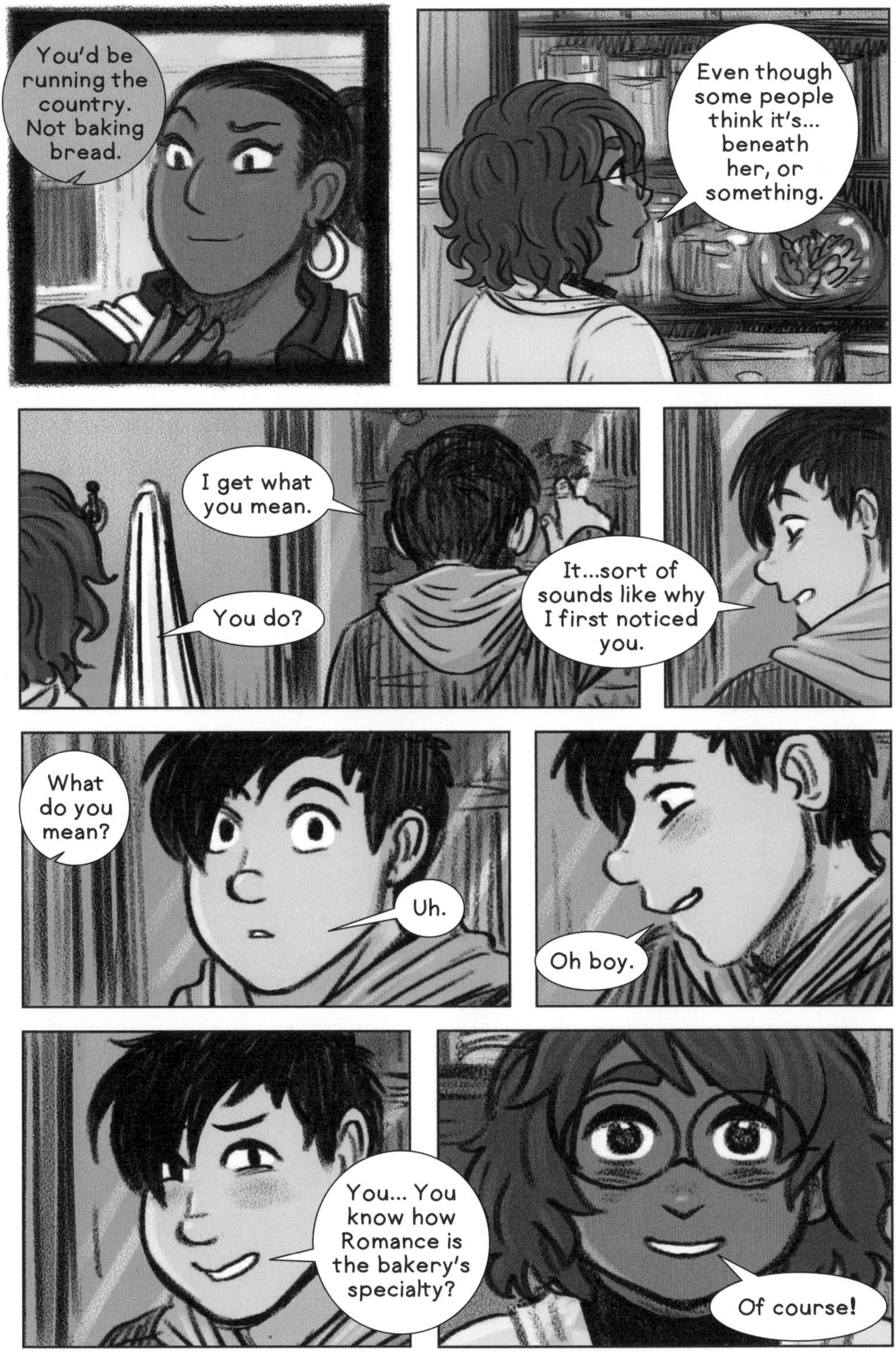
You'd be running the country. Not baking bread.
Even though some people think it's... beneath her, or something.
I get what you mean.
You do?
It...sort of sounds like why I first noticed you.
What do you mean?
Uh.
Oh boy.
You... You know how Romance is the bakery's specialty?
Of course!

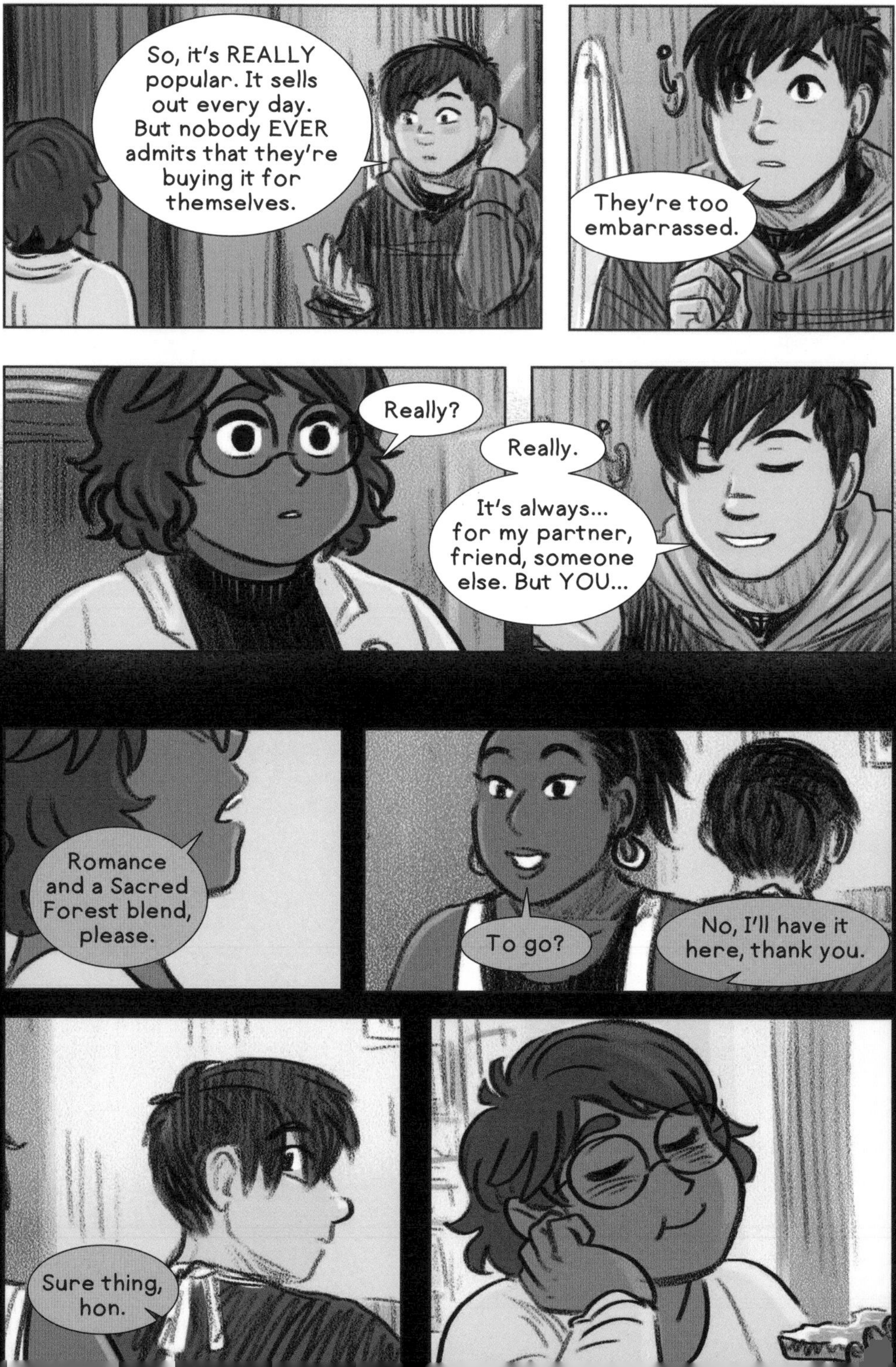
So, it's REALLY popular. It sells out every day. But nobody EVER admits that they're buying it for themselves.
They're too embarrassed.
Really?
Really.
It's always... for my partner, friend, someone else. But YOU...
Romance and a Sacred Forest blend, please.
To go?
No, I'll have it here, thank you.
Sure thing, hon.

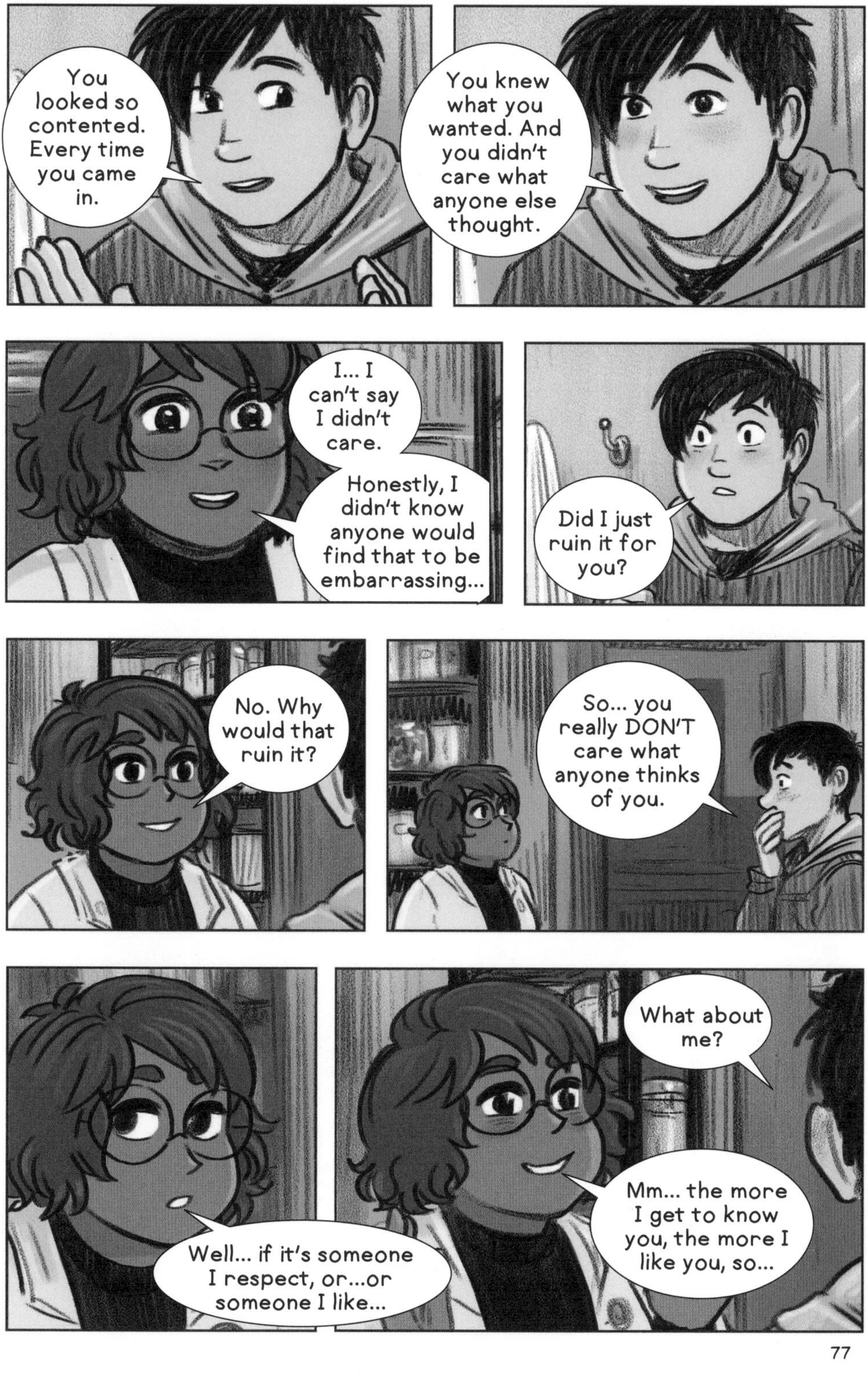
You looked so contented. Every time you came in.
You knew what you wanted. And you didn't care what anyone else thought.
I... I can't say I didn't care.
Honestly, I didn't know anyone would find that to be embarrassing...
Did I just ruin it for you?
No. Why would that ruin it?
So... you really DON'T care what anyone thinks of you.
Well... if it's someone I respect, or...or someone I like...
What about me?
Mm... the more I get to know you, the more I like you, so...

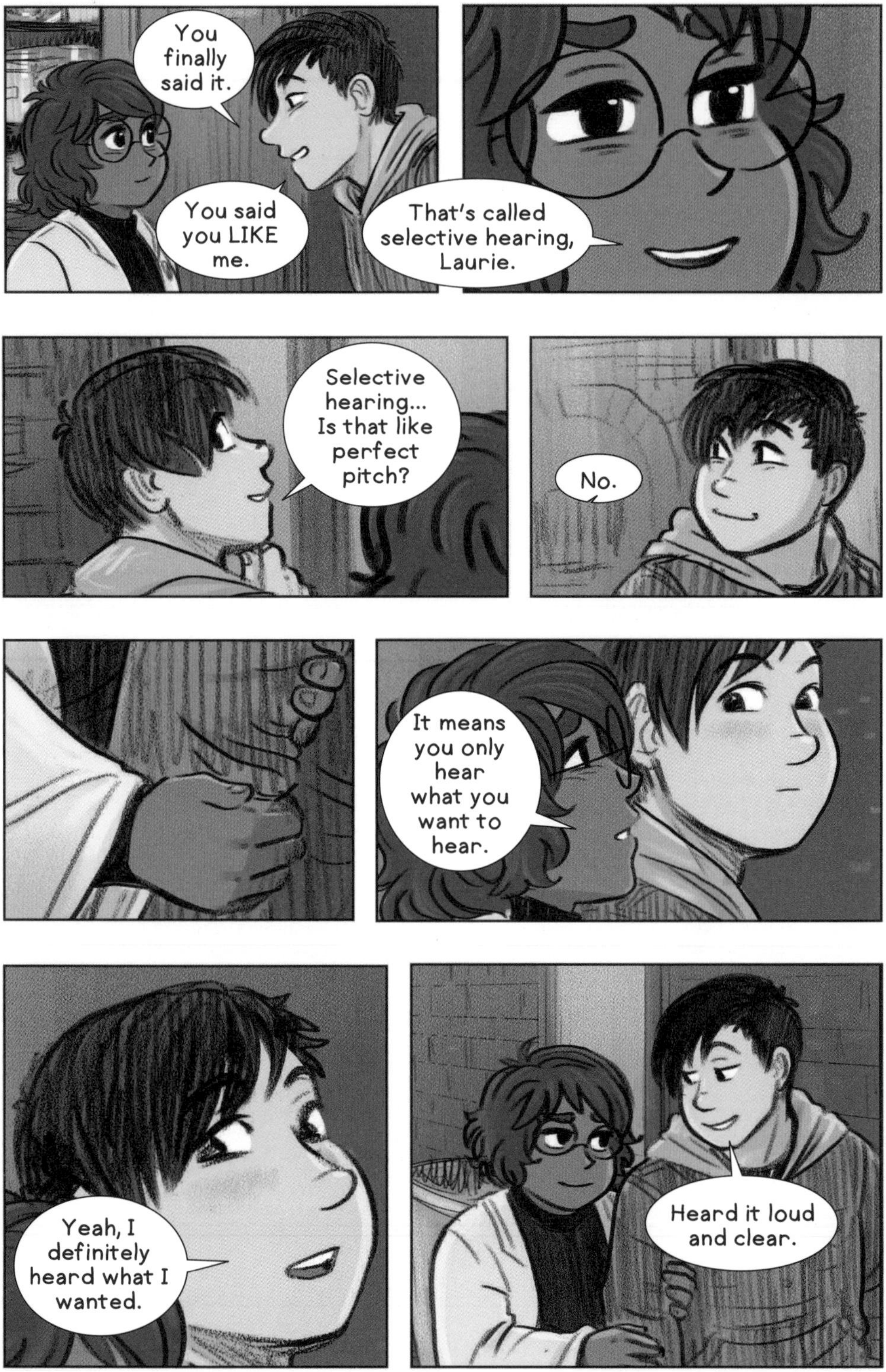
You finally said it.
You said you LIKE me.
That's called selective hearing, Laurie.
Selective hearing... Is that like perfect pitch?
No.
It means you only hear what you want to hear.
Yeah, I definitely heard what I wanted.
Heard it loud and clear.

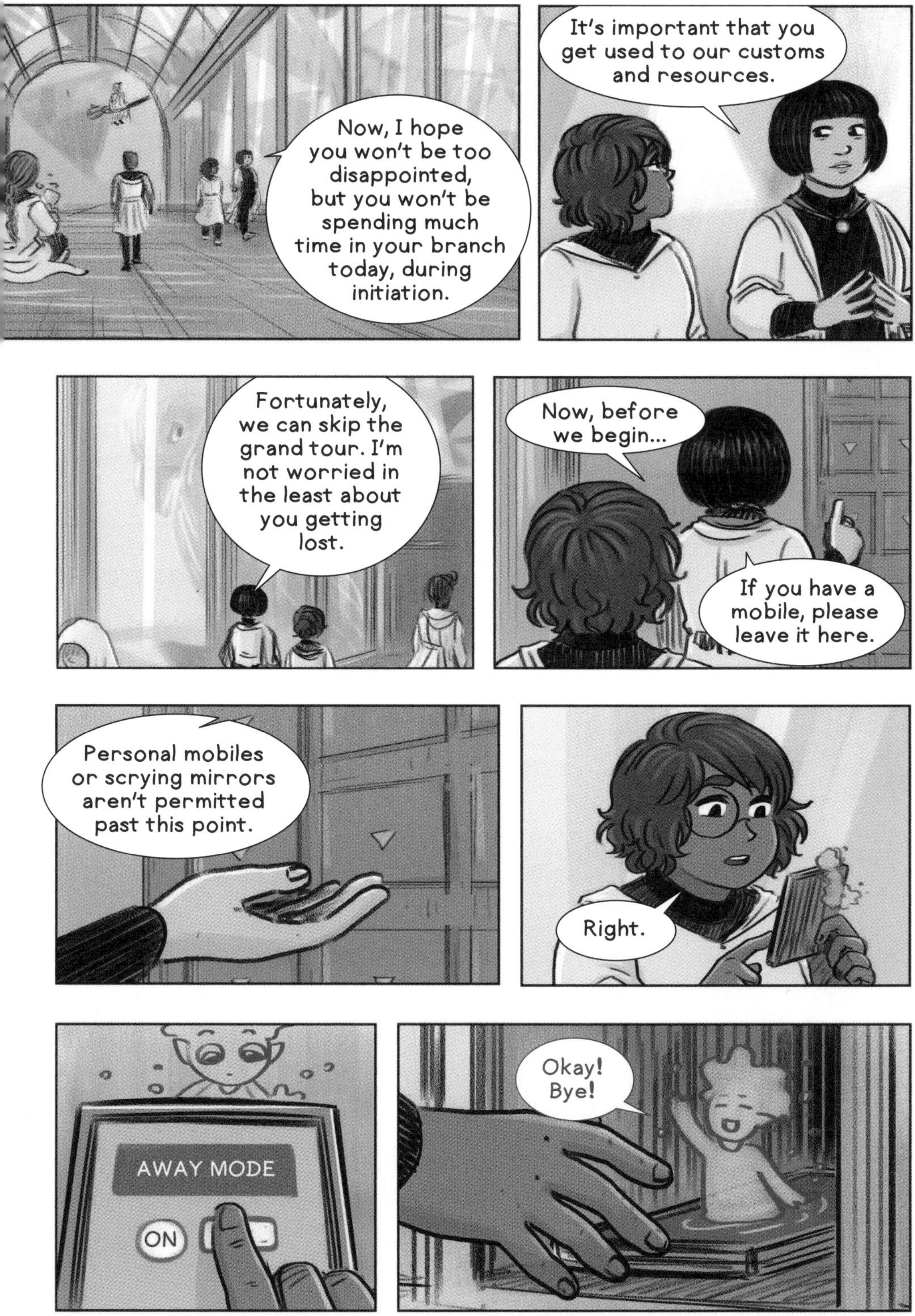
Now, I hope you won't be too disappointed, but you won't be spending much time in your branch today, during initiation.
It's important that you get used to our customs and resources.
Fortunately, we can skip the grand tour. I'm not worried in the least about you getting lost.
Now, before we begin...
If you have a mobile, please leave it here.
Personal mobiles or scrying mirrors aren't permitted past this point.
Right.
AWAY MODE
ON
Okay! Bye!

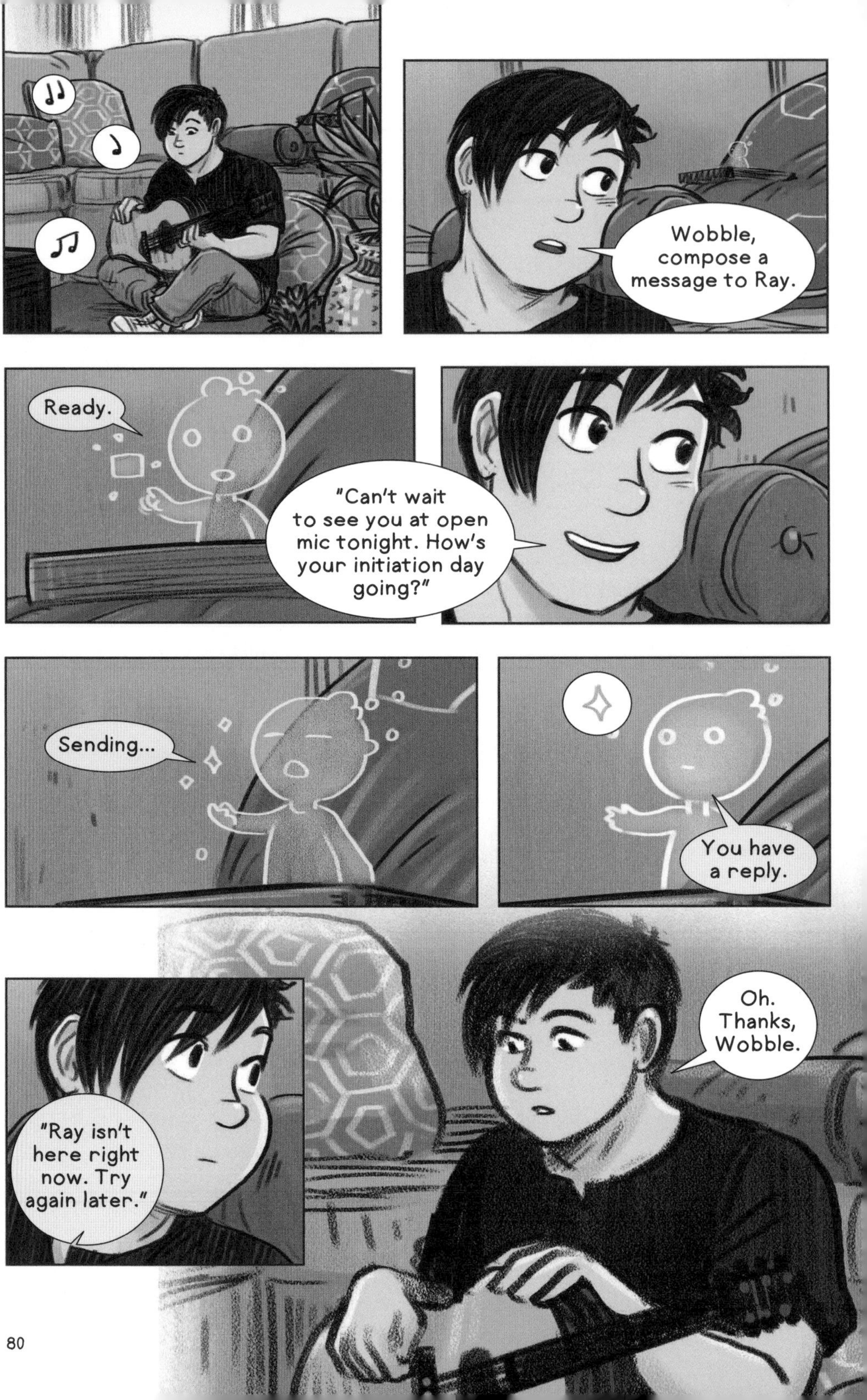
Wobble, compose a message to Ray.
Ready.
"Can't wait to see you at open mic tonight. How's your initiation day going?"
Sending...
You have a reply.
Oh. Thanks, Wobble.
"Ray isn't here right now. Try again later."

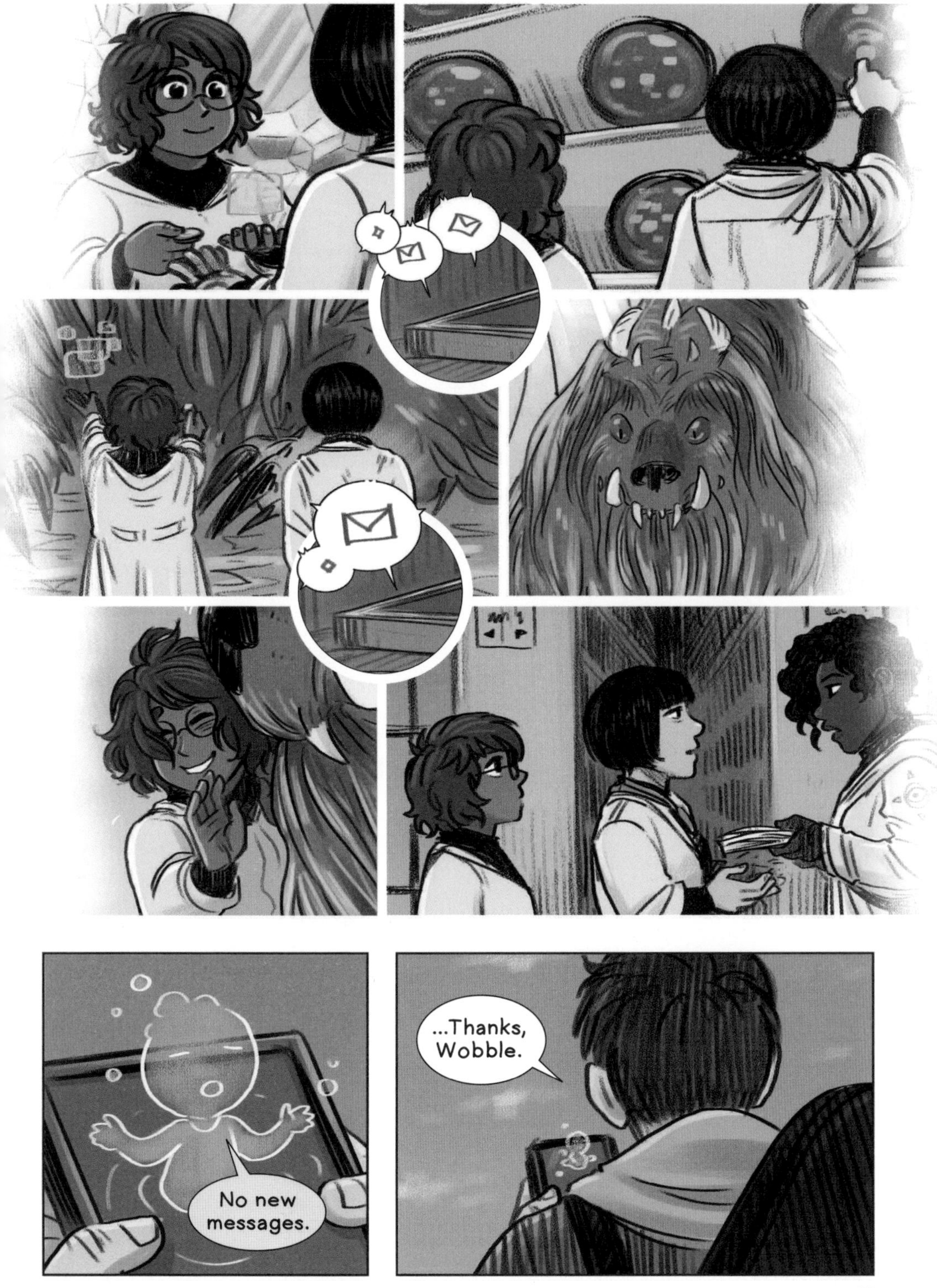
No new messages.
...Thanks, Wobble.

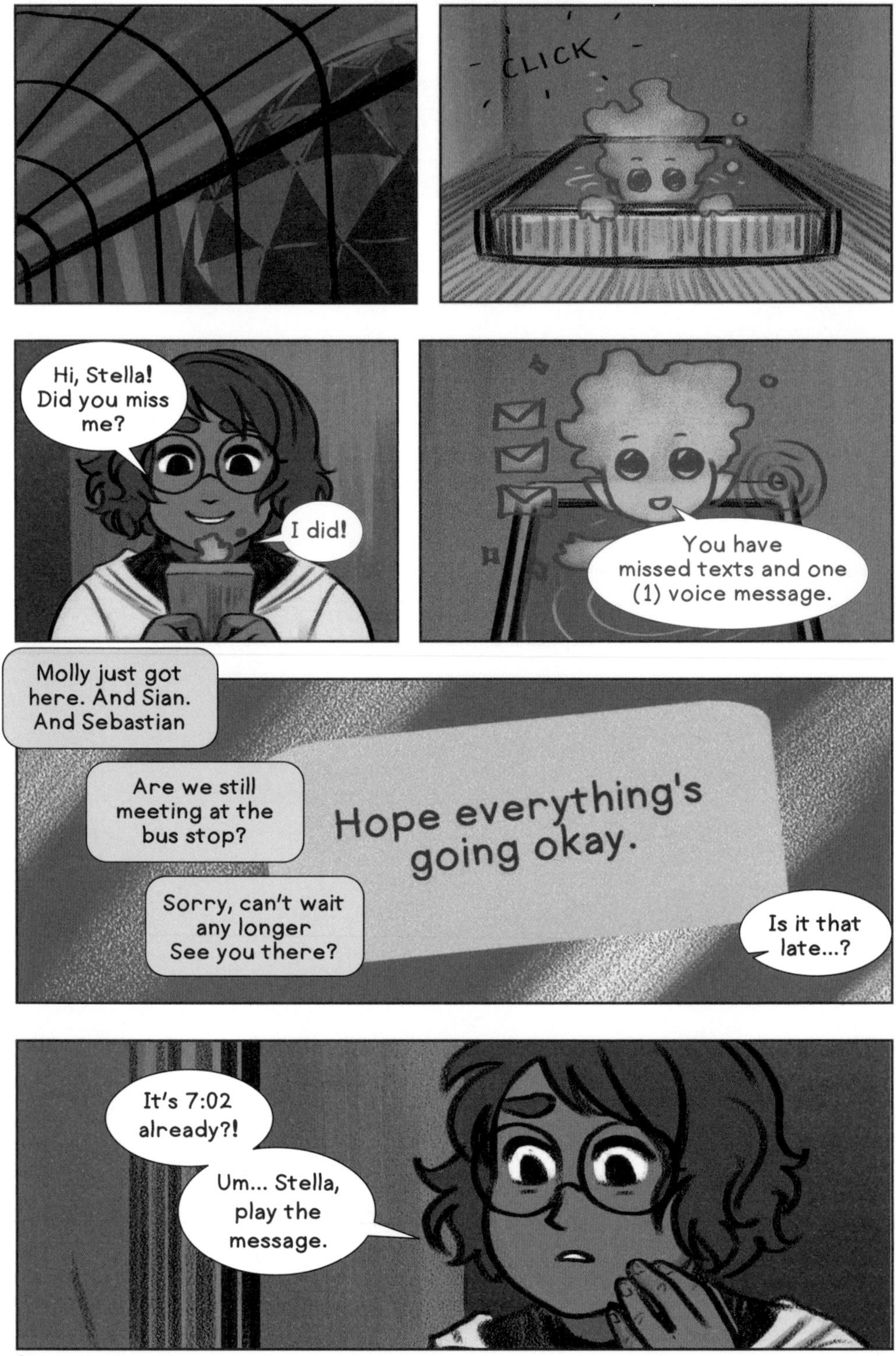
CLICK
Hi, Stella! Did you miss me?
I did!
You have missed texts and one (1) voice message.
Molly just got here. And Sian. And Sebastian
Are we still meeting at the bus stop?
Hope everything's going okay.
Sorry, can't wait any longer See you there?
Is it that late...?
It's 7:02 already?!
Um... Stella, play the message.

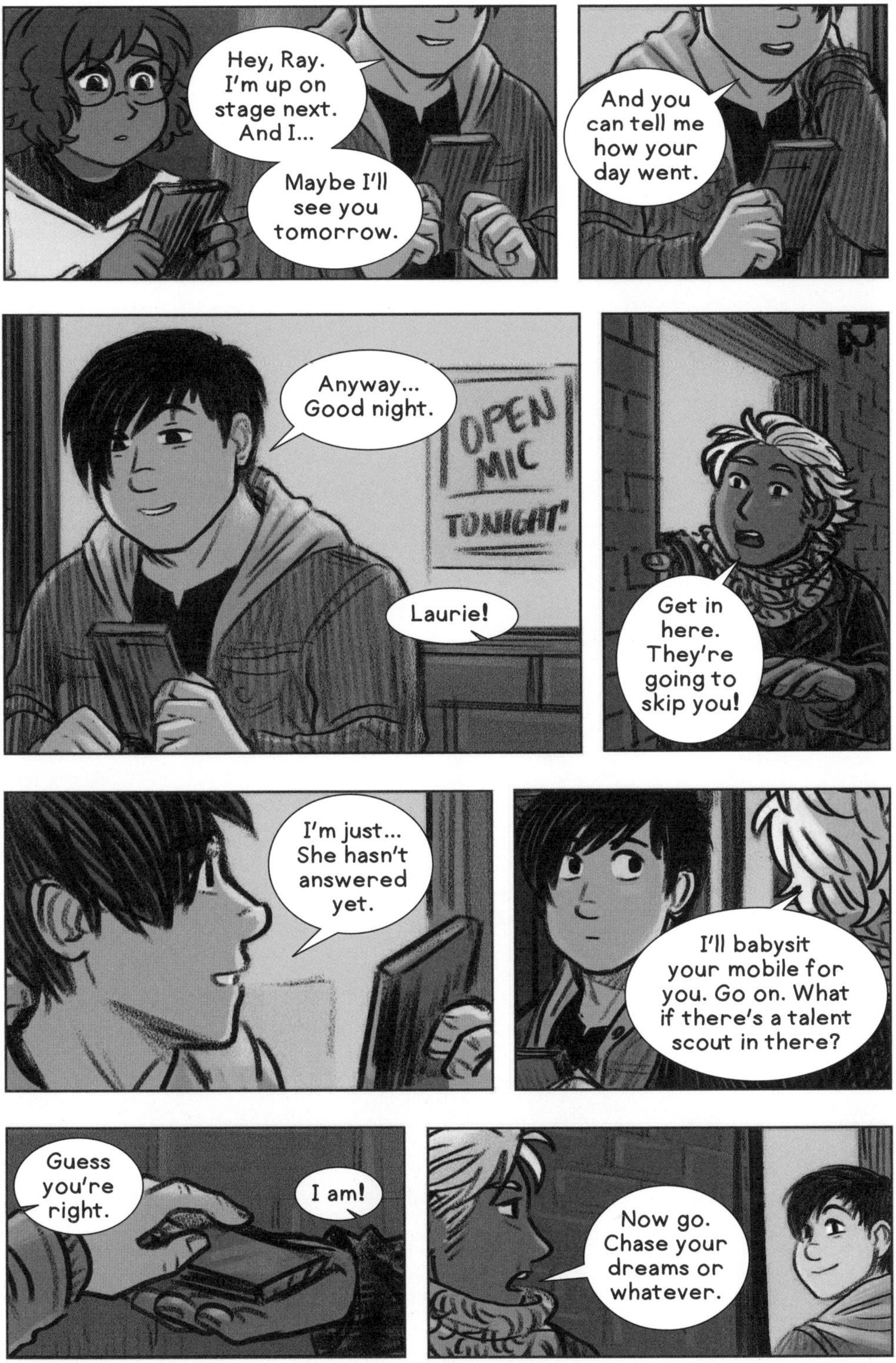
Hey, Ray. I'm up on stage next. And I...
Maybe I'll see you tomorrow.
And you can tell me how your day went.
Anyway... Good night.
OPEN MIC TONIGHT!
Laurie!
Get in here. They're going to skip you!
I'm just... She hasn't answered yet.
I'll babysit your mobile for you. Go on. What if there's a talent scout in there?
Guess you're right.
I am!
Now go. Chase your dreams or whatever.

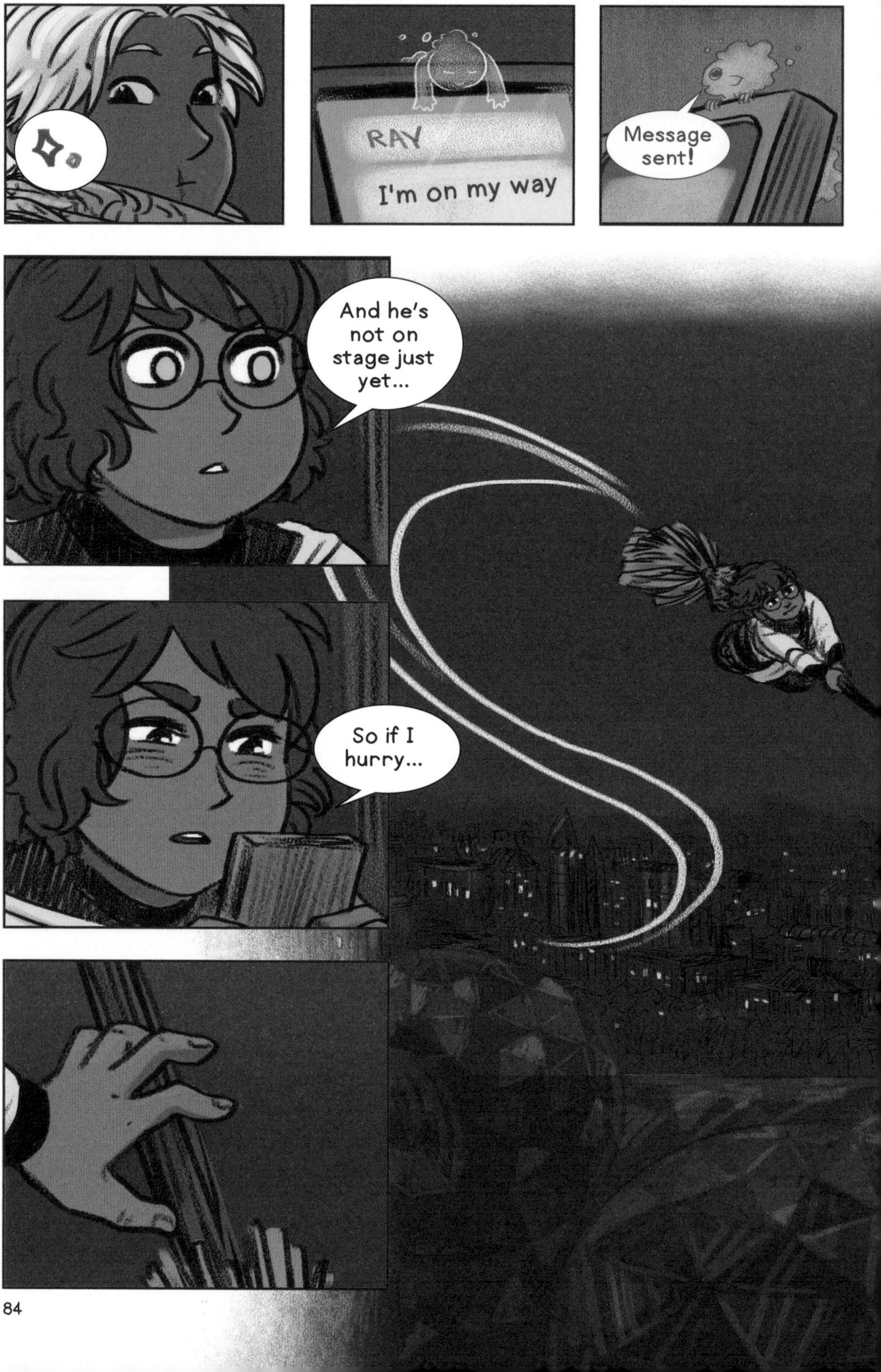
RAY
I'm on my way
Message sent!
And he's not on stage just yet...
So if I hurry...

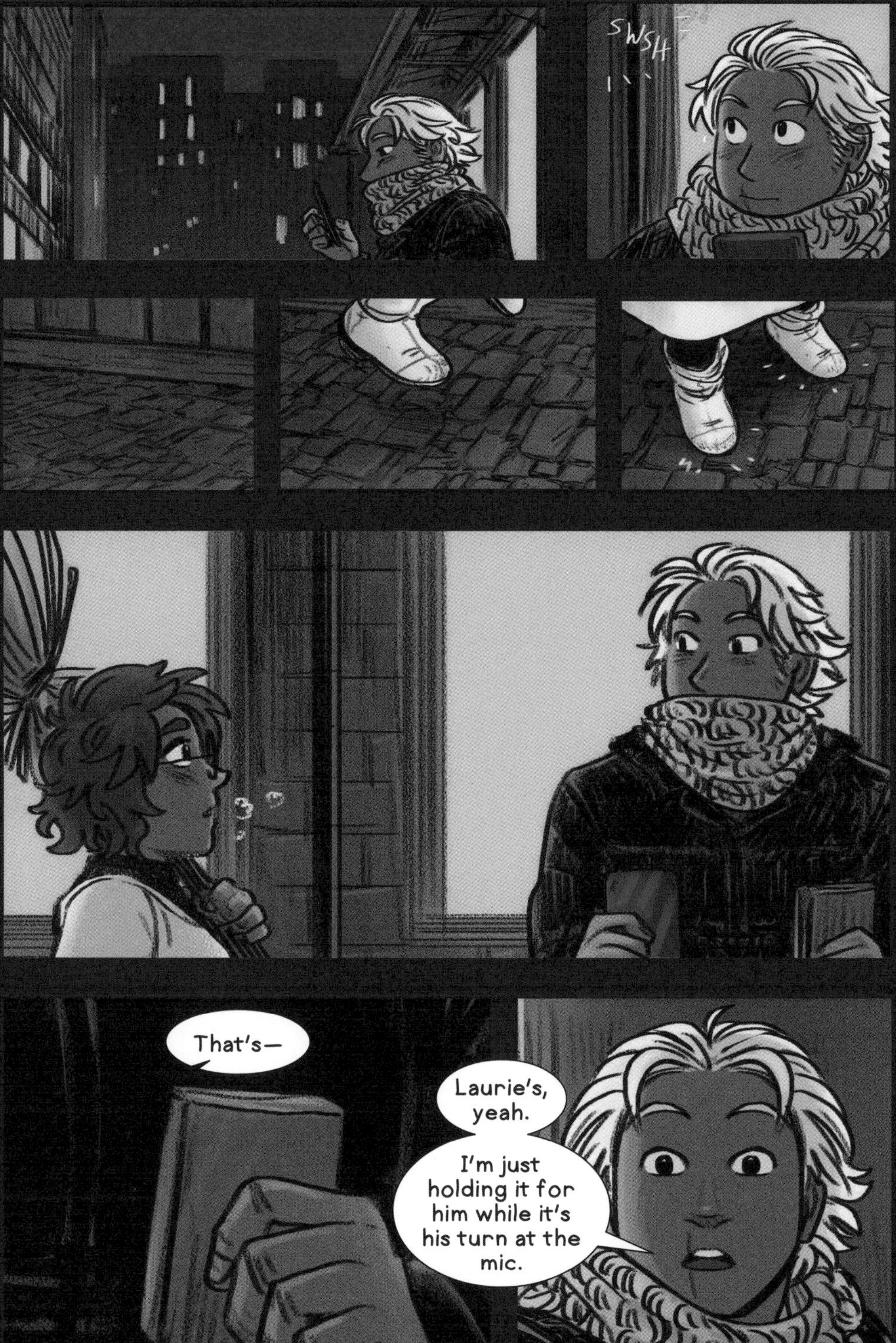
SWSH
That's—
Laurie's, yeah.
I'm just holding it for him while it's his turn at the mic.

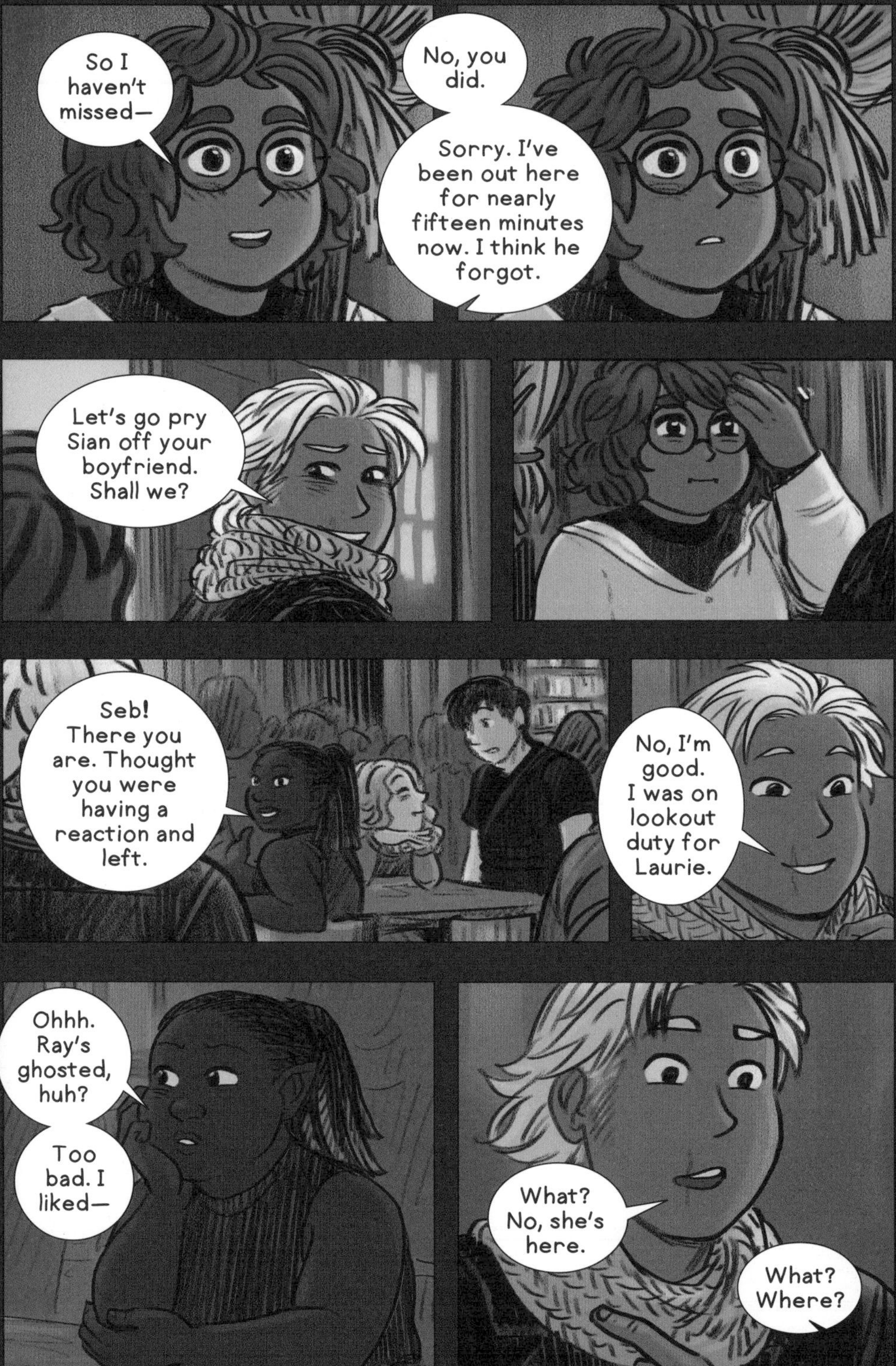
So I haven't missed—
No, you did.
Sorry. I've been out here for nearly fifteen minutes now. I think he forgot.
Let's go pry Sian off your boyfriend. Shall we?
Seb! There you are. Thought you were having a reaction and left.
No, I'm good. I was on lookout duty for Laurie.
Ohhh. Ray's ghosted, huh?
Too bad. I liked—
What? No, she's here.
What? Where?

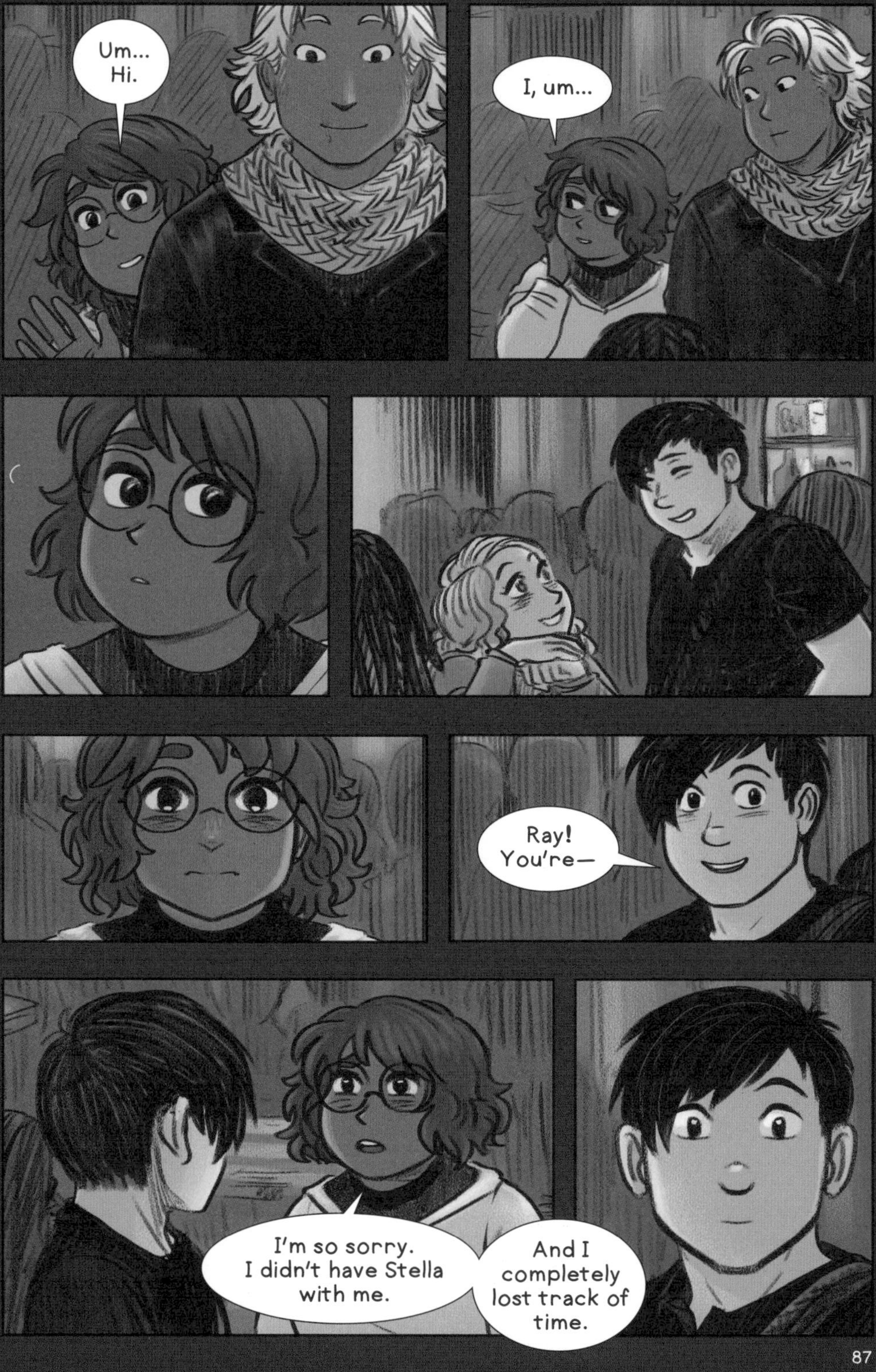
Um... Hi.
I, um...
Ray! You're—
I'm so sorry. I didn't have Stella with me.
And I completely lost track of time.

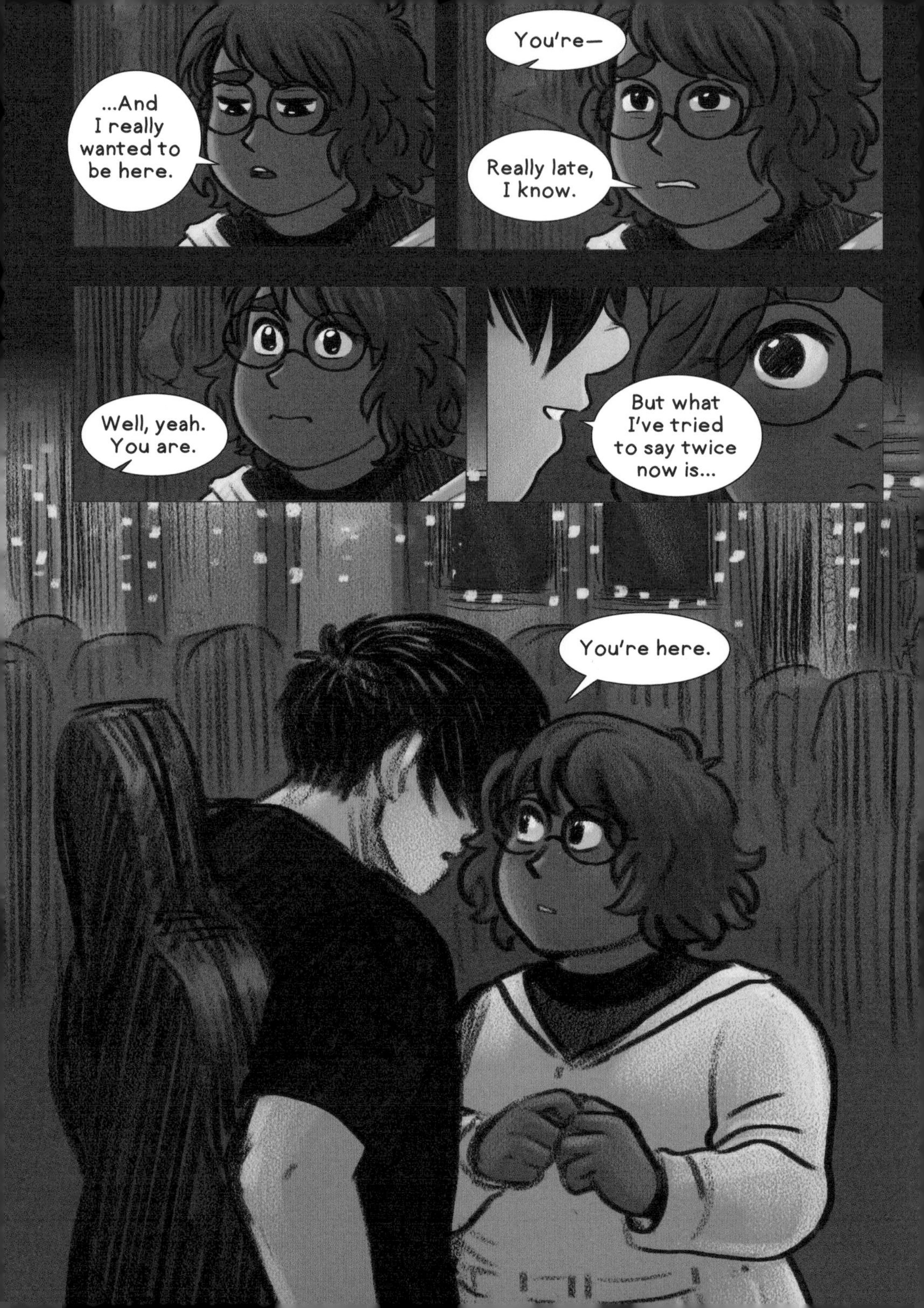
...And I really wanted to be here.
You're—
Really late, I know.
Well, yeah. You are.
But what I've tried to say twice now is...
You're here.

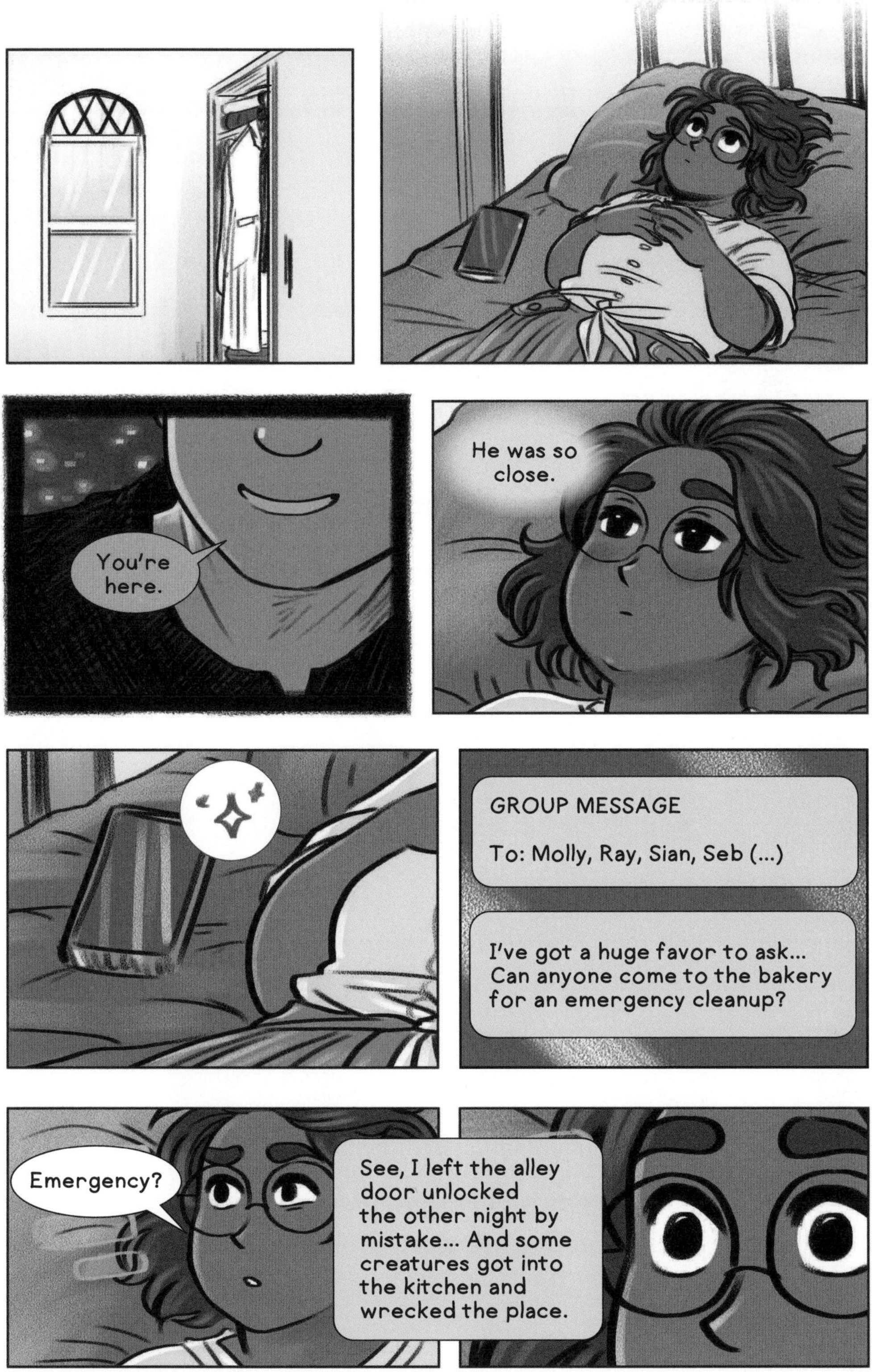
You're here.
He was so close.
GROUP MESSAGE
To: Molly, Ray, Sian, Seb (...)
I've got a huge favor to ask... Can anyone come to the bakery for an emergency cleanup?
Emergency?
See, I left the alley door unlocked the other night by mistake... And some creatures got into the kitchen and wrecked the place.

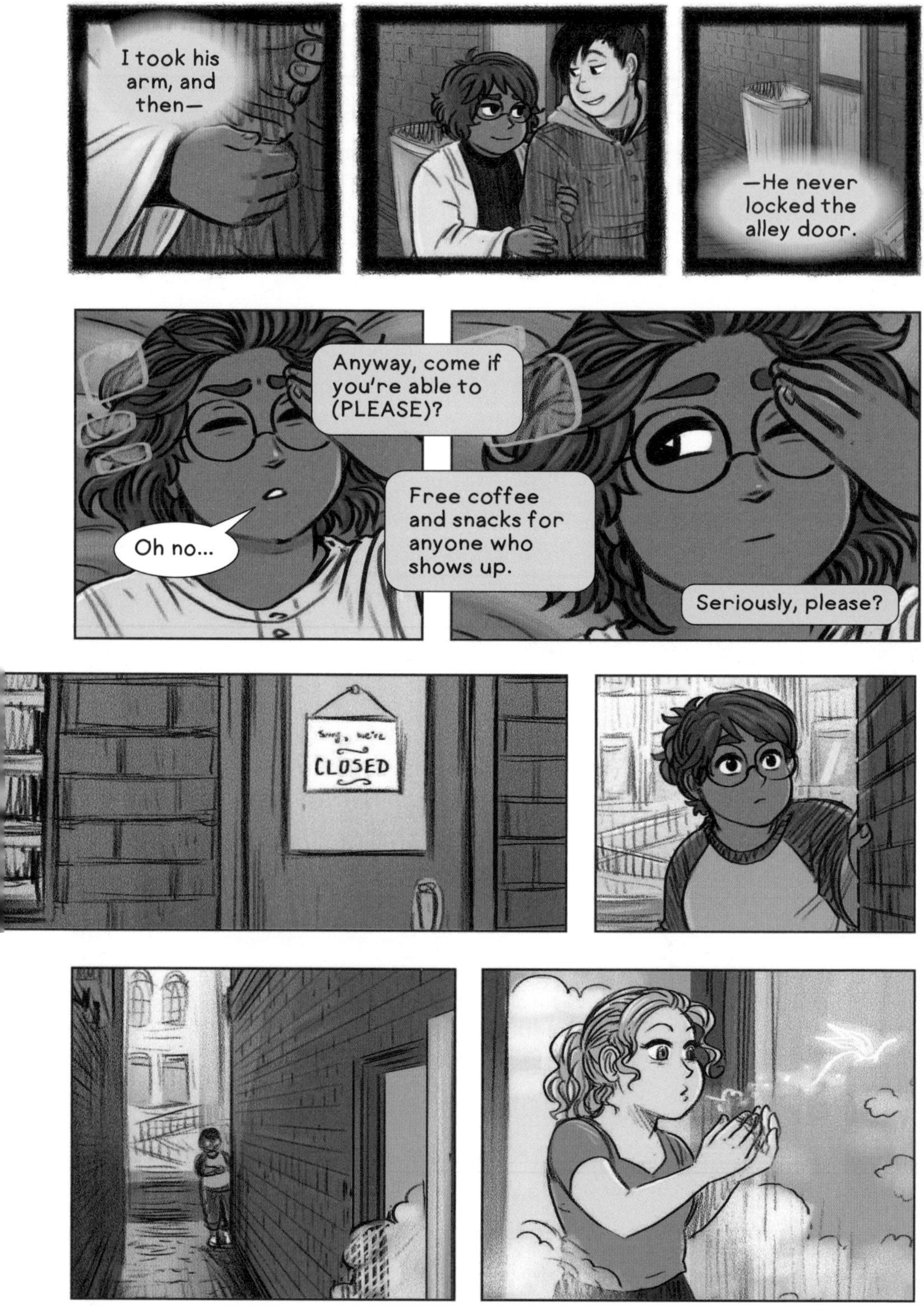
I took his arm, and then—
—He never locked the alley door.
Anyway, come if you're able to (PLEASE)?
Oh no...
Free coffee and snacks for anyone who shows up.
Seriously, please?
CLOSED

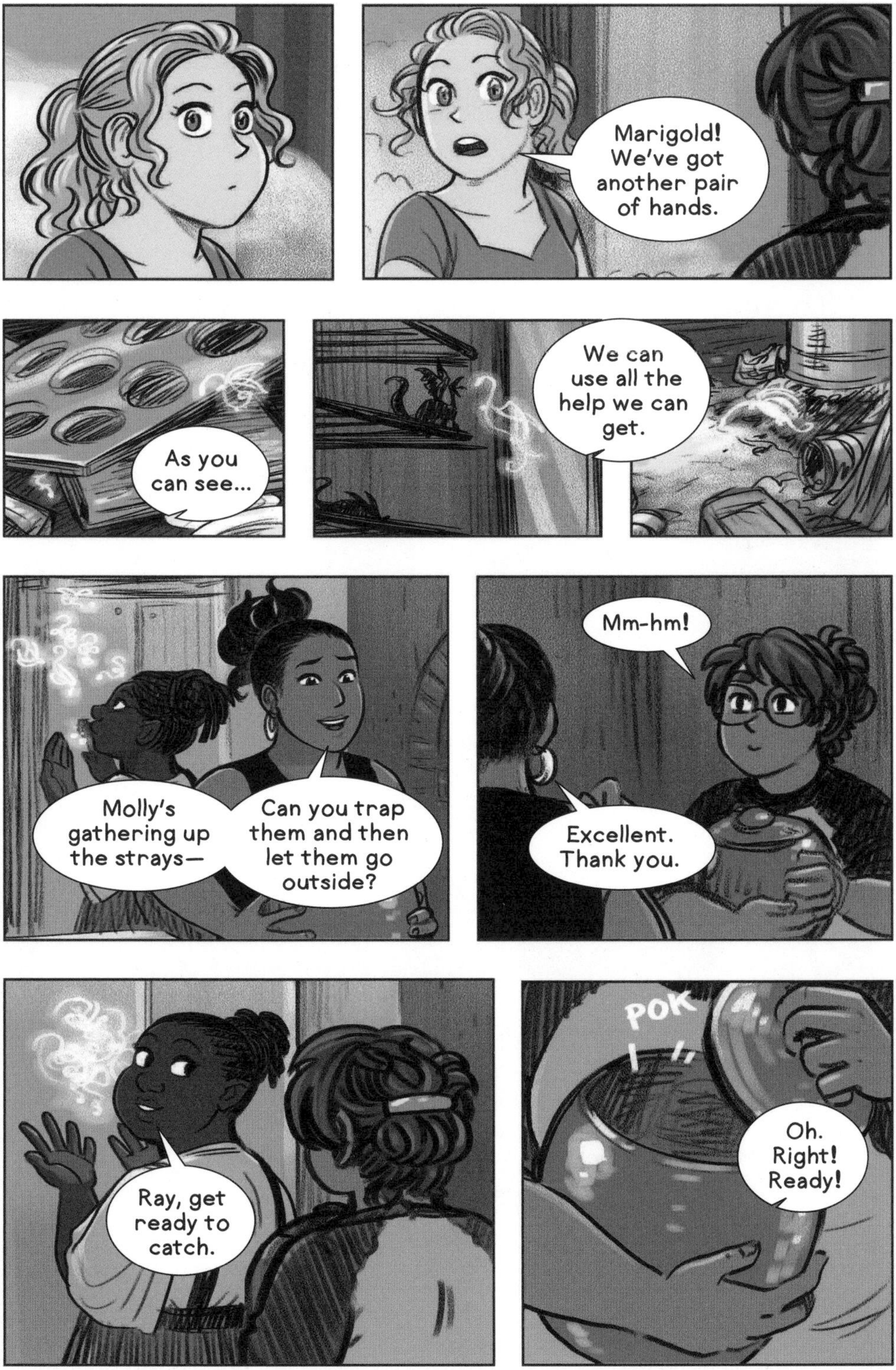
Marigold! We've got another pair of hands.
As you can see...
We can use all the help we can get.
Molly's gathering up the strays—
Can you trap them and then let them go outside?
Mm-hm!
Excellent. Thank you.
Ray, get ready to catch.
POK
Oh. Right! Ready!

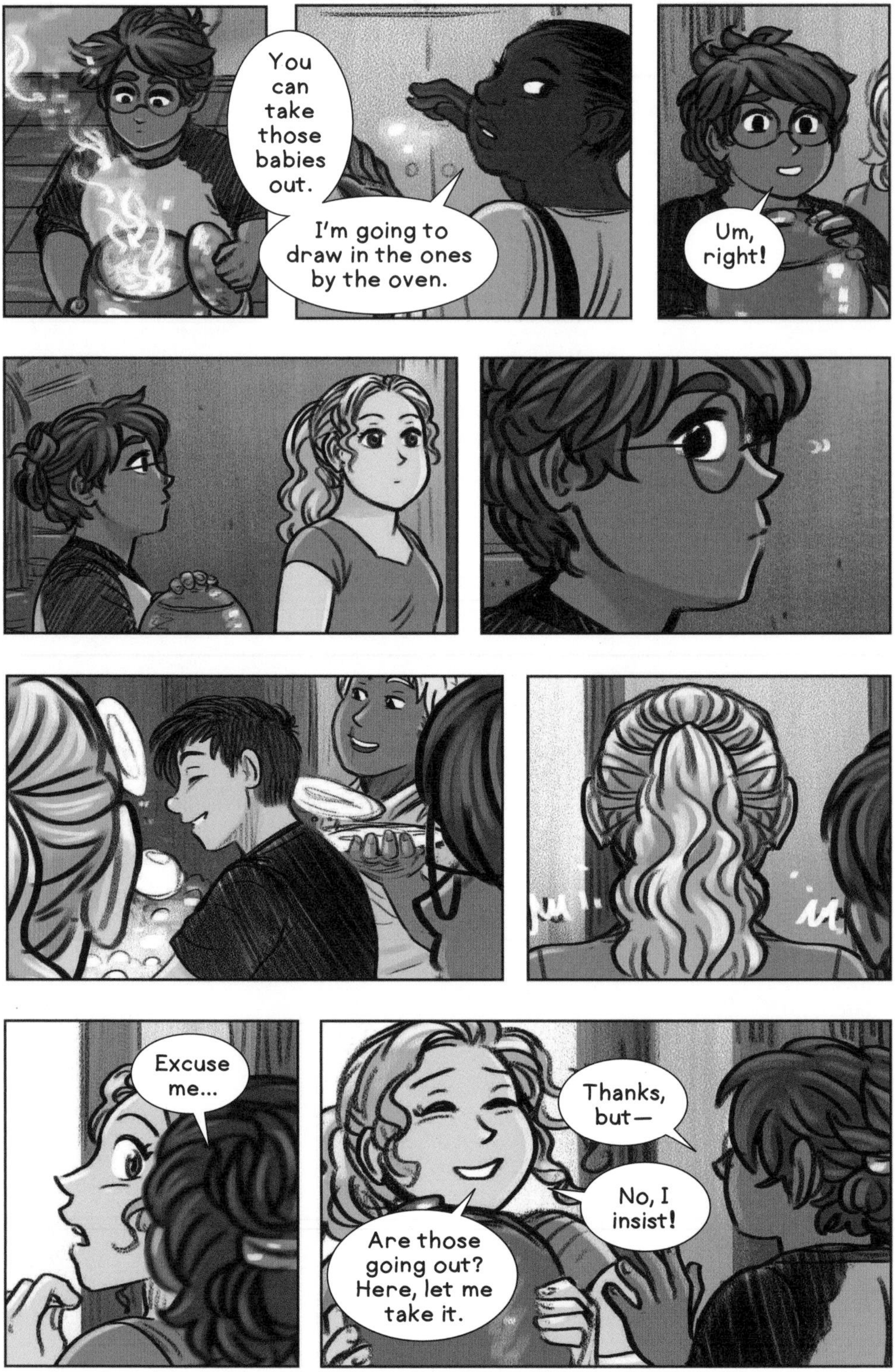
You can take those babies out.
I'm going to draw in the ones by the oven.
Um, right!
Excuse me...
Thanks, but—
Are those going out? Here, let me take it.
No, I insist!

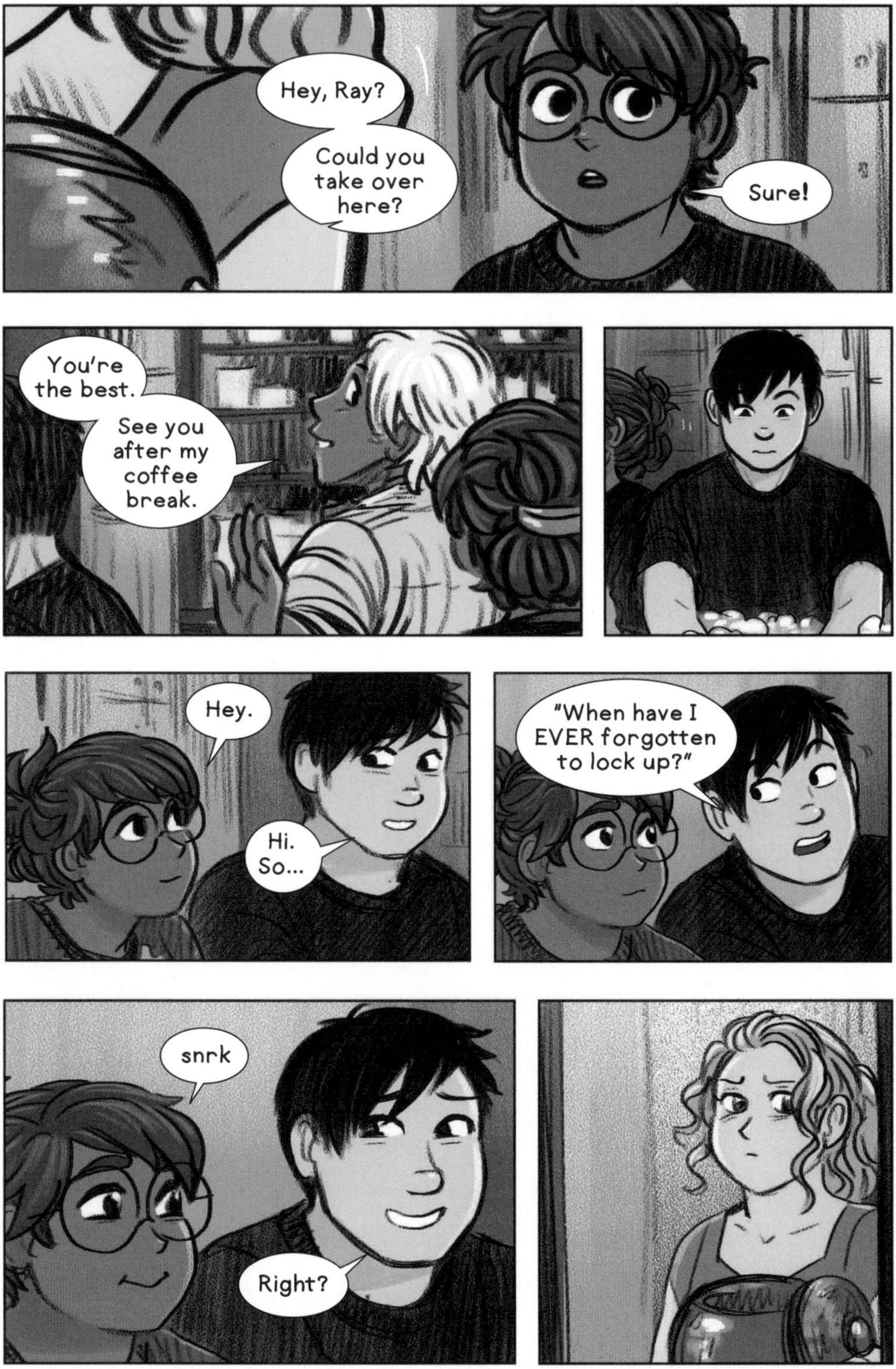
Hey, Ray?
Could you take over here?
Sure!
You're the best.
See you after my coffee break.
Hey.
Hi. So...
"When have I EVER forgotten to lock up?"
snrk
Right?

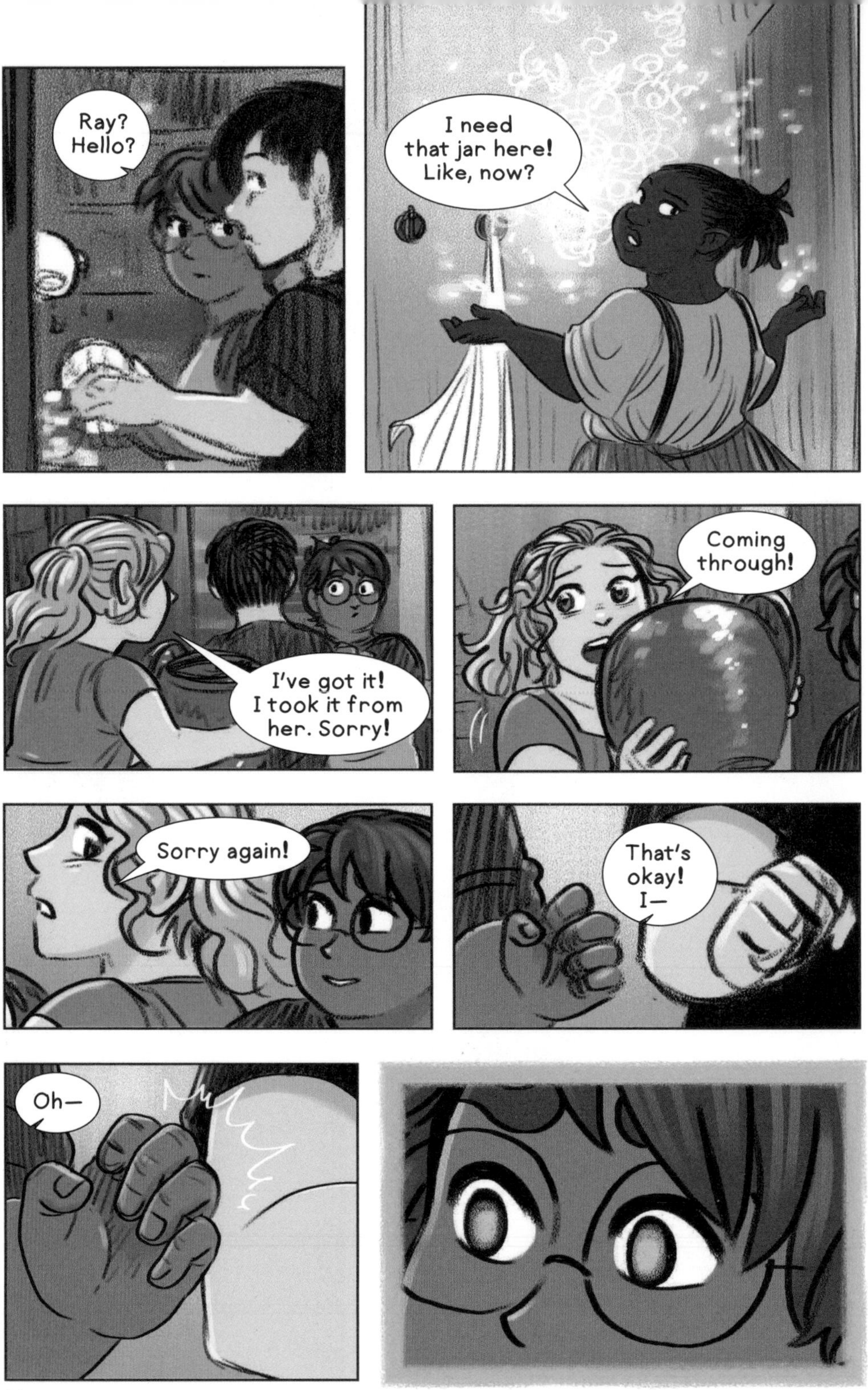
Ray? Hello?
I need that jar here! Like, now?
I've got it! I took it from her. Sorry!
Coming through!
Sorry again!
That's okay! I—
Oh—

I'm not a true seer. True seers have visions of the future.

In knowing what might come to be, they gain the ability to change it.

I tried. For years, I tried to learn how to do it... How to see the possibilities of the future.

Instead, all I achieved was increased accuracy.

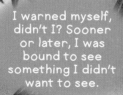

I warned myself, didn't I? Sooner or later, I was bound to see something I didn't want to see.

And this is it, isn't it? All perfectly accurate, down to every last detail.

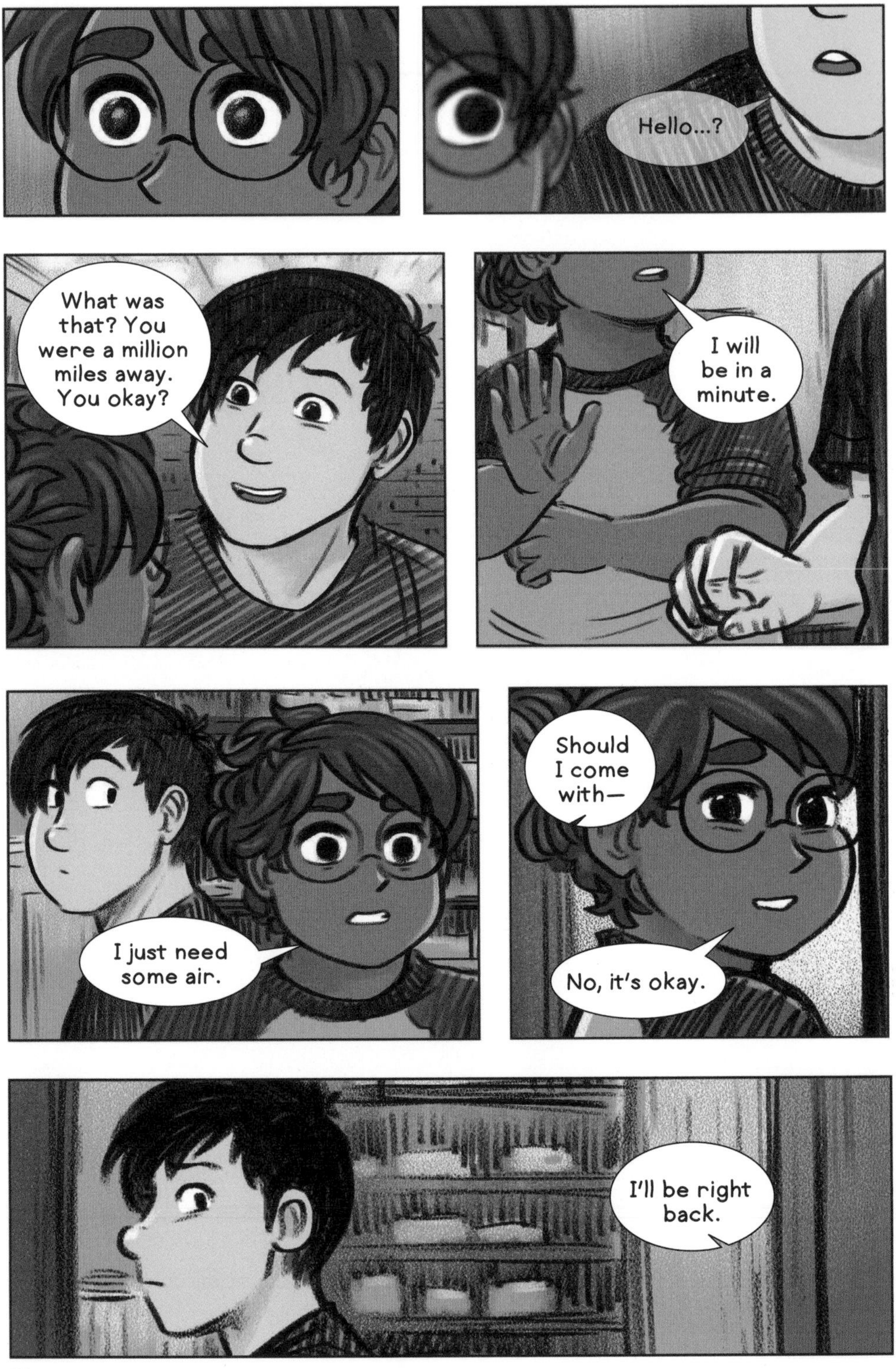
Hello...?
What was that? You were a million miles away. You okay?
I will be in a minute.
I just need some air.
Should I come with—
No, it's okay.
I'll be right back.

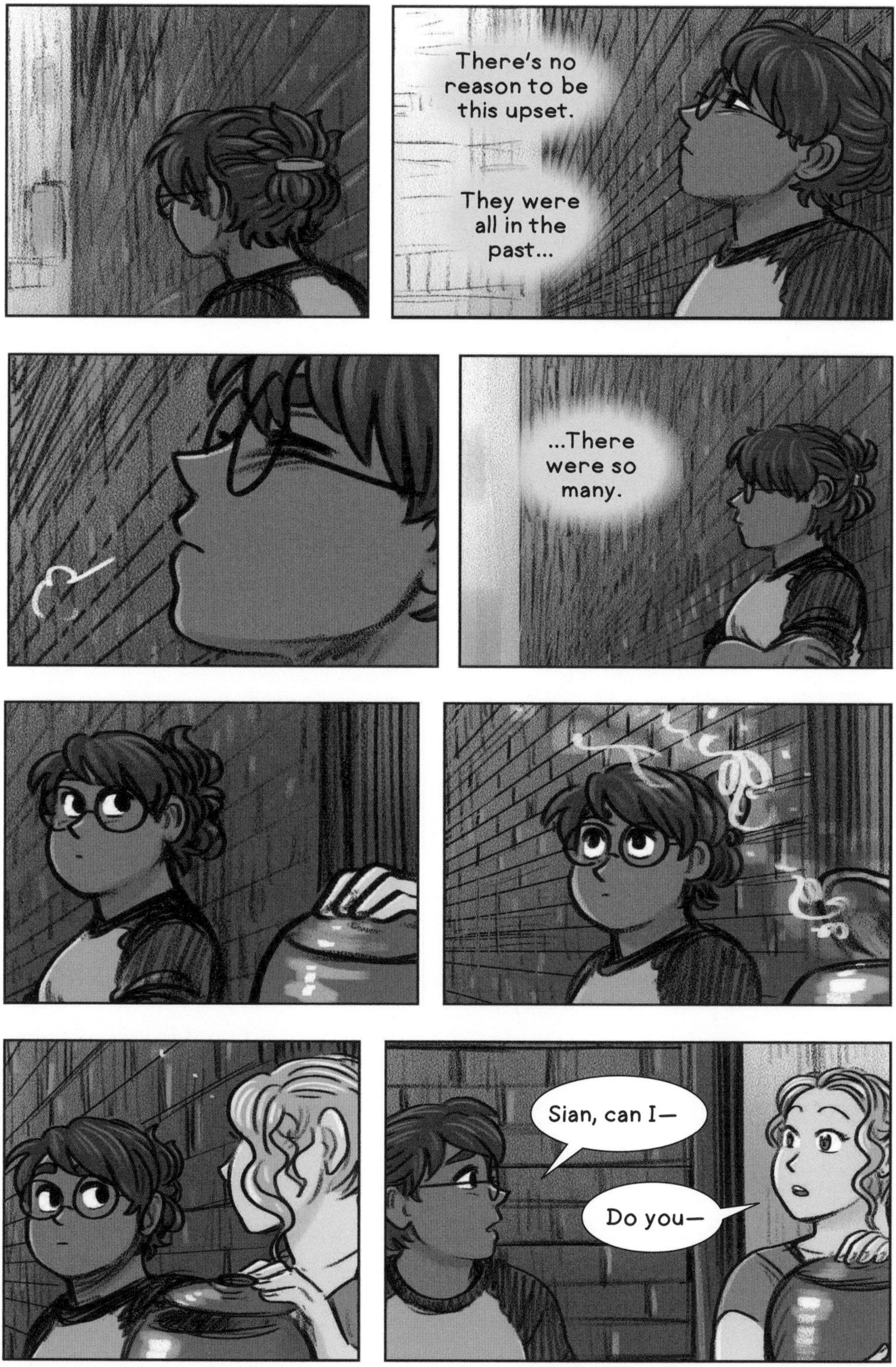
There's no reason to be this upset.
They were all in the past...
...There were so many.
Sian, can I—
Do you—

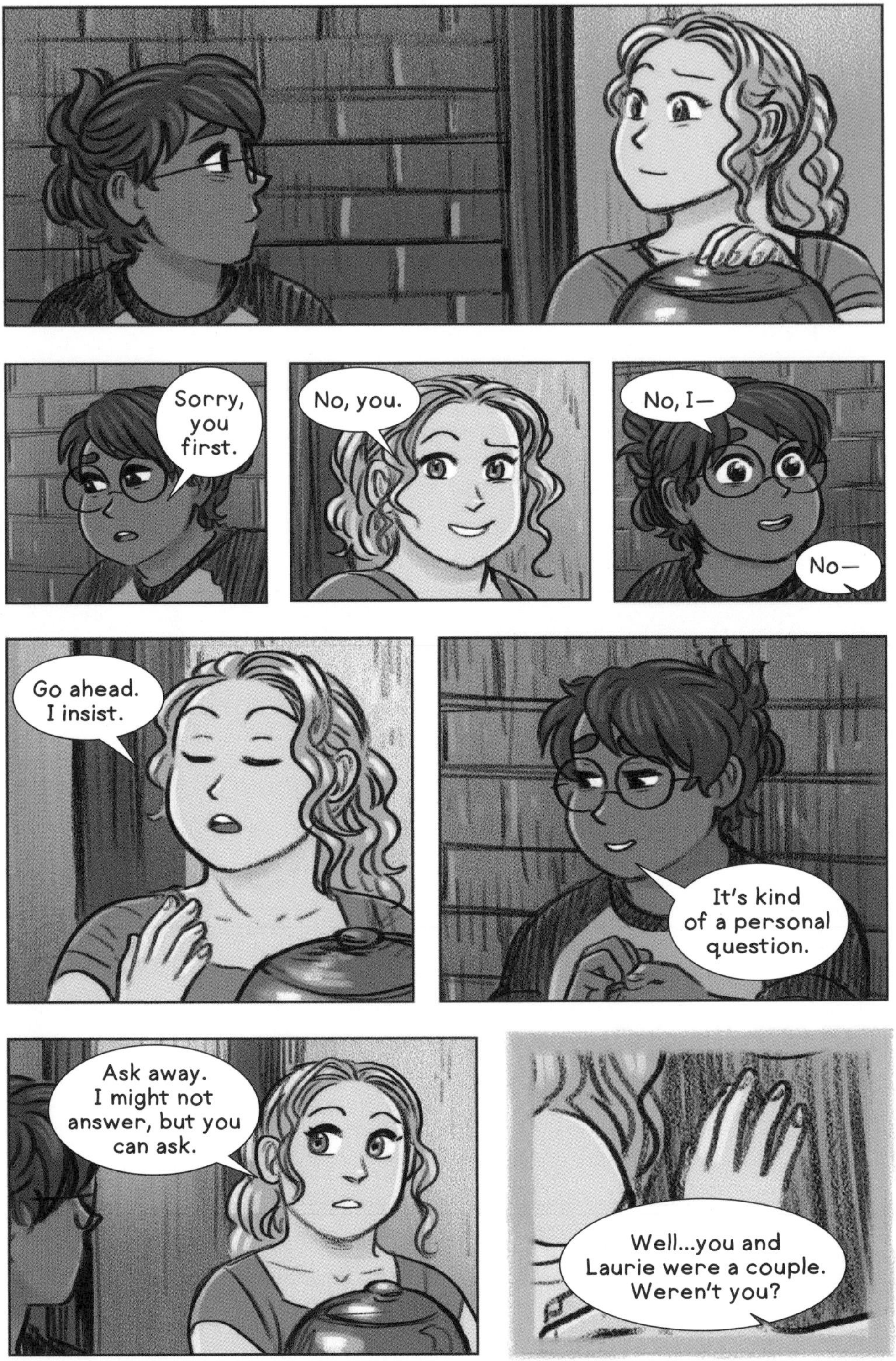

Sorry, you first.
No, you.
No, I—
No—
Go ahead. I insist.
It's kind of a personal question.
Ask away. I might not answer, but you can ask.
Well...you and Laurie were a couple. Weren't you?

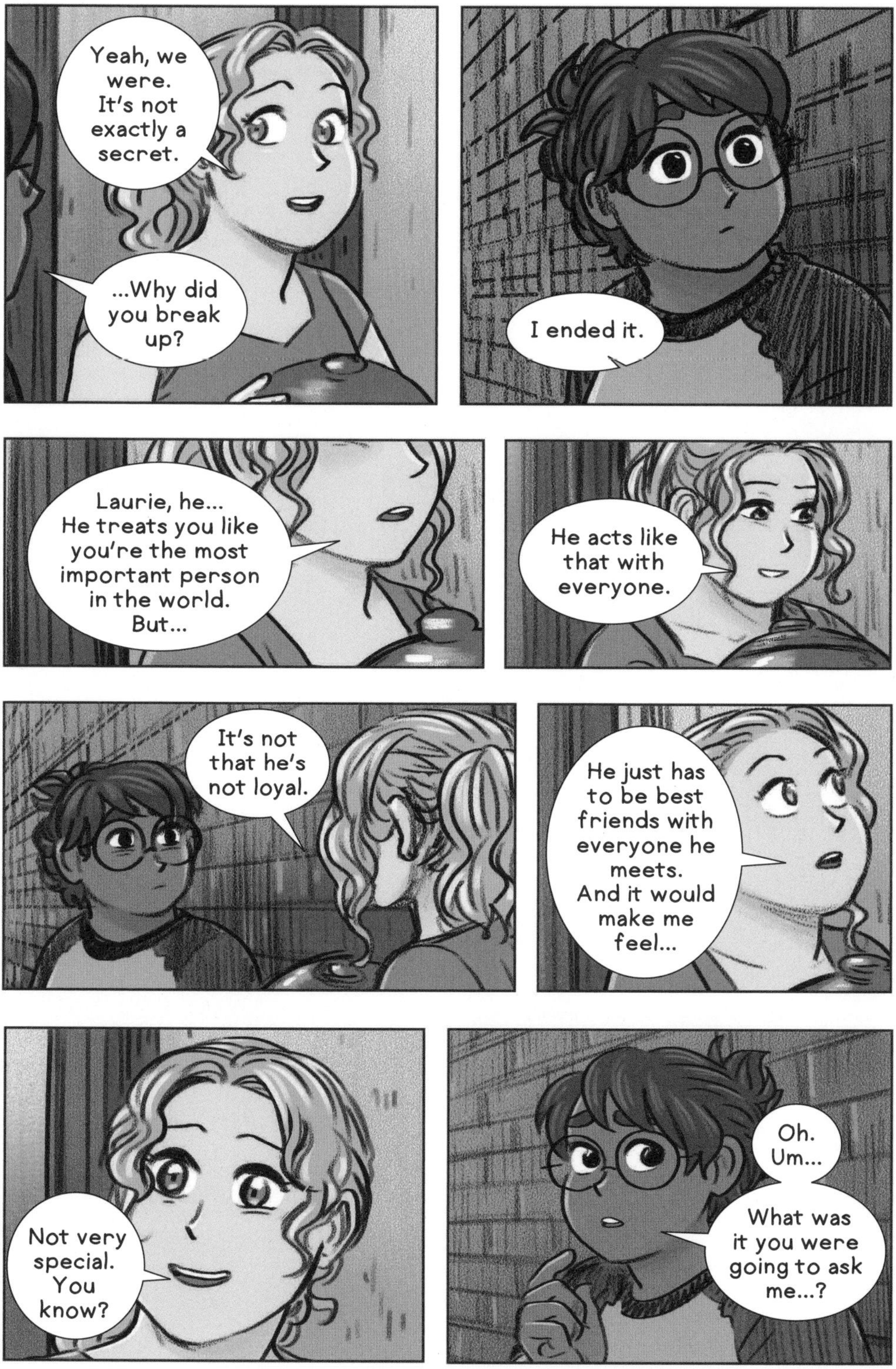
Yeah, we were. It's not exactly a secret.
...Why did you break up?
I ended it.
Laurie, he... He treats you like you're the most important person in the world. But...
He acts like that with everyone.
It's not that he's not loyal.
He just has to be best friends with everyone he meets. And it would make me feel...
Not very special. You know?
Oh. Um...
What was it you were going to ask me...?

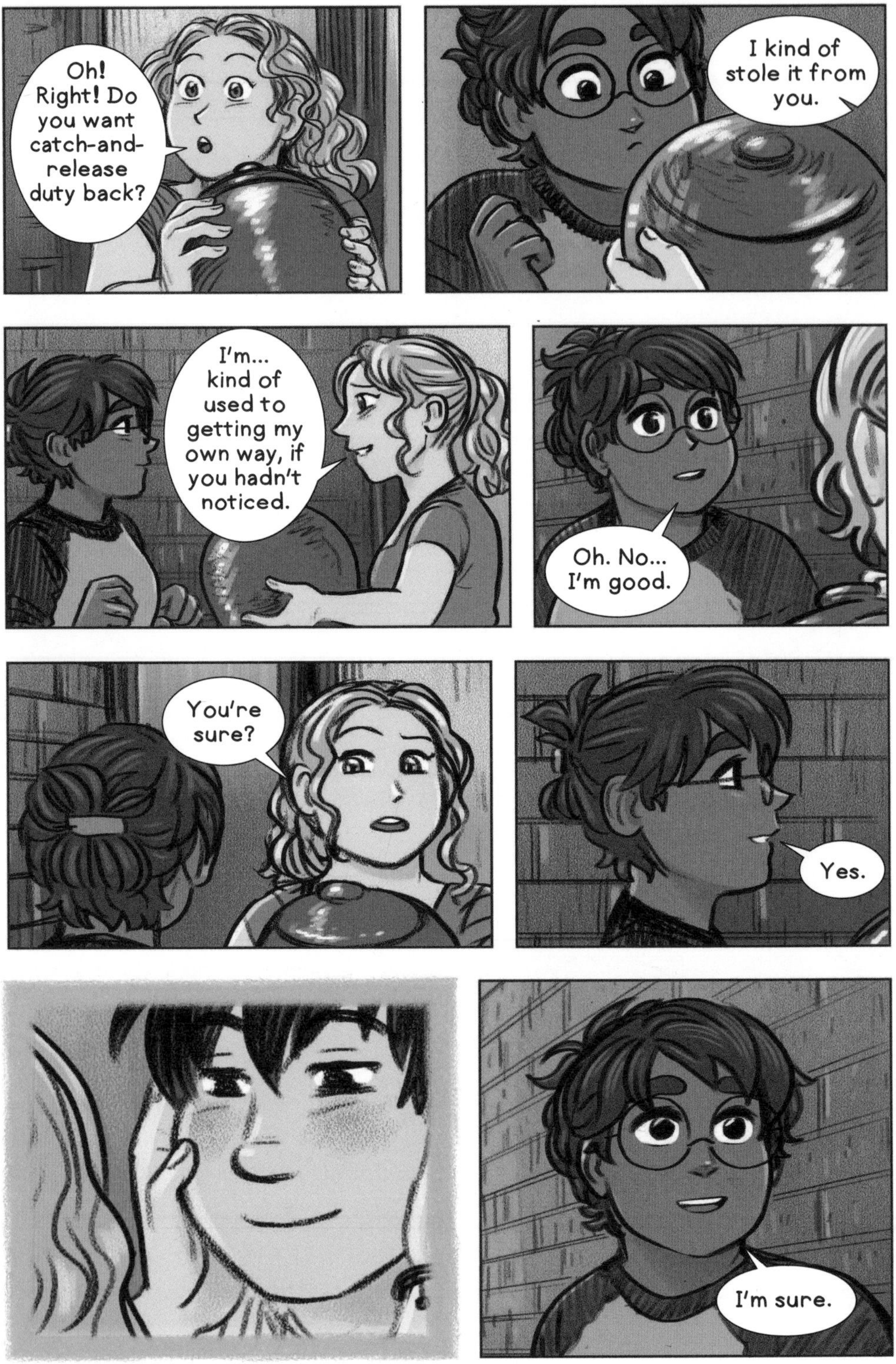
Oh! Right! Do you want catch-and-release duty back?
I kind of stole it from you.
I'm... kind of used to getting my own way, if you hadn't noticed.
Oh. No... I'm good.
You're sure?
Yes.
I'm sure.

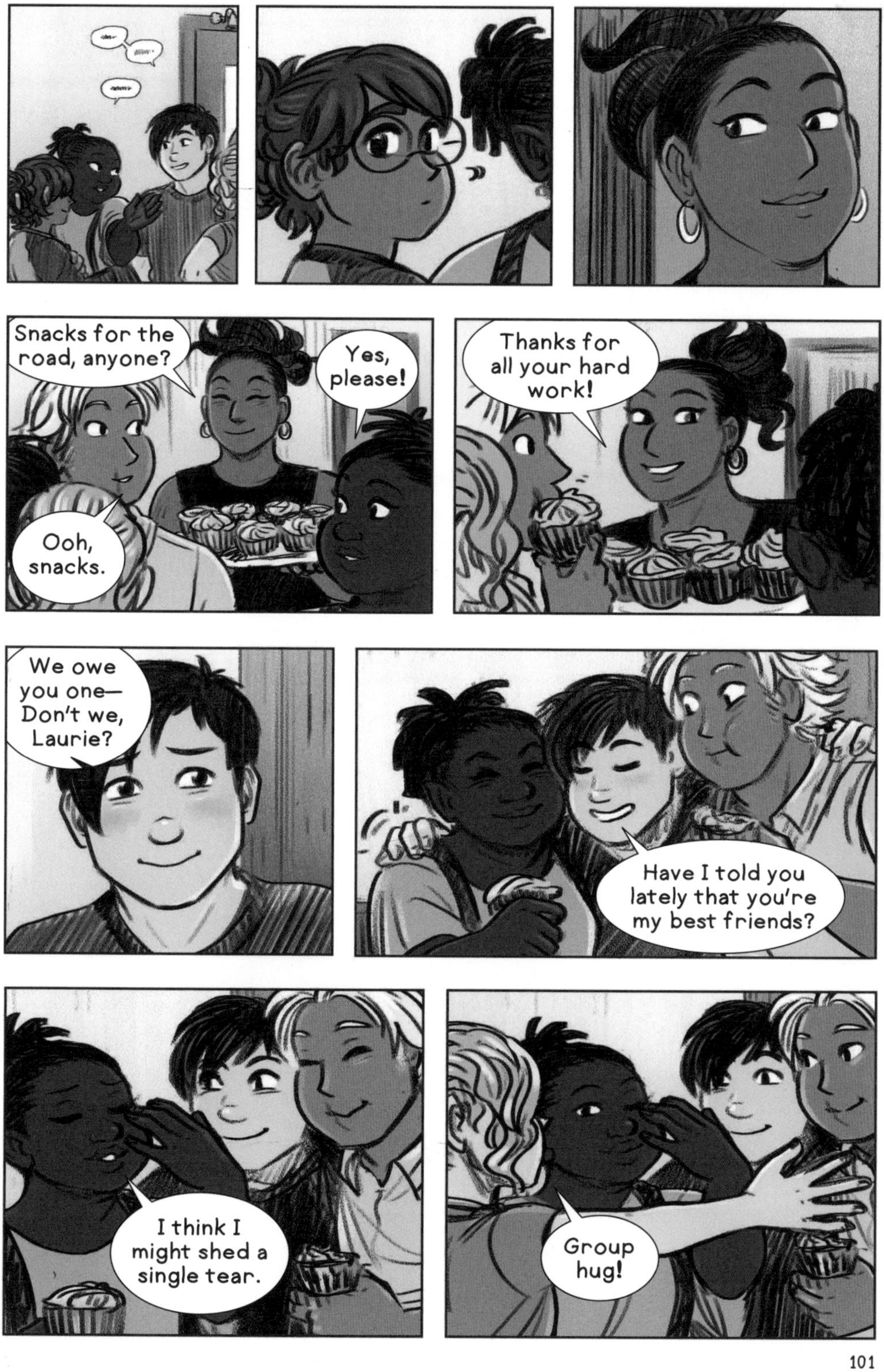
Snacks for the road, anyone?
Yes, please!
Ooh, snacks.
Thanks for all your hard work!
We owe you one—Don't we, Laurie?
Have I told you lately that you're my best friends?
I think I might shed a single tear.
Group hug!

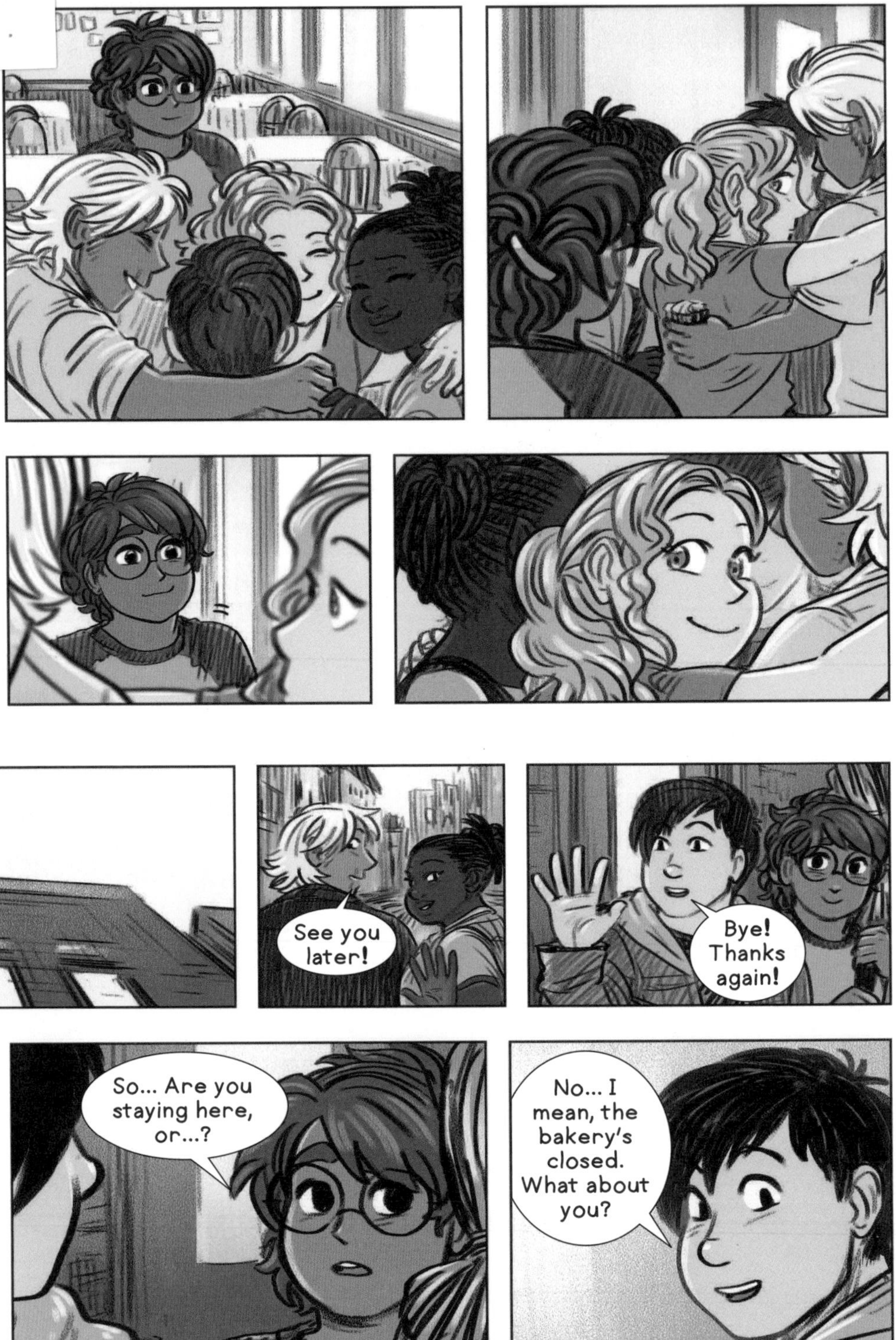
See you later!
Bye! Thanks again!
So... Are you staying here, or...?
No... I mean, the bakery's closed. What about you?

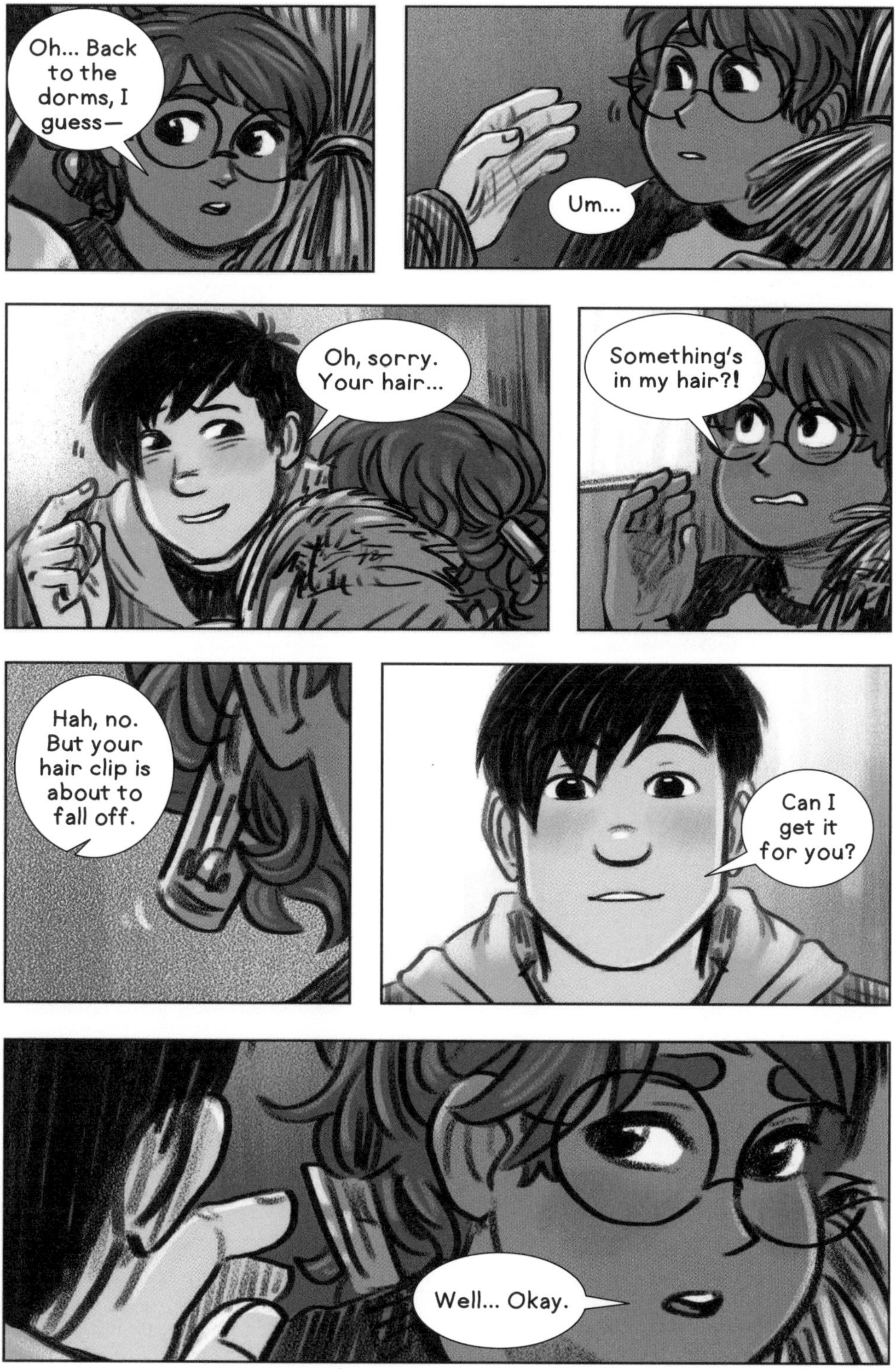
Oh... Back to the dorms, I guess—
Um...
Oh, sorry. Your hair...
Something's in my hair?!
Hah, no. But your hair clip is about to fall off.
Can I get it for you?
Well... Okay.

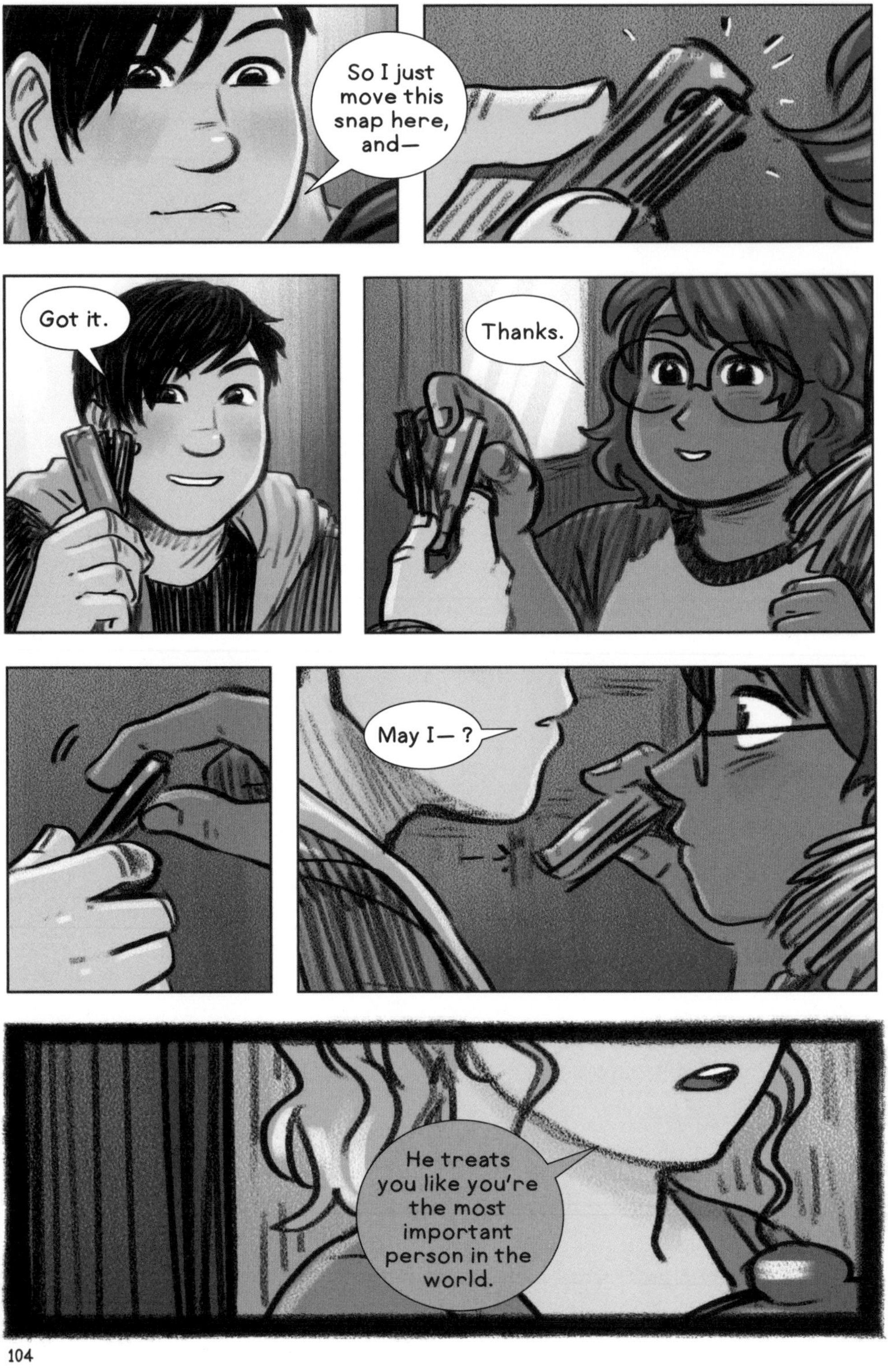
So I just move this snap here, and—
Got it.
Thanks.
May I— ?
He treats you like you're the most important person in the world.

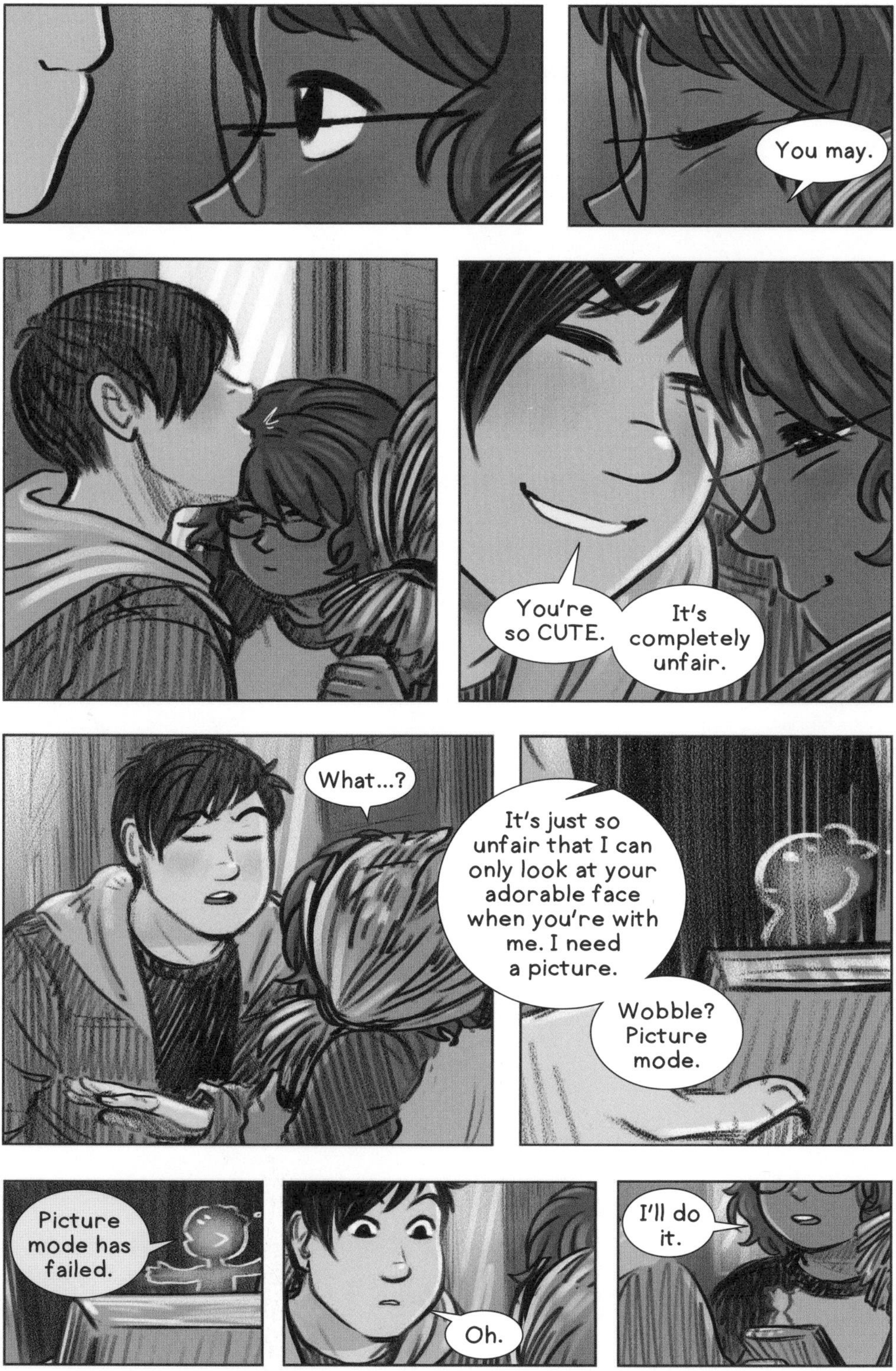
You may.
You're so CUTE.
It's completely unfair.
What...?
It's just so unfair that I can only look at your adorable face when you're with me. I need a picture.
Wobble? Picture mode.
Picture mode has failed.
Oh.
I'll do it.

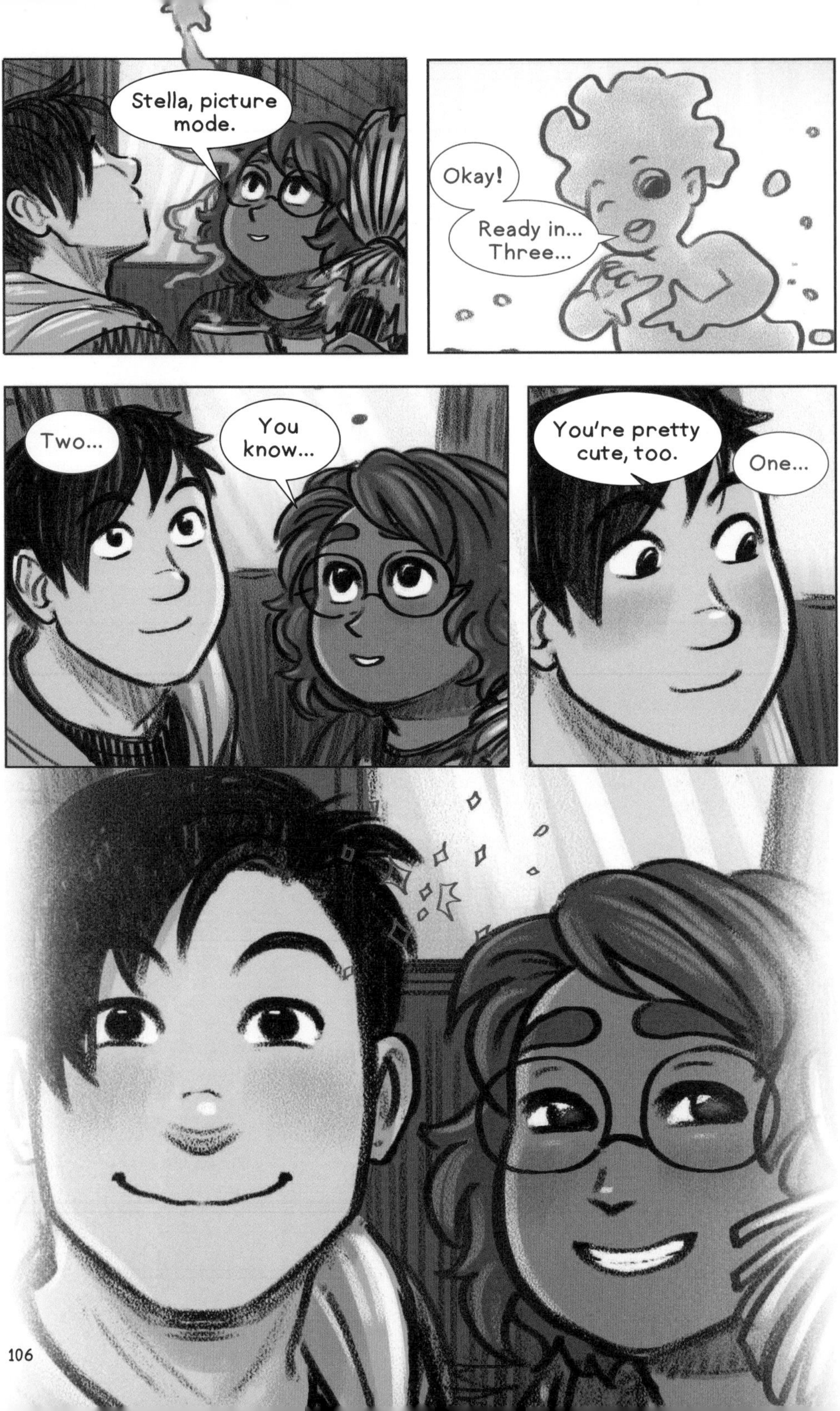
Stella, picture mode.
Okay!
Ready in... Three...
Two...
You know...
You're pretty cute, too.
One...

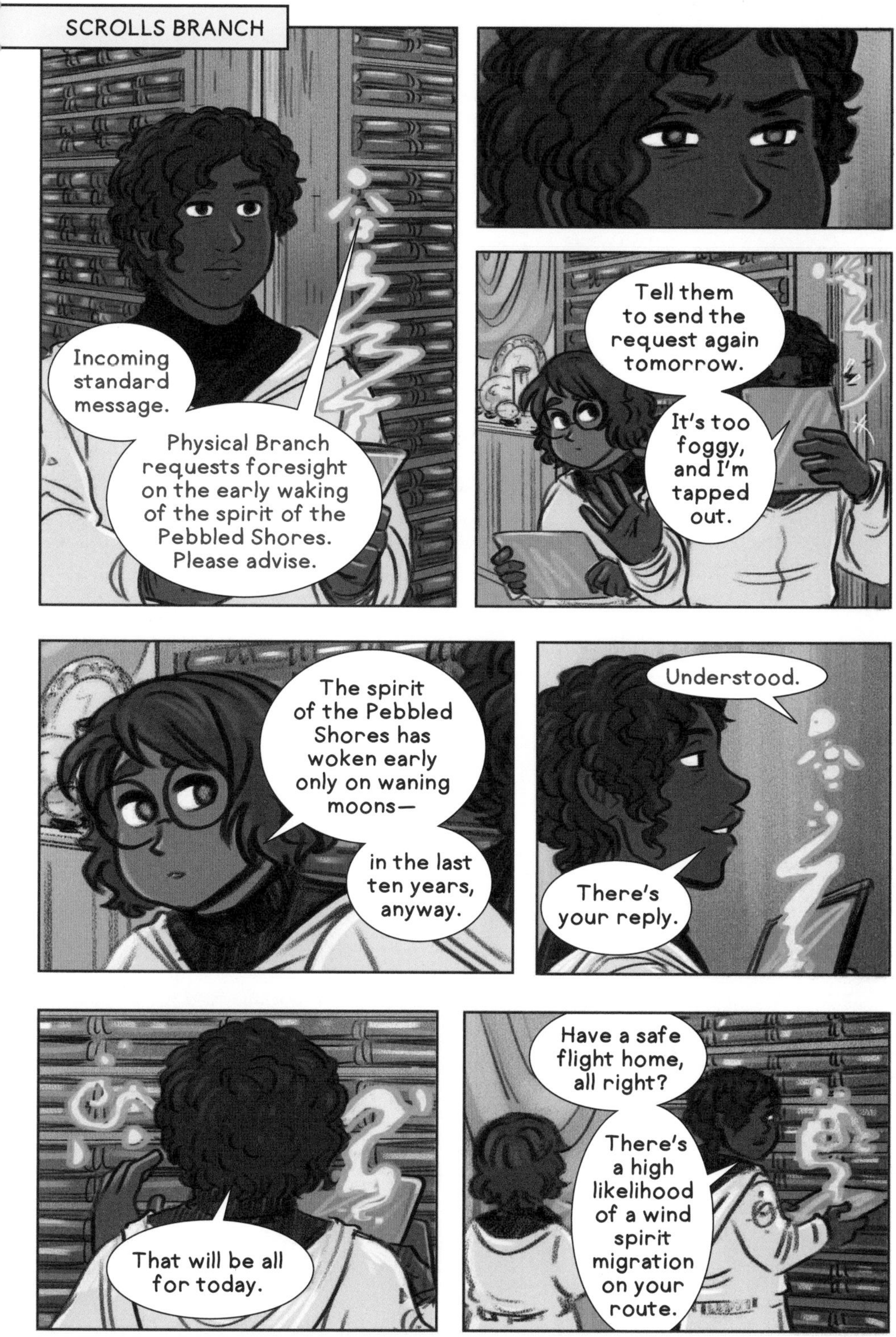
SCROLLS BRANCH
Incoming standard message.
Physical Branch requests foresight on the early waking of the spirit of the Pebbled Shores. Please advise.
Tell them to send the request again tomorrow.
It's too foggy, and I'm tapped out.
The spirit of the Pebbled Shores has woken early only on waning moons—
in the last ten years, anyway.
Understood.
There's your reply.
That will be all for today.
Have a safe flight home, all right?
There's a high likelihood of a wind spirit migration on your route.

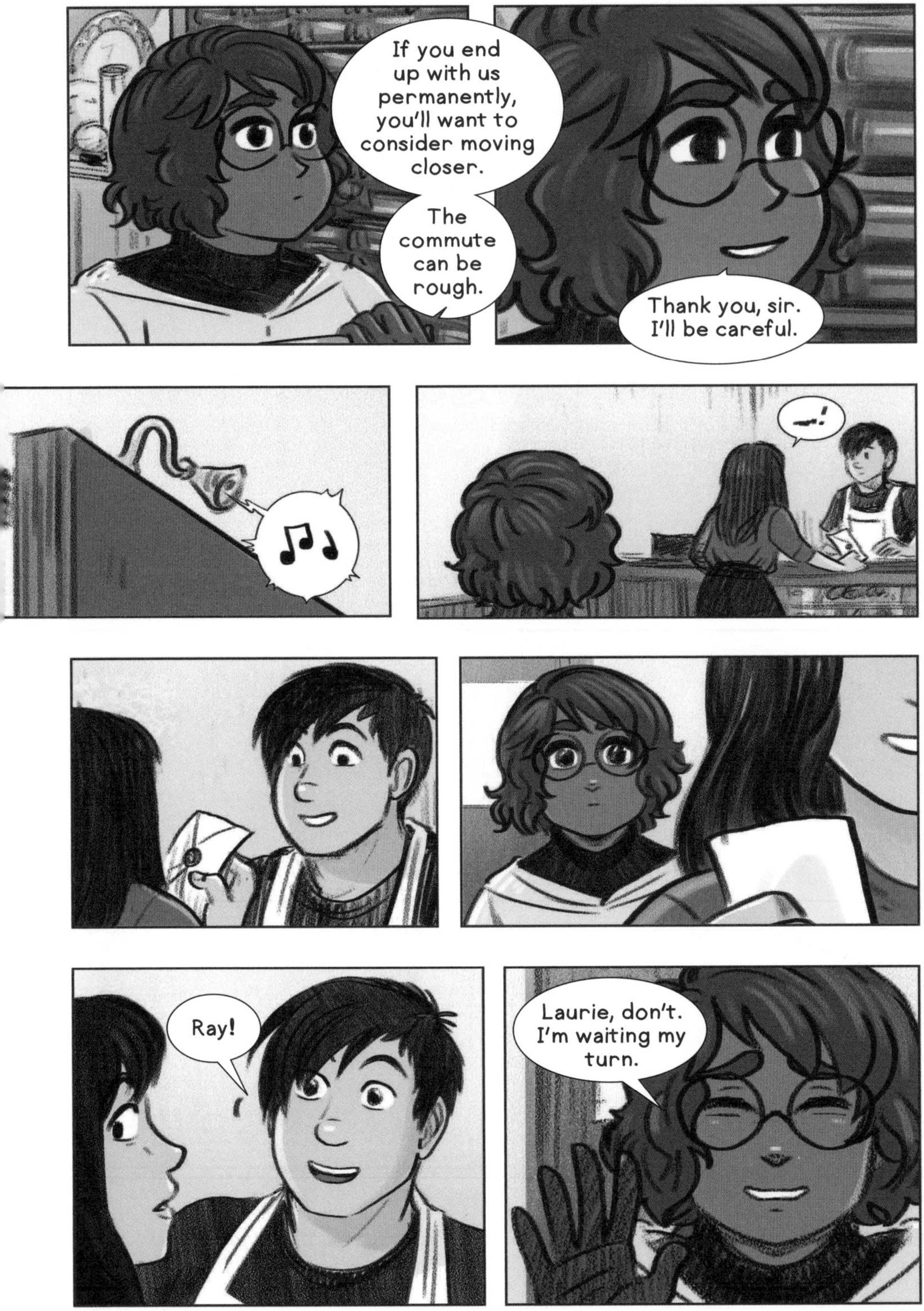
If you end up with us permanently, you'll want to consider moving closer.
The commute can be rough.
Thank you, sir. I'll be careful.
Ray!
Laurie, don't. I'm waiting my turn.

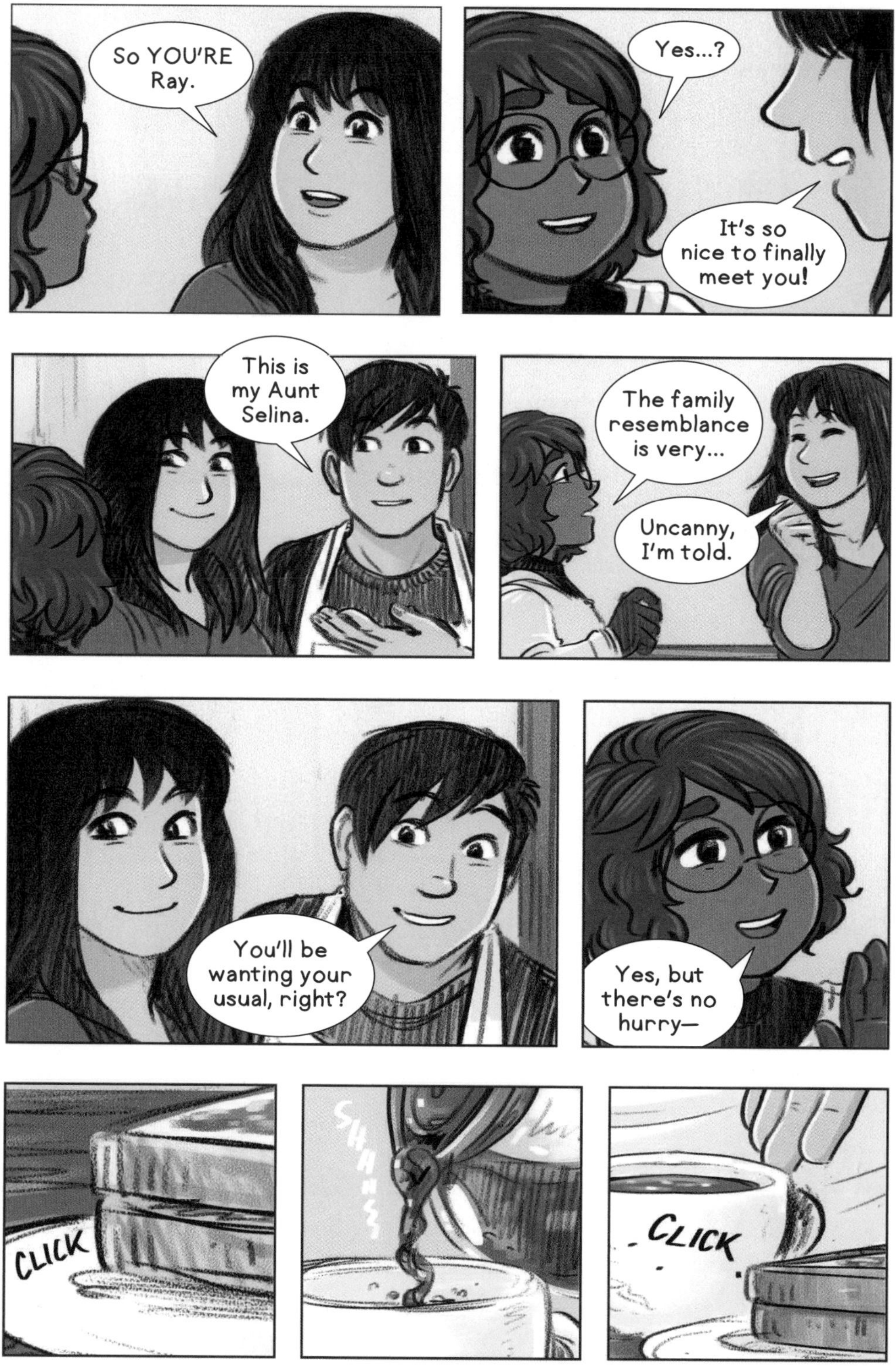
So YOU'RE Ray.
Yes...?
It's so nice to finally meet you!
This is my Aunt Selina.
The family resemblance is very...
Uncanny, I'm told.
You'll be wanting your usual, right?
Yes, but there's no hurry—
CLICK
SHHHSS
CLICK

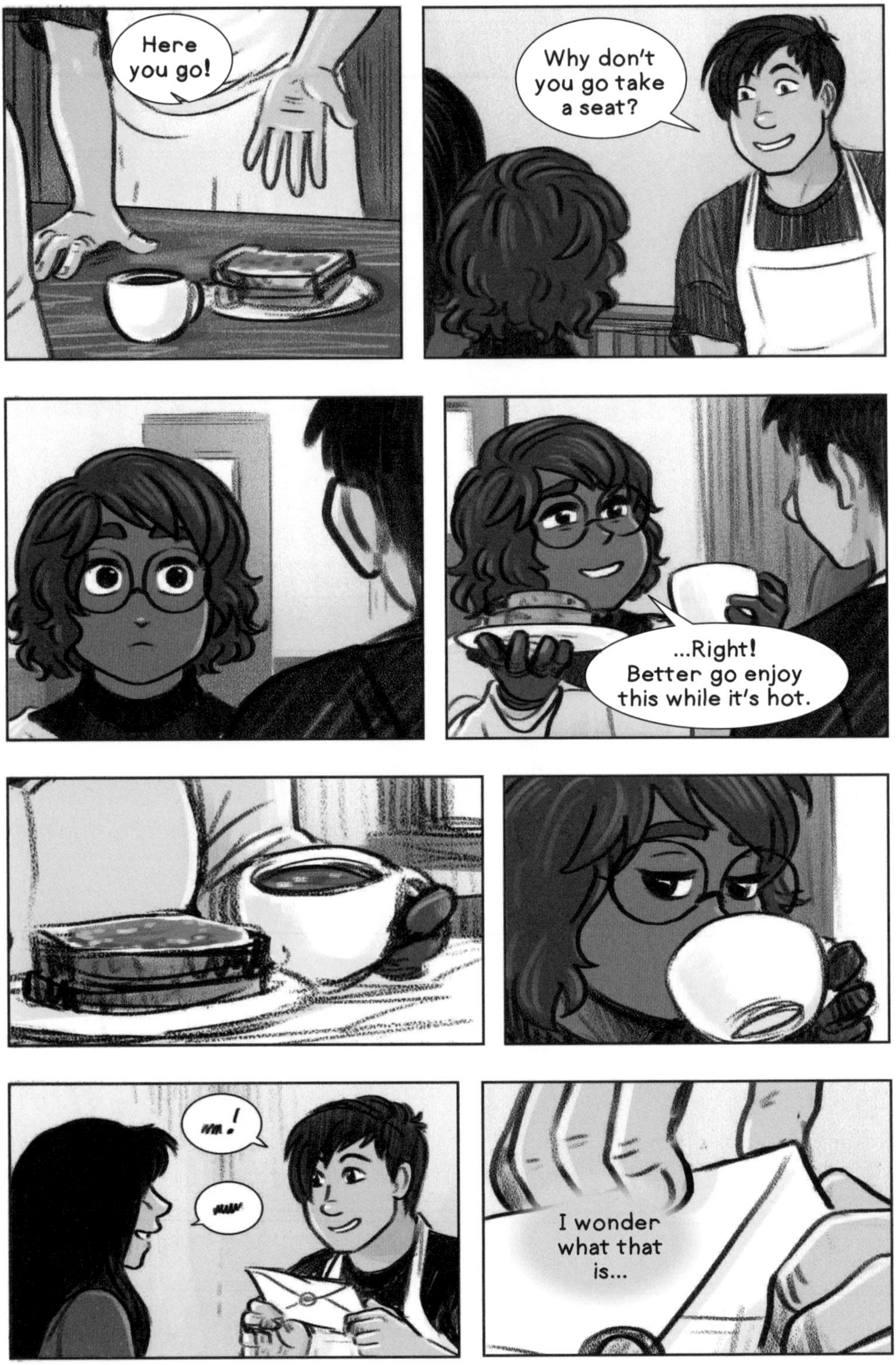
Here you go!
Why don't you go take a seat?
...Right! Better go enjoy this while it's hot.
I wonder what that is...

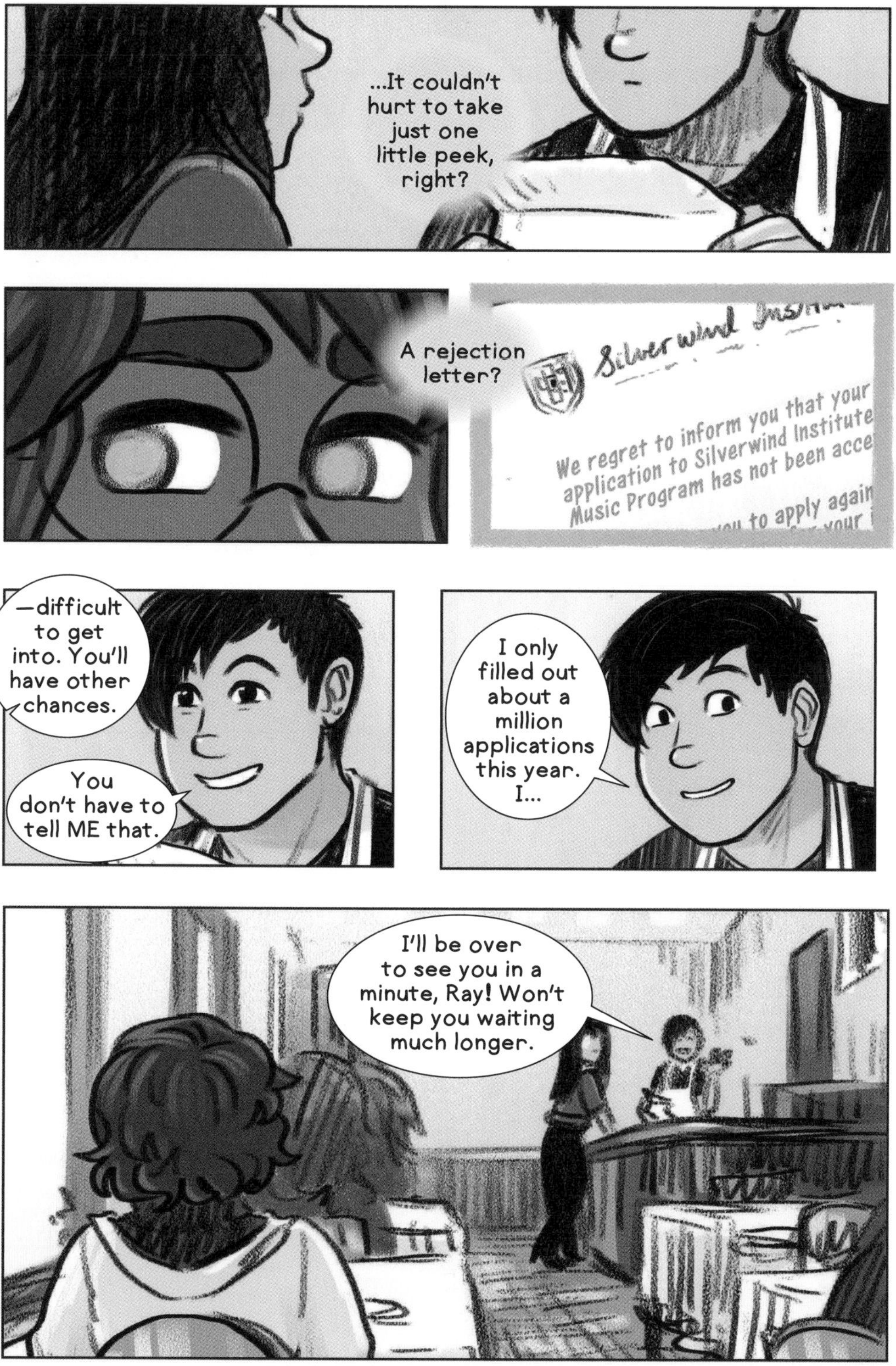
...It couldn't hurt to take just one little peek, right?
A rejection letter?
Silverwind
We regret to inform you that your
application to Silverwind Institute
Music Program has not been acce
—difficult to get into. You'll have other chances.
You don't have to tell ME that.
I only filled out about a million applications this year. I...
I'll be over to see you in a minute, Ray! Won't keep you waiting much longer.

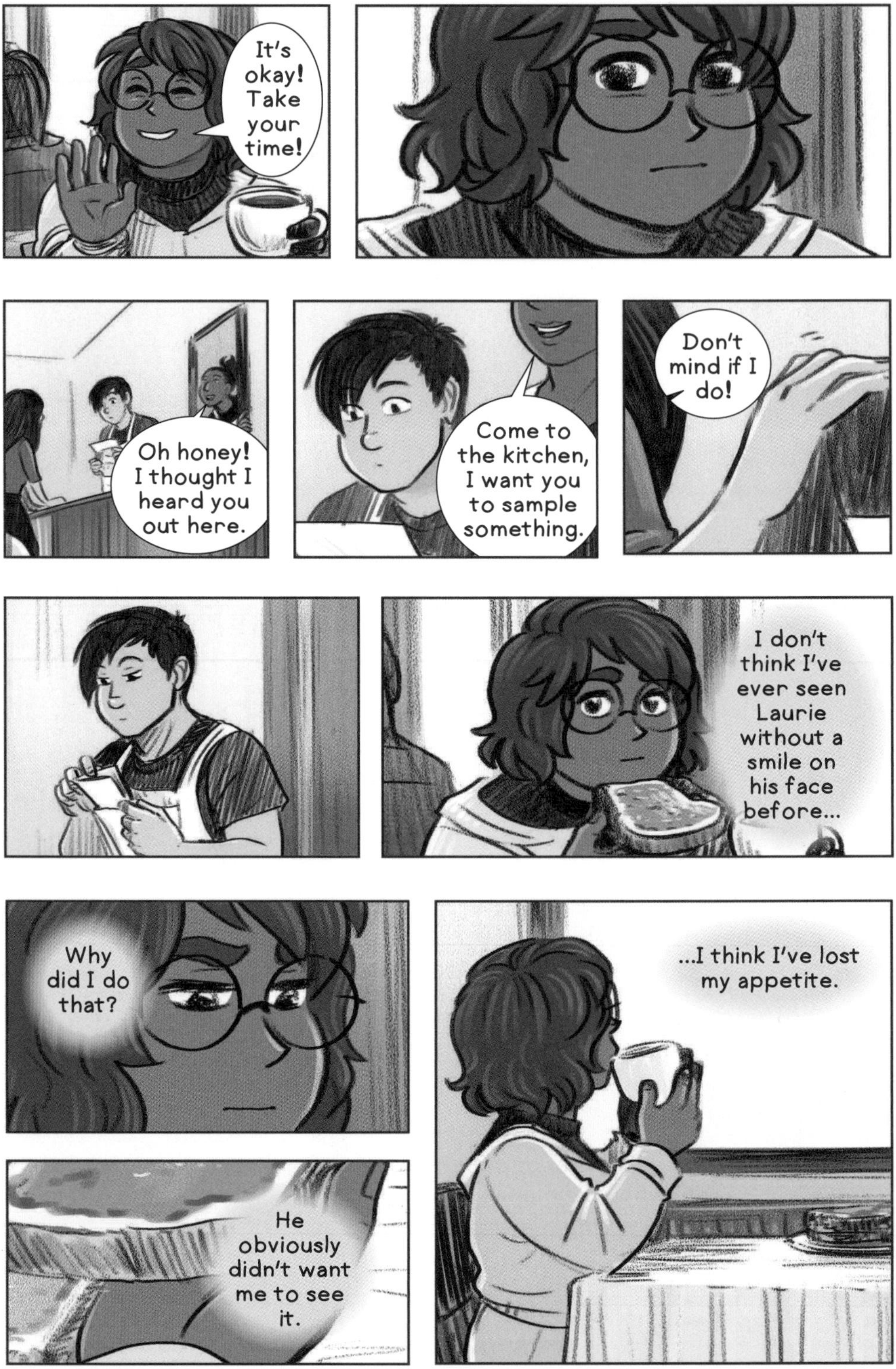
It's okay! Take your time!
Oh honey! I thought I heard you out here.
Come to the kitchen, I want you to sample something.
Don't mind if I do!
I don't think I've ever seen Laurie without a smile on his face before...
Why did I do that?
He obviously didn't want me to see it.
...I think I've lost my appetite.

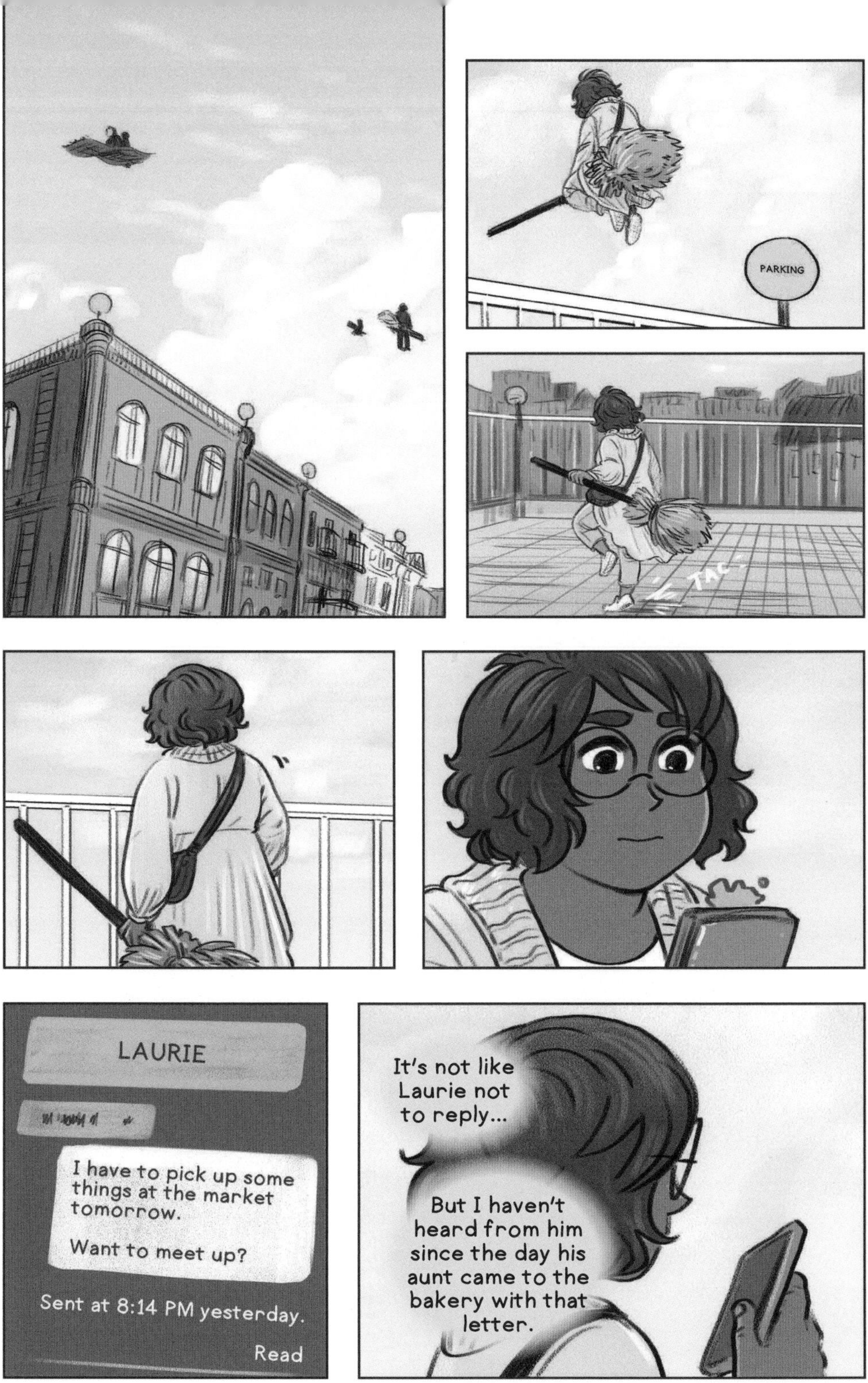
PARKING
TAC
LAURIE
I have to pick up some things at the market tomorrow.
Want to meet up?
Sent at 8:14 PM yesterday.
Read
It's not like Laurie not to reply...
But I haven't heard from him since the day his aunt came to the bakery with that letter.

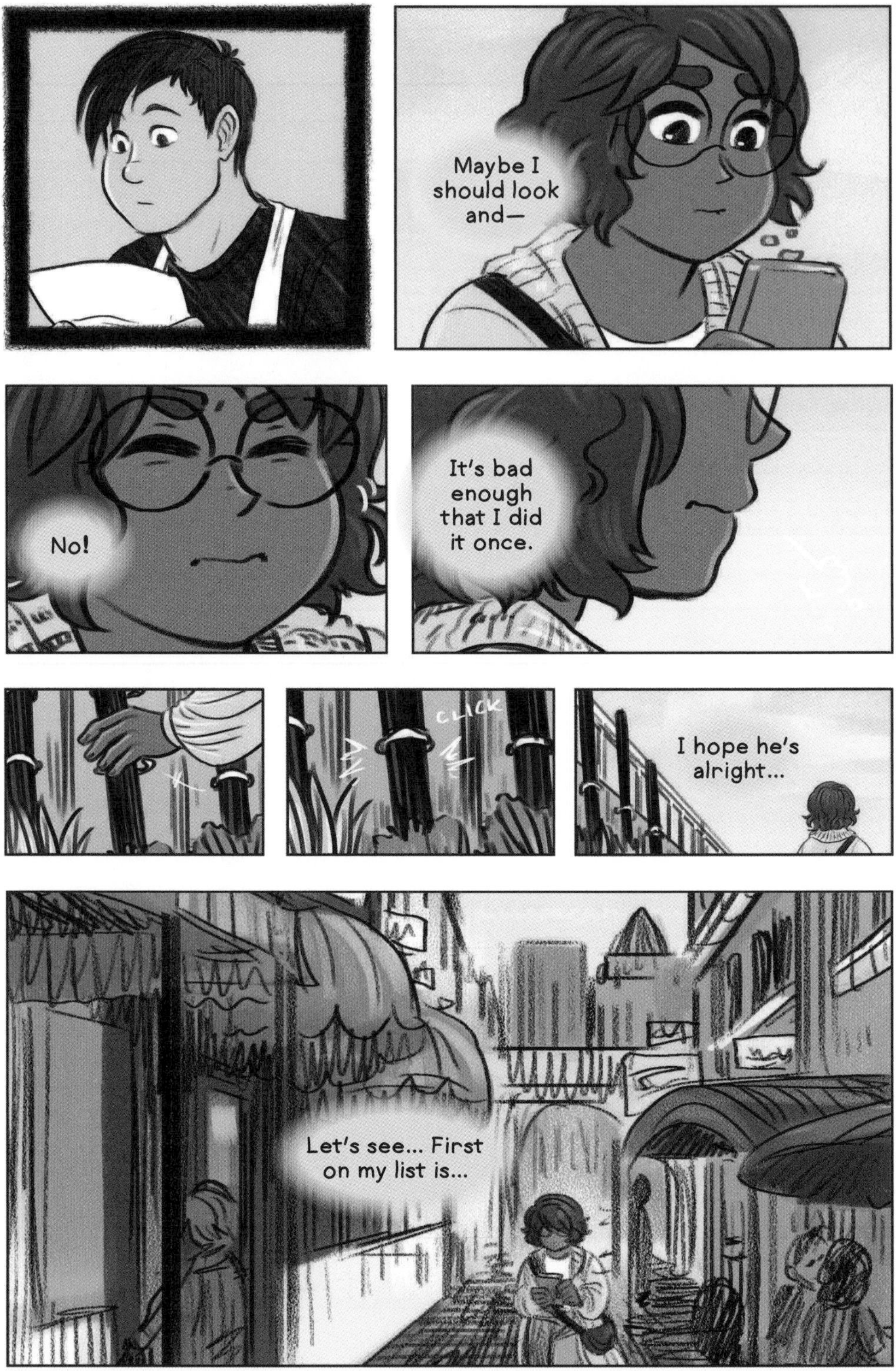
Maybe I should look and—
No!
It's bad enough that I did it once.
CLICK
I hope he's alright...
Let's see... First on my list is...

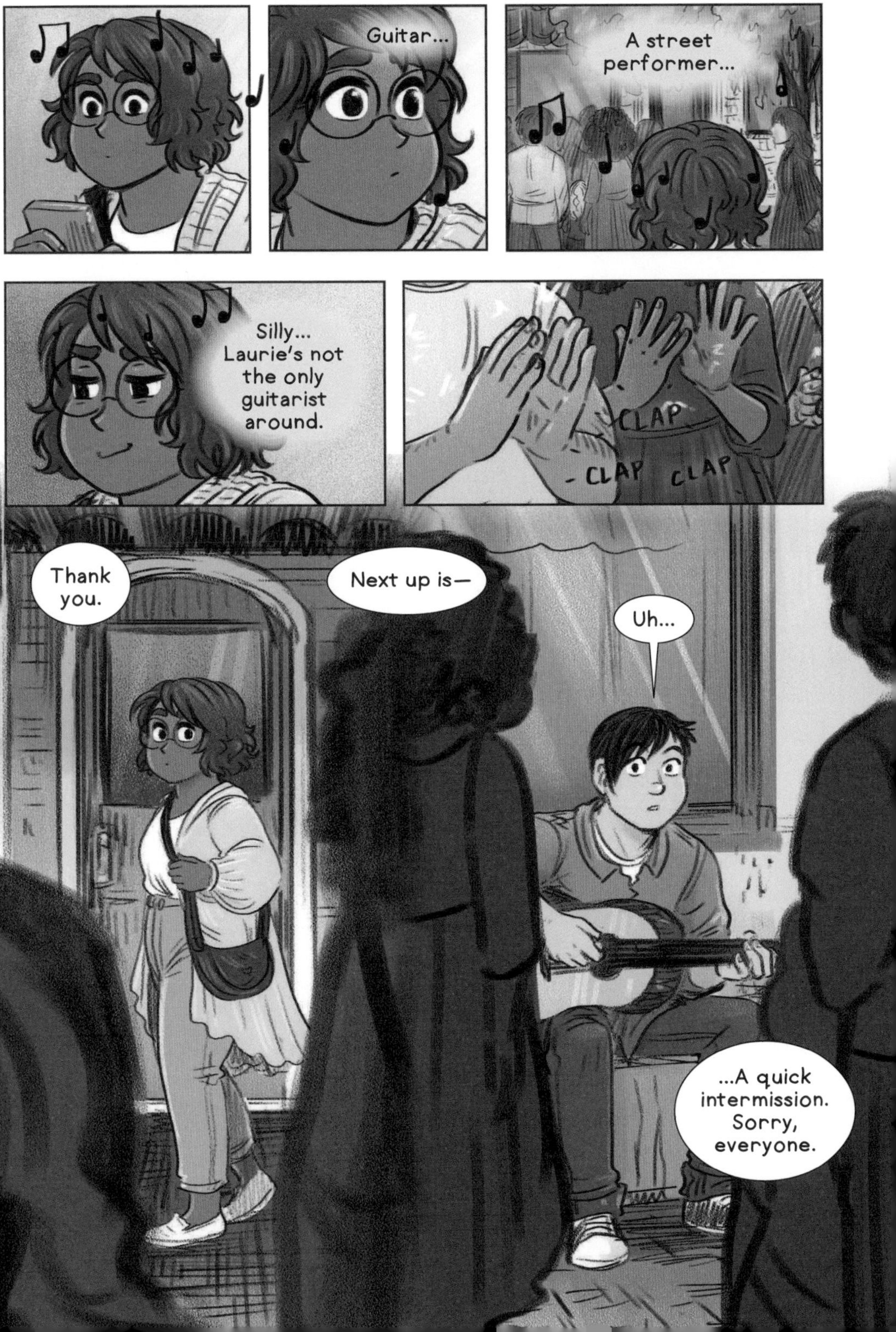
Guitar...
A street performer...
Silly... Laurie's not the only guitarist around.
CLAP
CLAP
CLAP
Thank you.
Next up is—
Uh...
...A quick intermission. Sorry, everyone.

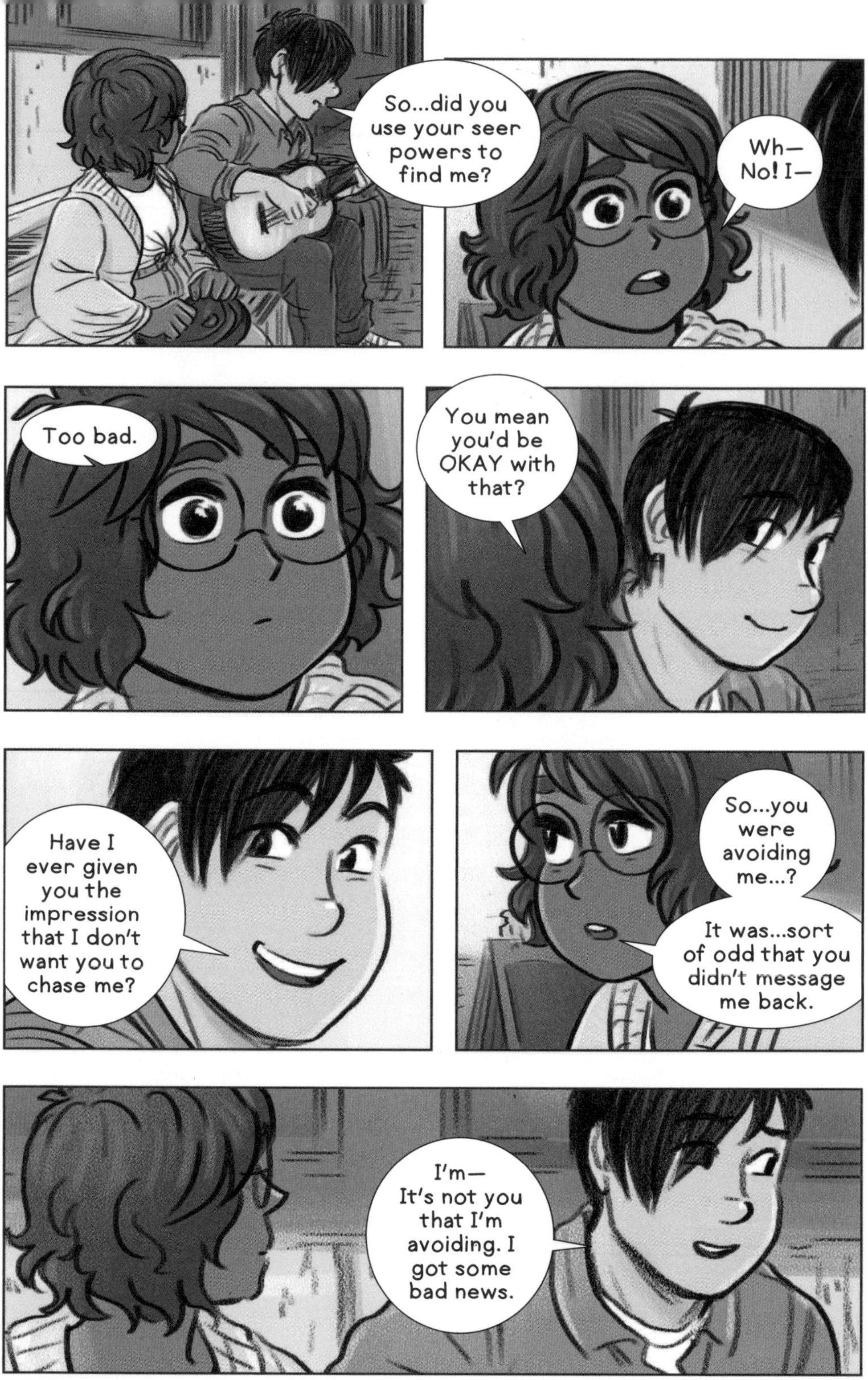
So...did you use your seer powers to find me?
Wh— No! I—
Too bad.
You mean you'd be OKAY with that?
Have I ever given you the impression that I don't want you to chase me?
So...you were avoiding me...?
It was...sort of odd that you didn't message me back.
I'm— It's not you that I'm avoiding. I got some bad news.

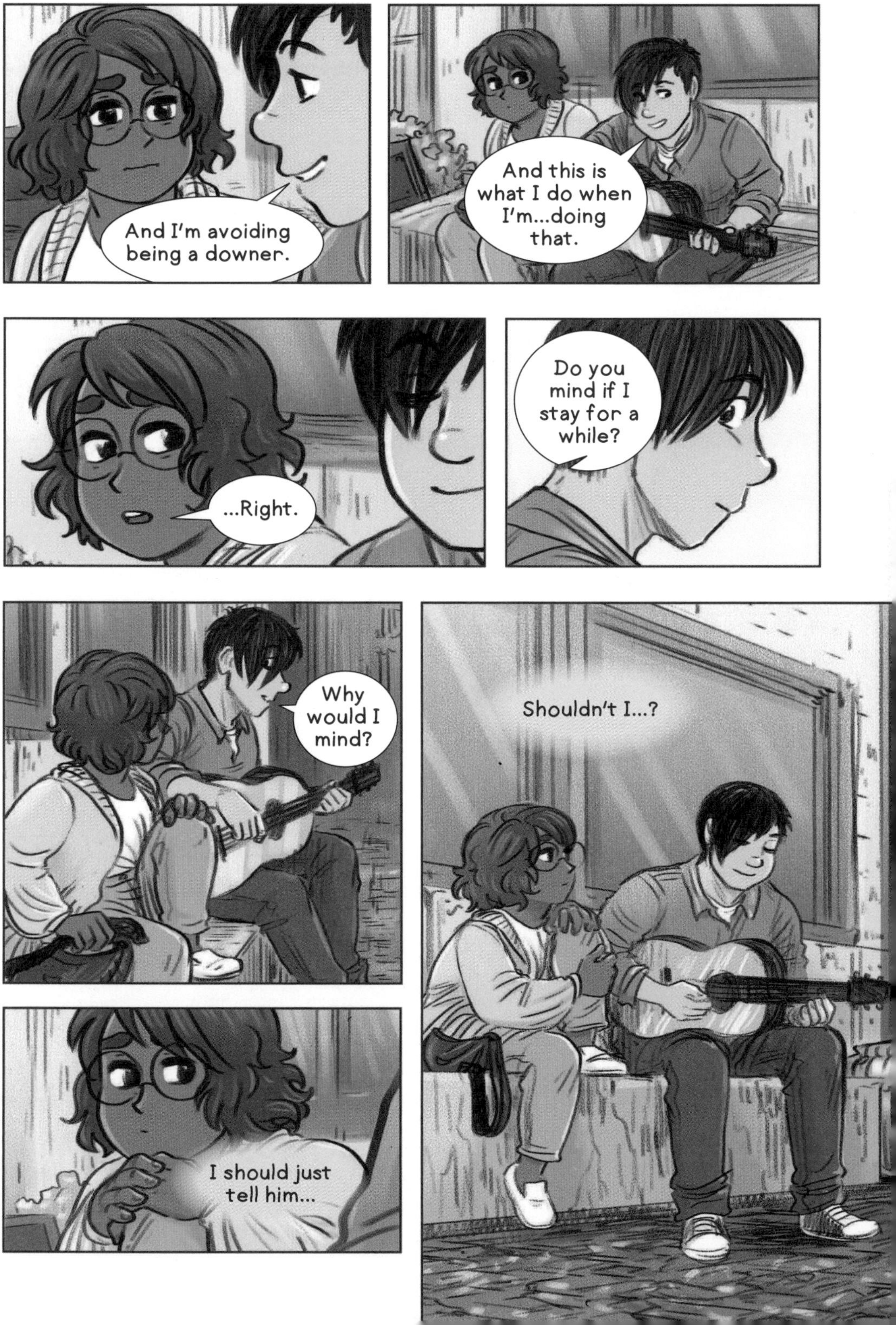
And I'm avoiding being a downer.
And this is what I do when I'm...doing that.
...Right.
Do you mind if I stay for a while?
Why would I mind?
I should just tell him...
Shouldn't I...?

CHAPTER 6

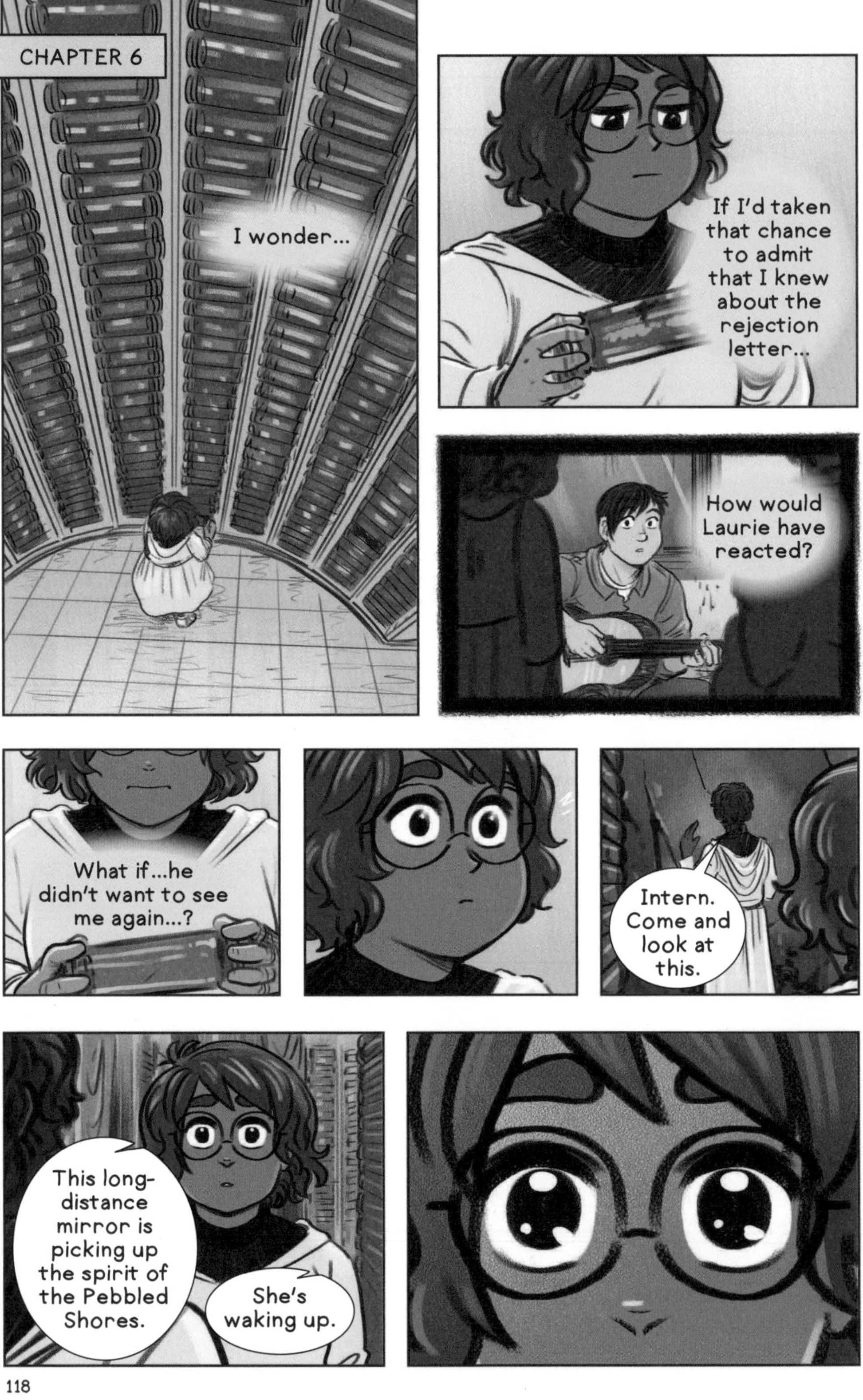
I wonder...
If I'd taken that chance to admit that I knew about the rejection letter...
How would Laurie have reacted?
What if...he didn't want to see me again...?
Intern. Come and look at this.
This long-distance mirror is picking up the spirit of the Pebbled Shores.
She's waking up.

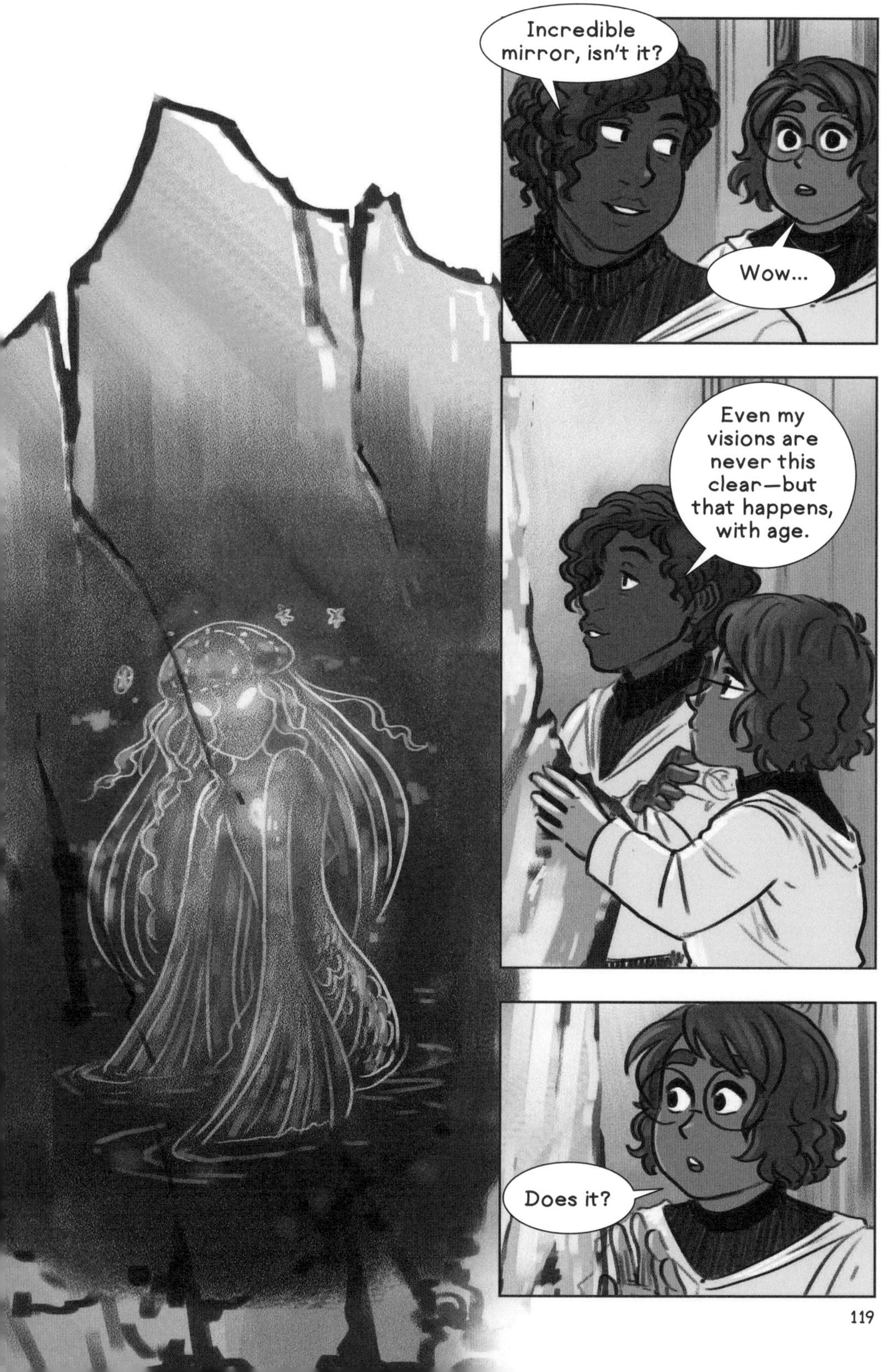
Incredible mirror, isn't it?
Wow...
Even my visions are never this clear—but that happens, with age.
Does it?

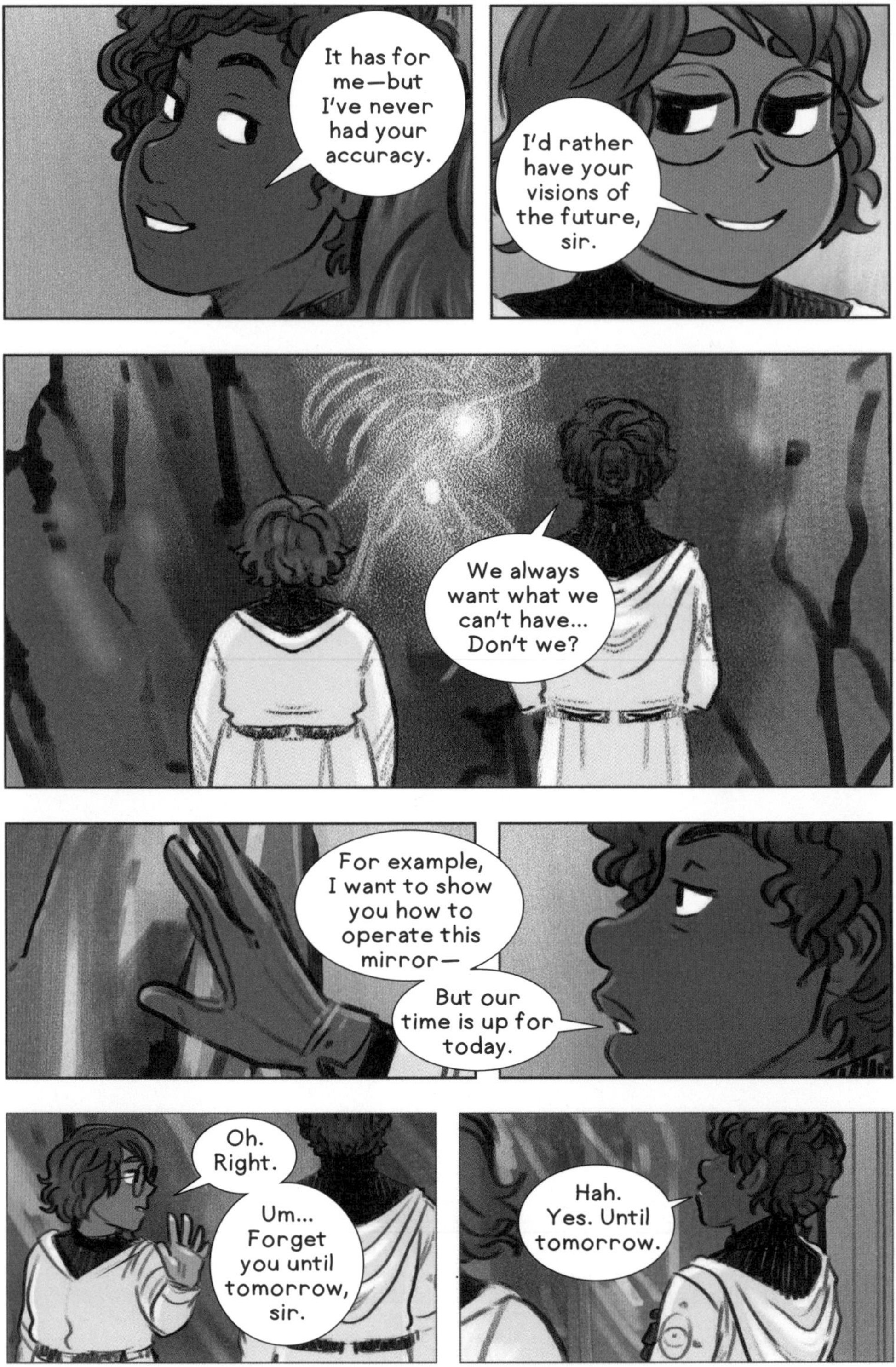
It has for me—but I've never had your accuracy.
I'd rather have your visions of the future, sir.
We always want what we can't have... Don't we?
For example, I want to show you how to operate this mirror—
But our time is up for today.
Oh. Right.
Um... Forget you until tomorrow, sir.
Hah. Yes. Until tomorrow.

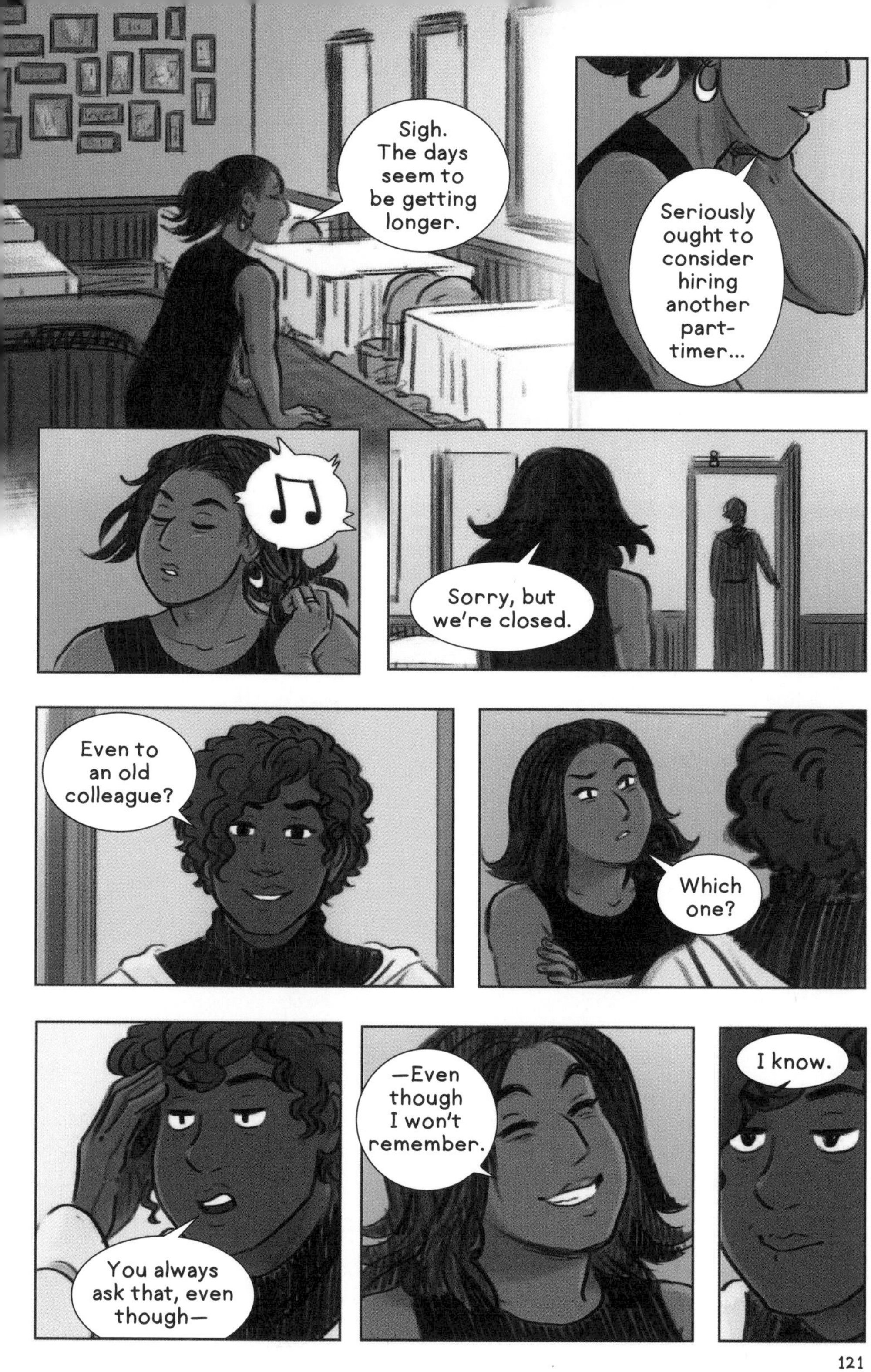
Sigh. The days seem to be getting longer.
Seriously ought to consider hiring another part-timer...
♫
Sorry, but we're closed.
Even to an old colleague?
Which one?
You always ask that, even though—
—Even though I won't remember.
I know.

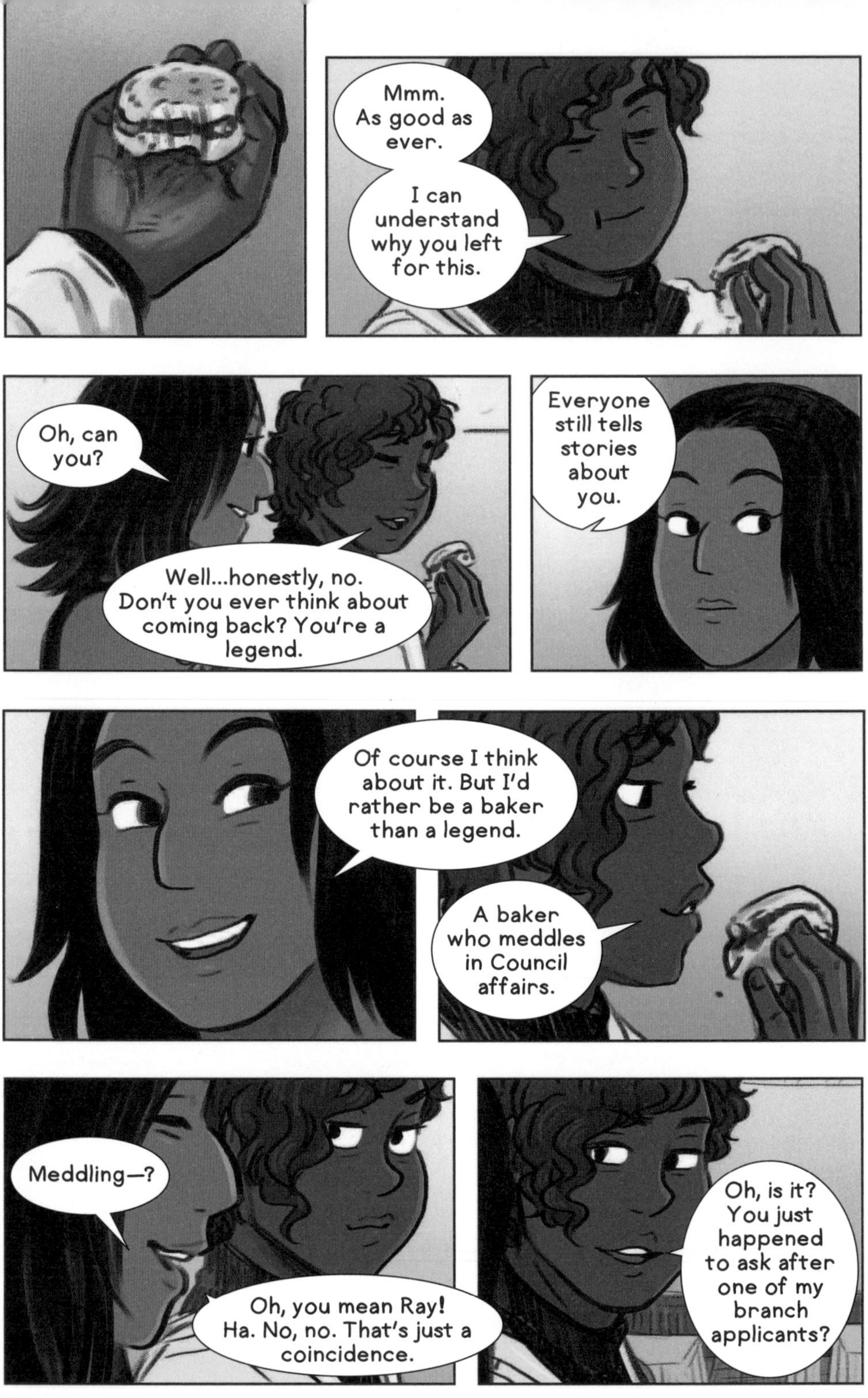

Mmm. As good as ever.
I can understand why you left for this.
Oh, can you?
Well...honestly, no. Don't you ever think about coming back? You're a legend.
Everyone still tells stories about you.
Of course I think about it. But I'd rather be a baker than a legend.
A baker who meddles in Council affairs.
Meddling—?
Oh, you mean Ray! Ha. No, no. That's just a coincidence.
Oh, is it? You just happened to ask after one of my branch applicants?

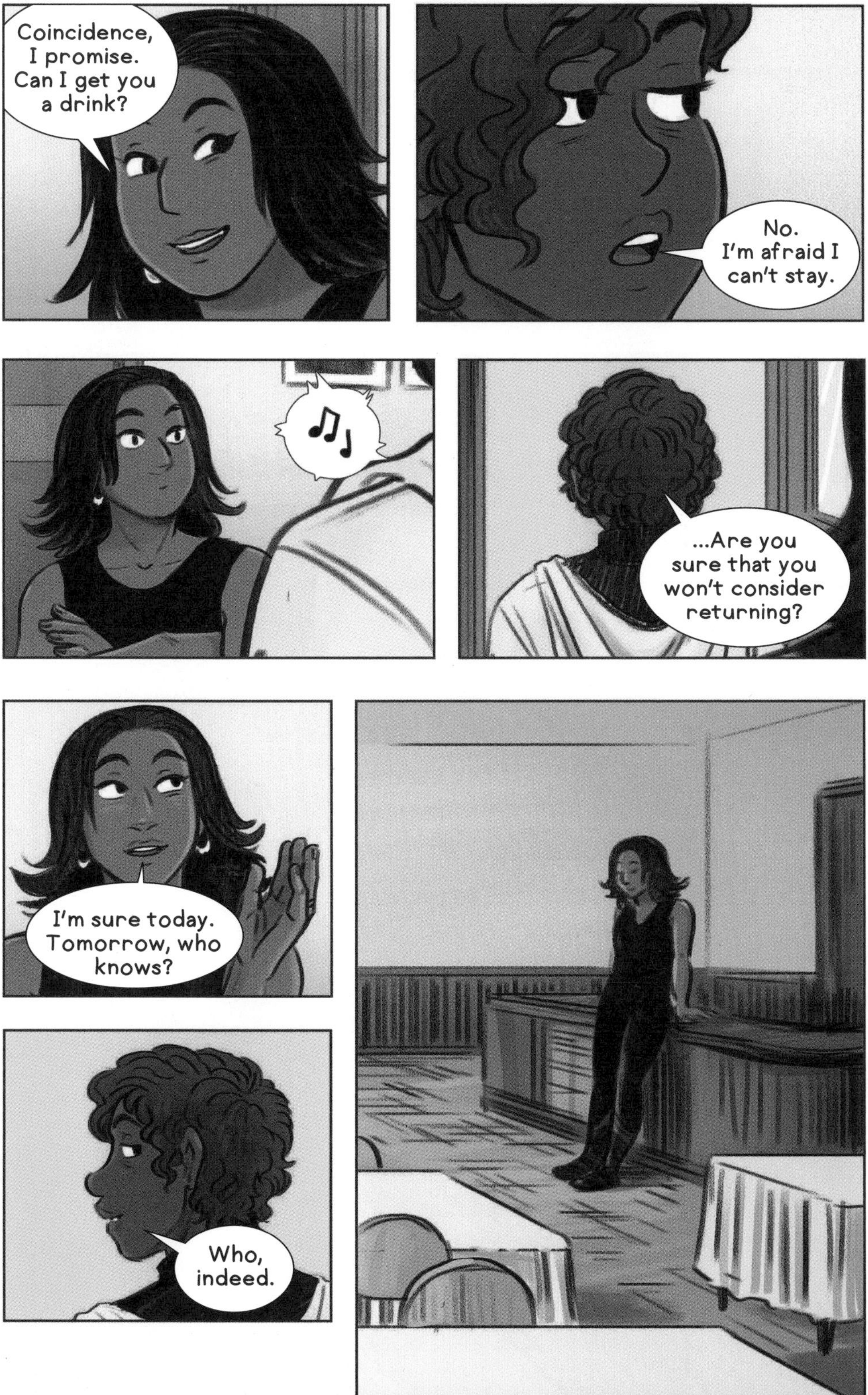
Coincidence, I promise. Can I get you a drink?
No. I'm afraid I can't stay.
...Are you sure that you won't consider returning?
I'm sure today. Tomorrow, who knows?
Who, indeed.

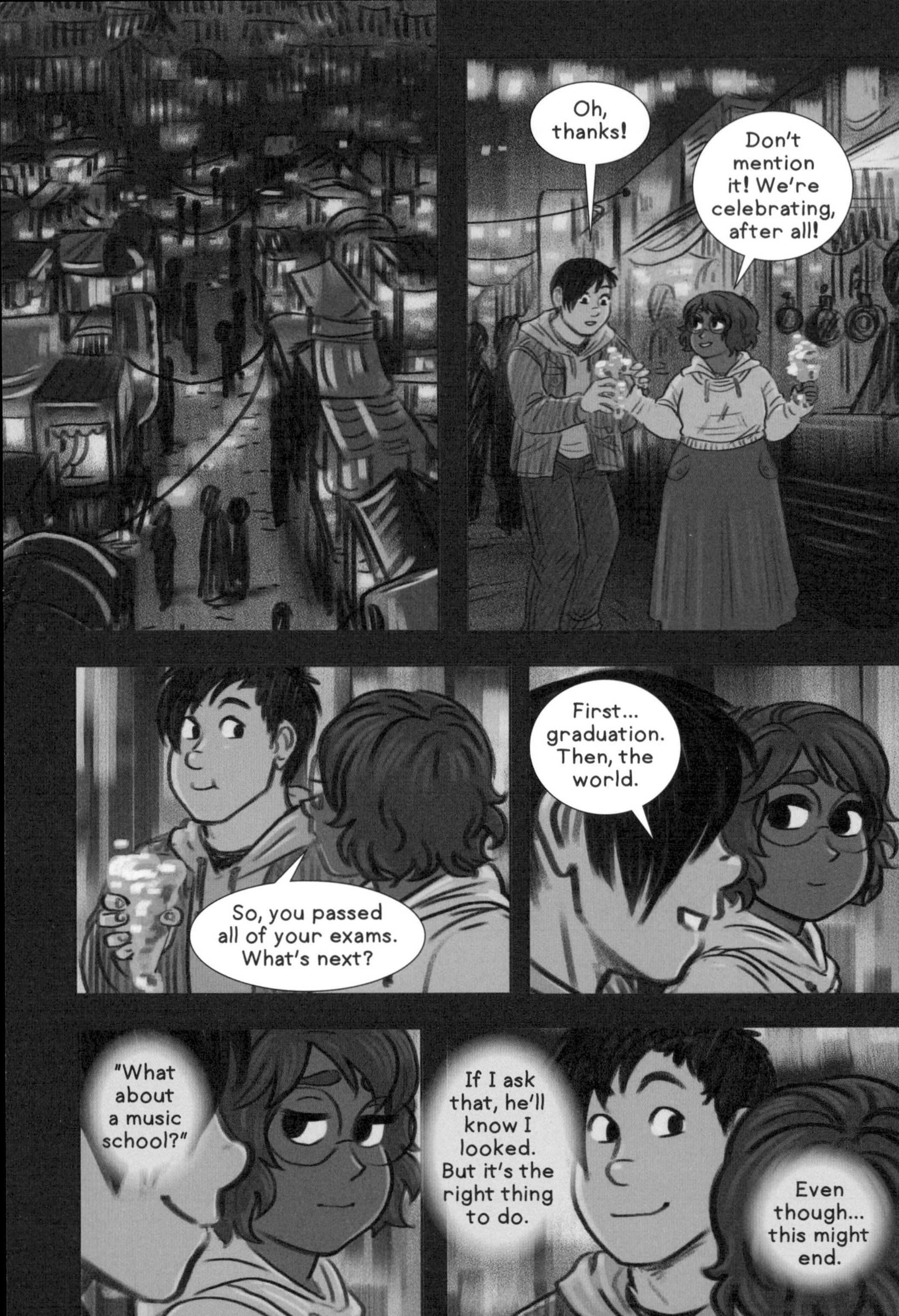
Oh, thanks!
Don't mention it! We're celebrating, after all!
So, you passed all of your exams. What's next?
First... graduation. Then, the world.
"What about a music school?"
If I ask that, he'll know I looked. But it's the right thing to do.
Even though... this might end.

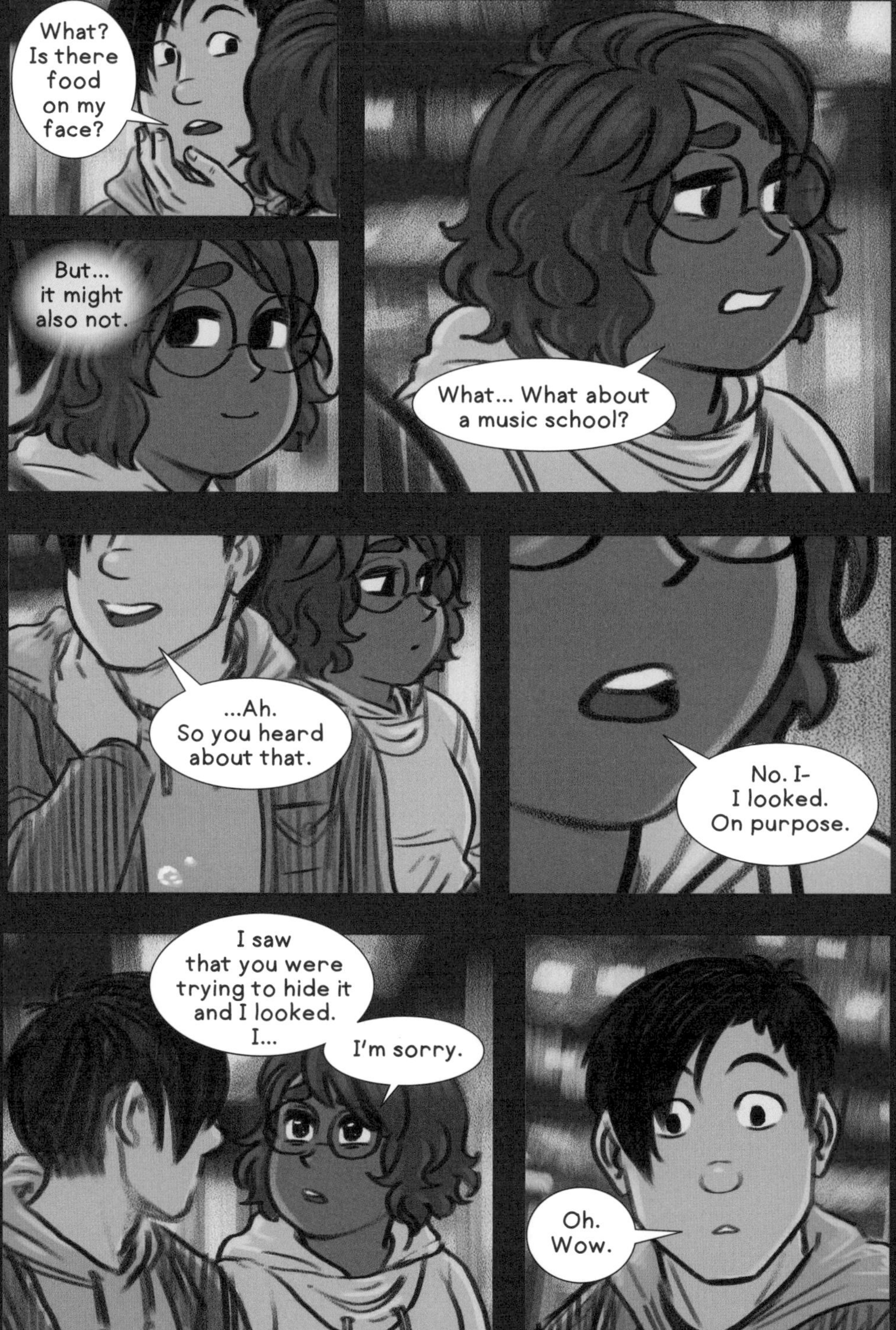
What? Is there food on my face?
But... it might also not.
What... What about a music school?
...Ah. So you heard about that.
No. I- I looked. On purpose.
I saw that you were trying to hide it and I looked. I...
I'm sorry.
Oh. Wow.

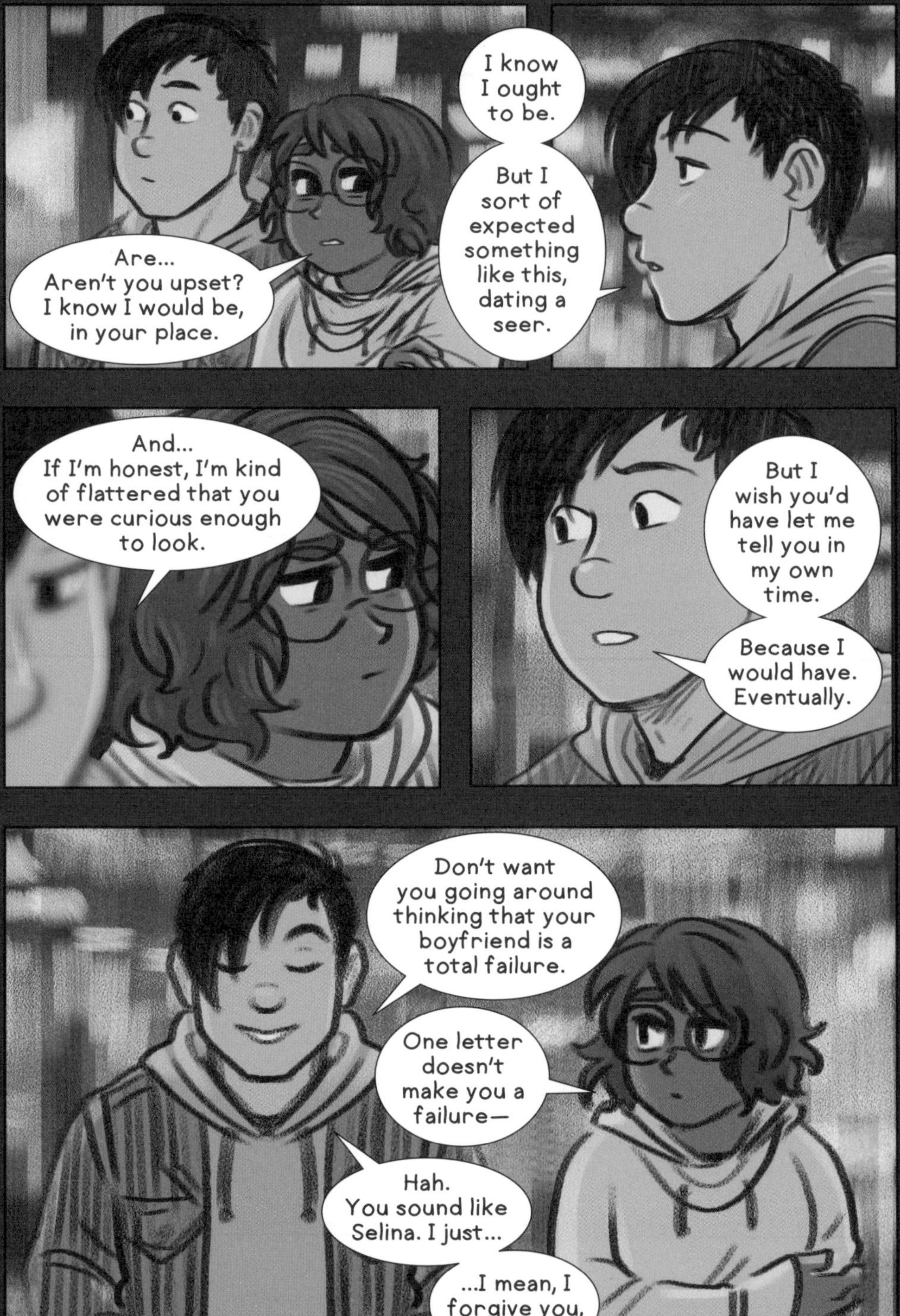
Are... Aren't you upset? I know I would be, in your place.
I know I ought to be.
But I sort of expected something like this, dating a seer.
And... If I'm honest, I'm kind of flattered that you were curious enough to look.
But I wish you'd have let me tell you in my own time.
Because I would have. Eventually.
Don't want you going around thinking that your boyfriend is a total failure.
One letter doesn't make you a failure—
Hah. You sound like Selina. I just...
...I mean, I forgive you, but...

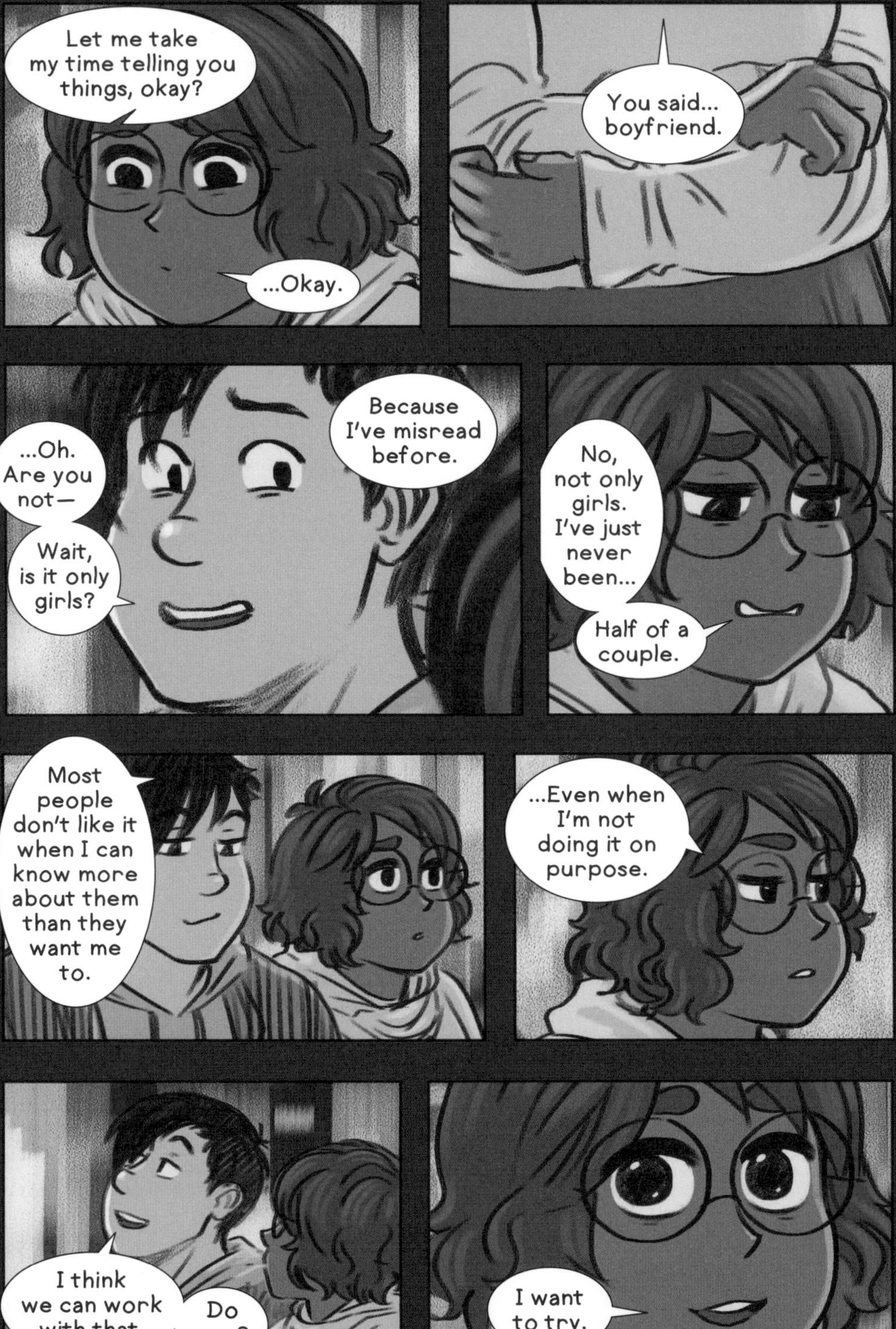
Let me take my time telling you things, okay?
...Okay.
You said... boyfriend.
...Oh. Are you not—
Because I've misread before.
Wait, is it only girls?
No, not only girls. I've just never been...
Half of a couple.
Most people don't like it when I can know more about them than they want me to.
...Even when I'm not doing it on purpose.
I think we can work with that.
Do you?
I want to try.

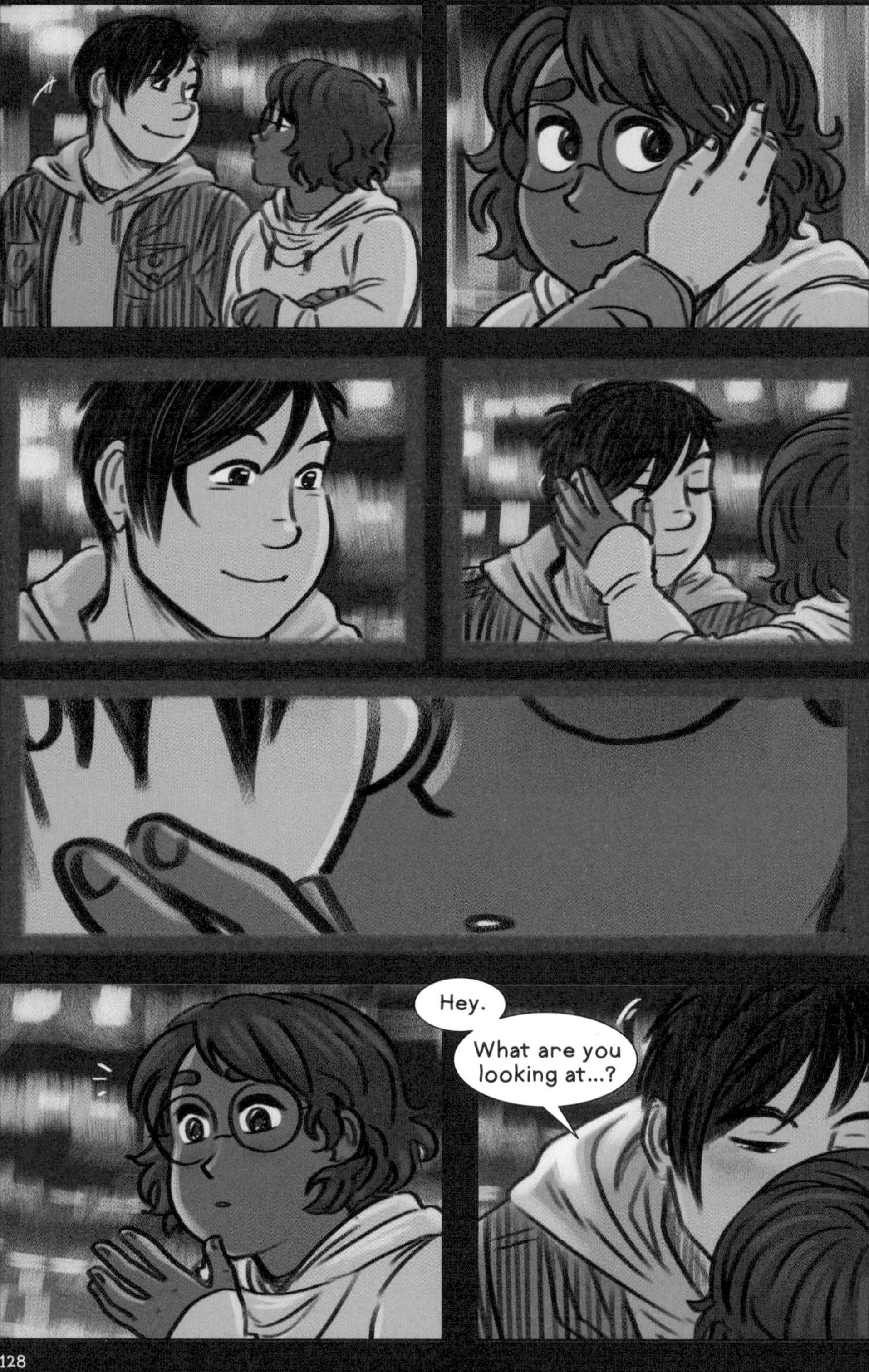
Hey.
What are you looking at...?

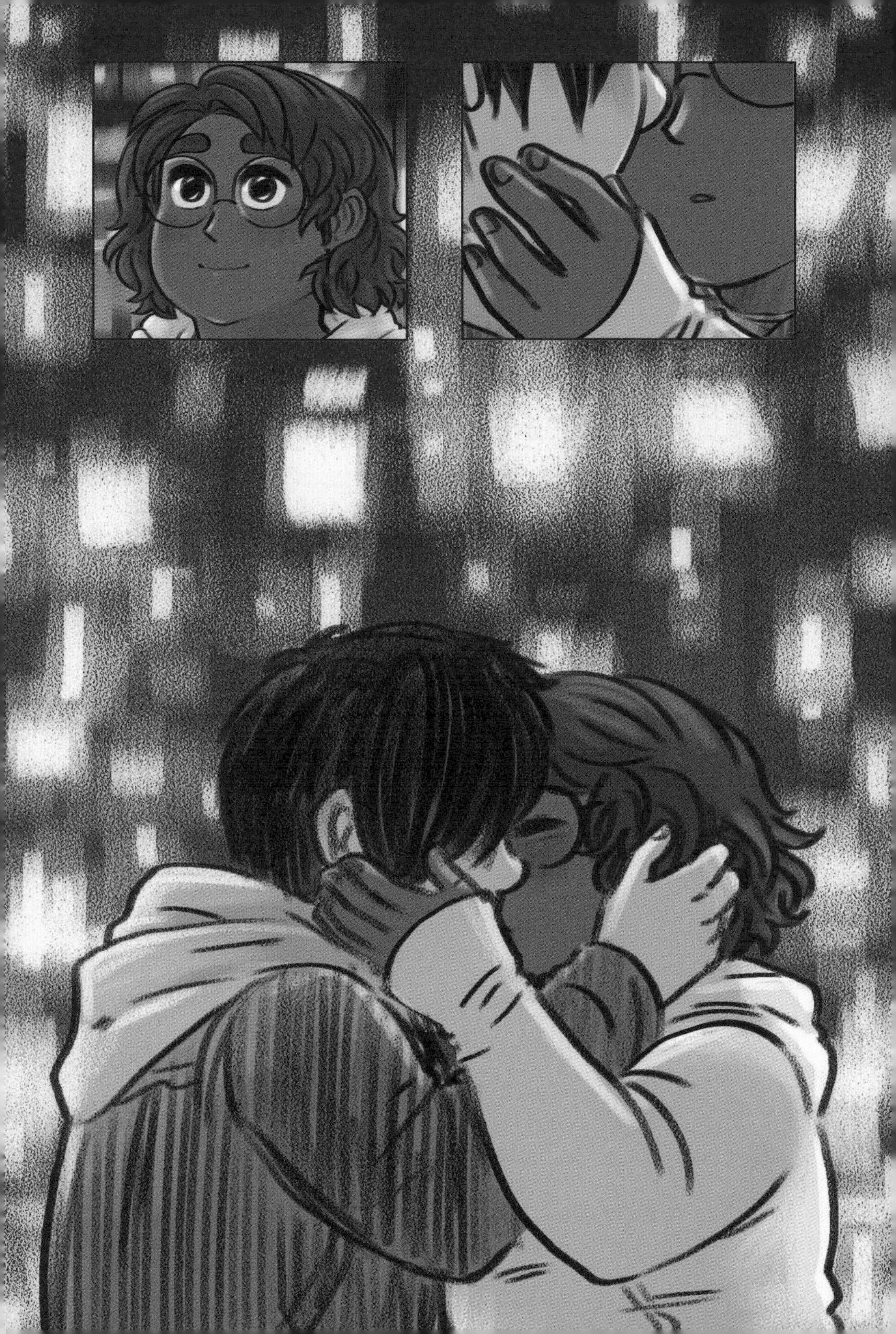

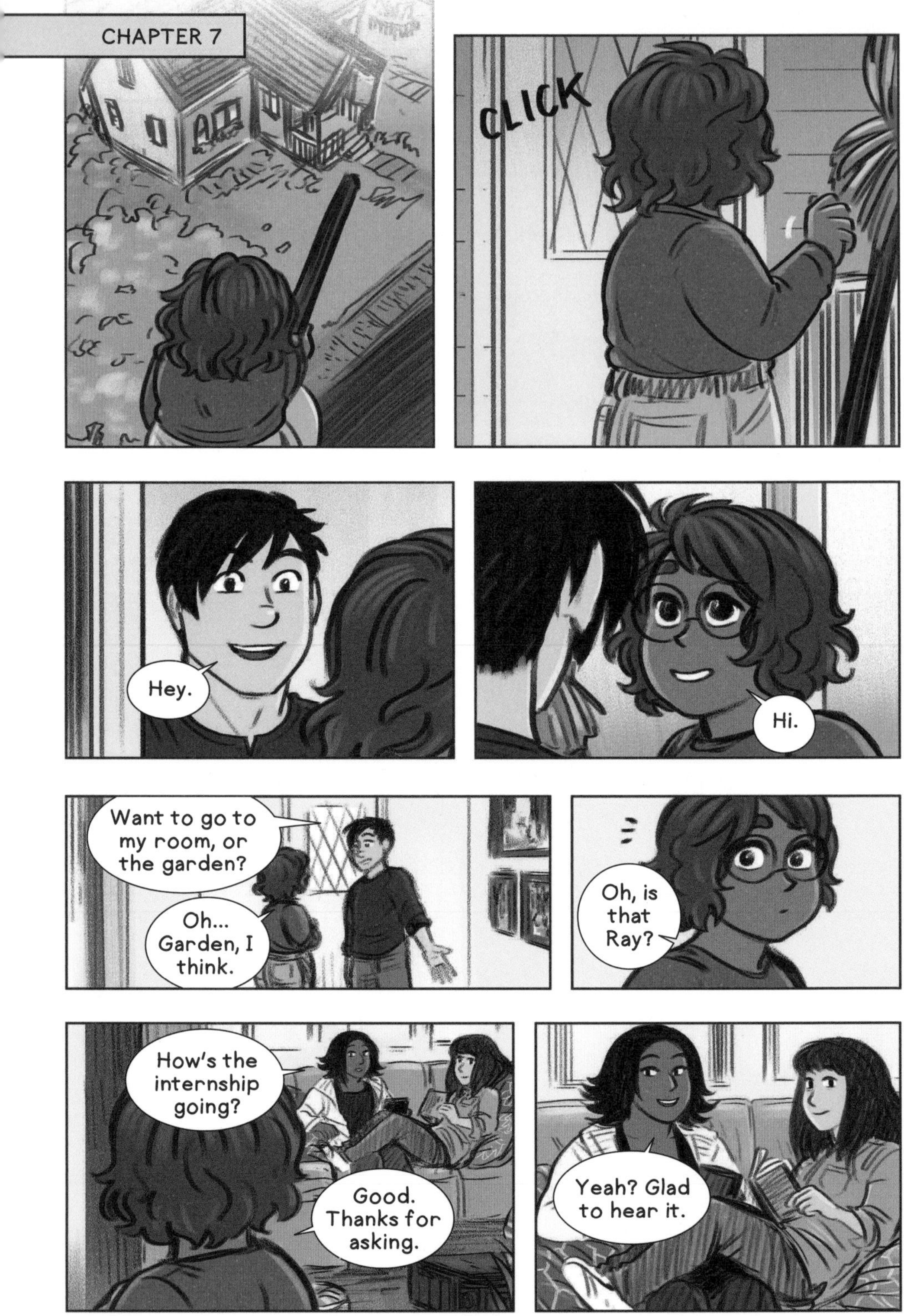
CHAPTER 7
CLICK
Hey.
Hi.
Want to go to my room, or the garden?
Oh... Garden, I think.
Oh, is that Ray?
How's the internship going?
Good. Thanks for asking.
Yeah? Glad to hear it.

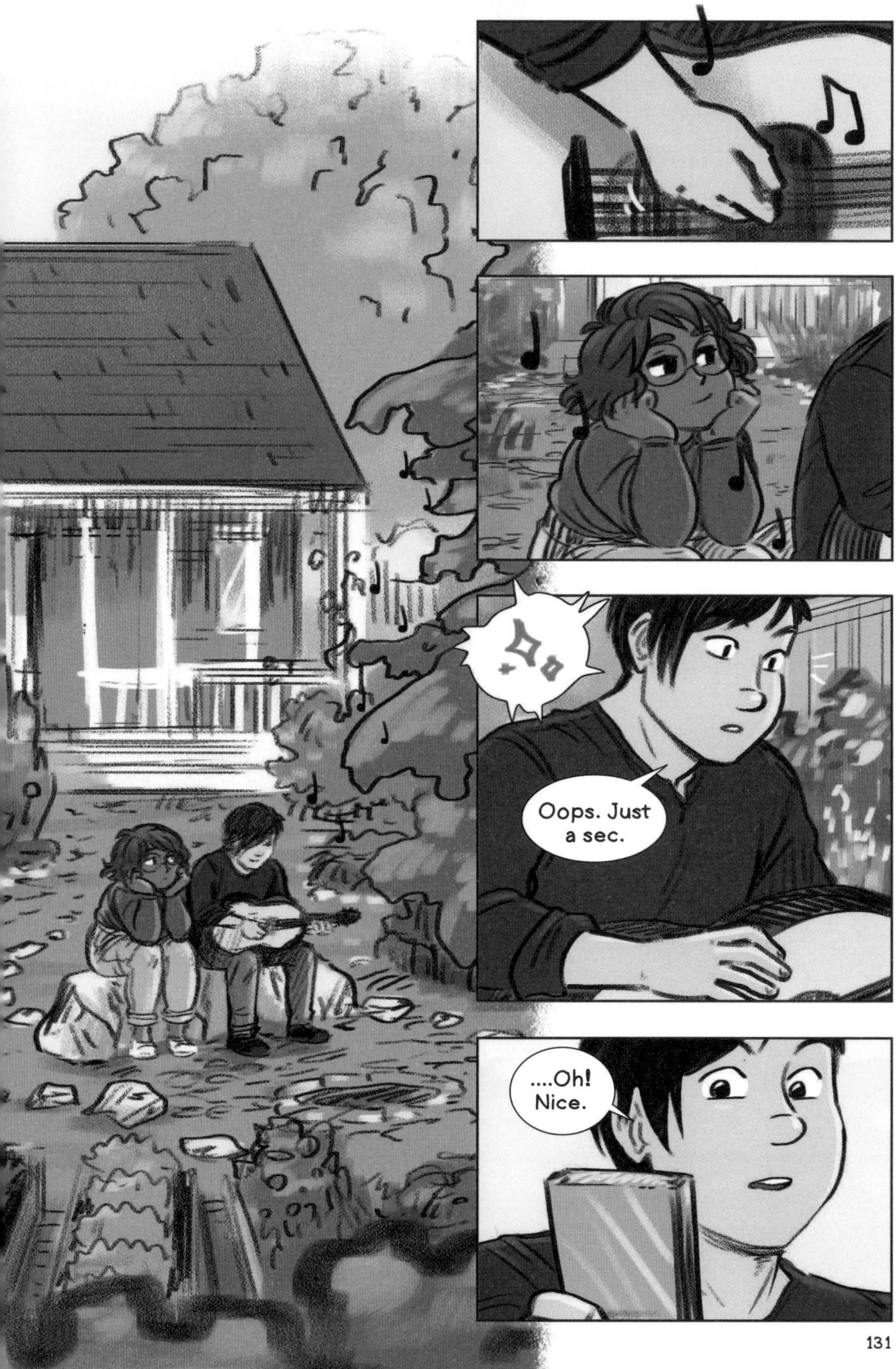
Oops. Just a sec.
....Oh! Nice.

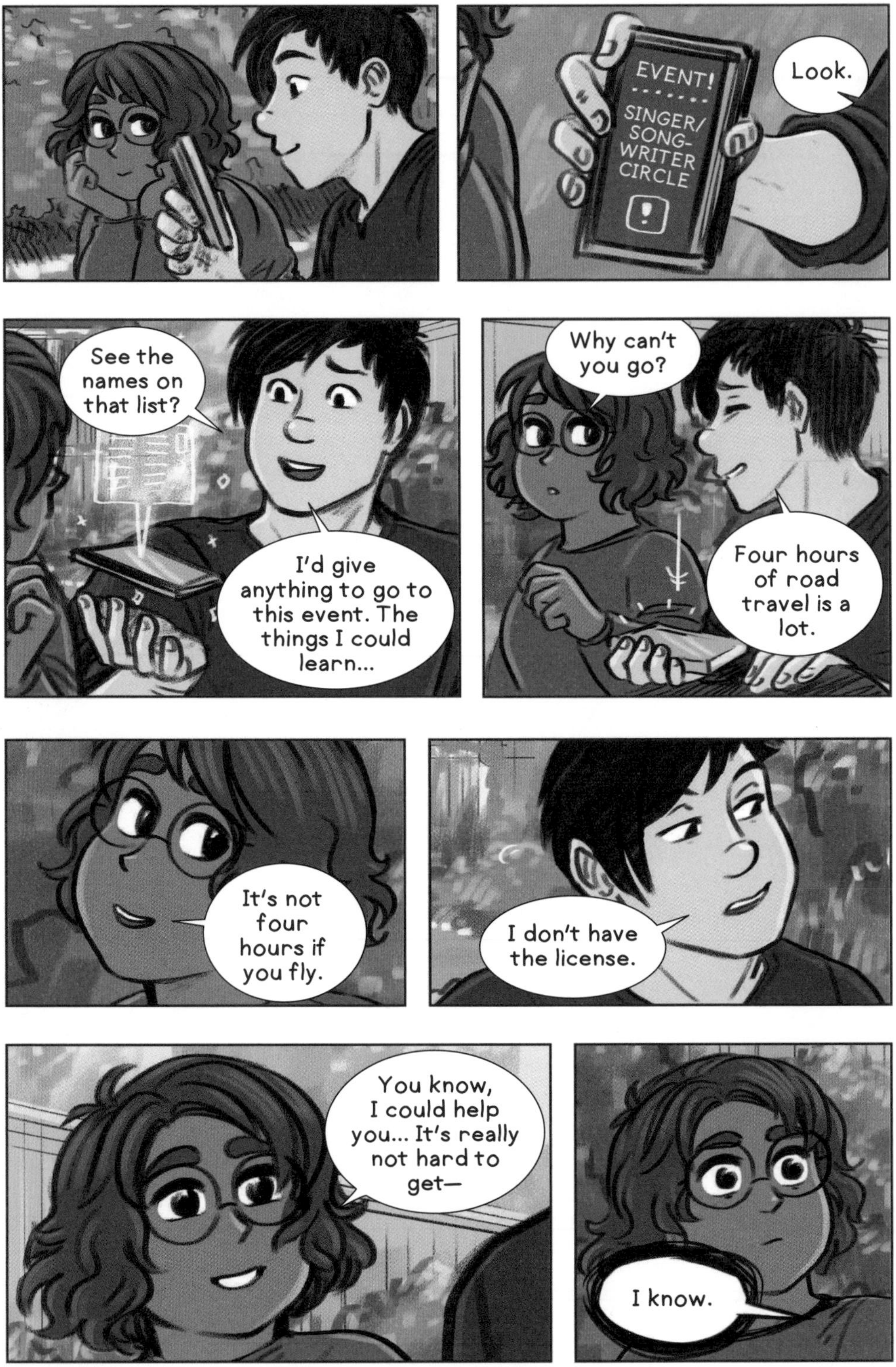
EVENT!
SINGER/ SONG-WRITER CIRCLE
Look.
See the names on that list?
I'd give anything to go to this event. The things I could learn...
Why can't you go?
Four hours of road travel is a lot.
It's not four hours if you fly.
I don't have the license.
You know, I could help you... It's really not hard to get—
I know.

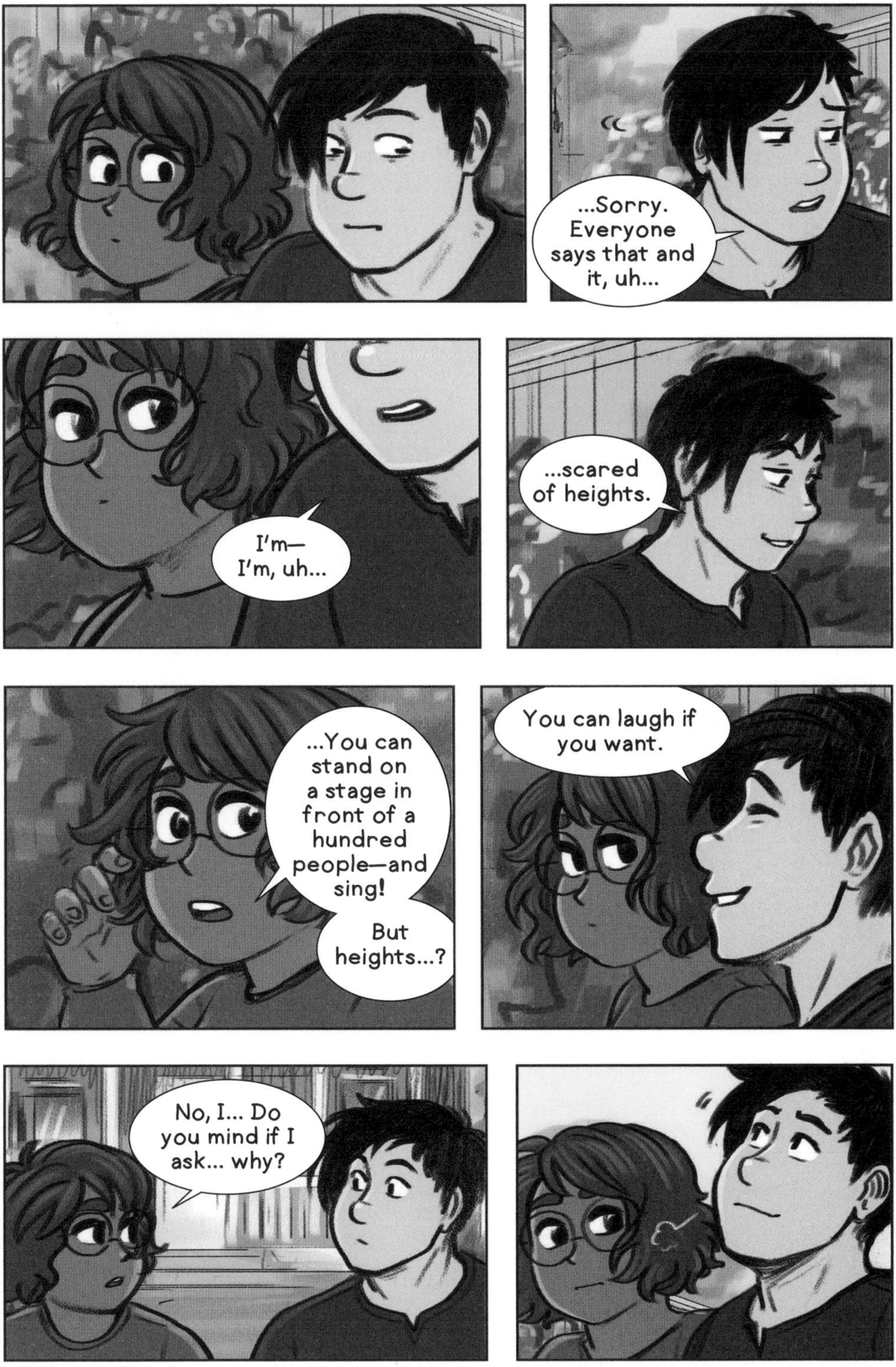
...Sorry. Everyone says that and it, uh...
I'm— I'm, uh...
...scared of heights.
...You can stand on a stage in front of a hundred people—and sing!
But heights...?
You can laugh if you want.
No, I... Do you mind if I ask... why?

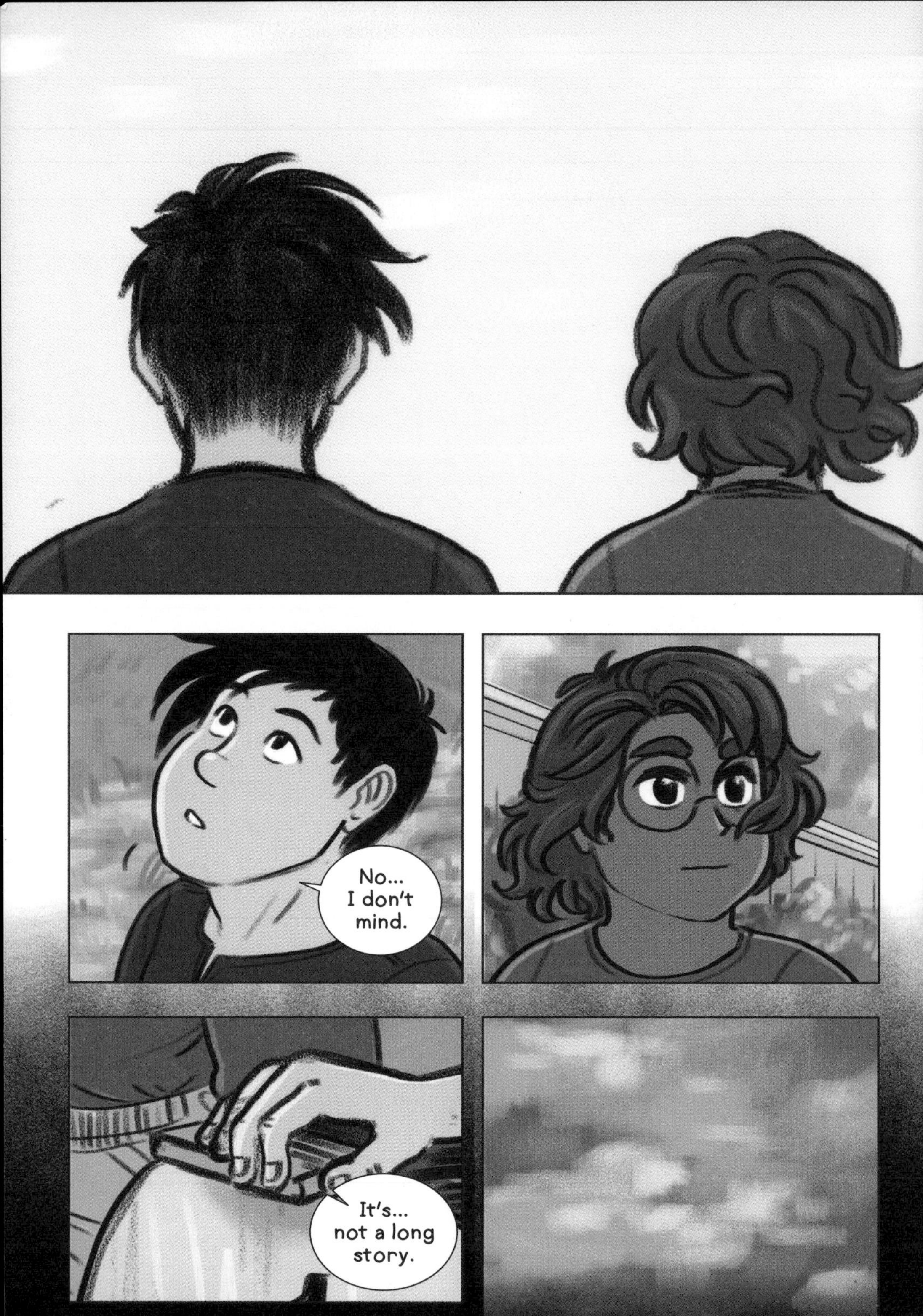
No... I don't mind.
It's... not a long story.

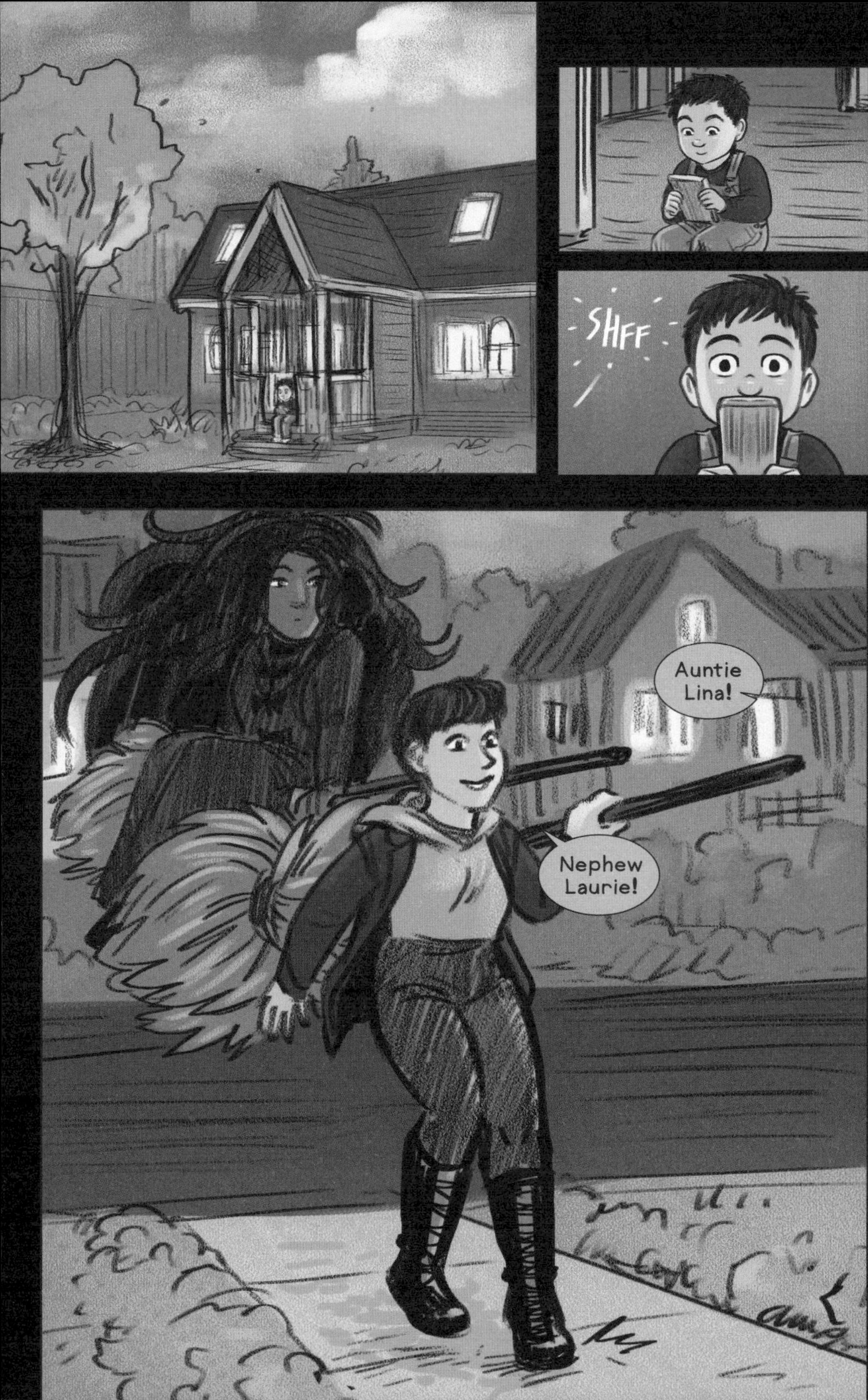
SHFF
Auntie Lina!
Nephew Laurie!

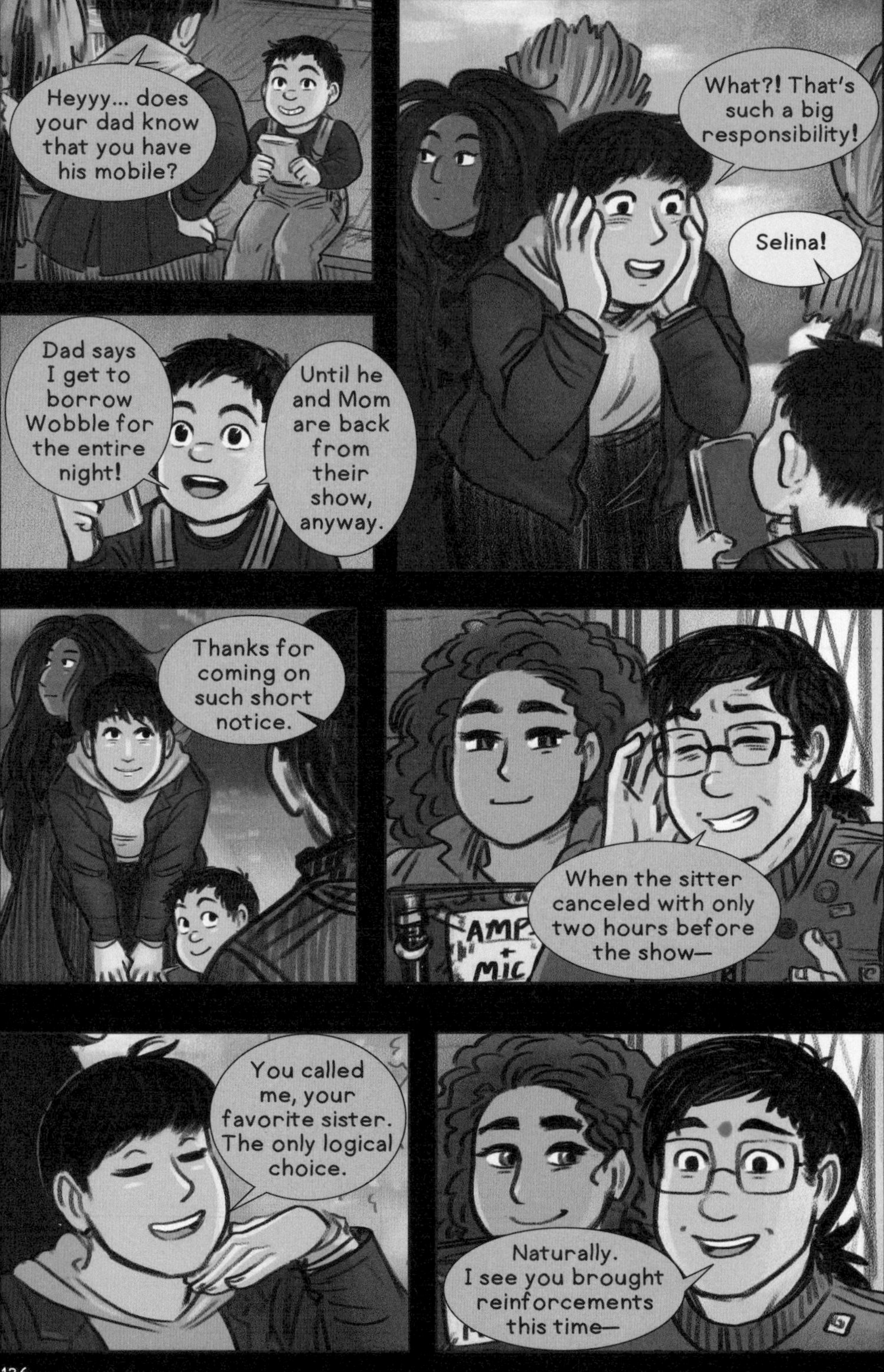
Heyyy... does your dad know that you have his mobile?
What?! That's such a big responsibility!
Selina!
Dad says I get to borrow Wobble for the entire night!
Until he and Mom are back from their show, anyway.
Thanks for coming on such short notice.
When the sitter canceled with only two hours before the show—
AMP + MIC
You called me, your favorite sister. The only logical choice.
Naturally. I see you brought reinforcements this time—

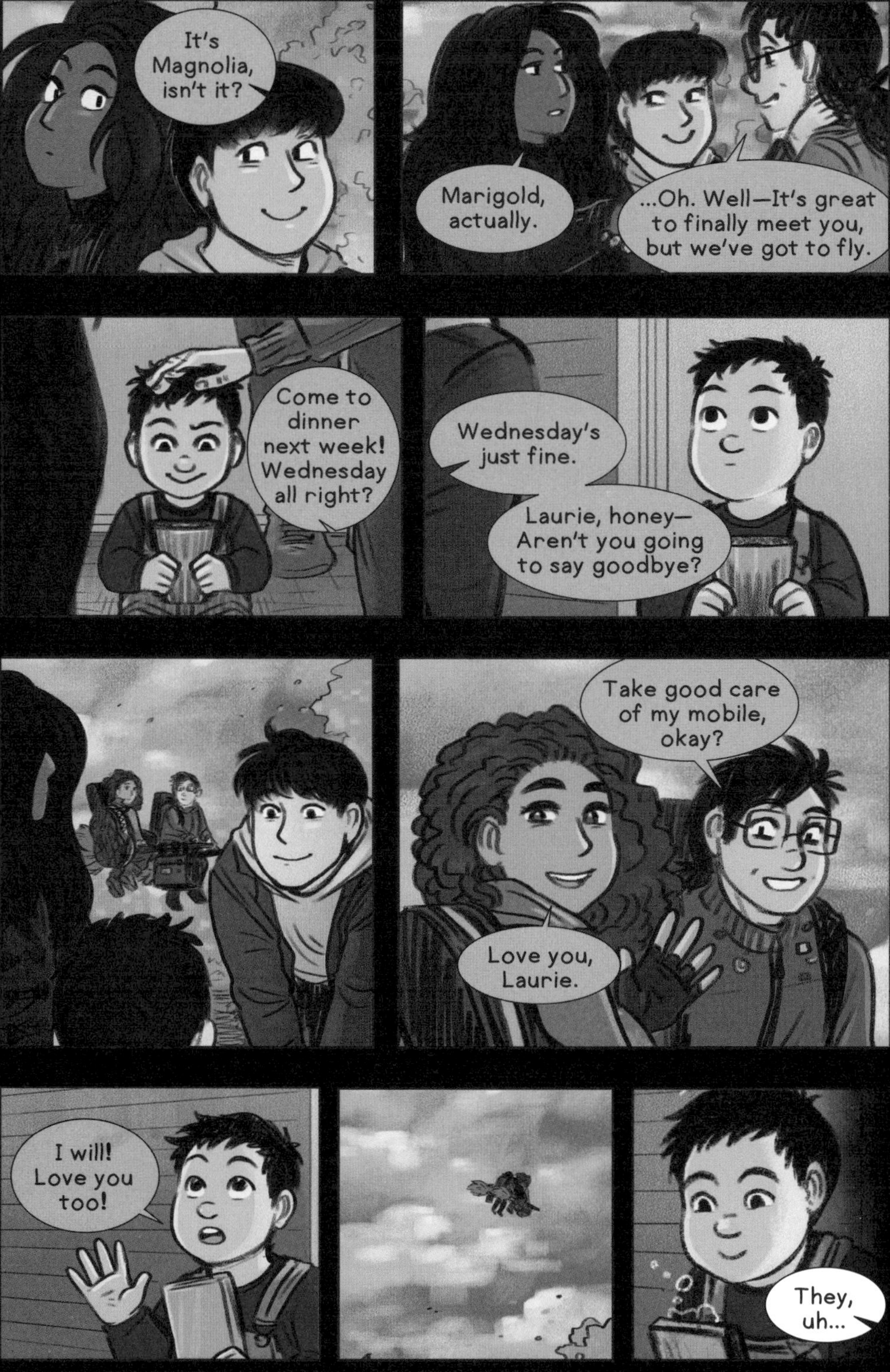
It's Magnolia, isn't it?
Marigold, actually.
...Oh. Well—It's great to finally meet you, but we've got to fly.
Come to dinner next week! Wednesday all right?
Wednesday's just fine.
Laurie, honey— Aren't you going to say goodbye?
Take good care of my mobile, okay?
Love you, Laurie.
I will! Love you too!
They, uh...

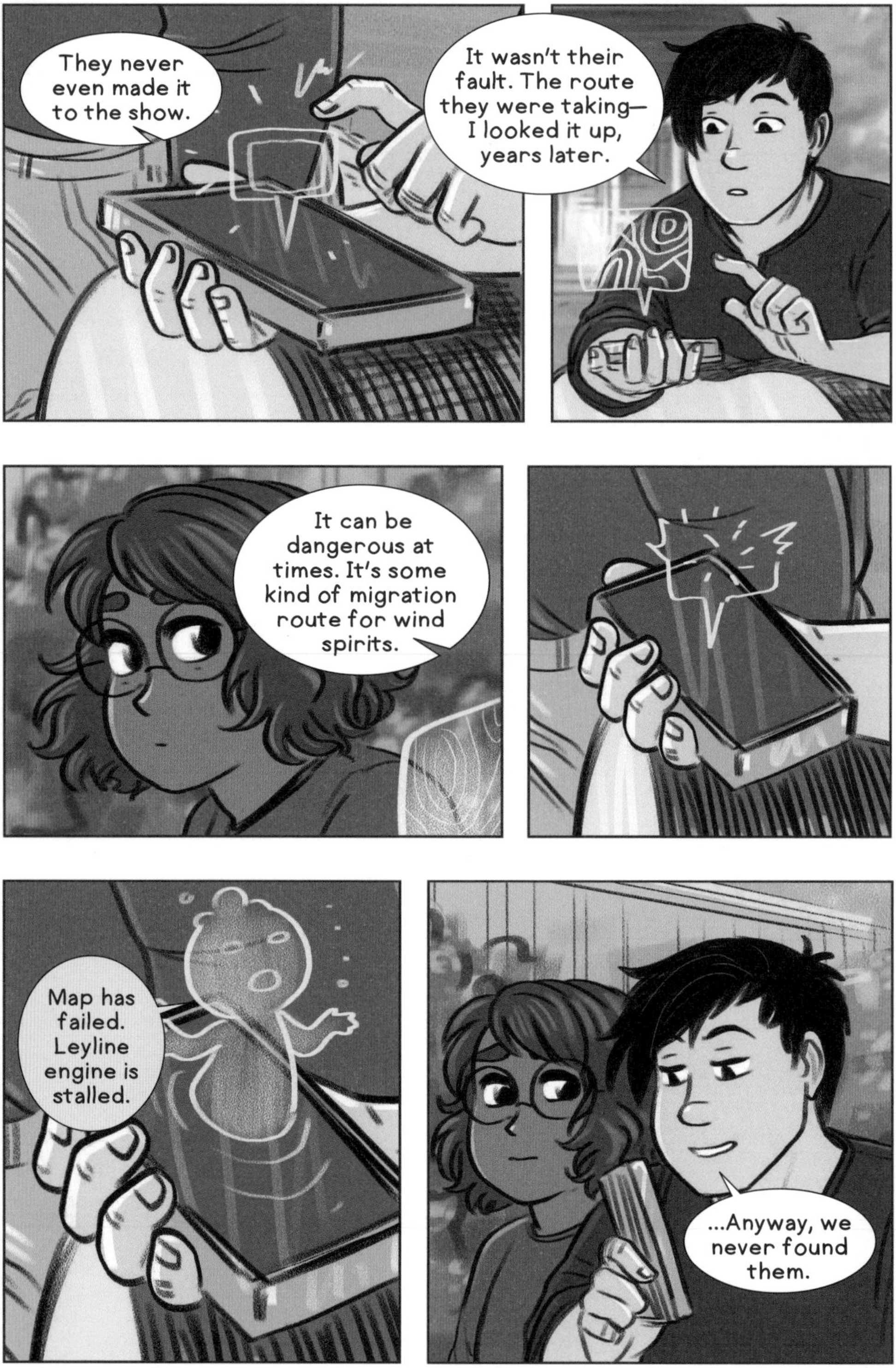
They never even made it to the show.
It wasn't their fault. The route they were taking—I looked it up, years later.
It can be dangerous at times. It's some kind of migration route for wind spirits.
Map has failed. Leyline engine is stalled.
...Anyway, we never found them.

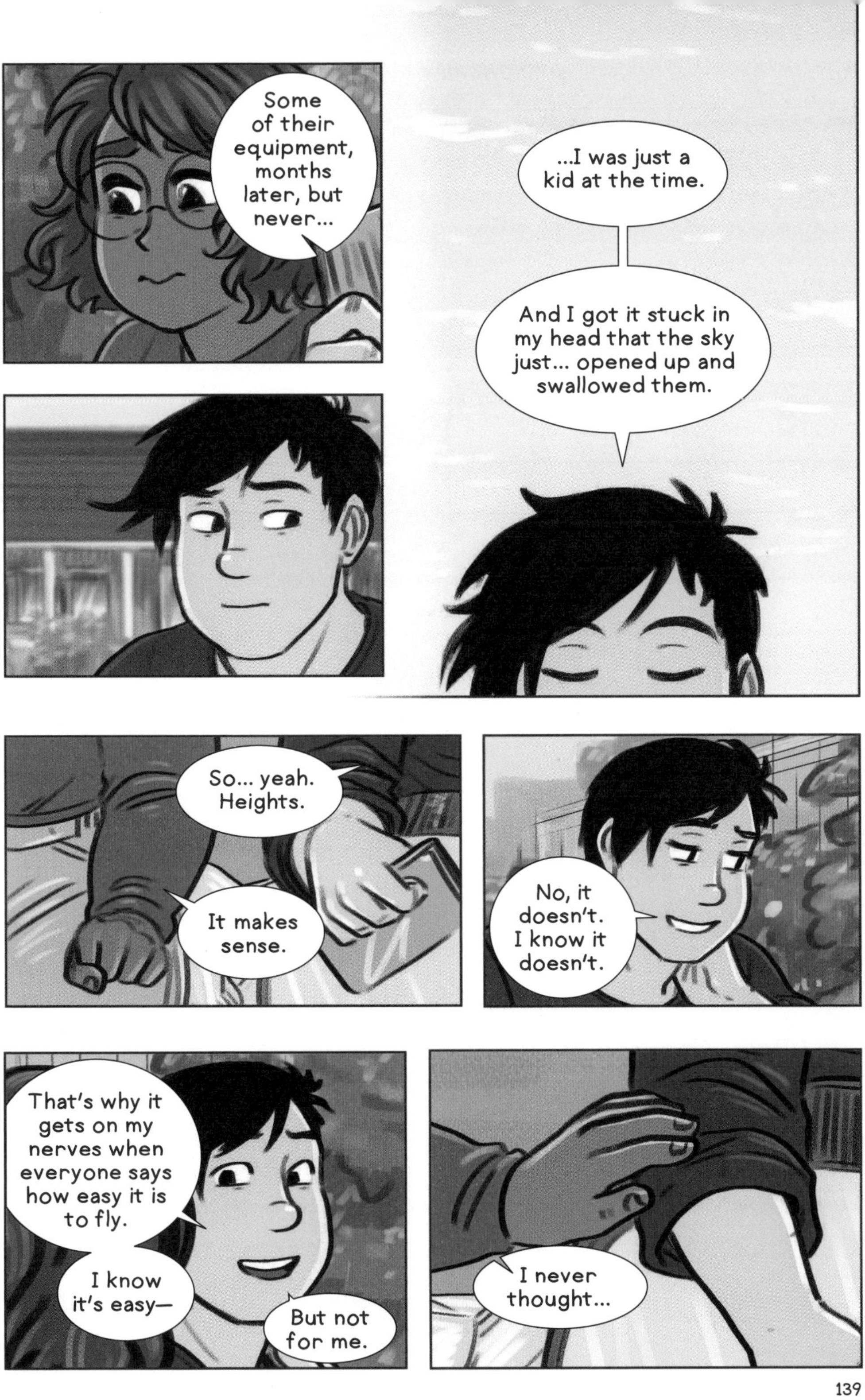
Some of their equipment, months later, but never...
...I was just a kid at the time.
And I got it stuck in my head that the sky just... opened up and swallowed them.
So... yeah. Heights.
It makes sense.
No, it doesn't. I know it doesn't.
That's why it gets on my nerves when everyone says how easy it is to fly.
I know it's easy—
But not for me.
I never thought...

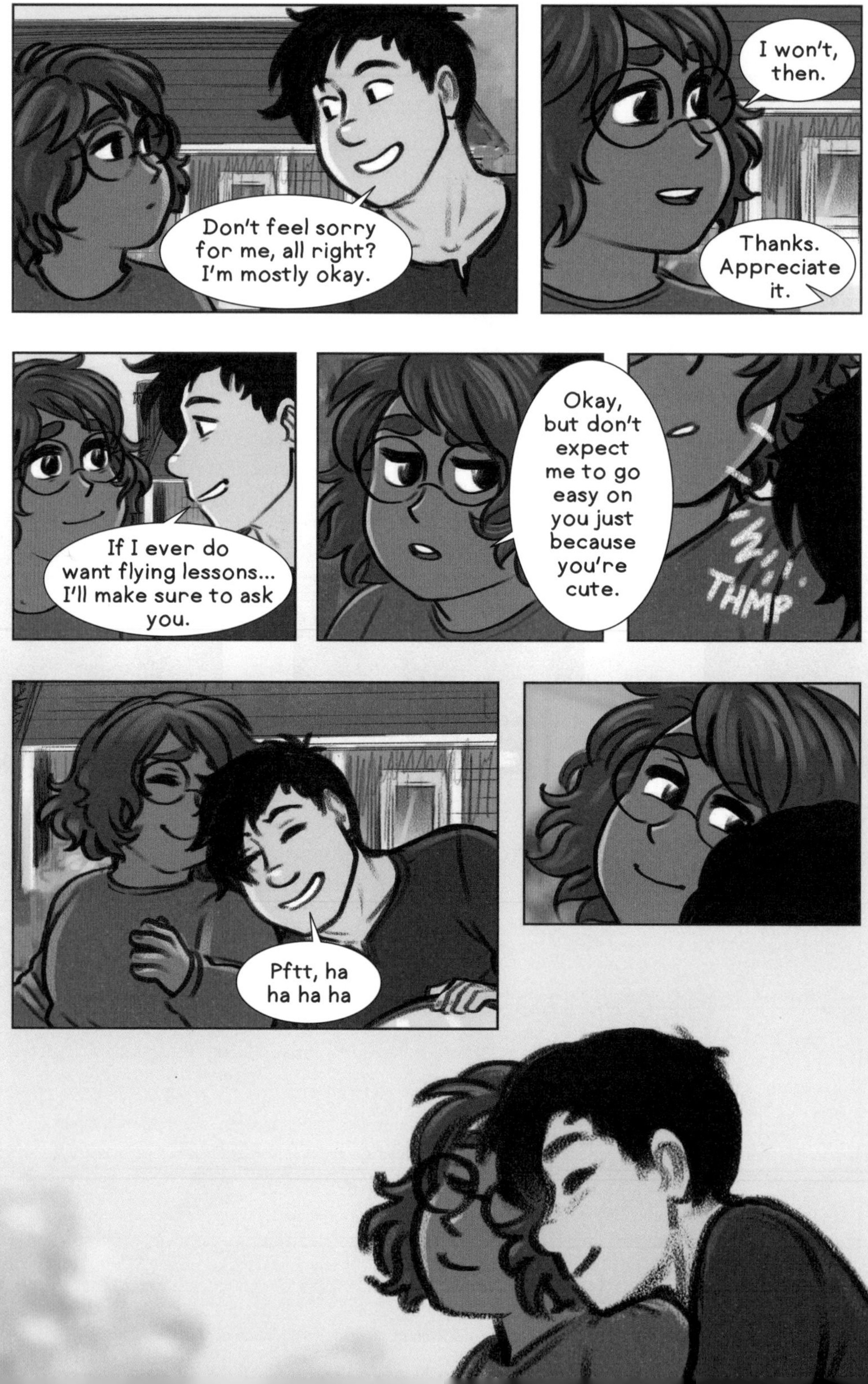
Don't feel sorry for me, all right? I'm mostly okay.
I won't, then.
Thanks. Appreciate it.
If I ever do want flying lessons... I'll make sure to ask you.
Okay, but don't expect me to go easy on you just because you're cute.
THMP
Pftt, ha ha ha ha

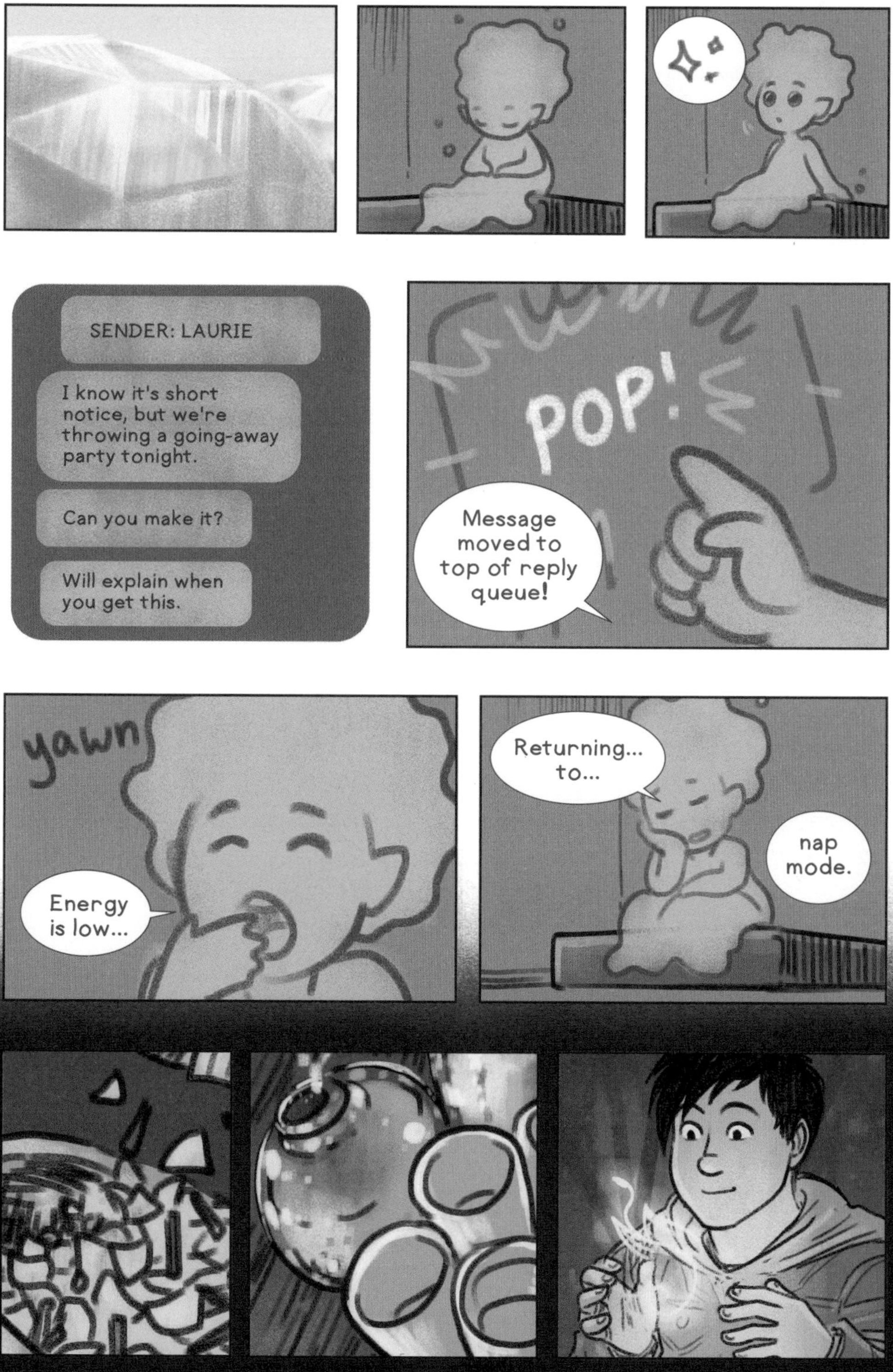
SENDER: LAURIE
I know it's short notice, but we're throwing a going-away party tonight.
Can you make it?
Will explain when you get this.
POP!
Message moved to top of reply queue!
yawn
Energy is low...
Returning... to...
nap mode.

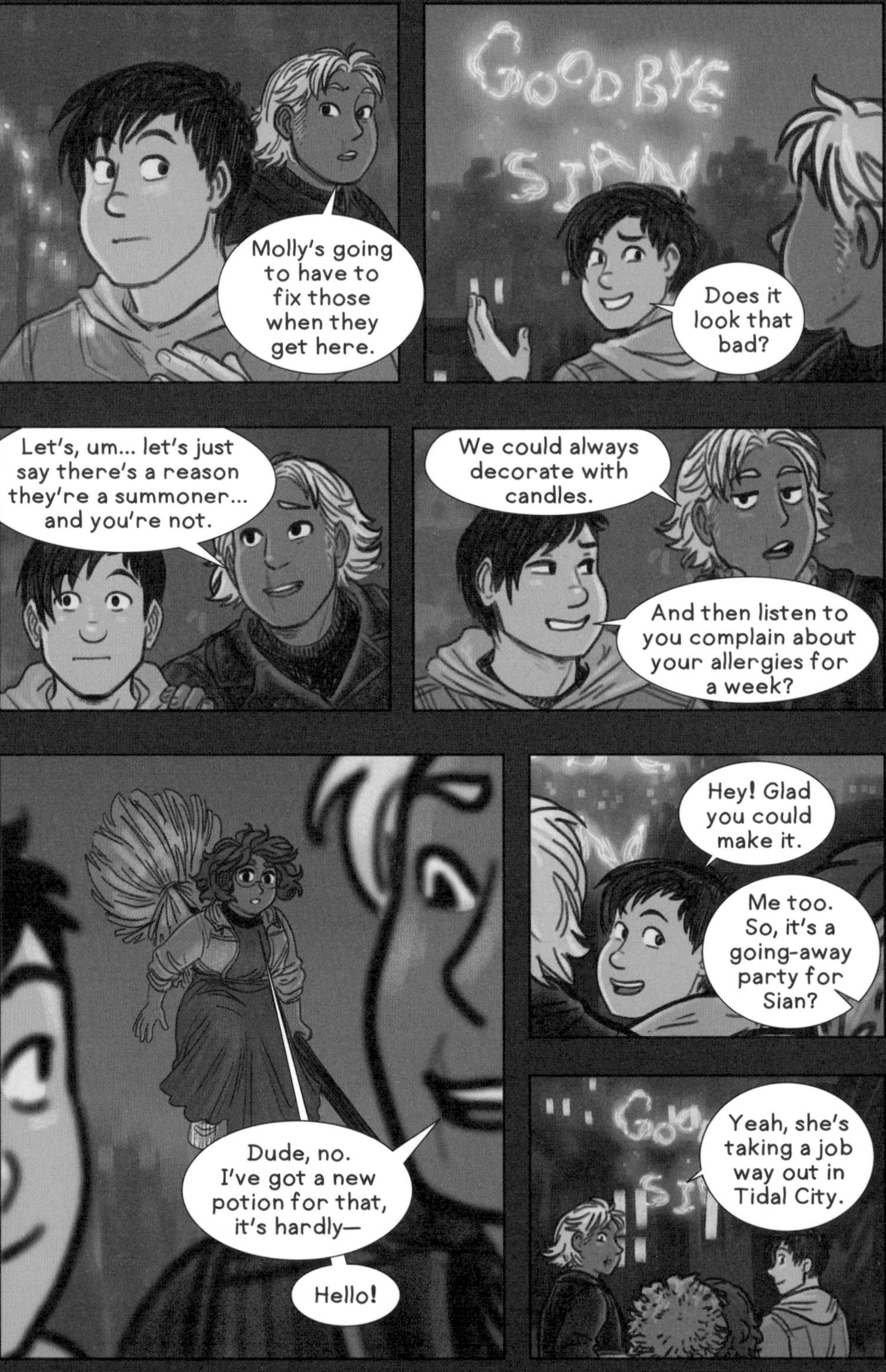
Molly's going to have to fix those when they get here.
GOODBYE SIAN
Does it look that bad?
Let's, um... let's just say there's a reason they're a summoner... and you're not.
We could always decorate with candles.
And then listen to you complain about your allergies for a week?
Dude, no. I've got a new potion for that, it's hardly—
Hello!
Hey! Glad you could make it.
Me too. So, it's a going-away party for Sian?
Yeah, she's taking a job way out in Tidal City.

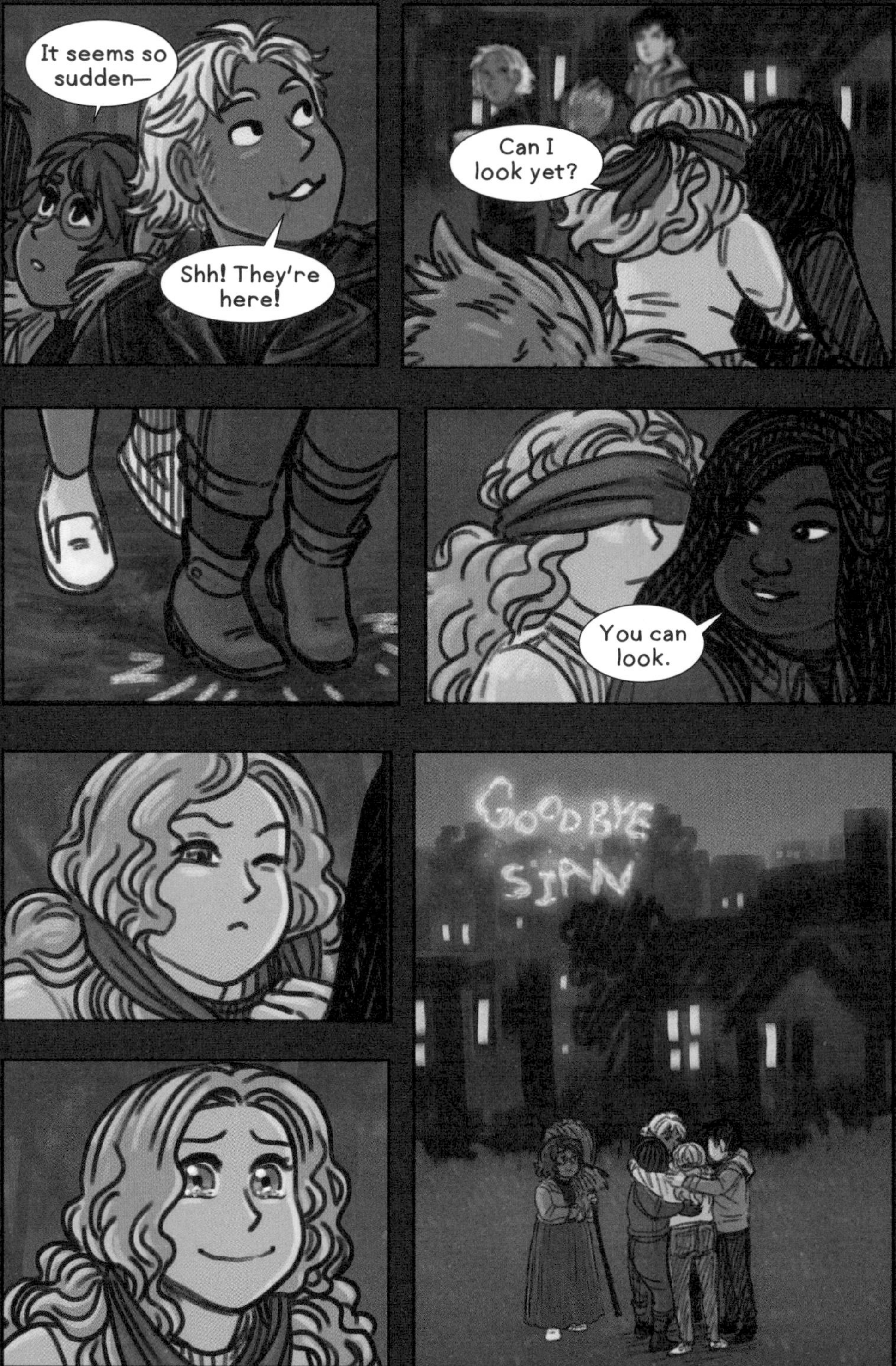
It seems so sudden—
Shh! They're here!
Can I look yet?
You can look.
GOODBYE SIAN

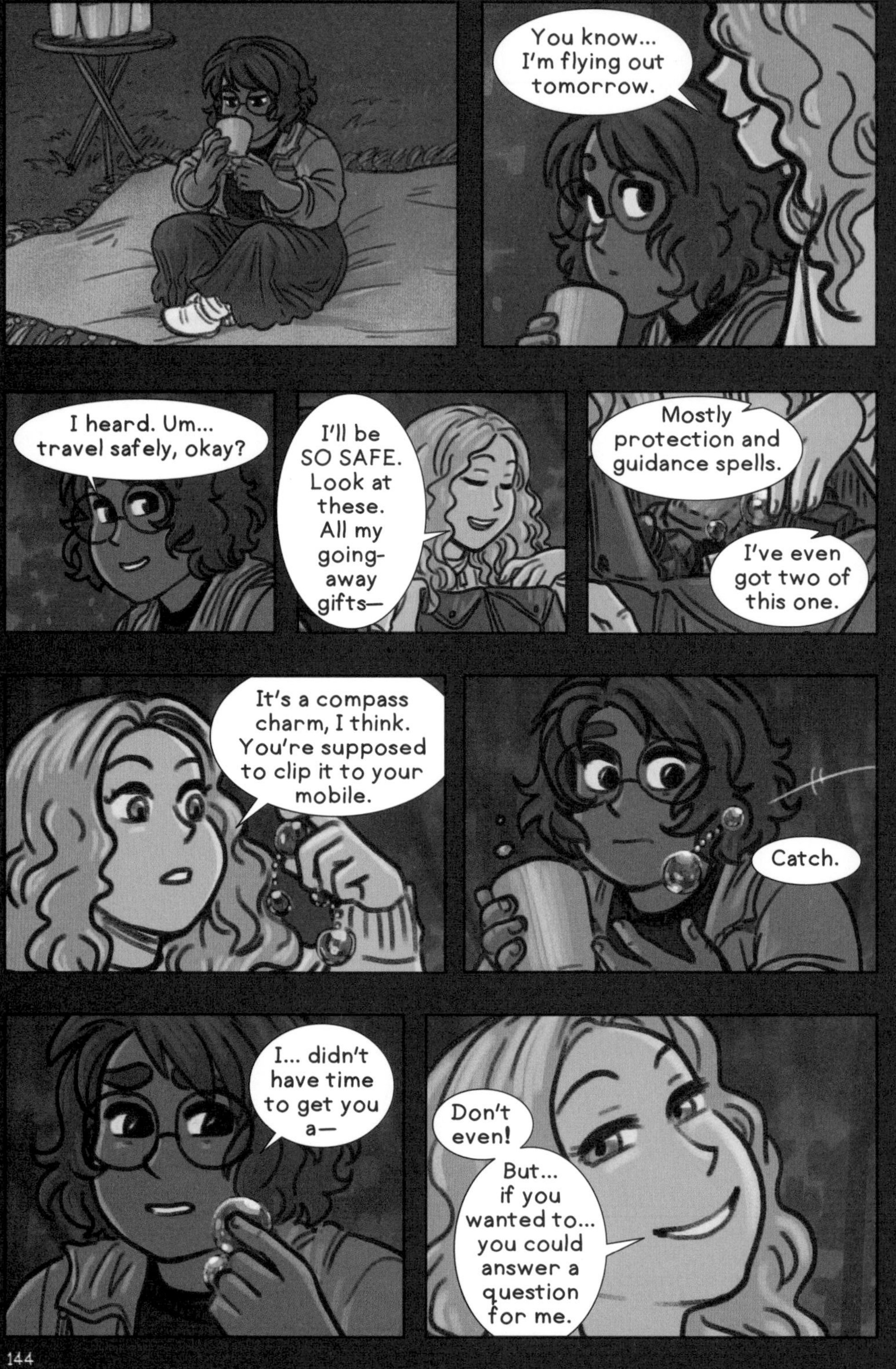
You know... I'm flying out tomorrow.
I heard. Um... travel safely, okay?
I'll be SO SAFE. Look at these. All my going-away gifts—
Mostly protection and guidance spells.
I've even got two of this one.
It's a compass charm, I think. You're supposed to clip it to your mobile.
Catch.
I... didn't have time to get you a—
Don't even!
But... if you wanted to... you could answer a question for me.

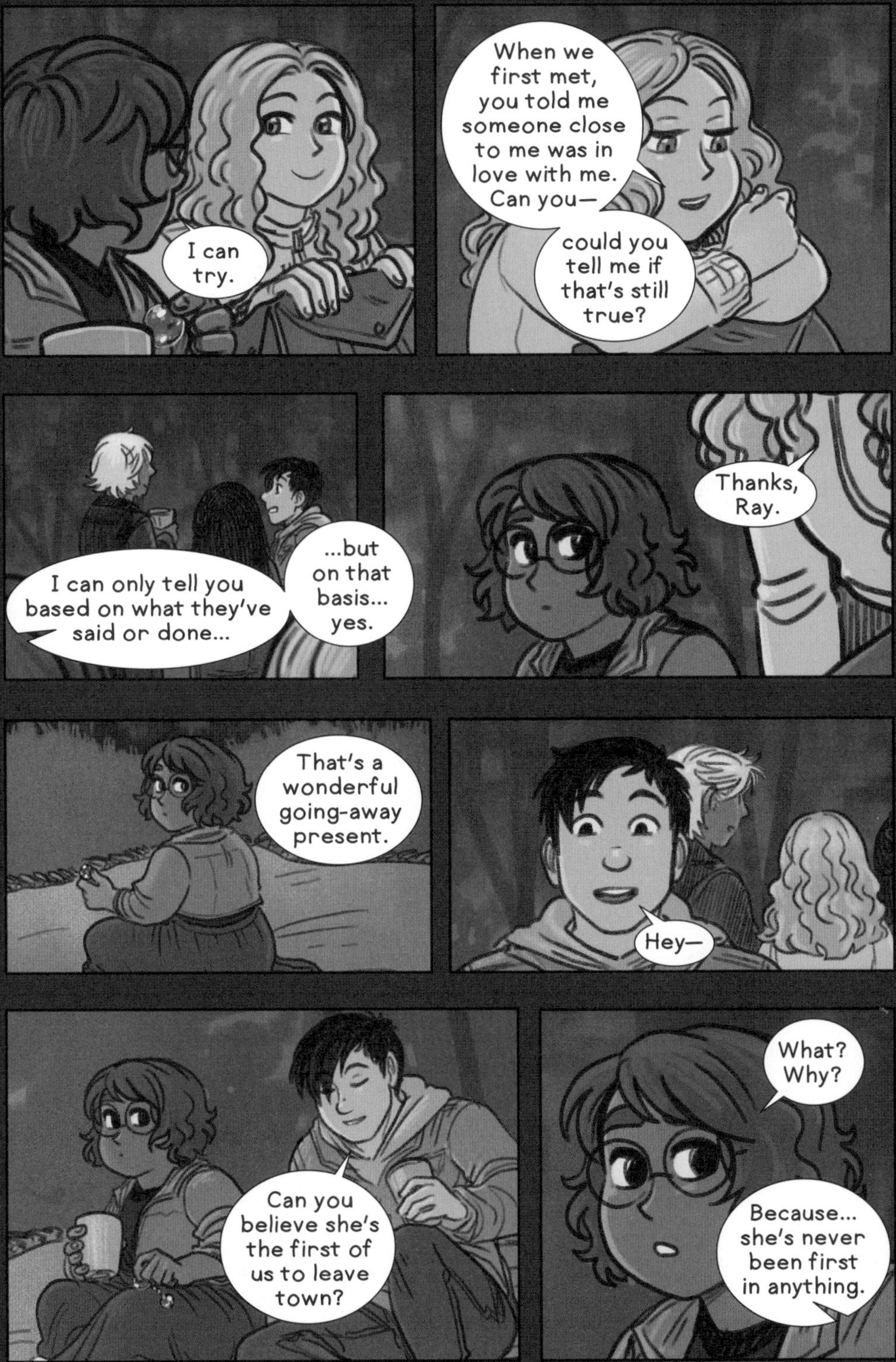
When we first met, you told me someone close to me was in love with me. Can you—
could you tell me if that's still true?
I can try.
I can only tell you based on what they've said or done...
...but on that basis... yes.
Thanks, Ray.
That's a wonderful going-away present.
Hey—
Can you believe she's the first of us to leave town?
What? Why?
Because... she's never been first in anything.

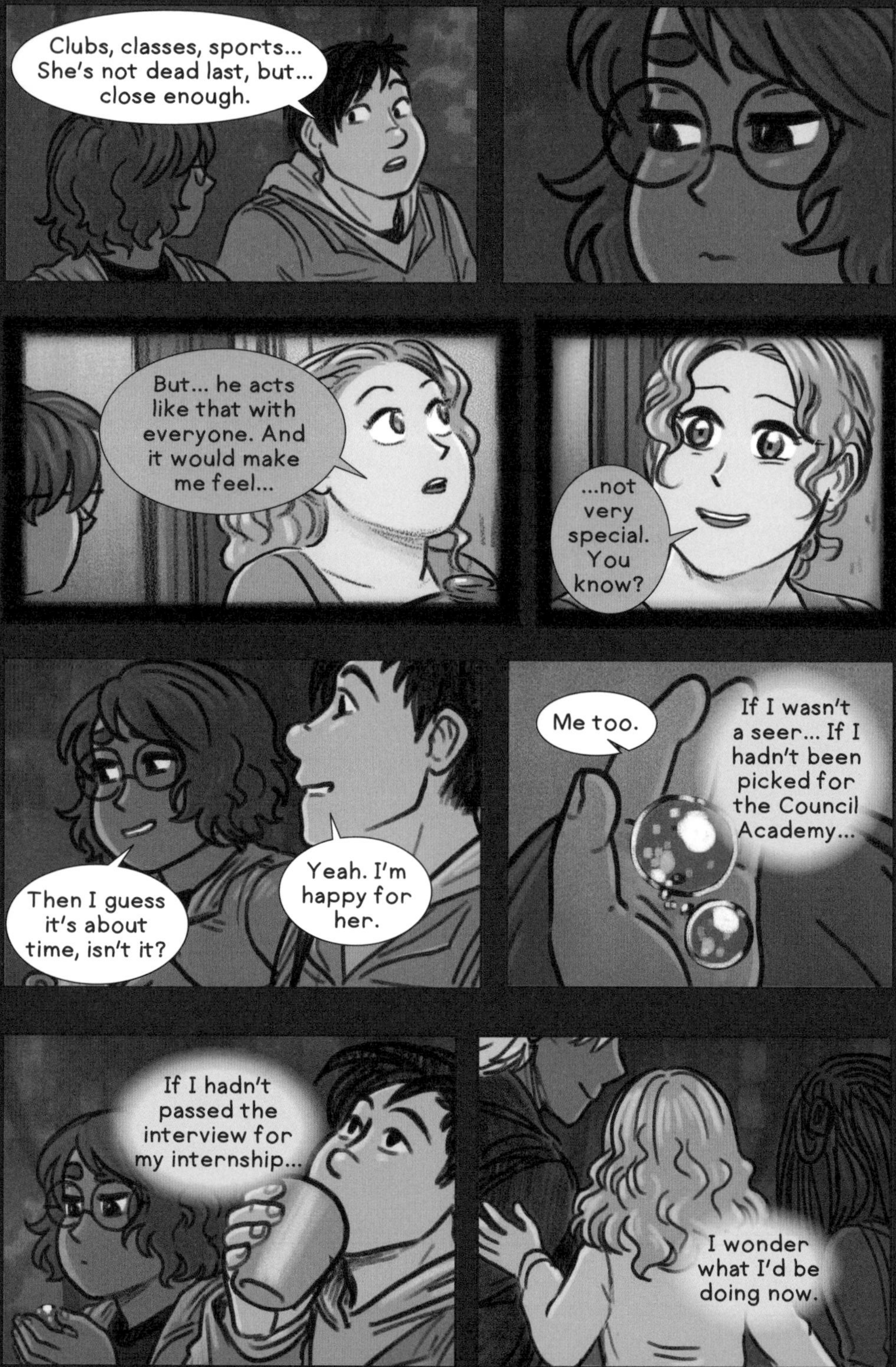
Clubs, classes, sports... She's not dead last, but... close enough.
But... he acts like that with everyone. And it would make me feel...
...not very special. You know?
Then I guess it's about time, isn't it?
Yeah. I'm happy for her.
Me too.
If I wasn't a seer... If I hadn't been picked for the Council Academy...
If I hadn't passed the interview for my internship...
I wonder what I'd be doing now.

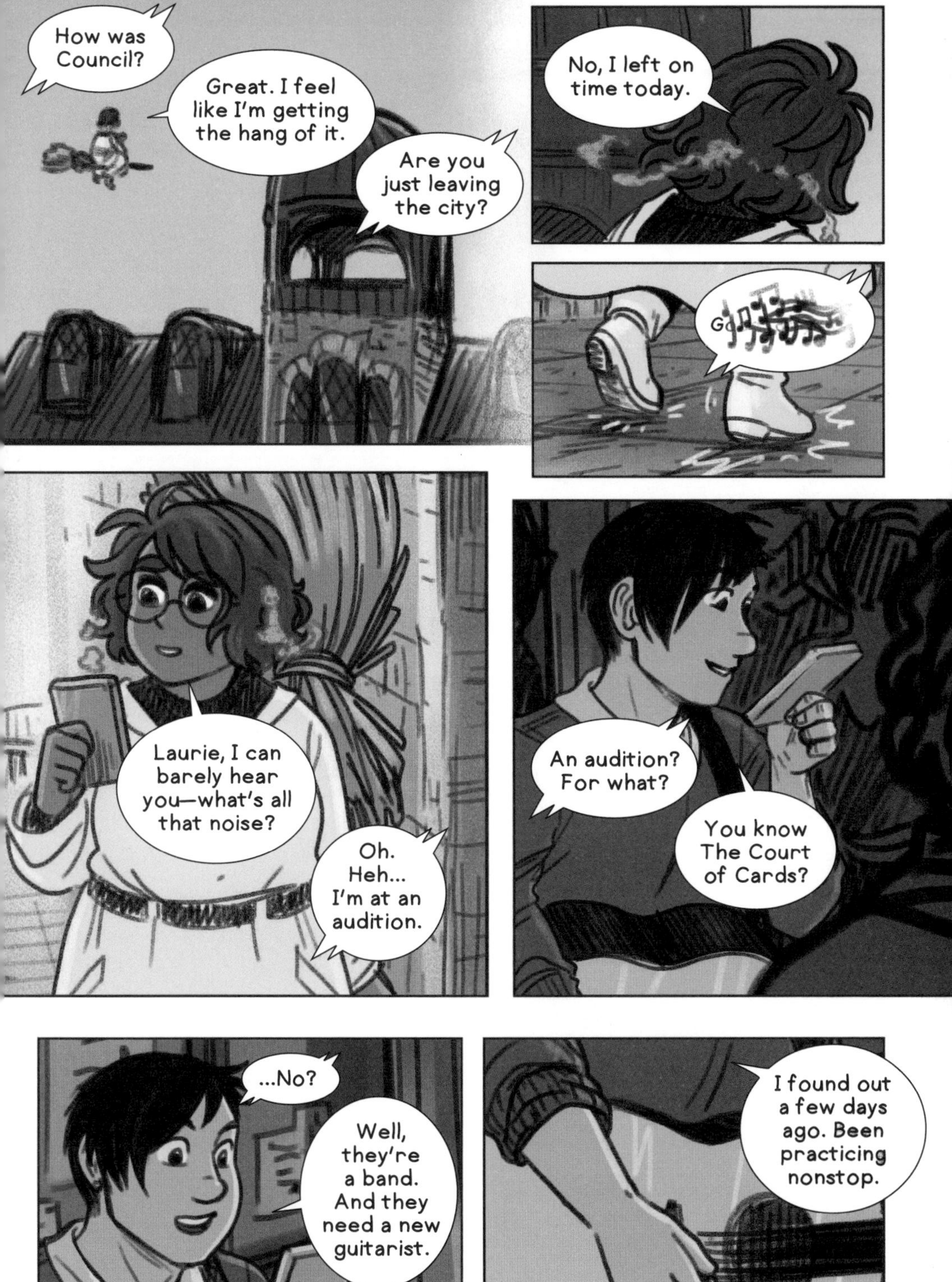
How was Council?
Great. I feel like I'm getting the hang of it.
Are you just leaving the city?
No, I left on time today.
Laurie, I can barely hear you—what's all that noise?
Oh. Heh... I'm at an audition.
An audition? For what?
You know The Court of Cards?
...No?
Well, they're a band. And they need a new guitarist.
I found out a few days ago. Been practicing nonstop.

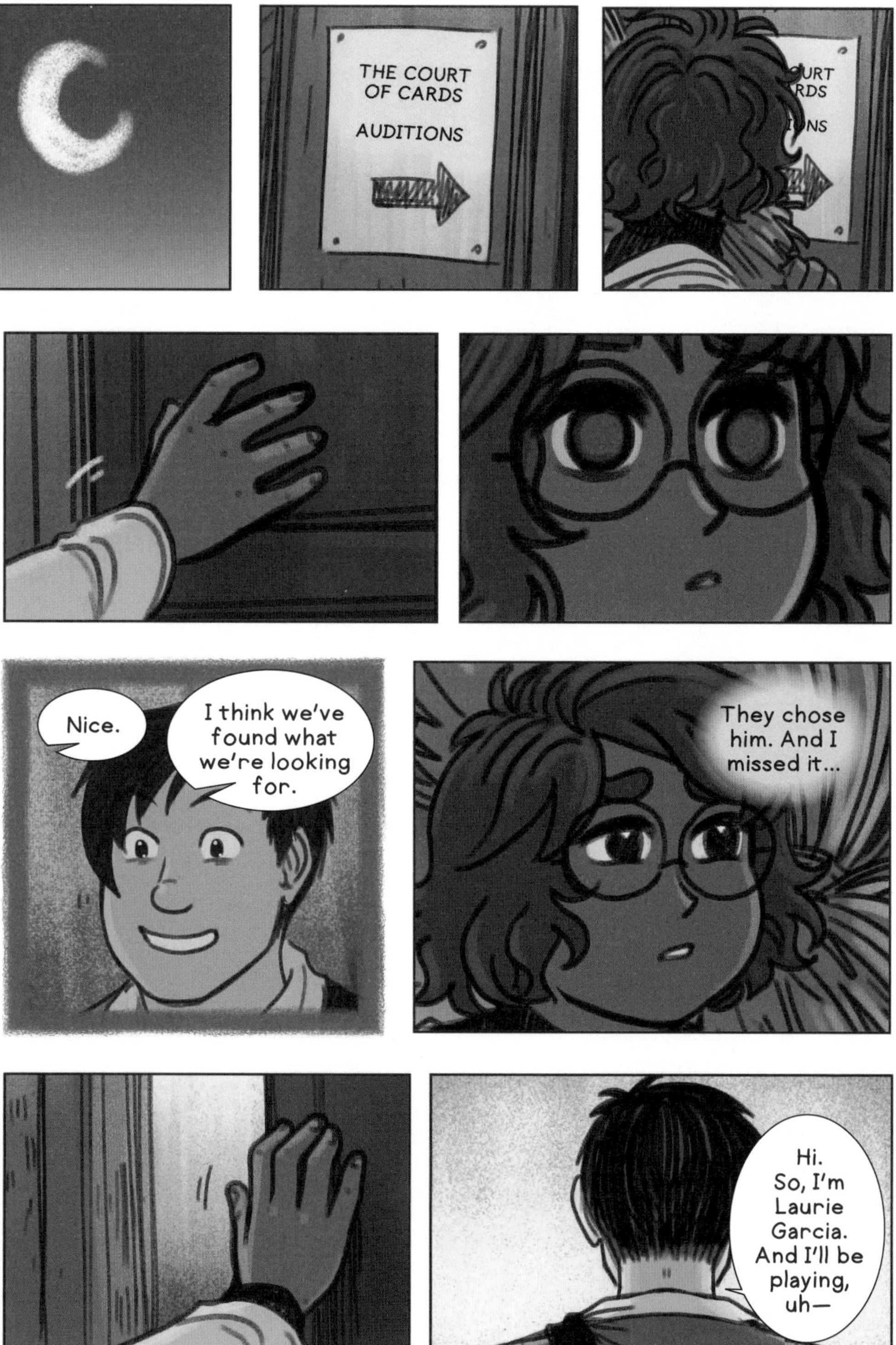
THE COURT
OF CARDS
AUDITIONS
Nice.
I think we've found what we're looking for.
They chose him. And I missed it...
Hi. So, I'm Laurie Garcia. And I'll be playing, uh—

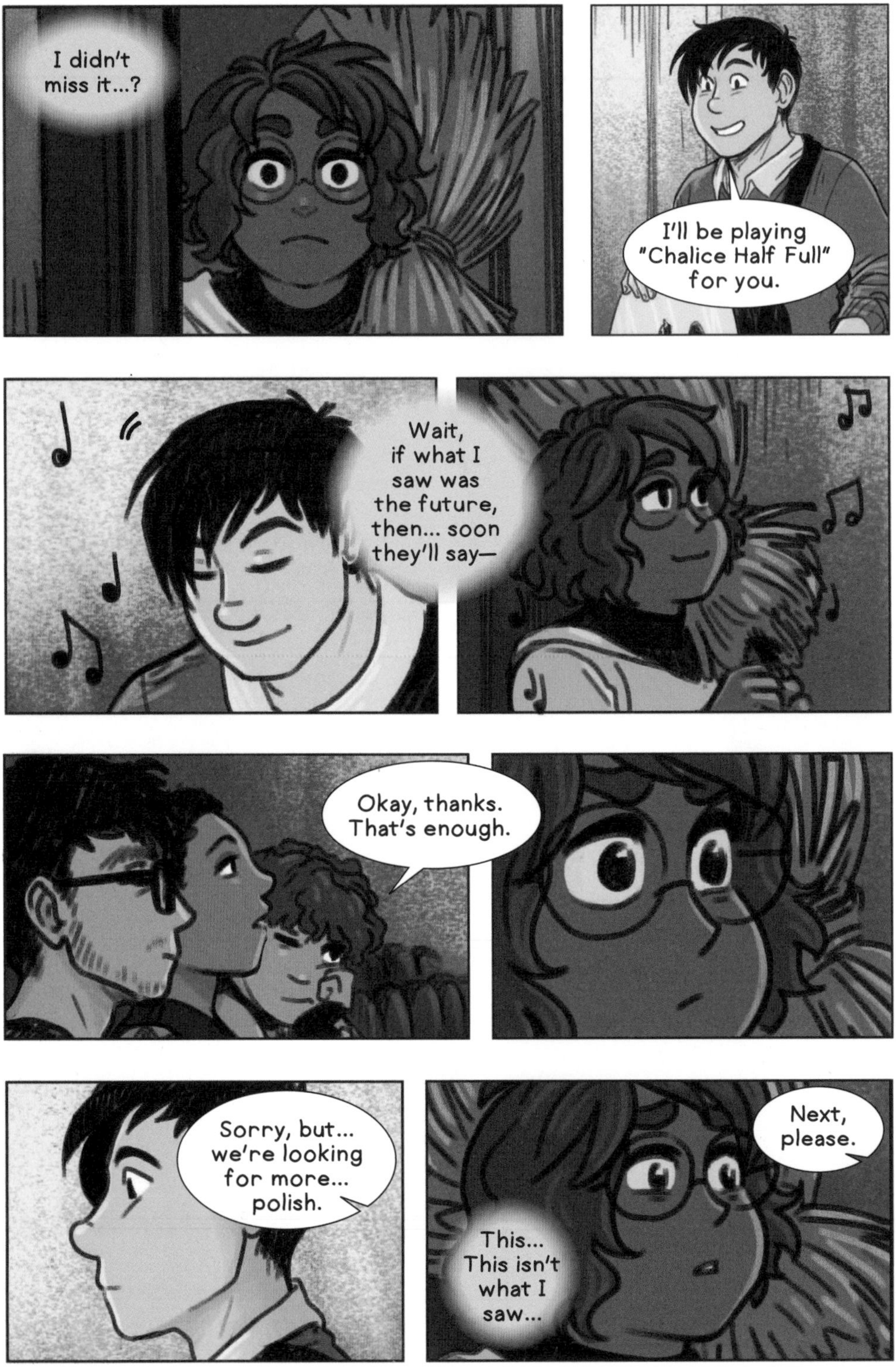
I didn't miss it...?
I'll be playing "Chalice Half Full" for you.
Wait, if what I saw was the future, then... soon they'll say—
Okay, thanks. That's enough.
Sorry, but... we're looking for more... polish.
Next, please.
This... This isn't what I saw...

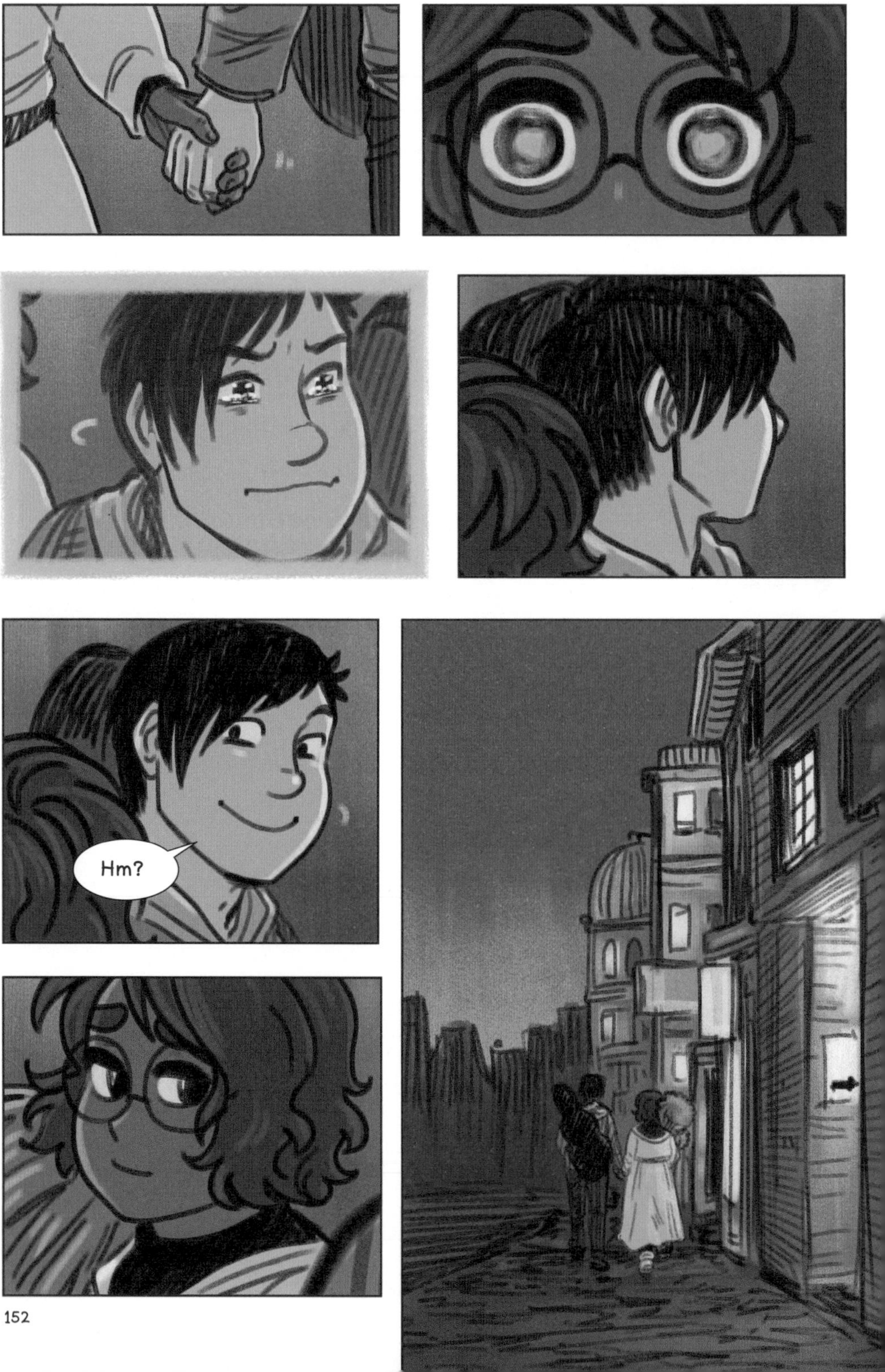
Hm?

153

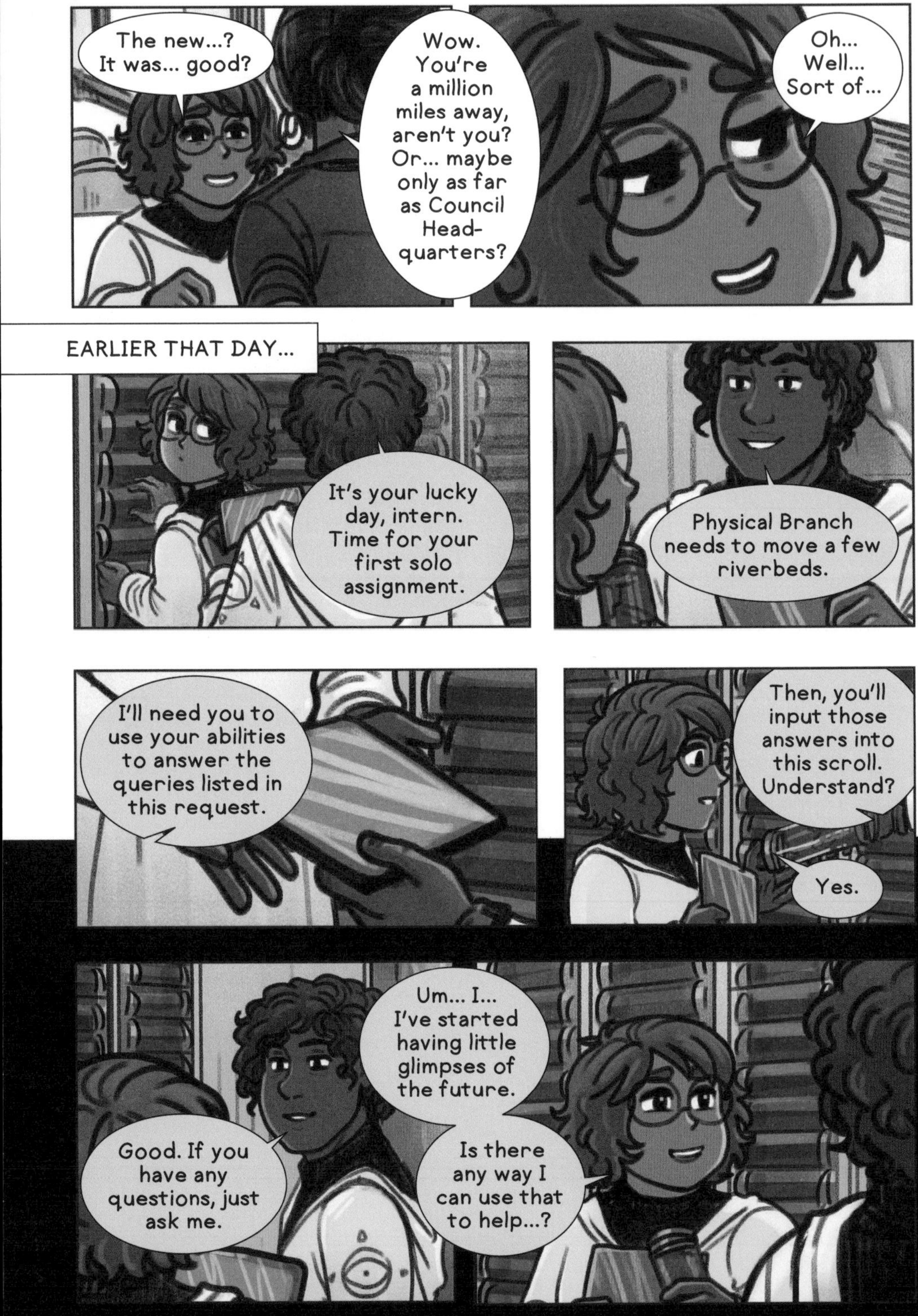

The new...? It was... good?
Wow. You're a million miles away, aren't you? Or... maybe only as far as Council Head-quarters?
Oh... Well... Sort of...
EARLIER THAT DAY...
It's your lucky day, intern. Time for your first solo assignment.
Physical Branch needs to move a few riverbeds.
I'll need you to use your abilities to answer the queries listed in this request.
Then, you'll input those answers into this scroll. Understand?
Yes.
Um... I... I've started having little glimpses of the future.
Good. If you have any questions, just ask me.
Is there any way I can use that to help...?

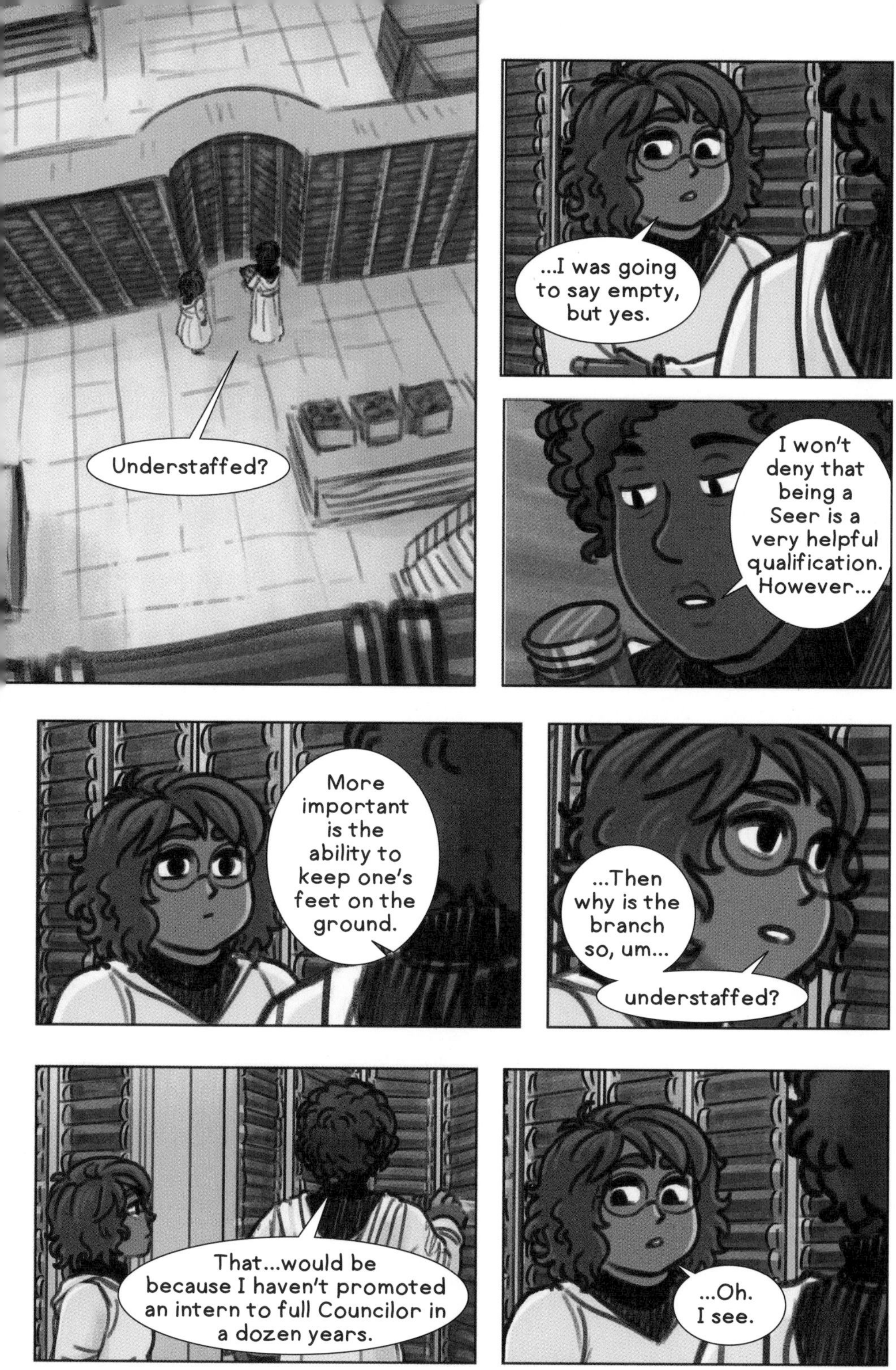
Understaffed?
...I was going to say empty, but yes.
I won't deny that being a Seer is a very helpful qualification. However...
More important is the ability to keep one's feet on the ground.
...Then why is the branch so, um...
understaffed?
That...would be because I haven't promoted an intern to full Councilor in a dozen years.
...Oh. I see.

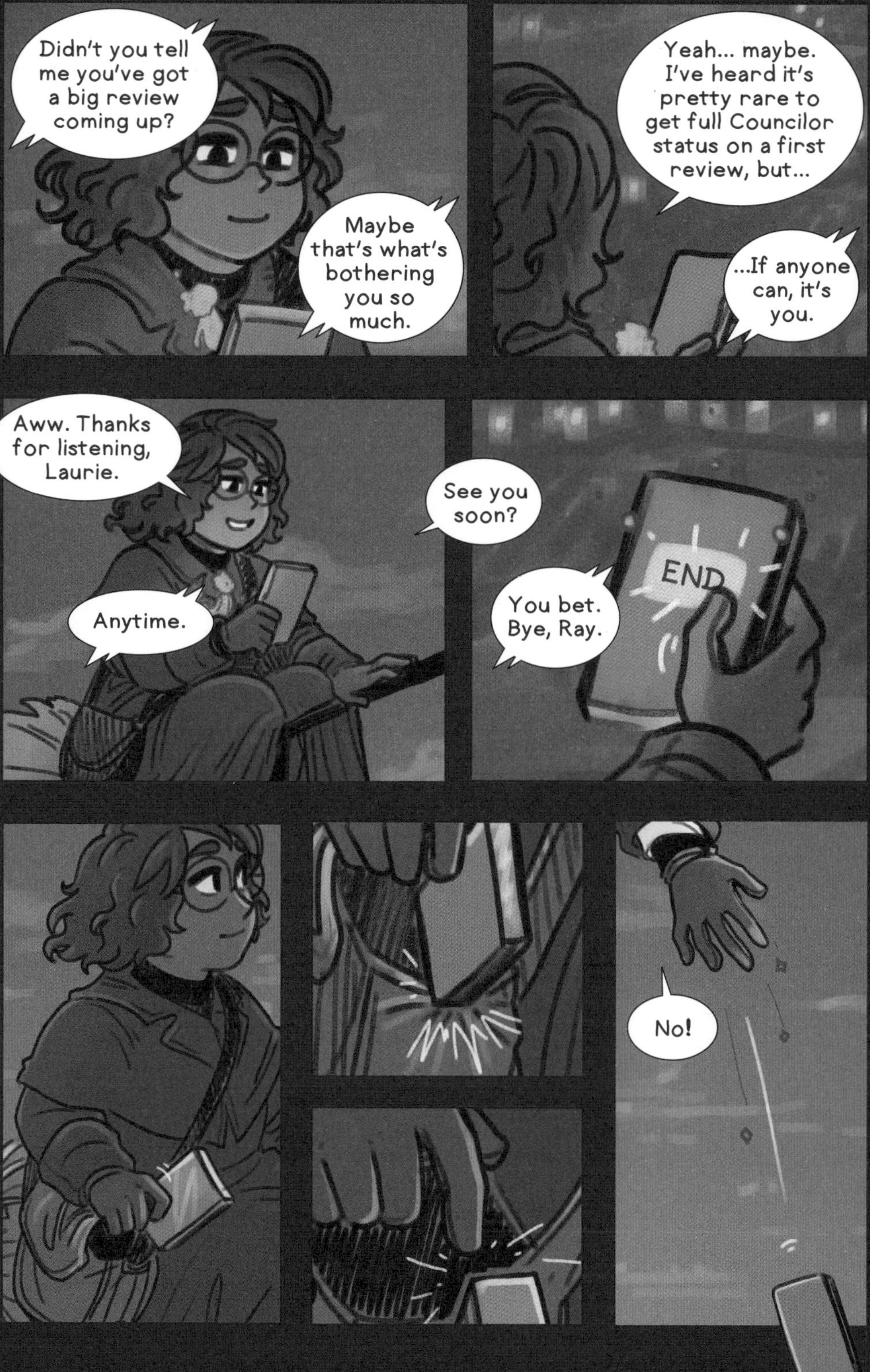
Didn't you tell me you've got a big review coming up?
Maybe that's what's bothering you so much.
Yeah... maybe. I've heard it's pretty rare to get full Councilor status on a first review, but...
...If anyone can, it's you.
Aww. Thanks for listening, Laurie.
Anytime.
See you soon?
You bet. Bye, Ray.
END
No!

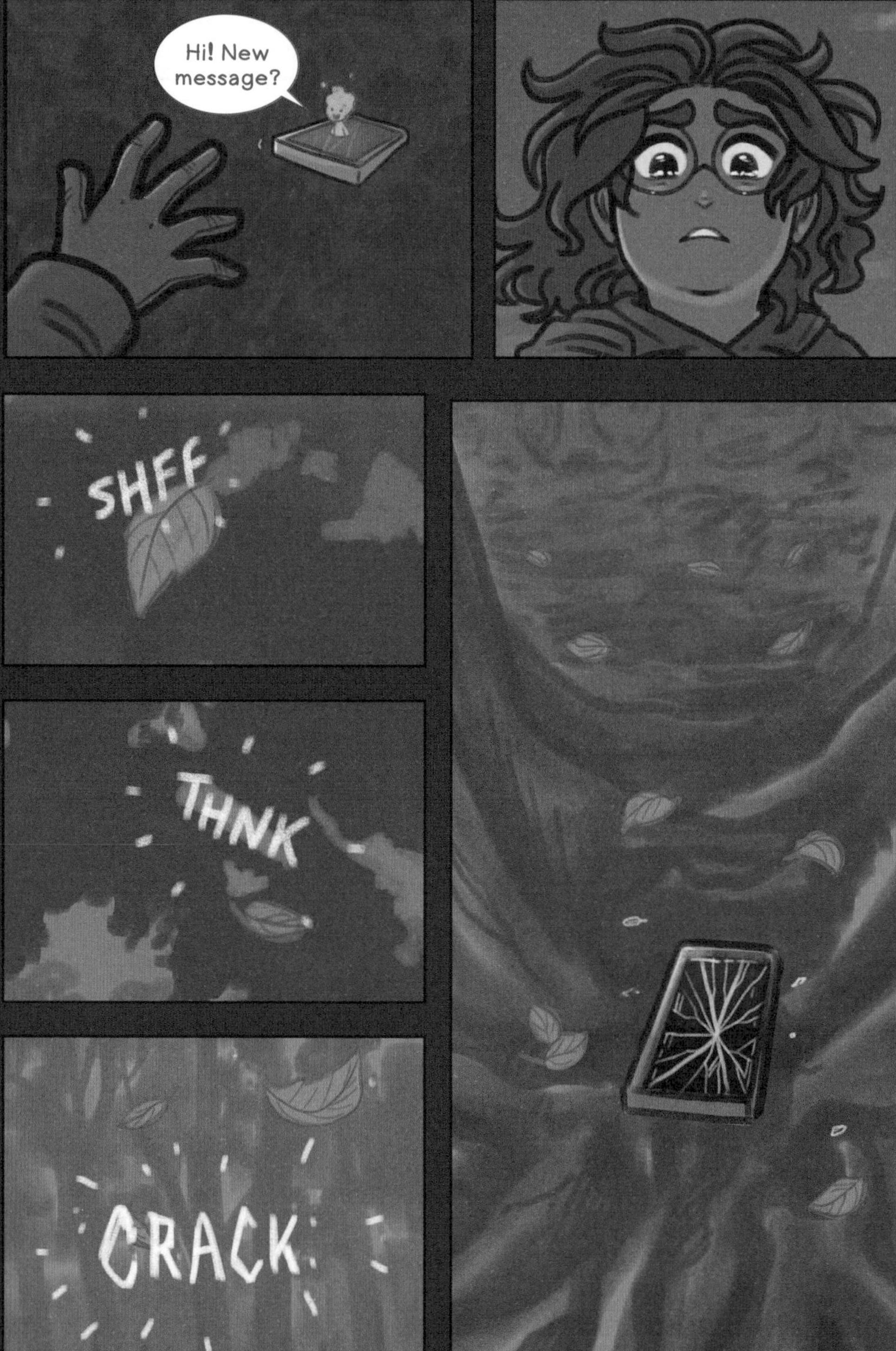

Hi! New message?
SHFF
THNK
CRACK

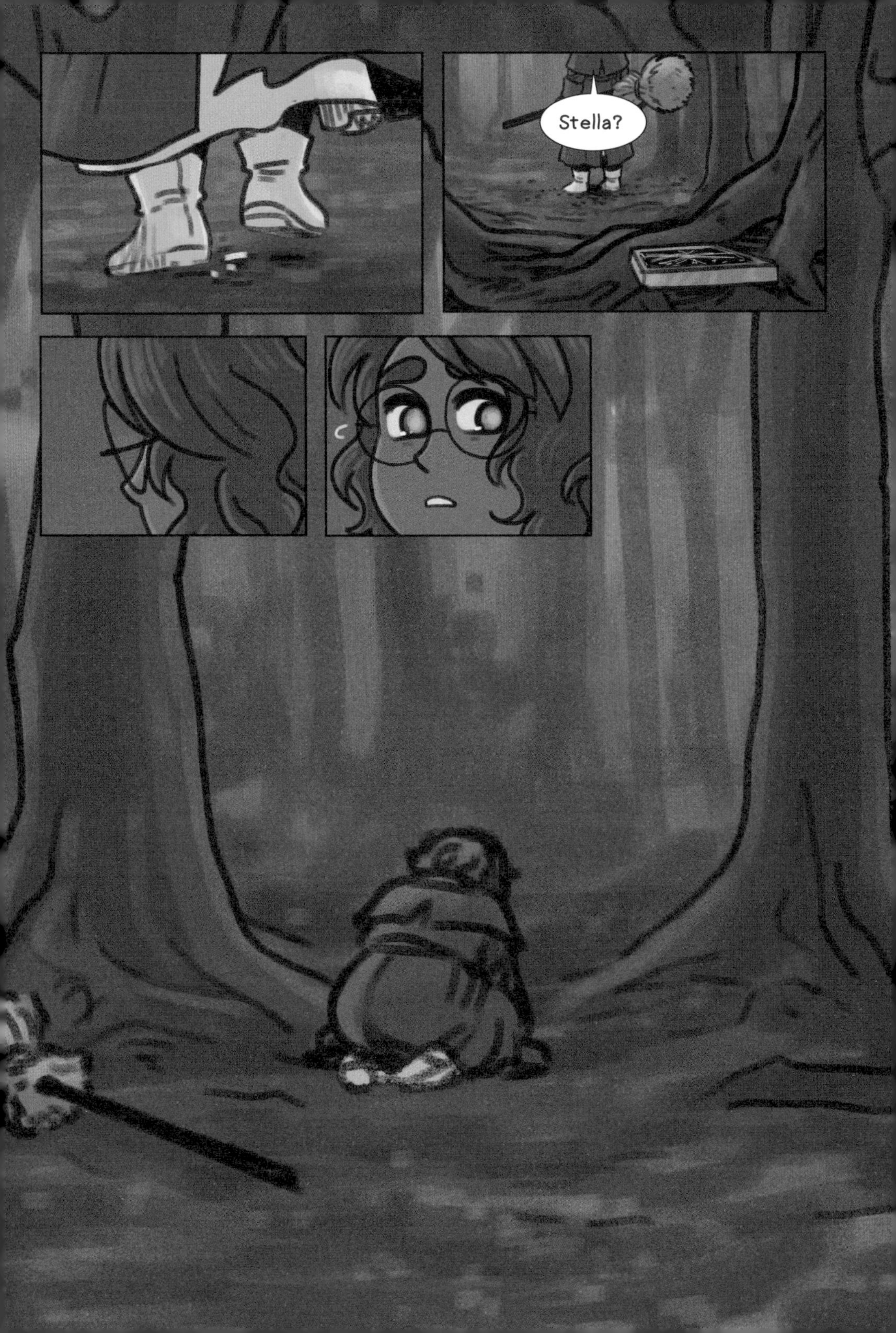
Stella?

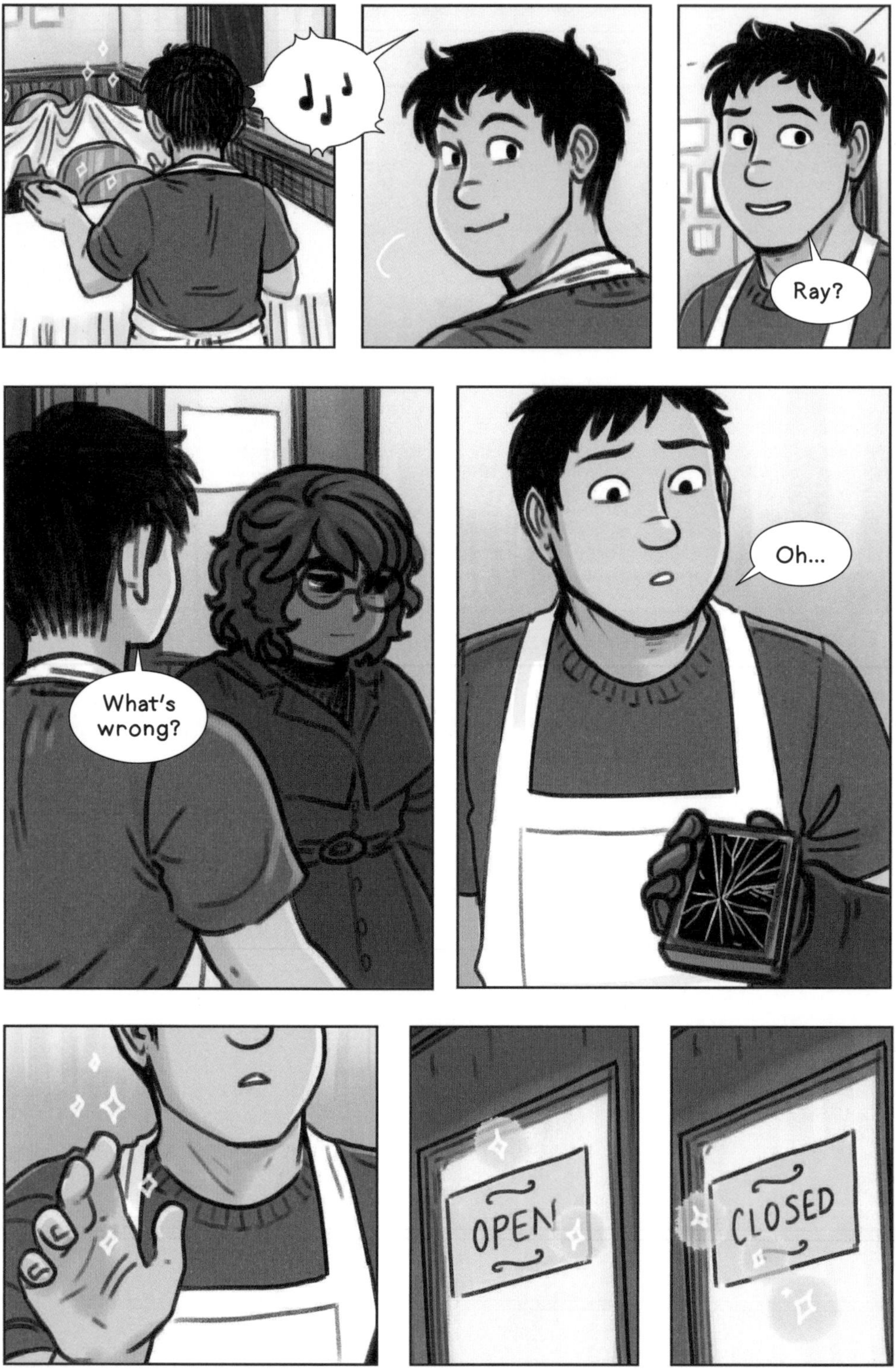
♩♩
Ray?
What's wrong?
Oh...
OPEN
CLOSED

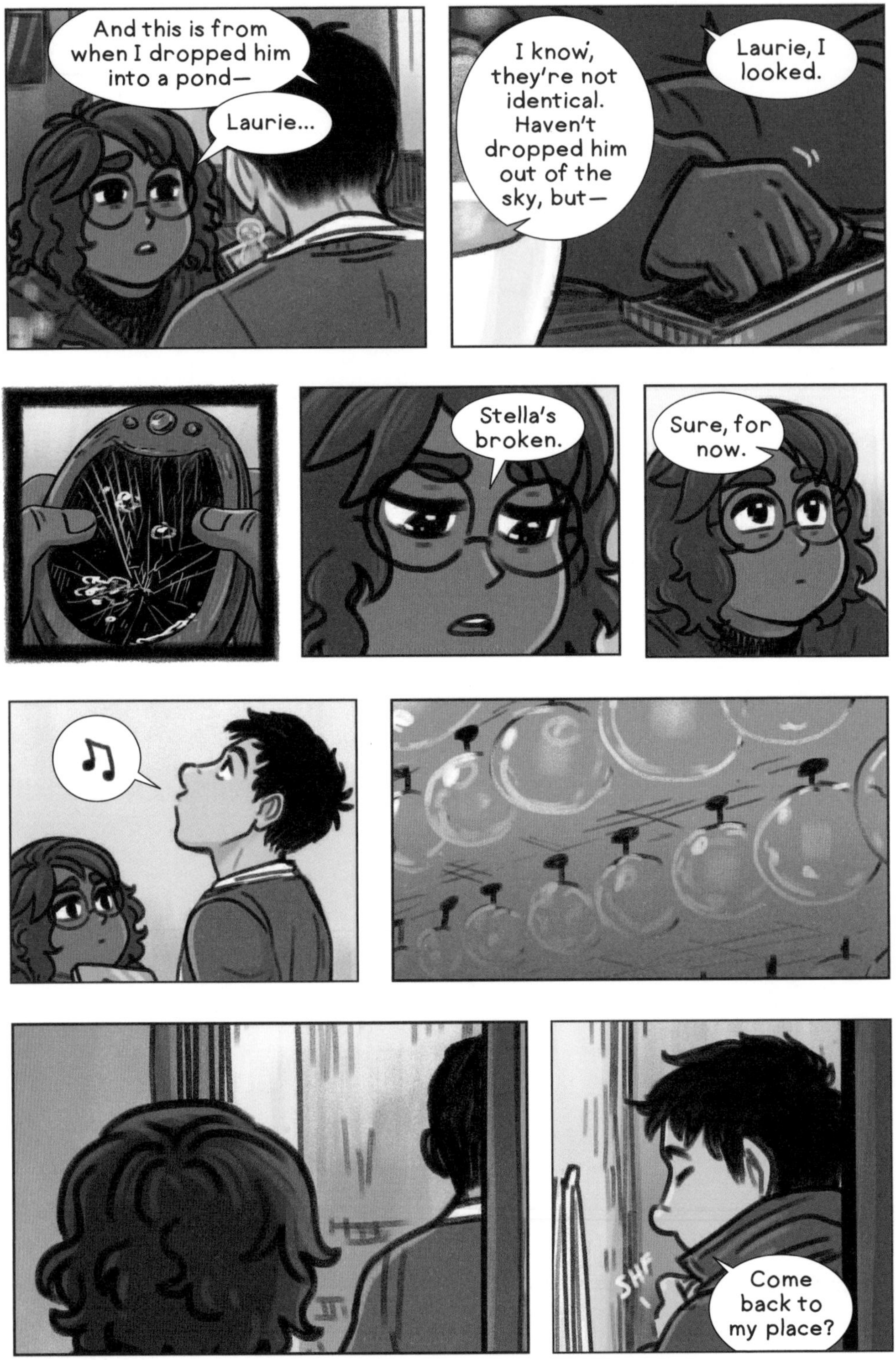

And this is from when I dropped him into a pond—
Laurie...
I know, they're not identical. Haven't dropped him out of the sky, but—
Laurie, I looked.
Stella's broken.
Sure, for now.
♫
SHF
Come back to my place?

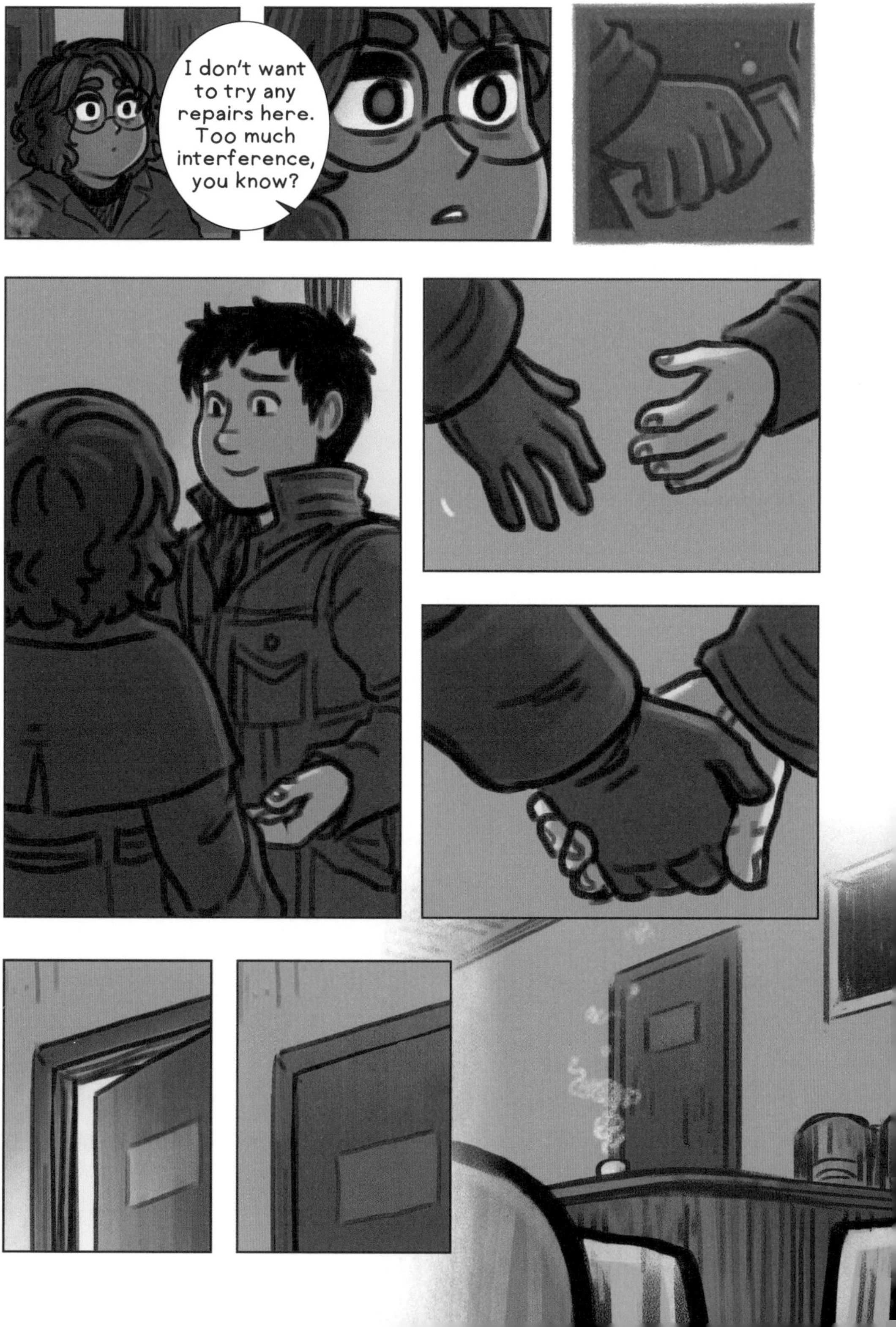
I don't want to try any repairs here. Too much interference, you know?

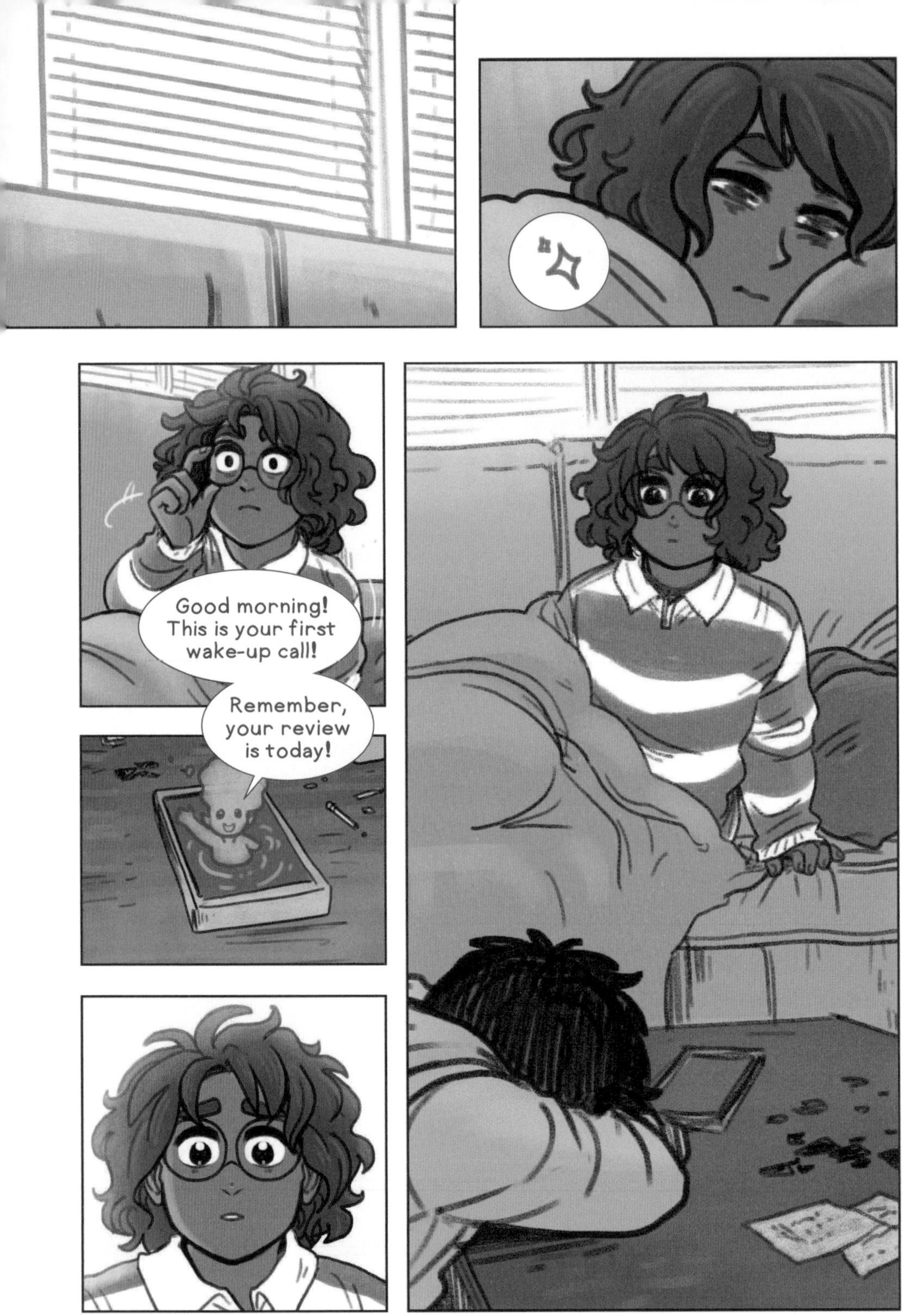
Good morning! This is your first wake-up call!
Remember, your review is today!

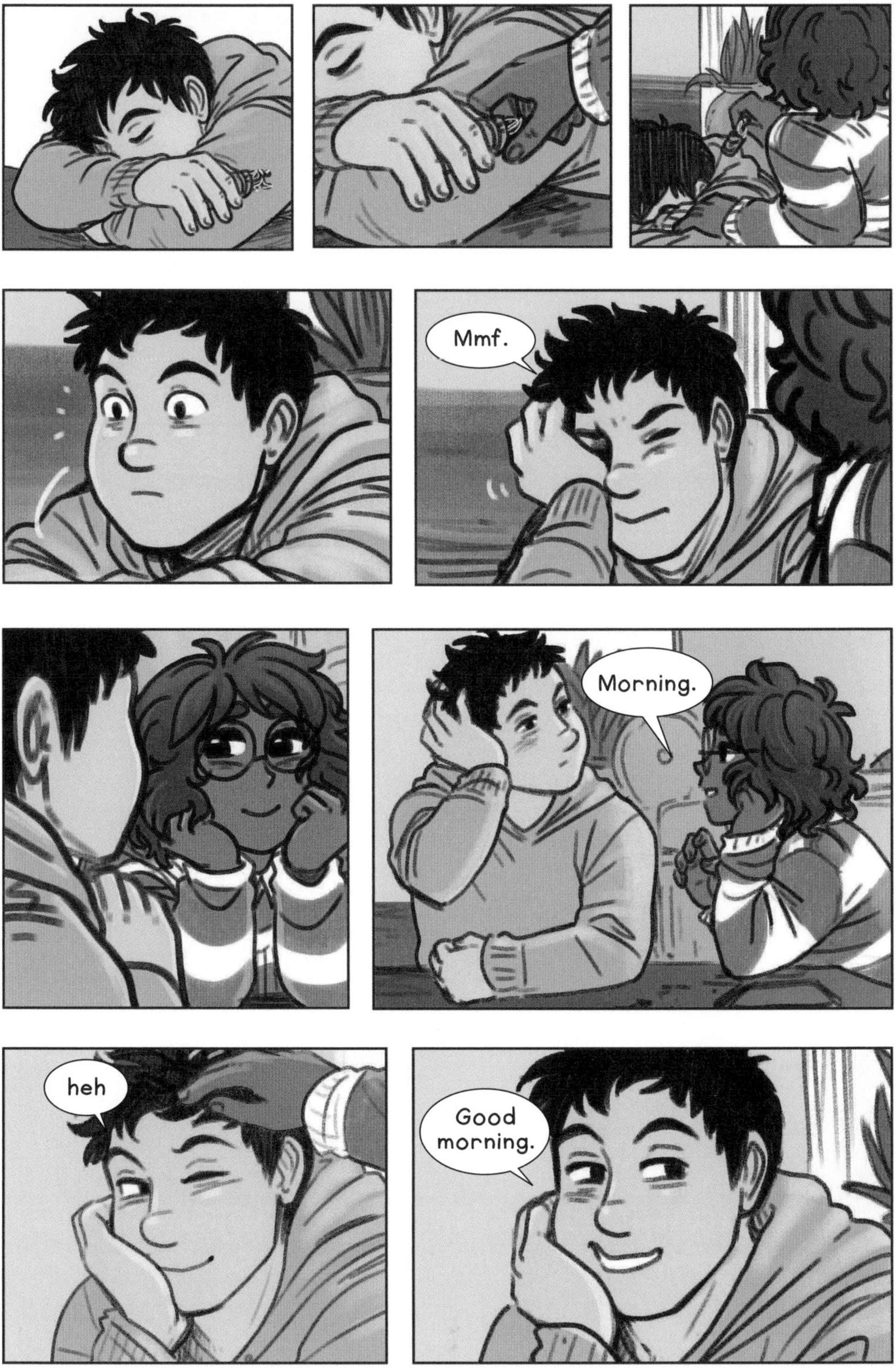

Mmf.
Morning.
heh
Good morning.

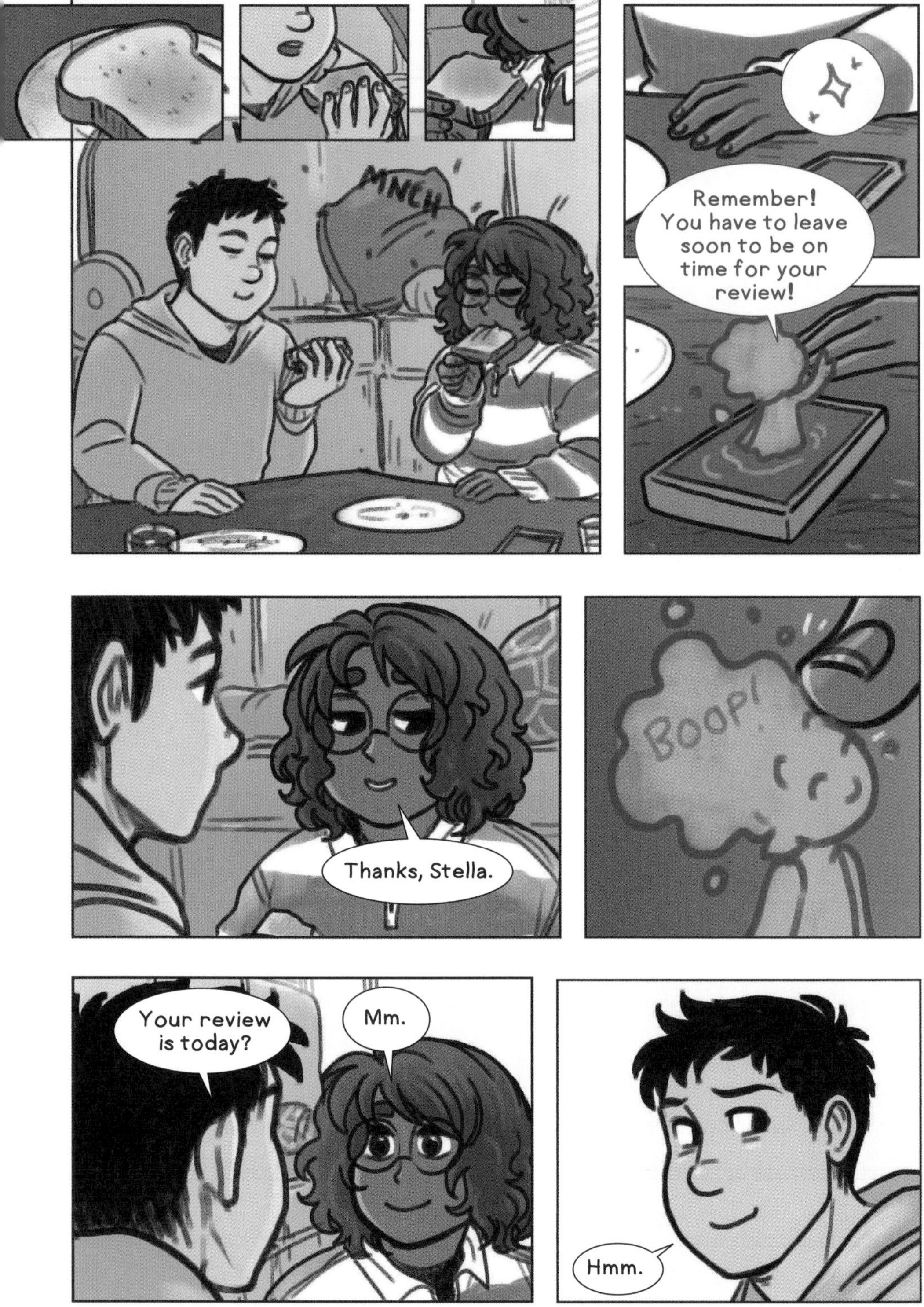
MNCH
Remember! You have to leave soon to be on time for your review!
BOOP!
Thanks, Stella.
Your review is today?
Mm.
Hmm.

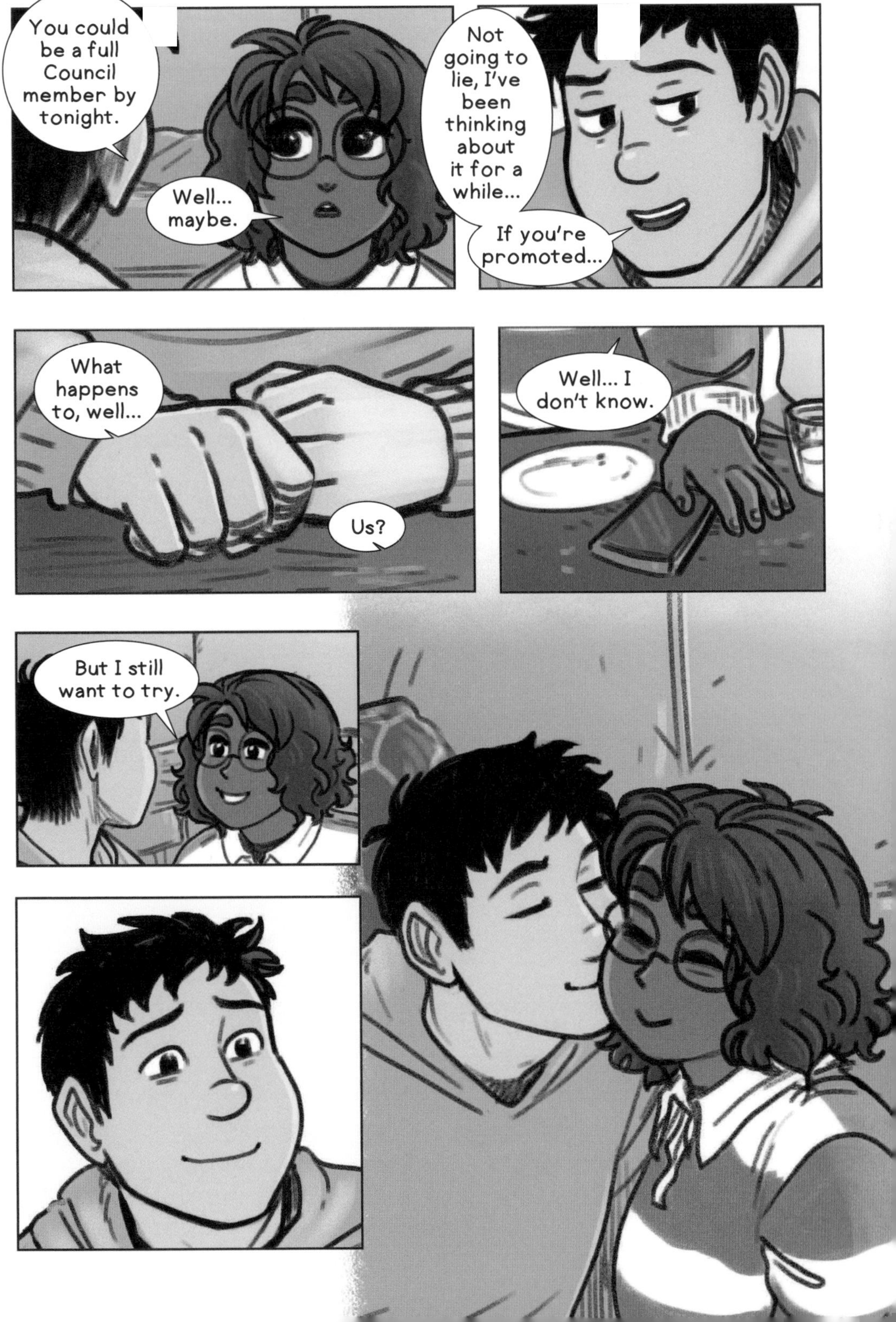
You could be a full Council member by tonight.
Well... maybe.
Not going to lie, I've been thinking about it for a while...
If you're promoted...
What happens to, well...
Us?
Well... I don't know.
But I still want to try.

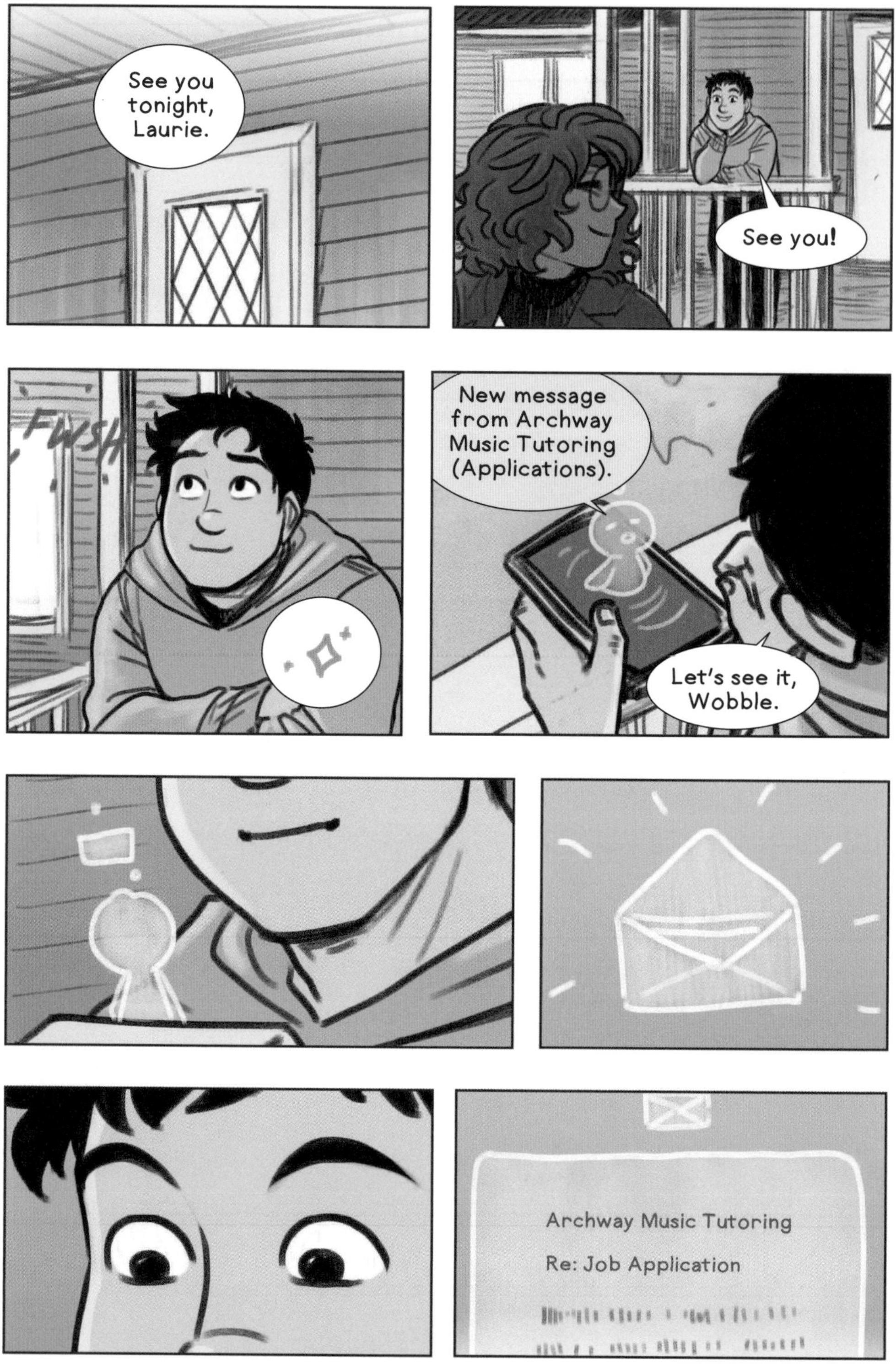
See you tonight, Laurie.
See you!
FWSH
New message from Archway Music Tutoring (Applications).
Let's see it, Wobble.
Archway Music Tutoring
Re: Job Application

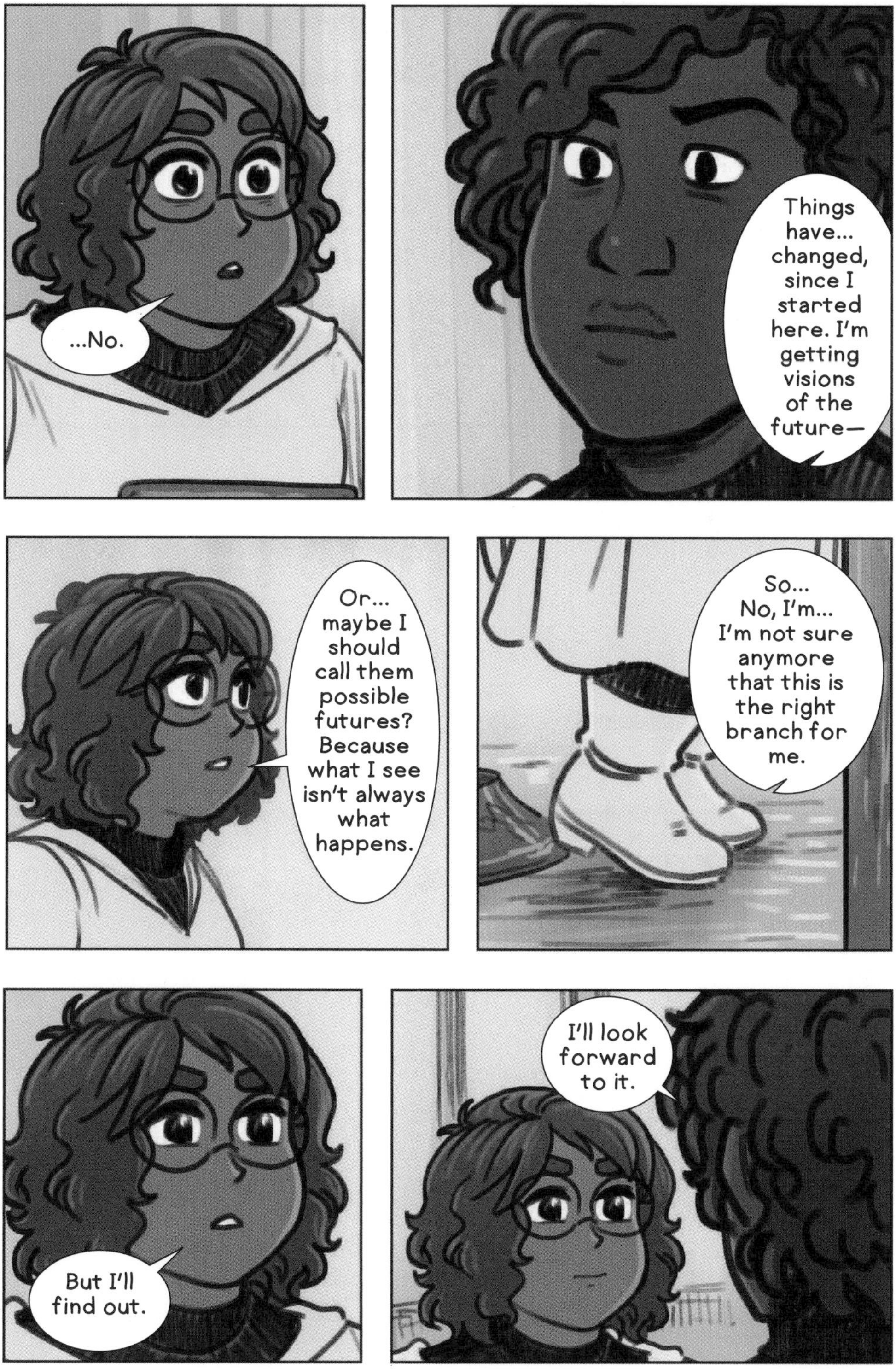
...No.
Things have... changed, since I started here. I'm getting visions of the future—
Or... maybe I should call them possible futures? Because what I see isn't always what happens.
So... No, I'm... I'm not sure anymore that this is the right branch for me.
But I'll find out.
I'll look forward to it.

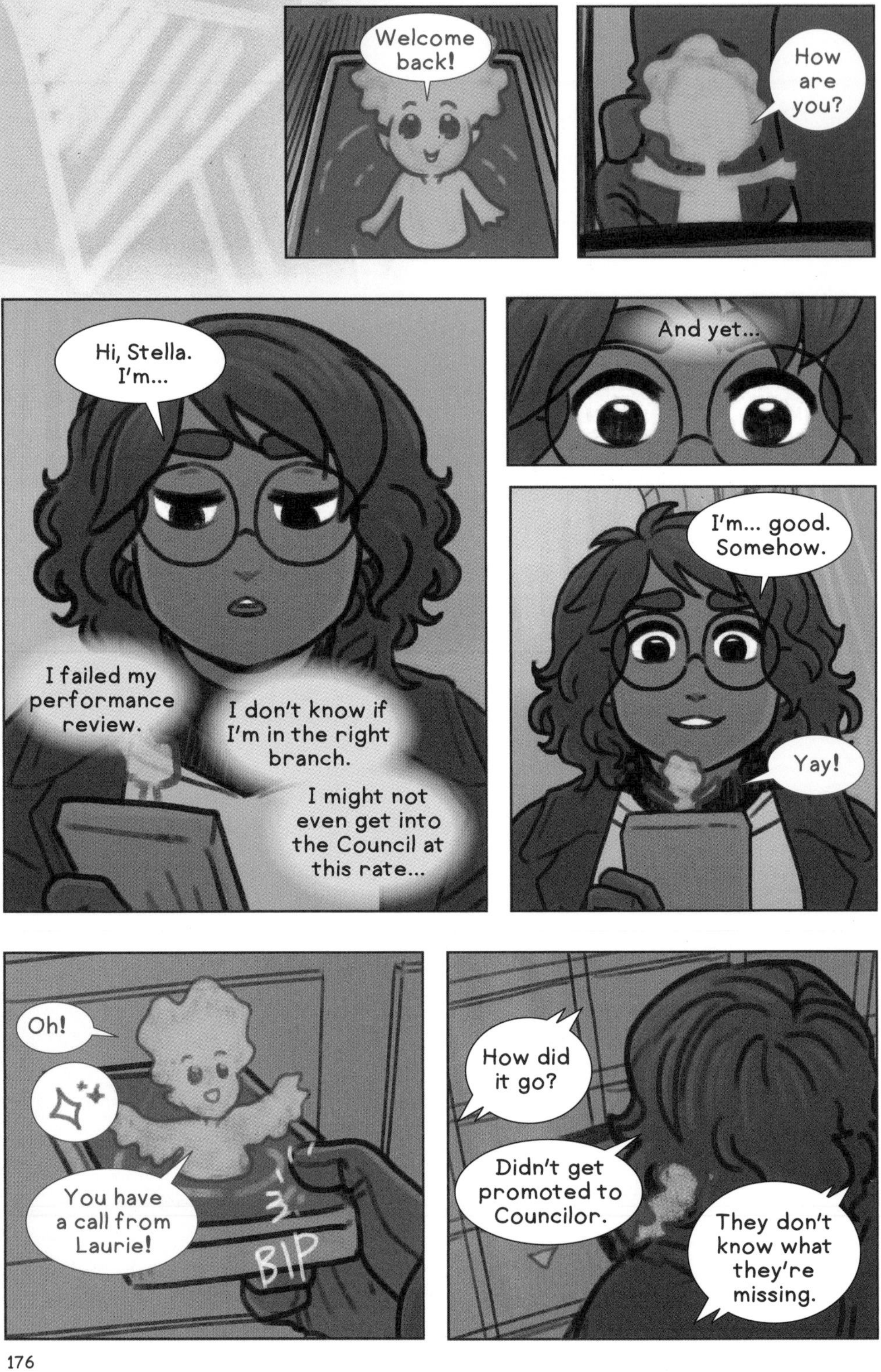
Welcome back!
How are you?
Hi, Stella. I'm...
I failed my performance review.
I don't know if I'm in the right branch.
I might not even get into the Council at this rate...
And yet...
I'm... good. Somehow.
Yay!
Oh!
You have a call from Laurie!
BIP
How did it go?
Didn't get promoted to Councilor.
They don't know what they're missing.

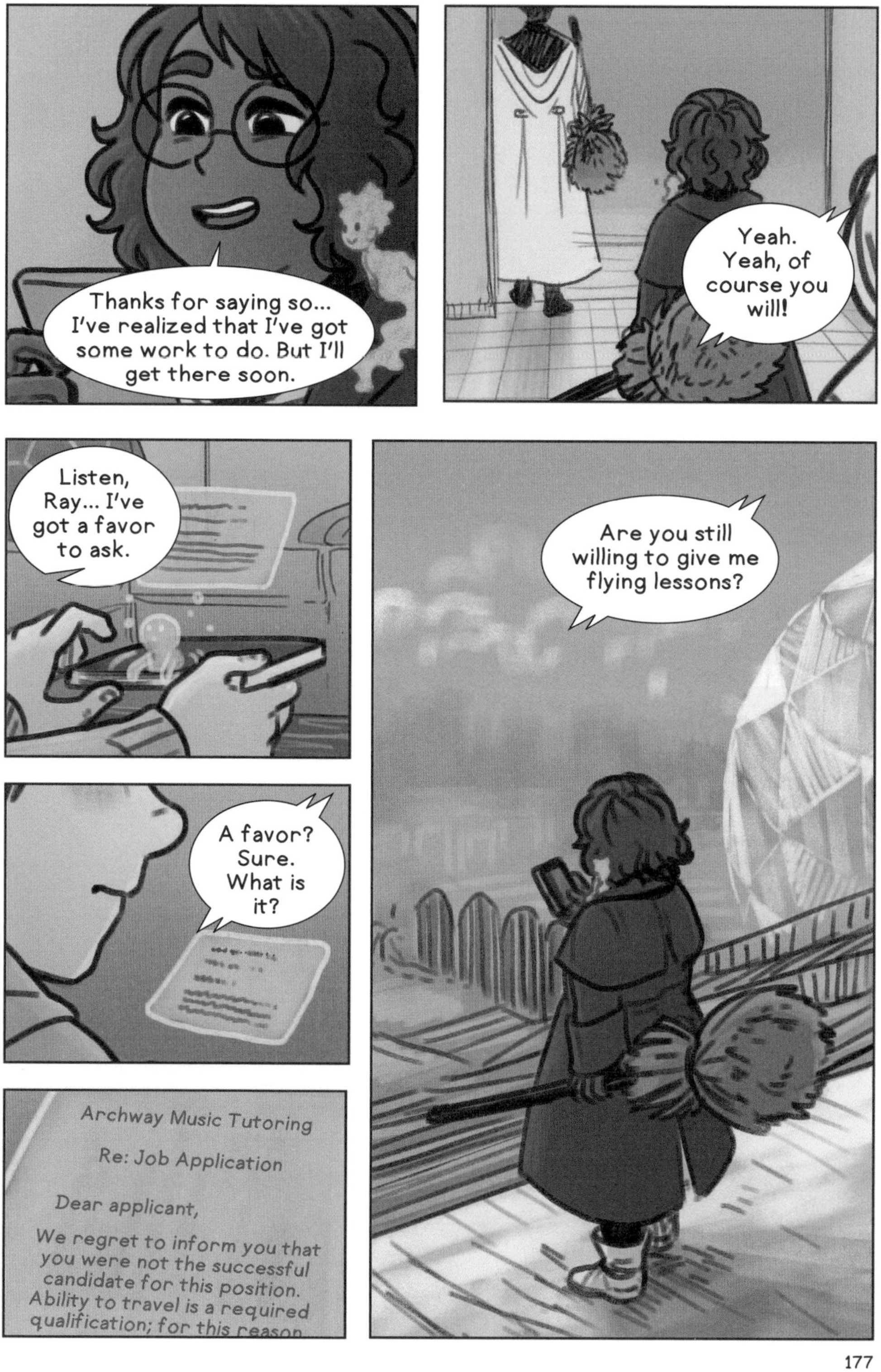
Thanks for saying so... I've realized that I've got some work to do. But I'll get there soon.
Yeah. Yeah, of course you will!
Listen, Ray... I've got a favor to ask.
A favor? Sure. What is it?
Archway Music Tutoring
Re: Job Application
Dear applicant,
We regret to inform you that you were not the successful candidate for this position. Ability to travel is a required qualification; for this reason
Are you still willing to give me flying lessons?

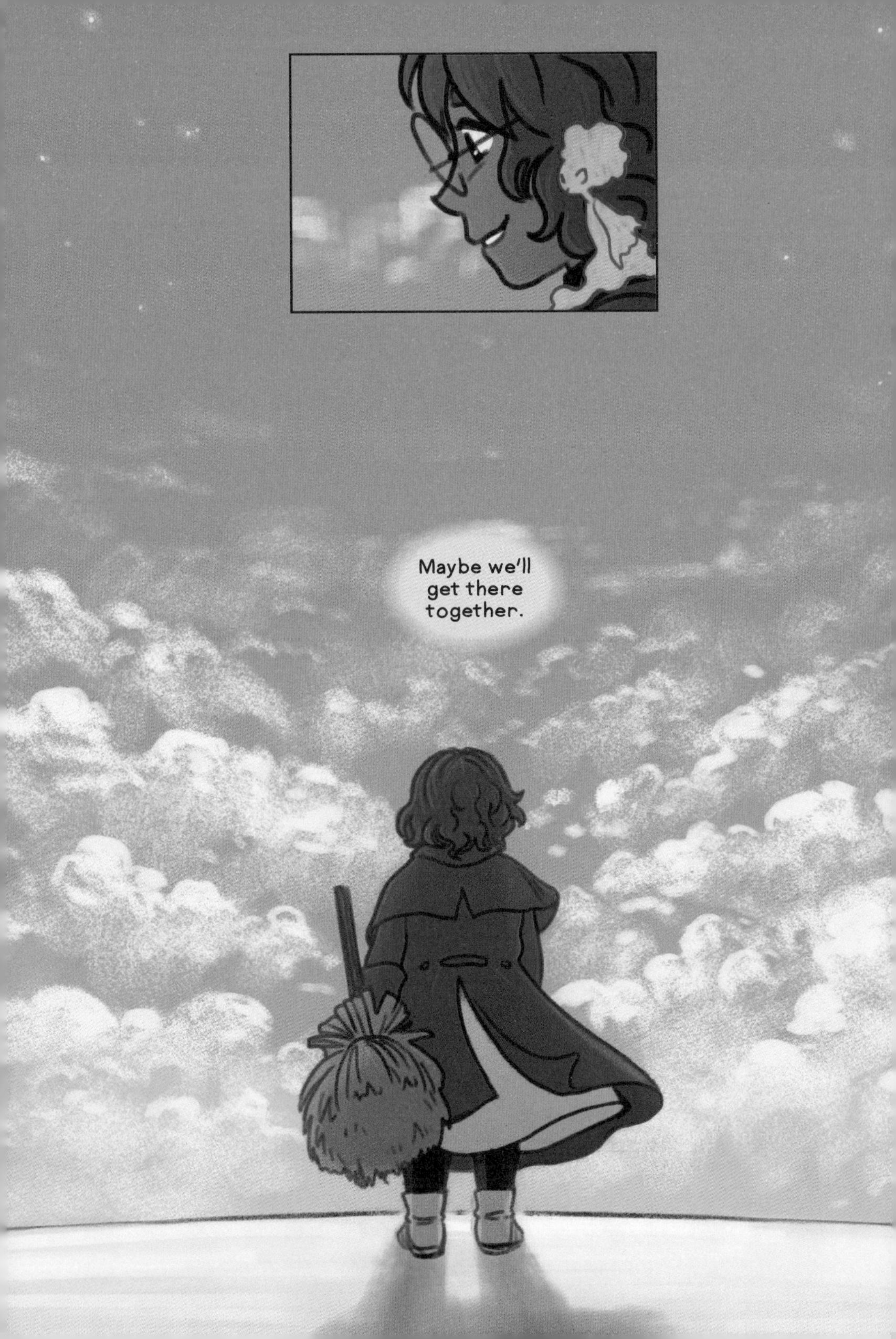
Maybe we'll get there together.

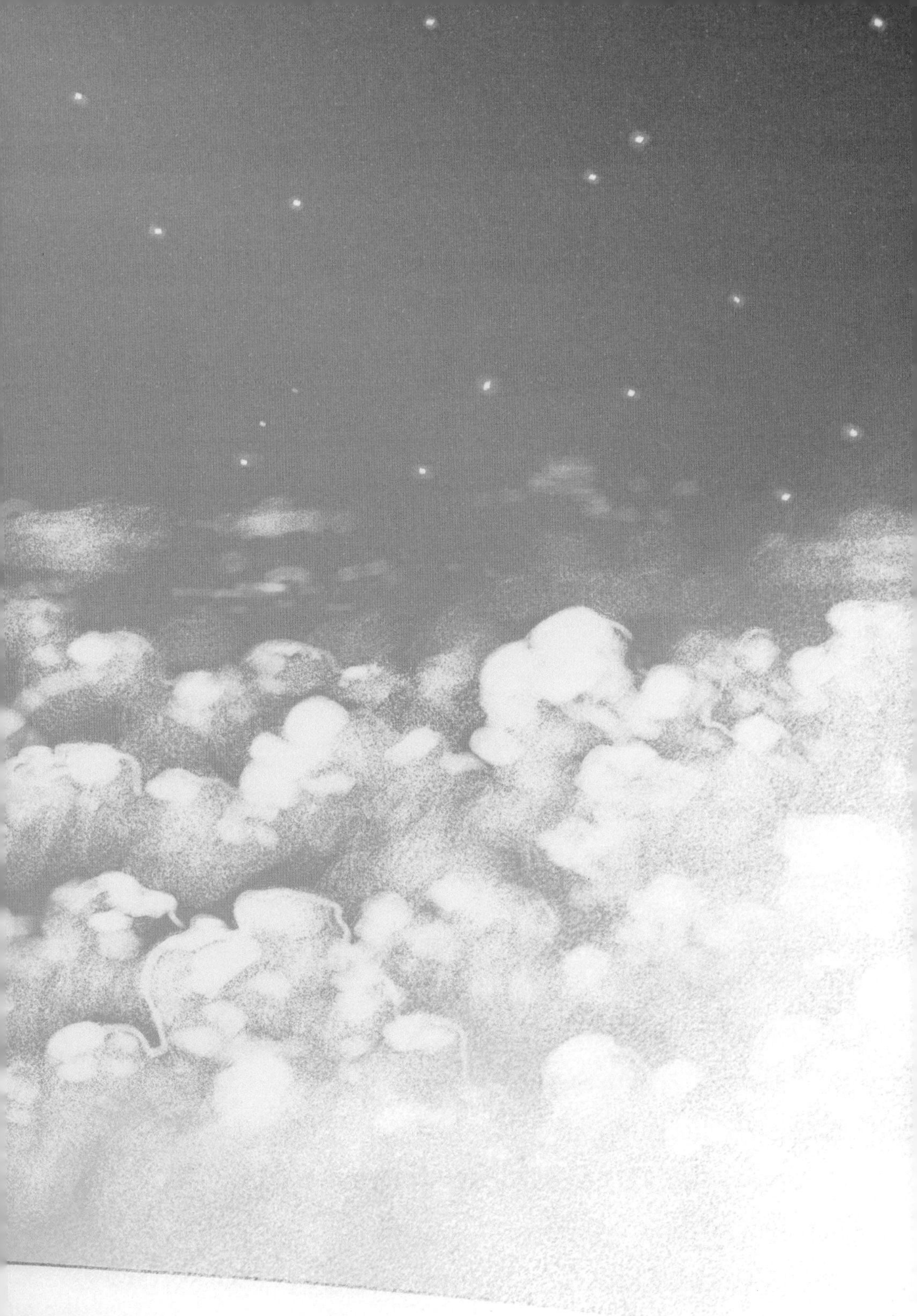

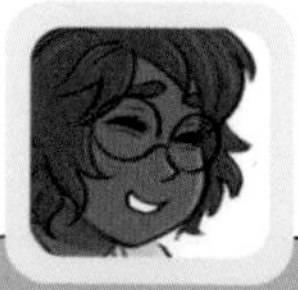

SEASON TWO

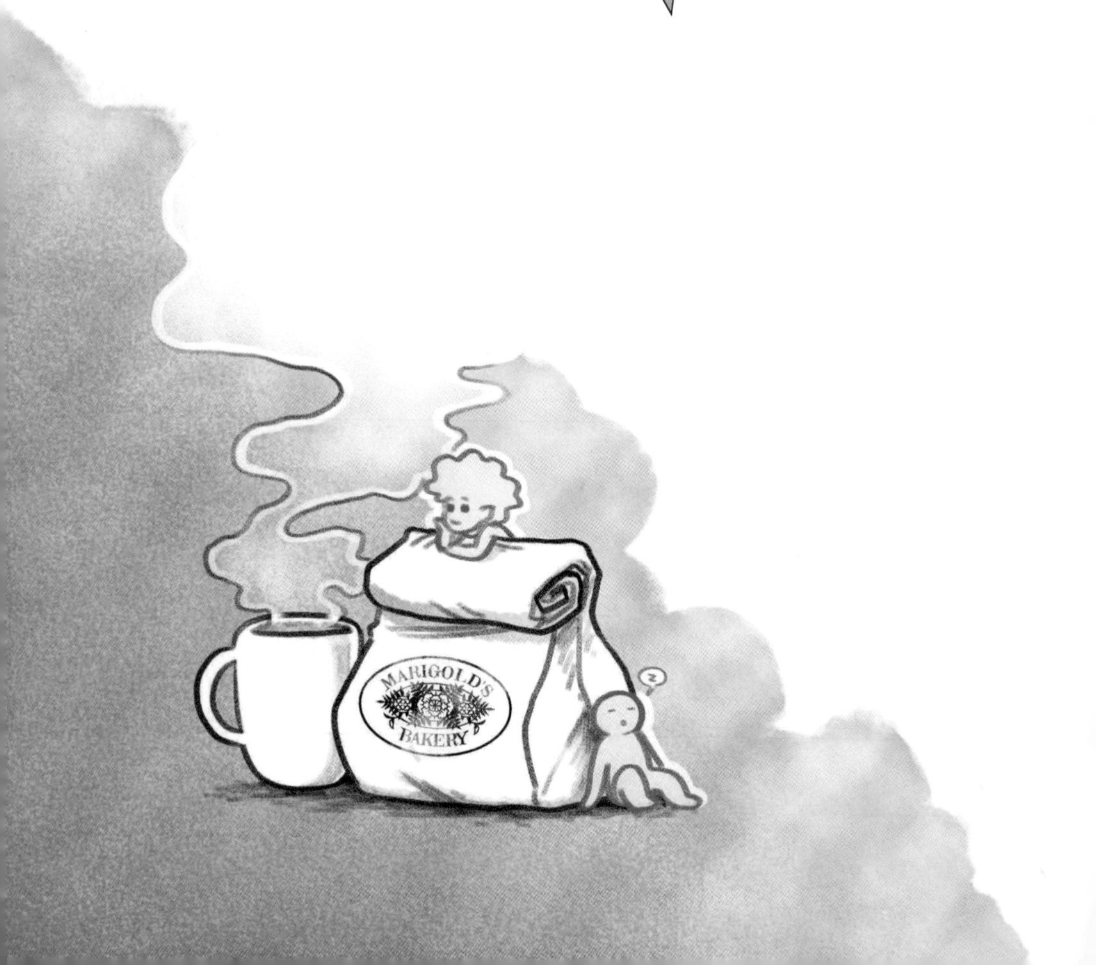
MARIGOLD'S
BAKERY

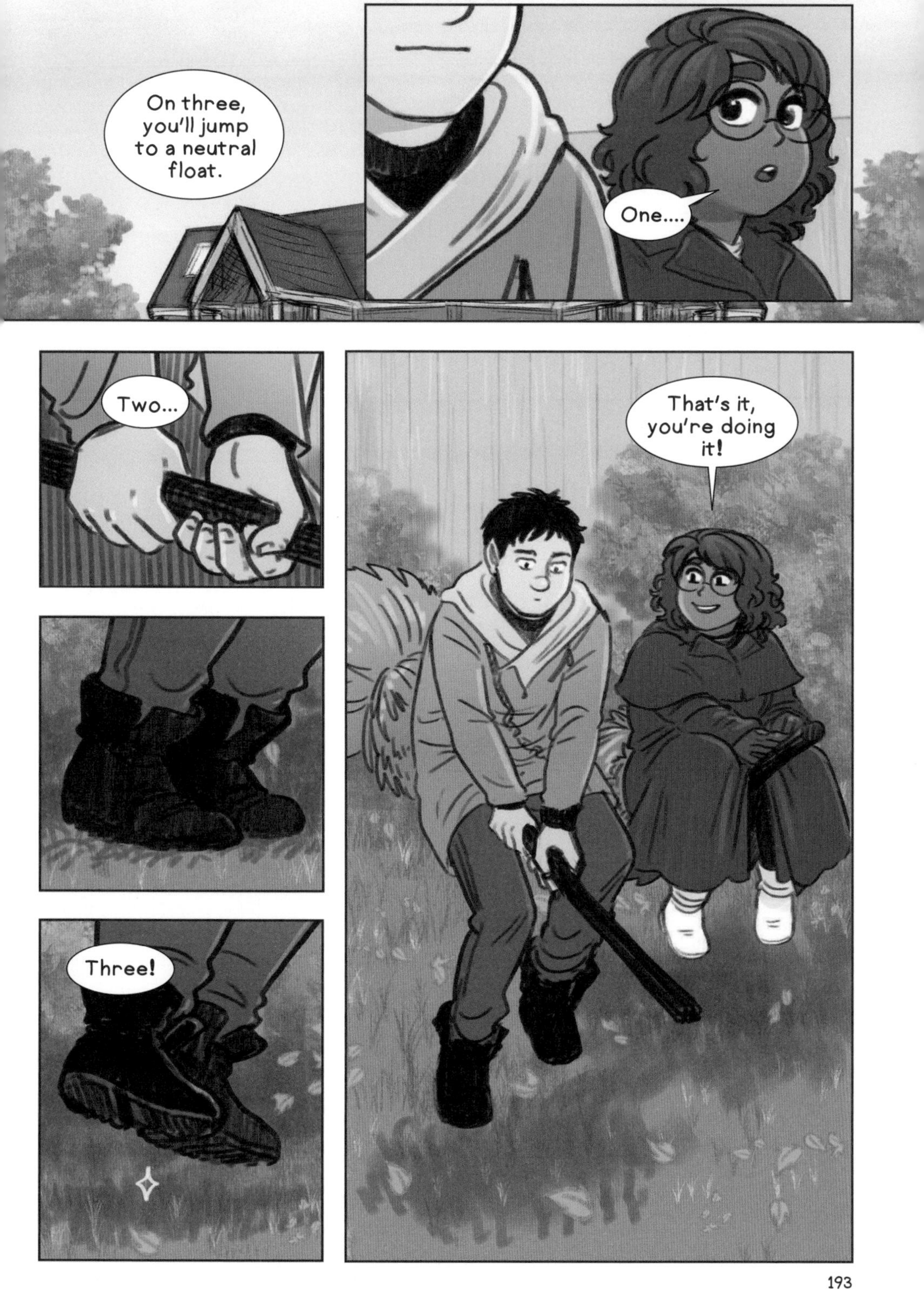
On three, you'll jump to a neutral float.
One....
Two...
Three!
That's it, you're doing it!

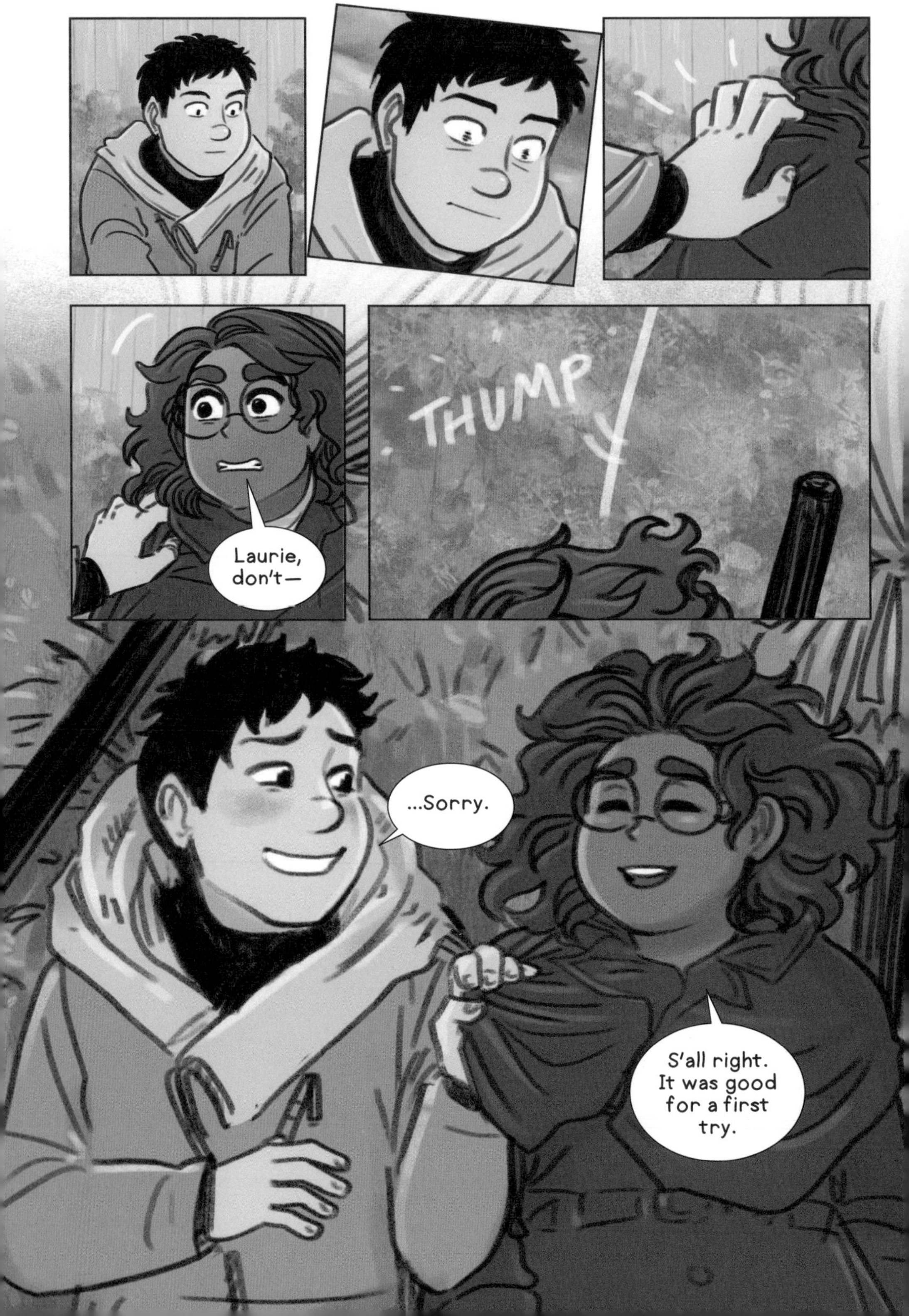
Laurie, don't—
THUMP
...Sorry.
S'all right. It was good for a first try.

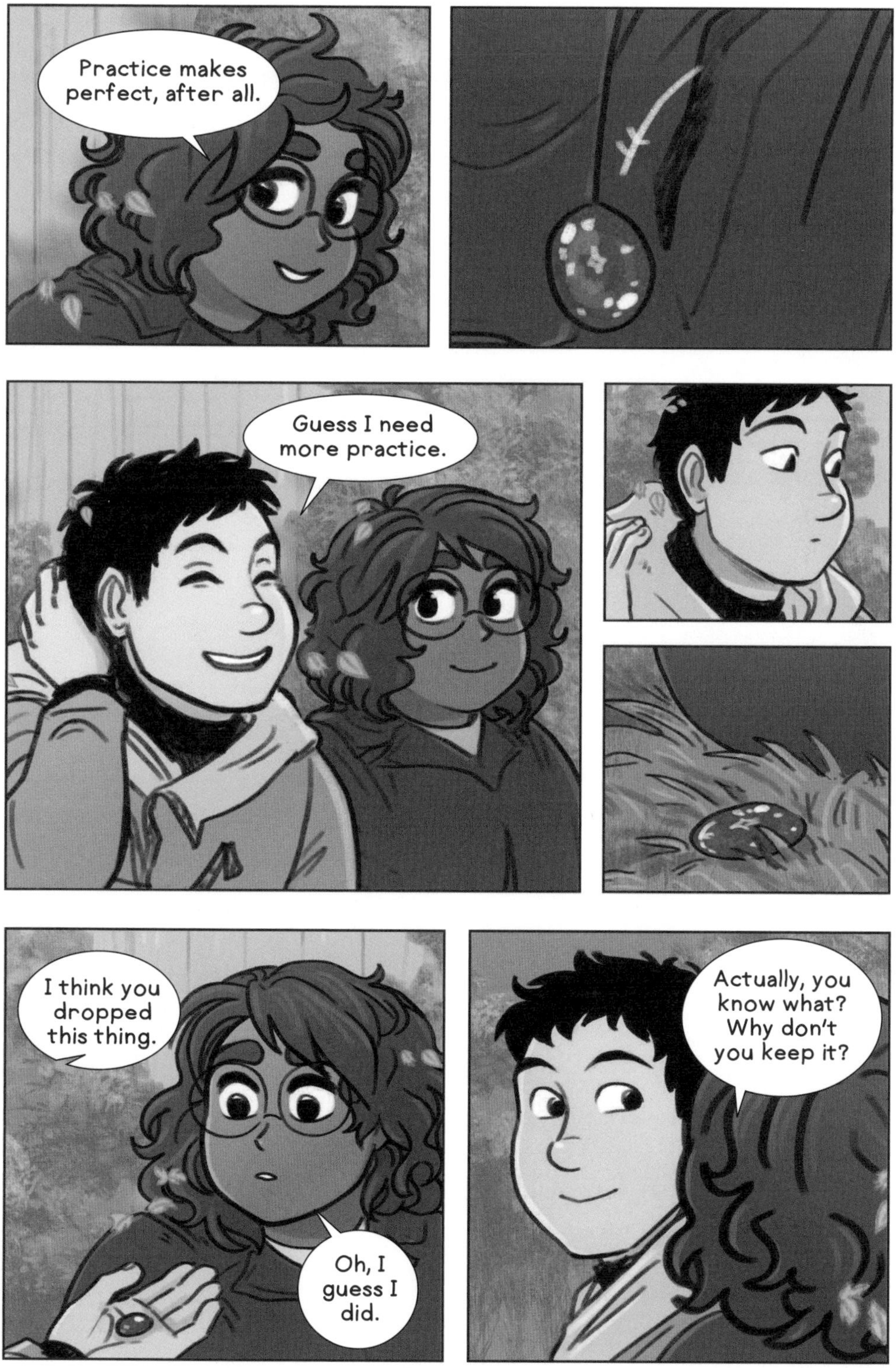
Practice makes perfect, after all.
Guess I need more practice.
I think you dropped this thing.
Oh, I guess I did.
Actually, you know what? Why don't you keep it?

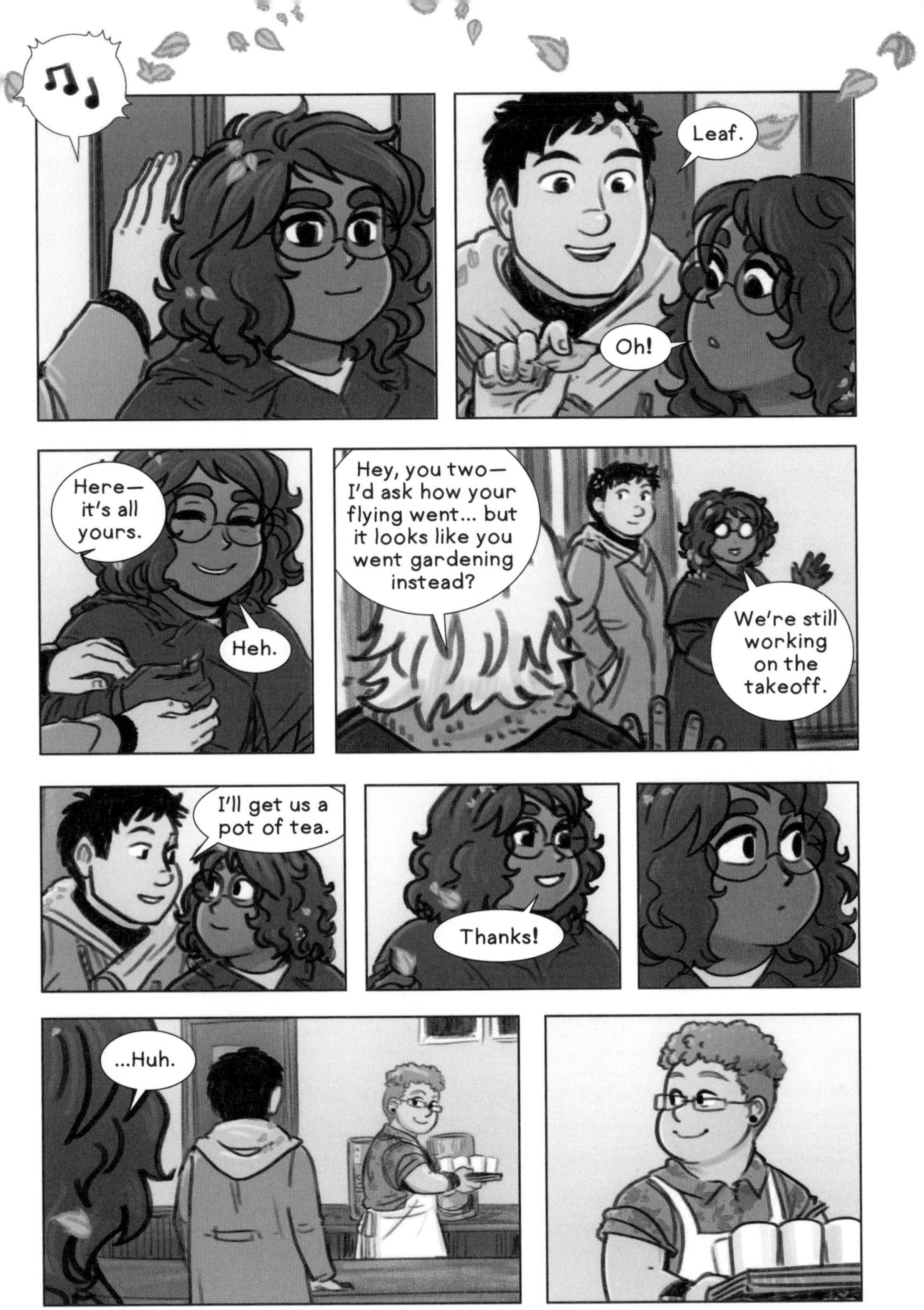
Leaf.
Oh!
Here—
it's all
yours.
Heh.
Hey, you two—
I'd ask how your
flying went... but
it looks like you
went gardening
instead?
We're still
working
on the
takeoff.
I'll get us a
pot of tea.
Thanks!
...Huh.

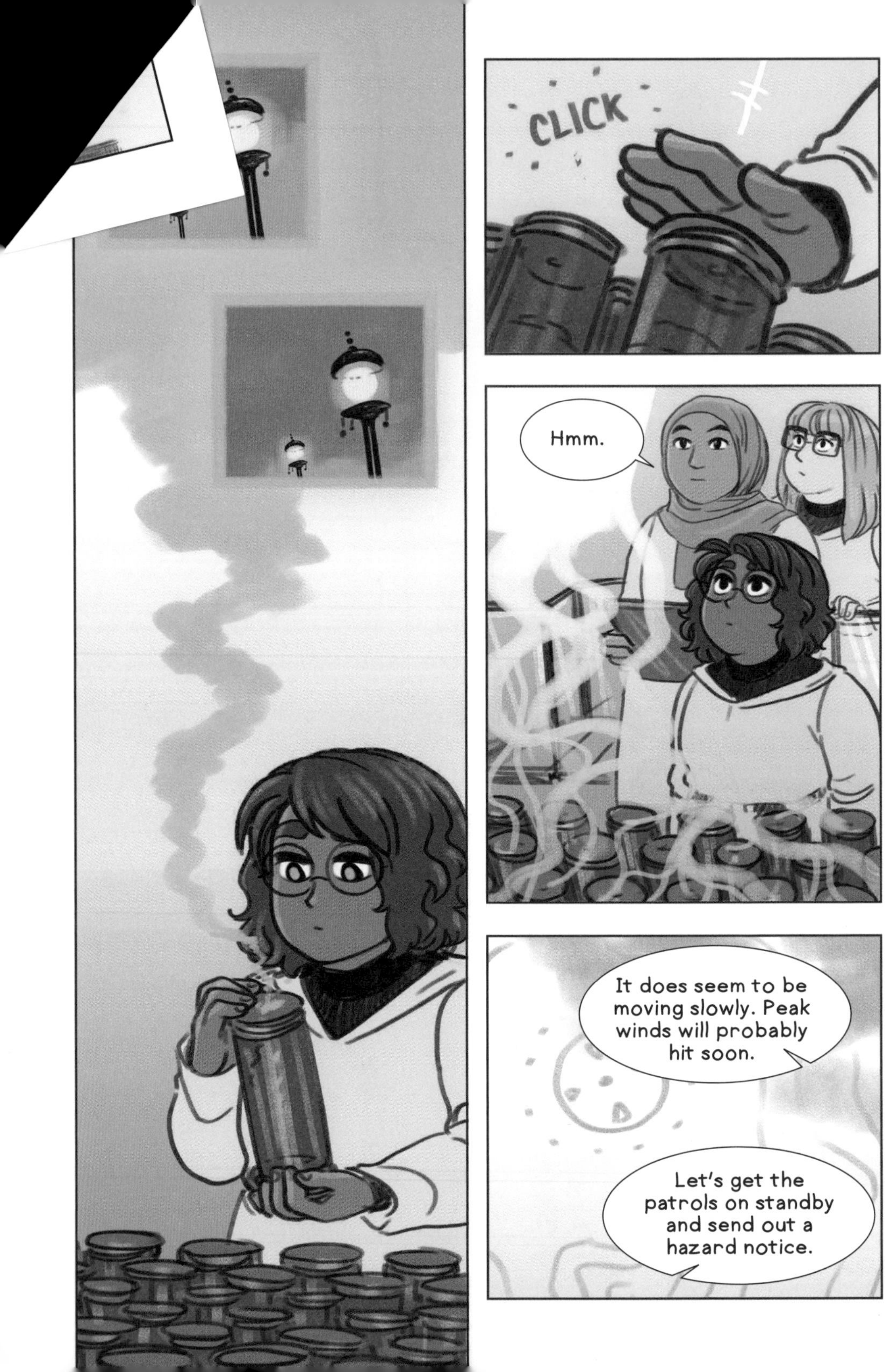
CLICK
Hmm.
It does seem to be moving slowly. Peak winds will probably hit soon.
Let's get the patrols on standby and send out a hazard notice.

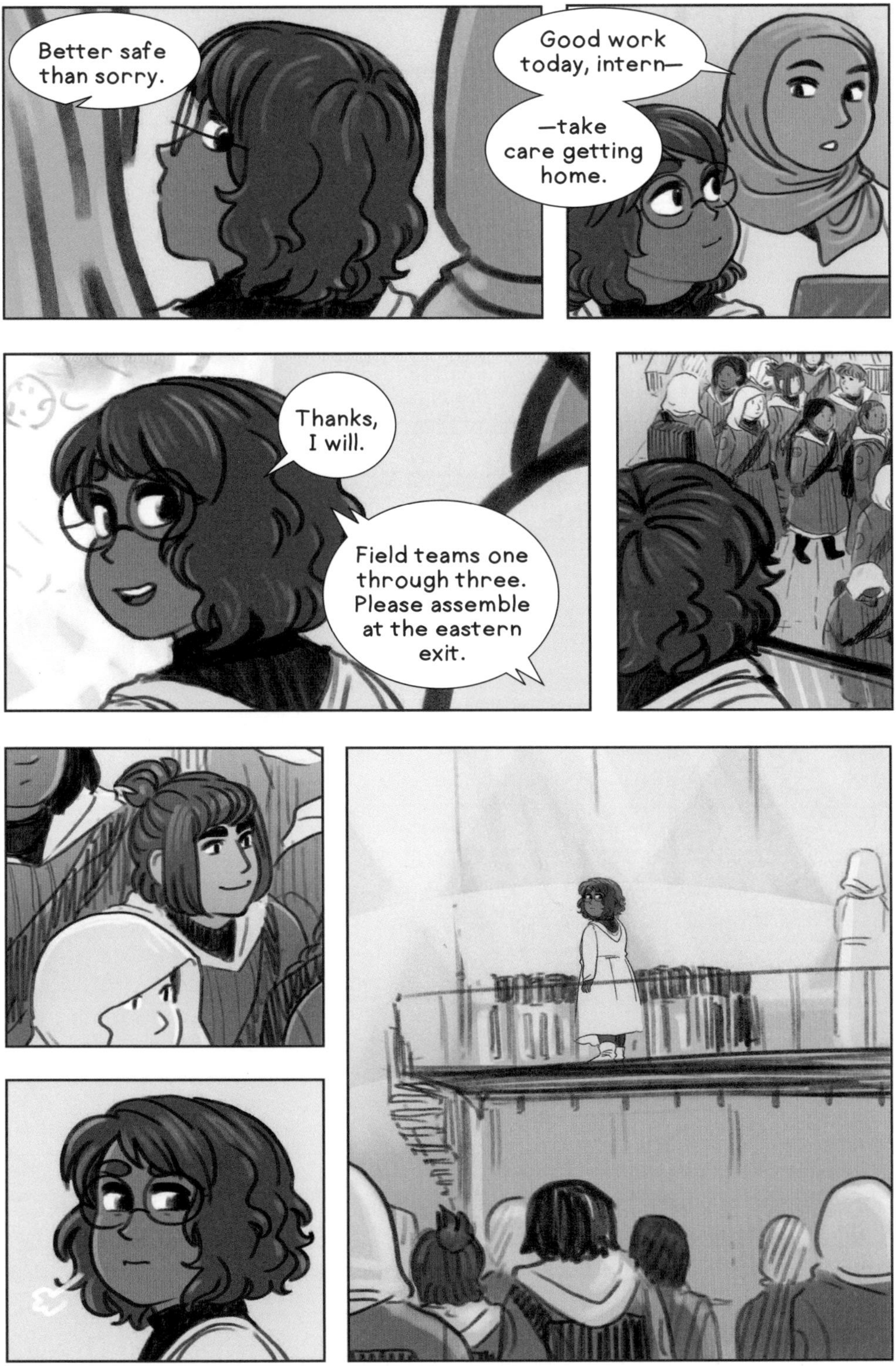
Better safe than sorry.
Good work today, intern—
—take care getting home.
Thanks, I will.
Field teams one through three. Please assemble at the eastern exit.

203

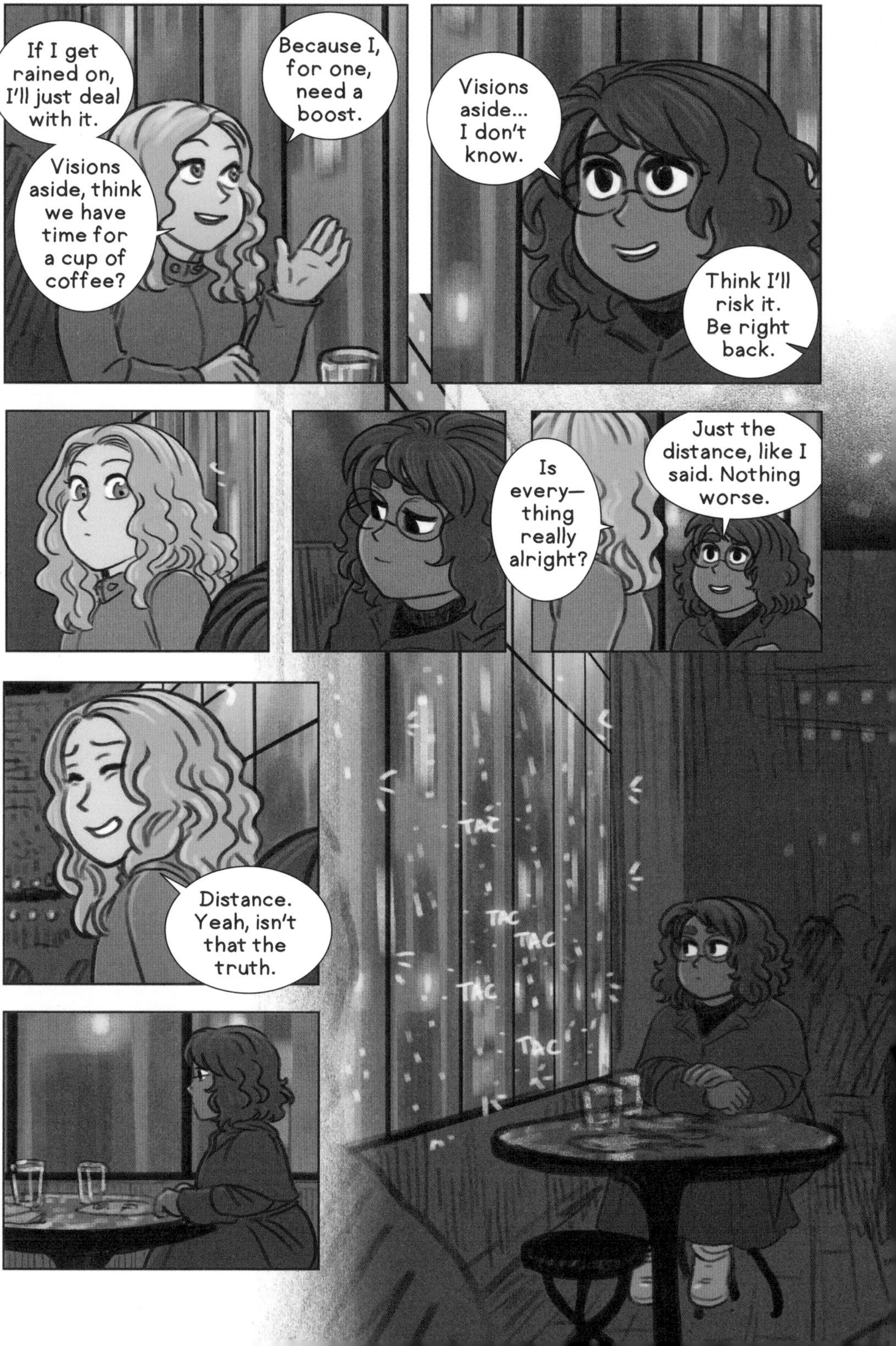
If I get rained on, I'll just deal with it.
Because I, for one, need a boost.
Visions aside, think we have time for a cup of coffee?
Visions aside... I don't know.
Think I'll risk it. Be right back.
Is every— thing really alright?
Just the distance, like I said. Nothing worse.
Distance. Yeah, isn't that the truth.
TAC
TAC
TAC
TAC
TAC

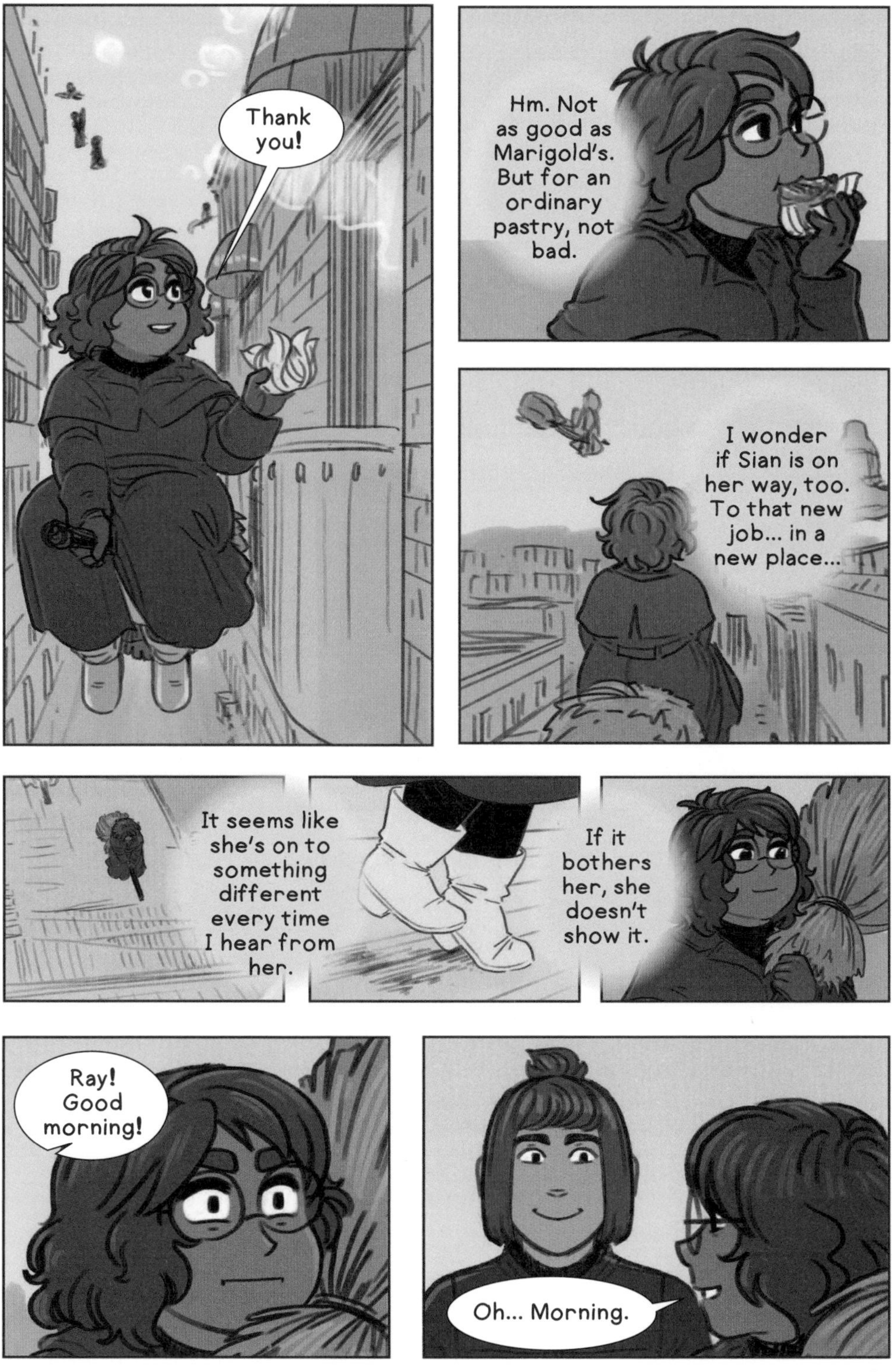
Thank you!
Hm. Not as good as Marigold's. But for an ordinary pastry, not bad.
I wonder if Sian is on her way, too. To that new job... in a new place...
It seems like she's on to something different every time I hear from her.
If it bothers her, she doesn't show it.
Ray! Good morning!
Oh... Morning.

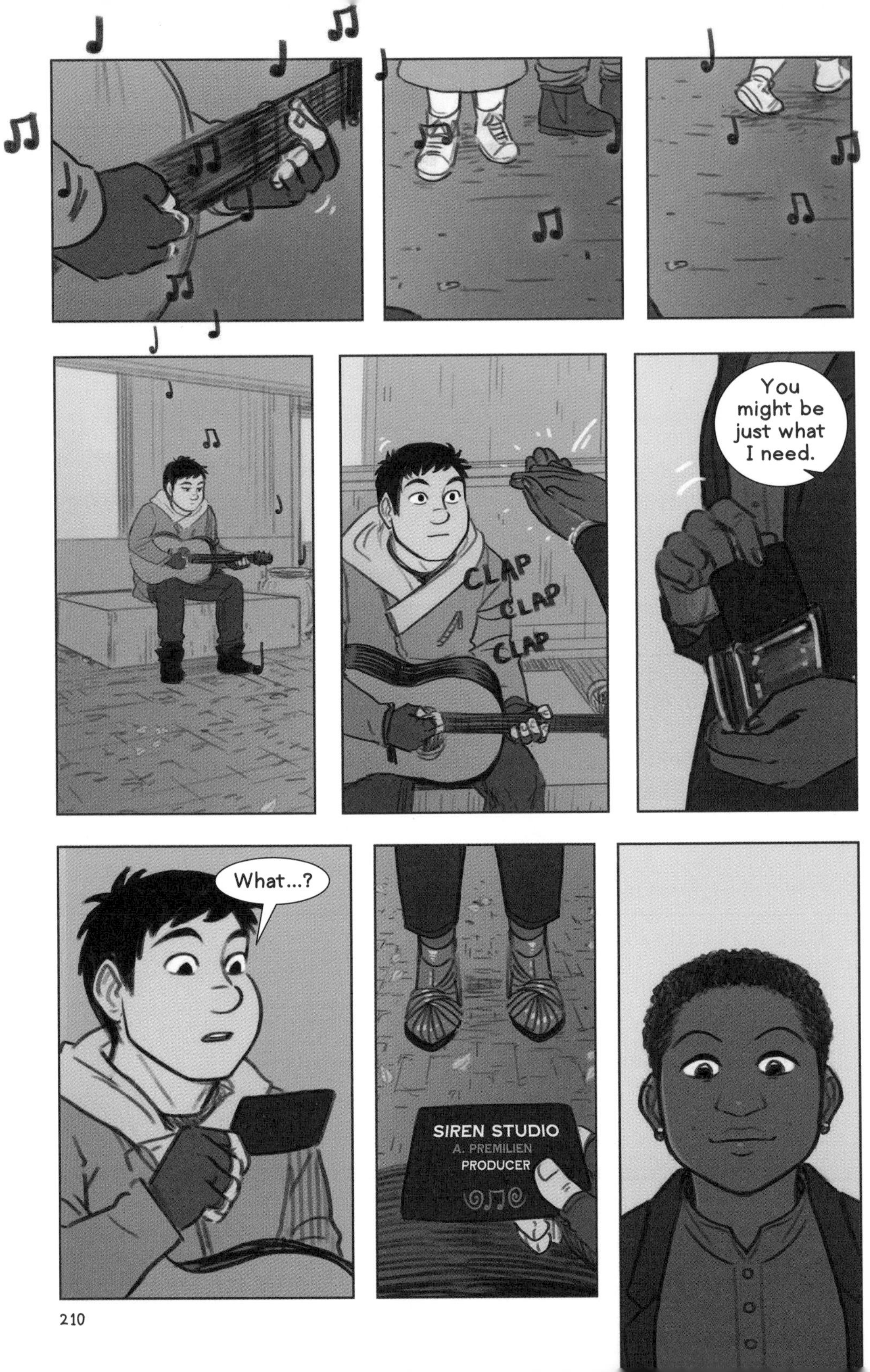
CLAP
CLAP
CLAP
You might be just what I need.
What...?
SIREN STUDIO
A. PREMILIEN
PRODUCER

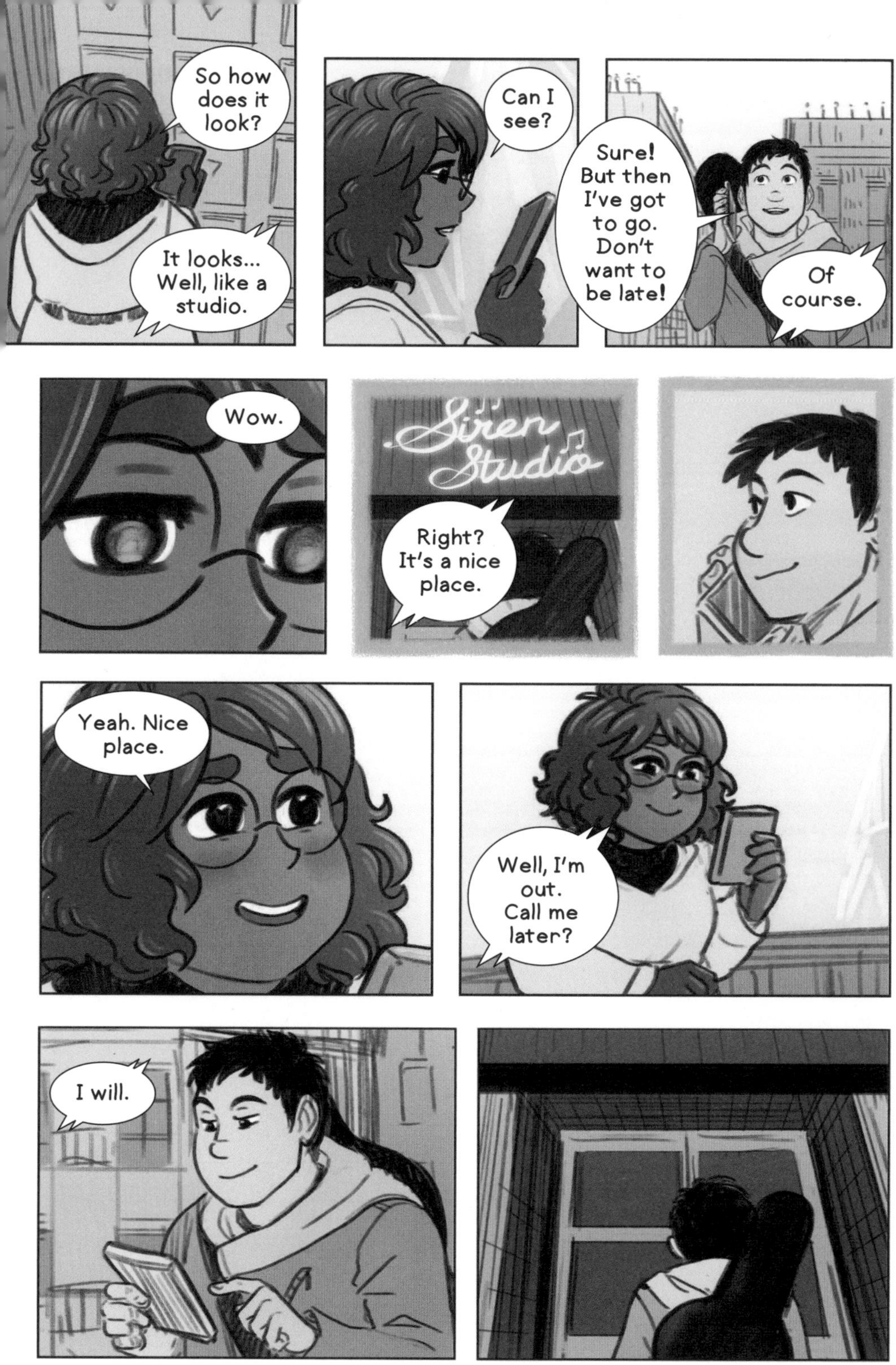
So how does it look?
It looks... Well, like a studio.
Can I see?
Sure! But then I've got to go. Don't want to be late!
Of course.
Wow.
Siren Studio
Right? It's a nice place.
Yeah. Nice place.
Well, I'm out. Call me later?
I will.

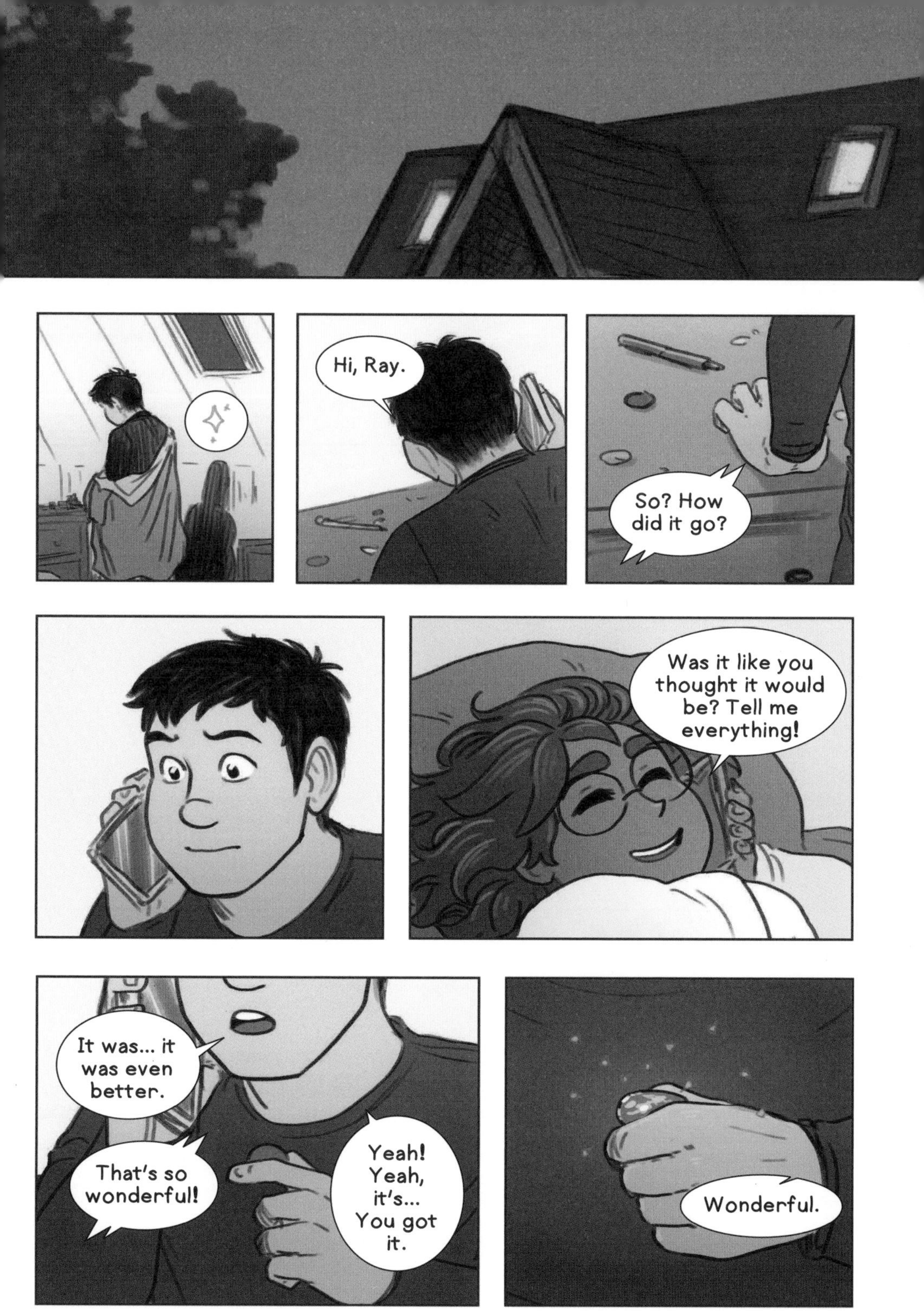
Hi, Ray.
So? How did it go?
Was it like you thought it would be? Tell me everything!
It was... it was even better.
That's so wonderful!
Yeah! Yeah, it's... You got it.
Wonderful.

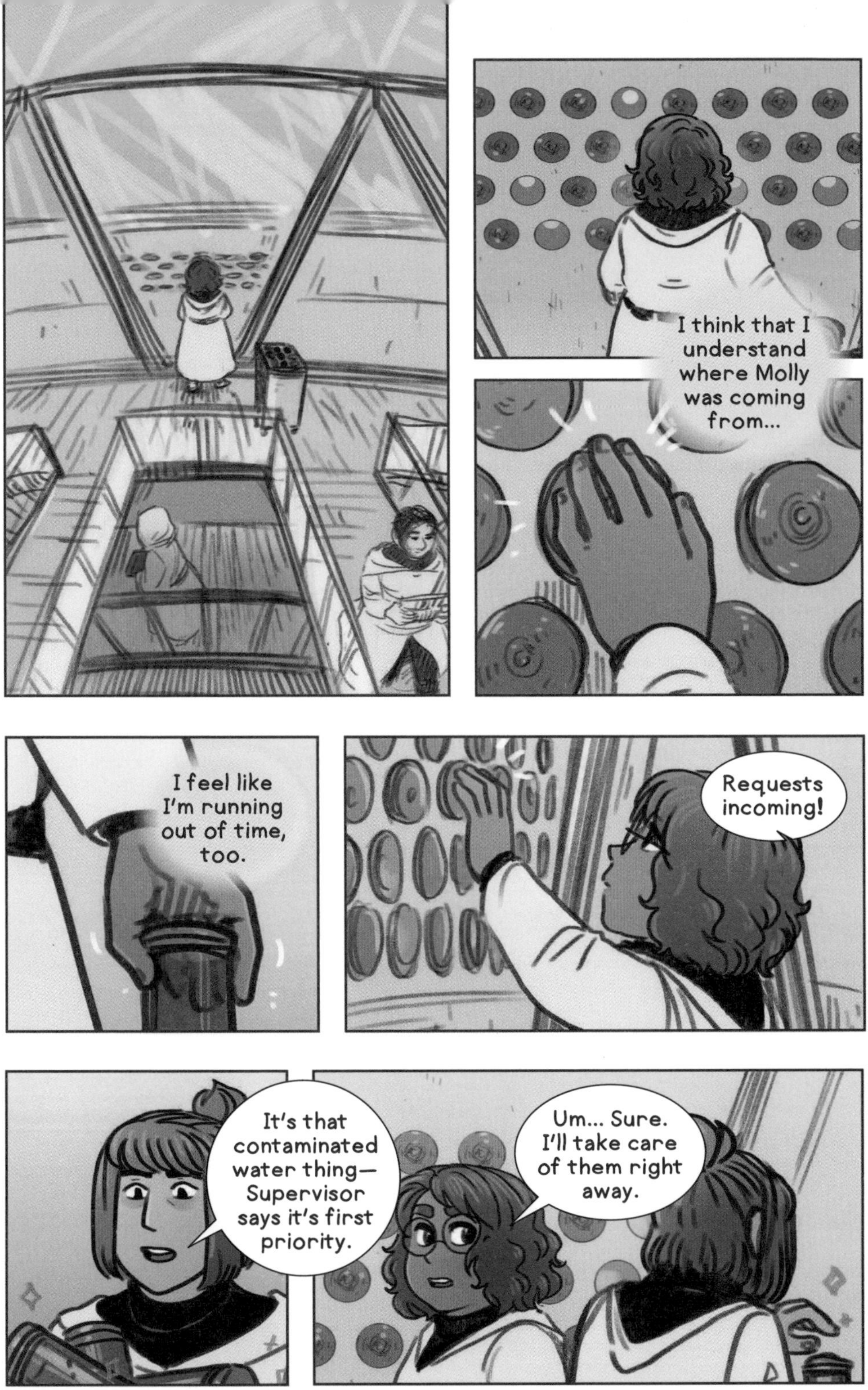
I think that I understand where Molly was coming from...
I feel like I'm running out of time, too.
Requests incoming!
It's that contaminated water thing—Supervisor says it's first priority.
Um... Sure. I'll take care of them right away.

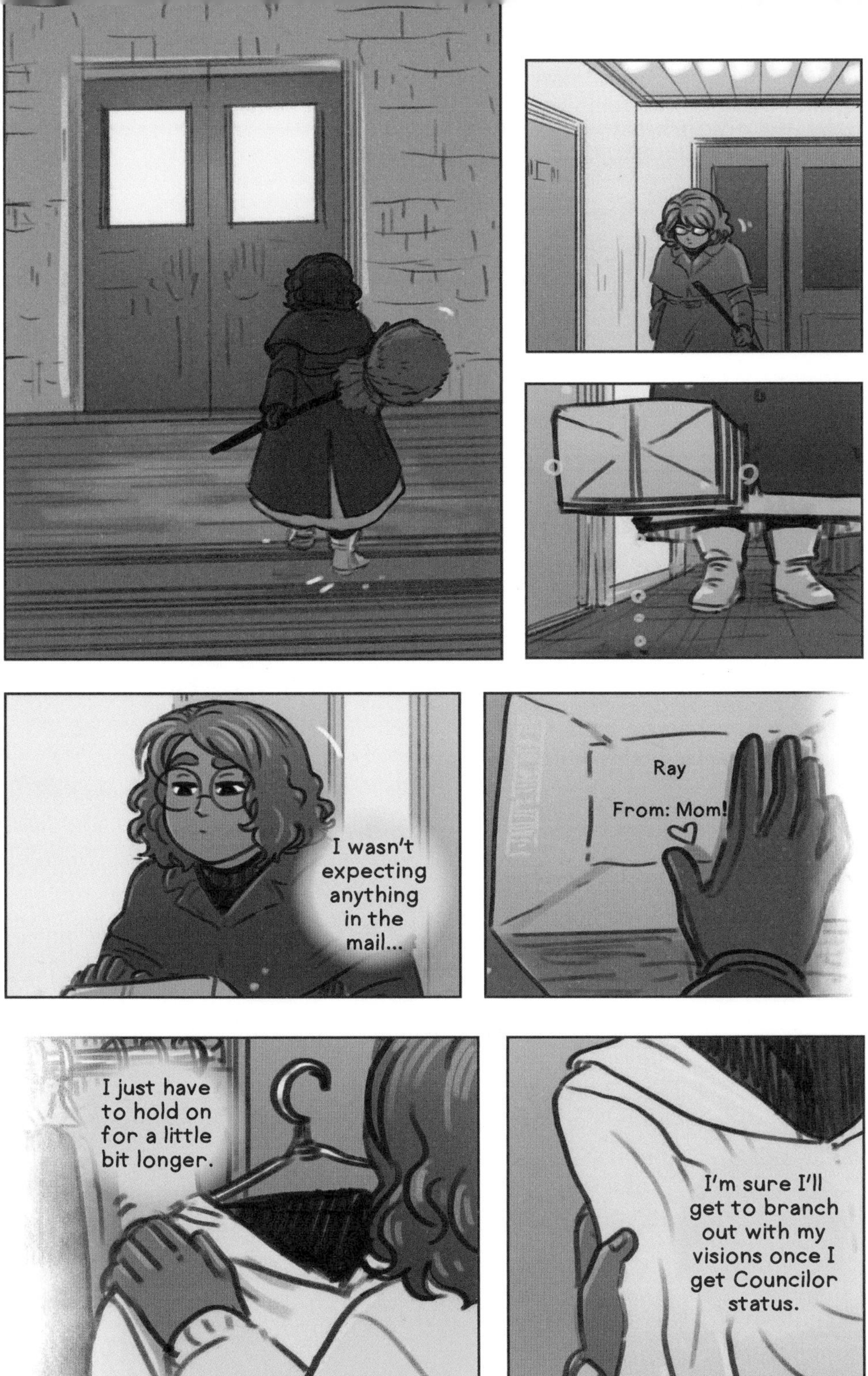
Ray
From: Mom!
I wasn't expecting anything in the mail...
I just have to hold on for a little bit longer.
I'm sure I'll get to branch out with my visions once I get Councilor status.

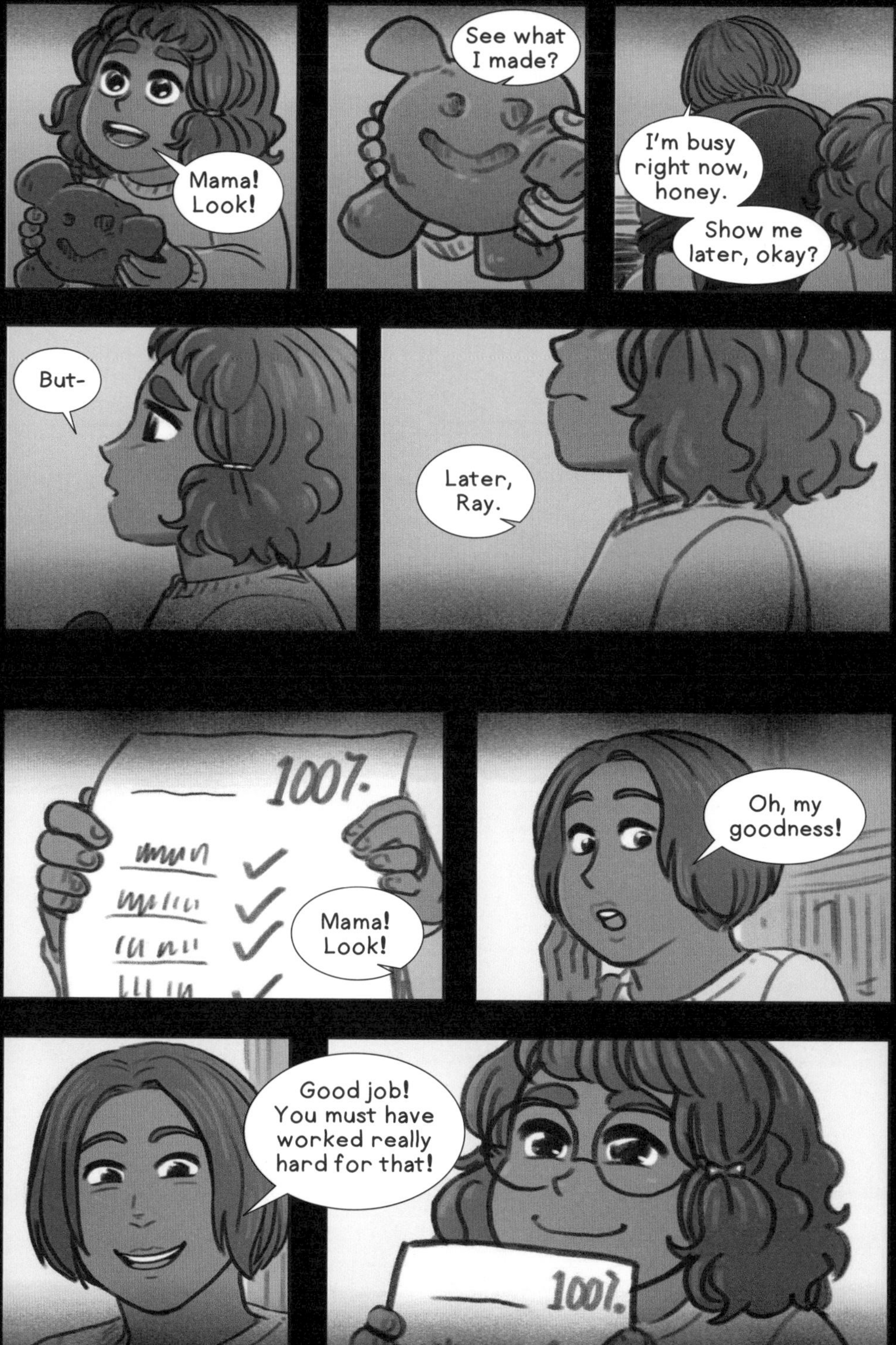
Mama! Look!
See what I made?
I'm busy right now, honey.
Show me later, okay?
But-
Later, Ray.
100%
Mama! Look!
Oh, my goodness!
Good job! You must have worked really hard for that!
100%

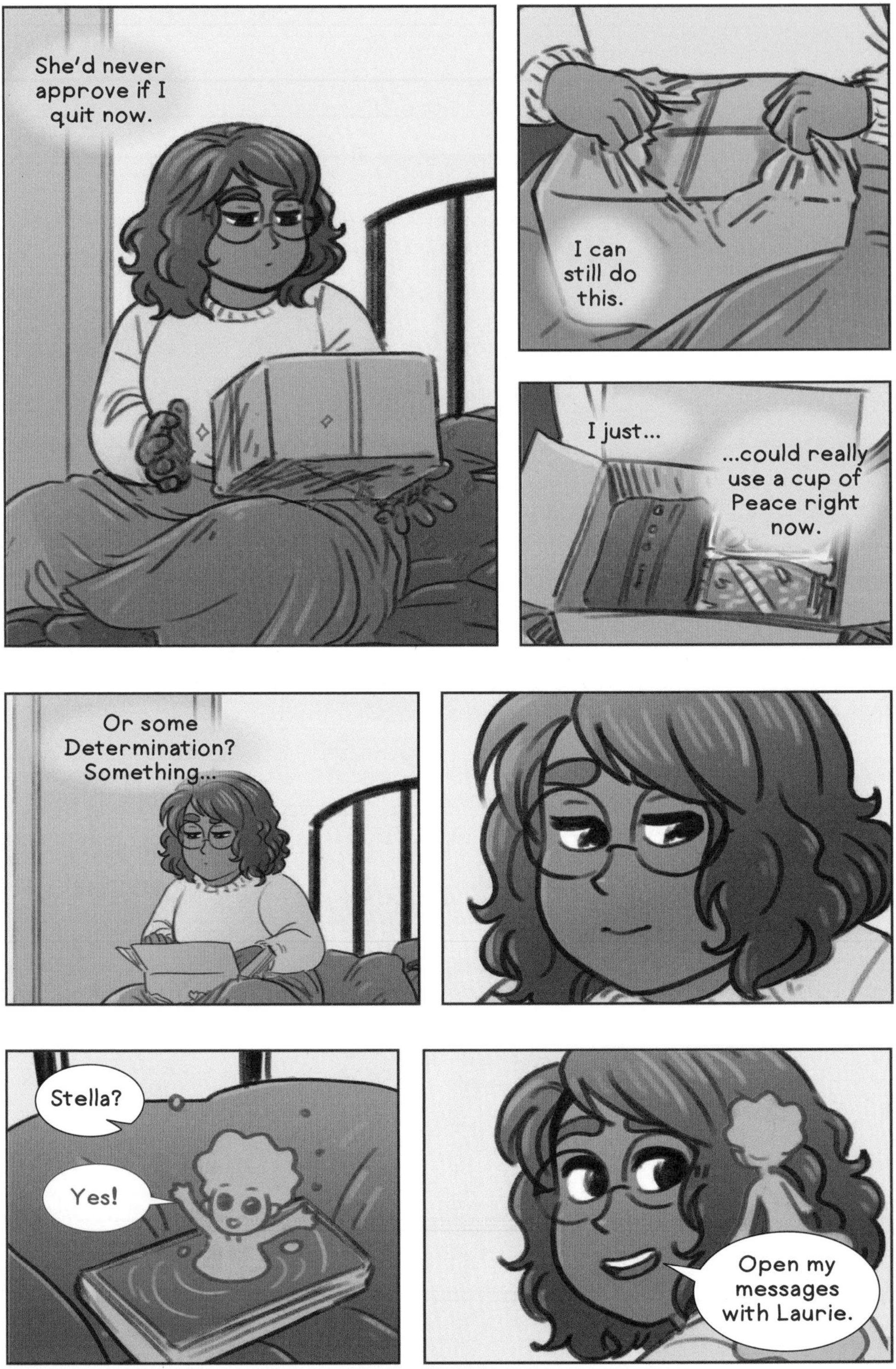
She'd never approve if I quit now.
I can still do this.
I just...
...could really use a cup of Peace right now.
Or some Determination? Something...
Stella?
Yes!
Open my messages with Laurie.

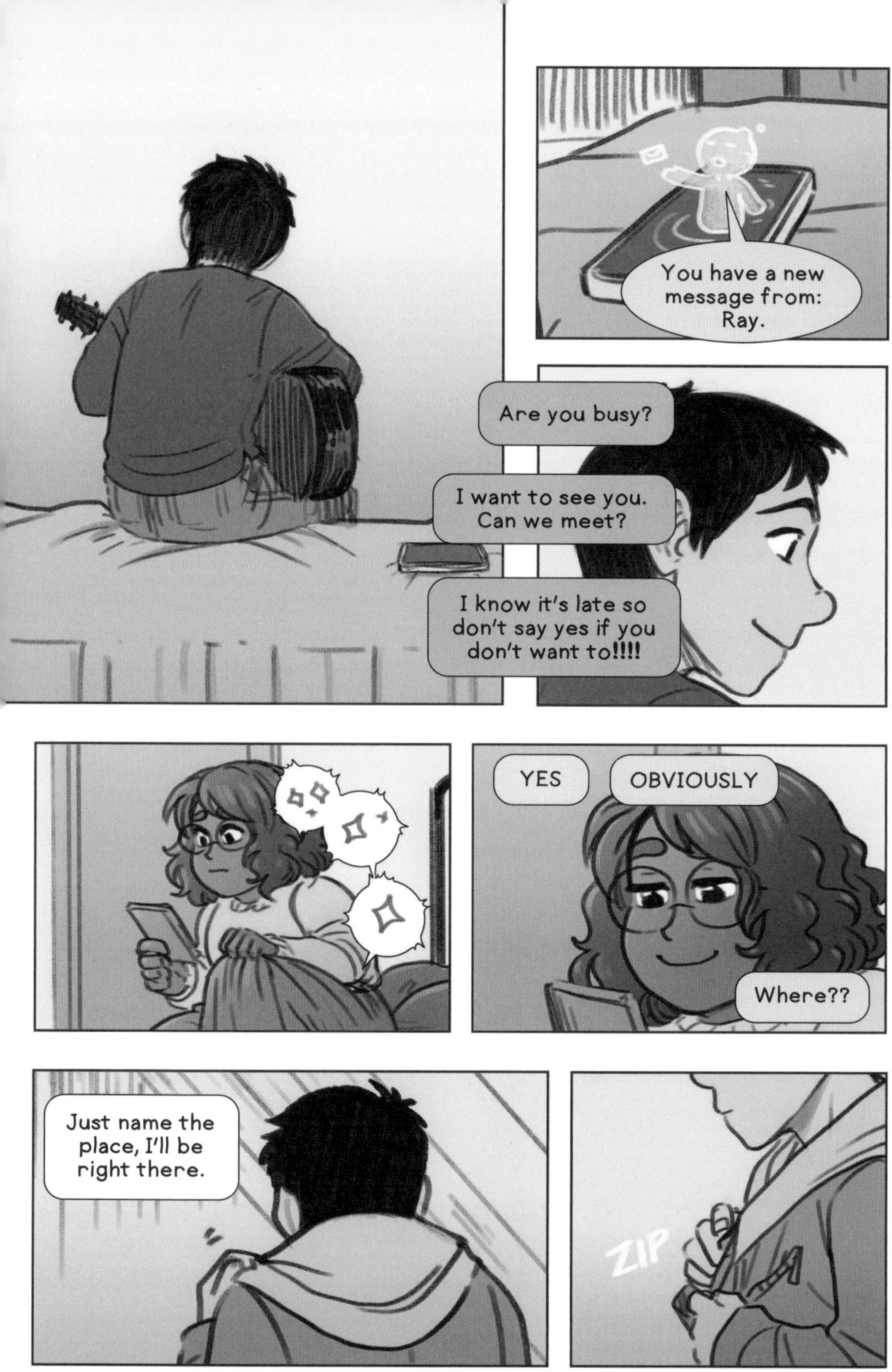
You have a new message from: Ray.
Are you busy?
I want to see you. Can we meet?
I know it's late so don't say yes if you don't want to!!!!
YES
OBVIOUSLY
Where??
Just name the place, I'll be right there.
ZIP

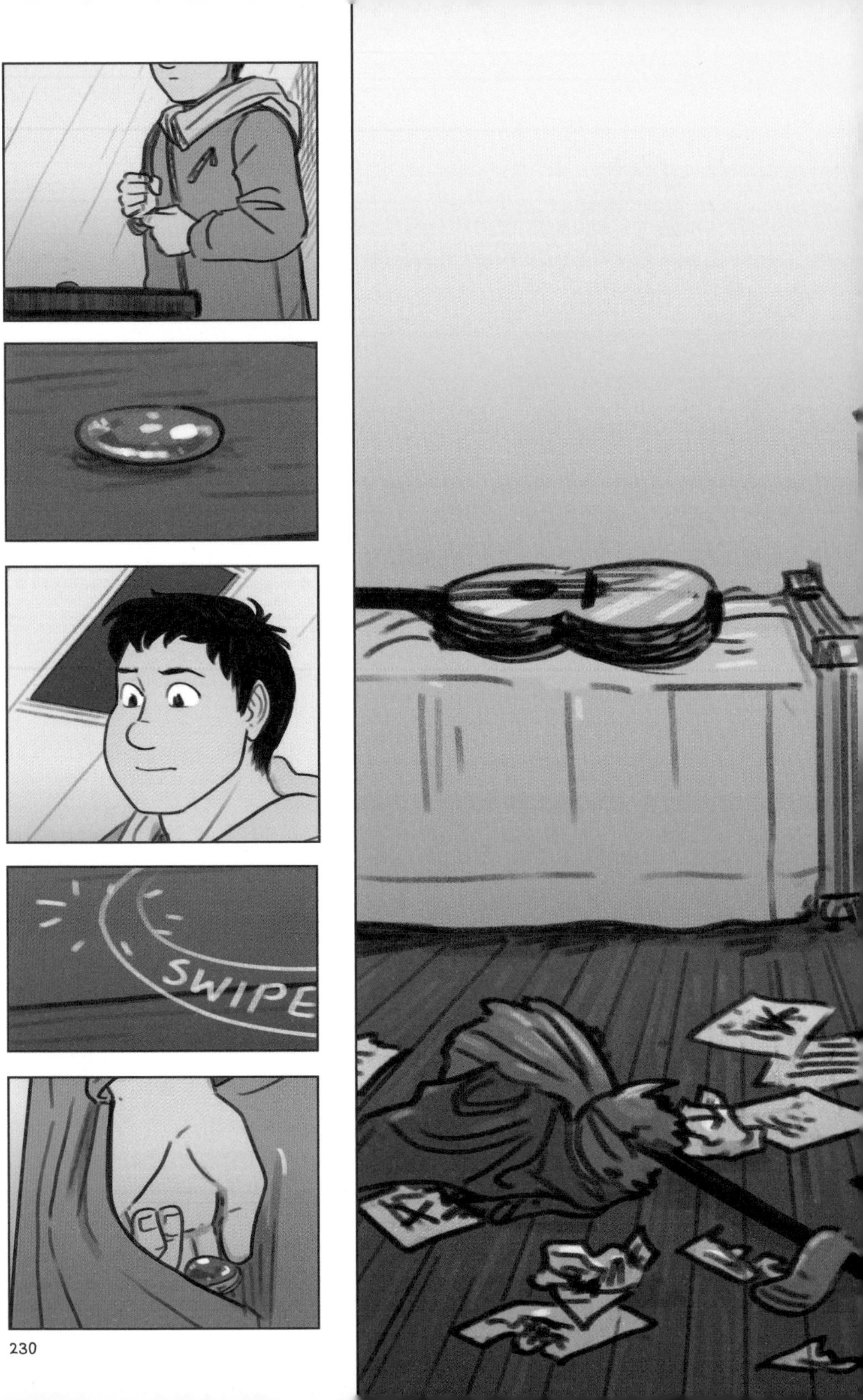
SWIPE

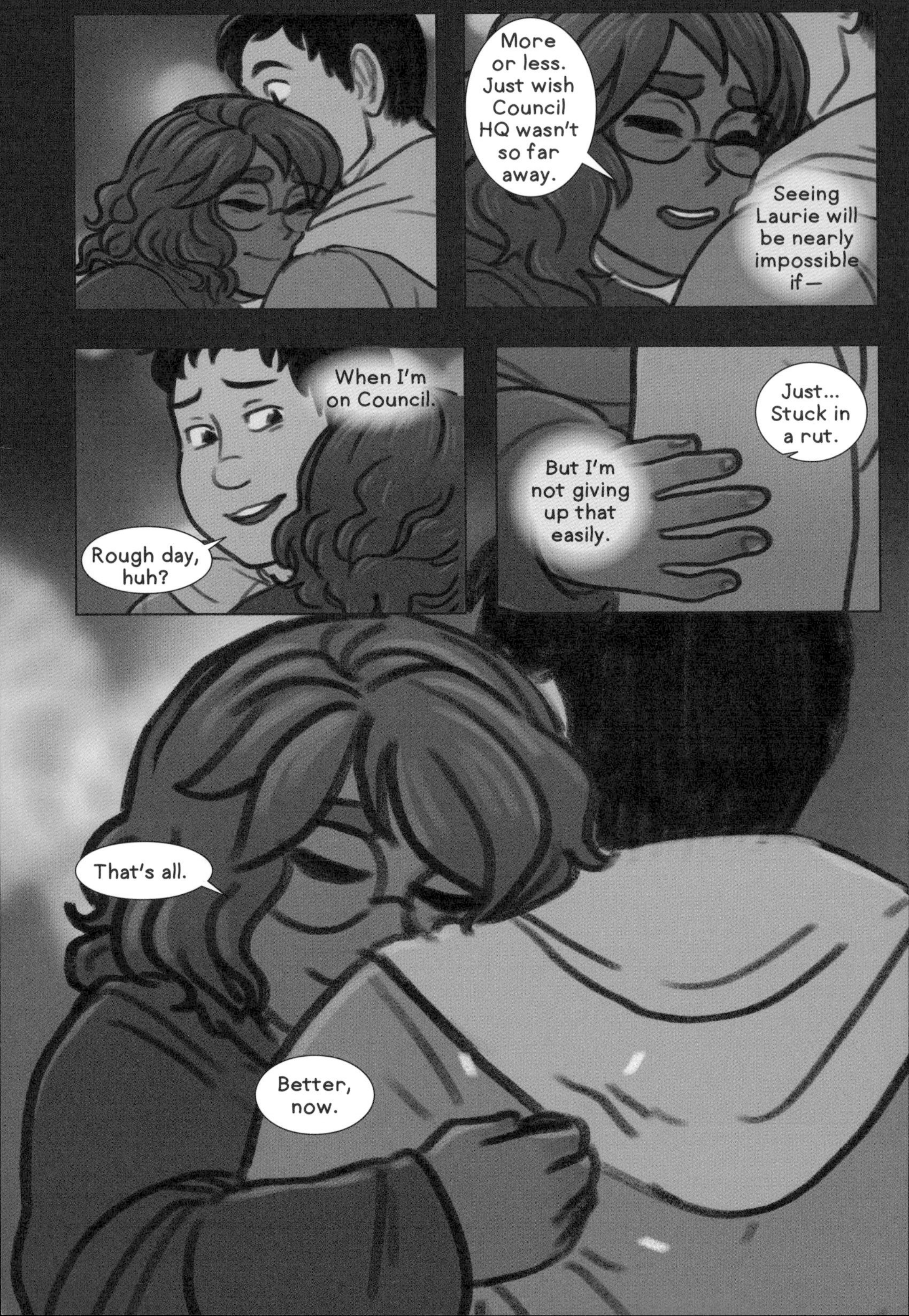
More or less. Just wish Council HQ wasn't so far away.
Seeing Laurie will be nearly impossible if—
When I'm on Council.
Rough day, huh?
Just... Stuck in a rut.
But I'm not giving up that easily.
That's all.
Better, now.

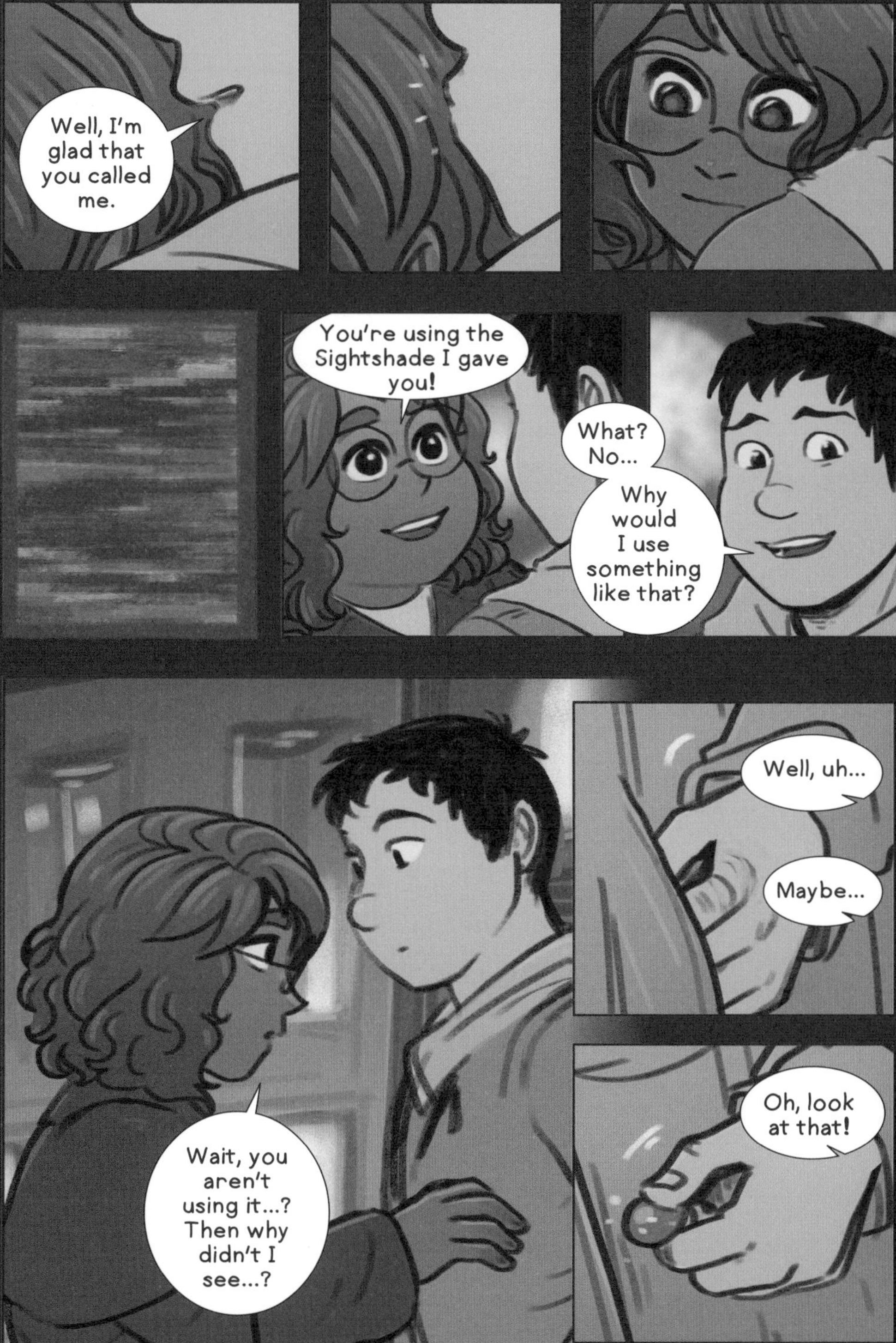
Well, I'm glad that you called me.
You're using the Sightshade I gave you!
What? No...
Why would I use something like that?
Wait, you aren't using it...? Then why didn't I see...?
Well, uh...
Maybe...
Oh, look at that!

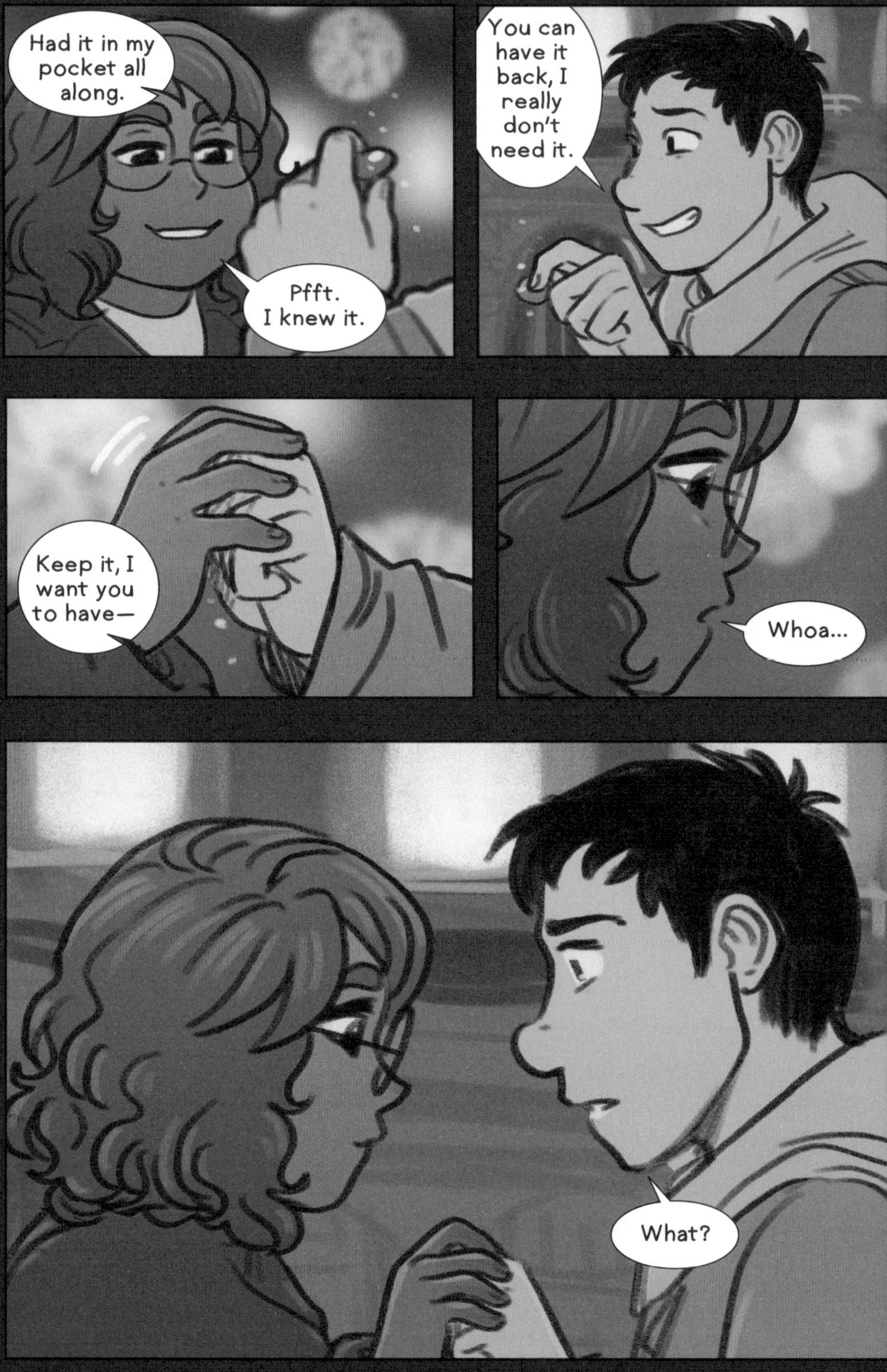
Had it in my pocket all along.
Pfft. I knew it.
You can have it back, I really don't need it.
Keep it, I want you to have—
Whoa...
What?

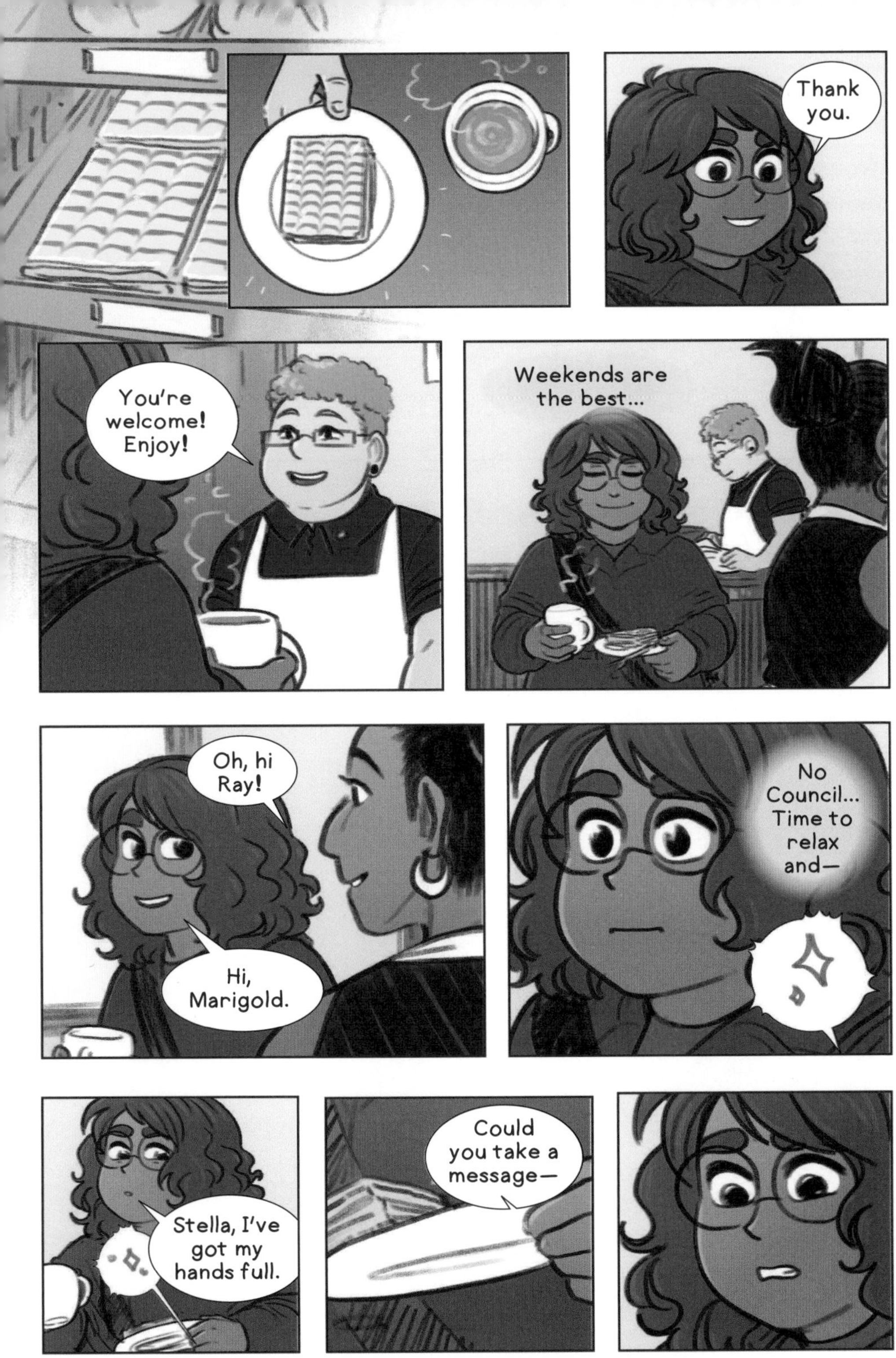

Thank you.
You're welcome! Enjoy!
Weekends are the best...
Oh, hi Ray!
Hi, Marigold.
No Council... Time to relax and—
Stella, I've got my hands full.
Could you take a message—

239

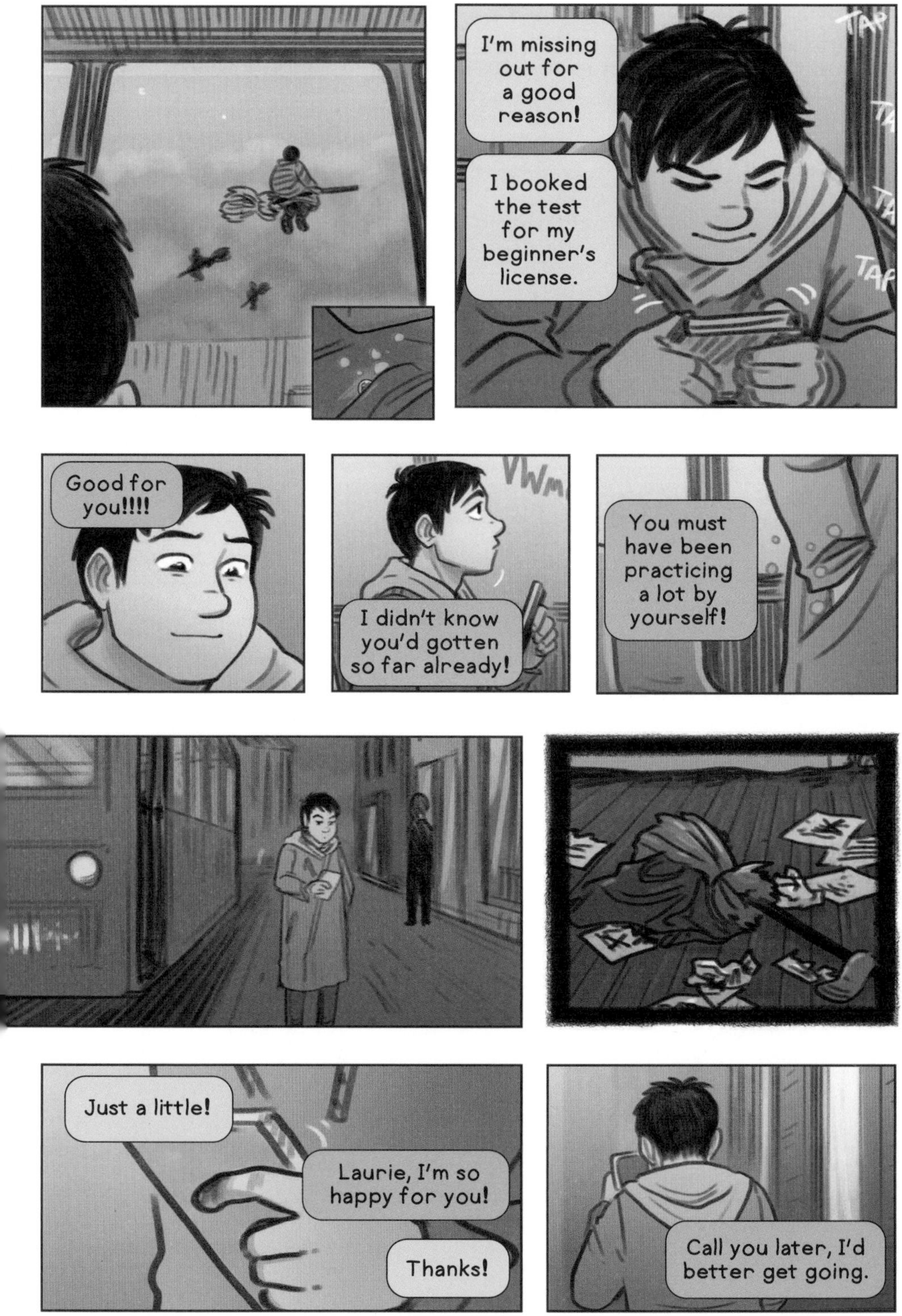
I'm missing out for a good reason!
I booked the test for my beginner's license.
TAP
TAP
TAP
TAP
Good for you!!!!
I didn't know you'd gotten so far already!
VWm
You must have been practicing a lot by yourself!
Just a little!
Laurie, I'm so happy for you!
Thanks!
Call you later, I'd better get going.

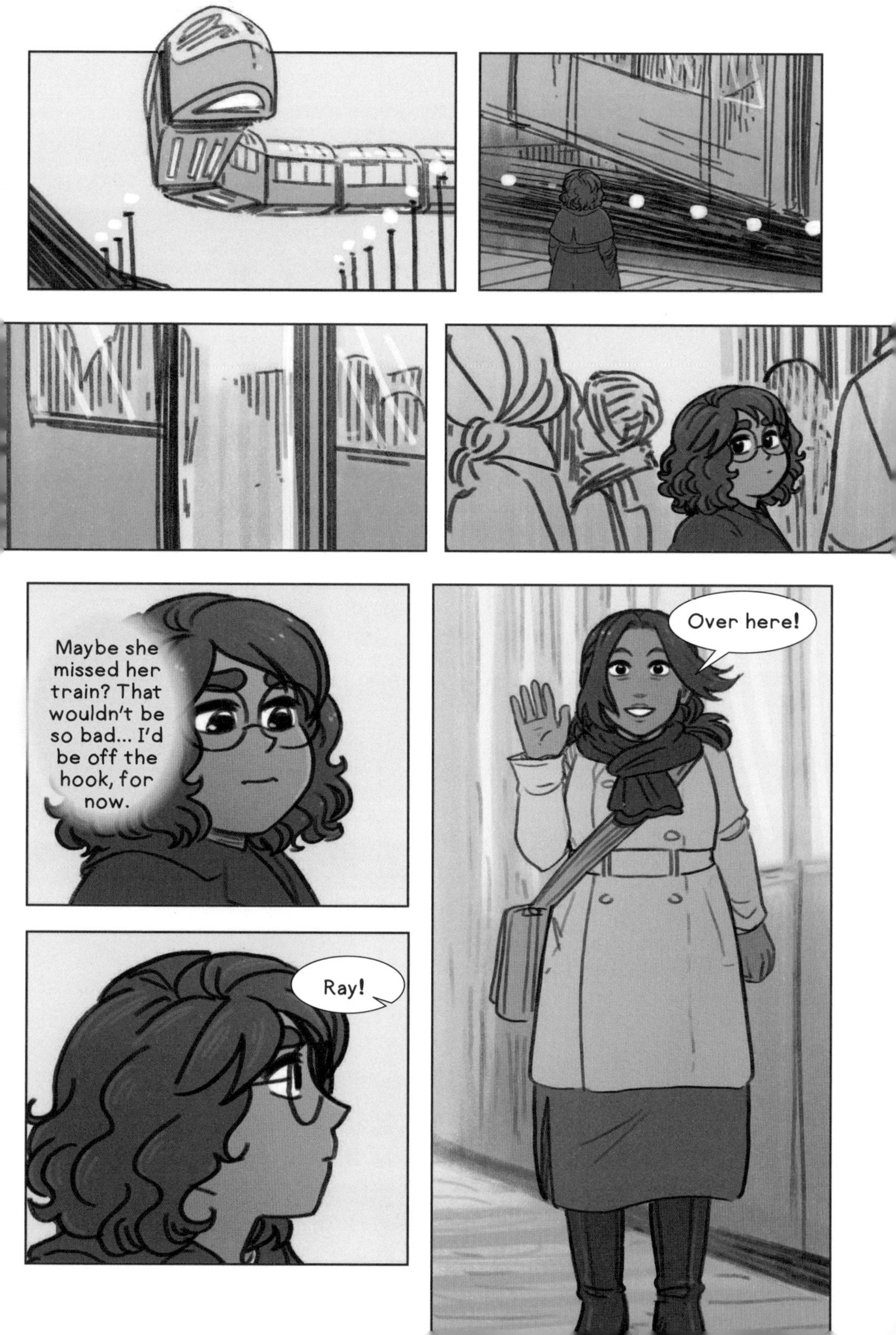
Maybe she missed her train? That wouldn't be so bad... I'd be off the hook, for now.
Ray!
Over here!

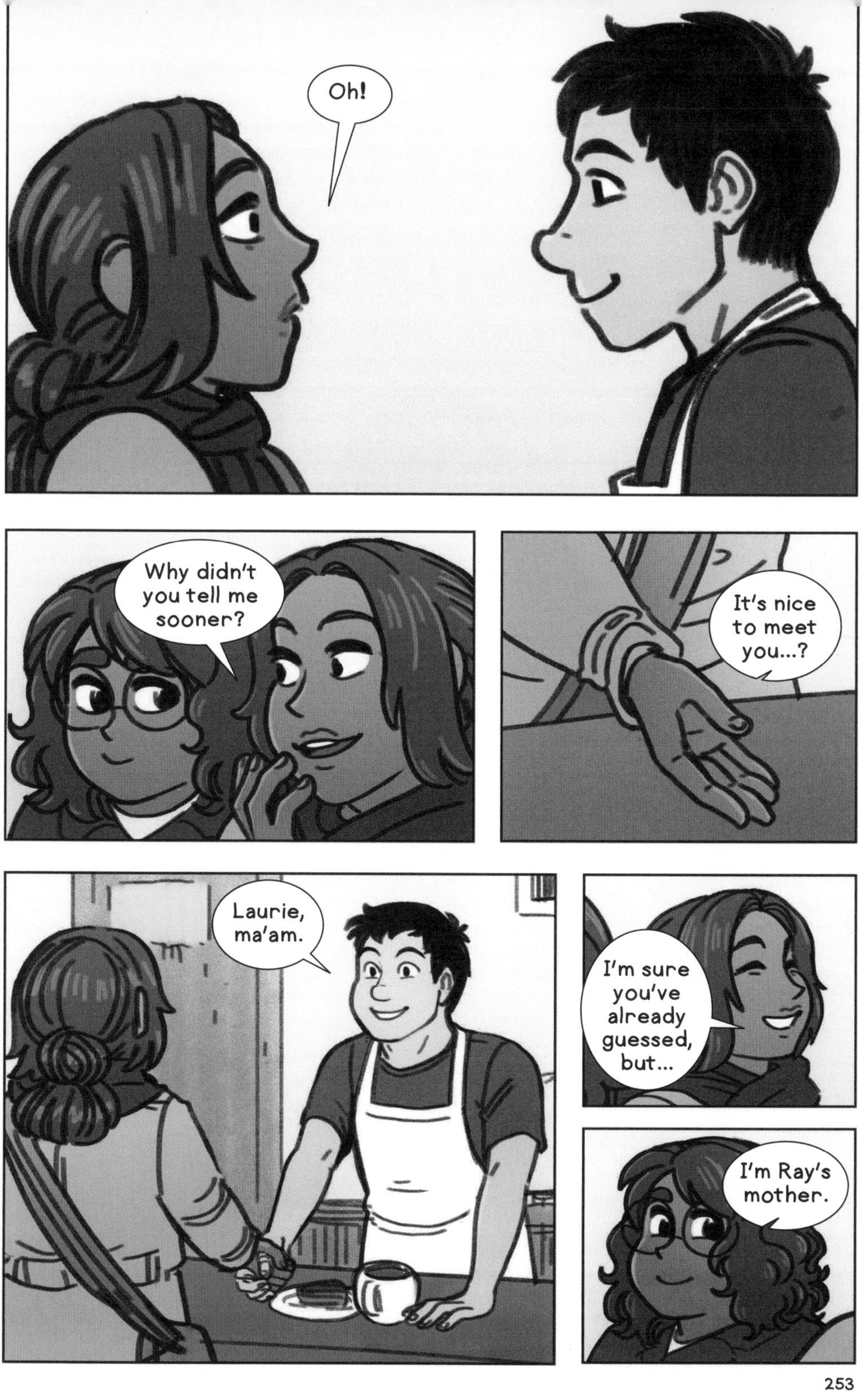
Oh!
Why didn't you tell me sooner?
It's nice to meet you...?
Laurie, ma'am.
I'm sure you've already guessed, but...
I'm Ray's mother.

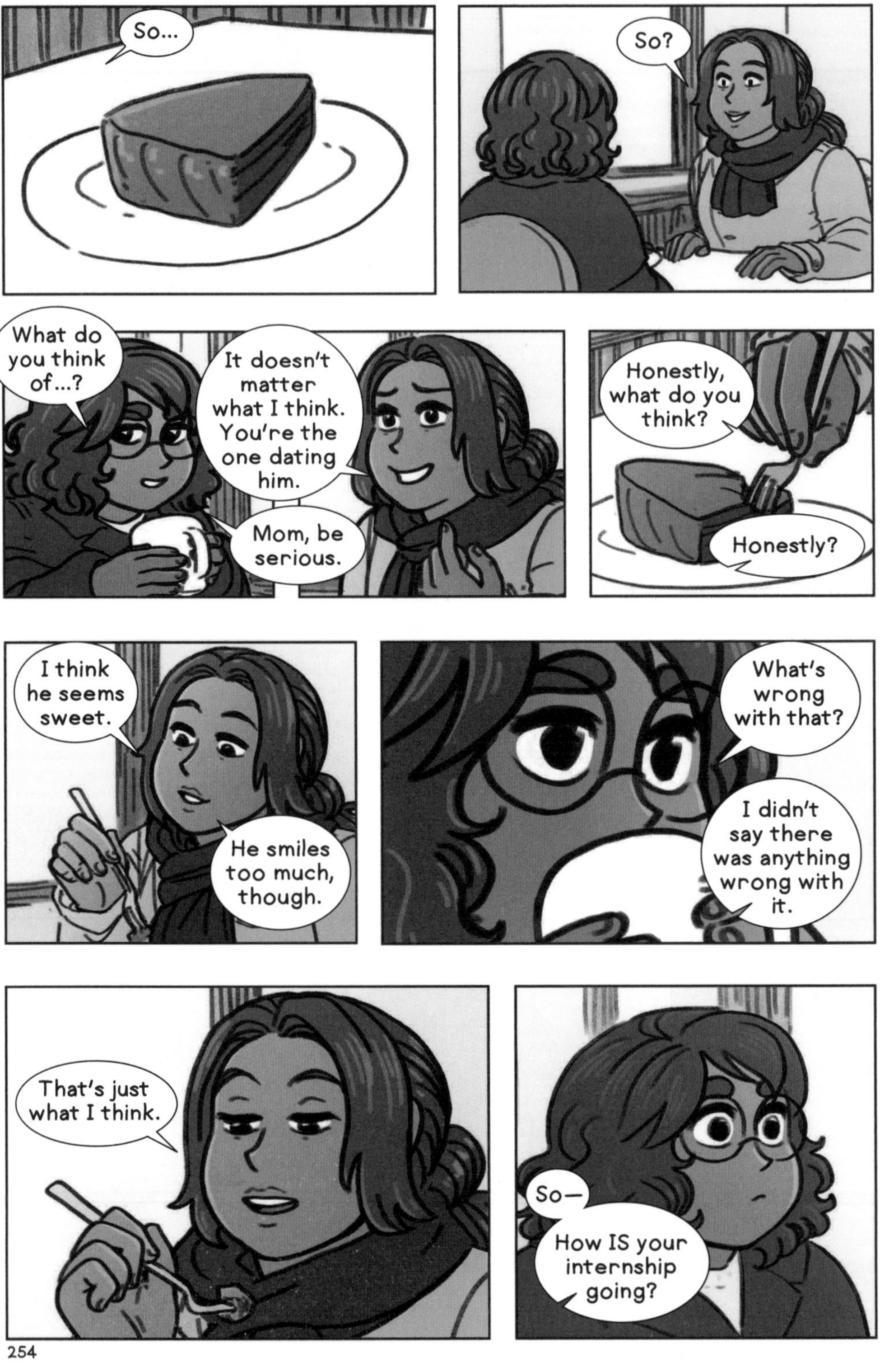

So...
So?
What do you think of...?
It doesn't matter what I think. You're the one dating him.
Mom, be serious.
Honestly, what do you think?
Honestly?
I think he seems sweet.
He smiles too much, though.
What's wrong with that?
I didn't say there was anything wrong with it.
That's just what I think.
So—
How IS your internship going?

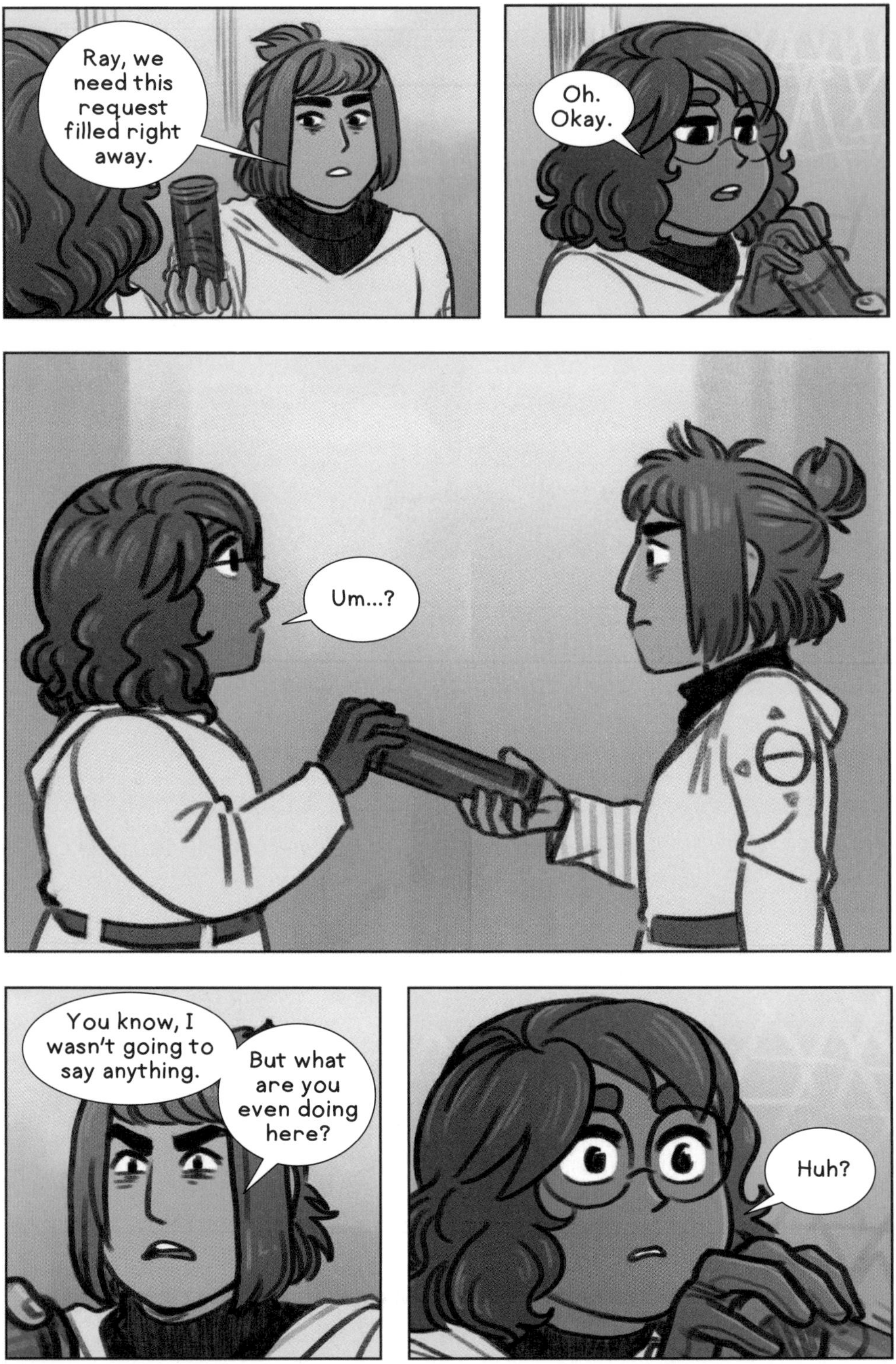

CHAPTER 11

Ray, we need this request filled right away.
Oh. Okay.
Um...?
You know, I wasn't going to say anything.
But what are you even doing here?
Huh?

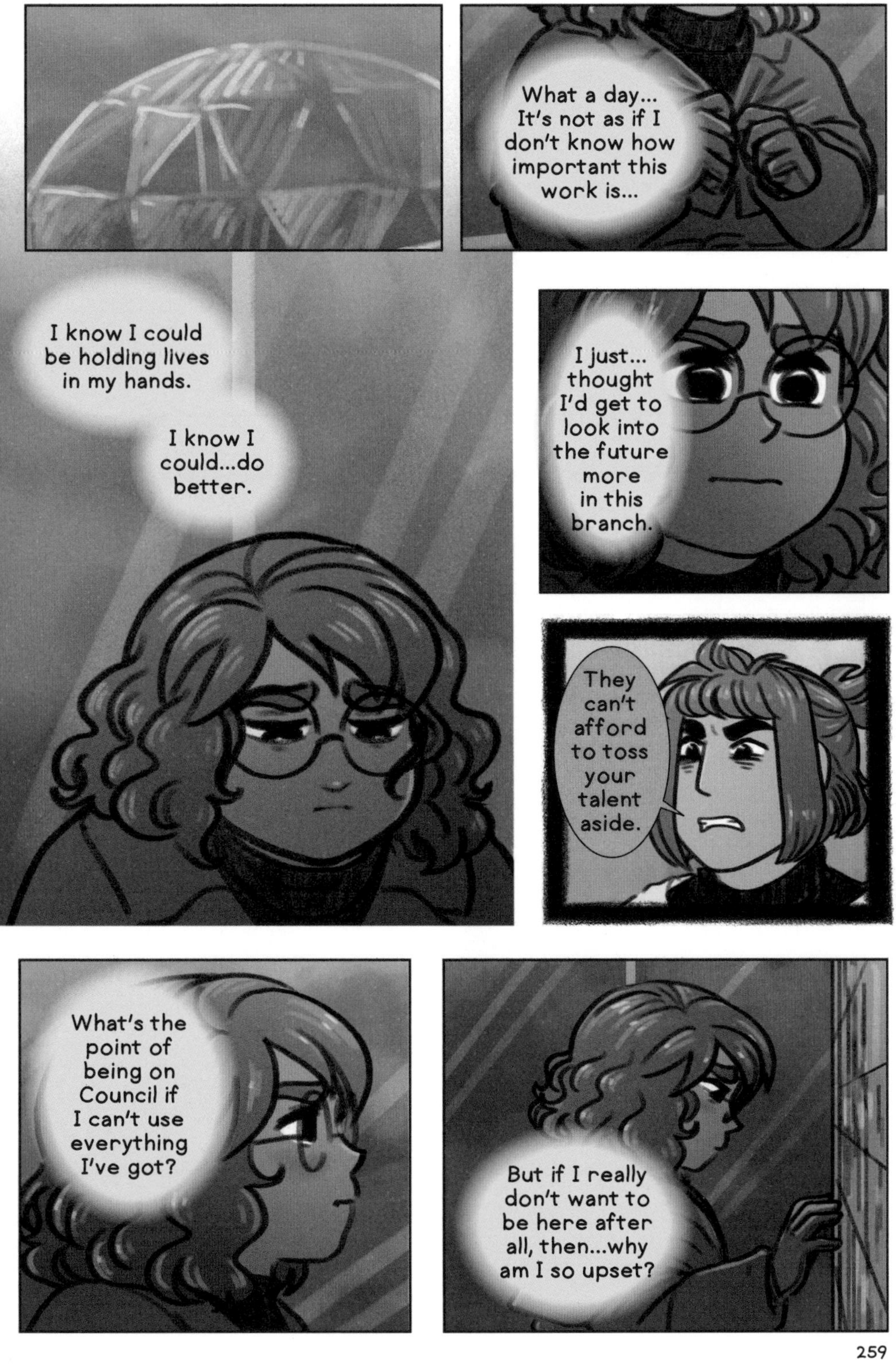
What a day... It's not as if I don't know how important this work is...
I know I could be holding lives in my hands.
I know I could...do better.
I just... thought I'd get to look into the future more in this branch.
They can't afford to toss your talent aside.
What's the point of being on Council if I can't use everything I've got?
But if I really don't want to be here after all, then...why am I so upset?

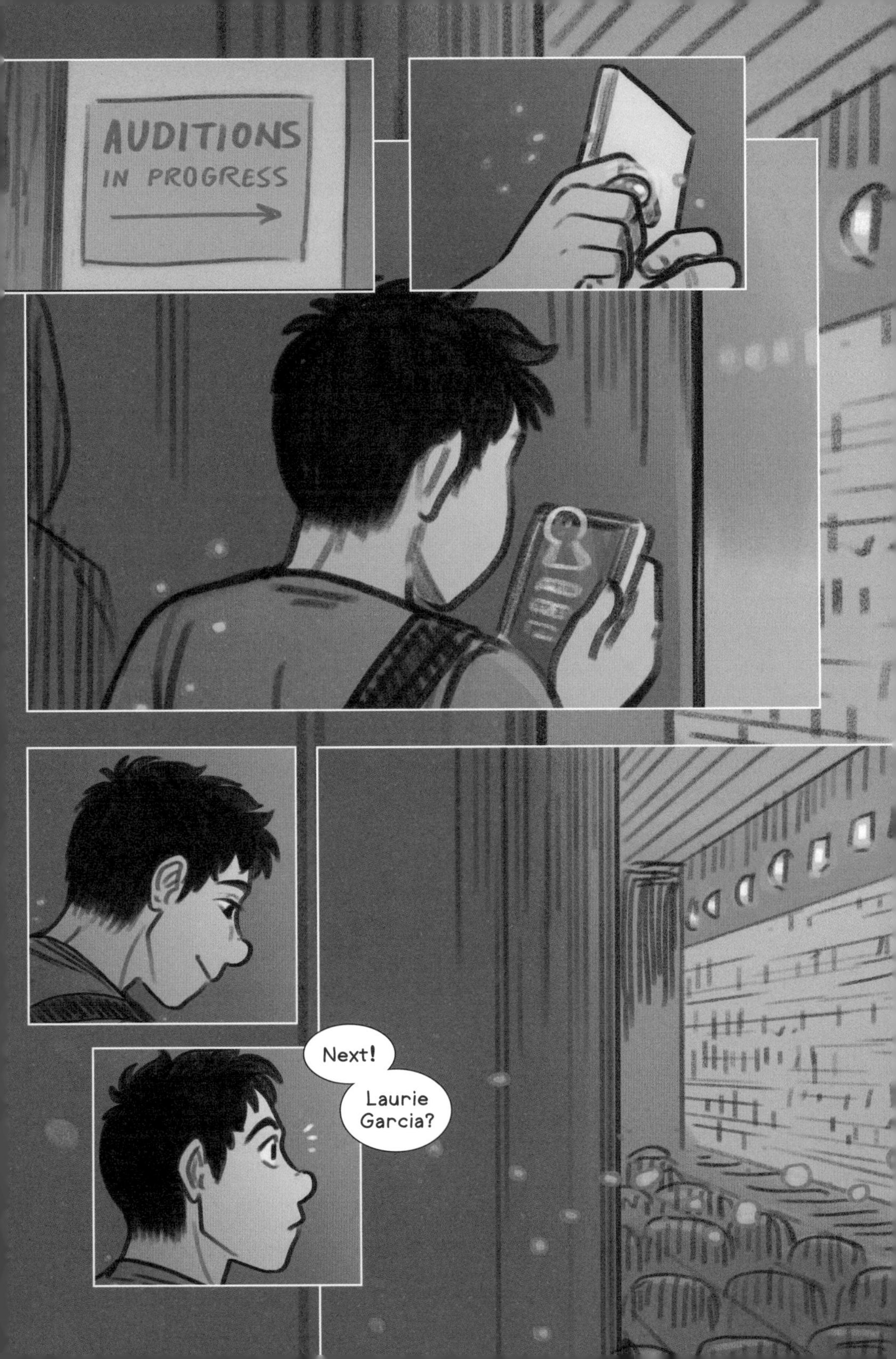
AUDITIONS
IN PROGRESS
Next!
Laurie
Garcia?

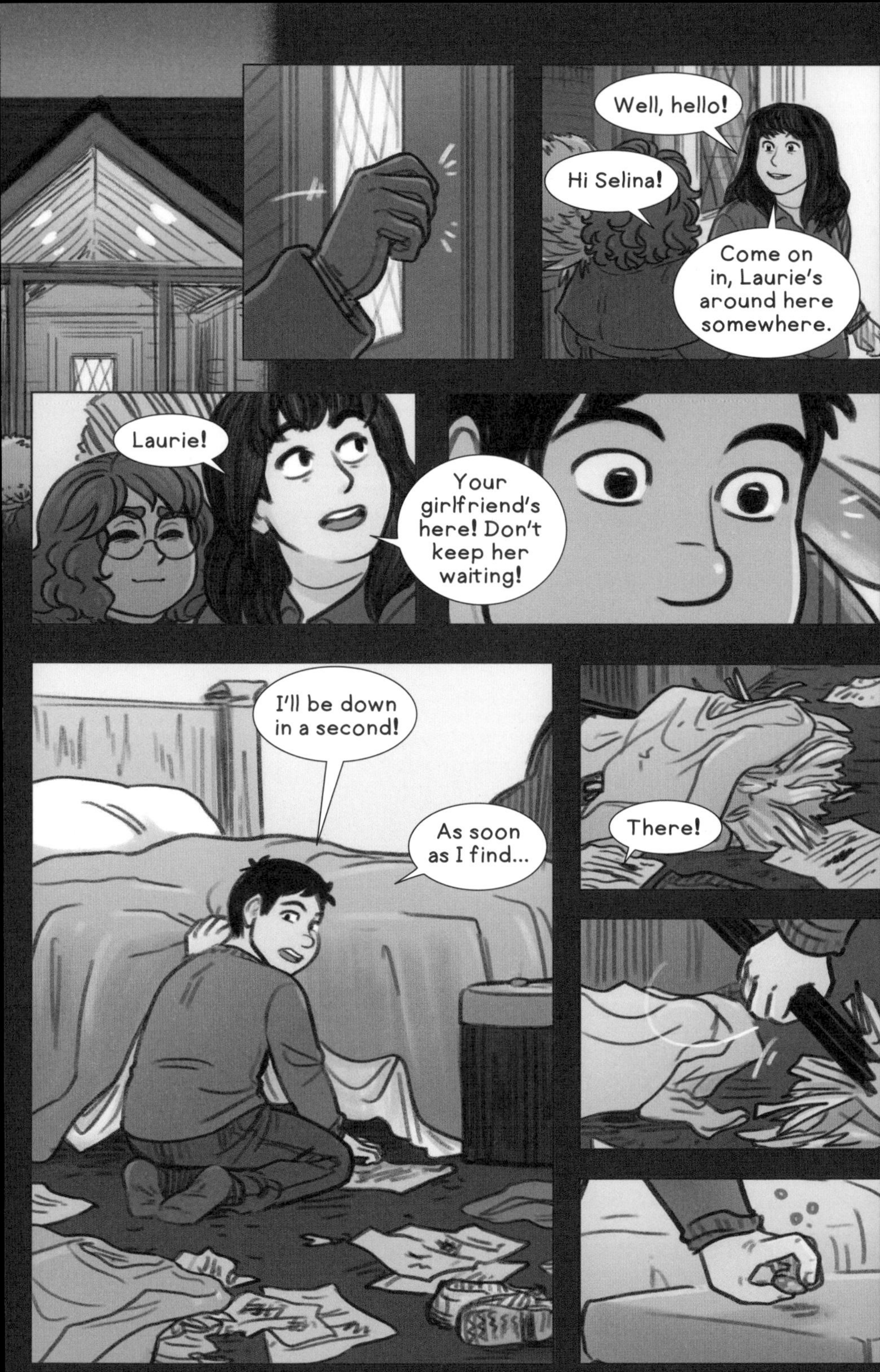
Well, hello!
Hi Selina!
Come on in, Laurie's around here somewhere.
Laurie!
Your girlfriend's here! Don't keep her waiting!
I'll be down in a second!
As soon as I find...
There!

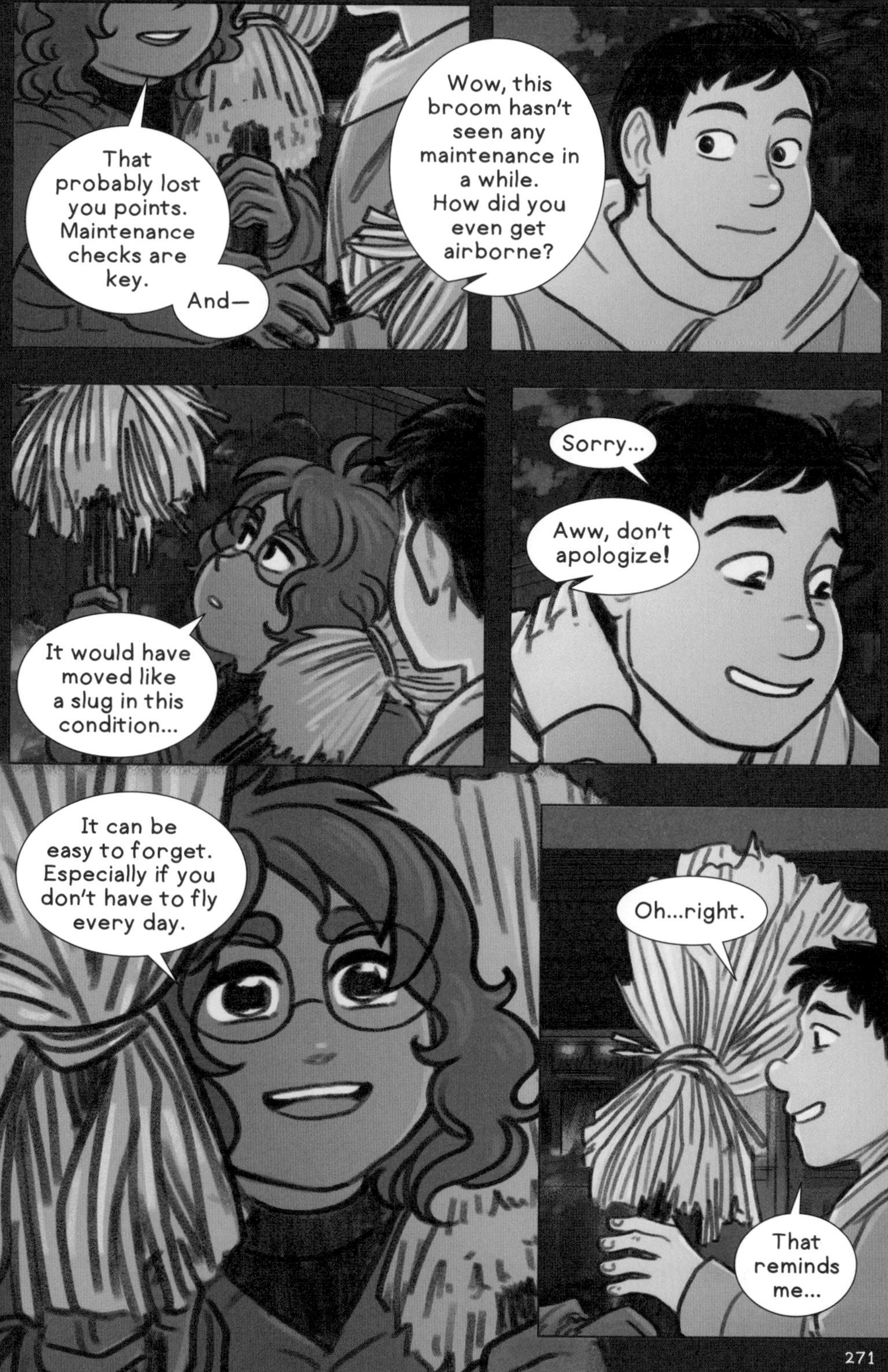
That probably lost you points. Maintenance checks are key.
And—
Wow, this broom hasn't seen any maintenance in a while. How did you even get airborne?
It would have moved like a slug in this condition...
Sorry...
Aww, don't apologize!
It can be easy to forget. Especially if you don't have to fly every day.
Oh...right.
That reminds me...

273

277

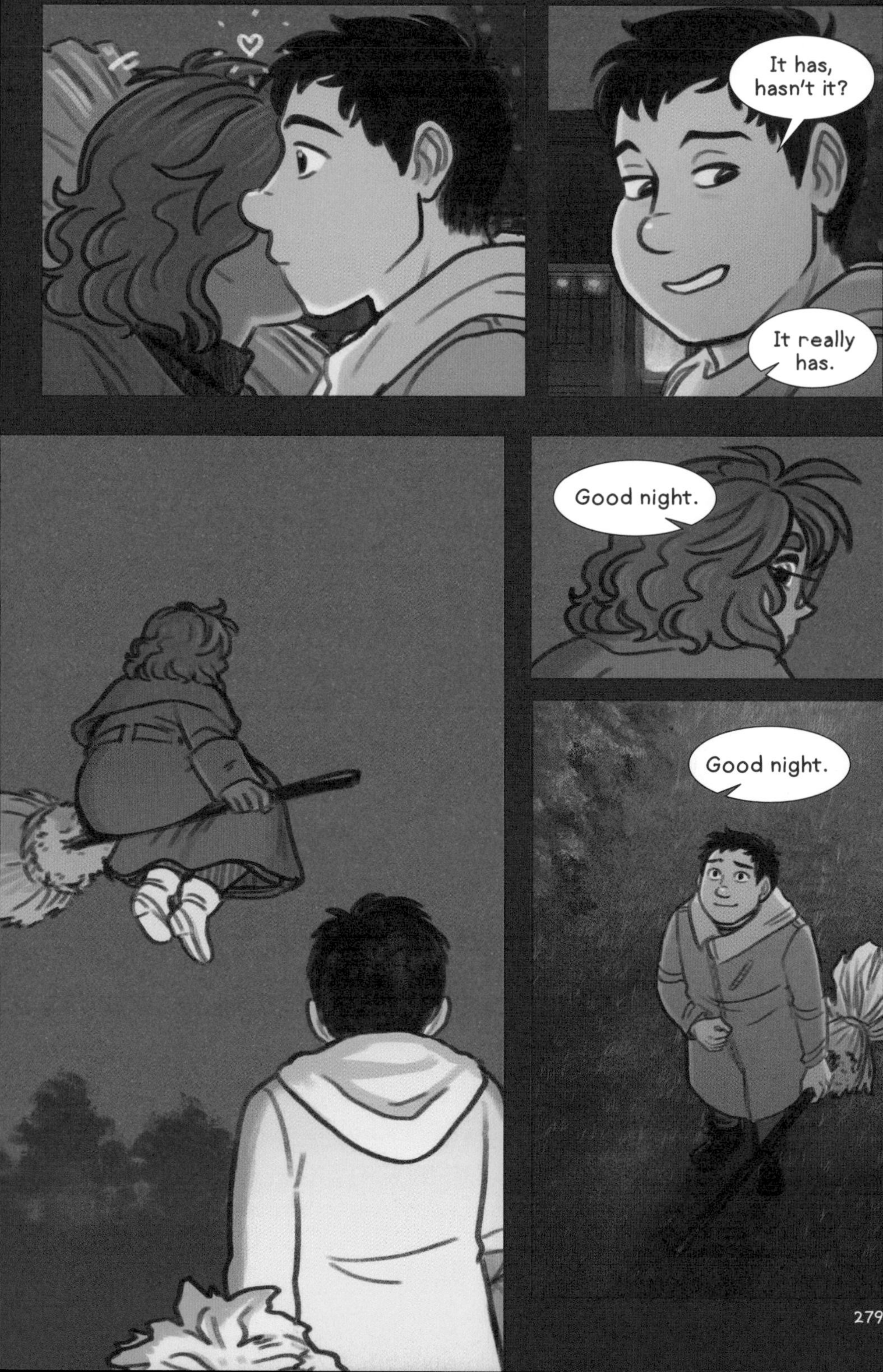
It has, hasn't it?
It really has.
Good night.
Good night.

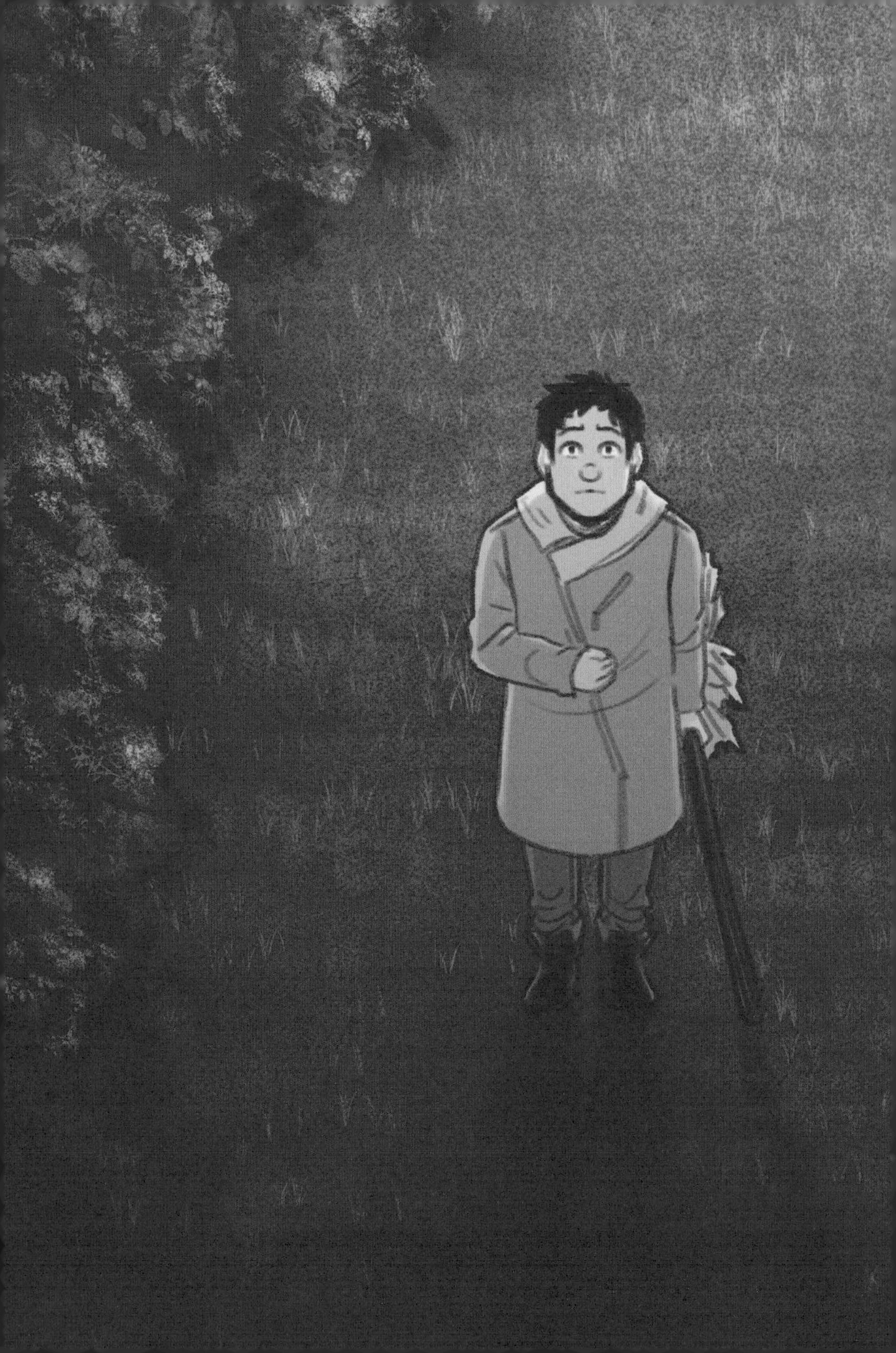

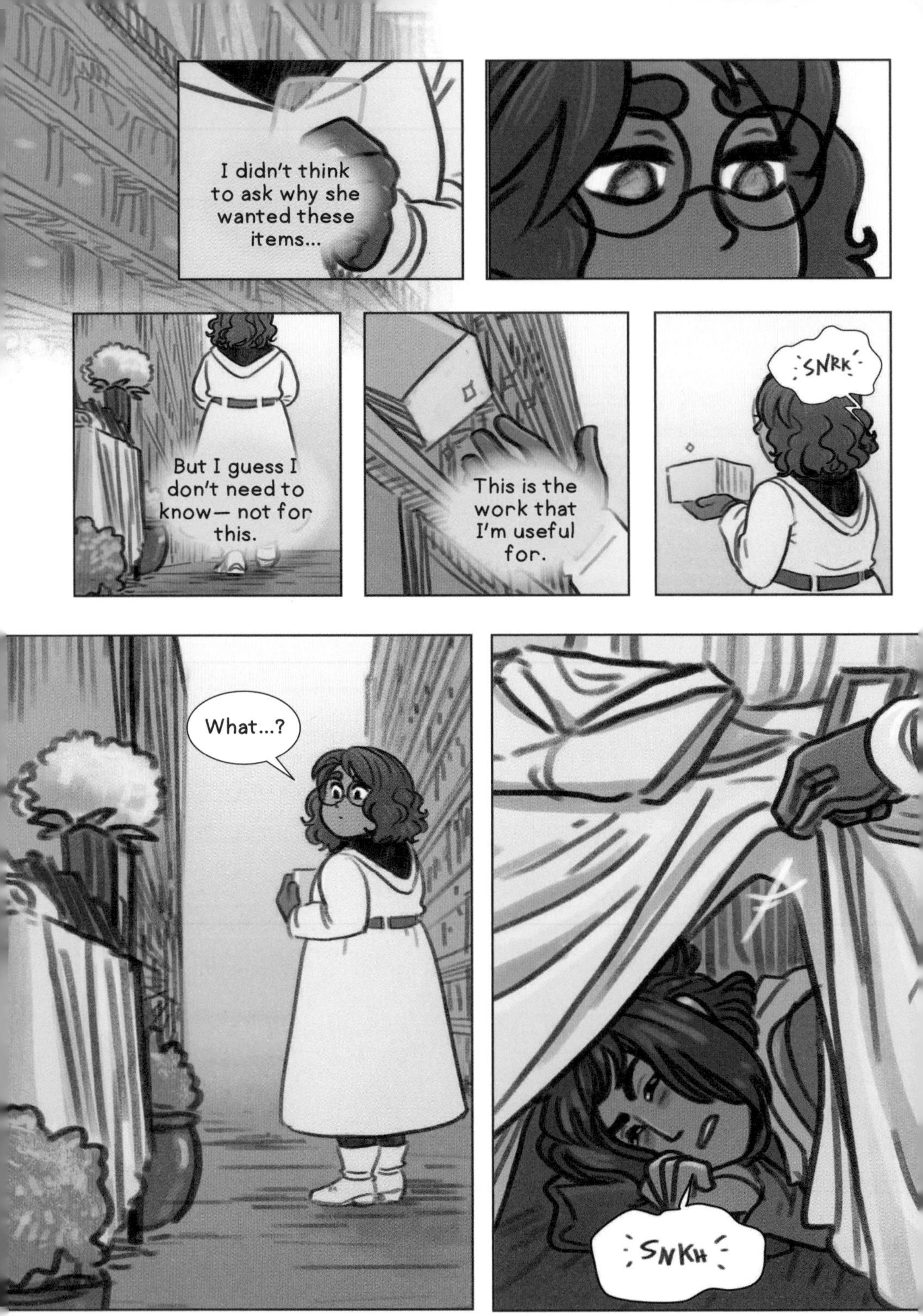
I didn't think to ask why she wanted these items...
But I guess I don't need to know— not for this.
This is the work that I'm useful for.
SNRK
What...?
SNKH

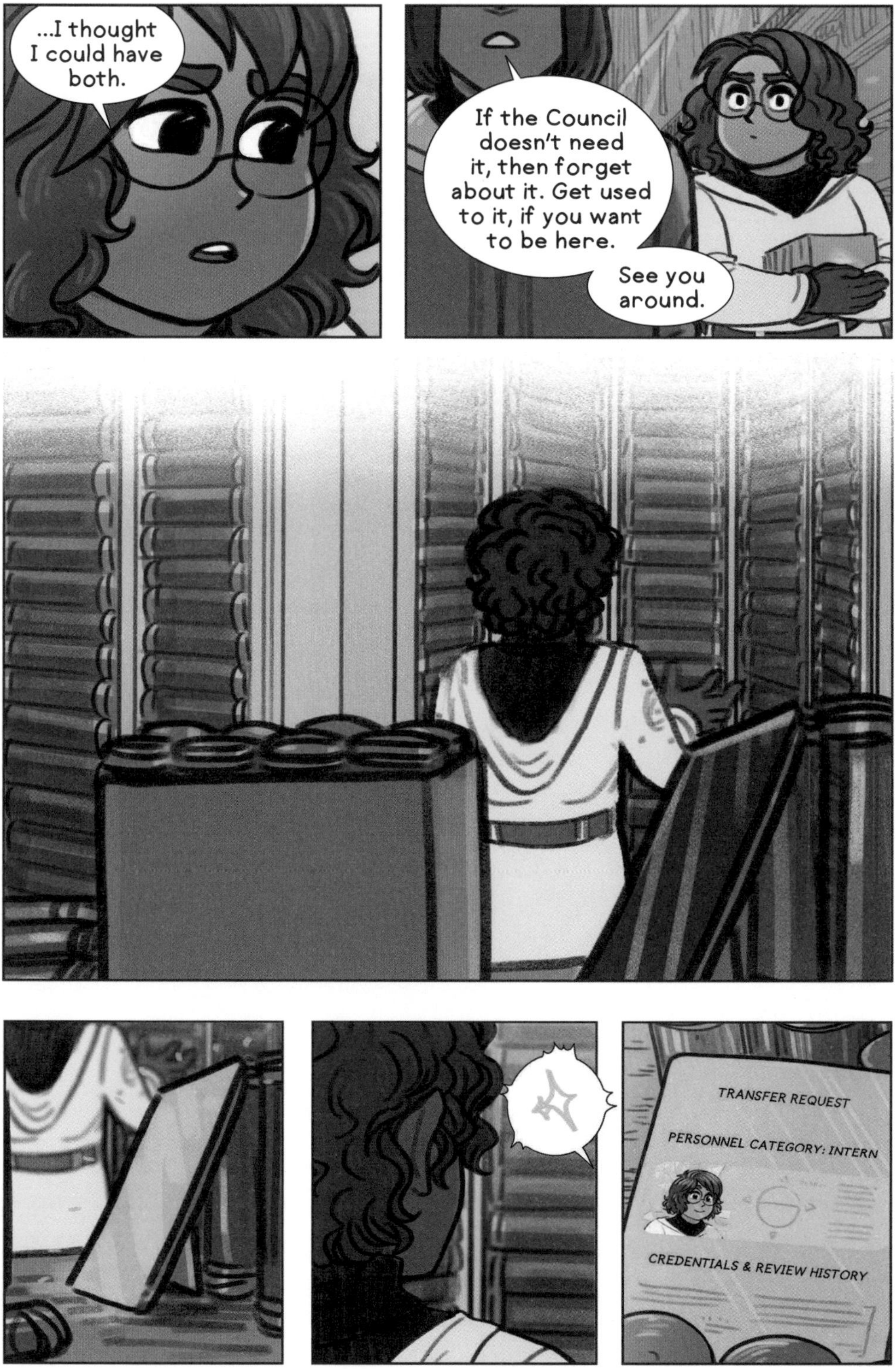

...I thought I could have both.
If the Council doesn't need it, then forget about it. Get used to it, if you want to be here.
See you around.
TRANSFER REQUEST
PERSONNEL CATEGORY: INTERN
CREDENTIALS & REVIEW HISTORY

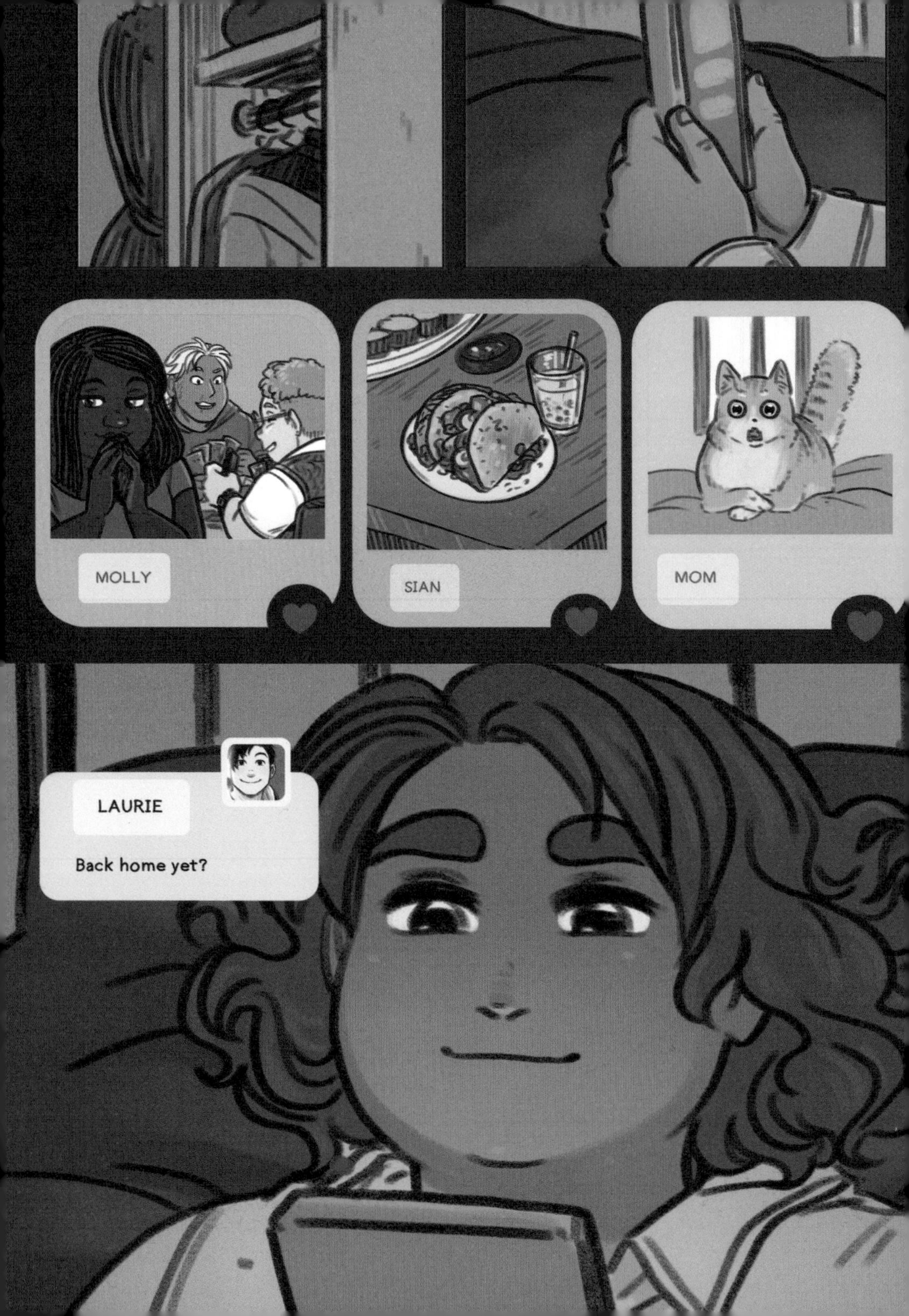
MOLLY
SIAN
MOM
LAURIE
Back home yet?

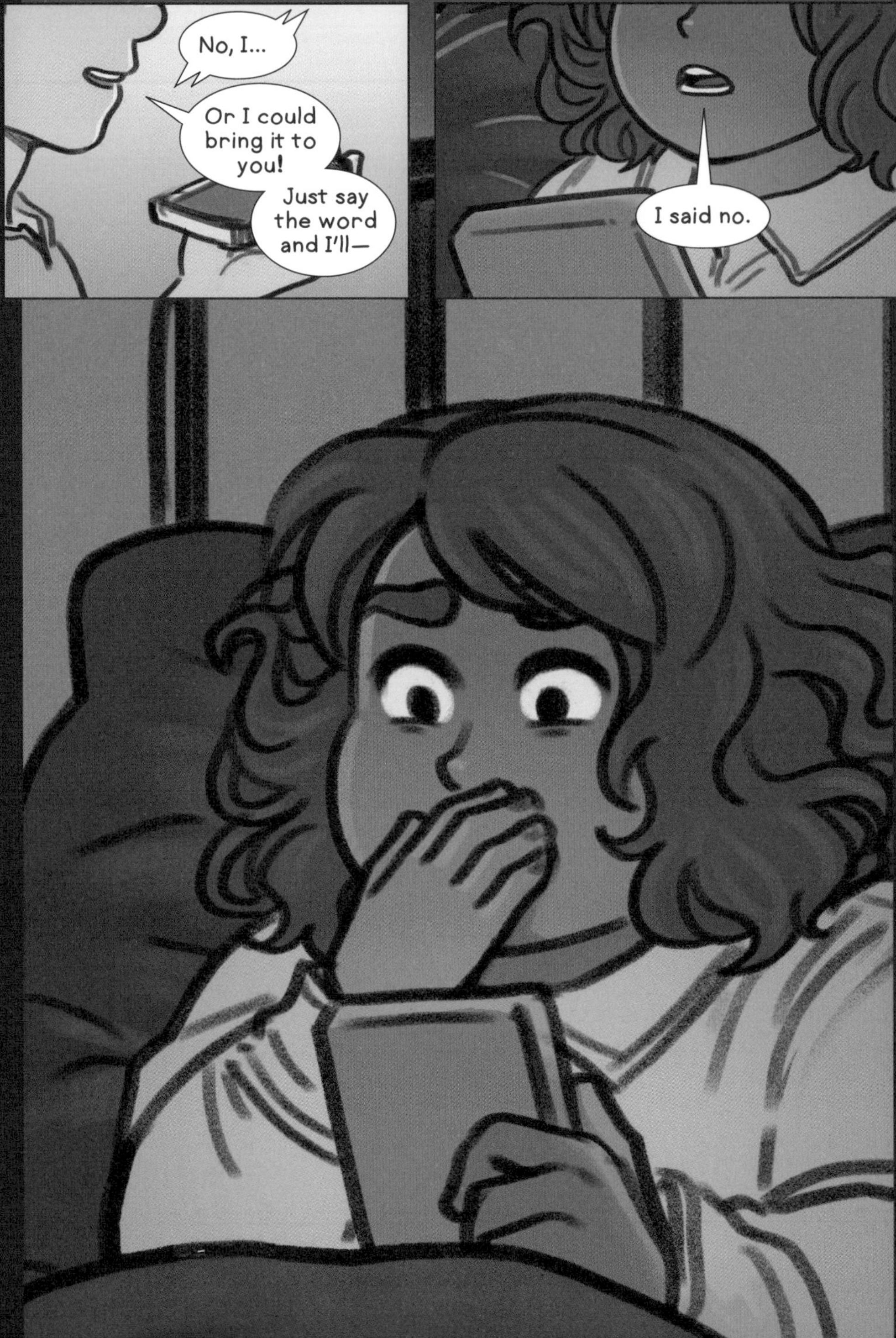
No, I...
Or I could bring it to you!
Just say the word and I'll—
I said no.

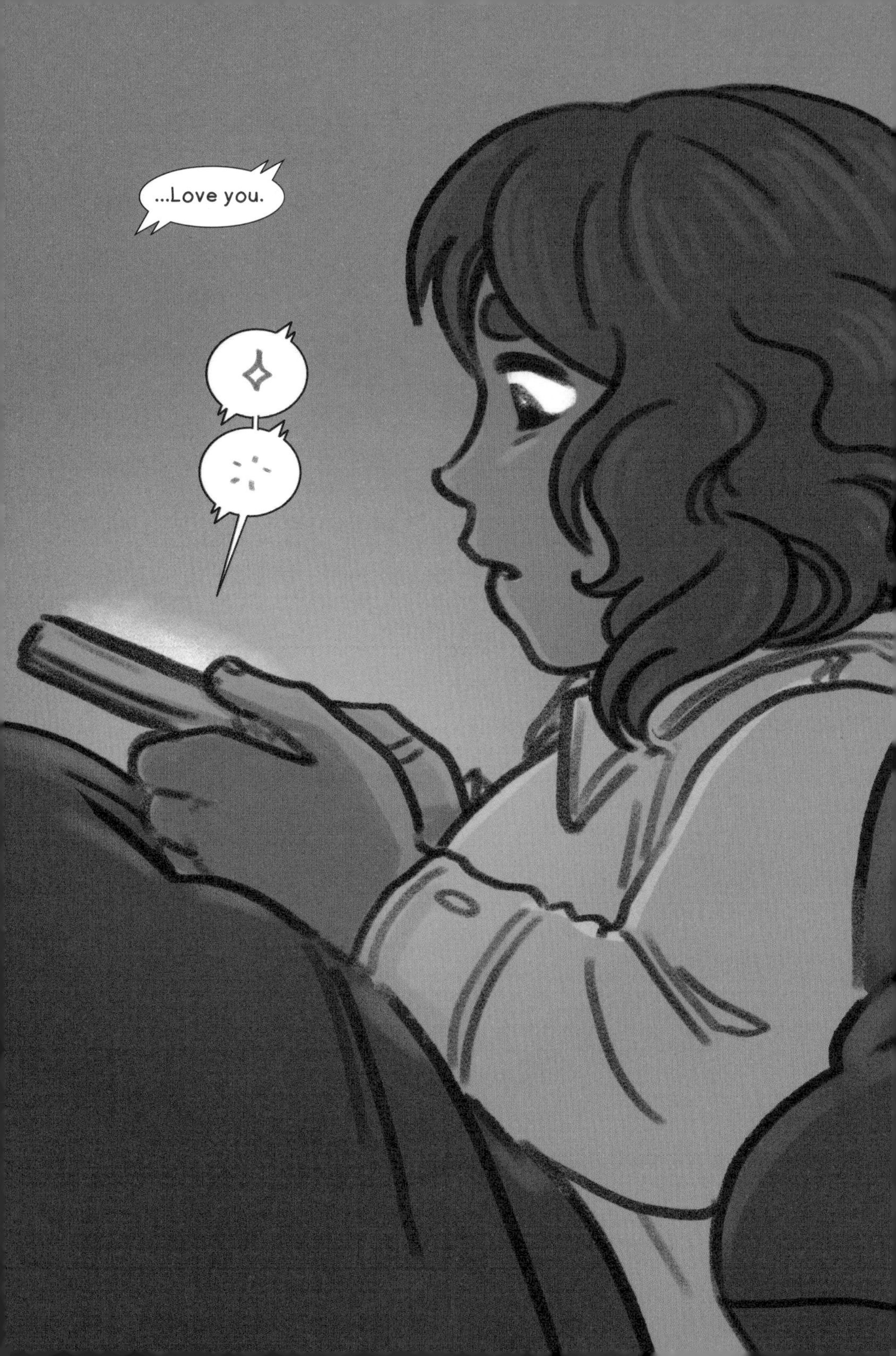
...Love you.

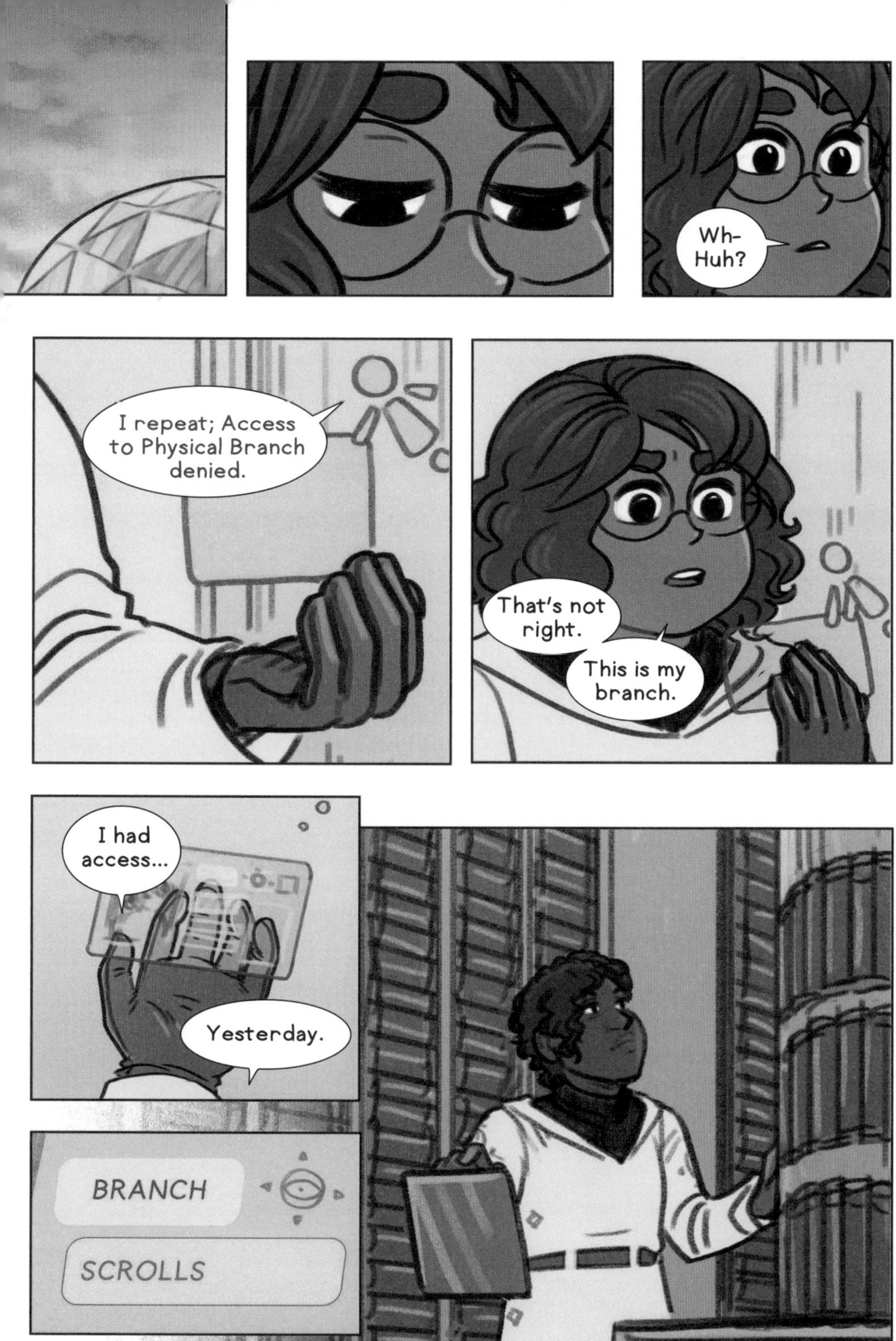
Wh-
Huh?
I repeat; Access to Physical Branch denied.
That's not right.
This is my branch.
I had access...
Yesterday.
BRANCH
SCROLLS

These are the archives. Past predictions and recordings.

Kept mainly for reference. Utterly useless if improperly catalogued.

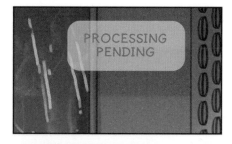

PROCESSING PENDING

This will be your project. You'll need to process all of these untagged scrolls.

It may not be exciting. But it's as essential as any prediction requests.

More, even.

...Of course.

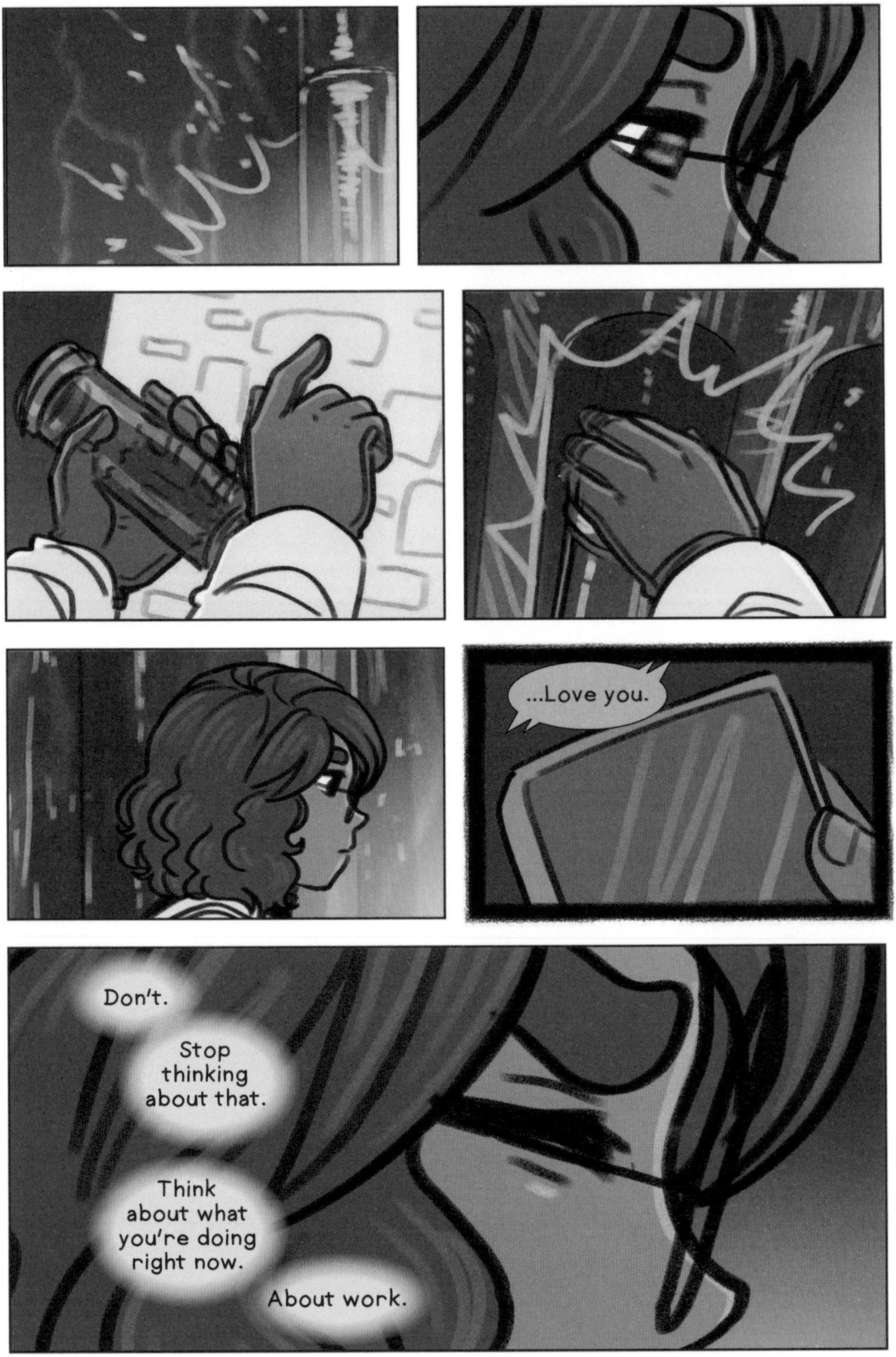
...Love you.
Don't.
Stop thinking about that.
Think about what you're doing right now.
About work.

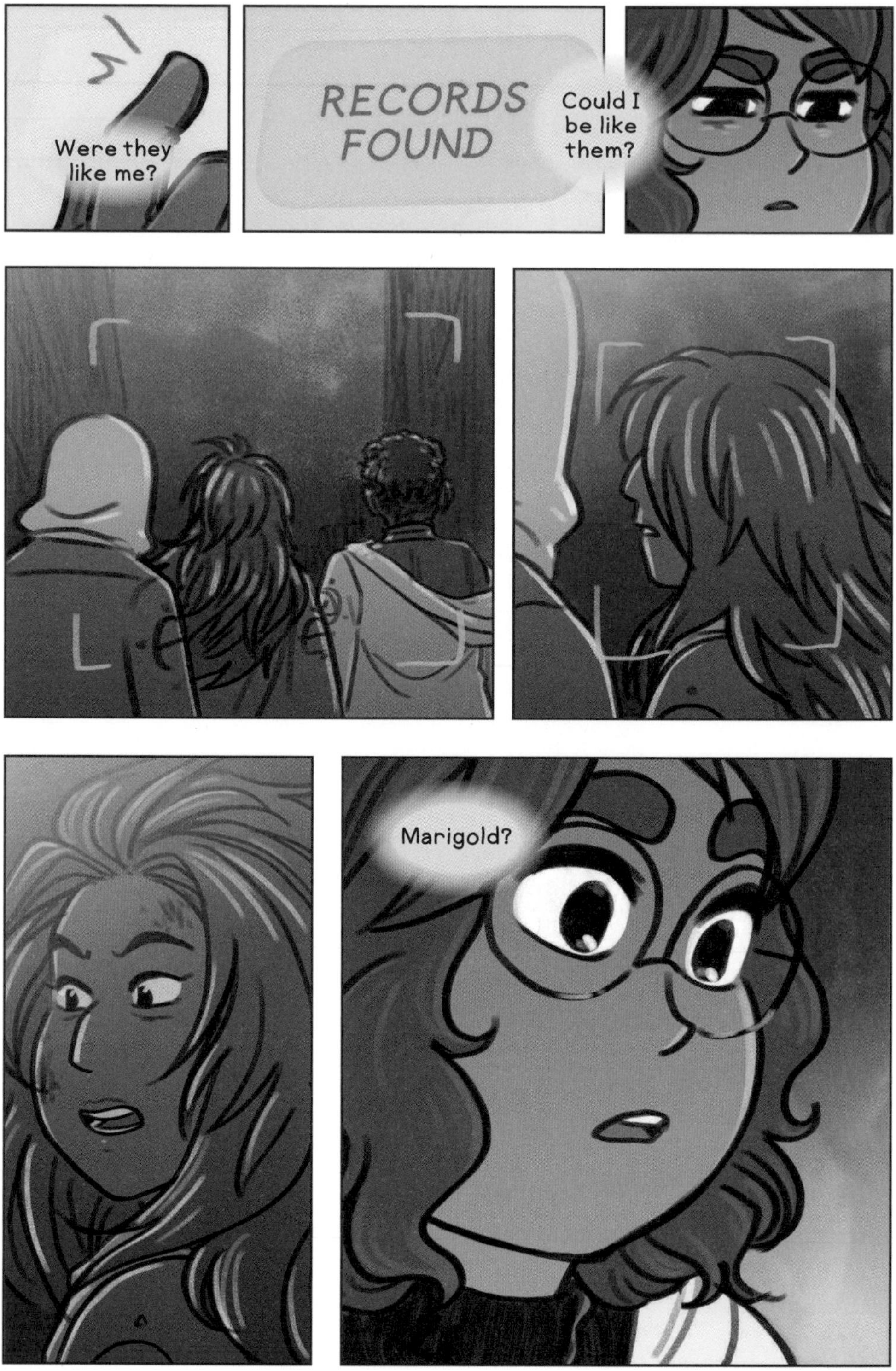

Were they like me?
RECORDS FOUND
Could I be like them?
Marigold?

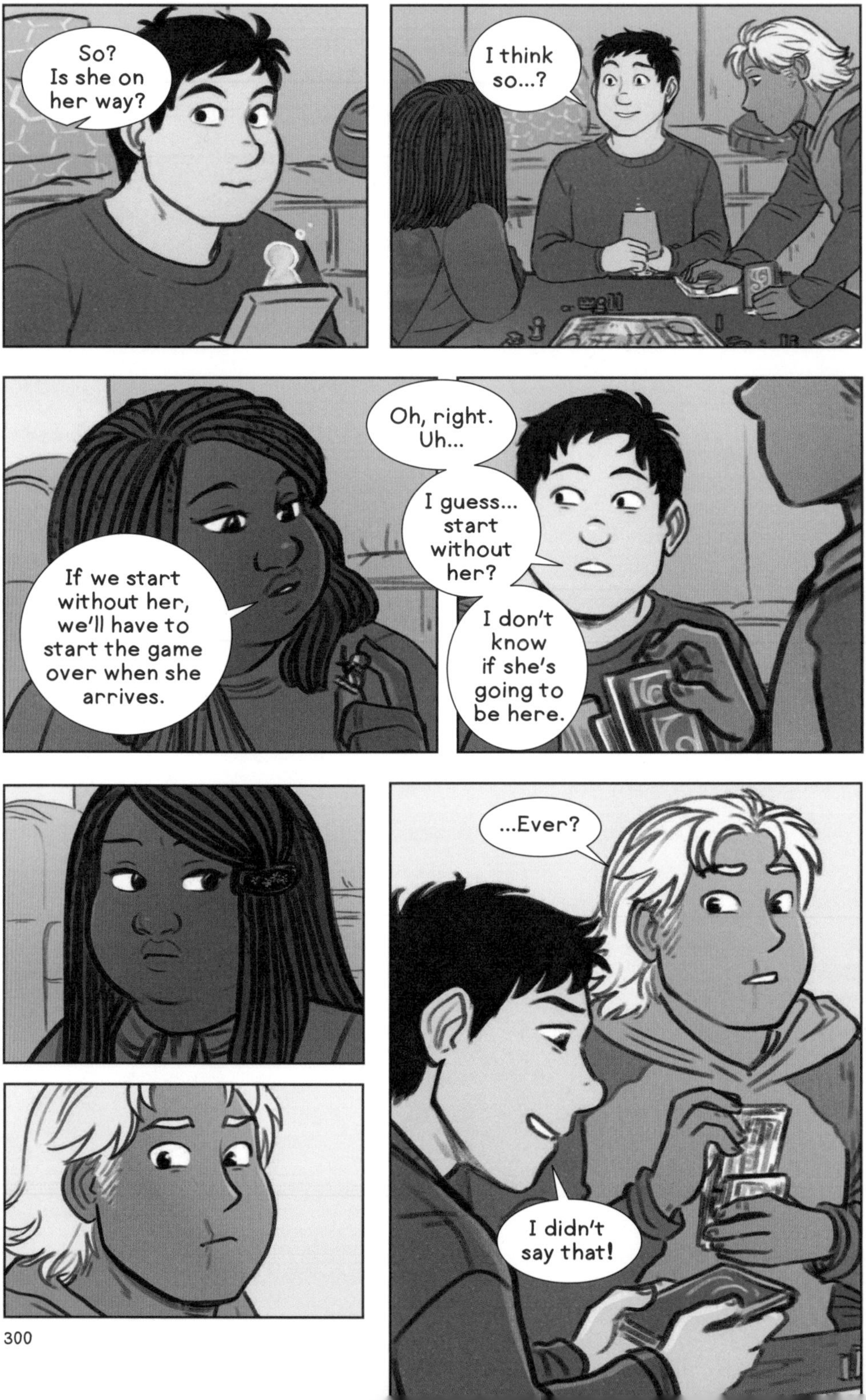
So?
Is she on her way?
I think so...?
Oh, right. Uh...
If we start without her, we'll have to start the game over when she arrives.
I guess... start without her?
I don't know if she's going to be here.
...Ever?
I didn't say that!

303

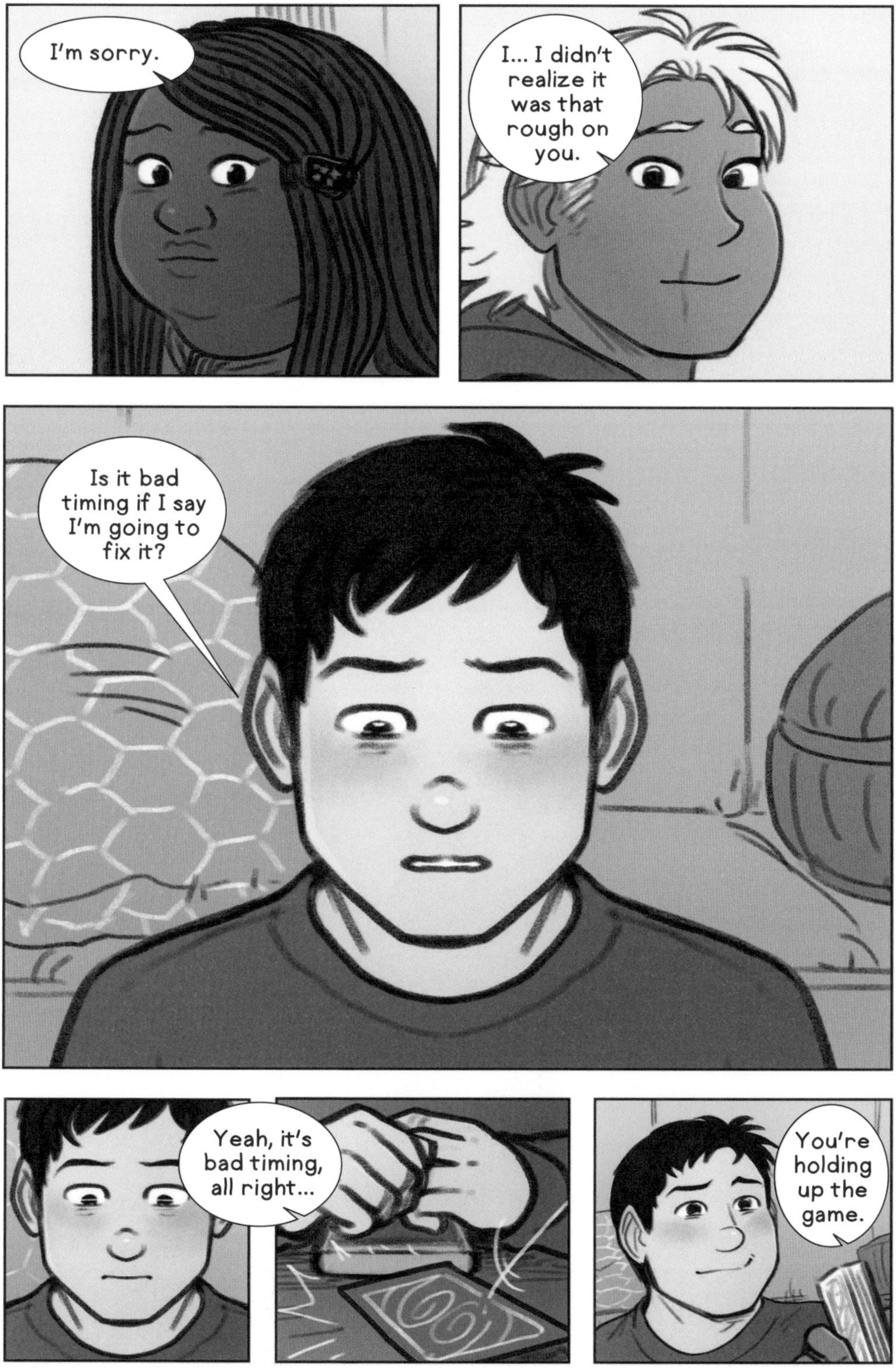
I'm sorry.
I... I didn't realize it was that rough on you.
Is it bad timing if I say I'm going to fix it?
Yeah, it's bad timing, all right...
You're holding up the game.

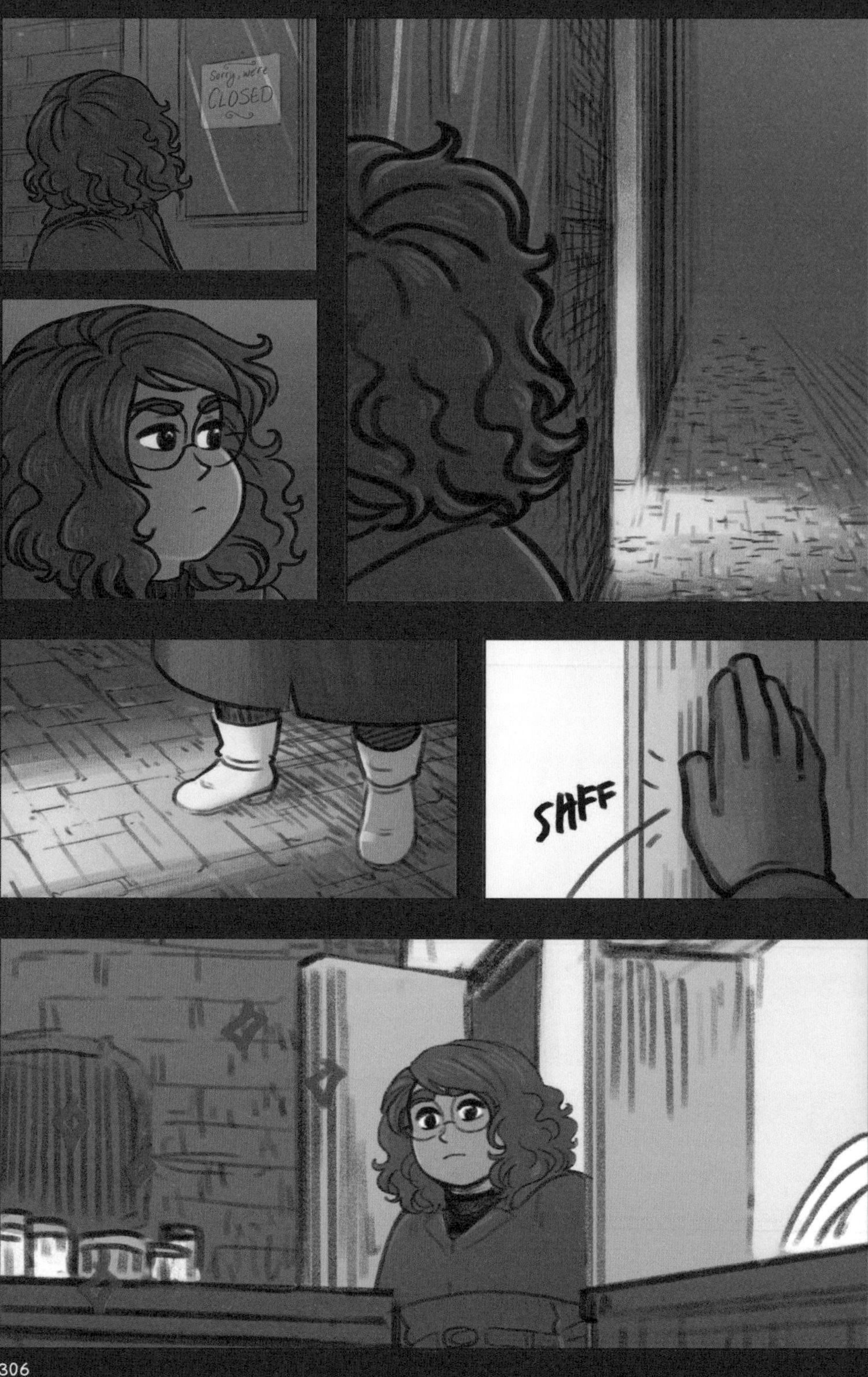
Sorry, we're
CLOSED
SHFF

Marigold?
Oh! Hi, Ray. If you're looking for Laurie, he's not here.
I'm not here to see Laurie. You used to be a Councilor, right?
Yes, but... I'm sure it's changed a bit since then. I resigned in—
You resigned in '05— after single-handedly repelling the largest recorded storm of the last century.
Is that what I did?
I suspected, but— hang on...
You shouldn't know any of that. Personnel files are classified.
I... take more memories home with me now. I got a security upgrade.

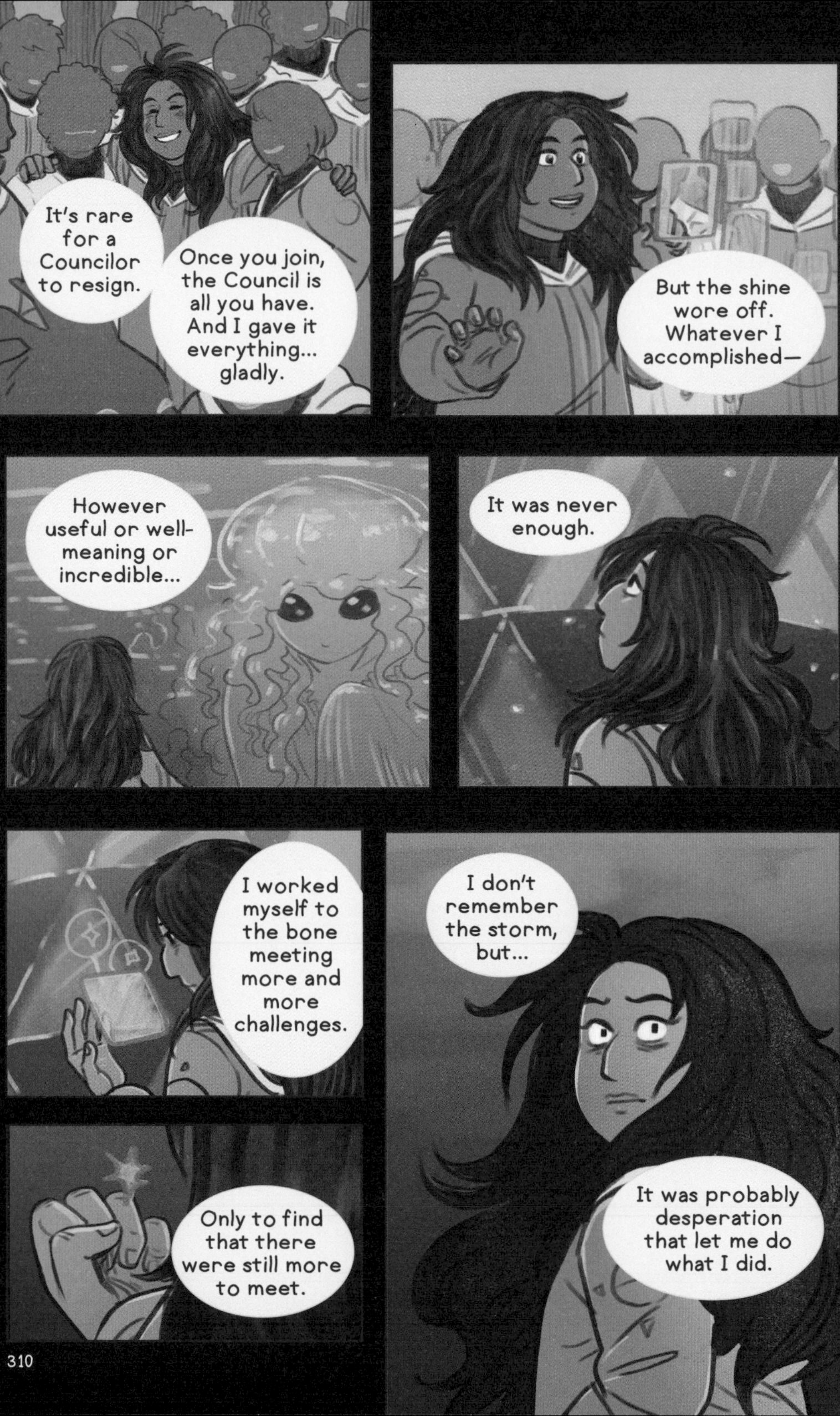
It's rare for a Councilor to resign.
Once you join, the Council is all you have. And I gave it everything... gladly.
But the shine wore off. Whatever I accomplished—
However useful or well-meaning or incredible...
It was never enough.
I worked myself to the bone meeting more and more challenges.
Only to find that there were still more to meet.
I don't remember the storm, but...
It was probably desperation that let me do what I did.

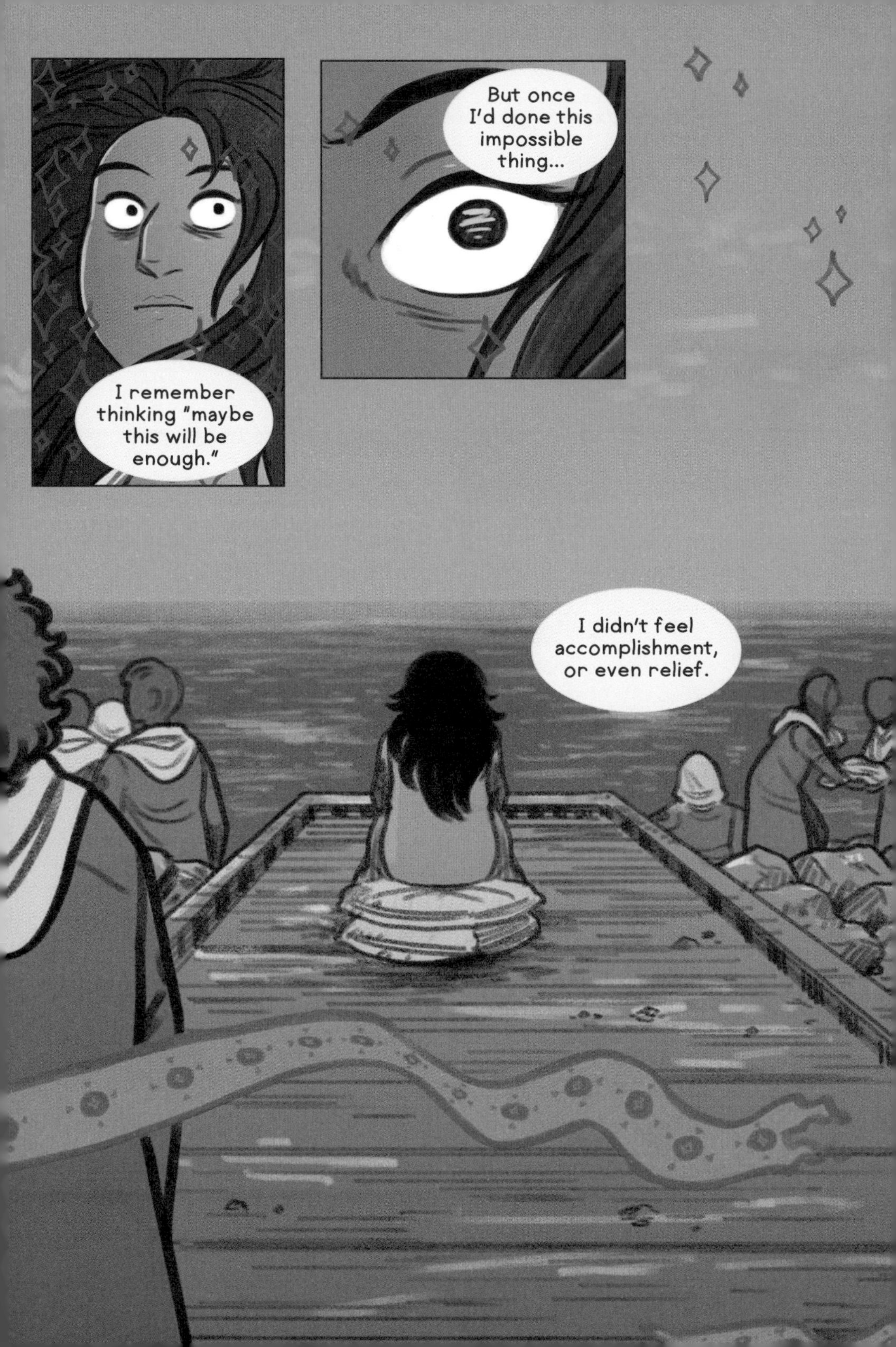
I remember thinking "maybe this will be enough."
But once I'd done this impossible thing...
I didn't feel accomplishment, or even relief.

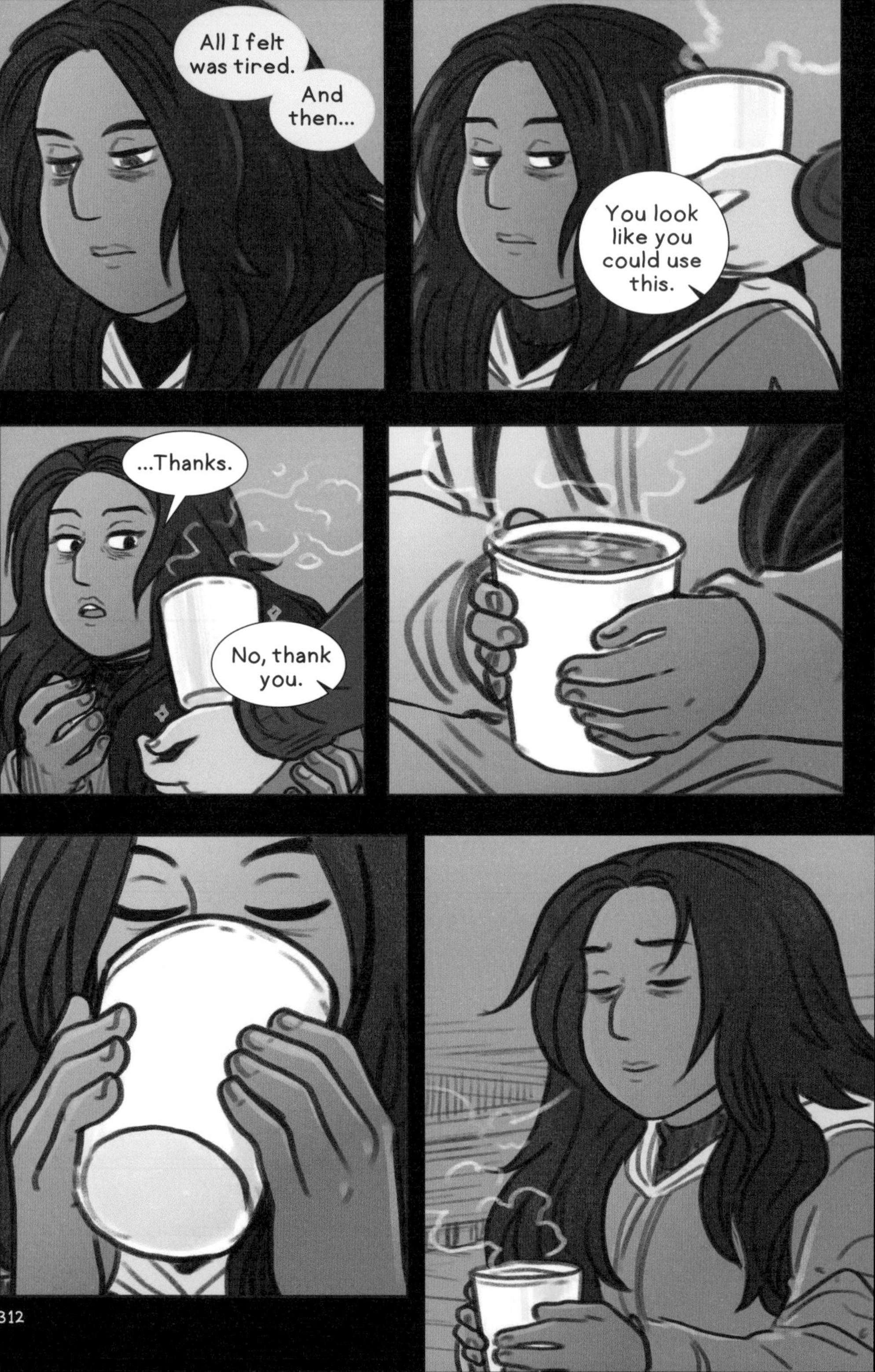
All I felt was tired.
And then...
You look like you could use this.
...Thanks.
No, thank you.

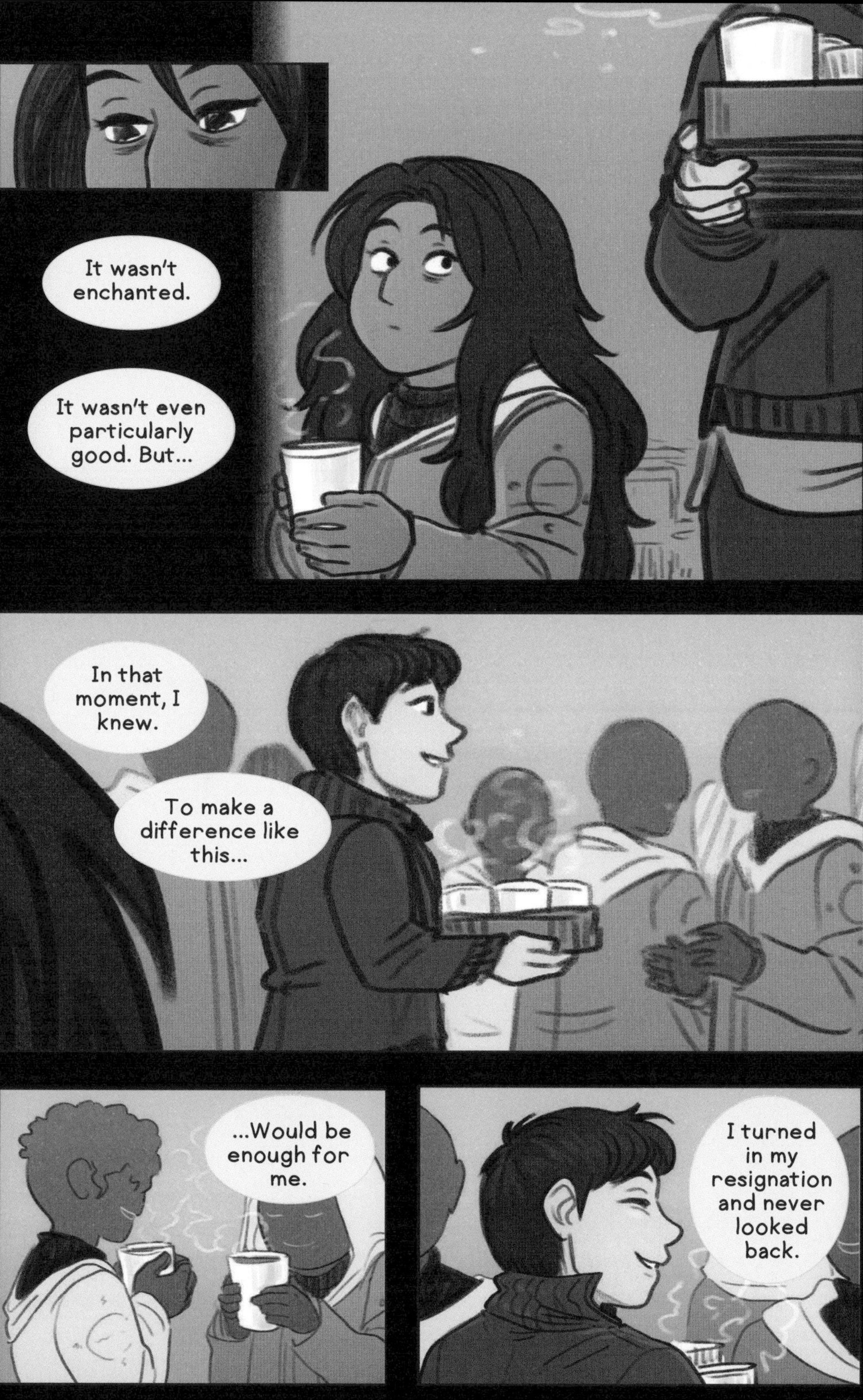
It wasn't enchanted.
It wasn't even particularly good. But...
In that moment, I knew.
To make a difference like this...
...Would be enough for me.
I turned in my resignation and never looked back.

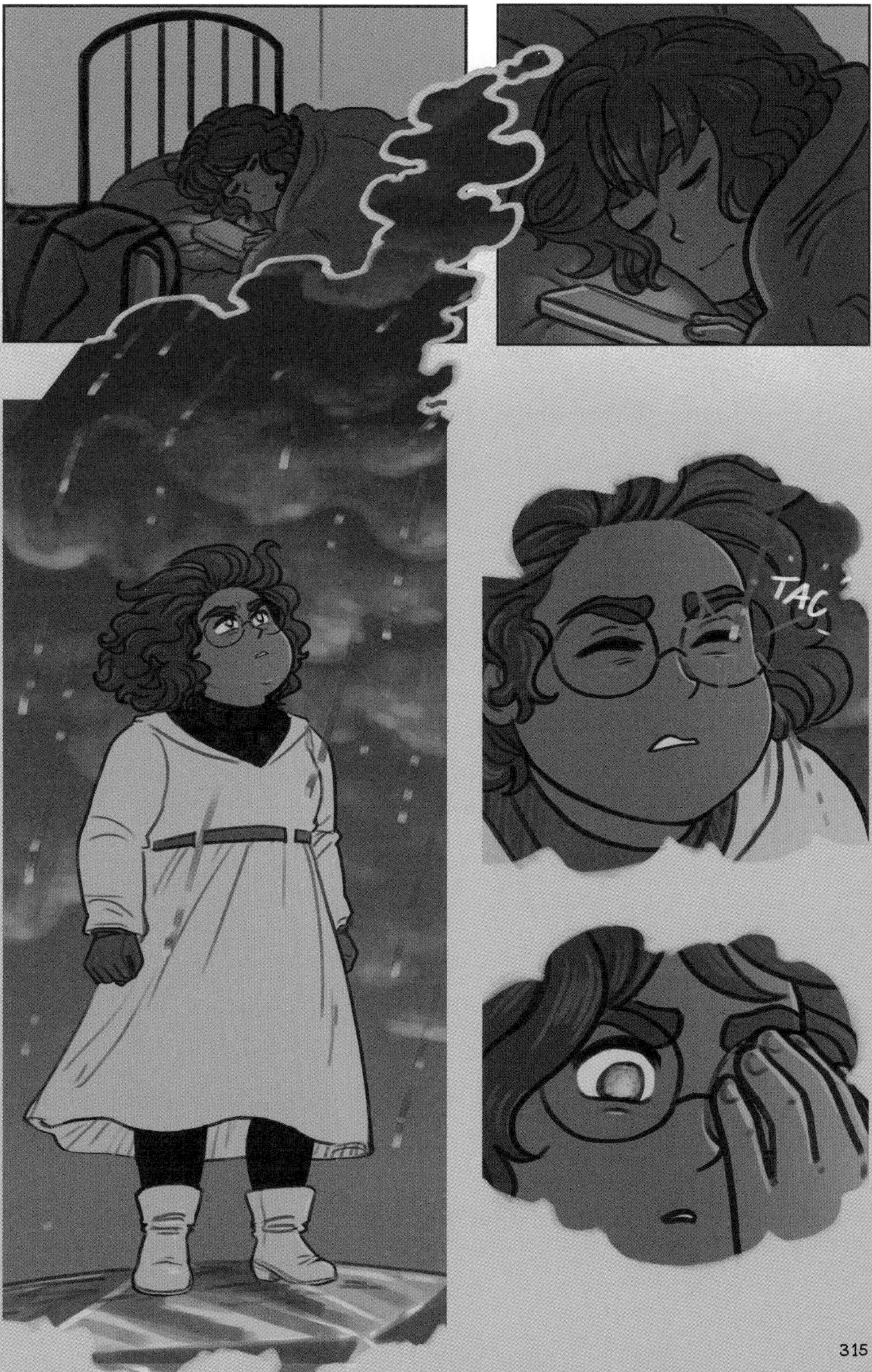
TAC

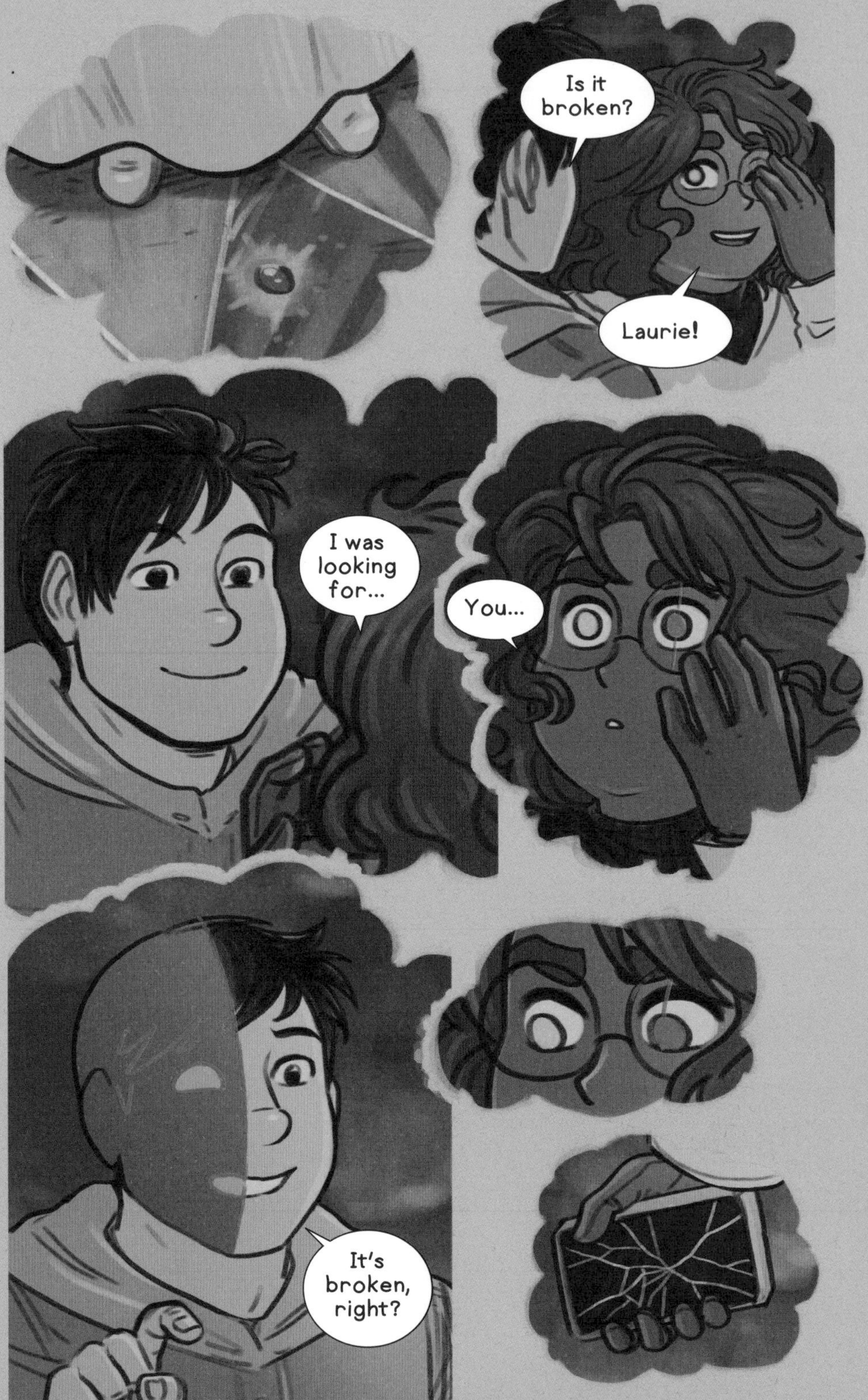
Is it broken?
Laurie!
I was looking for...
You...
It's broken, right?

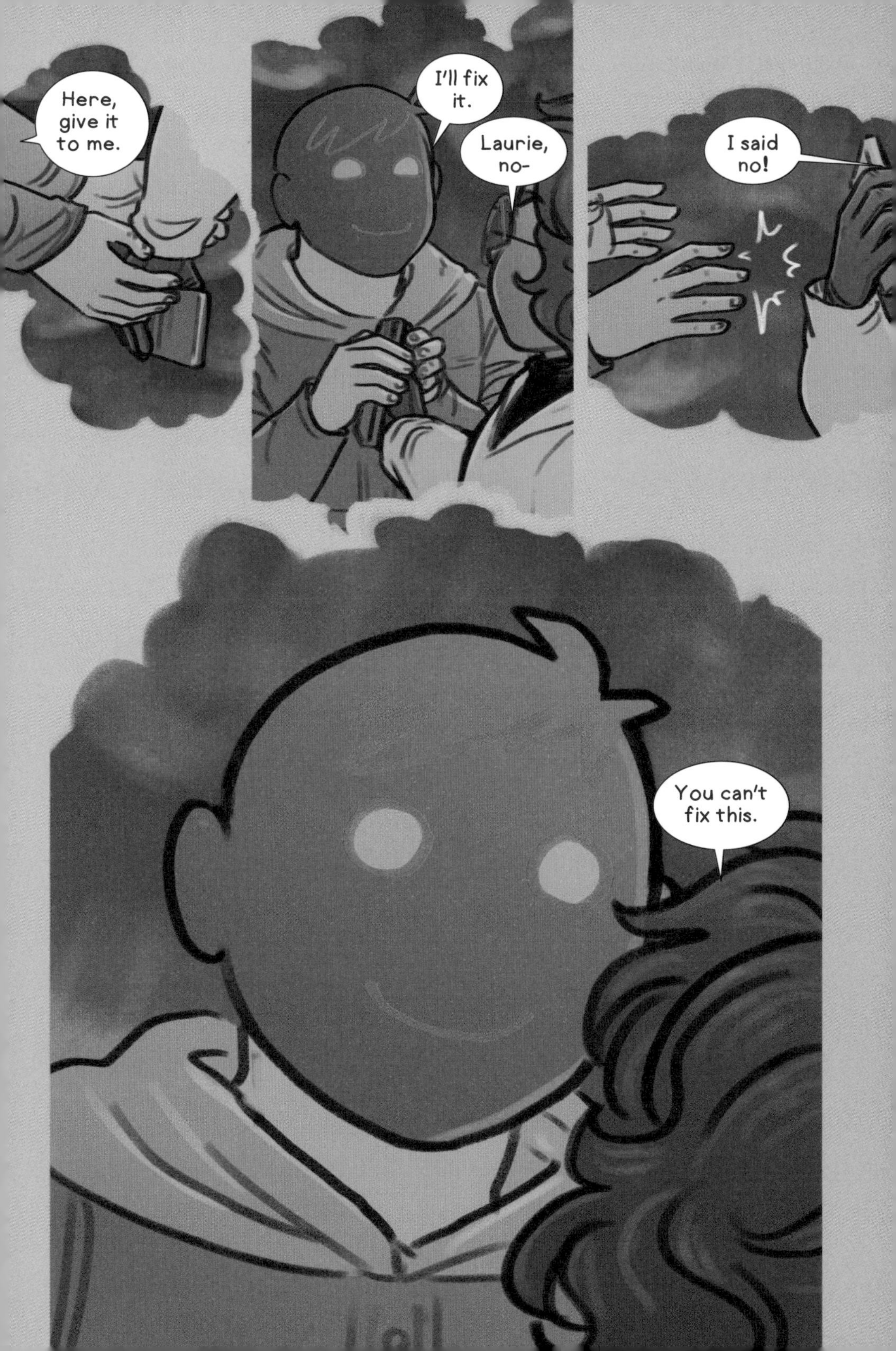
Here, give it to me.
I'll fix it.
Laurie, no-
I said no!
You can't fix this.

I miss him.
I miss the way we used to be.
Or...what I thought we used to be.
I thought there might be a future for us.
If I was wrong about what we used to have... I could be wrong about not having a future together, too, couldn't I?
But even if I am...what do I do?
I can't just hand it all over to Laurie and hope for the best this time.

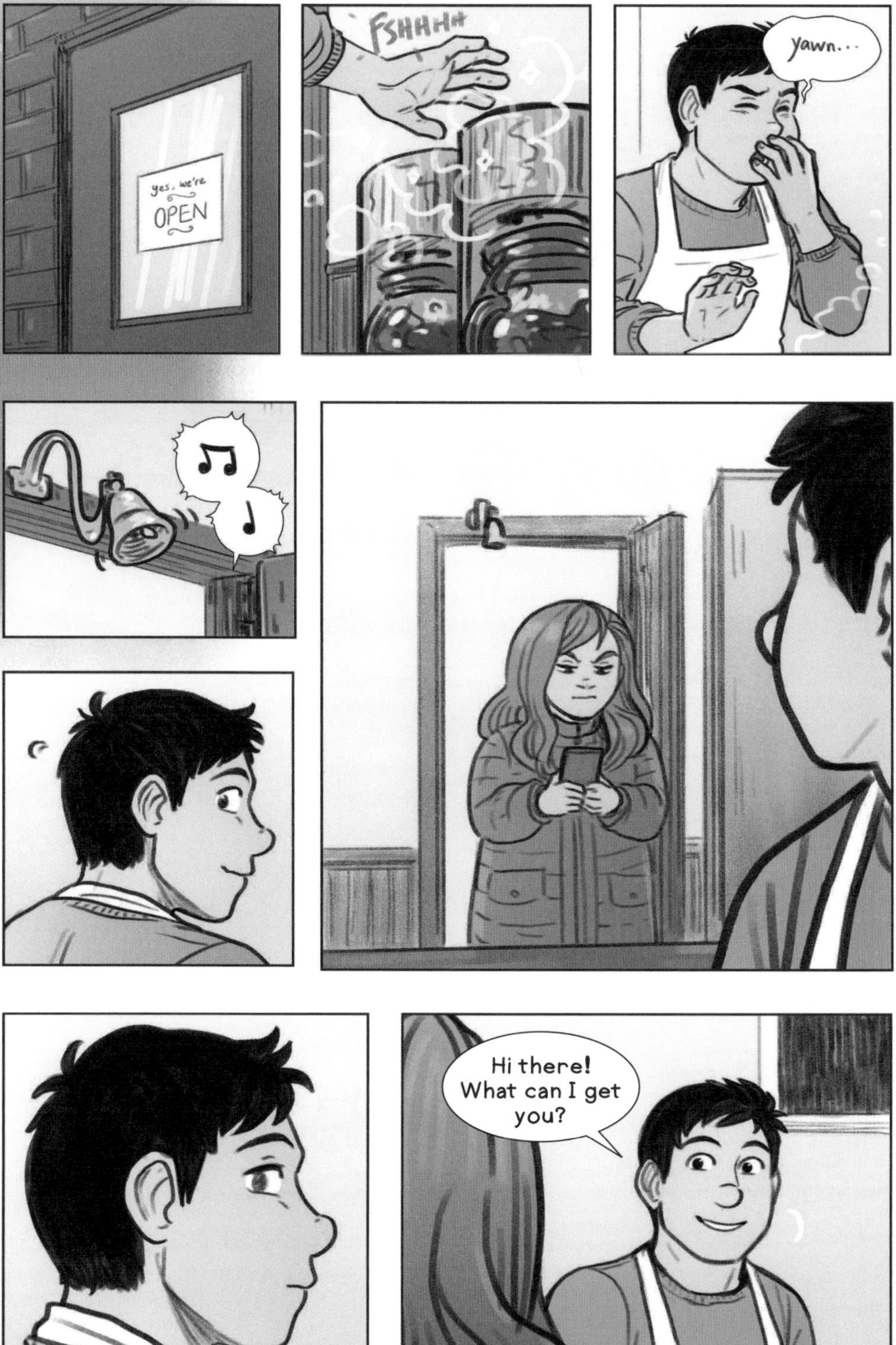
yes, we're
OPEN
FSHHHH
yawn...
Hi there!
What can I get you?

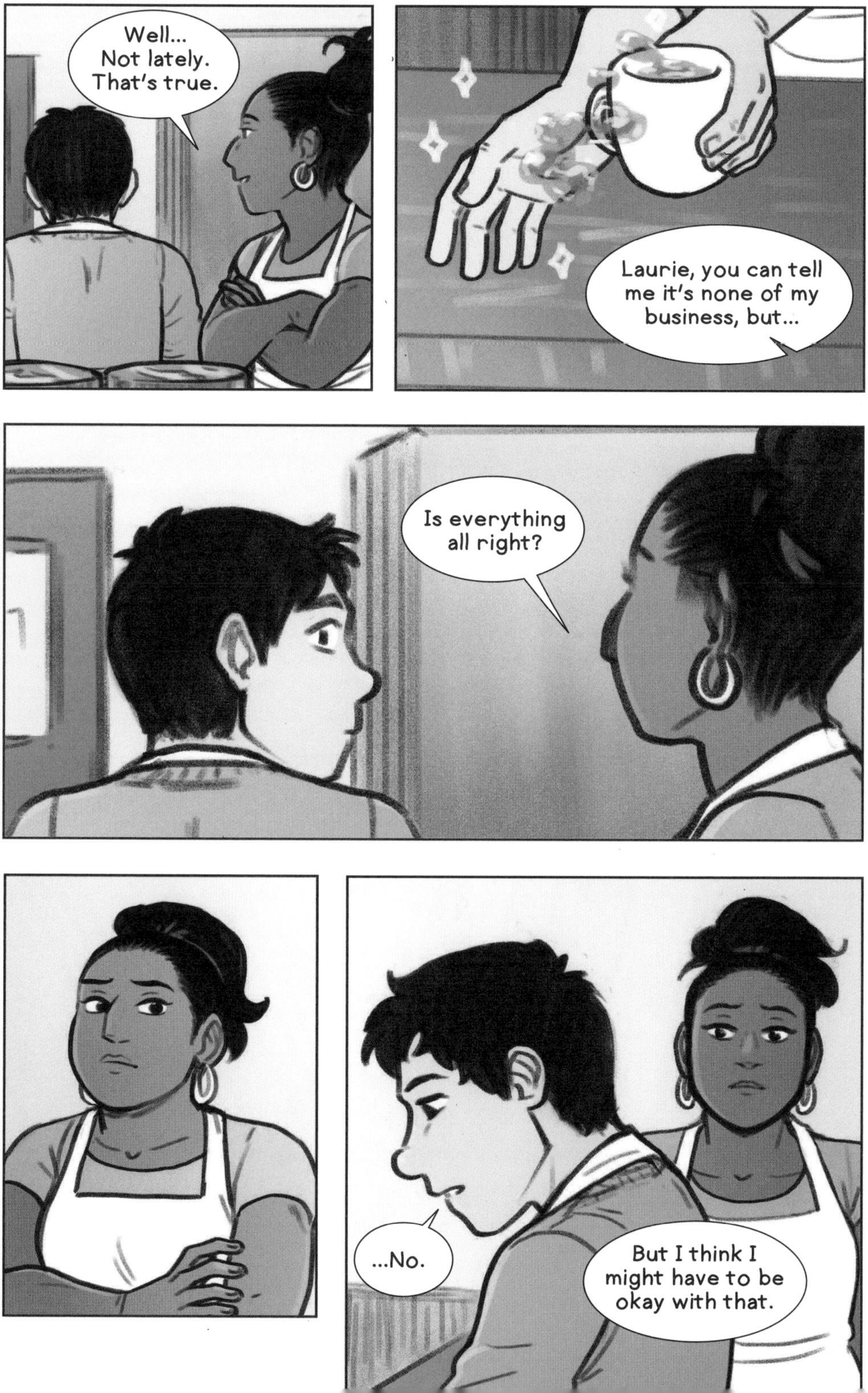
Well... Not lately. That's true.
Laurie, you can tell me it's none of my business, but...
Is everything all right?
...No.
But I think I might have to be okay with that.

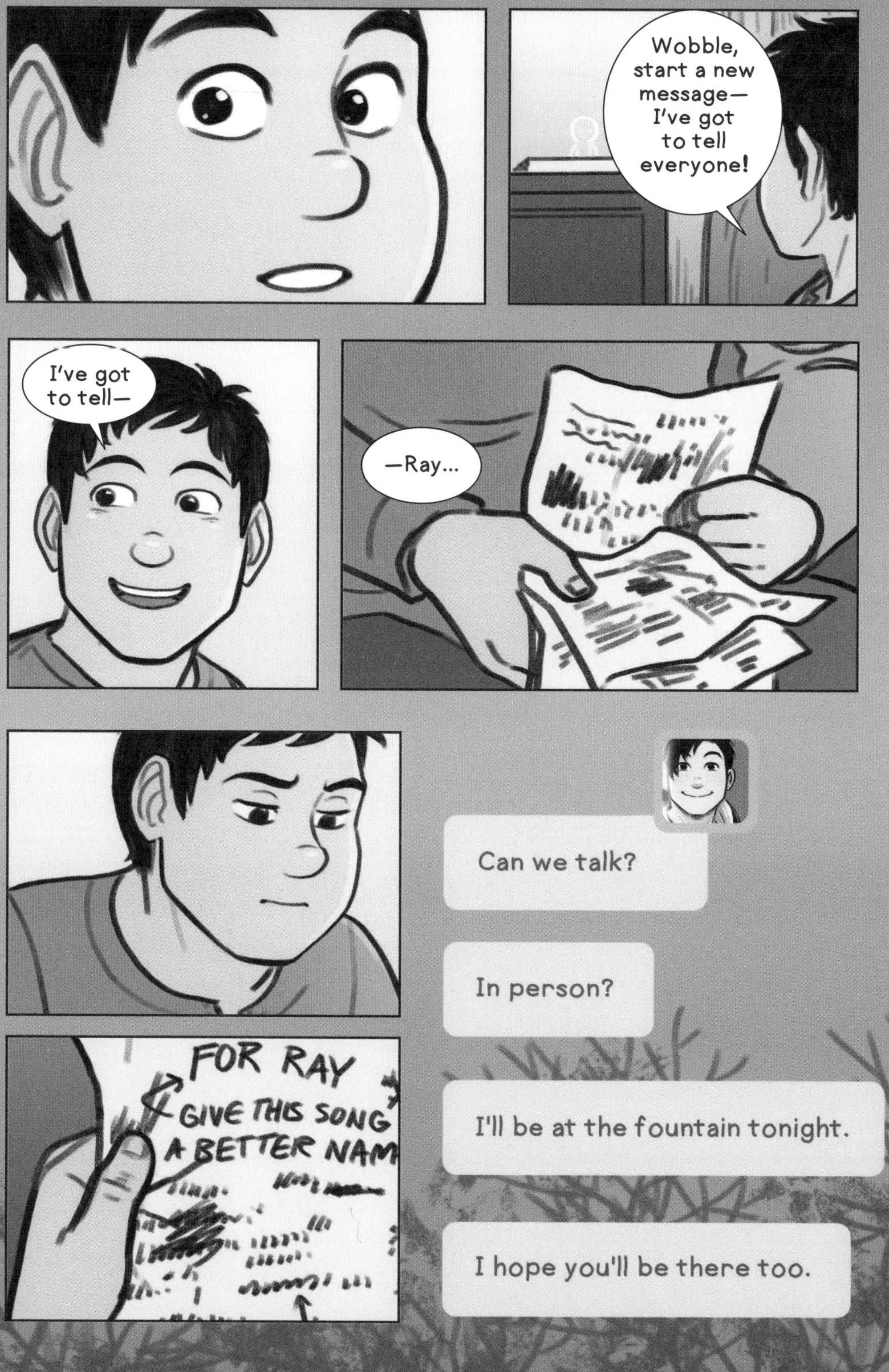
Wobble, start a new message— I've got to tell everyone!
I've got to tell—
—Ray...
Can we talk?
In person?
FOR RAY
GIVE THIS SONG A BETTER NAM
I'll be at the fountain tonight.
I hope you'll be there too.

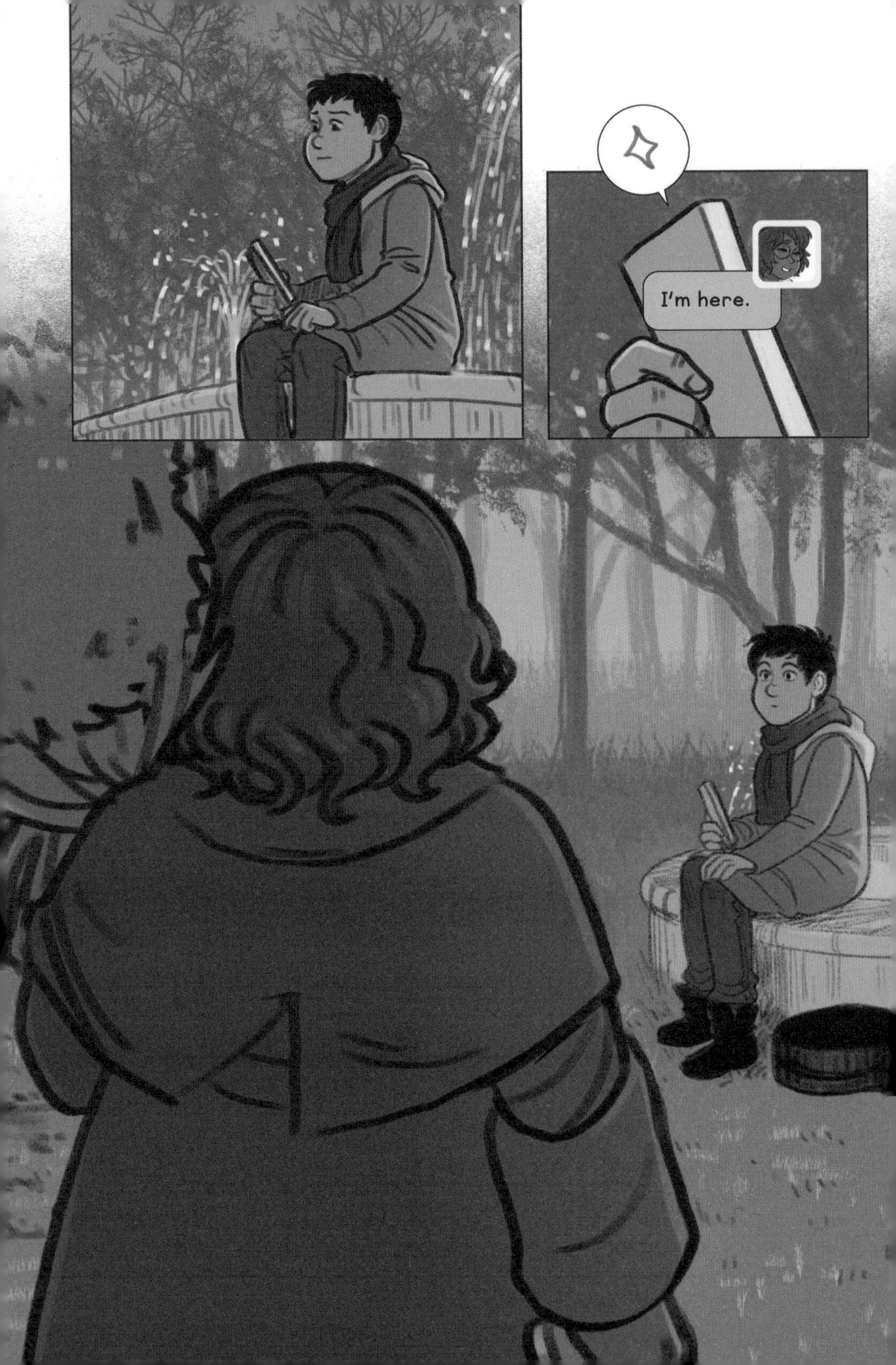
I'm here.

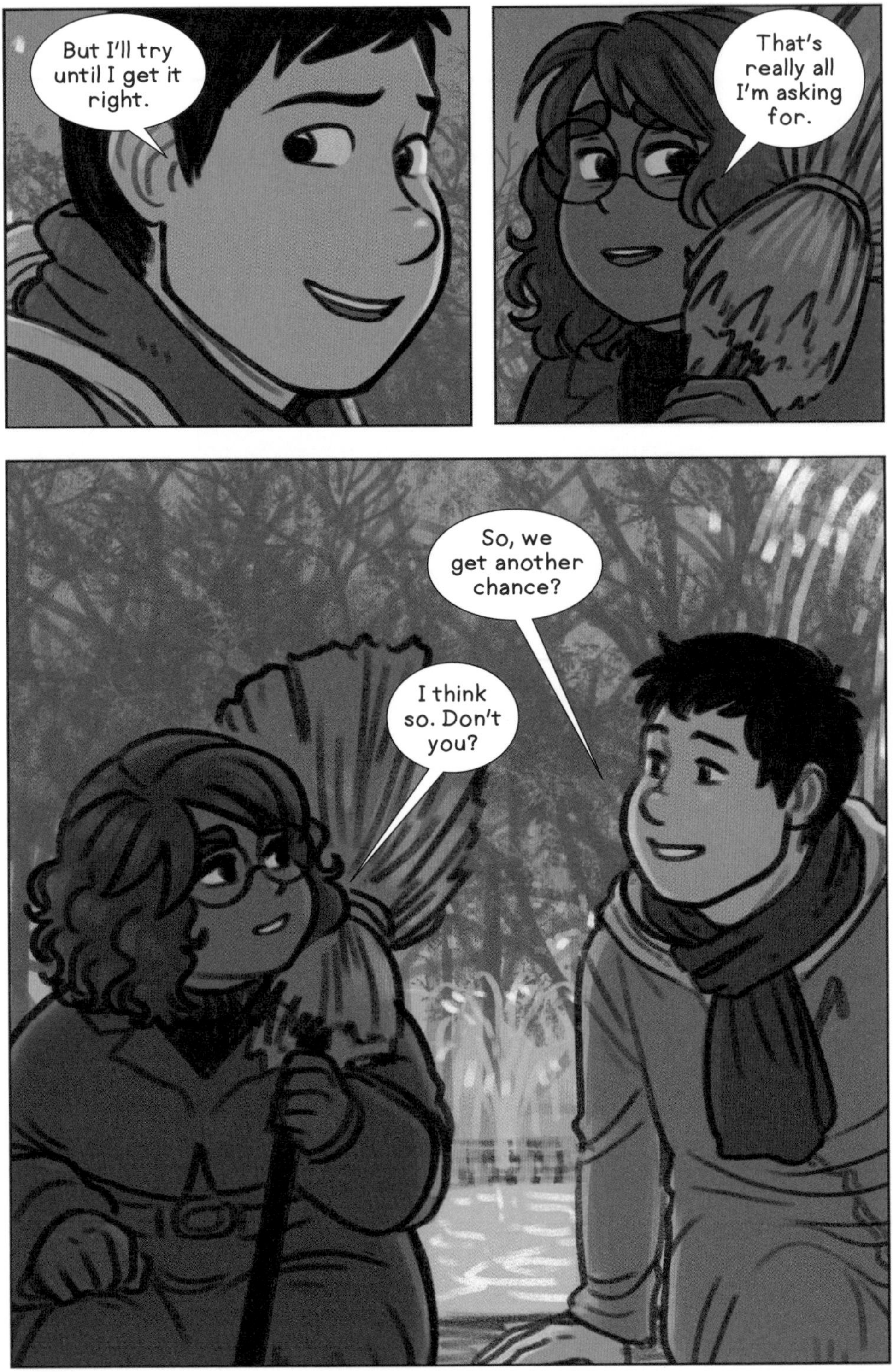
But I'll try until I get it right.
That's really all I'm asking for.
So, we get another chance?
I think so. Don't you?

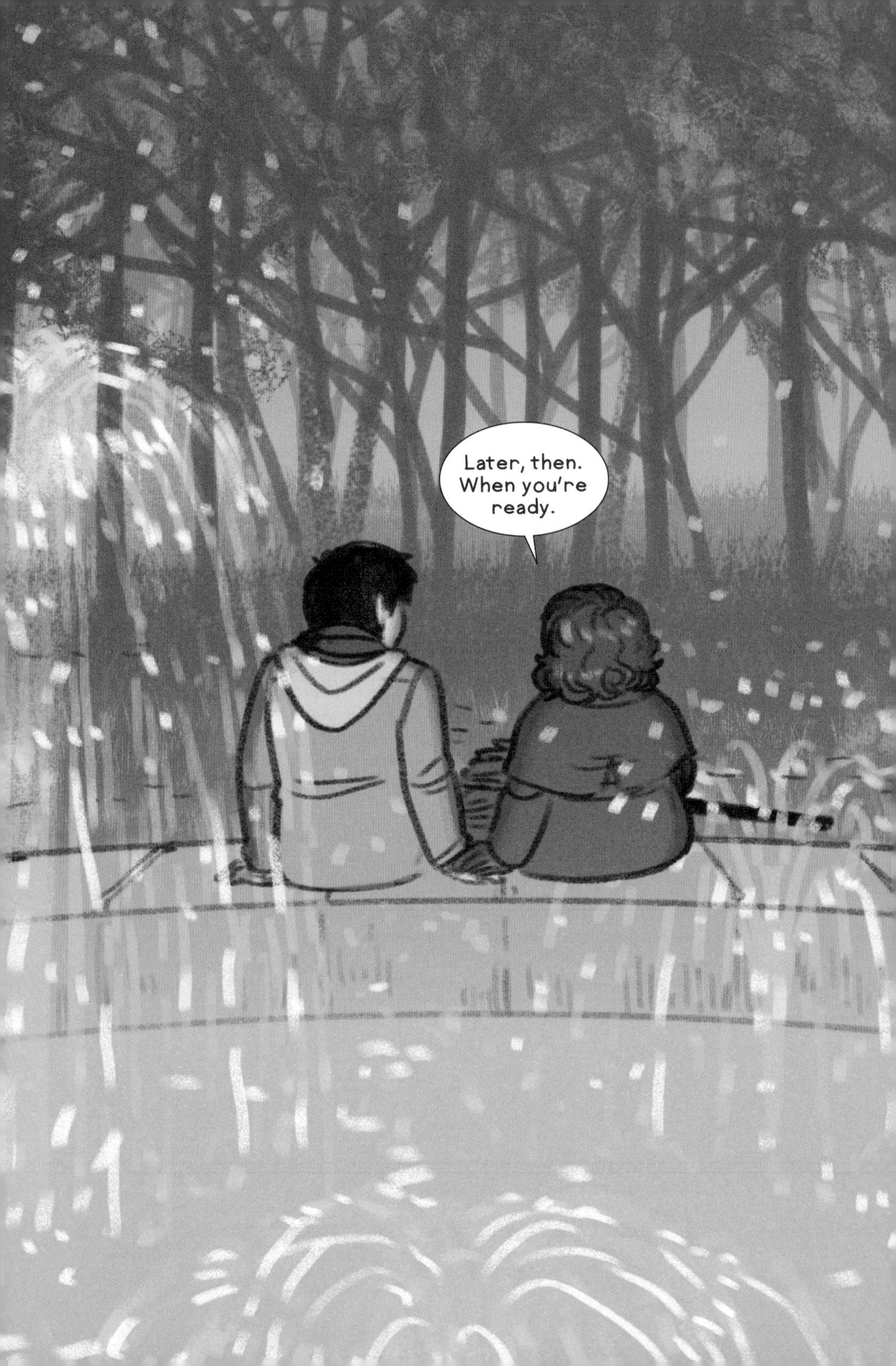
Later, then. When you're ready.

CHAPTER 13

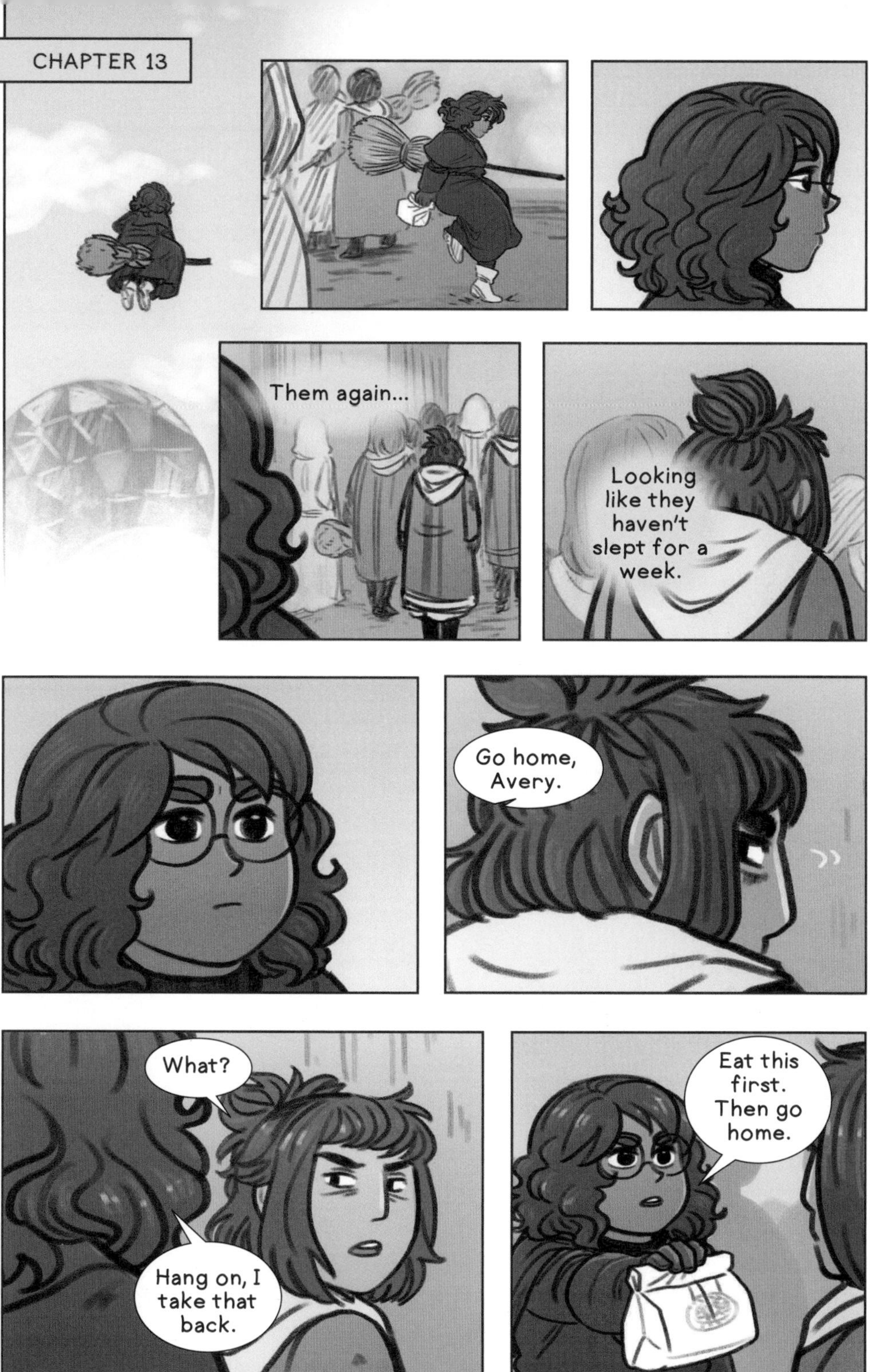
Them again...
Looking like they haven't slept for a week.
Go home, Avery.
What?
Hang on, I take that back.
Eat this first. Then go home.

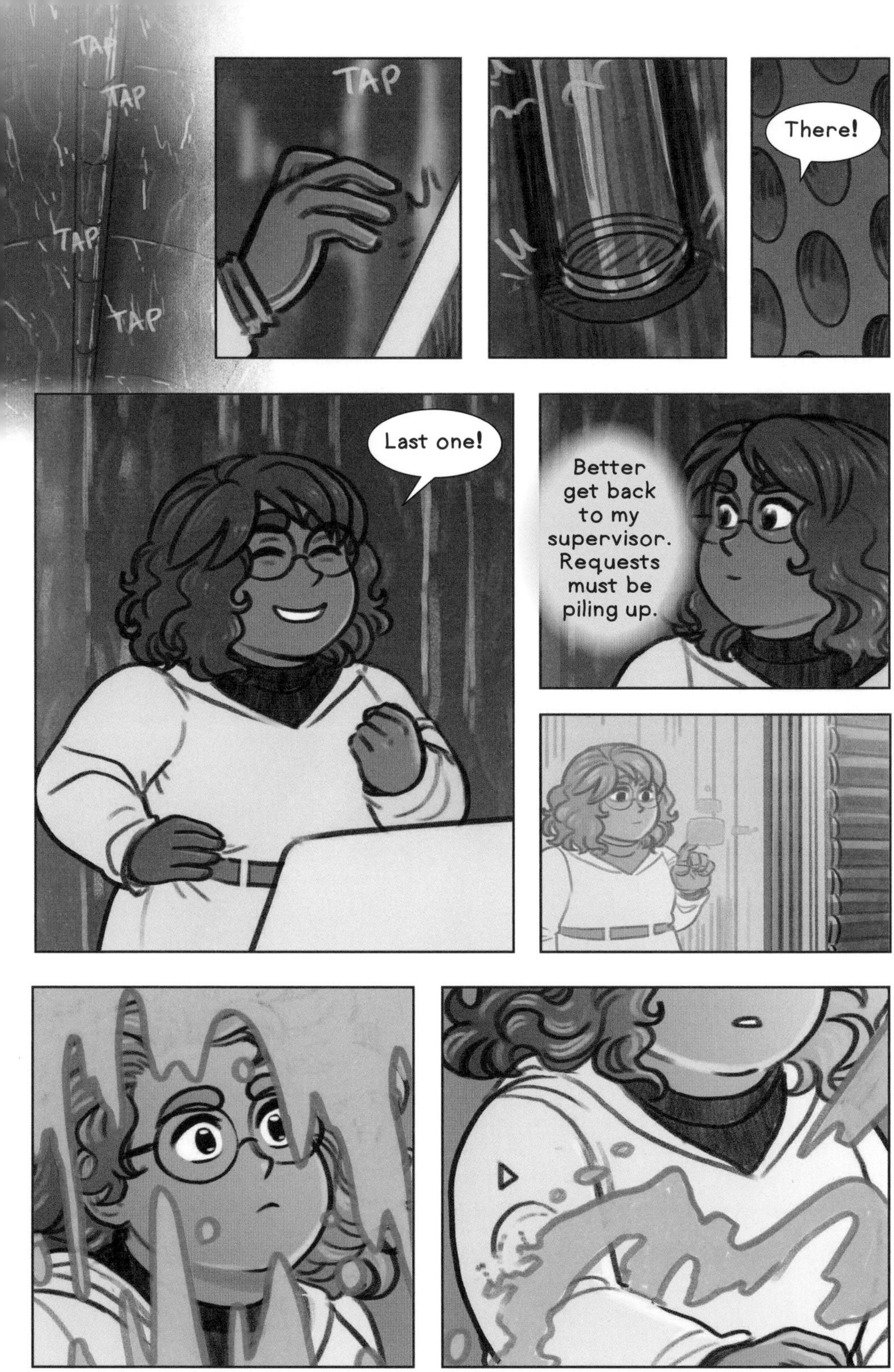
TAP
TAP
TAP
TAP
TAP
There!
Last one!
Better get back to my supervisor. Requests must be piling up.

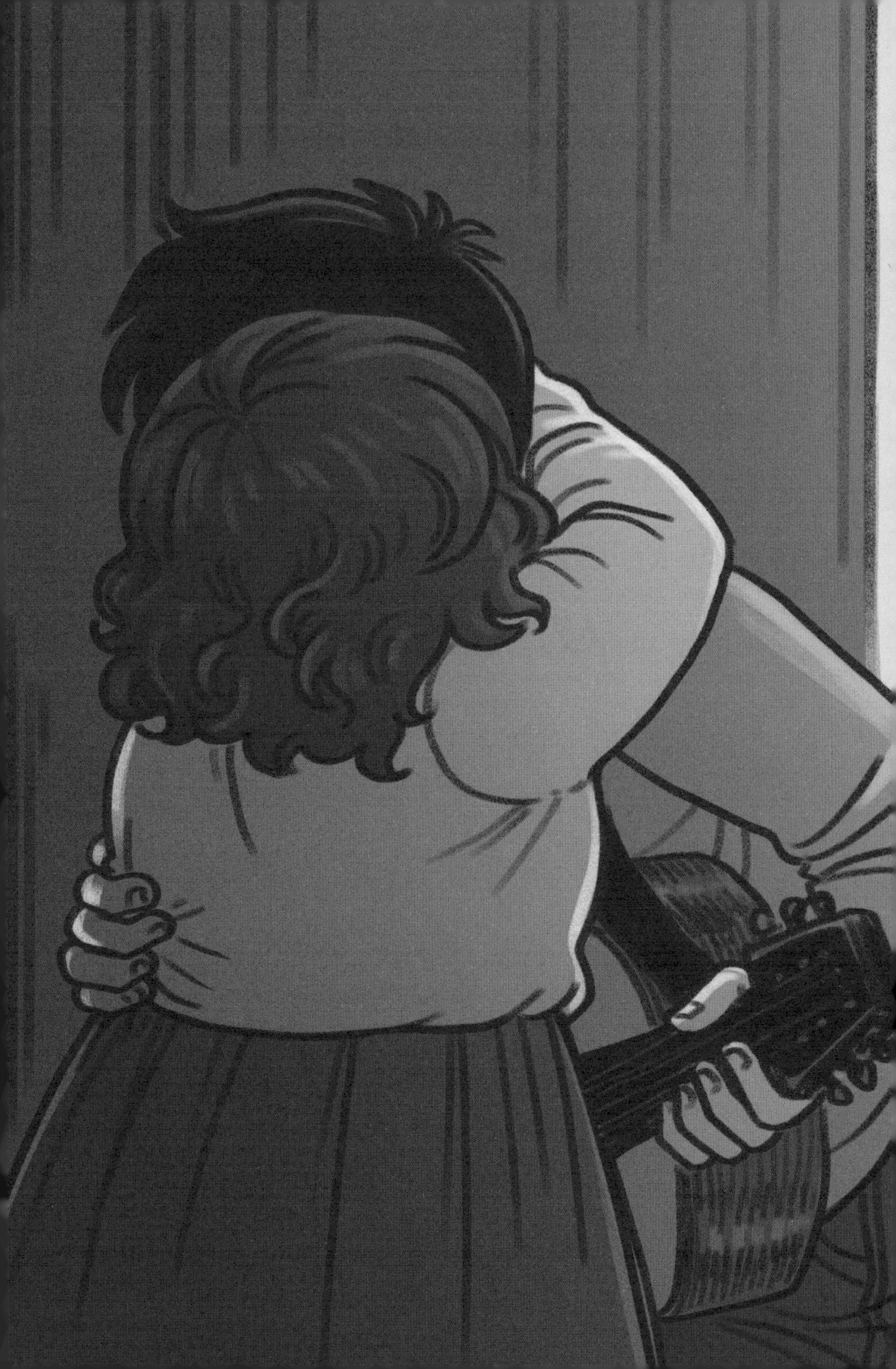

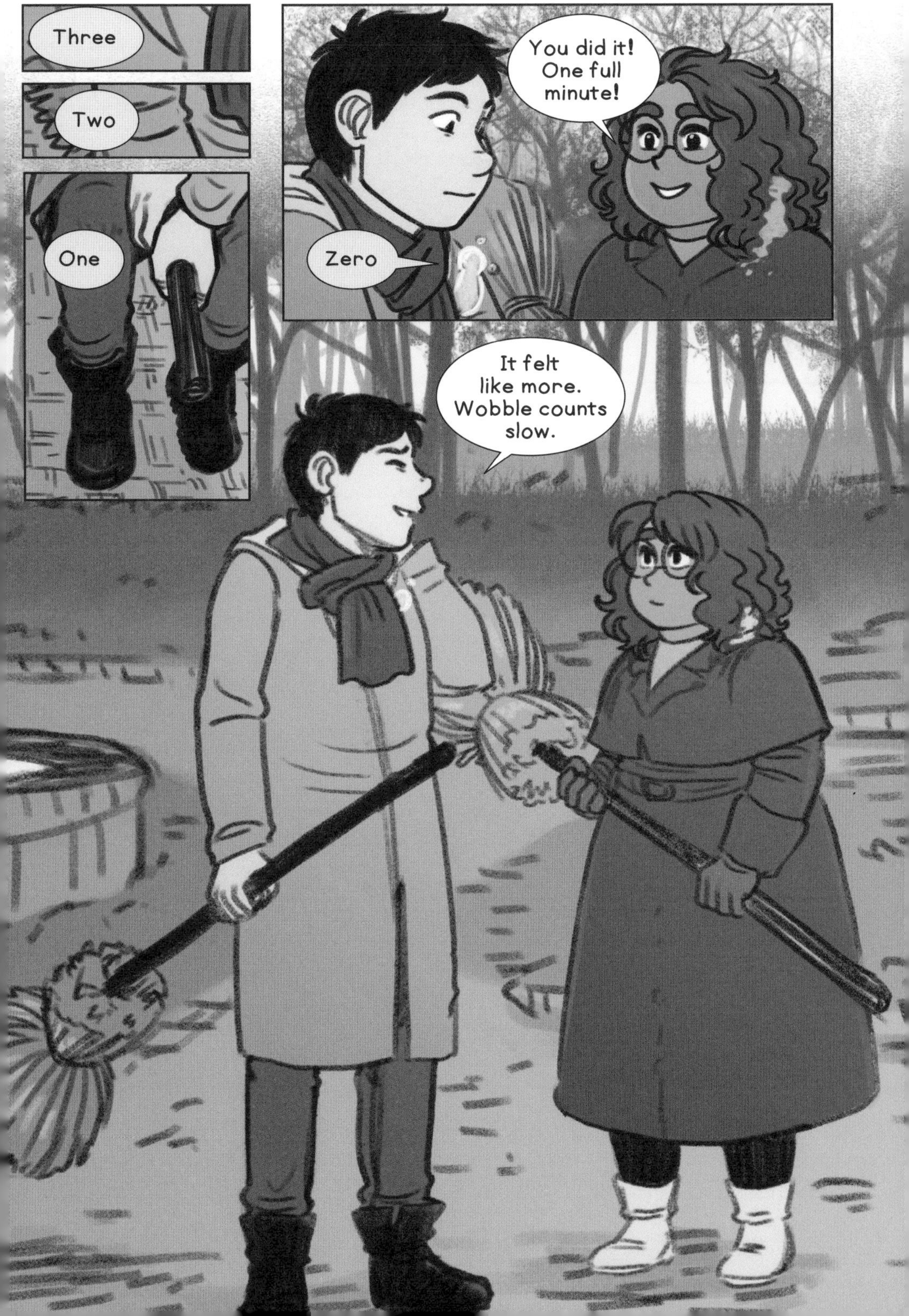
Three
Two
One
Zero
You did it! One full minute!
It felt like more. Wobble counts slow.

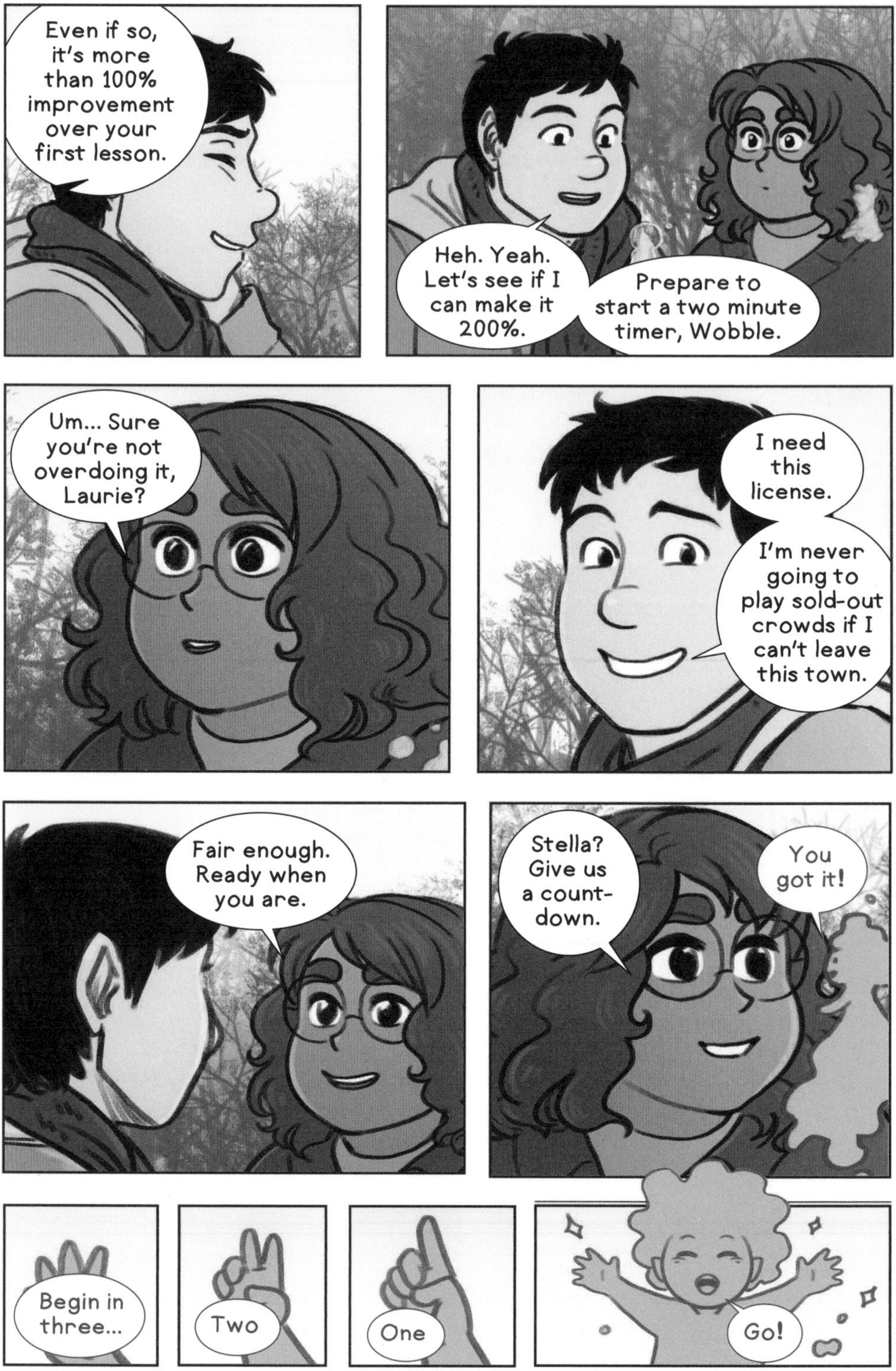

Even if so, it's more than 100% improvement over your first lesson.
Heh. Yeah. Let's see if I can make it 200%.
Prepare to start a two minute timer, Wobble.
Um... Sure you're not overdoing it, Laurie?
I need this license.
I'm never going to play sold-out crowds if I can't leave this town.
Fair enough. Ready when you are.
Stella? Give us a count-down.
You got it!
Begin in three...
Two
One
Go!

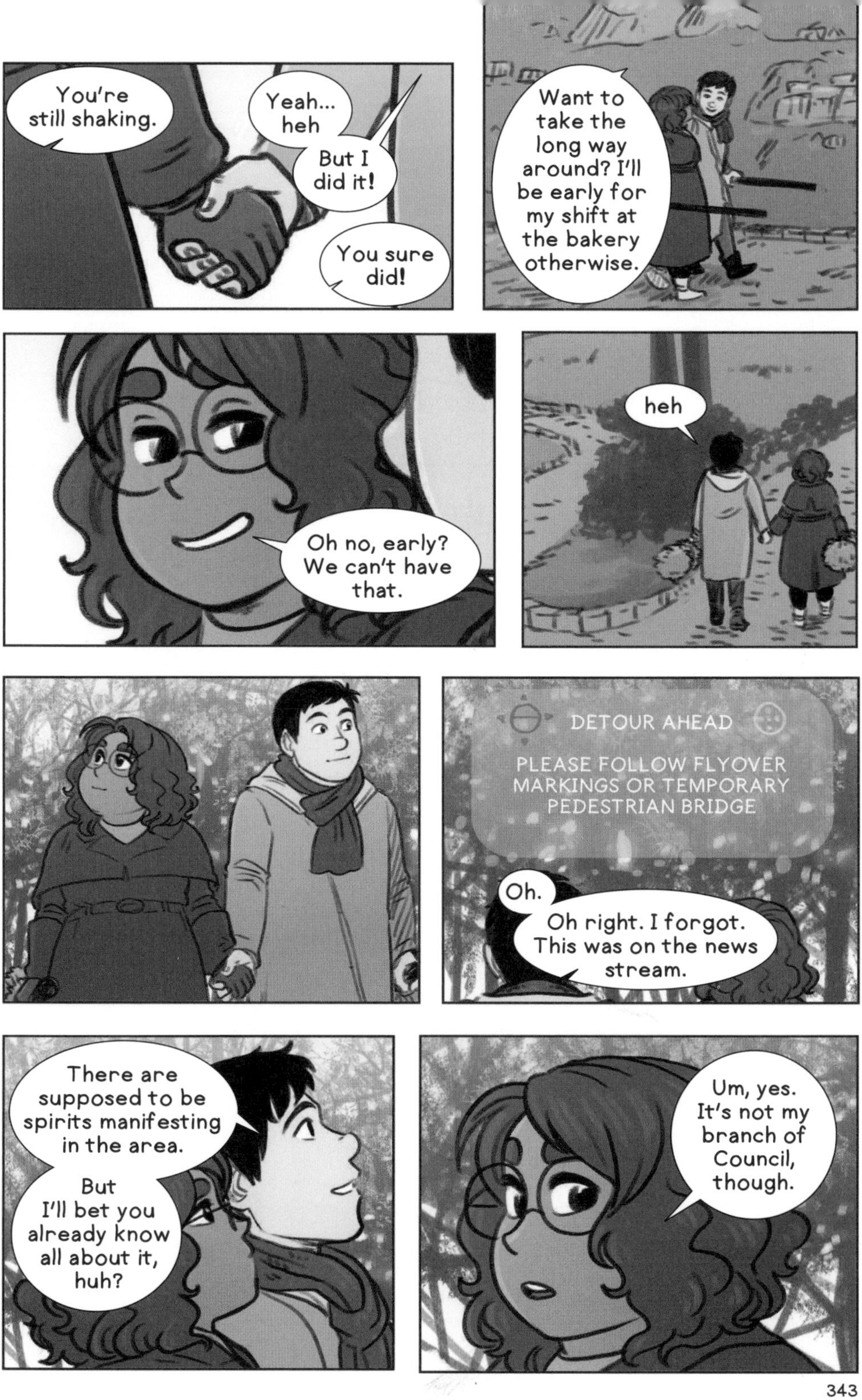
You're still shaking.
Yeah... heh
But I did it!
You sure did!
Want to take the long way around? I'll be early for my shift at the bakery otherwise.
Oh no, early? We can't have that.
heh
DETOUR AHEAD
PLEASE FOLLOW FLYOVER MARKINGS OR TEMPORARY PEDESTRIAN BRIDGE
Oh.
Oh right. I forgot. This was on the news stream.
There are supposed to be spirits manifesting in the area.
But I'll bet you already know all about it, huh?
Um, yes. It's not my branch of Council, though.

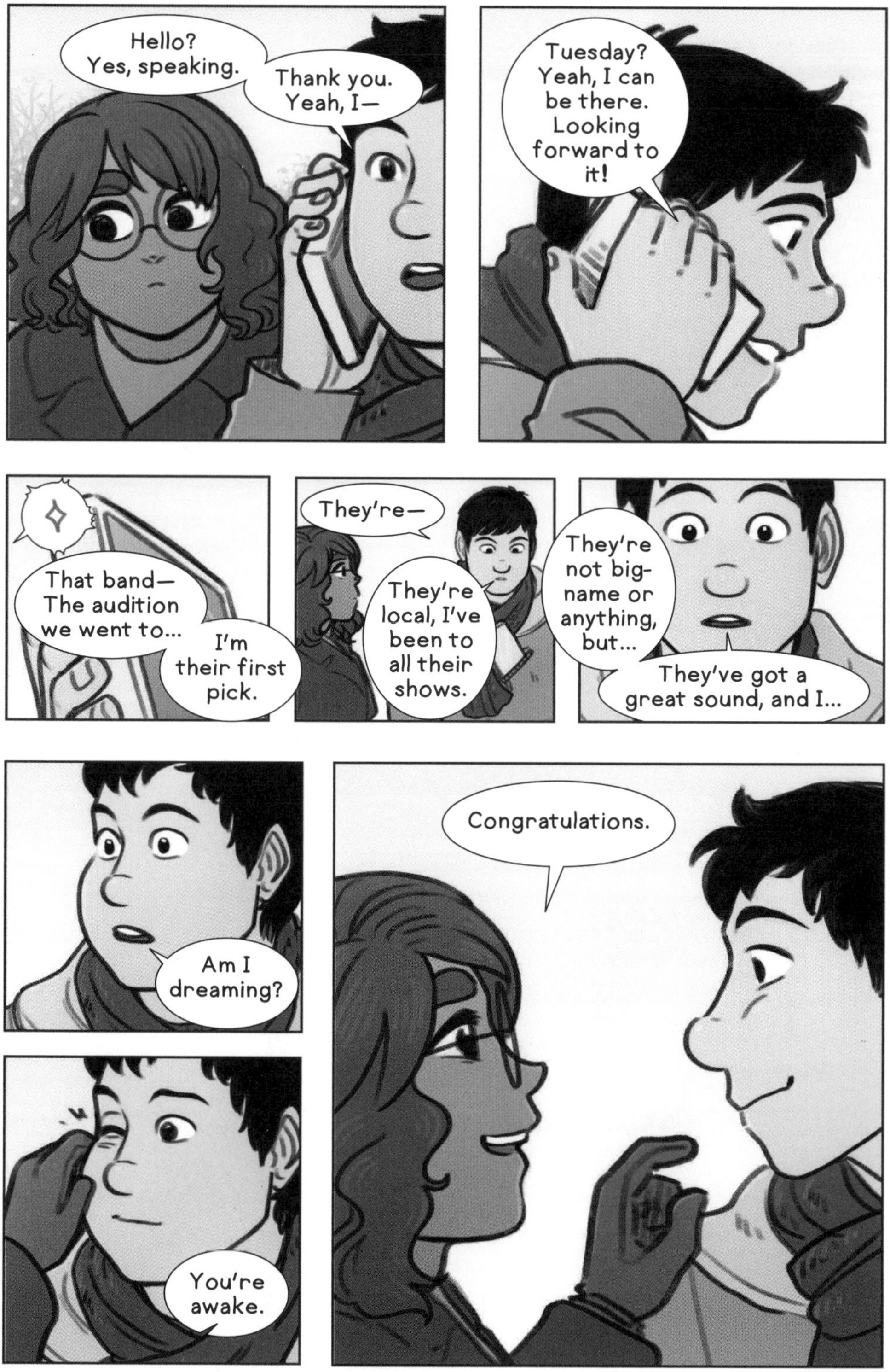
Hello?
Yes, speaking.
Thank you.
Yeah, I—
Tuesday?
Yeah, I can
be there.
Looking
forward to
it!
That band—
The audition
we went to...
I'm
their first
pick.
They're—
They're
local, I've
been to
all their
shows.
They're
not big-
name or
anything,
but...
They've got a
great sound, and I...
Am I
dreaming?
You're
awake.
Congratulations.

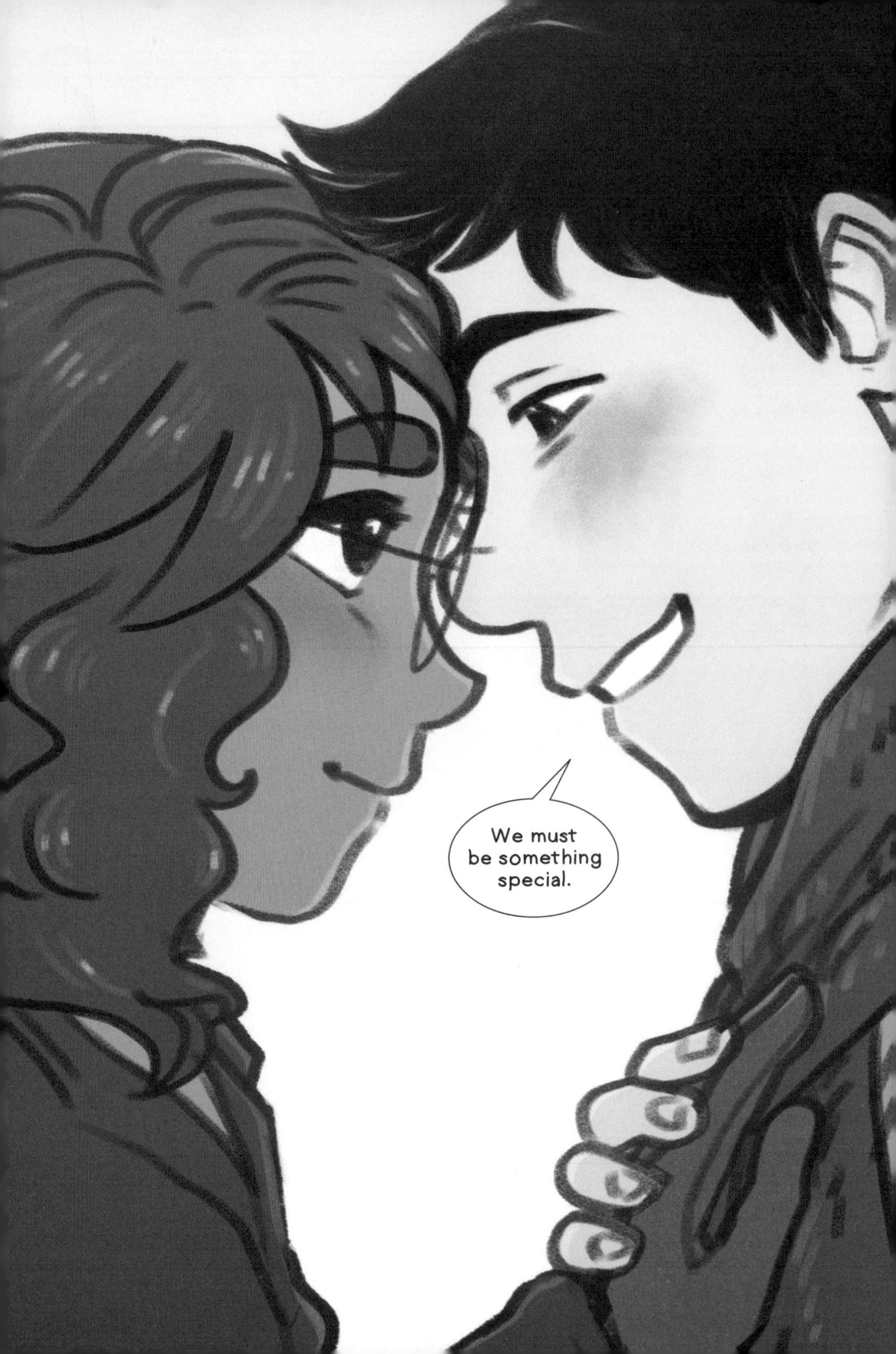
We must be something special.

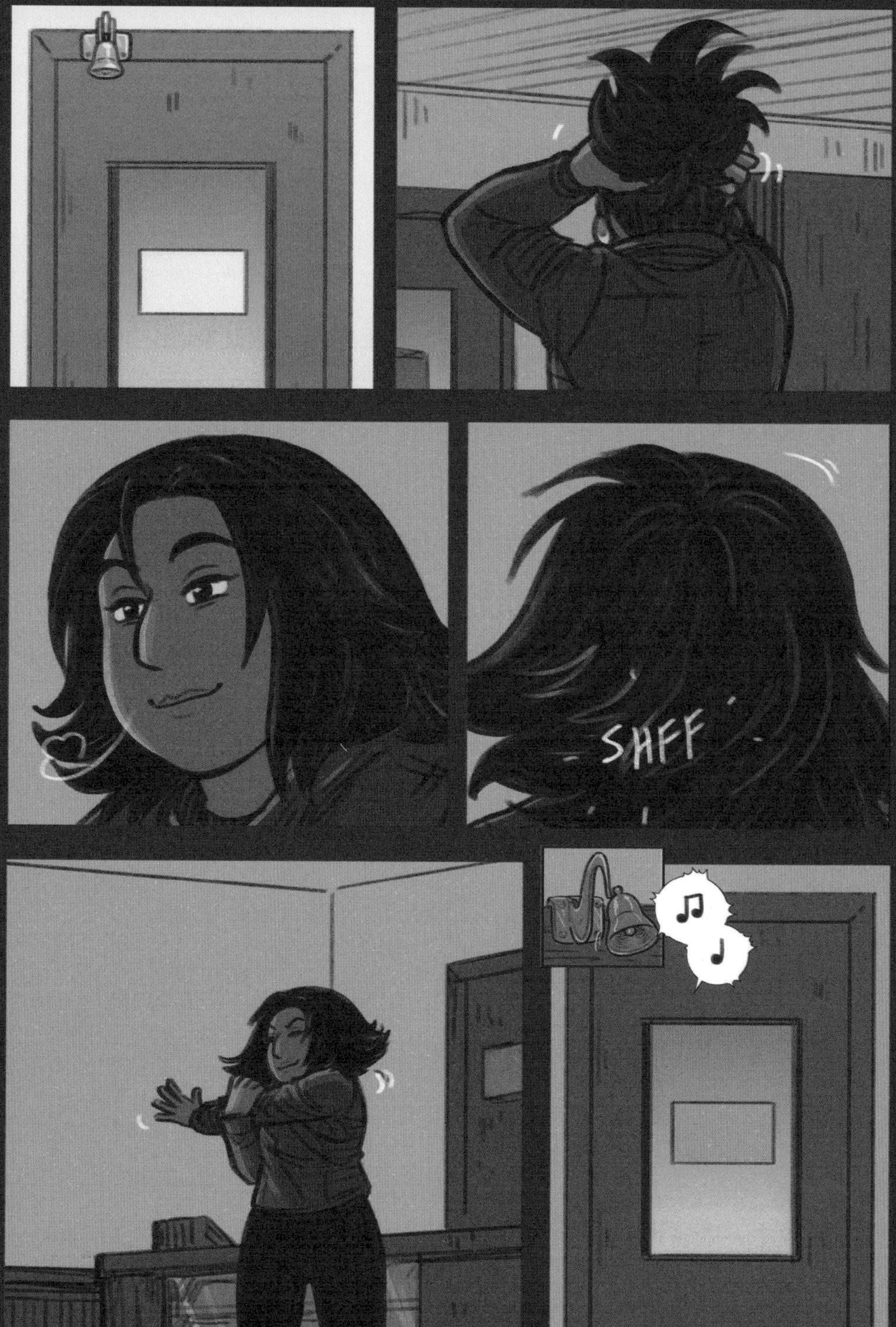
SHFF

352

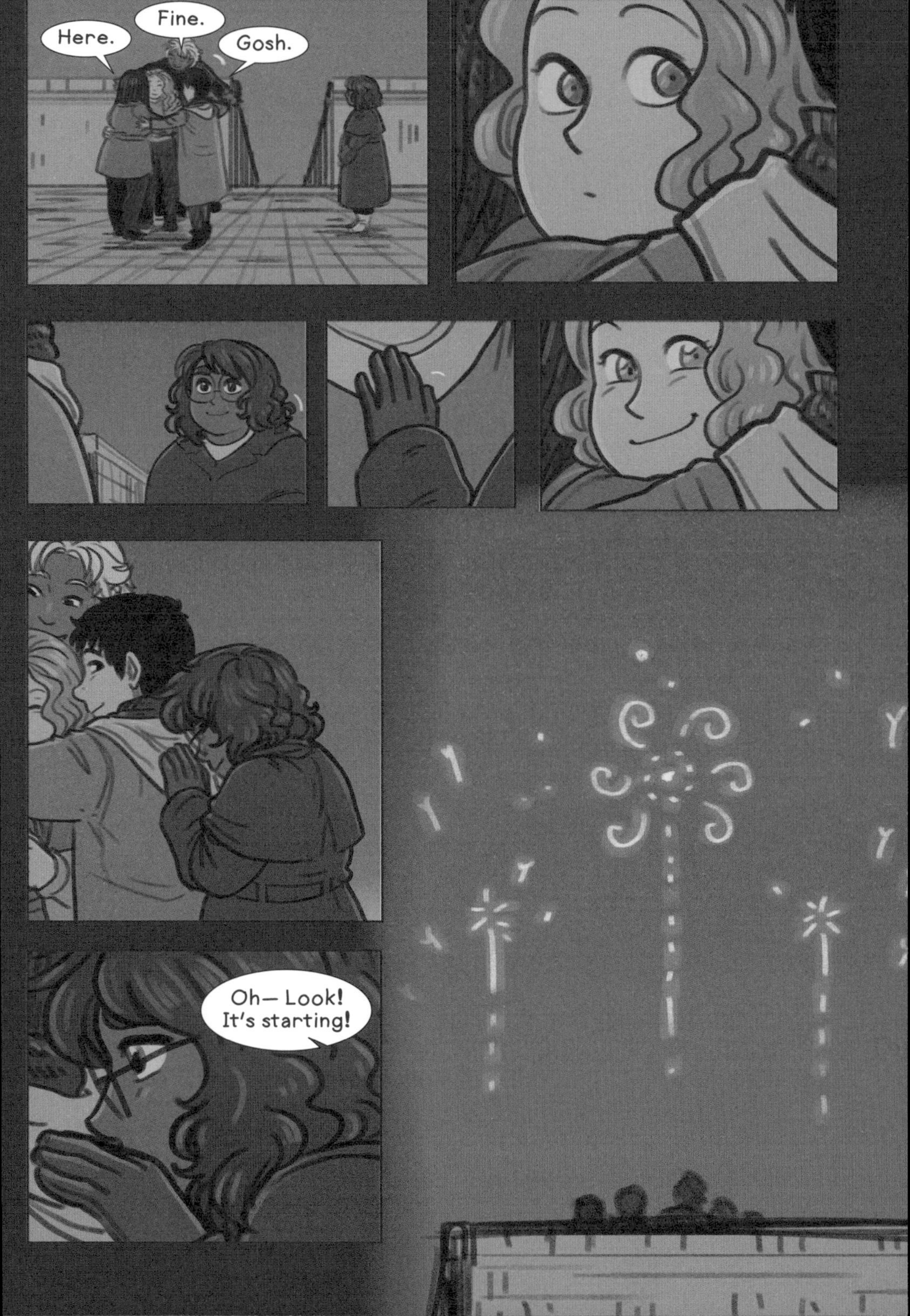
Here.
Fine.
Gosh.
Oh— Look! It's starting!

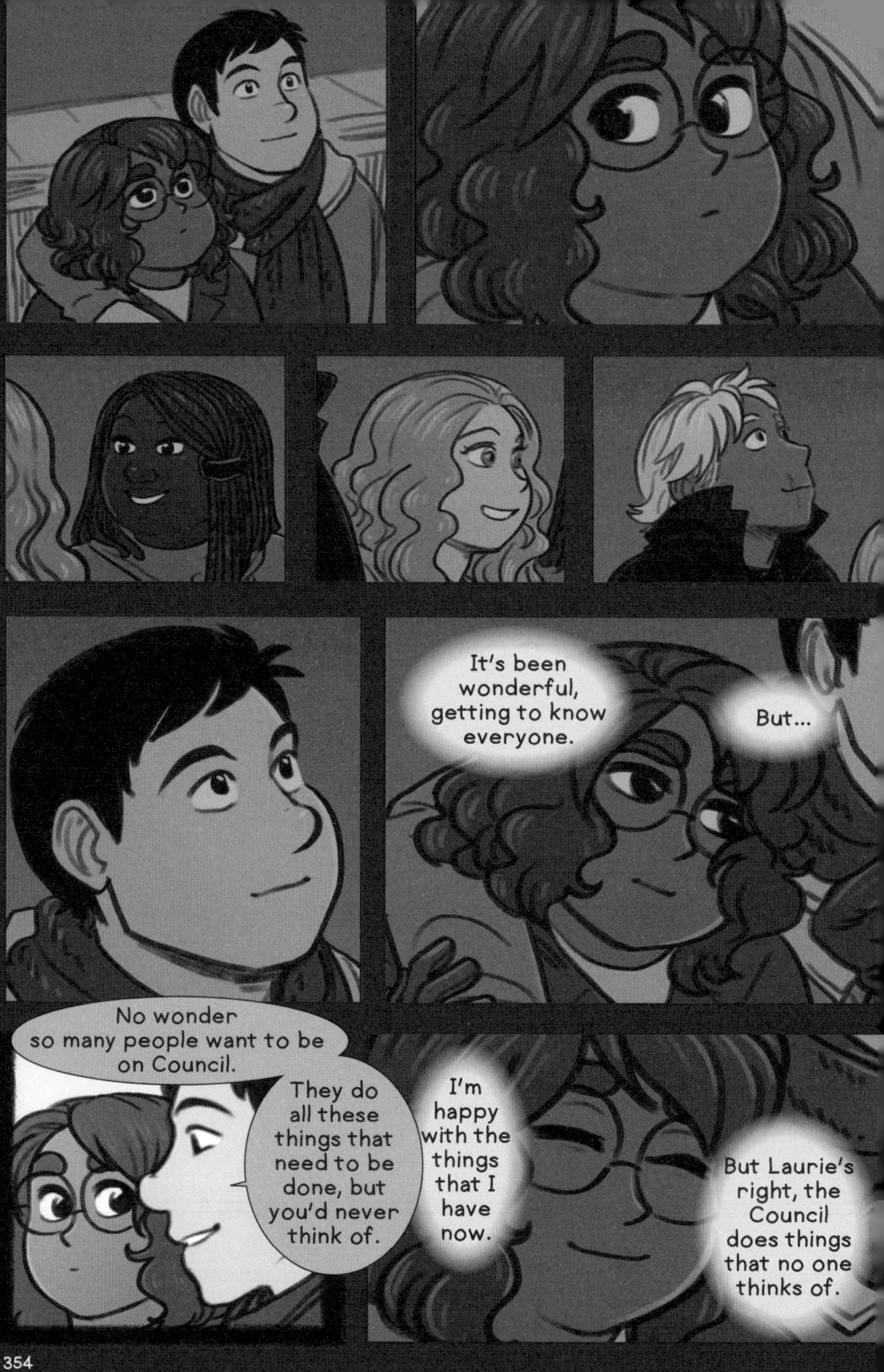

It's been wonderful, getting to know everyone.
But...
No wonder so many people want to be on Council.
They do all these things that need to be done, but you'd never think of.
I'm happy with the things that I have now.
But Laurie's right, the Council does things that no one thinks of.

If I don't join, I'll never know the best I could have done with all the Council has to offer.
I want to open the door to all of those possibilities. And if I didn't go for what I want—
I wouldn't be the person you liked in the first place.

CHAPTER 14

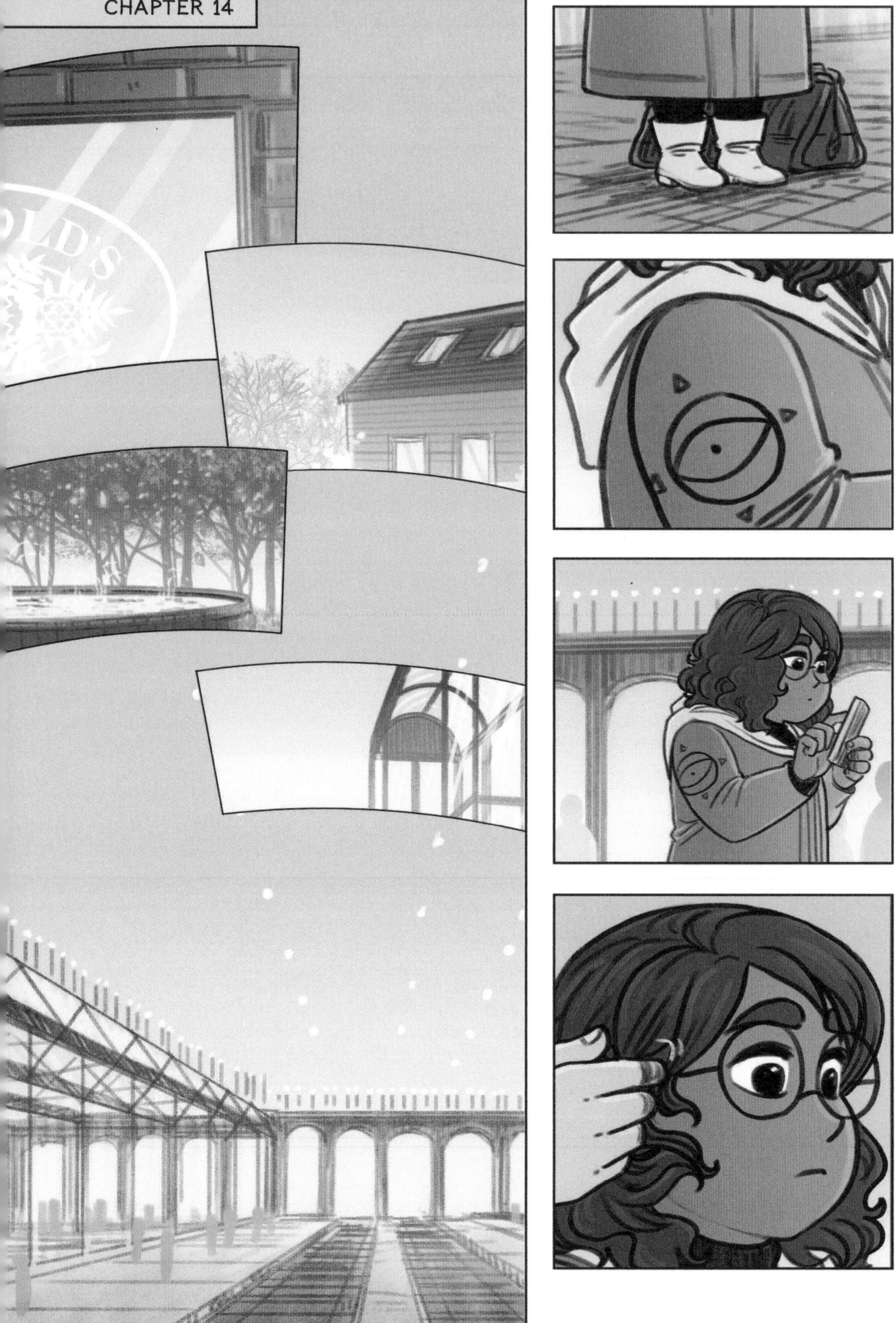

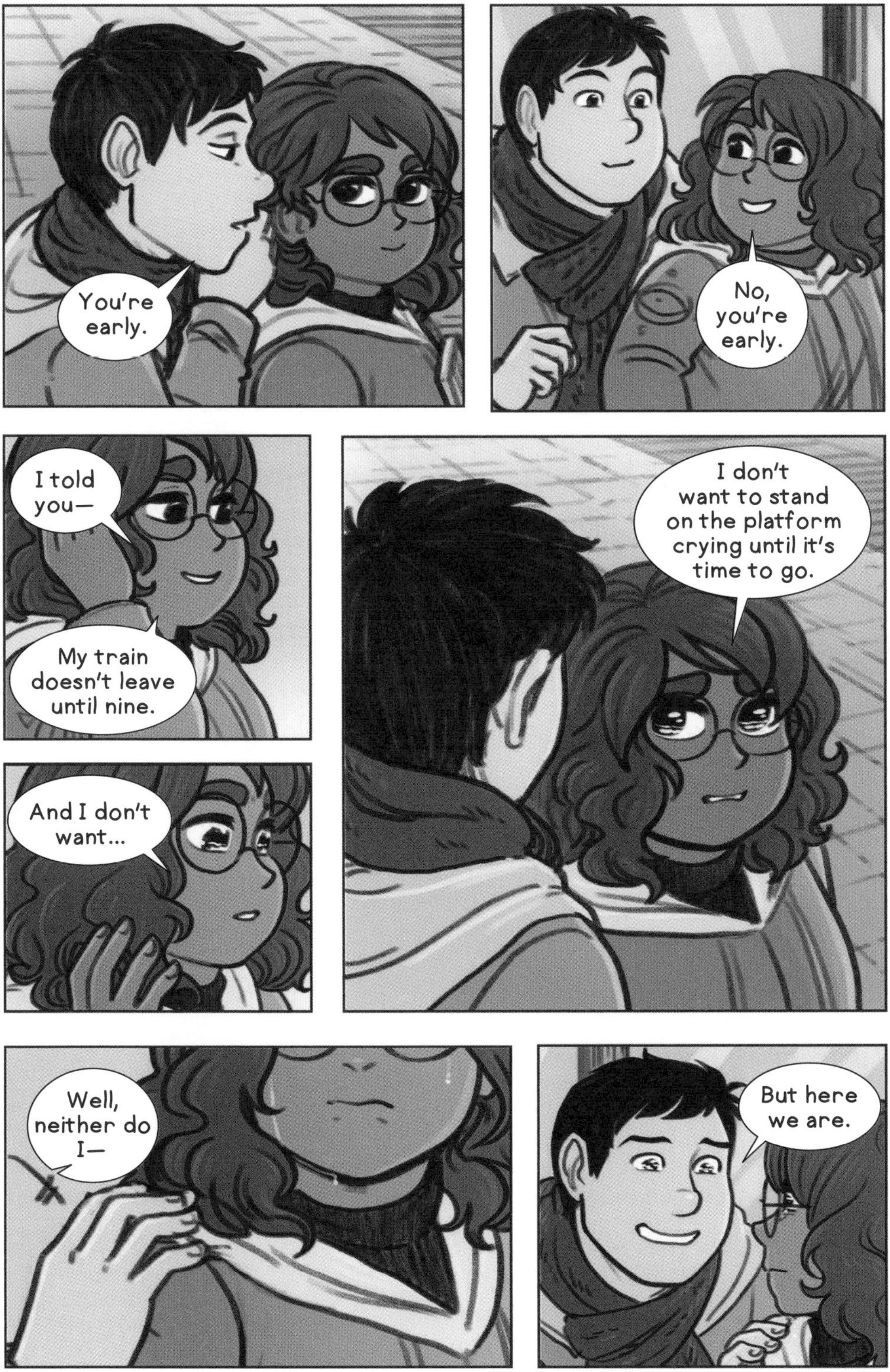
You're early.
No, you're early.
I told you—
My train doesn't leave until nine.
I don't want to stand on the platform crying until it's time to go.
And I don't want...
Well, neither do I—
But here we are.

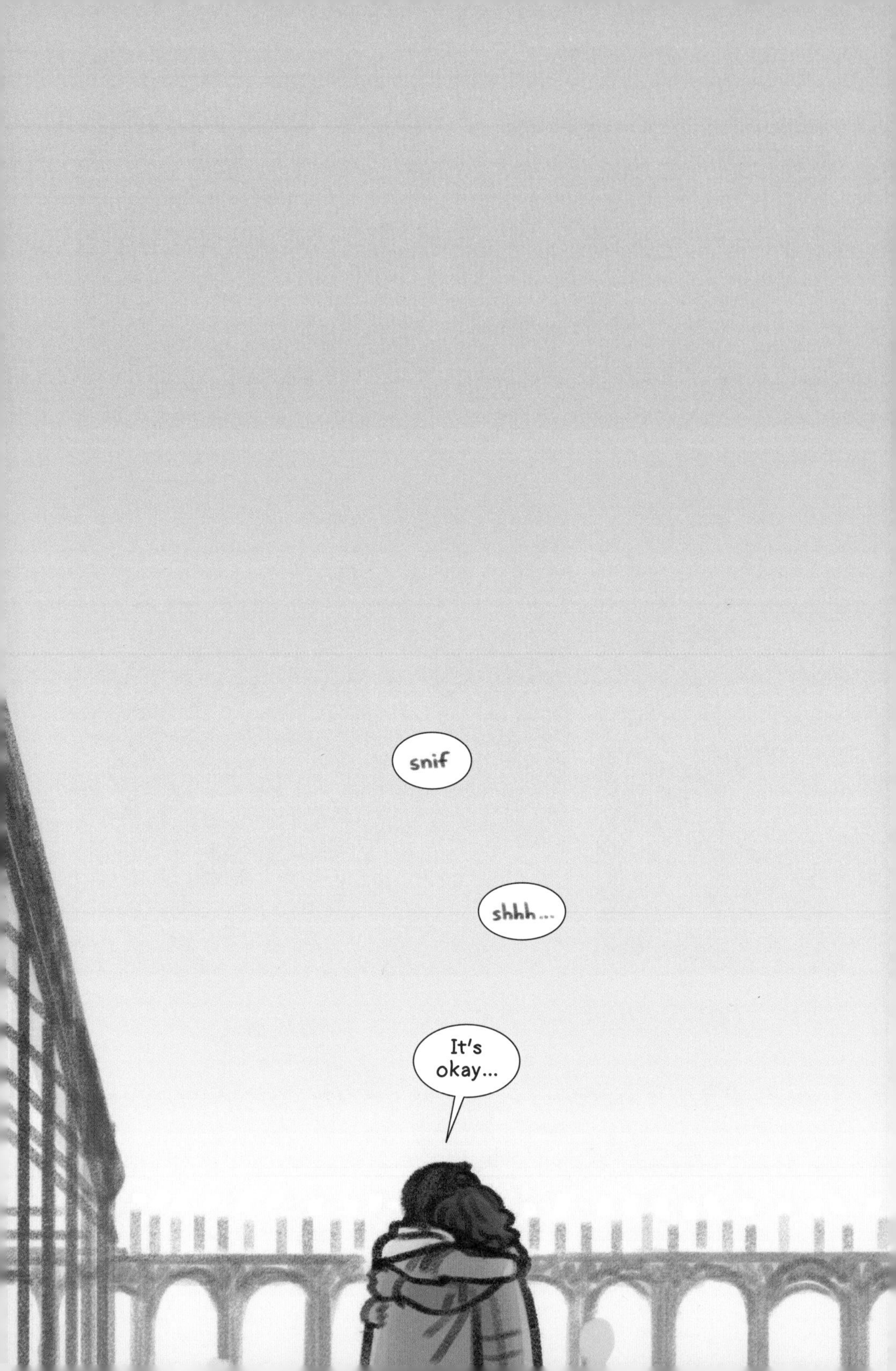
snif
shhh...
It's okay...

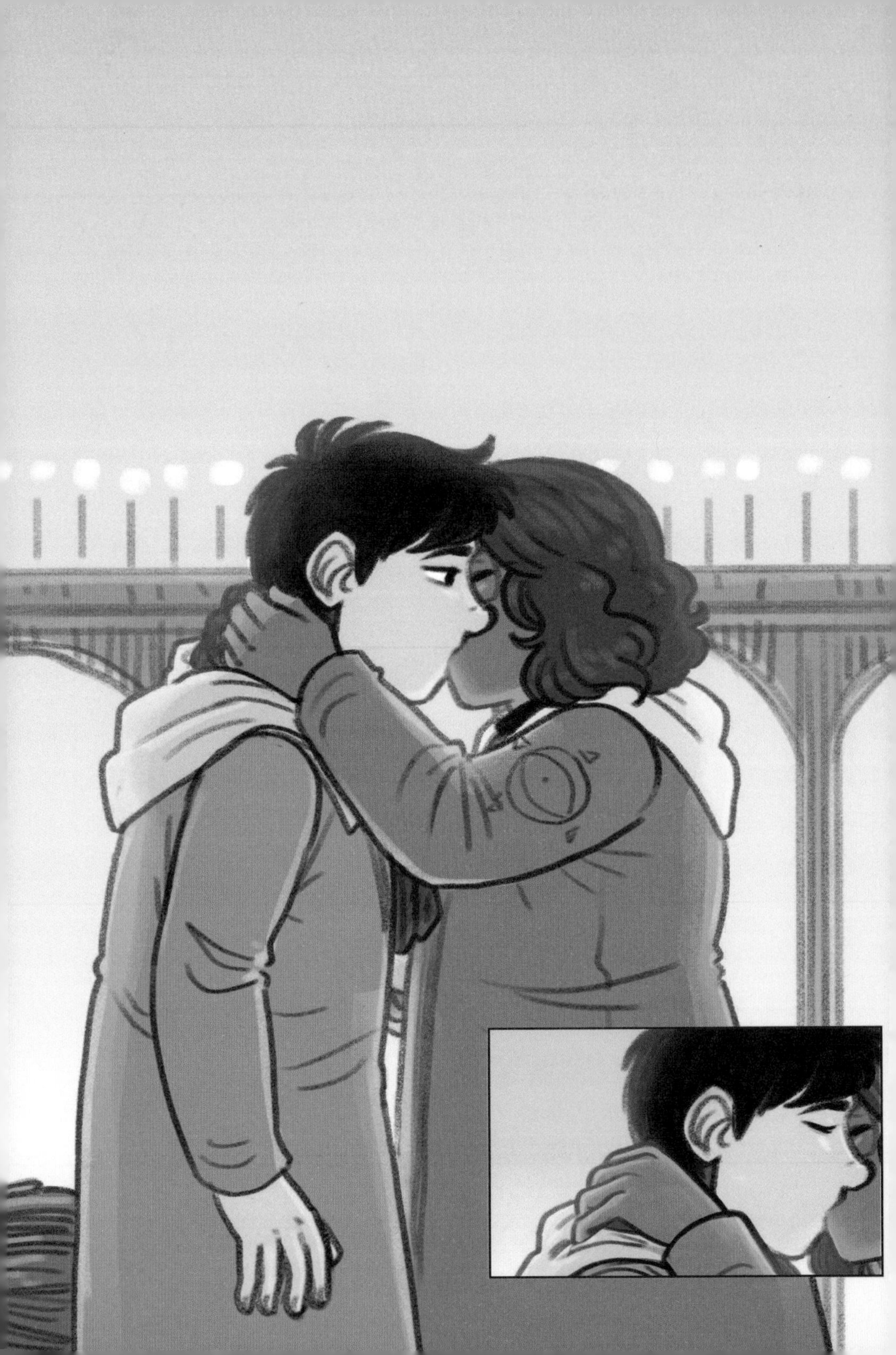

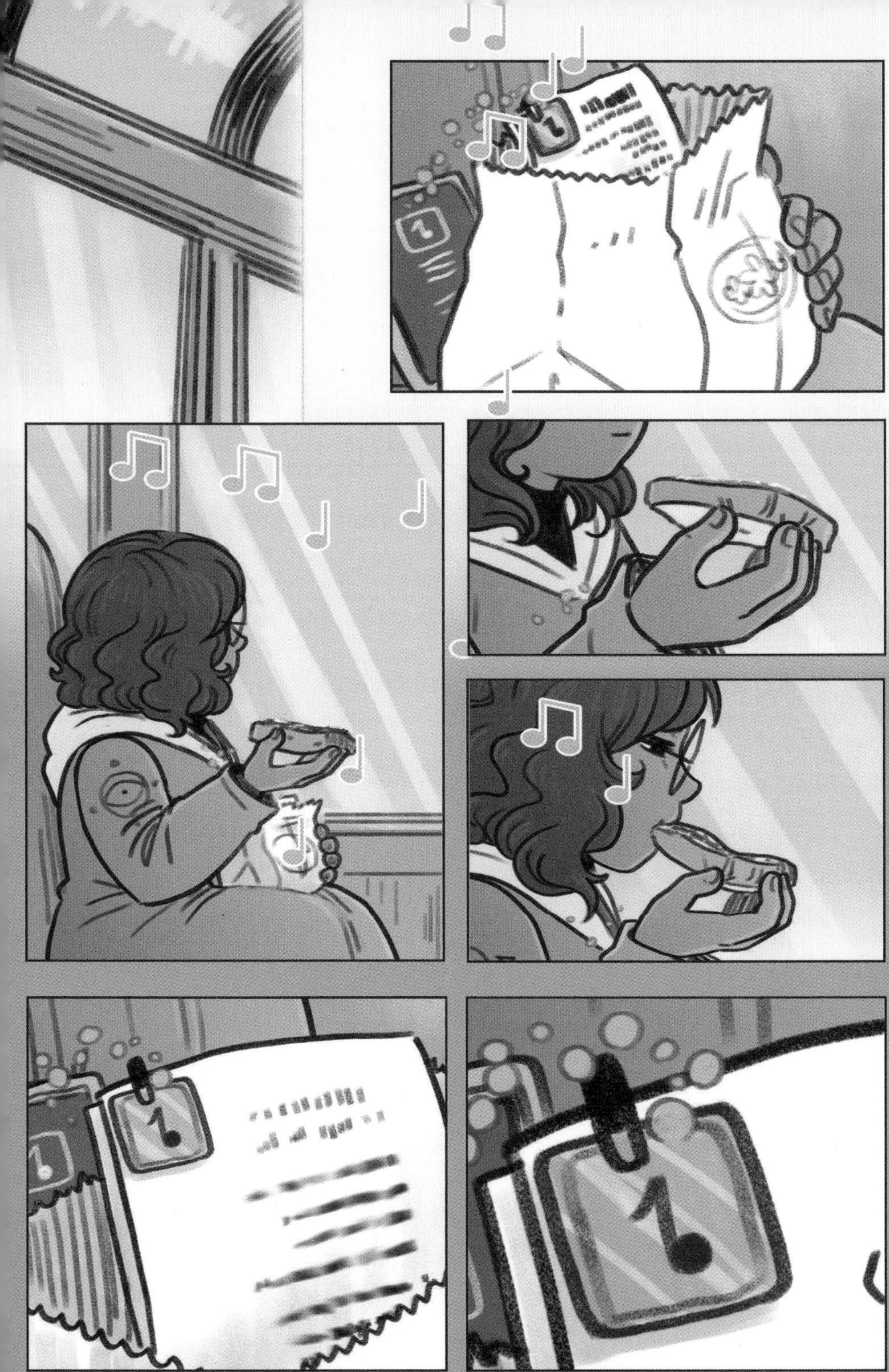

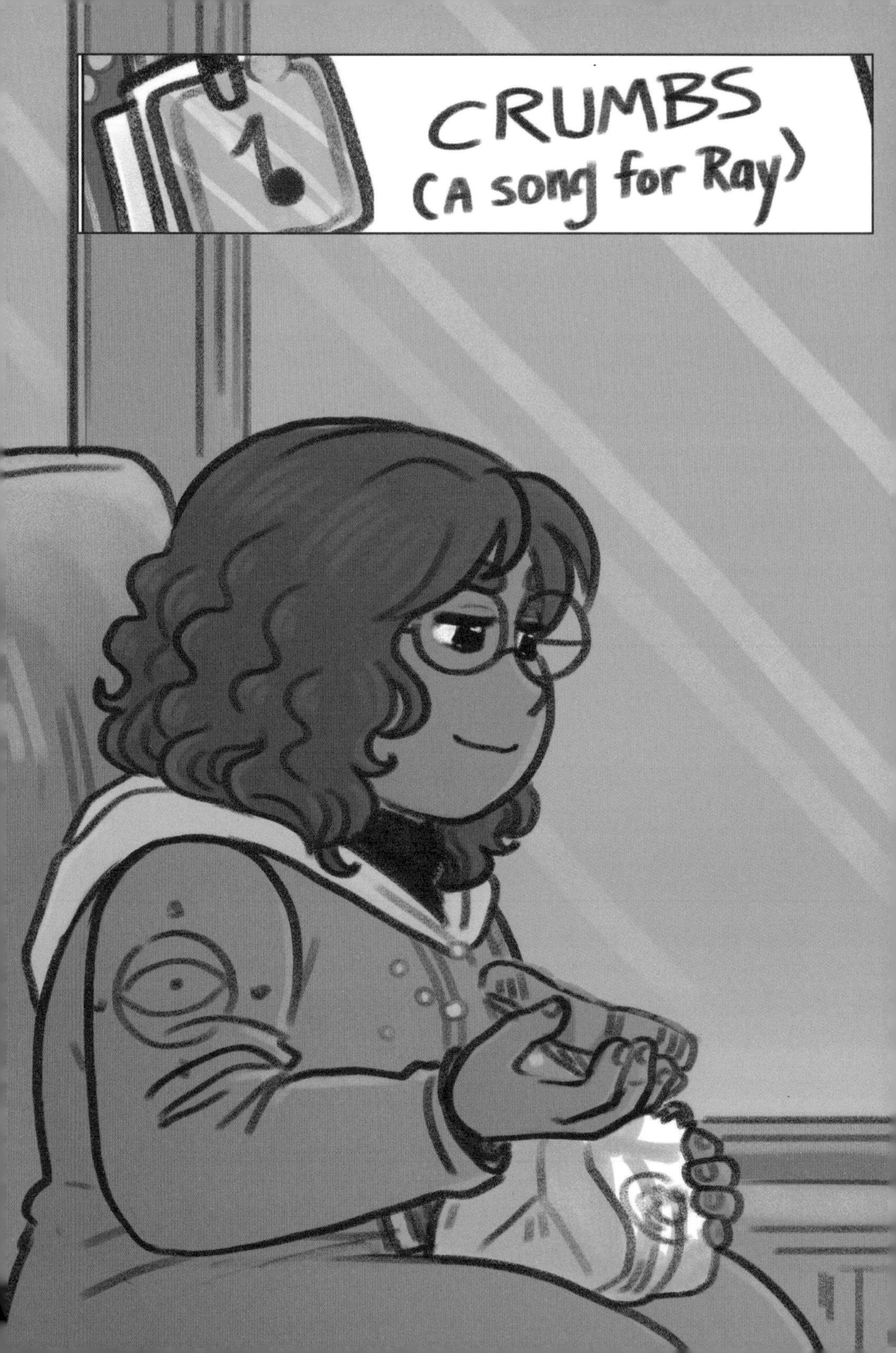
1
CRUMBS
(A song for Ray)

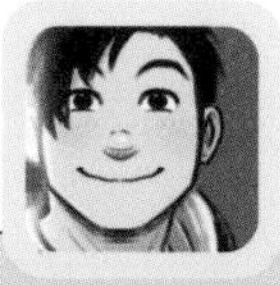

EPILOGUE

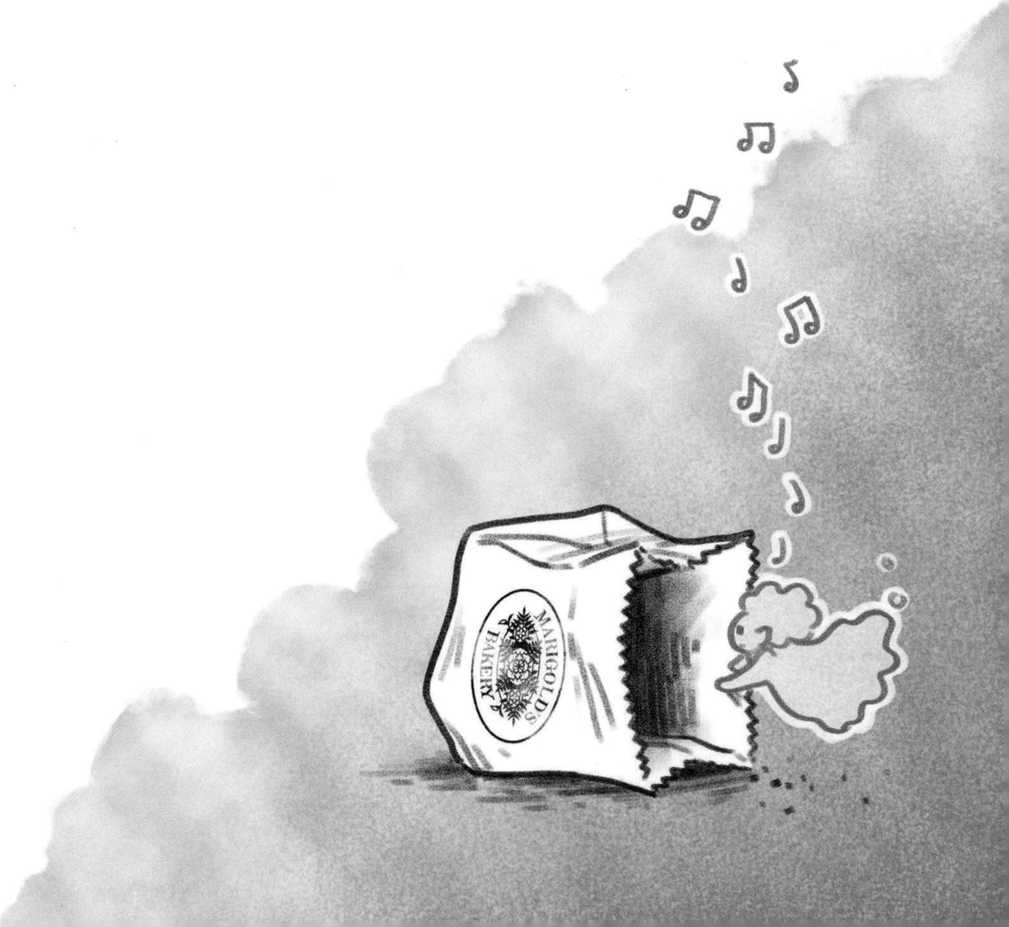
MARIGOLD'S BAKERY

The Assembly of the Higher Circle recognizes the Councilor from Scrolls.

Thank you, Councilors.

I move that we vote on the implementation of the resolution. Will anyone second the motion?

I second it.

The motion passes to a vote.

All in favor?

All opposed?

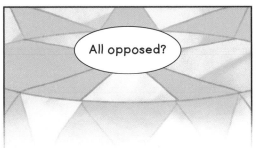

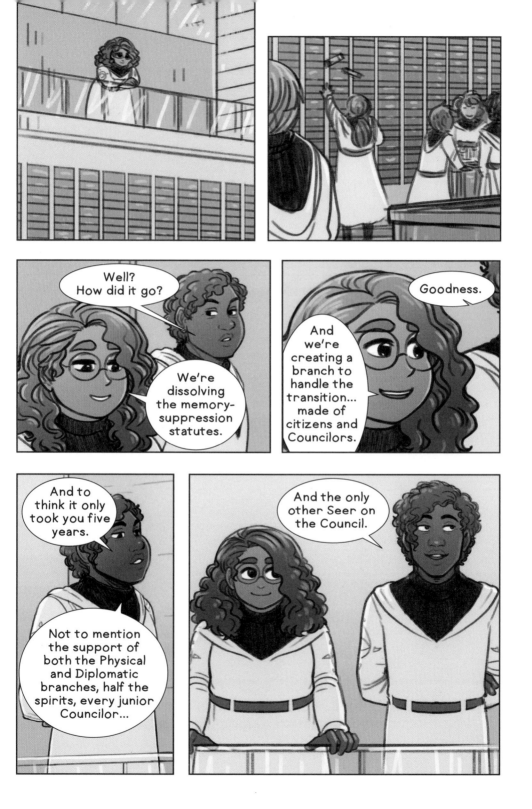

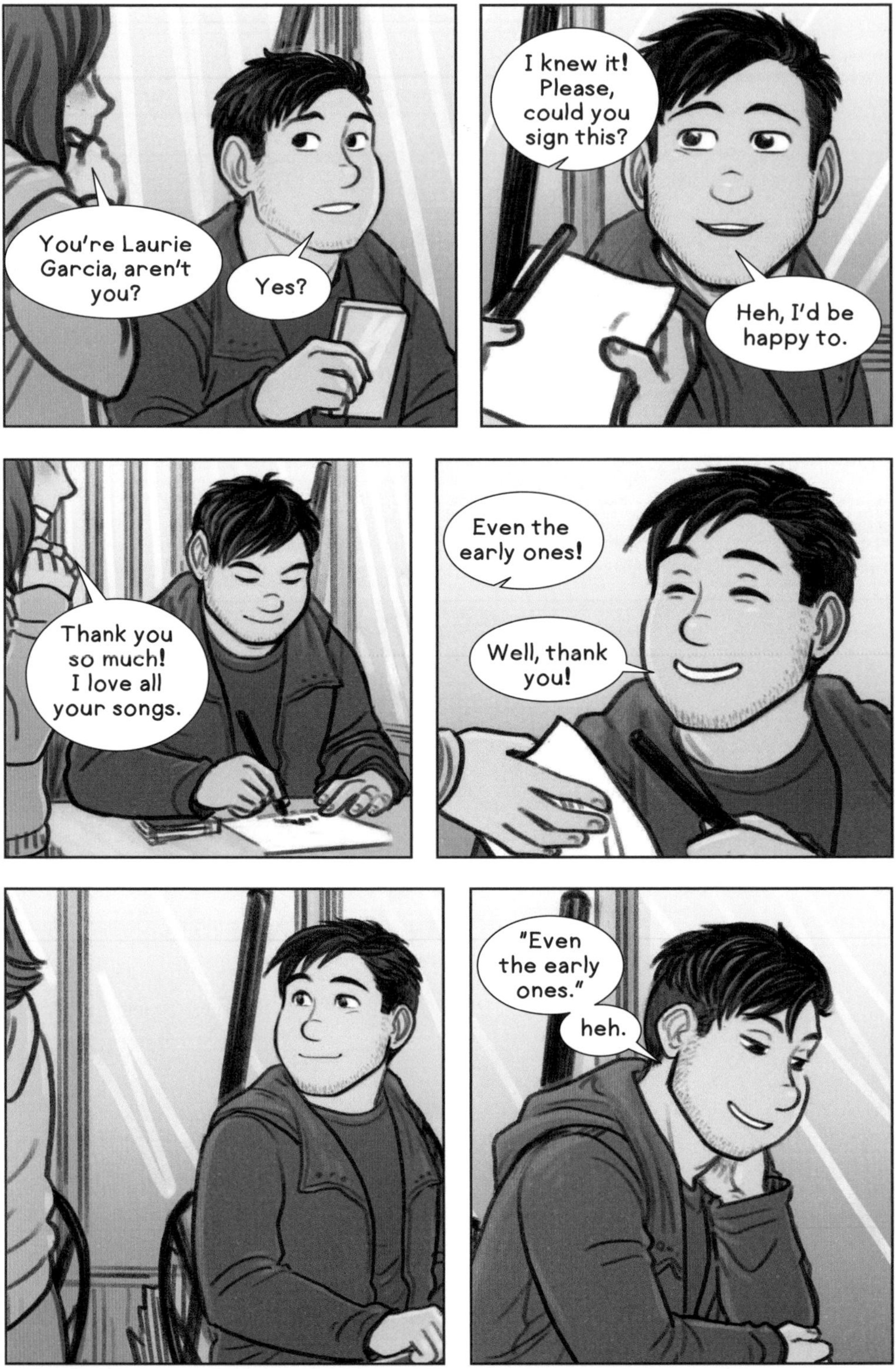
You're Laurie Garcia, aren't you?
Yes?
I knew it! Please, could you sign this?
Heh, I'd be happy to.
Thank you so much! I love all your songs.
Even the early ones!
Well, thank you!
"Even the early ones."
heh.

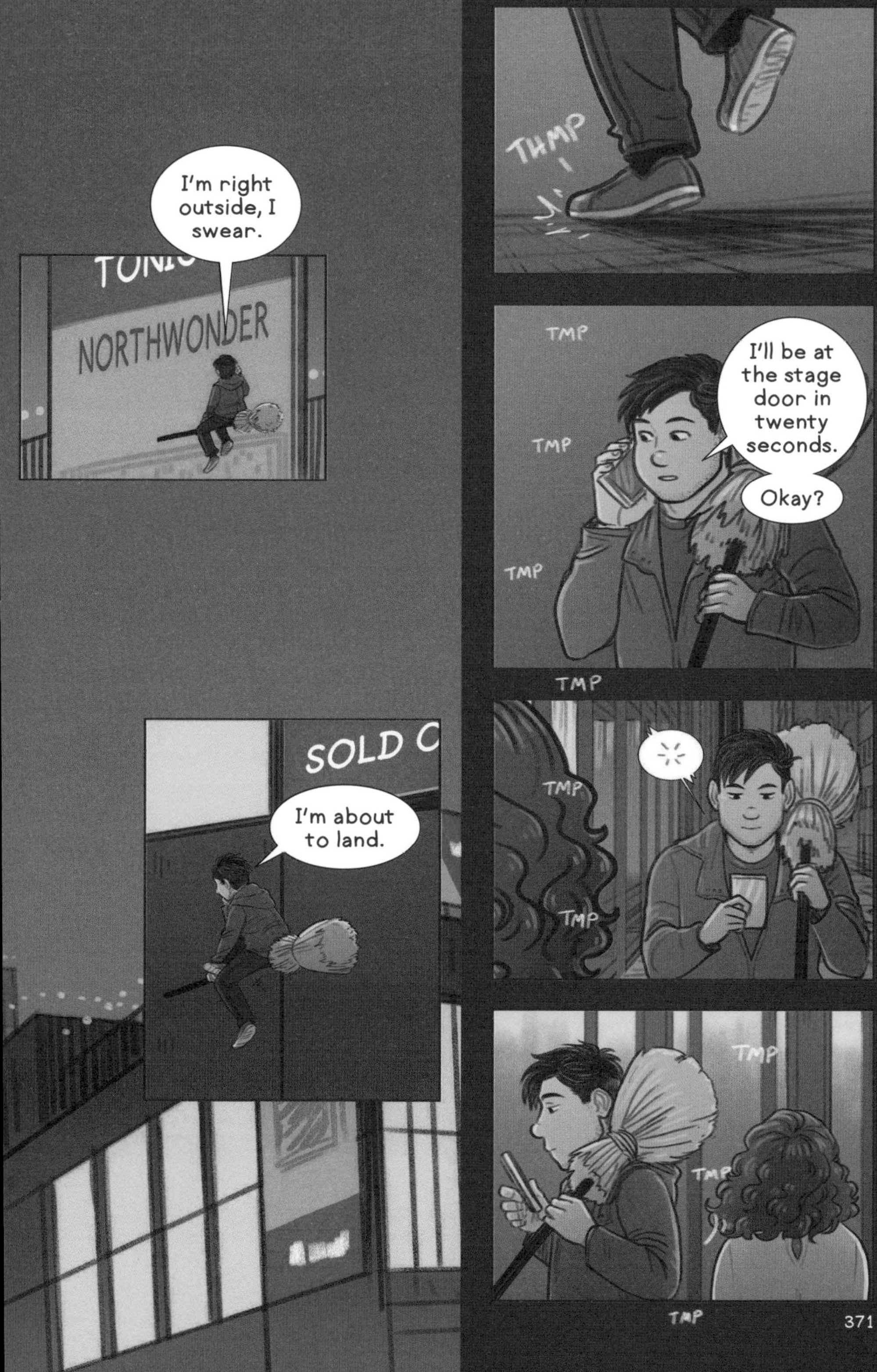
TONIC
NORTHWONDER
I'm right outside, I swear.
SOLD C
I'm about to land.
THMP
TMP
I'll be at the stage door in twenty seconds.
Okay?
TMP
TMP
TMP
TMP
TMP
TMP
TMP
TMP

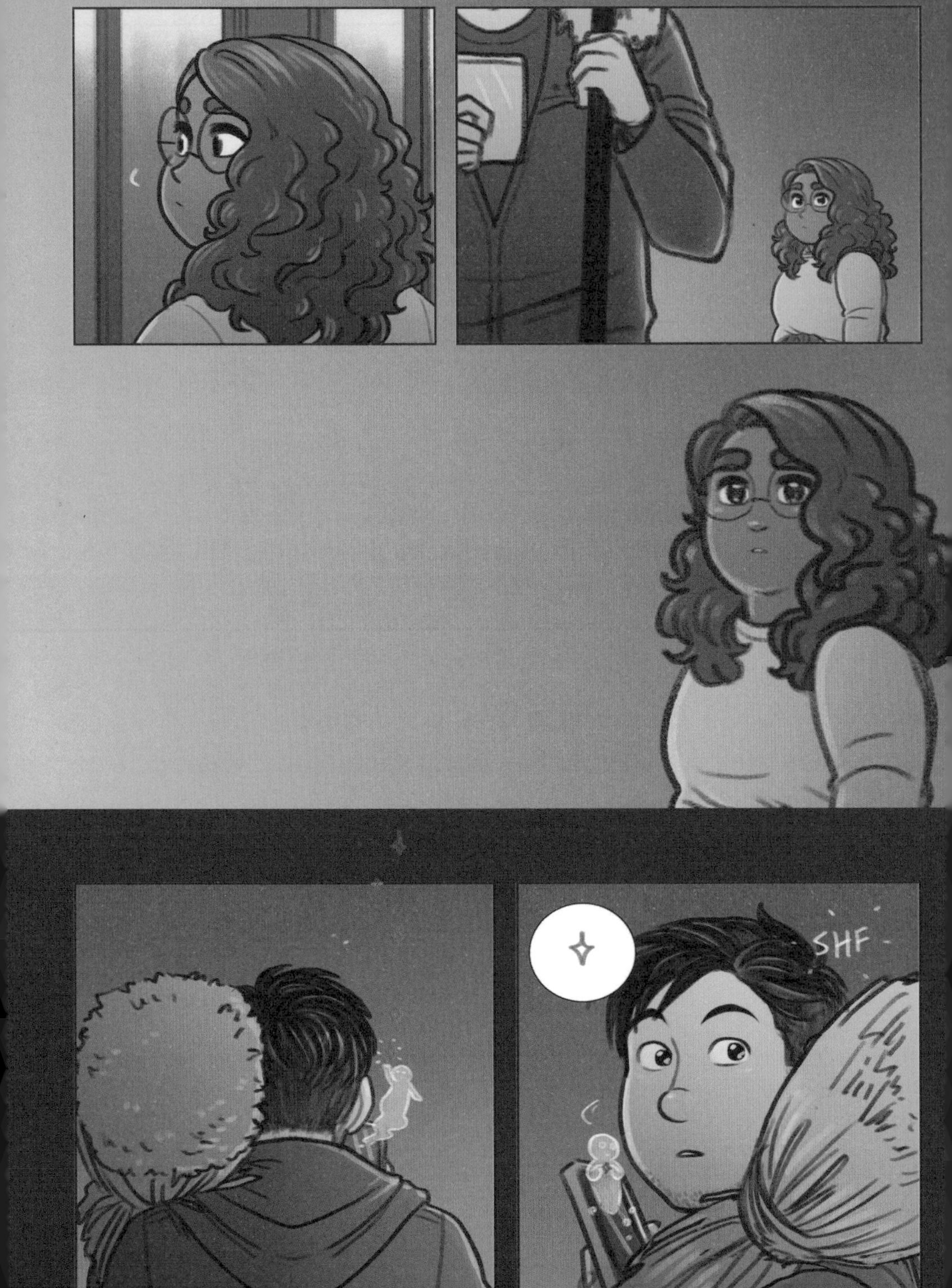
SHF

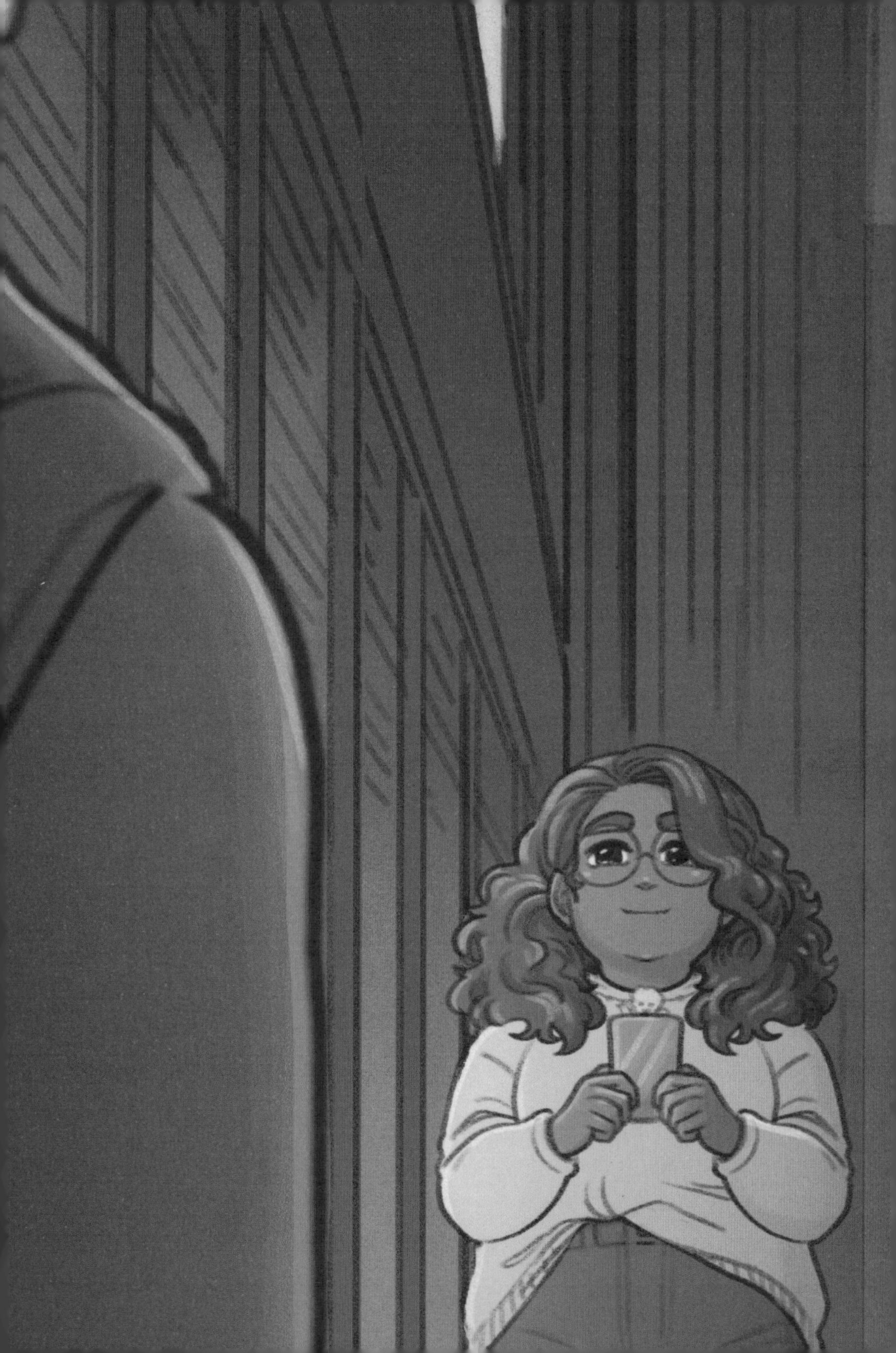

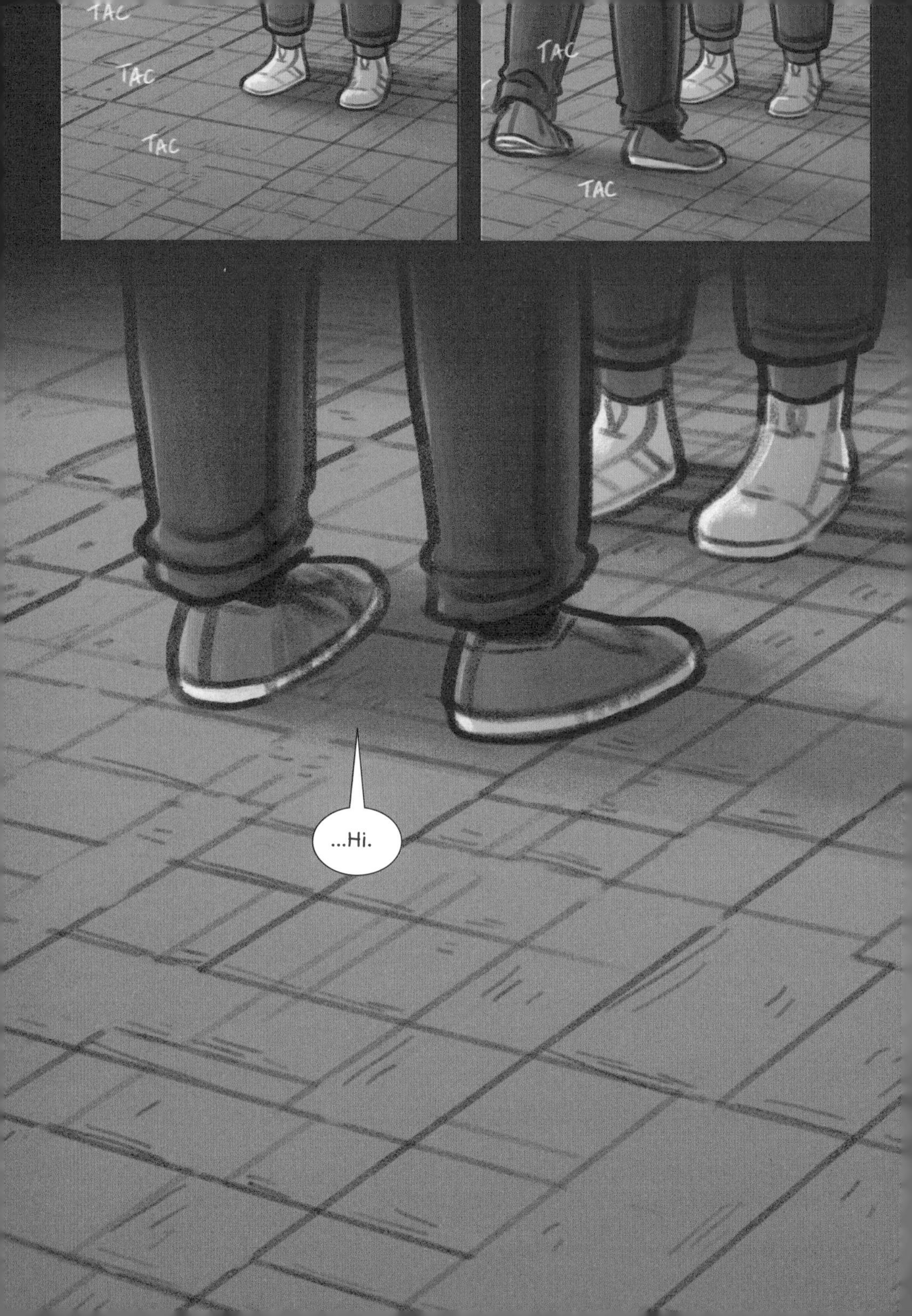
TAC
TAC
TAC
TAC
TAC
...Hi.

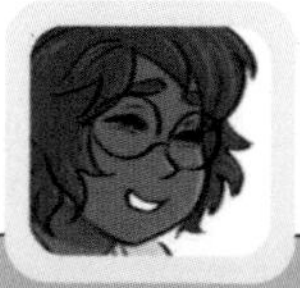

EXTRAS

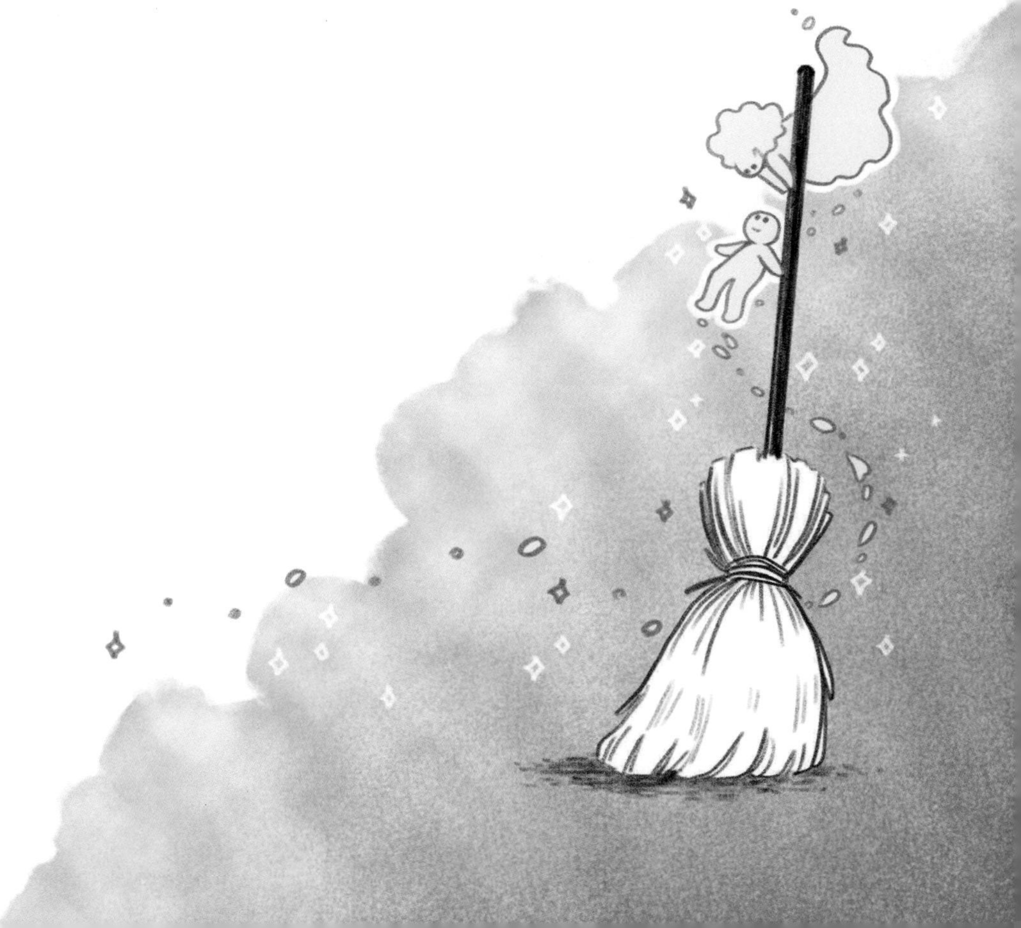

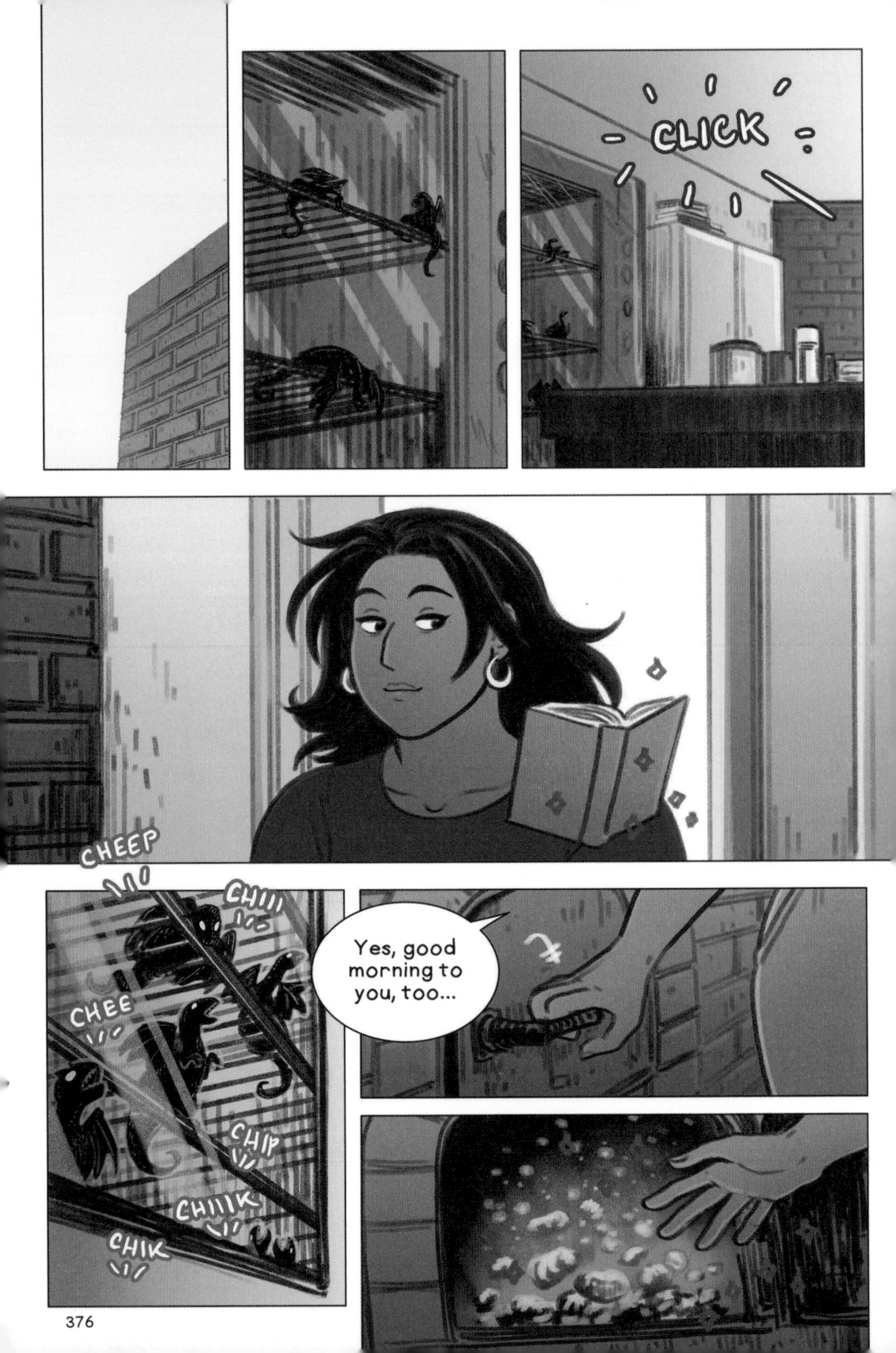
CLICK
CHEEP
CHIII
CHEE
Yes, good morning to you, too...
CHIP
CHIIIK
CHIK

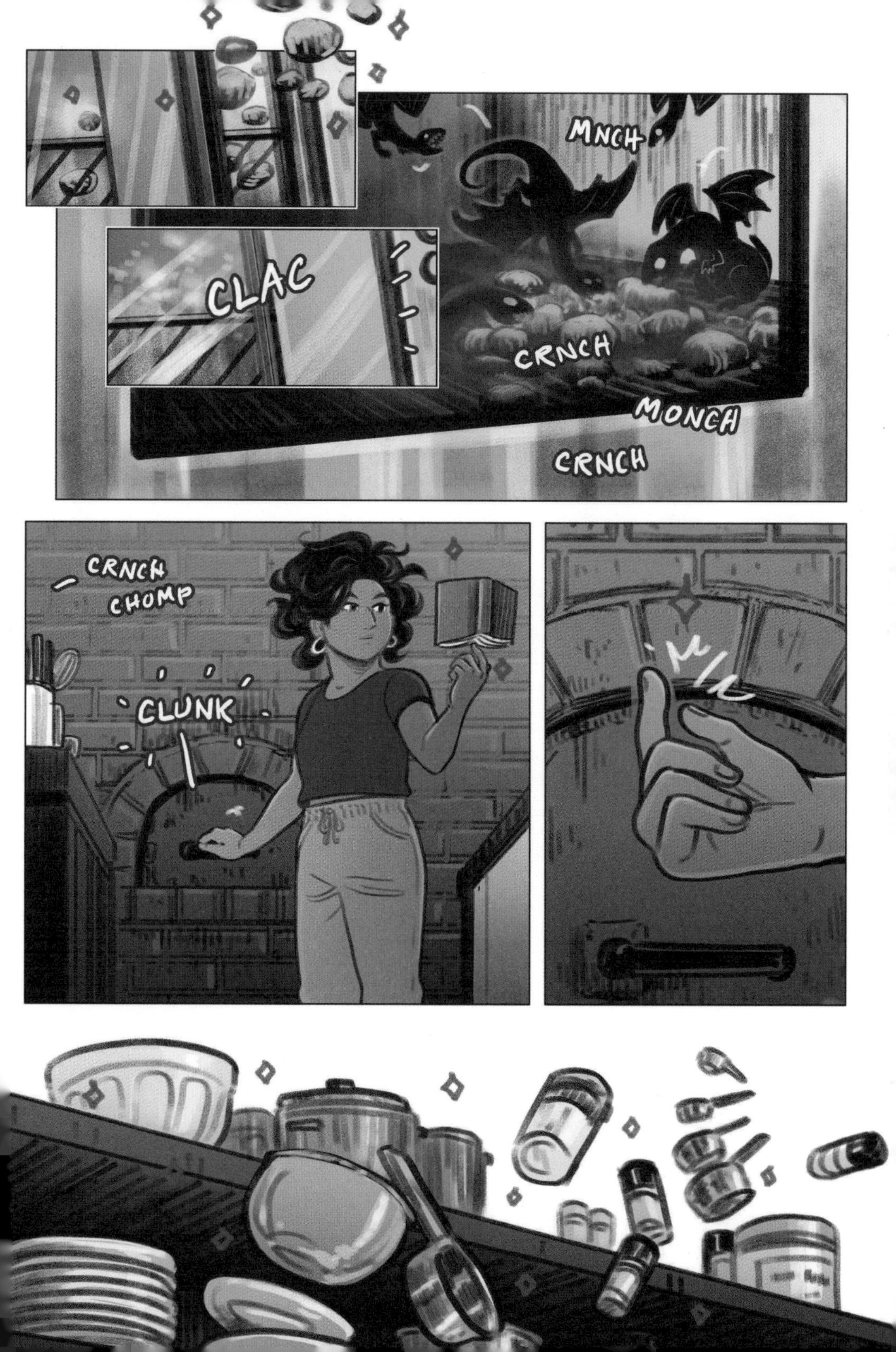
CLAC
MNCH
CRNCH
MONCH
CRNCH
CRNCH
CHOMP
CLUNK

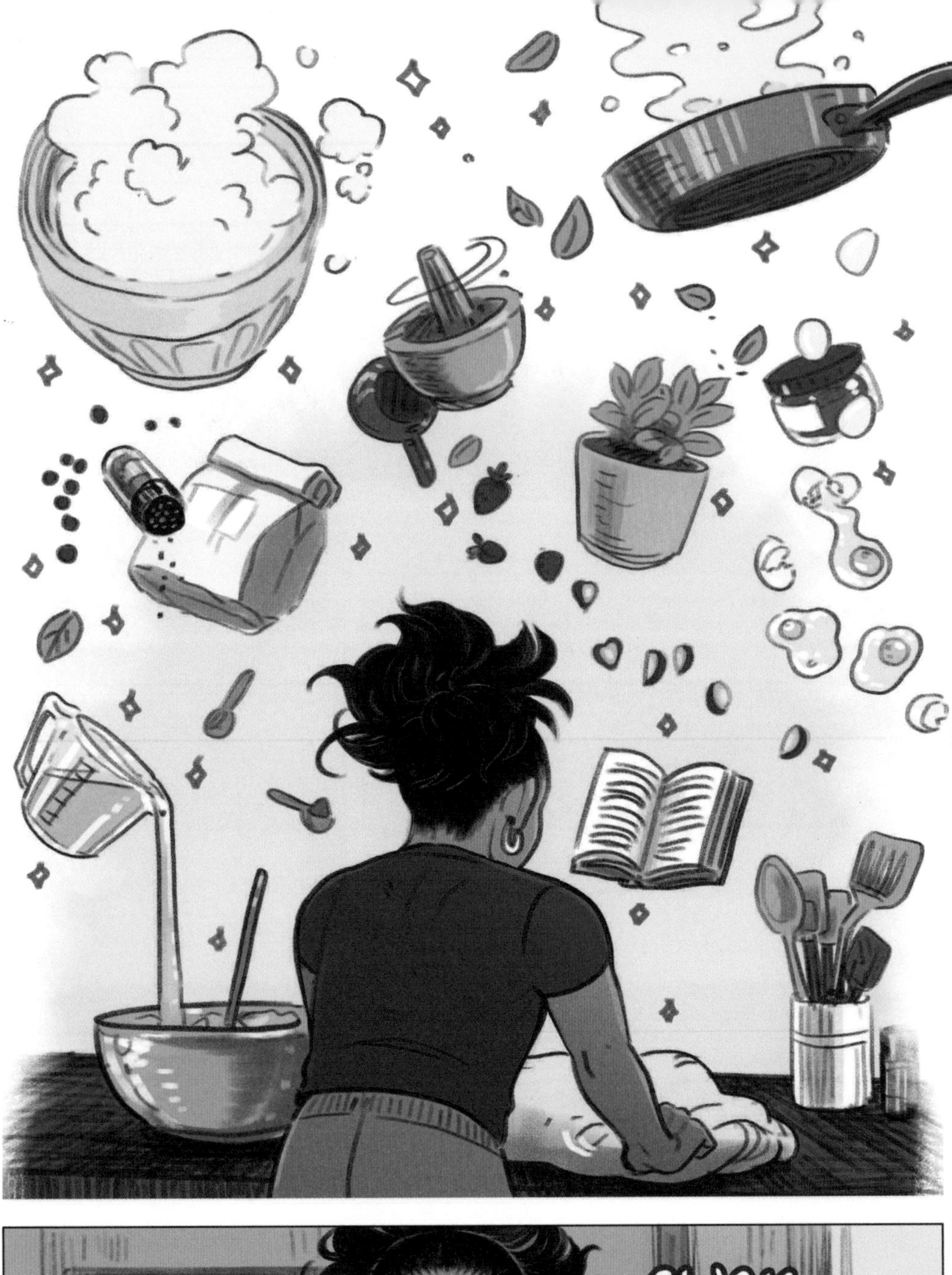

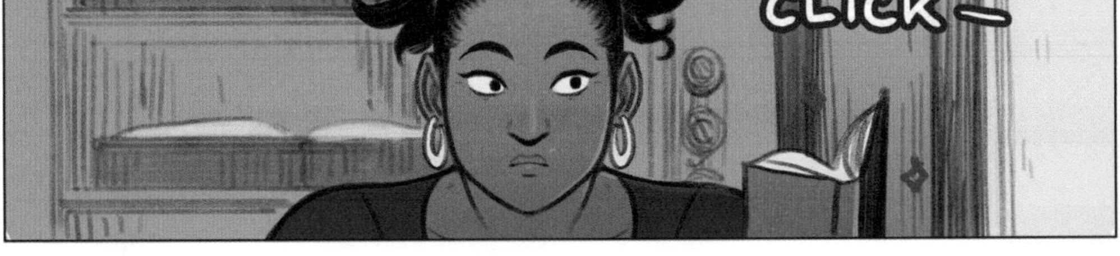
CLICK—

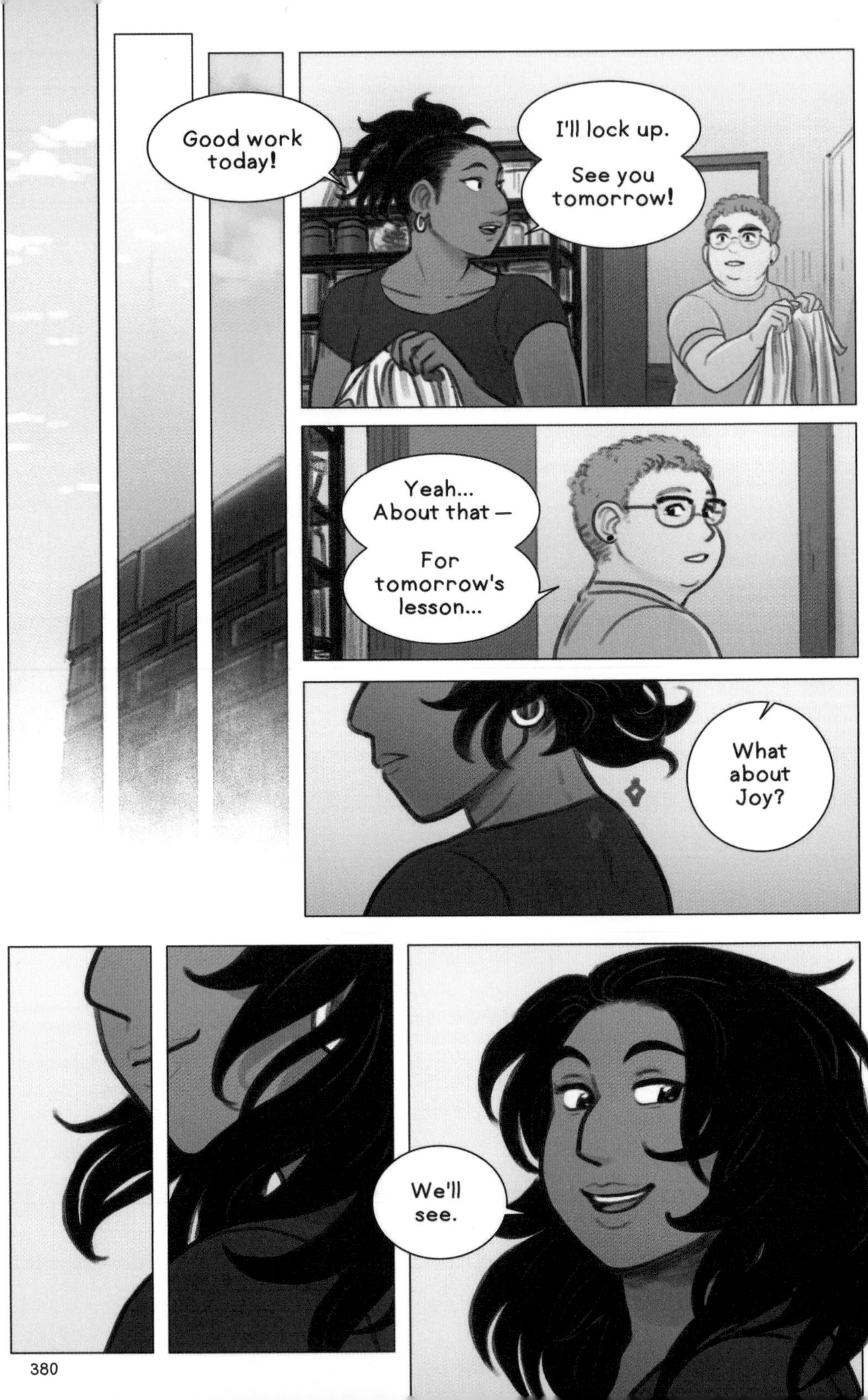
Good work today!
I'll lock up.
See you tomorrow!
Yeah... About that —
For tomorrow's lesson...
What about Joy?
We'll see.

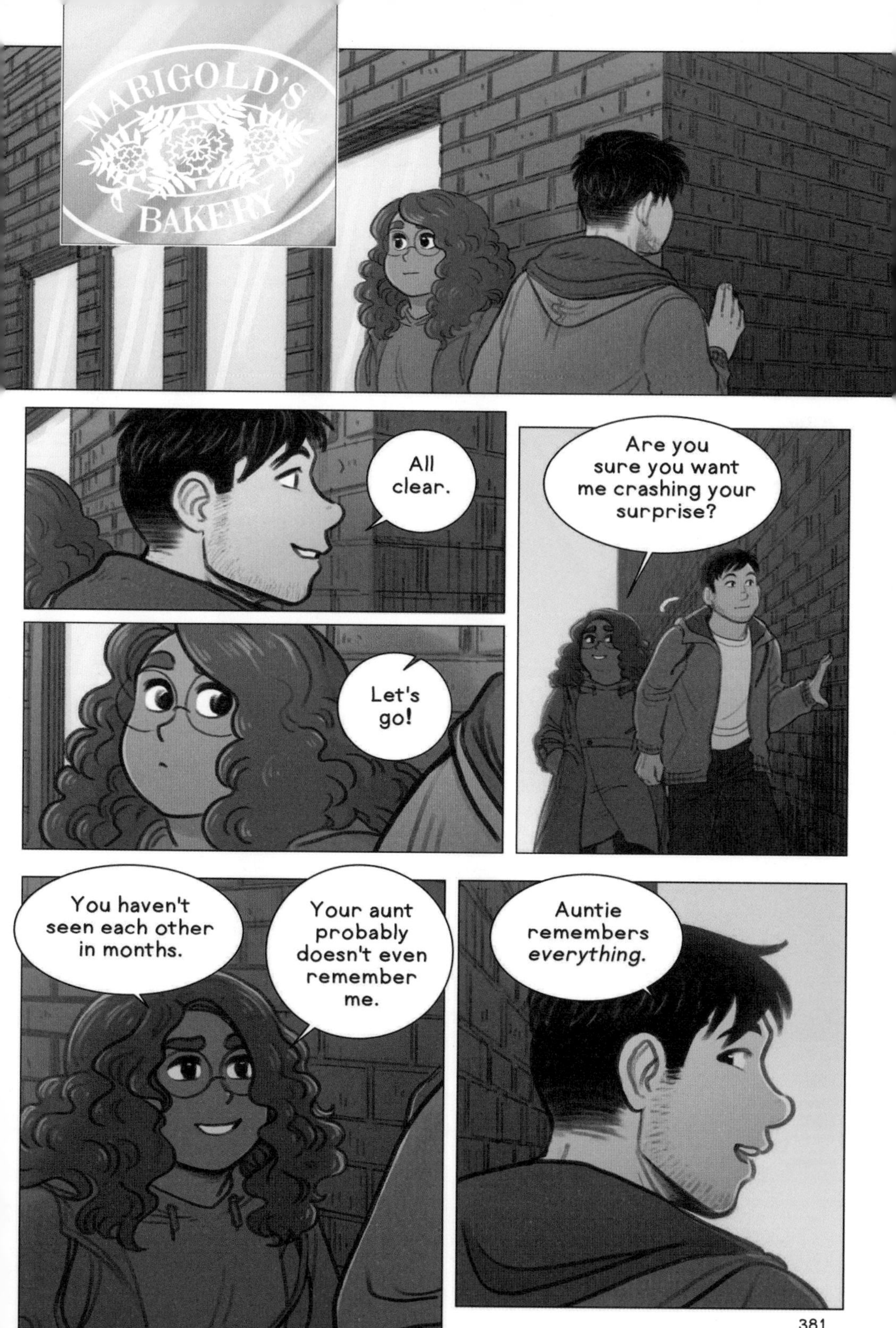
MARIGOLD'S BAKERY
All clear.
Let's go!
Are you sure you want me crashing your surprise?
You haven't seen each other in months.
Your aunt probably doesn't even remember me.
Auntie remembers *everything*.

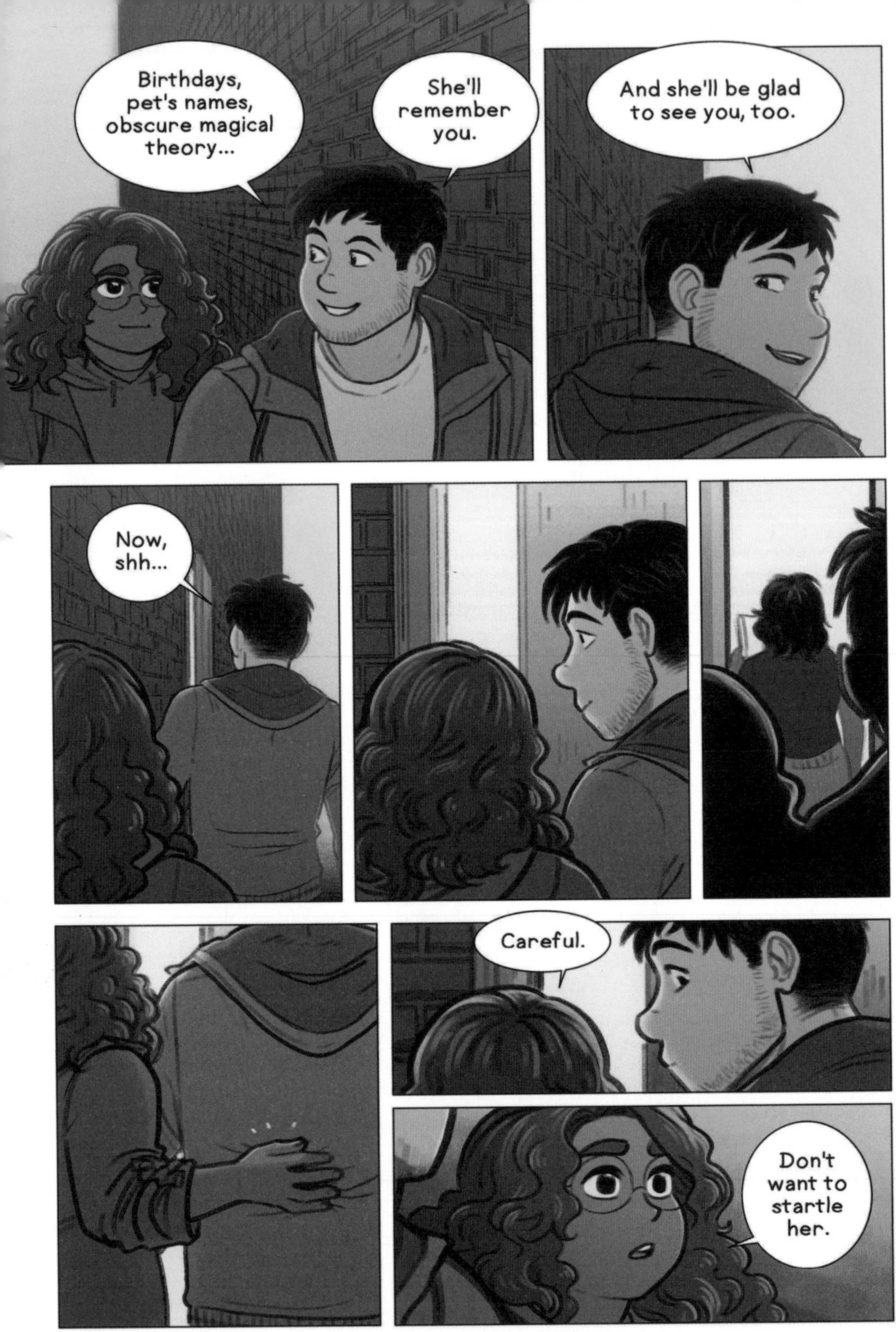
Birthdays, pet's names, obscure magical theory...
She'll remember you.
And she'll be glad to see you, too.
Now, shh...
Careful.
Don't want to startle her.

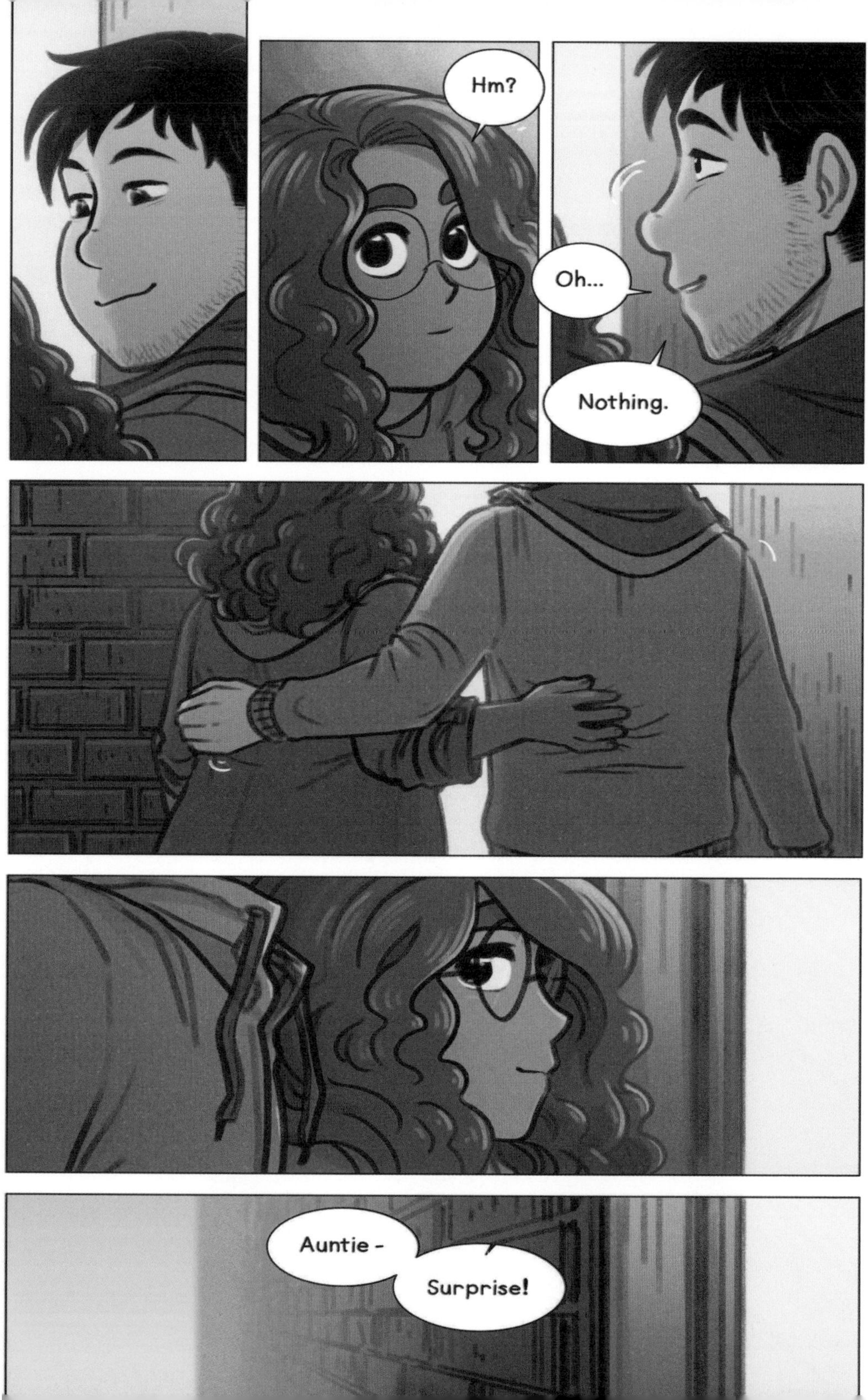
Hm?
Oh...
Nothing.
Auntie -
Surprise!

Acknowledgments

Maybe in some other enchanted world, books can be charmed into existence with a wish. In this world, it takes a bit more magic:

My family, who believed in and supported my comics, sight unseen.

H.B. Klein and my colleagues in webcomics, with their wealth of advice and their friendship.

Alakotila, who saved Crumbs from tripping on deadlines more times than I'd like to count.

And last but not least, Emilia Rhodes, Juliet Goodman, Celeste Knudsen, Alice Wang, Bones Leopard and the team at Etch, who did the heavy lifting of transforming over two thousand digital panels into these hundreds of pages.

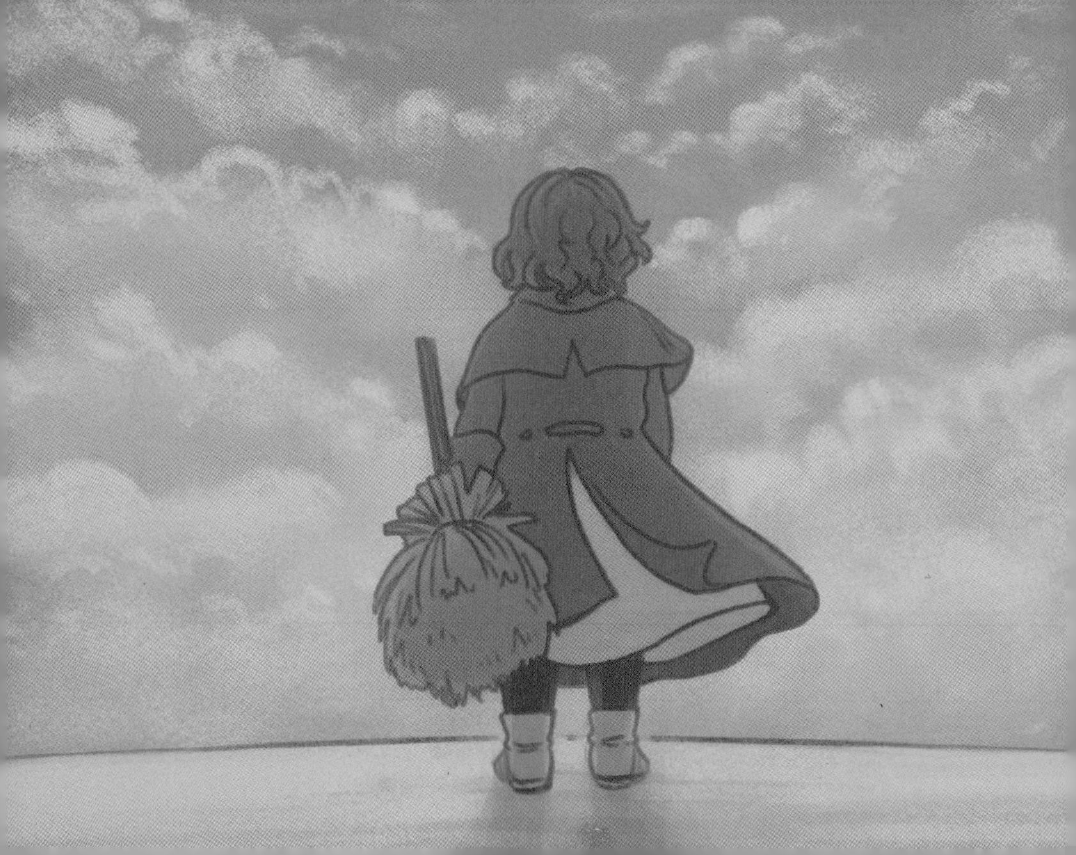